GALAXY ALIEN WARRIORS BOX SET

A SCIFI ALIEN WARRIOR ROMANCE

SEDONA VENEZ

WANT FREE SEDONA VENEZ BOOKS?

Sign up for Sedona Venez's Newsletter and receive FREE BOOKS. In addition to the free stories, you will also get special pricing, exclusive previews and news of new releases.

GET A FREE SEDONA VENEZ BOOK!

Join Sedona's mailing list to be the first to know of new releases, free books, special prices and other author giveaways.

https://sedonavenez.com/free-book

CRAZE

CHAPTER 1
MISTY

A faint chime caught my attention as I laced up my favorite purple sneakers. I looked at the small, antique clock hanging in the living room of my sparse Manhattan apartment and smiled. Ten on the nose…the perfect time to go for a run. The air had turned crisp outside, a light breeze freshening it, and the crowds had thinned enough to let me jog without stopping constantly.

Get a move on, Misty.

I was already tired, and if I went out too late, the October night would be too cold to exercise comfortably.

My nightly run was the first part of my three-step plan to unwind after another crazy day of overtime and eating at my desk. Part two would be a long, hot shower. It was Thursday night, so it was time to deep-condition my relaxed, waist-length black hair again. Part three would be pure entertainment. A campy science fiction movie from my collection, a slice of dark chocolate cake, and half a bottle of Chianti would see me through to my bedtime. Perfect, aside from the lack of a fellow night owl to share it with.

New York career women like me often didn't have time to date. We either met someone at work or at one of the places we grabbed food, went looking online, or endured long stretches without company.

Usually a combination. I had crappy luck in attracting good men, so I spent a lot of time without a lover.

My last date had been with a Wall Street finance douche who had taken me to an exclusive French restaurant. He had then berated our waitress to the point of tears barely ten minutes after I had met him.

I had watched him enjoy his petty bullying over how the wine had been served for just long enough to see him smile faintly when the server had started sobbing. Then I had excused myself and gone home. Inexpensive wine, meat loaf, and cat videos provided a much better night than Finance Douche would have.

He had blown up my texts with whining and trying to browbeat me into a second date. I had blocked his number, moved on...and reminded myself not even to look at another Wall Street suit again.

I pulled on my oversized purple hoodie and drew up the hood, hiding my hair under it and obscuring some of my curves. It was one of the comfiest things in my wardrobe and—deliberately—one of the least flattering except for the stretchy leggings I wore to run.

I liked my body. Lots of hard exercise in the last few years had turned me from chubby to voluptuous, with strong legs, arms I could go sleeveless with, and an ass I didn't mind looking at in a mirror. The problem was that Manhattan's creepy-guy population all seemed to "like" my body too.

There were a lot of creeps in Manhattan. Young, old, suited, homeless, weasel teenagers in sweatshirts and sideways caps, stumbling drunks, and "upstanding" men wearing wedding rings. They all had one thing in common besides all being male. Way too many of them caught a glimpse of a thick ass and double-D boobs and immediately decided to make pests of themselves...or worse.

I wore headphones on the street now to block them out, but sometimes a real shithead would just pull them off me so he could try to talk to me. I carried a pepper-foam spray, but when guys like that started into their catcalling bullshit, I never felt safe.

Hey, baby. Hey, baby. Back that up. You single? He makes you happy? I don't see a ring... Yeah, I love 'em thiiiiiick, baby...lemme get a handful of that... I'd love to take you home and fuck you hard...

Hey, why don't you want to talk to me? You stuck-up or something?

Bitch. Whore! Fat ass, you ain't even hot, I was just being nice! I should kick your ass!

Geez, lady, why you so nervous? Not all guys are bad. Though, if they say shit, well, you can't really blame them when you've got those great titties—Hey, where are you going? You frigid or something?

I would have learned to laugh at them were it not for their potential for violence. So far, I had just endured headphone grabs and a beer bottle thrown my way, but I knew a lot of women who had not been so lucky.

For a while, I had almost stopped running because I was so bothered by the harassment—and potential for worse. But it had been a favorite exercise of mine since I started jogging with my dad at the age of twelve, and I really didn't want to give it up.

So, I deliberately dressed down, covered my hair, and kept moving, knowing I would attract less attention that way. And four mornings a week, I went for kickboxing lessons at the local Y… just in case.

Locking the door, I bounded across the lobby and out of the complex, a concrete and stucco filing cabinet of a building that loomed eight stories over the street. My home for four years, paid for with my parents' life insurance. I had lost them in my sophomore year of college, and one of my million regrets about losing them was that I had never been able to show off my very first apartment to them.

I gazed up at it for a moment, before putting in my headphones, turning, and striding down the sidewalk toward Central Park. The Park was my favorite place for a run, and I was eager to spend some time clearing my head as I made a few loops around the reservoir.

I had more than earned the time at work today, that was for certain. As a first-year intern at the *New York Times*, I was constantly swamped—paperwork, filing, copying, office errands, helping to cover the phones…anything but writing or editing news articles.

I knew this dues-paying was part of the process of breaking in to the business, but all the drudgery took its toll after a while. I just wanted to write my own stories for once, but I knew I still had a lot of hard work ahead of me before I would ever get the opportunity.

The most famous publication in the American newspaper business had no room for whiners or slackers. So, every day, I worked my ass off, came home, took a run and a shower, and spent the rest of my night unwinding. Alone, usually. But, again, who had time to date?

My steps against the sidewalk kept a good tempo to the Lenny Kravitz playing through my earphones. As I entered the park, I reluctantly turned off my music, wrapping the earphones around my phone and tucking it deep into my hoodie's kangaroo pocket. I preferred to keep my ears open to the world around me once I reached the park, with its shadowy spots and deserted stretches.

I had only ever been mugged once, and he had left in disgust after discovering I was a penniless college student. Still, the run-in had taught me a serious lesson about being cautious. I had been lucky. The city could chew up and spit out a girl on her own like me if she wasn't careful.

Dangerous or not, I could still enjoy my time here. The night was perfect. Probably forty-five degrees and barely a need for my gloves. The moon hanging overhead was a clear, bright disc with no clouds to block it. I smiled to myself as I jogged over to the reservoir.

I had made half a circuit around that placid artificial lake when I started to realize something strange. New York never slept, the park was open until well past midnight, and yet I had not run into a single person since I entered the grounds.

"That's strange," I murmured quietly.

Where is everyone?

I ran on, keeping an eye out for any other people. Still nothing…a solid mile and a half that, except for me, was completely deserted. The wind had died, and the reservoir's water was as still as black glass under the moon. A dog barked in the distance, and I could hear traffic noises and the high wail of a police siren. But the park itself was as static as a painting. Even the crickets were silent.

About then, I noticed something strange on the dormant grass at the edge of the path. It was an irregular splotch, darker than the rest, the shape vaguely humanoid. As I slowly jogged past it, I realized it was a singed patch on the grass—as if someone's shadow had been burned into the lawn.

I was puzzling over it when a shock went through me. *I'm being watched.* The gut feeling made the hair on the back of my neck stand on end. My breath quickened. I stumbled to a stop and started looking around, trying to pinpoint the cause of this strange, hunted feeling. I saw nothing. But the feeling was getting worse by the second.

Get out of here. Get out of the park.

I could see a gate entrance between the trees a block away, and I made for it, breaking into a sprint. Whatever was going on in Central Park tonight, I wanted nothing to do with it.

I was ten paces from the gate when a shaft of hard white light broke over me like a spotlight. It felt like being hit with a sledgehammer. My muscles locked, and instead of falling, I was yanked upward suddenly, my feet leaving the ground.

For a moment, I stared helplessly out at the darkened, deserted park, smelling the dead grass burning under me, my heart pounding in my ears. *Help,* I thought, mind all but blank with terror. *Someone help me.* But I couldn't speak.

Then the light tore me into pieces.

∼

I awoke feeling very groggy. My muscles ached. It felt like I had slept wrong the entire night, and my mattress felt thin and hard for some reason. My whole body was sluggish, like I was suffering from a hangover.

How much of that Chianti did I drink last night?

I lay there rubbing my temples for a few moments before opening my eyes.

It's too damn bright.

The glaring lights forced me to close my eyelids again as pain shot through my head, making me gasp. I waited a moment before opening them again, this time in increments, allowing my eyes to adjust. Once my vision fully returned, my eyes grew wide in surprise.

What the hell? Where am I?

I was lying on my back on a thin, narrow mattress, barely more padded than the soles of my sneakers. The floor beneath it was some smooth gray metal, faintly warm to the touch. My body felt strange, a little bit too light, as if someone had turned gravity down a notch.

It looked as if I was in some sort of cargo hold, though I couldn't feel waves rocking it under me, so maybe I wasn't on a ship. But if it was a warehouse on land, why were the walls metal?

All around me, large, brightly colored containers had been stacked up, sometimes to the ceiling, and bolted together with heavy, dark metal brackets. Their corners had small but powerful lights attached to them, which threw a hard, bluish glow over everything.

To my shock, I saw a few more women huddled on the floor nearby. There were four of them, all of them white and wearing fall-weight clothes. They all looked both hungover and scared, and each one sat on her sleeping mat as if afraid to move from it.

What the hell is going on?

Quickly, I tried to get up, but I ended up banging my head on something. I looked up, blinking, and saw nothing but open air around me. I reached up tentatively and felt a barrier, invisible to the eye but as solid as a wall of heavy glass.

Horrified, I swung my hands around and found my fingertips contacting another solid wall about a foot away from each side of my sleeping mat. I was in the human equivalent of a dog crate—only one with invisible walls.

My heart hammered in my chest as my whole body shook, jolts of adrenaline running through me. *I've been kidnapped.* I remembered the light that had speared down, paralyzing me, lifting me, burning my shadow into the grass before pulling me apart. I had lost consciousness. Now I was whole and here…but trapped, along with the others.

I looked over at the nearest one, a doe-eyed blonde with a thin face and a heavy gray alpaca shawl. "Hey!" I hissed to her. She glanced my way but kept her head down, expression going even more nervous. "Hey. Over here! Can you hear me?" I called again softly. She looked up at me, then around, nodding distractedly. *Oh, thank God.* "Where are we?"

She opened her mouth to speak, but then suddenly looked up and went white as a sheet. Her mouth snapped shut, and she shook her head quickly and put her finger over her lips.

What is going on? "Damn it!" I slammed my palms against the invisible walls keeping me trapped, head pounding in frustration and confusion. But then I noticed something about my fellow captives that shocked me into silence.

On the sides of their necks, right under and behind their ears, a small, bright red light blinked every few seconds. It was round, about the size of a dime, and each one blinked in time with the others. *Marked,* I thought with growing horror. *They have been tagged like animals in a wildlife survey. Or maybe new pets being chipped…*

Cautiously, I reached up, feeling my own neck. *Oh God.* My whole body tensed as I felt a small, round disc embedded under my skin. I let my hand drop, numb with shock. "Fuck," I muttered under my breath.

Who the hell has us? Who has technology like this? The government? The Chinese? Who? I felt all over the walls of my invisible cage, searching for a seam or any weakness. Nothing.

I heard a weird slithering sound coming from somewhere nearby and looked around, but I couldn't see its source. Whatever it was made the other captives nervous.

Maybe I had lived in New York for too long, but when I got nervous, I got belligerent. Nothing made sense, and the only way I was going to get answers was by making some noise. I moved onto my knees and started to thump against the walls of my containment unit. "Hey! Let me the fuck out of this thing!"

I heard a tapping sound and looked over to see the blonde staring at me earnestly. She shook her head several times, and I saw a bruise developing on the side of her face. *What the hell?* I went quiet and realized that the slithering sound was growing closer, accompanied now by a thin, electronic whine.

My head swiveled to look as I caught sight of a large silver vehicle rounding the corner of one of the stacks of shipping containers. It looked like the upper part of a speedboat, just a cockpit, with walls and a control yoke in front, gliding along on a flat bottom. The floor vibrated slightly as it came nearer…and I caught sight of what was riding in it.

My heart started hammering, and a deep chill ran through my whole body as I got my first good look at my captors. Not military. Not Chinese. Not even human.

They were huge, each one about eight feet tall, but hunkered over, their burly, long-armed bodies reminding me of hairless gorillas. Their skin had a grayish-blue tinge like three-day-old bruises and was leathery-looking and covered in ropy veins.

Their faces were flat, noses mere bumps above single nostrils, and eyes small and black. Sparse manes of stiff, whitish hair grew around the edges of their faces, some of them decorated with beads carved from what looked like bone. Their ears were just holes in the sides of their heads, covered with membranes, like lizard ears. One was missing an eye and had a metal plate bolted to his skull over the socket.

They wore an assortment of beaded jewelry and belts hung with pouches, but were otherwise nude. And male. *Very, very male. Holy fuck.* I got an eyeful of gray dangly bits roughly the size and dimension of baby elephants' trunks before tearing my horrified gaze away.

Aliens. Those are aliens. Those are actual, extraterrestrial, high-tech, intelligent non-humans, and they've kidnapped all of us. I sat there with my heart pounding as I struggled to digest this fact.

There were four in all, drawn by the noise I had made. They peered at me curiously as their vehicle glided up to my cage. I stiffened with fear as the aliens disembarked and walked over to surround my invisible prison.

"Who…are you?" I asked almost breathlessly as I stared out at them. Frustration gave me a touch of courage. "What the fuck is going on?"

Then the aliens did something that scared me even more. A dry, rattling sound escaped from one of them, blooming up into a low hooting with a familiar cadence. The others joined in as they leered in at me, and I started to shake again as I realized what the noise was.

They were laughing.

CHAPTER 2
CRAZE

I kept my pace quick as I walked into the palace's vaulted throne room, ignoring the attendant scrambling to keep up with me. I had always lived a warrior's life, like my father before me, and had little use for servants.

The slim youth in my father's black and gold livery announced me with a bow, as if my parents could not see me quite plainly from their tall thrones. Then he hurried off into the pillared gallery to give us our privacy. I tossed a small crystal coin after him. He caught it in midair and nodded before vanishing.

The throne room was the information center of the palace, its towering stone walls arrayed with electronic relays, imagers, amplifiers, and communications devices which branched out on massive bundles of cable from the central gallery. There, enormous viewscreens flanked the low dais on which the thrones sat, each one showing a different view of our beloved home-world, Vixxia Prime.

I caught sight of two orbital images and the weather station atop Highlake Mountain as I approached the dais. It was carved from creamy white stone, like the thrones themselves and the stairs leading up to them.

The thrones, chiseled from a single piece of stone each and twice the height of their occupants, were positioned on a stage crafted in the shape of gigantic flower buds. Crystal chairs with deep fur cushions sat amid the buds, while the Emperor's and Empress's sensory helmets dangled from the ceiling, studded with multicolored lights which flashed in elaborate patterns.

My parents had sat upon those thrones for many years, their psychic abilities sustaining their bodies while their minds constantly monitored the home-world, its three moons, and the data transmissions being sent to and from their subordinates in a never-ending stream.

I had grown used to seeing them both up there—my father, black-armored, my mother, elaborately robed in gold. They remained still as stone, with their rows of silver braids growing almost to their feet. Their minds flew all over the world and beyond, but their bodies had become like living statues.

I stepped up onto the dais before them, hands behind my back and my stance ramrod-straight. I was glad I had bothered to rebraid my hair and polish my armor this morning after returning from weapons practice. This meeting was completely unexpected, and as the crown prince and co-leader of my father's armies, I had appearances to keep up.

"You summoned me, Mother, Father?" I called out to them, raising my voice to attract their attention from the constant data streams. My father blinked first and focused on me, his pale silver eyes brightening. A faint smile creased his face.

My mother opened her brilliant green eyes several seconds later, a look of annoyance flicking across her narrow, pale features before they went blank again. She had grown increasingly immersed in her endless watch over the years and disliked leaving it. I tried not to take her unimpressed look personally.

"We did, Craze. A Thezlum ship just crossed into our territory from the frontier zone. It's another slaver ship, and they're headed straight for the outer colonies. If we don't act quickly, they'll grab as many of our females as they can carry for their slave trade. I want you to intercept them before they get there." My father spoke plainly as he addressed me.

I nodded, my long silver hair falling over my shoulders as I bowed toward him in a sign of respect. The two narrow braids in front of each of my ears tinkled slightly as the gold rings binding them struck together. "It will be done."

"The Thezlums have been warned multiple times. Those gray savages think their conquest-god will bring them success against any enemy. I want the ship captured and the crew taken alive. Or, at least, mostly alive." My father was a realist.

"That will be more complicated than simply eradicating them," I mused.

My mother looked up, and her helmet lights flickered rapidly for a moment. "Chance of mission success rises to the high nineties if more than one ship takes part. Bring your brothers and a small company."

I nodded, meeting her gaze very briefly before it turned inward and she raised her face away from me again. "It will be done," I promised them, feeling a stab of deep annoyance at the Thezlums. Quickly, I keyed a message into my bracer, summoning my brothers to my chambers for a briefing.

Those kidnapping, slaving, mindlessly violent religious fanatics and their scumbag overlords had kept the frontier from pushing farther outward for two decades with their regular attacks on colonists. I was looking forward to teaching them a lesson.

My father sat back, nodding. "You are dismissed, my son. Go tell your brothers of my orders. I expect you all to return from a successful campaign." My father managed to give me another small smile before closing his eyes and going still again. My mother had not even waited that long. I knew she did not notice when I left.

My brothers were waiting for me in the small guesting-hall outside of my bedchambers, speaking with quiet excitement to one another as they theorized about the reason for my meeting. When I walked in, all four went quiet and turned to address me as I looked around at them.

Ragar was the middle son, an enormous brute of a Vixxian with our grandfather's flame-red hair and violet eyes. He was staring out one of the chamber's bubble-windows, bare arms folded across his black metal cuirass as he scowled about something. Probably his interrupted romance. He was the only one of us who had managed to attract a mate among the planet's rare fertile females. He was preoccupied with her and having sex with her—and with telling us about it. I pretended not to be jealous.

Nemesch, the youngest of us, leaned against the wall nearby, obscured as usual by a thin veil of shifting shadow. He had the strongest psychic abilities of all of us, but the problem was that he had trouble turning them off. His light-bending abilities could ward off the heaviest pulse weapons, but they also tended to ward off regular light from him, leaving him forever looking like the shadowy outline of a lean, muscular man a head shorter than me. Nemesch and I got on well; he was loyal to our father and acted as the palace spymaster as well as a warrior in his own right.

Lerolysi, the second youngest, paced the floor restlessly. He was a bit wild-looking, his hair white like mine but unbound and falling in disarray down his muscular back. He was the only one of us who disdained armor, aside from his thick, black, scale-hide leggings, boots, and gauntlets. His sword already hung from his hip, and there was a hopeful gleam in his green eyes. Lysi lived for battle, even more than I, his many scars were a testament to that. He was a bit of a savage, but honorable and kind to his loved ones. We were the closest thing to friends among my brothers.

Finally, there was my twin brother, Sephir. Ironically, we didn't look much alike and were opposite in personality. His hair was an unusual steel gray, which he wore in narrow braids like our father, and his eyes were a deep ruby color. He had inherited my mother's thin features, which looked both cruel and strangely ascetic on a man. Armored save for his helmet, he lounged on one of the long, gray-padded benches lining the walls, looking tremendously bored.

He spoke up first as I walked in, barely turning his blood-drop eyes to me. "So, big brother, what did the old man have to say?"

I scowled before I could stop myself. Second in birth meant second-in-command, and sarcastic, power-hungry Sephir took advantage of his position a lot. He was our mother's favorite and the only one she spoke to often, even if she did it through network feeds. Sephir often disrespected and undermined both our father and me, if only with words. I didn't like him or trust him. He knew it, and it amused him.

"Thezlum slavers raiding the border colonies again. They will reach the outer ones in half a standard day. We are to intercept and capture the ship and its crew and return with them as prisoners."

"Capture? Ugh." Sephir rolled his eyes and looked away from me. "That sounds like a lot more work. Why not just blast them into space junk again?"

I forced myself to speak patiently. "Because every time we blast one of their slaver ships into space junk, their idiot religious censors cover up the disaster and tell everyone back on Thezlum Prime that the gods called the crew home as a reward for sufficient victories. Taking them alive as hostages forces their government to face facts. Or so our father hopes."

"So he hopes." Sephir smirked, and I stared at him hard for a moment before looking around at the others.

"Do we all have to go? I'm meeting Azunki this afternoon. I'd hate to disappoint her," Ragar said with a smirk on his face as his chest swelled with pride.

We all eyed him with resentment. With the female population of Vixxia Prime numbering around one to every nine males, thanks to androgen-producing chemicals in the soil, pickings were slim where romance and sex were concerned. The rest of us were left with occasional hookups, mismatched relationships that collapsed quickly, and sex droids. Ragar missed absolutely no opportunities to rub that in.

"If Ragar doesn't have to go, I don't want to go either." Sephir sounded petulant. I was tempted to backhand him, but I simply gave him a grim look.

"All of us are going, and that's final," I interjected. "It is our duty as royals to protect the empire from threats like the Thezlums." My voice was unyielding as I scrutinized my siblings, my deep blue eyes glowing as I asserted my dominance as the eldest brother.

I heard a collective sigh that I quickly silenced with a glare. "I don't want to hear another complaint. Ragar, you can wait a few hours to have sex, for pity's sake. And as for you, Sephir, you need the combat practice. Your aim is falling off."

Ragar's ear-tips went nearly as red as his hair as the younger brothers snickered at him. Sephir, meanwhile, glared in indignation but finally tossed his braids back over his shoulder and forced the smirk back onto his face. "Fine."

I grabbed my sword, the double-edged Exredilan, and walked out, my brothers falling into step behind me. Armor creaked, Ragar let out a heavy, dramatic sigh, and Sephir started humming tunelessly. But they were with me, and that was enough.

With that, we all stepped outside into the palace courtyard. The palace was built in a series of ring-shaped plazas, which mounted up in a graceful curve, with the courtyard spread out for many ship-lengths within the lowest-level walls. Like all our warriors, my brothers and I had our chambers set within the lowest ring, so we could access the launchpad complex for our attack ships easily.

Aside from the warriors' quarters, the outer ring housed several other administrative buildings, like the Council Chambers and embassies for the five other, single-planet species that served our empire. But the courtyard remained the main draw, for everything from formal gatherings to mounted sports. Beyond the rolling moss-lawn that surrounded the central plaza, the Imperial shipyard shimmered like a forest of sleek silver rockets.

My ship, the *Solrei*, stood among the tallest there, its flight wings folded against its gleaming body. The ramp was already down, my crew busily seeing the boarding troops inside. I strode up the ramp with my brothers on my heels, trying to ignore the surge of excitement that built in me as I prepared myself for another space battle. I had to stay cool-headed, even when we were in the thick of it.

The insides of the ship were all sleek, organic lines and pale metal surfaces, with a matte finish inside avoiding distracting glare. After a decade as her captain, I knew every inch of her, from the central corridor to the engine room. *It feels good to be home.* "Everyone, gear up and take your stations," I directed as we rode a set of lift-discs up to the bridge.

Once we stepped off on the bridge level, we went straight to our lockers to retrieve what armor and weapons we weren't already wearing. I had gone before my parents in my black-and-gold battle armor, and I now attached gravity plates to the soles of my boots and strapped my pistols to my hips beside my sword. A control gauntlet with my uplink to the ship and my parents' data feed came next, along with a psychic amplifier set into a simple gold band that I laid across my brow. The command cloak with my father's crest went on last and then the rifle-sling over my shoulders. I was ready.

Sephir was already ready, his plain black cloak hanging perfectly, and his ruby eyes staring back at me in amusement. The long, slim blade that he carried into battle radiated heat, the air around it rippling slightly. He disdained rifles, preferring instead to use his powers when his enemies were at a distance.

Ragar, on the other hand, loved firearms of every kind and was currently standing there in cloak and armor, trying to decide between four enormous rifles. Sephir had once actually managed to make me laugh by suggesting Ragar's overemphasis on his cock and its use heavily influenced his weapon choices. "Hmm," he rumbled.

"Oh, for pity's sake, take the rail gun. It's your favorite." Lysi's mailed fist clanked as it bonked against our brother's armored shoulder. Ragar lifted an eyebrow and turned his head, and our wild-haired younger brother shrugged and grinned. "You know I'm right."

"Shouldn't you put on the rest of your blast armor?" Ragar replied, eyebrow still dangerously lifted as his gaze flicked over Lysi's naked, battle-scarred chest.

Lysi just grinned, showing his sharpened canines. "No need for them. They just slow me down." He wasn't kidding. If I liked a good fight, and Ragar channeled his aggression through heavy firearms, Lysi was a pure berserker. Enhanced by his powers, his combat skills carried him from one end of a fight to the other, and his body count was almost always higher than the rest of ours—even though he paid for it by taking the most wounds as well.

Lysi's only weapons besides a backup blaster at his hip were the two arm-length, curved swords he carried. Their black blades went translucent as smoke when they were activated, blurred by the speed of their vibrations. They could cut through hull metal.

"Ridiculous," Ragar grumbled. "How many times am I going to have to carry you away from a battle before you'll wear some proper protection? Stupid kid."

"You've got just three years on me, old man!" Lysi laughed and ducked when Ragar took a halfhearted swing at him.

"Here we go again," Nemesch sighed from within his cloud of shadows as he closed his locker. I couldn't tell what weapons he was carrying or whether he still wore the same armor he had before the darkness from his power seepage had swallowed him completely. But he was both smart and practical, and I trusted his judgment.

Sephir leaned against the wall and snickered as he listened to Ragar's and Lysi's sarcastic comments at each other heat up. He made no move to intervene, instead shooting a mocking look my way.

Some of my crewmen were filing past as Ragar finally took a swing at Lysi. Lysi leaped clear over his arm and grabbed a support strut arching above, swinging a booted foot at Ragar's helmet. *Clang.* My navigator, a blue-scaled Brennian who barely came up to my shoulder, jumped slightly and scurried to his post.

"Well, then, why don't you take *all four* rifles with you?" Lysi laughed as he dropped before Ragar could hit him in the stomach.

"I would, if I could fire all four at once!" Ragar got frustrated with all our brother's jumping around and reached for the rail gun.

"Enough," I called out, and both brothers stopped and looked over at me. I eyed them. "We have a mission to complete. You can beat each other silly later."

Lysi rolled his eyes, but he turned and walked over to his seat beside our shadowed brother at the weapons control station. Ragar grumbled, grabbed his rail gun, and stuffed it in his back sling, eyeing me in annoyance once, before heading for his own seat on Nemesch's other side.

"You know, you aren't emperor yet, Craze," Sephir commented as he reclined in his seat. His lip curled as he stared challengingly at me, steel-colored hair falling over one eye.

Sephir had always been my rival for everything and had created a scandal when he dropped out of military service upon learning he could never surpass me in rank. I had lost much of my respect for him that day, and he had never done a thing to earn it back. Nevertheless, we were of the same blood, and therefore, I had no choice but to work with him, especially during missions of this caliber.

"No, but I am commander of this ship and this mission. Or did you forget that?" I questioned.

Sephir just widened his smirk and spread his hands. "Whatever my Lord Commander wishes."

"In that case, put in a gag for the rest of the mission. Or just shut up and get in your seat." Turning away from him, I walked over to my command chair and swept my cloak aside to sit down in it.

I spread my fingers, and sparks started to jump between them, glowing a blinding blue. I started to sense the ship around me, as if it were an extension of my own body, as I extended my electrical field into its systems. My power was like my parents', in that I could communicate with machines, but I had learned several offensive uses for it as well.

Closing my eyes, I started to power on the individual systems one by one. The ship hummed to life as the crystals that powered the ship came to life in the depths of Engineering. I waited for a moment as the data systems went through their respective boot sequences. The control panel in front of me lit up brightly, and multicolored script started to scroll from right to left across it as the systems did a self-diagnostic.

"Final lift-off preparations have commenced," I announced through the ship speakers. "All personnel assume their seats and safety harnesses."

I didn't have to wait long for compliance. Collaboration was essential to man a Vixxian ship, and everyone on my crew knew it. From navigation and weapon control, to engineering and life support, each subsystem required its own pair of hands. I had worked hard to gather the best team possible. Usually, the only wild cards on any given mission were my own brothers.

That sometimes got a bit embarrassing, but even it had not cost us any victories.

"I want a clean takedown of the ship," I said as I flipped switches and checked readouts. Even though we were physically superior to the Thezlum slavers, we couldn't afford to get sloppy. Overtaking, boarding, and seizing control of a ship that would be actively trying to destroy us was never a straightforward or easy task.

I sat back and closed my eyes again, mentally instructing the data systems to start the countdown to lift-off. "Good. It's just a short hyperspace jump once we leave the atmosphere. If we all work together on this, we should be home in time to enjoy our free evening," I added in, hoping it would motivate them.

CHAPTER 3
MISTY

The aliens snickered at my pleas for freedom as I pounded on the walls of my enclosure. They began speaking to one another in a strange, croaking language I couldn't understand. I sighed and sat down, realizing my cries for release amused them. Blood boiled in my veins as I stared out at them helplessly, my face defiant but my mind still hazy with shock at my situation.

If I get out of this, I can't go home and tell my friends at the New York *freaking* Times *that aliens kidnapped me. I'll end up in a basket on the doorstep of some crackpot tabloid publisher with a layoff notice and a letter of recommendation.* I was trying to convince myself that it was a "when" not an "if." But that was hard to do when four leathery gray hulks from another world had me in a cage I couldn't even stand up in.

I didn't even want to contemplate what they might be planning to do to me. The fact that they had tagged me and the others like animals and were keeping us in cages in a cargo bay didn't inspire confidence. In fact, it made me sure that even if I escaped this place, I would find literally nothing outside. This wasn't a ship hold. It was a spaceship hold. And since I had no idea how to pilot their tech, I would have been trapped even if they had put me in the alien equivalent of a presidential suite.

Abruptly, one of the aliens pulled what looked like a small television remote from his belt pouch and pressed a button on it. The enclosure around me shimmered, and for a moment, I could see the force fields—or whatever—that made up its walls. The shimmering concentrated on the roof of the structure, which flashed briefly…and then disappeared.

I stood up, and my back popped from being able to stretch for the first time in hours. The relief made me think they were showing a small act of mercy. But then the one with the remote shot out a crusty-looking three-fingered hand and grabbed me by the back of my leggings.

I let out a cry of shock as he lifted me unceremoniously out of my prison and set me on the ground. He peered at me a moment—then croaked at one of the others, who nodded. That huge hand clamped around my forearm, and the alien started dragging me to their vehicle.

"Let go of me!" I screamed loudly as I tried to fight that terrible grip, but it only tightened painfully until I stopped struggling. The others followed us as he pulled me into the vehicle. They surrounded me, and he dropped his hand away, leaving my whole arm throbbing. I held it gingerly as we lifted off.

Except for the one driving, they were all staring at me. No…leering at me. Their black eyes had a greedy look, their too-wide mouths smirked or grinned. Most disturbingly of all, the elephants' trunks between their thighs were stirring to life. I tried to ignore all the twitching and swelling going on. Dealing with massive alien boners on top of everything else was just too horrifying.

The implications sickened me, and that immediately had me looking around for anything I might be able to use as a weapon. Maybe one of the long knives on their belts? *I might be able to grab one if I get lucky.*

First, though, I would have to wait for them to drop their guard, and they were still too intensely interested in me for that. Maybe they would start talking again, or better yet, bickering.

To keep my sanity as I waited for my opening, I looked past them instead of at them, watching where we were going now.

The cargo bay was huge, and I saw many more cages like my own, occupied by an assortment of captives, both human and alien. The only thing they all had in common was that every one of them was obviously female.

That is a very bad sign. I started shivering and jerked away when one of them ran a rough hand over my hair. "Fuck off!" Fear fueled my anger, and my thoughts started getting bloody. *I will defend myself. They might have caught me, but I can make them regret it.* If all else failed, I could back-fist one of them in their gigantic balls and take his knife that way.

The one who had pulled my hair growled and reached over to grab me by the neck, but one of the others barked something at him and he let me go. He continued to eye me. Skin crawling, I went back to watching our surroundings.

A huge, round door opened, letting us out into a blocky hallway of dull, greenish metal. A musky stink hit me as we left the relatively open air of the cargo bay. The hall was crowded with more of these beastly looking aliens. They parted for the vehicle as it slid along the floor, passing several open doorways on one side of the hall…and after a little while, a series of square viewports on the other.

I glimpsed star-studded blackness outside and swallowed, stomach dropping. *Sometimes I hate being right.*

Finally, we slid to a stop outside one of the alcoves, and they disembarked, dragging me with them. I went quietly, my eye on the nearest one's belt knife. I was still waiting for my moment. But when I saw where they were taking me, I reached for the knife at once.

Multiple hands grabbed me and yanked me off my feet. I screamed, kicking and struggling, my panic destroying my focus for a moment. One of them slung me over his shoulder and carried me toward the small surgical theater in the center of the room, ignoring me while I squirmed and pounded on his back. "Let go of me! Leave me alone! Help! Somebody fucking help!"

My voice echoed uselessly off the walls as he dropped me onto the massive metal table, hard enough to drive the air from my lungs. I struck out at him, but he grabbed my wrists and pulled them down against the table. Metal rings sprouted from the surface and snapped closed around my wrists.

The metal was cold enough that I felt it through my leggings. I started shivering from that and fear as two of them bent over me, reaching for me. I lashed out with both feet, straining my back, and struck one in the midsection. He stumbled back, and the other hesitated before backing off slightly.

The other two stepped up to the table, one of them shouting at me in his grunting, barking language. I flinched away from him while he continued to yell, my head and heart pounding with terror. *I must get off this ship.* I kicked out again, but one of them grabbed my legs and pinned them against the steel, and I felt a set of rings close around my ankles as well.

The alien with the remote walked around to my head and bent over me, looking me over. I winced and squinted up at him, head turned partly away, leery of the thin lines of drool hanging from his jutting jaw. He was smirking, giving me a clear view of his sharp teeth. My body tensed in fear. I tried to keep my cool, but as I lay spread-eagled on the table, completely vulnerable, it was all I could do not to panic.

I embarrassed myself by begging. "Please…you don't have to do this. What are you going to do with me?"

Unexpectedly, I felt one of the aliens slide their filthy claws over my thigh, the ragged, greenish tips catching on the legging. "Don't touch me!" I freaked out, thrashing, twisting my wrists and ankles against the cuffs, but it was hopeless.

My breathing had gone thready from fear. I craned my neck, following my captors' every move as they watched me and muttered to each other. *What are they going to do to me?*

My mind went back over every bad alien movie I had ever seen. The possibilities were not comforting. Would they probe me? Would they dissect me? I swallowed, throat tight, unable to do anything but wait and see.

Slowly, one of them reached for me with a small object held in a set of tweezers. It reminded me of the SIM card from my phone.

"What is that? What are you going to do with it? Don't you dare touch me." I tried to scream, but all that came out was a whisper.

They cackled, amused by my terror. I cursed as the one with the tweezers grabbed me by the head and turned it forcibly, pinning me down. I couldn't move. I trembled, my heart threatening to beat out of my chest.

I felt a sting behind my right earlobe. "Ow!" I yelped as the alien straightened up and moved away.

"Do you understand us now, *human*?" the one I had kicked asked. He was the biggest member of the group and looked like their leader. His skin was a touch darker than the others, and he had the most scars. The others seemed to defer to him a little.

"I…yes, I can understand you now. What did you do?" I blurted out in disbelief.

His smirk widened slightly. "We implanted you with what we call a 'Slaver's Friend.' It allows you to understand and speak any language in the galaxy. Customers won't buy a slave who can't understand their orders."

"I am not going to be anyone's slave! Let go of me. Now," I hissed at them. "Or I'll make sure you pay for it."

The leader snorted, his sharp teeth showing. "Not a chance. We have captured you and plan to sell you on the slave market. The Dragicans are opening another brothel and are paying us top dollar for a hundred head of females. I have no intention of finding out what they do to those who don't fulfill their quotas. I can't imagine it being very…pleasant."

I glared up at him and squirmed against the steel rings. "Neither is what I'm going to do to you when I get out of this, you son of a—"

He barked out a loud laugh. "Spirited! Our clients are going to enjoy very much breaking you down. In any case, I imagine you will fetch a handsome profit for your…" He paused, running a grotesque finger across my cheek, making me cringe. "…glowing beauty," he crooned as he leaned in even closer. His breath smelled like he had been munching on rotten garbage.

I waited until he was close enough to kiss me—and then head-butted him hard in the nose.

He gurgled with pain and stumbled back, holding his face. His single nostril was now drizzling purplish blood onto his hands. "Ah! My face! You little bitch!"

The other three had frozen when I struck, their jaws dropping.

Then one of them roared with laughter, and the others started snickering. "That is the funniest thing I have seen in this sector!" one of them tittered, reminding me of a frat boy after too much bad beer.

Their leader spluttered, wiping blood from his face. "Put her back in her containment. She is too disruptive. Withhold food for two days. See if that won't take some of the fight out of her."

Obediently, the aliens unfastened me from the table and dragged me toward the vehicle. I was going back to my solitary prison…and once they locked me into it, I had no chance at all of escape.

Desperation took hold, and I managed to squirm away briefly, tearing the sleeve of my hoodie. Recalling everything I had learned in kickboxing class, I swung my left leg and managed to kick one of the aliens in the stomach.

He grunted and stumbled back, and I took my chance. I ran full speed out into the hallway, looking around desperately for a place to hide from them.

Unfortunately, my freedom was short-lived. Within moments, I felt a tingling sensation run up the length of my spine, and my knees buckled. I stumbled, grabbing for the disc under the skin of my neck, and my fingers prickled when they brushed against it. Body feeling like lead, I collapsed to the floor, completely limp.

Effortlessly, they carried me back into the hover-sled and drove back to the cargo bay. I was angry with myself for not putting up a better fight. But the aliens cheated. Something in that beacon they had put in me could be used to paralyze me, and God only knew what else.

I must find a way out of here, or they'll send me to a goddamn interplanetary whorehouse where I'll be dealing with giant alien cocks all fucking day. But I couldn't move.

The aliens dropped me into my force field prison, and one of them hit the button to seal me in. I was starting to get feeling back in my limbs, but I couldn't quite move yet.

The three aliens that had brought me back were turning away when an ear-piercing explosion from somewhere in the ship startled all of us. The whole cargo bay shook violently. Klaxons started whooping, and I heard shouts from the hallway.

Another explosion shook the ship violently enough to knock one of the aliens off his feet. Some of the towers of shipping containers started to sway and creak dangerously. Luckily, I was already in my enclosure, protected by the thick force field.

Even so, I was trapped.

All I could do was watch as the aliens ran around, the lights started to flicker, and more thunderous booms shook the floor. "What is it?" one of the aliens shouted to another as he struggled to keep his balance.

The other checked a readout on a heavy bracer on his forearm and looked up. "It's the Imperials!"

"How did they get here so fast—" the first one started. Before he could even finish his sentence, something slammed into the ship so hard that the floor tilted violently, and the cargo containers started to fall. One of them broke free of its clamps and tumbled over, crushing the alien, and then knocking one corner into my cage as it came to a rest.

My cage flew into the air, and I went tumbling around inside of it as if caught in a washing machine. Then it hit the floor several paces away, and my head slammed against the force field. Everything went black.

CHAPTER 4
CRAZE

"Target in sight, my brother," Lysi stated as the enemy ship came into range on the view-screen. I analyzed the ship through the *Solrei's* sensors and shook my head. Sometimes I wondered if religious fanaticism really was enough to motivate their constant attempts at raids in the face of our overwhelming military superiority. The Thezlums were also as dumb as livestock, but I couldn't understand their lack of self-preservation instincts. How many raids had they tried in the last moon-cycle? Three? *Ridiculous. It's like they want to die.*

"Their escort is tiny. Thirty single-pilot fighters." I looked around at them.

Sephir lifted an eyebrow. "Should we pick them off first?"

"No. They are insects. Fire on the main ship's engine array. We'll sever it and leave them drifting." I checked the scanners. "Full crew complement, plus a score of other life forms. They've already grabbed some people."

"We don't have time to go on a rescue mission—" Sephir started, and I glared at him.

"We can't afford not to if they've taken any of our colonists. Their protection is part of our duty." *Something I know you don't care much about, you selfish slacker.* I looked at the silhouette seated between us.

"Nemesch, block any incoming energy blasts. Let them drain their crystals hammering at us."

I looked to Ragar and Lysi, thinking of something that would use their conflict to our advantage. "As for you two, I propose a contest. Whoever captures the most crew members alive once we breach the hull wins."

Lysi grinned fiercely. "I'll win."

Ragar smiled slightly and gave me a shrewd look. "What's the prize?"

"The loser has to praise the winner's work in front of our father." I fought down a grin as their eyes widened.

"Oh no. No way in all of space am I kissing your butt in front of the Emperor," Ragar boomed at our brother, who started snickering.

"I can see how nervous this is making you. Good, good." Lysi folded his arms, eyes dancing. "Better get your concession speech ready."

"Same to you," Ragar growled, and I couldn't help but smile a little.

There's that handled. "Once we breach, Nemesch will lead the main party of boarding troops and shield them with his powers. The reserve will stay aboard in case any of the Thezlums try to get cute and escape in our ship. Lysi and Ragar will free-range and meet back up with the main body once we attack the bridge."

"So, what about me?" Sephir asked in a bored tone.

"Go with Nemesch," I replied shortly. "Try not to get shot."

I turned away from him as his face started to redden. "Since there's a question of my stretching resources too thin, I will take our medic and a small team and personally rescue the captives from their cargo bay."

"Well, that's politic of you," came the snide response.

I turned to Sephir. "Are you and I going to have a problem over my orders? Because if so, now's the time. If you drag your feet once we're in the thick of it, it will get you killed."

"Your concern for me is touching," he sneered in response.

"Which is it, Sephir? Or would you rather wait on my ship and hide from battle altogether?" There came that familiar feeling again, the growing desire to backhand him so hard he bounced off the far wall.

His eyes flashed briefly—but then he just put his smirk back on and waved a hand casually. "Fine, fine, I'll help Nemesch babysit the ordinary people. Let's get on with it already."

I snorted and shook my head, then looked back at my three brothers at the gunnery console. "Take aim on the engine array. Secondary targets are the large weapon pods. Don't worry about the fighters unless they try a suicide run. Their beam weapons can't get through Nemesch's powers."

My brothers tapped buttons and peered at their instrument readouts, setting the targeting systems. "Ready," Ragar said after a few seconds.

"On my count, fire all batteries," I ordered, my voice level as I focused my attention. I knew we had to be precise to cripple their ship in a single strike. "Three…two…one…Now!" My voice rose to a shout as we fired a volley of missiles which streaked away on the viewscreen, seeking out the Thezlum vessel.

With a bright white explosion, the target spacecraft's huge, funnel-shaped propulsors sheared off and drifted away in chunks of half-melted metal. The fighters peeled away and headed toward us. Nemesch closed his eyes and focused as they started to fire blazing streaks of solid light at us. He began breathing heavily from the effort as the pulse beams faded away before they reached us.

Our shields flashed brightly as the Thezlum freighter trained its weapons on us and loosed a barrage of missiles. "All weapons on secondary target!" I yelled, and Ragar and Lysi set back to work. Our missiles shattered the weapon pods within a few more seconds.

"That's it! They're crippled," Lysi crowed, jumping up and down in his seat like an excited boy. "And the fighters are running!"

"So much for the glory of their battle-god," Sephir sneered as the fighters flew off at top speed for the border. "Do we let them go?"

"Their fleeing can only hurt morale. Let them run away with their tails between their legs," My voice dripped with disdain as I watched them go. "Cowards."

"I knew those Thezlums didn't stand a chance against us," Ragar declared, broad face full of pride. "Now, let's go over there and reap the spoils."

"Chances are they have little of value besides the innocent people we're rescuing," I pointed out.

He let out a laugh. "I was talking about the contest!" He looked at Lysi mockingly. "Hope you've been working on that speech."

"It's fun watching you delude yourself," my wild brother replied with his broad grin.

I leaned to speak into the communicator grid again. "All personnel prepare for boarding procedures. Reroute seventy-five percent of shield strength to forward sectors." The energy shields around us brightened to a luminescent shimmer. "Deploy breaching ram." I heard a rumble of heavy machinery as a massive lance extended from the nose of the rocket. "I want everyone geared and ready in thirty seconds."

I stood and walked up to my armor locker again, grabbing another piece of equipment, a helmet, shaped to fit over my psi-enhancer. Gold-chased black metal shimmered as I turned it in my hands. The unbreakable visor was retracted, and its power lights dark. My late grandfather, a mighty warrior and brilliant general who had been a legend among our troops, had willed it to me from his personal armory.

I aspired to be like him, and so far, I was off to a good start. Even at the young age of twenty-eight, I had led my people to victory multiple times against raiders, pirates, and invading troops. I was the rightful heir to the throne, and I had made many friends among soldiers, diplomats, nobles, and advocates for the common folk alike. Though I wasn't a braggart like Ragar or Lysi, I was proud of my accomplishments.

I pulled the helmet on, and the visor slid down over my face. I noticed a few of my brothers pulling on their helmets as well. Returning to my seat, I fastened my safety harness, took a deep breath, and then shouted an order. "Ramming speed!"

The ship shook slightly as our target started to grow rapidly in the view-screen. "Breach the forward quarter!" I ordered, and I saw my navigator hurriedly tapping a series of keys. The cargo bay was amidships, and breaching there would have put the captives at risk.

I braced myself as we slammed into the freighter's third-rate shield barrier, collapsing it, and powered through the hull beyond with its ram. The retro propulsors fired just in time to keep us from punching a hole through the ship. I only felt a hard jolt as we stopped, inertial dampers keeping us from splattering ourselves over the inside of the ship.

"That's it!" I jumped up and drew my sword and one pistol. "Everyone to the ram for boarding!"

The chaos of the initial missile impacts had apparently kept the Thezlums from regrouping properly yet. As I raced down the corridor of the breaching ram toward the freighter's interior, I caught a few racing past the breach in a panic but none forming up to fight. *It's just like the fighters outside. These beasts fancy themselves to be true warriors, but they panic the moment they face a real threat.*

Good. Makes my job easier.

"Careful, now. Keep up your guard," I warned my siblings and my troops, mostly young and promising warriors who followed me faithfully. Then we emerged into the dim light and animal stench of the Thezlum ship, and chaos erupted.

Boarding was always a dangerous job. Nemesch led the way, the shadows around him devouring the bolts from the Thezlum energy weapons. The troops fired back then, knocking the defenders out quickly with stun bolts and clearing the hallway. Ragar and Lysi charged, Lysi laughing madly, and Sephir simply sauntered after the shield wall of troops, looking bored.

"Split up and search every inch of this ship," I instructed, and everyone dutifully went their separate ways. I checked my small cadre of six soldiers and two medics, all in blast armor, and then turned and headed down the hall opposite from where my brothers and the other troops were going. The Thezlums always scrambled to protect their command crew on the bridge in a situation like this. They were so predictable that sometimes I wondered if their rulers put them through mental programming.

Meanwhile, I advanced toward the cargo hold, my helmet taking readouts of our surroundings and feeding me a cascade of data through my amplifier. Now and again, we ran across a few Thezlums, but most did not bother to offer any resistance, trying to turn and run instead.

Finally, I reached the entrance to the cargo bay. It was locked down, the iris closed. "Stand back," I told the others and stepped forward, laying my hand on the control box. One of the Thezlums had had the foresight to put an energy bolt through it, trying to lock us out and away from their precious contraband. But they hadn't counted on my power.

I let my mind slide into the damaged circuitry to the control crystal in its center, which was still intact. I struggled briefly with the clunky Thezlum programming, and then the iris rumbled open, letting through a blast of cold, relatively clean air. "That's it. Split up into two-man teams and search the place for those captives. Medics, you're with me."

The commlink in my helmet hummed faintly. "Craze, this is Ragar. We've got something weird here up on the bridge."

I paused, checking all around me before stopping just inside the iris. "Go ahead."

"We got decent resistance on the lower levels, but it thinned out the farther forward and up we went. The bridge is deserted, brother." His rumbling voice dripped with disappointment.

"Lysi must be beside himself. Do you think they abandoned ship as we were preparing to board?" I had not sensed any escape pod launches during our charge, but the Thezlums had matter-transmission technologies beyond ours.

"It seems likely." He let out a quiet grumble. "Well, with the cargo and all, I think we could get good salvage off this thing. How many captives survived?"

"I'll let you know as soon as I know." I signed off and waved the medics on, moving down the center of the cargo bay as the others moved along the walls on either side.

I kept up the search, peering at the cargo containers now and again as we checked every corner and nook of the mazelike room. Strange that they had left the cargo unguarded, instead fleeing without it and leaving behind their rank and file to slow us down. Were the Thezlums getting smart…or were they getting advice from somewhere?

My commlink hummed again. "Sir, we've found some survivors." The grim tone in the young soldier's voice told me that they had found some dead as well.

"Hold your position. I'll be right there." I nodded to the medics, and we turned and hurried toward the far wall. I traced the soldier's signal around a stack of half-tumbled cargo containers and glimpsed him standing near a few smallish figures that were sprawled on the floor.

"What's the situation?" I demanded as the soldier looked up at our approach. My power detected a force-cage around each of the figures, invisible to the naked eye. Their confines were disturbingly small, and all occupants were female.

"Four injured, two unconscious, five dead. Looks like they left with the others, unless they have them stashed away in stasis somewhere in here." His salute was a little stiff. "Looks like most of the injuries were from being tossed around in the attack. But someone detonated the tracker discs embedded in the necks of the dead ones. Looks like they were trying to get rid of their cargo before they could be freed." This clearly disturbed him, his face was almost as white as his hair.

"Spite," I muttered and looked around at the survivors. "I'll get them out of the cages. Medics, I want you to tend to the wounded and then run a life-scan search of this entire area. All the containers. We have missing people, and they may be Imperial citizens."

I started walking around to each of the force-cages, laying a hand atop them and focusing my energy-control powers long enough to deactivate the shield projector for each one.

The captive women were a mix of races, all quite beautiful in their often exotic ways. One was a youthful Brennian female, her scales almost violet, and vestigial wings draping iridescent sails down her back. Another was Toranian, her hair, skin, and eyes dyed golden, green, and orange, the colors mixing in almost hypnotic patterns. I caught myself staring at her three pert, bare breasts and looked away quickly. Both women were banged up and unconscious from the missile impacts, leaving me feeling a bit guilty. I freed them and waved the medics over to them.

I didn't recognize the race that the rest of the captives seemed to belong to. They were smaller than Vixxians, their skin of similar texture but darker on average, with a variety of hair and flesh colors that were mostly various shades of brown, pink, and gold.

"What race are these people?" I asked our Vixxian medic as he walked by.

He looked them over briefly and shrugged. "Human. They're a fringe world, well past the Frontier, in lawless space. The Thezlums harvest those worlds for a lot of their slaves. Most of them haven't gone too far past their own planetary atmospheres, and Earth is no exception. More than half the population still thinks that life only exists on their planet."

"That must make them easy pickings for the slavers." The human women were quite…attractive, even compared to the others. Vixxian women suffered from hormone problems thanks to the androgen issue, and they were usually slim, small-breasted and -hipped, and infertile.

Apparently, if anything, humans suffered from the opposite problem. My eyes widened while they swept over the four survivors one at a time as I released them from their cages. Their curves seemed almost exaggerated compared to what I was used to, rich hips, lush hair, satiny skin, bountiful breasts… *Lysi is going to make a fool of himself around these girls,* I thought as I walked up to the last cage. I was suddenly wishing that my armored codpiece was a bit…roomier. *Maybe I will too if I'm not careful.*

I looked down at the last human as I freed her…and found myself suddenly staring. *Hold that thought…*

The other humans had been pale-skinned, two with pink complexions and one with amber. But the lovely lady in the last cage was far darker, her skin a deep bronze-brown, and her features fuller and softer-looking. Her hair was a sleek, rippling black, and her curves were even more robust than those of her fellows. My eyes fixed on the mounds of her breasts beneath her soft purple tunic, and the ache from my trapped erection suddenly got so bad that I let out a little grunt of discomfort.

Shaking off my entrancement, I quickly realized that blood was matted into her hair just above one temple. *She must have knocked her head when the cage got thrown around. Don't those idiot Thezlums ever secure their cargo properly? Or their prisoners, for that matter?* I felt a surge of anger that sent blue sparks dancing along my hands. I quickly controlled it, but it gnawed at my belly as I crouched down beside the alien beauty.

I slid my visor up then removed my gauntlets, hanging them on my belt. Gently, I scooped the unconscious woman up off the cold floor. As our skin made contact, I felt an electric tingle run all through me, and I caught my breath. Then I chided myself for getting distracted and started looking her over for further injuries. Aside from a few bruises, the gash on her head and her unconsciousness seemed to be the only problems.

I held her gingerly in my arms as I drank in her beauty. Leaning down, I smelled something divine that I couldn't quite place. It was light and airy, reminding me of blooming season. And under it, mixing with the faint tang of her blood, was a delicate musk that made my heart speed up.

I smiled to myself as I wrapped my arms around her tightly, feeling the suppleness of her body. A surge of arousal raged through me, and I shivered, suddenly preoccupied with a vision of her in my bed. *Her limbs wrapped around mine, her breasts pressed warm against my chest as I thrust into her… Stop. It's not the time.* It took everything I had in me to tear my eyes away from her and call a medic over.

The slim young Vixxian closed his violet eyes and ran a psychic scan, muttering rapidly about his observations as he did so. "The concussion isn't very bad, but she has some other complications. We'll need to close the gash on her head now. Other than that, she has several bruises, a minor case of transport shock, and mild dehydration." He looked up at me calmly. "With assistance from your healing acceleration abilities, she should be back on her feet after a few hours' sleep."

"Good. I'll tend to her, then. You deal with the other wounded." I stared down at her face for a moment longer, then shifted my grip on her and laid my hand over the wound. The skin of my palm prickled as one of my secondary powers kicked in in response to her injury. She let out a soft whimper and arched her neck slightly. I felt a drop of sweat run down my back under my armor, but I forced myself to focus on healing her. The smell of blood faded slightly, and when I drew my hand away, the gash was gone.

I turned to my team, who had finished their sweep of this section of the cargo bay and gathered while I had worked on the woman's wound. "I want you to take all the captives and help them to our ship. We are taking them back to Vixxia Prime," I informed them. "And make sure there are no more slaves on this damn freighter."

"Yes, sir," the medic who had helped me tend to my lovely charge replied. "What about that one?"

"I will…see to this one." I looked down at her, knowing that my distraction was obvious to my men but unable to draw myself away. "Perhaps she knows something about the circumstances of her capture that will explain the Thezlums' change in tactics."

With that, I walked back out, heading to my ship with the lovely female in my arms. I glanced down at her now and again and felt my heart pound. I had never been this attracted to anyone at first sight before. It intrigued me. I should have been worried about the vanishing crew and missing slaves…but all I could do as I carried her back was wonder how she would react to me when she finally opened her eyes.

CHAPTER 5
MISTY

I woke up slowly and found myself afraid to open my eyes. After what had happened last time, I was damn worried about what I would see when I did so. I tried to tell myself that I was being ridiculous, but my heart started pounding and I took a minute to just lie there, sorting out what I could of my surroundings while pretending to still be asleep.

I was warm for the first time since I had left my apartment. I was lying on a mattress that was properly soft, even if the texture of the fabric covering it felt a little slick and strange. A thick blanket of some fluffy material covered me up to my chin, and someone had undressed me and put me in a thigh-length gown of the same stuff.

The air smelled clean here, with a faint tinge of what smelled like spicy incense. And best of all…it was quiet. No rumble of ship engines. No big, creepy elephant-skinned aliens barking at me. I screwed up my courage and opened my eyes, only to find myself in a strange new place.

Everything around me was pale, clear, or iridescently metallic, with organic curves, as clean and beautiful as the other place had been filthy and ugly. The oval-shaped bed I lay on was more like a beanbag or gigantic pillow, and it sat next to a dressing table and a slim wardrobe of some kind. Round windows with glass that bulged outward like bubbles lined two of the walls, letting in sunlight.

Am I back on Earth? Or is this another planet entirely?

I blinked a few times, trying to clear my vision as my mind attempted to recall what had happened. *Why am I here? Why does my head hurt like hell?* I was thirsty too. Last thing I remembered, I had been in a cage in that cargo hold, and suddenly things had started shaking and flying around…

I hit my head. That's it. I'm surprised I survived. I sat up and looked around further—and my eyes grew big with fright. *Oh, shit.*

Sitting right there on a tufted seat at the foot of my bed, another alien watched me intently. I froze, staring at him, taking in white hair, lots of muscles, and a cloak like a medieval prince. *At least this one is wearing clothes.* But that didn't make him any less intimidating. Especially since he was maybe seven feet tall, had at least two weapons on him, and was built like a truck.

I jumped back as fast as I could, immediately remembering what the other aliens had done to me. My legs tangled in the blanket, and I fell off the bed, once again hitting my head—this time, against the damn dressing table. "Ow! Oh…dammit…" I rolled over, holding my head.

"Careful," the alien called out in a smooth voice, a little laugh at the bottom of his tone. I glared up at him—and our eyes met for the first time.

I felt a jolt go through me as I realized the guy I was looking at was about as far from my kidnappers as any being could be. Big and muscular was where the resemblance ended, in fact. Those deep blue eyes in that pale face, that long and soft-looking hair with the braids at the temples, that powerfully built body and those well-carved features… Even the funky points on his ears made him seem more attractive. *Wow.* With my luck, he was hostile too and just toying with me, but…

He came over to me slowly. "Can you understand me?"

"Yeah, they put a chip…thing in me. Translates stuff." I rubbed the tiny lump, which was barely more noticeable to me than a mole. It was the bigger bump—the one that flashed with red light—that really creeped me out.

"I see. That's lucky. I don't think you'd want me to come after you with an implant gun right now. Here, let me help you up." He tried to offer me a hand, and I took it after a moment's hesitation. But my legs collapsed under me as soon as I tried to stand, and I started falling. The alien reacted quickly, scooping me into his arms as if on instinct. I blinked in shock, but…this was an awful lot nicer than the way the other aliens had handled me.

He slowly leaned me against his body. I felt the rippling muscle of his chest and a surprisingly fast heartbeat through the slick black material of his sleeveless tunic. Instantly, I felt my body relax against his as he held me as if I were weightless. The fear that he was planning me harm dissolved as I felt for the first time in my life what it was like to be treated gently by a man big enough to snap me in half.

Hesitantly, I looked up. As I did, he leaned down and kissed the top of my head. I let out a little yelp of shock at the brush of those surprisingly soft lips, and then just blinked up at him in confusion.

Wait a second. What did I miss here?

At once, the pain that had settled in the back of my skull vanished. "You hit your head pretty hard back there. You should be more careful." That honey-like voice made my toes curl even harder.

Damn. Who is this guy?

"Yes, well, the last time I woke up and an alien was looking at me, I had just been kidnapped, tagged like an animal, and thrown in a cage." I reached up to touch my head where I had hit it. No more bleeding, but the skin still felt a little tender. "How did you…?"

"Apparently, your race has no significant regenerative abilities. I can accelerate what an individual does have through physical contact." A faint hint of flirtation entered his tone. "I could enhance them further, but that would require that we be…intimate."

My breath caught in my throat at the idea, and I couldn't properly answer. I couldn't stop myself from staring at him, completely enthralled by his good looks. My body felt like it was on fire. *Who is this guy—and how can he have such an effect on me?* "Wow," I mumbled under my breath before I could restrain myself.

The unknown alien peered down at me, the multiple gold rings in his pointed ears tinkling slightly as his head tilted. "Are you all right?" he asked, concern drawing his narrow silver brows together.

"Yes. Or, I will be." I couldn't feel much pain at all anymore, and the strength was returning to my legs. Not that I really wanted him to set me down yet. Being in his arms was just too damn comfortable. "But where am I? Who are you? What happened to the ship I was on? All I remember is that the ship came under attack. The whole cargo bay shook, and one of the containers fell and knocked into my cage. I got bounced around a lot, and then everything went black."

The stranger sighed and settled onto the edge of the bed, loosening his grip so that I could move away if I wished. I didn't, and he blinked and smiled faintly. Delicately, he rested his hands on my stomach, letting them linger there as a rush of heat gathered in my belly. I didn't know whether it was from his touch or from his power, but I wanted it to keep going.

"Let me explain," he answered calmly. His face had a serious expression. "You were captured by Thezlums. They are infamous for scavenging the galaxy for slaves to sell on the black market. They work under the authority of the Dragicans, who run the intergalactic slave trade."

"That's exactly what they said…more or less. They did mention they were going to sell me, and they talked about the Dragicans." As a goddamned sex slave. The horror of what I had just escaped made me shudder as it crept up on me.

"Yes. Their next stop was going to be a raid on some of our outer colonies. My brothers and I came to capture the ship, only to discover you and the other captives." He frowned slightly. "One of the other humans didn't make it, and the others are still recovering. I hope they weren't personal friends of yours."

"No, total strangers. We weren't captured as a group. I think they grabbed a bunch of people from Central Park using those…beams." I rubbed my temple, sighing through my nose as I struggled to process everything enough to explain it.

To think that I simply had been out jogging not so long ago, and now, in such a short amount of time, I had met two alien species. *What is going on? Am I even awake, or am I dreaming?* Deep down, I knew that I was conscious and that I needed to get away from wherever I was and return home. *I should be running away and looking for some way to escape back to my life.* But as close encounters came…I liked this one a lot. It left me conflicted.

Obviously, I couldn't just walk outside and catch a cab back to Earth. If I really was stuck on some alien planet, I had no other choice but to work with this strange man and his people. I needed to persuade them to help me get home. "My name's Misty," I said warmly, trying to draw him out. "What's yours?"

He finished whatever he was doing and drew his hands back, leaving me disappointed. I couldn't remember ever enjoying a man's touch that much. But then he gave me an apologetic little smile and inclined his head. "Ah, my manners are lacking. I apologize. Prince Craze, heir to the throne of the Vixxian Empire at your service." The alien finished his statement with a look of pride on his face.

"Wait…so you are a prince? And you saved me?" I paused. "What is this, a fairy tale or something?" I muttered under my breath. *Parts of this sure feel like it. He even rescued me from monsters.*

"Hmm?" he asked, lifting a well-groomed white eyebrow in my direction. "What's a fairy tale?" The pointy-eared nonhuman could have passed for an elf on steroids.

"It's a type of story from my homeland, about magical creatures and strange adventures." I looked at him with hopeful eyes. I had to convince him to get me home. "Craze, if you are the prince…then you must have influence, right? You can get me back to Earth, can't you?"

He gazed at me wistfully for a moment and reached up very briefly, brushing a long-fingered hand down my hair so delicately that I barely felt it. I blinked up at him, tingling, emotions tangled, and felt my heart sink when he shook his head apologetically.

"I wish I could, but there's an unpleasant complication, which would have to be resolved before we sent you home. That tracking disc in your neck."

I reached up to touch the foreign object under my skin and shuddered. "What about it?"

"Not only do we have no idea what the health effects being stuck with it long-term would be, but you wouldn't be able to explain its presence to your fellow humans. And since it glows, it will be rather difficult to hide. But the worst part is that now that you're tagged, the Thezlums can track you anywhere. You and your associates would simply be picked up again the next time they made a sweep of your world." He winced slightly in sympathy. "Until those trackers are eradicated, the safest place for you is here, well behind the Imperial frontier and under my protection."

I gave him as warm and diplomatic a smile as I could manage under the circumstances. "As wonderful as that sounds, especially the company..." I saw a gleam in his eye as I flirted back a little, and I pushed on with a bit of reluctance. "I really need to get back to my responsibilities at home. Can you get this...tracker thing...out of me?"

He brushed aside my hair and peered at the disc. I felt his breath blow lightly against the back of my neck, and I clamped my knees together hard, heartbeat speeding up.

A few seconds later, he sighed. "These tracker discs are an upgrade from the ones the slavers have been using for years. They're booby-trapped. We attempted surgical removal of the discs on one of your fellow prisoners. It detonated a small charge, which opened her artery. She bled out before healing acceleration could save her." His smile faded as he told the gruesome story, and I found myself shivering. "I had hoped that you were outfitted with one of the older trackers, but I'm afraid that's not the case."

My stomach dropped further. I was starting to feel sick. "So... what can I do?"

"I think breakfast would be a good start. And then perhaps I can answer some more questions for you." He gave me a warm smile, which I wanted to return but couldn't.

As attractive as he was, and even though I owed him for saving me, his company couldn't make up for the fact of my being trapped here.

My whole plan to get his help escaping had shattered in seconds. *What am I supposed to do now? Am I really stuck on some unknown planet with a bunch of aliens, while a bunch of other aliens will hunt me down if I leave? How can I fix this? And can I trust Craze to help when I'm not even sure if I can trust myself around him?*

CHAPTER 6
CRAZE

I peered into the woman's dark eyes, feeling my heart speeding up at the mere sight of her. Tenderly, I rested my hand on hers, giving it a slight squeeze as my skin tingled on contact. The mix of fascination, raw lust, and protectiveness I felt eclipsed almost any emotion I had ever felt in my life. At that moment, I knew I couldn't lose her.

I found myself pleading my case almost reflexively. "But do not be saddened. Vixxia Prime is a wonderful planet, and I will not let any harm come to you. You will not want for company—or anything you need."

I saw the conflict in her eyes. She seemed as shocked by my sudden interest as I was, and clearly, she wanted to go home. Yet, she hadn't pulled away from me once, and I kept hearing her breath catch when I touched her.

"Look," she said finally, a sad smile on her face. "You're nice, you saved my life, and you're really hot. And I truly appreciate the offer. But you can't expect me not to want to get home or not to ask for help finding a way."

I paused, gathering my breath. "I know this must be a lot for you to process, but please, try to understand." I pressed her hand a little harder. "The Thezlums are one of the few races capable of faster-than-light travel. It's one of the areas where they exceed even us. And it is they who have whatever technology or technique is needed to safely remove those discs. We would need access to both technologies to get you and your fellow humans home safely."

Even if we succeeded in all of that, I still wouldn't want to send her home. But I did recognize that, ultimately, it was her choice. I was just hoping that the difficulty of achieving it would help her settle her mind about staying instead. I knew I could offer her a good life here. And—for reasons I could not fully understand—I very much wanted to.

Maybe I can find other ways to persuade her, I thought, as my gaze swept over her again. She was so soft and warm against me...and neither of us seemed to want to move away. The bed was right there. Perhaps we could simply—

"Wait. You *do* have access to one of their ships. The one you rescued me from." She looked back at me with faint excitement and hope in her eyes, and my heart sank.

"That is true. We might be able to salvage at least some of the technology that we need from there...if I can get approval for the salvage mission. My father did not want the usual salvage teams to go near it. It's too close to the frontier."

My parents could be glacially slow about approving nonessential but risky missions, but that could only work in my favor. It would give me time to woo this fascinating woman properly.

"But it means there's a chance." She brightened, and I felt a stab of guilt at my ulterior motives.

"Yes, there is, and a very good one at that. It simply takes time to make a case to my Emperor. But if I can convince him that we might be able to reverse-engineer their transporters and other technologies, I think he'll be interested." My mouth was dry, and my cock throbbed insistently against my thigh.

"I...I can live with that, then, if you'll at least try." She swallowed and nodded, looking worried but determined.

She clearly loves her home-world. But perhaps I can still win her heart away from it. "Please, let me introduce you to my parents, the Emperor and Empress. I am sure they would be delighted to meet you. They have already met the other women we rescued from the wreckage. We have a shortage of compatible females on this world thanks to an environmental issue. I know my parents are quite interested in offering them a place here, and I'm certain they would make you the same offer."

Misty nibbled the corner of her lip. I could see the hesitation in her expression. "I don't know. Things like this…expecting me to decide right away, when I have a chance of getting back to everything I know…"

I sighed. "I swear by all the honor I have gained in battle, I will make every effort to help you get home if you choose to do so. I will also be doing my best to show you the merits of staying, however." I couldn't help my flirtatious look, and I saw her glance away shyly, a tiny smile on her lips.

"Oh, will you?" she murmured, voice gone a little throaty and amused, eyes gleaming beneath her thick black lashes.

Before I could answer, there was a loud rapping at the door. "Come in," I answered, recognizing that gauntleted fist.

In a flourish, the door opened, and Ragar strode into the room. "I thought I'd find you curled up with one of the refugees." He gave me an annoyed look. "You didn't even stick around long enough to judge the contest between Lysi and me! Where are your priorities?"

I bristled immediately, with a vehemence that startled the both of us. "You dare come into my quarters and make accusations of poor judgment?" I barked, moving away from Misty and standing to challenge him. *He's one to go off about priorities when he wanted to beg off the entire mission to go have more of the sex he can have anytime he wants!*

"The Emperor and Empress want to see you," Ragar answered as he rubbed the back of his neck. "They sent me with the message. Don't be so defensive, Craze. The contest was your idea, and you still have duties to the rest of us." His gaze turned toward Misty, who looked away from him shyly. "No matter how fetching the distraction is."

I felt my ears prickle with embarrassment at his comment. "Ragar, I haven't forgotten about the contest. I'll see you and Lysi about it as soon as we've checked in with the throne room." Normally, I would have challenged him to a sparring match and knocked him on his ass a few times to remind him not to question me, but Misty was already on edge, and something about being around her made me want to curb my more violent urges.

His eyebrows rose at the calmness of my reply, and he glanced between Misty and me incredulously. Then he seemed to relax and inclined his head. "I'll tell them you're on your way, then."

"You do that." I saw him out and then turned back to Misty, who had stood up and was looking down at her short sleeping-gown. The fluffy white cloth looked particularly fetching against her ebony skin, and I had to fight down another surge of desire. "What's the matter?" I asked, gaze tracing down the curves of her legs.

"I can't go like this. Where are my clothes?" She sounded so worried that I laughed a little and couldn't help but tease her.

"What's wrong with that?" I indicated the gown.

She put her fists on her hips and then gestured at herself. "Uh, well, I'm barefoot, I'm bare-assed, and almost my entire legs are showing—"

"Yes, and they're very fetching legs indeed. So, what's the problem?" I blinked at her rapidly, and her consternation turned into amusement and a touch of annoyance.

"Dammit, be serious!" She tossed a pillow at me. "I'm not visiting your parents in a fucking spa wrap, and that's final."

I caught it and tossed it back on the bed, then walked up to her. "Hmm. Well, you could always take it off, if you'd prefer that."

She let out a little squeak of outrage and reached up to give me a playful smack on the chest. I caught her wrist gently but firmly. That tingle shot through me again, and from the sudden dilation of her eyes, I knew she felt it too. A connection.

I moved closer to her, staring down at her, stopping just close enough for her breasts to brush delightfully against my lower chest. She relaxed in my grip, looking back at me with wide, suddenly bright eyes. Her lips parted ever so slightly. Our eyes locked for a moment— and then she yelped in shock as my palms sparked reflexively with bluish energy.

"What's wrong with your hands?" she asked, backing away in fright as she saw the little flashes of electricity fly from one fingertip to another.

A little frustrated, I looked down. "I'm sorry. Psionic of my strength sometimes experience power leakage. It happens when I'm feeling… strongly about something. It won't hurt you."

She relaxed slightly, then tilted her head curiously. "Is that normal?"

"Of course. Don't you have psychic abilities on your planet?" I inquired, a little bewildered. Every Vixxian was born with their own unique set of talents, ranging from peasants divining with forked sticks, to members of the Imperial Family controlling starships with their minds.

It seemed strange that this foreign being couldn't recognize one of the most common Vixxian traits. Then again, maybe it shouldn't have. Although I had never met any, I had heard of races that didn't boast any mastery of psi ability. Perhaps they had it latently; such things had never been studied. But about one in ten sapient races in our region of space couldn't so much as move a feather with their minds.

She simply shook her head at me, and I had to quash a surge of pity. Another reason for the Thezlums to target humans, they could not defend themselves well without weapons. "We only have legends of things like that. But then again…we only have legends of aliens as well."

At least she had an open mind. "It is equal parts inborn talent and a whole lot of training and discipline. Fine control requires years of practice. May I demonstrate?" I held out a hand and looked to her.

Misty gave that curious little head-tilt again, her silky hair spilling over her shoulder, "Go ahead."

I closed my eyes and concentrated my energy. Slowly, my sword Exredilan slid free of its brackets on the wall and levitated over to my palm as the sparks of electricity adhered around it like a tether.

"Wow," she whispered in astonishment. "That's quite amazing. More so than anything I've ever seen on Earth, that's for sure." She gave me a bashful look.

I smiled to myself. Maybe I was making a good enough impression to catch her interest. I was determined to keep trying until I did. "Come. Let me introduce you to the Emperor and Empress. They must be eager to meet you if they sent Ragar as their messenger."

"Who is he anyway?" she questioned, with a sweet purity in her voice that sent my heart thundering in my chest.

"He is my brother. The middle of all my siblings. There are four of them, and they're rather…diverse. Don't worry. In time, you will meet them all." I went over to my clothes press and opened it, pulling out a box which I handed to her. "Here, I… took the liberty of having some clothes made for you."

"Thank you." She took the box from me and set it on the bed, pulling it open. Her eyes widened slightly as she pulled out the filmy, pale pink gown beneath. Matching soft boots and a sheer set of stockings completed the outfit. "It's beautiful."

"You are quite welcome. There's a changing-alcove behind that curtain." I had no idea what she would look like in Vixxian clothing, but I thought the touch of formality would help her make a good impression on my parents. I just wished I had had time to procure some jewels to go with it, though her round little ears didn't look like they would take much decoration. I would have loved to dangle something gorgeous and eye-catching just above those gorgeous and eye-catching breasts. To dazzle her a little, as she had dazzled me.

When she returned from behind the curtain, however, I saw that she needed no adornment. I stared; I couldn't help it. On a slim, boyish Vixxian woman, the dress would have floated ethereally. But Misty's spectacular body pushed rebelliously against the confining fabric, its delicacy only emphasizing the robust curves just beneath.

The bed's right there… I thought again, feeling my cock straining the crotch of my leather leggings. "You look magnificent," I breathed, hoping she didn't notice the proud bulge. Hoping even more that my *parents* didn't notice it, or worse, my brothers.

I took her hand. That same jolt of pleasure went through me again, and I wondered what it would feel like to place my hands on her hips and pull her close. "Come. The transport to the throne room is down this hallway."

We entered the main corridor of the lowest ring of the palace, which ran around its inner wall. With a measured step, I guided her toward the transport tube. She would have to ride close to me when we took a disc up to the top level since she had no psi ability to command them. But I certainly didn't mind that. Not a bit.

I could have traversed the halls of this palace with my eyes closed. That was fortunate, for right now, I found myself thoroughly distracted by Misty's beauty. The luscious curves of her ass. The radiance of her skin. Those big, liquid eyes. She was simply too enthralling for me to look away.

After a too-brief ride up the tube with her in my arms, we arrived at the twin-gilded doors of the throne room. "I'm nervous," she admitted, swallowing as she stared at the door.

"Don't be," I reassured quickly. "I am here with you." But deep down, I wondered what my parents would make of her.

CHAPTER 7
MISTY

I went mute with awe as I entered the throne room. The mixture of Medieval-looking carved stone and the high-tech screens and computer equipment jarred me a little. I had never seen anything like it —especially on this scale. The throne room was as large as a small airplane hangar.

The room centered on two tall stone and crystal thrones on a low dais crammed with esoteric-looking computer equipment. They were occupied by two regal individuals who almost seemed like statues at first. In appearance, they both closely resembled Craze, with flowing pale hair and pointed ears. The male wore black armor and a rich golden cloak, his female companion wore an elaborate cloth-of-gold gown and an even richer cloak, edged in golden fur.

They had blank looks on their faces as Craze approached their thrones with me. But first the male, then the female blinked, seeming to come out of a trance, and looked down at me slowly.

"Who is this?" the man asked, scrutinizing me.

"This is Misty, of Earth. She was one of the captives we saved from the Thezlum ship, Father," Craze answered in a confident but respectful tone.

I glanced between them. *I thought they were eager to meet me, but now they're acting like they didn't expect a visitor. Did Craze lie about that, or did his brother?* I would have to find out. It worried me a little. Craze was so hot and so friendly. But could he have an ulterior motive?

The Empress was staring at me, I realized with a sudden shock. Her expressionlessness had given way to a faint look of curiosity, but a cold one, as if she were examining some curious new insect she had found instead of a person. I shuddered slightly and stepped closer to Craze. *What is wrong with her? What is wrong with both of them? And why did they send that Ragar guy to summon us if they weren't expecting me?*

"As for you, young lady." The Emperor leaned forward, tugging thoughtfully at his narrow, braided beard. "What is your name, and what do you have to say for yourself?"

I squared my shoulders and looked up at him. "My name is Misty Kendrick, and I want to go home."

I felt Craze stiffen next to me, and I frowned slightly, confused. But I had only been honest.

The Emperor nodded thoughtfully, and he and his wife exchanged glances. "Interesting. Though we have made a very generous resettlement offer to the other humans among the refugees, all have made the same request. Is your home-world so pleasant to you?"

His face and voice held only the shallowest curiosity. He didn't seem fully capable of feeling emotions. I wondered if it was some disease…or perhaps it was something that happened naturally to Vixxians as they aged. I glanced at Craze and, suddenly, fiercely, hoped it was the latter. I had not known him long, but the idea that he might suddenly lose his heart horrified me.

I cleared my throat. "Well, Your Imperial Majesty…" I hesitated. *Did I get the title right? I don't even know if this stupid chip thing the Thezlums stuck in me is translating correctly.* "Earth isn't perfect, but it's home. I don't have…" I trailed off suddenly. *I don't have family there, or many friends, or a lover, or even a pet. Just a job where I do scut work all day and dream of being recognized.* My chin trembled. "I…"

The Empress's head tilted slightly, her brilliant green eyes not blinking enough.

"Go on, child," the Emperor said, his voice holding what small warmth he seemed able to muster.

"Earth isn't perfect, but it's home. A home that I was kidnapped from. And as much as I appreciate the rescue…" I glanced Craze's way and found him watching me like a hawk, "I, at least, want to be able to stay or go of my own free will."

The Empress sat back slightly, and when she spoke, her low voice had a strangely brittle edge to it. "Freedom is important. We do not keep hostages here outside of prisoners of war." She turned her jewel-colored eyes to her companion, her expression never changing. He returned her gaze, one eyebrow arching slightly, and she nodded once. "We must consider her appeal, my husband."

"Hmm." The Emperor tugged his beard again. He seemed to grow more animated as the conversation continued, almost as if his soul had been elsewhere and was just now returning bit by bit to his body. Even his skin had regained some of its color. "The matter of returning you safely, and without further molestation by the Thezlum slavers, is a very complicated problem. The solution may not be easy, quick, or safe to come by. Nevertheless, I will give all consideration to your request." He turned his eyes to his son. "Per our discussion, I will confer with our science ministry about the possibility of drawing…inspiration from technology seized from the Thezlum craft."

I blinked and looked at Craze, who glanced at me and then away. *They already had the conversation about stealing the other aliens' transport technology? But he was with me the whole time! How did he tell his father in that short time, without leaving my presence?*

Craze inclined his head, silky hair slipping off his shoulder and hanging in a curtain beside his face. I couldn't see his expression for a moment. "Thank you, Father."

"Very well, then. Keep our human friend here safe for the time being, while I see what can be done. But…remember your place as the Imperial heir, Craze," the Emperor said with an edge to his voice that unnerved me and made even Craze swallow.

"As you wish, Father," Craze said without missing a beat. He bowed to his parents, I followed suit clumsily, and when I straightened, I noticed the Emperor's eyebrows were nearly at his hairline and a small smile was lingering on his face. I looked down and belatedly remembered I wasn't in my hoodie anymore. *Oh, shit. Oops. That would be why girls in cleavage-baring dresses curtsy.*

The moment of total ridiculousness in the middle of the tense scene almost broke me, and I stifled a giggle. *Well, I guess the old guy's a bit livelier than I thought.*

And at least he seemed marginally sympathetic. The Empress on the other hand… I didn't know if she disliked me or disliked being pulled from whatever bizarre trance she had been in when I had walked in. Her icy curiosity had made me feel like a lab specimen, and I wondered with creeping horror if she had been this way for all of Craze's childhood.

"Is that all?" The Emperor turned to his son, who nodded his head.

"You are dismissed." The Empress barely glanced at us as she spoke. She was already going into a trance again, eyes glazing over, and her posture painstakingly straight, as if there was some sort of apparatus keeping her upright. I started to wonder if she was wired into the surrounding computer network in some way.

At her command, Craze grabbed my hand. "Come. I will show you around the palace." Again, I felt energy prickle through my skin. My heart beat faster at the sensation. *Why is this alien making me feel this way? Is someone who isn't even human really turning me on? Let's face facts, Misty. He could have anything in his pants, from a cloaca to tentacles.*

I let him lead me. He seemed lost in thought right now as well, and I had a lot to think about. *Can I trust him with my body, or at all?* I didn't even know if their race was good or evil. For all I knew, these Vixxian people could be just as cruel in their own way as the apelike aliens that had kidnapped me.

There was something…wrong…with the Empress, though everyone around her seemed to treat her behavior as perfectly normal. I knew that it wasn't, and the fact that I couldn't read her attitude toward me at all only made things worse.

Her husband seemed much more present, but even he had been strangely remote. And the reluctance I felt from Craze whenever I spoke of leaving made it more confusing. How much like humans were these beings, really, when it came to emotion and morals?

Nervously, I gnawed at my lip, trying to process this information, but as Craze led me along and quietly pointed out different parts of the palace, I couldn't deny the heat gathering between my legs just from holding his hand and breathing in his sharp, masculine musk. I couldn't lie to myself. Deep down, I knew I found this alien incredibly attractive. I could think of a dozen things I wanted to do to him, and with him. I just didn't know what to do about those feelings.

I could always just take him to bed and see what happens. I wasn't all that into casual sex, normally. Every time I'd tried it back in New York City, I had ended up with some idiot who came in two minutes and left me unsatisfied. Thanks to fuckboy culture, half of them asked for anal within five minutes of meeting me. *Yes. Maybe the problem was that the guys on offer really didn't do much for me, even before we went to bed.*

Craze, though…who had rescued me, who could have broken me but was always gentle. Craze, who stared at me like a starving man when he thought I wasn't looking. He made my toes curl with barely a touch. If I were going to make an exception to my rushing-into-sex rule, it would be the alien hunk next to me.

What would fucking him even be like?

So far, the only thing I knew about how Vixxians related to each other came from the crazy contrast between Craze's touchy-feely affection and the icy, almost mechanical formalities of the throne room. I didn't yet know how sexuality played out with these aliens, any more than I knew what Craze was packing in that leather codpiece. *But I'm just itching to find out.*

As we walked through the corridors, these thoughts kept me preoccupied. I barely registered the gathering-halls, audience chambers, or even the ride back down on that weird floating disc. *Being held close to Craze's body again on the ride down, however, I remembered every second of.* Eventually, I snapped out of it and looked around. *Are we back on the bottom floor? I can't even tell anymore.*

I couldn't recognize anything around me from the walk up. "Where are we going?" I asked as we sped up a little. Without answering, Craze stopped before a set of heavy, bluish metal doors. He turned and pushed them open, and welcome sunlight and clear, crisp air flooded over me as we stepped outside. "Wow…" I breathed as we walked out onto a thick lawn of blue-green moss.

The courtyard at the base of the palace, surrounded by its lowest ring, was enormous, containing acres and acres of land. I could have gotten in my usual exercise just by running across to the far end and back. Flowering vines in a rainbow of colors climbed the walls, giving off a rich, sweet scent. Maybe a quarter of the land here was devoted to a gigantic network of launchpads occupied by immense silver rockets. The rest rambled freely, the lawn crisscrossed by shining stone paths and dominated by a large central plaza.

"Do you like it?" Craze chuckled as he tugged me toward the plaza. At a distance, all around the palace walls, iridescent metal buildings soared into the sky. Brightly dressed aliens from multiple races wandered the courtyard, alone or in small groups that chatted together as they walked. I couldn't stop gawking at all the sights and sounds, my mind trying to process everything.

"What are we doing out here?" I finally asked, watching as a tiny Vixxian kid bounded past with a dog-sized purple lizard grunting happily at his heels. It was like a day in the park here…on another planet. I couldn't ever forget that part.

"I want to show you something," he whispered, his voice hushed as if he was letting me in on a secret. I shivered as I felt butterflies develop in my stomach. I didn't know what this alien was planning, but for some reason, it excited me.

I followed him faithfully, suddenly eager for this new adventure. Now that I was free and out in the sun and air, I was starting to wonder if living on this planet would be all that bad. After all, it was much more interesting than my mundane life on Earth. *But also weirder, more dangerous, and a ton less familiar. I can't forget that part just because it's nice now.*

But it had been depressing to look back at my life on Earth and realize I wouldn't be leaving much of anything behind. Besides the job I might one day have if I worked long and hard enough, anyway. But what kind of life would I have here if I stayed? *So far, besides the nice weather and not being in the cargo hold of that slaver ship, the only reason for me to like the place is Craze.*

Looking up at him and feeling that flush of heat run through me again, though, I had to admit that it was a compelling reason.

Halfway across the field, Craze took a side path that led to the depths of a strange-looking stand of trees. There were bent in odd formations, as if shaped by constant high winds, and their broad hand-sized leaves were a plum color. Bright orange, pear-shaped fruit hung from the lower boughs, almost glowing in the dim light. At times, it was all too much to look at.

Abruptly, we stopped in front of a large canopy of leaves that had tangled together to form a gatelike structure.

"I come here when I want to be alone, but now I want to share it with you." Craze's voice held a hint of tenderness as he uttered the words. Once again, I found myself shivering in reaction to him.

Oh man. I didn't know he had a romantic streak. This just keeps getting harder and harder to resist. I looked back at him, at the way his dark blue eyes shone as he gazed at me, and I had to smile. *This isn't just lust for him. Does he have a crush on me?*

That made him more endearing and made it easier to relax around him. If it had been simply lust, I might have felt in danger. But when he smiled at me like that, I knew he meant me no harm, after all. Quite the opposite, in fact. As we crossed through the archway, we continued to hold hands. The touch of his skin on mine alone was enough to make me feel so alive.

As Craze led me through the canopy, I gasped as I saw the beautiful sight before us. In front of me, beyond a narrow strip of fields and an even narrower beach of transparent pebbles, stretched a lake with water that looked and glittered like quicksilver in the bright sunlight pouring into the clearing. Pastel-colored flowers surrounded the lake, dancing in the gentle breeze. They sent up a rich, spicy scent that mixed beautifully with the earthy smell of the trees and moss. Crystal wind chimes hung from the trees closest to the lake, along with multi-colored ribbons. I could hear the soft chiming from them whenever the wind gusted.

"Where are we?" I murmured, mesmerized by the setting.

"This is Silviana's Center. It is believed that the great goddess who created Vixxia Prime emerged from this lake."

"So, this is a…shrine?" I looked down into the water, which shimmered over that bed of multicolored clear pebbles. Slim fish darted in its depths, changing their colors like octopi to blend in with the lake bed. Sometimes, only their golden eyes and trailing silvery fins showed. It was so far off from the church my mom had dragged me to for a few years that only the reverent hush to the site helped me to recognize it as such.

"Only members of the clergy or the Imperial Family are allowed here. Along with our guests, of course." He led me out into the clearing and settled down on the thick moss, lounging there with his eyelids at half-mast. "Come. Lie down beside me."

I bit the corner of my lip as my heart thumped in response. I couldn't believe how attracted I was to this alien. He had the perfect mix of exotic and familiar features. Many of his characteristics were human, but at the same time, he had this charming uniqueness, with his silver hair and impossibly blue eyes. His body could have passed for human…at least, what I had seen of it so far. A very tall, absolutely ripped human, anyway.

Naturally, I lay down beside him. I felt my cheeks growing hot as my eyes wandered down to his crotch. The leather was straining over a familiarly prominent bulge. Momentarily, I once again wondered what he had packing down there. After a few moments, I slammed my eyes shut, trying to clear my mind. No. I couldn't think about such things.

"You know, Vixxians are a unique race. We possess the strongest psychic powers in the known galaxy." He held out his palm. Again, it sparked with energy as he gazed into my eyes. My body shook as he captured me with his fierce look. It felt like the whole world had stopped. "But not only that, we can also lend our abilities to others… for a time."

I stared back at him, intrigued. He had shared his healing abilities with me by touching me, but I had no idea how he could possibly transfer control of such a power over to me. "How is it done? And… how long does it last?" The prospect of having powers of my own for a while intrigued me almost as much as being close to him did.

"It can be extended for a fair amount of time, but only when we are regularly…intimate," he admitted, his eyes glowing with silent desire.

I stared back at him, suddenly unable to catch my breath. What he was suggesting was nothing short of miraculous, and gaining it...and a potential edge in this unknown place...involved doing things I had already admitted to myself that I wanted to do. But did I dare take the plunge and agree?

CHAPTER 8
CRAZE

"Really?" Misty rolled toward me, moving closer as she tossed her hair back over her shoulder. I suddenly found myself distracted by the flash of her smooth, dark throat and the way her scent mixed with the odors of the spice-flowers around us.

"Yes," I answered, trying to keep my composure as she moved even closer and her breasts gently brushed against my chest. I was so sick of being mashed by the damned codpiece by now that I wanted to tear it off to give my poor cock proper room, but I held myself steady, wary of scaring her off.

"Show me." Her voice was steady as she made the request, her eyes bright. "I want to see if it can work on me too."

"You do understand that we must become lovers for this to happen," I clarified. I was so horny that it hurt, but I still did not want to take advantage of her in any way.

Suddenly, a grin appeared on her face, and her expression shifted to one of desire. Before I could stop her, she leaned forward and pressed her lips softly against mine, catching me off guard. "Show me," she demanded again, her eyes sparkling with enthusiasm as she placed her hand on my chest.

I took a shuddering breath as I felt my lust for her catch fire inside of me. Swiftly, I took her into my arms. "As you wish," I rasped and pulled her into a tight embrace, our hips pressing together in a way that made my trapped cock throb hard with impatience. I rolled us over so that she lay on top of me, the warm mounds of her breasts rubbing hard against my chest. Her legs straddled me as I felt her body quiver with excitement.

We kissed for a long time, my mouth exploring hers, my thin lips sliding and clinging against her full ones, while my hands glided over her back, down to her hips, and finally over the twin mounds of her perfect ass. I groaned into her mouth as I squeezed and kneaded her cheeks, and she whimpered and rocked her hips against me.

I quickly flipped us over and lay on top of her, pinning her down in the deep, soft moss. I took a moment to consider her dark eyes before I leaned down and ran my lips along the delicate skin of her neck and jawline. She tasted so sweet. My tongue instantly darted out of my mouth, teasing over the pulse in her neck before I kissed her fervently again.

My head pounded in time with my cock as I kissed and licked and nibbled from her ears down to the hollow of her throat, then lower, darting a tongue between her breasts. She squirmed, whimpering, her hands sometimes exploring my back, sometimes tangling in her hair as she whimpered encouragement.

My life had left me frustrated where women were concerned. Like most Vixxian males, I had owned more than one sexbot to try to deal with my unfulfilled urges. We always excused them, saying we were practicing for our wives. But "practice" wasn't why I had worn out three of them in the span of five years.

Frustration had taken its toll, and not just on my sexbots. Only once had I made a real connection with anyone before now, and that had ended in disaster. Now, however, that didn't matter. Now, I had this sweet-faced, soft-bodied goddess lying underneath me.

In my lust, my hands tightened around her wrists. "You asked for this," I whispered and kissed her hard, darting my tongue into her mouth. She tasted like copper and mint, and I felt the breath from her nostrils shiver against my cheek. She squirmed just a little under me, then gave in, her lips moving in response against mine.

This place was sacred and secluded by the tangled copse around it, but it was also just a short walk from the bustling plaza. Someone might hear. Someone might see.

The idea of that—the risk of it—only excited me more.

As we made out, I felt a thin trickle of my psychic power sliding into her where our lips met. She moaned out at the sensation, her whole body tensing and straining with pleasure beneath me. I smiled to myself as I let go of one of her wrists and ran my fingers down her body, letting them dance across her skin and the thin, smooth fabric of her gown.

I slid my fingers inside her overflowing bodice and finally felt the silky skin of her breast under my hand. Her nipple tightened at my touch. I ran my fingers over it and started alternately kneading and caressing as I ravaged her mouth.

Tiny whimpers of pleasure vibrated in her throat as she reached up impatiently with the hand not gripping my hair by the roots and pushed the dress off her shoulders.

Breath shuddering as well, I propped myself up one-handed and leaned down, letting my lips move across her collarbone. Slowly, they settled on her breast as I started to kiss it lightly, moving slowly toward her nipple.

Her back arched. "Stop teasing," she moaned, half plea and half order. Her fingers tugged at my hair as I blew my warm breath over her taut nipple. Then I fastened my lips over it firmly and started to suck.

She groaned, hips rocking under me as I ran my other hand down to stroke her other breast. Her heart beat fiercely against me as I kept pleasuring her, and I felt my head get light even as the ache in my groin spread hotly to my belly and thighs.

Finally, I raised my head to look down into her eyes, which were wide and dilated and drunk-looking with lust and pleasure. It was a beautiful sight, and I let out a soft groan, shaking suddenly with the instinctive need to claim her as my own.

I set my mouth on the muscle of her shoulder, and my teeth sank lightly into her flesh, just enough to break the skin. She cried out, arching her back, her hand in my hair pulling me closer. Pleased, I started to lap at the wound. The small amount of pheromone on my tongue worked to add to our growing connection.

I had to give her every reason I could think of to stay with me. I knew this instinctively, as thoroughly as I knew my need for air or food. I understood a little now why Ragar was always so preoccupied, and I wondered if that would be me from now on.

I certainly hoped so.

I put everything I had into pleasing her, exploring her with my hand as my mouth kept tonguing and suckling her breasts. I undressed her as I went, untying laces and unfastening stays, revealing increasingly warm skin until she lay gloriously nude under me.

I sat up, chest heaving, my heart thundering. *Someone could walk in on us here,* I reminded myself again, but that tiny voice of reason got lost in a torrent of lust as I stared down at her. Letting out a low rumble of desire, I stripped off my tunic and unbuckled my belt, kicking off boots and shoving down my trousers. It left me in a simple loincloth, which strained to hold my furious erection.

Her eyes were wild, ravenous, as she gazed at my bulging loincloth and then reached up for me, sliding her hands over my chest before tugging at my shoulders. Smiling, I returned to my effort to give her the kind of sex she wouldn't want to live without after.

My explorations soon had her trembling under me, her breath coming in little sips and her eyes glazed with pleasure and lust. I paid attention to the places where my stroking made her gasp loudest: her spine, the hollows of her hips, the firm globes of her ass, her neck, and her inner thighs. Finally, my hand slipped between us to caress the sleek, short-curled mound between her thighs.

I ran my fingertips over her plump sex, surprised and glad to find it familiar territory instead of something completely alien. I hadn't quite been sure about humans—though I had doubted the Dragicans would accept sex slaves without compatible bodies. Was it wrong to be glad that her strange misadventure had brought her to me? Perhaps, but I couldn't help it. Especially not now, as the heady tang of her arousal tickled my nostrils.

She squirmed and rolled her hips against my hand as I stroked the edges of her damp slit, then slipped my fingertips just inside to caress her soft inner flesh. She moaned louder and parted her legs, then whimpered when I teased her lips open and started exploring the soft, slick folds within.

I slipped two fingers into her easily, my cock shuddering with need as I felt those hot, sleek walls clinging to me. My thumb slipped upward, finding the soft nub of her clit beneath its hood, and gently rocked against it as I thrust my fingers in and out of her.

I watched her face as her eyes rolled closed and her whole body started to tense and relax in time with my movements. Her hips rocked against my hand, her nails dug softly into the skin of my back, and her voice had gone from soft pants to little cries that rose in volume and desperation as I went on.

I couldn't hold out, and increasingly, I felt that she couldn't either. Her legs were now wrapped around my waist as I pulled her closer. Our hips rubbed together, and I forcefully pressed my cloth-covered cock against her so she could feel my aching length brush her thigh. She moaned out, arching her back even more. "Please..." she begged, her voice sounding desperate as her fingers found their way into my hair, pulling at it again.

Her eagerness nearly drove me over the edge by itself, but I controlled my lust with an iron will. I knew I had to please her intensely before my own explosion forced a rest.

Moving down her body, I knelt between her legs, taking in the beautiful sight of her slick, swollen cunt. Gently, I ran my hands along the length of her stomach and down her thighs, teasing her as I rubbed small circles into her flesh, gradually coaxing her legs wide open.

I licked my lips in anticipation before I plunged down, taking her hips into my hands and hoisting her up. She moaned loudly as her legs rested on my shoulders, and my tongue slipped in between the lips of her pussy.

I heard her nails dig roughly into the moss as she squirmed under me. "Oh God..." she gasped and stretched out, head back, long shudders rolling through her. Her reaction was so violent that I wondered if human men hadn't developed this trick.

Yet another reason for her to stay around, I thought with a devious little smile before I started caressing her soft folds with the tip of my tongue. Her whole body jerked, and she let out a cry as if I had stabbed her. Then she fell back against the moss again, whimpering. "Don't stop…" she begged, and I dove in with greater fervor, rewarded by her rising cries and the juices that poured from her.

I closed my eyes, surrendering myself to the delights of tasting her flesh, my tongue lapping and swirling as her scent rose around me. I knew, as I buried my face in her sex and heard her voice go ragged and shaky with pleasure, that I would never get enough. I was addicted.

I teased her, keeping her on the edge of ecstasy for as long as either of us could endure. Finally, my cock ached so much with need that I couldn't carry on.

With a desperate groan, I pulled away from her and leaned back, tearing at the ties of my loincloth. She was left on the ground, panting for air, little whimpers of pleasure and frustration escaping from her parted lips. I smiled, knowing she had been overwhelmed. I could see it in the glazed-over look in her eyes. Then she reached for me, and I tore away the constraining cloth in my impatience.

Her eyes moved to my cock standing against my belly. I had no idea what the men of her species looked like, but from what her face told me, she seemed impressed. Satisfied by her expression, I rested my hand on my organ, now quite thick and purple-tipped.

"Oh God…" Misty groaned. I grinned with pride at her reaction and even more at her next words. "Please…Craze…I want you," she begged, her dark eyes imploring me to continue.

I knew I couldn't deny her, and I took care to fit my throbbing head inside of her in preparation. She squirmed under me, trying to push more of my cock inside of her. Gasping, I rammed my hips forward, plunging my cock inside of her, filling every inch. She wailed and started to writhe under me, lifting her hips to meet mine. Overtaken by lust, I pumped my cock in and out of her, my grunts becoming animal-istic as I lost all control. In my desire, I reached forward and harshly grabbed one of her breasts, kneading it between my strong fingers.

CHAPTER 9
MISTY

I screamed in pleasure as I felt his cock spread my flesh wide. I had never taken someone so big in my entire life. And he seemed to be getting bigger every time he shoved himself inside of me. Or maybe I was just going crazy from being this turned on. My whole body was racked with longing for my climax as he continued to assault my wet, hungry cunt, going harder and harder with each thrust.

"Fuck!" I screamed as he dug his sharp nails into my hip. I was almost there…and the more he drove me toward it without pushing me over, the wilder I got. My nails dug into his back and scratched deep, and my voice was starting to scare the birds out of the trees.

As for Craze, he was so far gone that he might have kept fucking me even if someone had walked up and stabbed him. Unrelentingly, he ravished my tight womanhood, harsh groans pushing out of him every time our hips met. My juices spilled down my thighs as I felt myself coming a hair closer to the edge of orgasm with each thrust.

Suddenly, he leaned down, sinking his teeth into the side of my neck. I screamed as white-hot pleasure filled my body, coursing through my veins until my heart struggled to keep up. My cries aroused him further. He pounded away at me in ways that would have hurt like hell if I hadn't been wet and hungry for him. But he had made sure that I was.

My back arched and my breasts bounced as my body was pleasured increasingly with each passing second. A thin layer of sweat covered my skin. All too soon, it was too much for me to handle, and I lost all control. My scream sent a flock of birds out of the trees as I came so hard it almost hurt. "Yes! Yes!" Another long moan and I collapsed under him, whole body tingling.

Still, Craze relentlessly continued his rampage, his free hand all over me, sharp nails leaving thin lines of pain along my skin that only excited me more. Then it trailed down between us, and he started kneading the top of my mound as he kept pounding away at me. I felt myself melt into him. Never had I felt this good with a man. I wanted more. "Fuck. Keep going. Don't stop."

Craze couldn't respond. His lips were now locked around my breast, sucking hard on my nipple as his skilled tongue toyed with it until I felt my body start to tense deliciously again. Goose bumps formed on my skin as my fingers tangled in his hair to pull him even closer. Wanting to feel him more, I began gyrating my hips.

Craze growled with pleasure in response and rammed himself into me even harder. My whole body shuddered as I orgasmed hard again, the folds of my cunt tightening around him in long spasms. A silent scream strained my throat as I rolled my head back and forth on the moss.

It felt like he would split me in half at any moment. My fingers dug into his skin as I felt my muscles tightening in excitement around him yet again. I could feel the thick moss being crushed underneath me as he pounded into me with all his strength. One of his hands was propped on my right shoulder now. His grip almost hurt, but my mind was already overwhelmed with pleasure, and I just didn't care.

"Misty!" he suddenly screamed out, howling my name as I felt him tense up. My own body quivered with delight upon hearing his cry. As he slammed his cock deep into me and ground his hips against me, I moaned into his throat, my body taking off a third time.

Only when I came down from ecstasy did I notice the burning heat on my right breast. I looked down to see his palm resting there. I tried to pull away, but he kept me pinned against the moss. His face was close to my neck, and he raised it just enough to lock his gaze with mine. "You're mine," he hissed, eyes burning, before finally climbing over the edge. His head arched back, eyes closed, mouth dropping open in a long groan that sounded almost agonized. Then he pulled me up against him, wrapping his arms tight around me.

I shook with pleasure as my whole body was enveloped in a deep warmth. I felt like I was floating. To my amazement, when I looked down, we were levitating a few feet off the moss. My eyes went big. "Craze," I breathed in disbelief. I attempted to get his attention, but his head was now resting on my left breast as he regained his composure. "Um…Craze? Babe? We're airborne."

He did not answer me, and yet we slowly started to float back to the ground. His feet landed firmly on the soft ground, and he gingerly eased us back down onto the moss. *Phew,* I thought, *that was weird.*

He made a low, contented sound in his throat as he lifted his head. Ever so slowly, he took his hand away from my right breast. I gasped when I saw a deep, azure symbol like a linked double spiral etched into my skin. It glowed brightly for a second before dulling down to a shimmer. It was strikingly beautiful. "What…is that?"

He still didn't speak. His arms wrapped around me reflexively, pulling me close until my body was nestled against his. I felt his still hard cock resting against my thigh. As I came down from our frenzy, I found myself shocked and a little embarrassed with myself. I couldn't believe what we had done—in semi-public, no less. But even that didn't change a simple fact: I had never felt that good in my entire life.

"Craze," I murmured once more and lifted my head to look at him. His silver hair was draped over his body, glimmering in the bright sunlight. I smiled before gently running a finger through his luxurious locks. He really did look like a prince from some fairy tale. As I uncovered his face, I noticed he was fast asleep. *Aw. Poor guy. Almost seems like he went without as long as I had.* I chuckled before cuddling against him.

Even in his sleep, his arm tightened around my body in a protective embrace. Gradually, I leaned forward and kissed his cheek ever so slightly. Never would I have thought that the best sex of my life would have been spent with an alien. I smiled at the thought, pleasure still racing through my veins. I closed my eyes and rested my head on his shoulder. A faint voice in the back of my head reminded me that someone might discover us, but I was too exhausted to listen. Soon, I surrendered myself to sleep.

CHAPTER 10
CRAZE

When I awoke, the cool of evening had settled over the lake, and the glowfish were coming out to dance in the water like stars. Night birds called in the trees, and I heard the distant rumble of one of our rockets taking off. The sweat had dried on my skin, but in the shadows beneath the trees, a chill was starting to seep into my bones.

I instantly sensed the presence of my new companion by my side. Misty was breathing softly and slowly as she curled against me, her head pillowed on my shoulder. Her eyes were closed in sleep, and I propped myself up on one elbow to watch her. I leaned down and kissed her lips softly, then ventured farther down her body until my lips rested on the psychic brand that I had marked on her breast.

She was now mine. Forever. *She'll have to feel it too. I know she will.* I congratulated myself on finding her—and on a successful mating against all odds. Surely now, she would decide to stay…and make a life with me.

As my tongue traced out my personal insignia on her skin, she started to wake up. I pulled my tongue away as I held her closer, waiting for her eyes to open. As they did, I pressed my lips to hers lightly. "Good evening, beautiful," I purred as my fingers caressed her hair.

She tilted her head at me curiously before her eyes grew wide with surprise. "What happened?" She quirked her head to look down at herself, before sitting up with a bewildered expression on her face.

I looked at her quizzically, trying to figure out what she meant. *Had she really forgotten our wonderful time together?* "We copulated," I answered, getting a little closer, letting my already hardening cock slide against her skin and hoping it would jog her memory.

She snorted and shook her head, relaxing slightly. "I know. But, last night…you were so rough with me… Yet I feel completely fine. You scratched me all over and you even bit me, but I don't have a single wound on my body." Her words stumbled out of her mouth as she tried to explain herself. "Just…this…" She brushed her hand over my sigil. "Which you still haven't explained."

I chuckled. "Ah. I understand your confusion now. As I said before, during intimacy, a Vixxian can lend their magical abilities to their mate. My healing is so accelerated as to make me impervious to physical damage. So, while our bodies were connected, we shared that quality. Therefore, I can be as rough as I'd like with you, and you'll never get hurt," I said slyly. "Though, of course, the actual limit is up to you."

She looked up at me with doe-like eyes. I leaned forward and kissed her, hoping it would put her mind at ease. She just wrapped her arms around me before rolling on top of me. "Well, okay, then."

I was pleasantly surprised by her boldness. Usually, Vixxian women were so cold-blooded and slow to start. Misty was also tiny compared to me, but apparently, all her wariness of me had dissolved. It felt nice to have a woman in my life again who wasn't afraid of me—or afraid to take control. "Oh. Well, then."

She grinned down at me. "Any problems?"

I shook my head, flashing a grin, my eyebrows up. "Oh, no problem. No problem at all."

"Good. Now, one more question." Her mouth drew near my ear as her lips caressed my lobe. She nibbled on it before her fingers touched the tip of my golden ear cuffs. "Well, two," she added with an amused look on her face.

"Yes?" I raised an eyebrow in her direction as my arms wrapped around her, my hands resting on the small of her back. I was already hungry for her again and impatient to bury myself inside of her. But the calm firmness of her gaze made me hold off. I needed to make certain her mind was put at ease.

Especially since I was just more than a little bit sneaky. I kept trying to justify it in my own head. But once I had realized that she was both attracted to me and curious about the chance to share my powers, I simply hadn't been able to resist. *And possibly premature as well. But I'll happily live with any potential mistakes. This feels too right.*

"What's this symbol thing on my breast?" She hoisted herself up slightly, showing off the bright blue emblem that was now a permanent part of her skin. "I'm not sure I'm feeling the whole 'instant tattoo' thing, though it is pretty."

"Ah. That is my insignia. When Vixxians get intimate, they mark their lovers. They form a pact with them," I explained, hoping that the concept would translate properly. But as I saw her eyebrows climbing toward her hairline, I wondered if it actually had.

"So, it's like marriage?" she asked, shock and embarrassment on her face. "Shouldn't we have talked this over before you just went ahead and—"

"Marriage?" I responded in confusion. I had never heard the word before, and even with the translator chip working properly behind her ear, it still seemed foreign to me.

My shock seemed to mollify her, as if she suddenly realized that we were having a mix-up over our terms. "Yes. When two lovers come together and get married. You know?" She seemed to have a hard time trying to define it as her brows furrowed together. Her tone was deeply confused, as if what I was asking her to explain should have been obvious to anyone.

"I have never heard of such a ceremony. The pact that I refer to allows you to access a portion of my powers. We mark our mates, and in marking them, both stake a claim and offer a gift of our powers. Had you the ability, your touch would have marked me as well." I did my best to keep my voice reassuring. She seemed unnerved by the mark, perhaps concerned the encounter had gone too far.

"Oh." She chewed her lip, still seeming a little dubious, and I wondered how much trouble I was in with her. Sometimes women would carry things for a while to try to keep the peace…but their anger would grow secretly. "I didn't know things would turn out like this."

"Is it…different with the men of Earth?" I could only guess that, from her reaction to me, Earth matings were singularly unsatisfying. But then again, that might simply have been her experience.

"Has been for me. But, uh…yes, usually committing to one another long term takes time and planning." She gave me a small but rueful smile. "Now I'm just wondering what I got myself into."

"An adventure," I purred at her, kissing her hand, and she giggled. But then my smile faded, and I tilted my head.

"What was your second question?"

She was about to inquire about what I could only assume was another fact about our culture, when the ground began to rumble. It was just a slight vibration at first. I looked around, trying to locate the source of the disturbance, when all of a sudden, a loud explosion sounded nearby. Echoing screams could be heard all around as black smoke billowed into the sky.

What? How did attackers get past the orbital sentries without an alarm sounding? I grabbed our clothes and helped her up, and we ran for the shelter of the trees. Once we had a substantial tree between the fight and ourselves, I wrapped my arms around her. "Do not fear. The palace shields should deploy momentarily. And I will protect you."

Misty tensed up in my arms, and I held her securely against my body. I peered into the sky as the dome-shaped shield lit it up suddenly, and my eyes narrowed in disgust as I saw three stubby gray Thezlum warships skid harmlessly off its surface. I cursed under my breath.

"What's going on?" Misty's voice was high and shaky with panic, and I cupped the back of her head comfortingly.

"It seems the Thezlums are attempting a rescue of their captured crew," I growled, mind racing. "I don't know how they got this far into our atmosphere without being spotted, but I must help deal with them." She looked up at me, and I kissed her forehead. "I'm sorry. My transferred powers will protect you in my absence."

"But...I don't know how to use them or what they are," she protested.

I tilted her head up and kissed her lips. "They will activate by instinct to protect you. It's how psychic abilities generally manifest—through stress. You will be fine. Come. Let's get dressed, and then I must meet with my family and troops."

"Oh." She looked at me a little dubiously. Possessing no experience with psychic powers, she was taking a leap of faith by trusting my words, and I knew it. But after a moment, she steeled herself and lifted her chin. "Okay. Not like I can expect you to stick with me when you have the city to defend anyway."

Struggling back into our clothes, we watched as the ships circled the dome, constantly testing its integrity with their weapons. They didn't seem to be getting anywhere now, but I had no idea how much damage the initial strike had done. I snatched my discarded cloak from the ground and wrapped it around Misty's body. Then we ran as fast as we could for the edge of the copse and the path back to my chambers beyond.

As leader of the Vixxian military, I was responsible for the protection of my planet. But at the same time, my mind was still fogged with the aftereffects of my passionate night with Misty. I took a deep breath and noticed my reflection in the lake. I uttered a soft prayer to the Goddess Silviana as I stood there. *Watch over her while I am gone.*

It struck me as strange that I had connected with this alien woman so quickly. But I was too overcome by desire to think about that before. Now I was too busy trying to get her to safety so I could turn my mind to the defense of my world.

"Are you going out into space again after them?" Misty sounded panicked as we heard renewed screams nearby, followed by another loud explosion.

The ground rumbled underneath us. One of the attacking ships had tried ramming its way through the shield dome, only to crash against it and land somewhere in the city beyond the barricade. Loaded with fuel and ordnances, it had exploded on impact, the fireball still rising skyward as I looked up. "The citywide shield never came up. Everyone outside the palace is still at risk!"

Effortlessly, I grabbed Misty and hoisted her up on my back. I held on to her firm thighs as I gazed at the city, now engulfed in flames. "Hang on." I started running, bolting across the moss field toward the door we had entered by yesterday afternoon. "We've got a saboteur among us. First the orbital sensors, then the planet-side sensors, and now the city shield. Somebody planned this. Somebody here planned it."

"A mole of some kind?" She hung on firmly, hands gripping my shoulders and knees clasping my thighs.

"No, worse," I growled. "A traitor."

I spared a glance upward—and froze for a moment in sheer horror. The sky was black with Thezlum attack craft. It seemed that this was more than a small division trying to rescue the captives. It was a damned invasion.

"Oh God—why are there so many? What is this?" Misty demanded, holding on to me tightly.

I started running again. "War."

CHAPTER 11
CRAZE

Misty hung firmly to my shoulders as I carried her back indoors as fast as I could run. The palace dome was holding, but that wouldn't help anyone outside. I could still smell the smoke and hear the screams and alarm klaxons sounding out in the city.

My fingers tightened around Misty's thighs as blood boiled in my veins. I couldn't believe the normally cowardly Thezlums had the audacity to attack us like this. Had the Dragicans forced them into it, or was something else going on? Whatever the case, they would pay dearly for this attack. And so would whoever had let them into our airspace.

"Is there anything I can do?" Misty whispered as her arms tightened around my neck reflexively, nearly choking me. I ignored her question as I stopped at the door and laid my palm against the lock, giving it a mental command. My hand stung as a small genetic sample was taken, and the lock-down bolts to the stout double doors clunked back open.

I set Misty down, my mind racing. "Hide in my chambers. The palace walls are heavily armored." Looking up, I saw that the palace cannons had started firing on the various Thezlum ships still hanging overhead. Narrowing my eyes, I searched for the enemy's leading vessel. To my astonishment, it didn't bear a Dragican standard on its side, just a black mark where its standard had been lasered off.

It was a rogue ship. Either the Thezlum raiders had mutinied, or a third party had manipulated or conquered them and was now using them to carry out this attack. My jaw clenched as I pushed open the door. This situation just kept getting more complicated.

"Craze, these Thezlum guys can't beat your shields. Except for the crashes in town, they can't get anything through, and your guns keep blowing them away. Why do they keep coming?" Misty asked. There was a thin frown on her face, and her brown eyes searched mine desperately.

"Fanaticism. That and their usual bosses ensure loyalty with planet-killing weapons." I grabbed her hand firmly and guided her into the palace. "I'll keep my suite communicator open so that you can contact me once the all clear is given. Don't use it before that. I'll need to concentrate."

"I understand." I looked up, frowning, noticing Ragar's tall figure standing outside my door in full armor. He turned and strode our direction when he saw me.

"There you are! Where in space have you been? If you want to play around—" He stopped when he saw my face. "What is it?"

"The Thezlum squadron leader's ship has a burnt standard." I came to a stop as we drew close to each other, with Misty hanging back a little behind me.

His eyes widened. "Pirates?"

"Or outlaws, yes. We haven't heard any news of a rebellion from our spies in the Dragican court, but for all we know, these troops are part of a smaller mutiny." I stared hard into his eyes, speaking gravely as I tried to impart just how bad this could be.

"Or, someone else is manipulating them. What's the effect of them breaking with the Dragicans?" Ragar tugged his pointed beard thoughtfully.

"If they've broken with the Dragicans, it means they no longer have any outside motive to limit their fanaticism. They remain cowardly, but all they have to do is muster the courage to drop a bomb or jump in an escape pod after aiming their attack craft at our cities." I watched my brother's eyes widen as the implications of this sank in, and he nodded gravely.

"Our father wishes to see you immediately. Bring the girl. The Queen has requested it." Ragar was liked least of all of us by our mother and rarely spoke of her as a relation.

I exchanged glances with Misty, who nodded and fell into step beside me as we turned to stride quickly down the hall. Despite the circumstances, she followed me faithfully as I hurried toward the throne room with my brother.

I burst through the doors with the others on my heels. Inside, the rest of my family was already gathered.

"Craze. What kept you?" my father accused the moment he laid eyes on me. Then his eyes flicked over to take in Misty, wrapped in my cloak, and narrowed angrily.

I was about to defend myself and Misty when he shocked me by unfastening the data-transfer helmet from his head and sitting forward on his throne. Beside him, my mother still sat like a statue, keeping her helmet on, but her eyes had come alive, and she watched him curiously.

He looked around at all of us, his eyes more fiercely animated than I had seen in a decade. "The Thezlum are acting as suicide troops, and they'll overload our shield systems eventually. Every time they bounce a fighter off our shields, the wreckage lands in the capital."

"Has there been no progress in getting their shields back on-line?" I looked over at my mother, who gave a tiny nod.

"Your mother is investigating the program alterations that sabotaged shield activation. Meanwhile, I need every ship in the air, from atmospheric fighters to the big rockets." He fixed his fierce look back on me. "Board *Solrei* and get rid of them. The army is already mobilized and ready to follow your command." His eyes locked with mine, and I nodded in recognition. The responsibility to restore peace back to our planet now rested on my shoulders. I knew I couldn't let everyone down.

"I'll need to armor up," I apologized, and he snorted and looked away from me. His eyes flicked over to his mate and narrowed slightly again.

Sephir spoke up in a mocking tone in his stead. "Well, at least you did us the courtesy of covering up at all before you came in with… her." My other brothers snorted, and Ragar sighed and poked Sephir with his elbow. "Ow. Well? I don't know about you, but I have no desire whatsoever to get an eyeful of my idiot brother's—"

"Funny how you're cheery enough to crack jokes when the Capitol is in flames, you dishonorable brat," I growled in response.

The laughter stopped dead, and the smile dropped off Sephir's face so fast it was as if I had spat in it. But, really, his making jokes at a time like this was too audacious—and suspicious, as well.

"Enough of this." Suddenly, my father got up from his throne and clambered stiffly down the stairs. My brothers and I exchanged surprised glances as he did. He had not risen from his seat for over a year, and that had become common for him. "Father?" I inquired as I approached him, offering him a hand if he needed assistance.

He pushed my hand aside and straightened himself out. Even though he was hundreds of years old, he had a reputation as one of the strongest Vixxian warriors. His physique was well built and powerful, with dense muscles and a compact stature. He only came up to my shoulder, unlike my willowy mother, but it was from him that his sons had all gained their warrior strength.

I eyed him suspiciously, wondering what he was about to do. We had not suffered an invasion since I was a green cadet, and back then, he had led our armada on his own. "This rogue attack must have some ulterior motive besides freeing the imprisoned Thezlums. This all started when we intercepted that slaver ship." He paced in a small circle, hands behind his back—then he looked up, raising his voice. "Nemesch. Ragar. Get my ship ready." His voice was firm as he gave the command. My two brothers looked at each other, dumbfounded. My father had not manned his own ship in over a century.

"Are you sure about this, Father? We can handle the attack on our own," I assured him, hoping he would take my advice.

"That was an order." Nemesch and Ragar jumped to fall into step behind our father as he walked off the dais and strode toward the main doors. "This whole attack is a diversion." He strode out of the throne room, his legendary sword swinging by his side and my two younger brothers rushing after him. I looked at my mother for confirmation, but she just sat on her throne with her usual detached expression.

"Does anyone have any idea what he meant?" I looked to Lysi and, reluctantly, to Sephir.

Lysi shrugged, looking wistfully after Ragar's departing back. "Don't know, big brother. Wish Father hadn't dragged Ragar away. Wanted a chance for a rematch of our little contest…in midair!" He was an accomplished dogfighter in single-man skimmers and as blood-thirsty there as he was hand-to-hand.

"You'll get your chance." I looked over at Sephir, who had been silent since my outburst about his inappropriate humor.

He folded his arms almost dramatically and sniffed. "I'm sure that I don't know."

"Hmph. Well, that's useless." I looked down at the human by my side. "Misty." My new mate looked at me, her brows furrowed together. No doubt all of this came as a great jumble to her. "No time for further explanation. My father may be on to something." I just had no idea what yet. "I have to go with my brothers and command the *Solrei*. I want you to stay here with my mother. The palace's defenses are the best in the galaxy. You are perfectly safe." I rested my hand on her delicate shoulder, and my eyes lingered on the curve of her breast where my mark just peeked out at the edge of her bodice.

"You can't just leave me here," she answered quickly, her eyes growing large as she tried to convince me to let her come along. I thought she was being clingy, until I noticed her nervous glances toward my mother. It was a sad thing that my mother had reached the point where much of her personality was permanently melded with our world's data streams. She had always been remote, but now she was strange enough that she even unnerved me sometimes.

Yet she had specifically requested Misty's presence, and I could not disobey such a direct request. At least I could more or less trust that my mother meant my new mate no harm. I would not have left her with Sephir.

Fortunately, he was coming along with me, where I could keep an eye on him.

I shook my head solemnly. "I cannot risk you getting hurt. The

Thezlum raiders may be lesser creatures, but they are fierce warriors nonetheless. They will not hesitate to kill you, and I can't take that chance." I removed my hand before I leaned down and gently kissed her full lips, letting a bit more of my psychic power flow into her through her sigil. She moaned softly, bringing a smile to my face. I wanted nothing more than to stay with her and hold her in my arms, but my planet needed me. "I'll see you soon."

Without another word, I left the room, Lysi and Sephir following me. I sighed and cleared my mind as I strode out. I had to push away thoughts of Misty, or I would only be distracted on the battlefield. *She will be safe here.* Taking deep, calming breaths, I finally emptied my mind.

Determined, I made my way to the palace courtyard and started running toward the shipyard. I boarded my vessel with my brothers, to find my crewmen ready at their stations. I nodded at them as I got in my own seat.

The Thezlum raiders were about to regret ever crossing our borders. And once they were driven away, I would find out where my father thought the real battle lay…and discover who among us was a traitor.

My mother sent a burst of data through our ship's relays, presenting us with a hologram of the unknown ship and a scrolling list of stats on the main view-screen. I patched the image through to the rest of the ship and started issuing orders. "Their lead vessel is a rogue one. It's an antique, but it's had a lot of illegal modifications. None of our interceptors has been able to get past its shielding. It's up to us to cripple that ship and take in whoever is commanding it." I informed my crew while I mentally prepared the rest of the ship's systems. As they all hummed to life, I knew we couldn't lose.

CHAPTER 12
MISTY

I watched Craze leave with a bitter taste in my mouth. My stomach sank, like a large boulder had lodged itself inside of me. I didn't know what risks Craze would be facing out there, but from the sounds of the explosions and sirens that kept echoing through the air, it didn't sound good.

Suddenly, there was a loud boom, which shook the entire foundation of the palace. I let out a little yip as I felt my skin crawling with a mixture of fear and excitement. *Are we safe here? I don't have access to that communicator thing Craze was going to show me in his quarters. How is he going to check in with me?*

"Girl. Come sit down," a toneless, slightly dreamy voice called out behind me.

I turned around quickly. I had nearly forgotten the Empress was still in the room. Probably because she spent most of her time imitating part of the computer network. I wondered if this was a normal lifestyle for some Vixxians, or whether she had some kind of tech obsession, like an internet addiction taken to a horrible extreme. It might have been the first, but as I hesitated to walk back up onto the dais, it felt like the second.

Hesitantly, I stepped up to the base of her throne. "Sit." She waved her arm toward the Emperor's throne, shocking me.

"Are you sure it's okay for me to sit there?" I stammered.

"Yes," she answered plainly. "I will not repeat myself." Her voice was devoid of emotion as her expressionless face peered in my direction. She gave me the creeps. I could already feel a chill embrace my body as goose bumps covered every inch of my skin.

No. This can't possibly be normal. Is her family under pressure to pretend that it is? Is Craze afraid of explaining the truth to me? Another mystery. This place is full of them.

Without further prompting, I climbed the narrow stairs and sat down on the throne.

It was as hard as a rock. I shifted my weight, trying to find a comfortable position, but it was useless. What I had taken for padding had an odd, prickly surface to it. It felt like there were tiny needles being pressed into my ass. *What is this? How does the Emperor sit here all day? Is he a masochist? Or are these prickly things somehow part of the computer interface?*

"How has Vixxia Prime been treating you?" The Empress posed the question as she rested one of her hands on her knees, her posture relaxing just enough that I could see the cables trailing from the back and top of her globular, visor-less helmet. She craned her neck, glancing down at me with those blank, unfocused eyes.

Why is she suddenly making small talk in the middle of a crisis? She must have had another reason for summoning me, and it doesn't seem like she'd much care about putting me at ease. I forced a polite smile. "It's been good. I can't complain. I do miss Earth, but Craze has treated me very well." I chose my words carefully, trying not to insult their hospitality or reveal too much of my relationship with her son.

I certainly wasn't going to point out that we had ended up fucking like wild animals at the local sacred shrine, or that we had been going for seconds when the damn raiders had attacked.

Her smile was a dispassionate twitch of her lips. It was like watching a robot imitate a human expression. Her eerie calm continued as another explosion shook the palace. "Very good. Tell me, what is this Earth of yours like?" She didn't even bother to look at me as she asked.

"My people don't even have a unified world government yet. If nations aren't fighting each other, they're having a coup or a revolution or a stolen election. It's crowded. It's polluted, and most of the ecosystem is in danger. But it's still home." *Wow, that sounded like I was bad-mouthing my own home-world after asking them to go out of their way to get me back to it. I hope I don't seem crazy to them.*

The Empress had gone quiet. I followed her gaze to one of the large view-screens. It provided a satellite view of the ongoing battle. Missiles, laser beams, and explosions colored the sky in fiery reds and foggy whites. In an odd way, it was almost beautiful. Terrifying as well, thinking of Craze out in the middle of all that. I sat there, mesmerized by the sight. "Wow…"

"Are you impressed with the Vixxian fleet?" she inquired, turning her head to study my face with those cold eyes.

"On my planet, we don't have spaceships. Well, at least, none of such caliber. In fact, we have never met another sentient species," I explained as I continued to watch the battle. "That and the whole kidnapping-and-slavery thing are why the other humans and I were so freaked out when we got here." I had almost forgotten about the other refugees in my preoccupation with Craze. "Are they all right?"

"Their life signs remain stable despite their health issues, but none of the three is out of the infirmary yet. Two had injuries from the space battle, like yourself, but more extensive. The third was given a disease —" Faint distaste flashed across her face "—by someone aboard the Thezlum slaver ship."

"Oh." *I hope the Vixxians have good therapists…and really good antibiotics.* I suddenly realized how lucky I had been that those gray *things* had decided I was too feisty to toy with.

"They will be seen to quickly enough. Our healers are the finest in the galaxy. They have maintained this body of mine for…far too long." An ironic smile flickered across her face suddenly, startling me.

"I have seen something of what they can do. I came here with injuries myself." I couldn't help but squirm on that uncomfortable seat. Did the Emperor simply heal so fast that it never registered with him? *I would be ready for a new ass in a couple of hours.* "I believe you." *About that, anyway.*

"Yes, I noticed how my son Craze tended to your wounds himself. And how he's barely been without you since." Her voice was as remote as ever, but her eyes had finally focused—on my face, which she stared at as if watching for every microexpression.

I felt my cheeks heat up at her scrutiny. *She knows.* I didn't know if it was some weird psychic power of hers, something she had used the data streams to determine—maybe even through any security cameras they might have—or the weird Vixxian equivalent of mother's intuition. But she knew. And now I had to face the music.

Oh, crap. "It's a little hard to explain, and parts of it I'm still figuring out myself." My heart started beating hard, and I suddenly wished even more that Craze were there. The Empress had suddenly gone from all android to half android, half overcurious and overprotective potential mother-in-law. *I am in no way ready for this.*

"Has he marked you?" she asked me in that low, neutral voice, but I saw her eyes locked on the bit of sigil that peeked out of my cleavage. I knew she was testing my honesty. She already knew the answer.

"He has. But I don't really know what it means. He suggested we become lovers, but…it seems to mean different things in your culture than in mine." While being similar in comforting, intriguing ways. But not familiar enough. I still felt lost, and never more so than when this strange being turned her eyes to me and asked these questions.

I suddenly realized that the whole reason she had had me come to sit near her, on her level, was so she could get a closer look at the markings on my breast. *Oh. Damn. Well, glad I caught that and didn't try to lie.*

"Craze is very, very like his father," she said, and to my absolute shock, a note of sadness and regret entered her voice. "The men of his family have certain habits that have apparently passed down from father to son." She looked down at her hands, and as she did so, I saw another sigil, with the same shimmering blue coloring, on the side of her neck under her hair.

"I'm sorry, I'm not sure what you mean." At least now she seemed to be…engaged…in the conversation, instead of drifting above it from somewhere remote and occasionally sending messages from that place through her mouth.

She reached up and touched the sigil. "Vixxians mate for life, you see. We occasionally do have more casual lovers, but they are not… spoken of in polite company. Especially once one passes a certain age." The faint sadness in her face deepened slightly, filling my head with a million questions. I concentrated on the few that had a prayer of getting answered.

"Is that why he's been on me this whole time to stay?" It suddenly made a lot more sense. But why had he fallen so fast?

The corner of her mouth tugged upward. "My eldest son is a romantic fool. He has offered his heart twice in his life to women. The first time, I'm afraid, things ended…badly. This time, I am hoping that a union will bring you both some small happiness."

I didn't know what to say. I knew from the sadness in her face that her own whirlwind marriage perhaps hadn't turned out the way she had hoped. "Then you think I should stay as well."

"Well, he's hardly in a position to return to Earth with you." The tiny bit of sarcasm in her voice was a relief to hear. Then her green eyes fixed on the sigil on my breast again, and she sighed almost silently. "Once a Vixxian male has marked his mate, she can draw on his power so long as he still loves her. In addition, the mark means that he can always find her, no matter where she goes." The note of sadness deepened into despair for a moment. "It has its benefits, but…it will cost you your freedom."

I stared mutely at the space battle with her for almost a minute as I struggled with this. This woman had been with her husband for at least three decades, if not a lot more. I didn't know if she had once loved him and enjoyed their rushed-into mating as much as I felt a similar sensation blooming inside of me for Craze. But as she stared back at me, I realized that any former joy had long since turned to ashes for her.

"Are they cruel?" I worried aloud.

"Oh no," she replied, some of the sadness retreating as her icy composure crept back like a glacier. "They merely profess lifelong love quickly, and then, though they may hold out a long time, they fall short of their own ideals."

"But isn't that everyone, to some degree?"

What in the world have I gotten myself into here? I'm genuinely starting to get scared.

Another small twitch of a smile. "Oh yes, of course it is. But the difference is that the Vixxian idea of love does not make allowances for the fact that it ends."

If that's true, how is it that Craze broke up with someone once? I started to wonder how much of what this strange being was telling me was meant to be manipulative, and how much was simply tainted by her own bad experiences.

Except… What happened if she was right?

"What do you think I should do?" I asked hesitantly.

"Well," she said thoughtfully, "There is always a way to escape the bond if need be. Another Vixxian could challenge him for you."

"Whoa. Hold on. He's the only Vixxian I even like enough to think about trying this whole 'mating for life' thing with." I squirmed again on the seat and finally shoved a fold of the cloak Craze had given me under my ass, just to give myself a little padding.

"Well, I doubt you would say that if a few more eligible males showed an interest. As much as I love my son, he's not the only one of my issue who finds you fetching, and one of his rivals is significantly stabler and less apt to just…push you into things." That little twitch-smile again.

"I'm sorry, what are you talking about?" I felt a little baffled…and then a little worried.

Why is she trying to steer me away from Craze? Is it because she worries about history repeating itself as it did with her, or is she trying to keep the Crown Prince from bringing alien blood into their line?

They were a royal family, after all. If they were anything like humans about such things, they would probably frown on mixing their blood with someone not of their race. If, of course, humans and Vixxians could interbreed at all. "I haven't even really met anyone else yet. None of your other sons has even trulyspoken to me."

"That is only because my dear eldest has made sure to command all your time," she replied, a note of tiredness in her voice. "I know he can be quite charming. But one other of my sons has shown an interest…"

I knew she was being manipulative, and it left me wary. But her words stirred up my own doubts. I knew the cleverest way to lie was to mix it with the truth, and as delightful as my time with Craze had been, it didn't change the fact that he hadn't really given me a choice in the matter.

My hand drifted to the sigil, and I thought of where he had rescued me from—and their intentions. *The Dragicans would have had me fucking a whole lot of aliens unwillingly for the rest of a probably very, very short life. Craze, I would have wanted anyway, but he did push far and fast. And from the way the Empress is acting over her husband doing something similar... maybe it isn't all that normal for her race, after all.*

"Who?" I asked finally.

"His name is Sephir, and you probably saw him when you came in. Dark gray hair, red eyes?" That tiny twitch of a smile again. It looked completely fake and lifeless, like someone had sent electricity through a dead frog to make it kick.

Dark gray hair, red eyes, total asshole, hates Craze? Hmm. Something weird was going on. The investigative journalist in me was sure of it. "I noticed him. What did he say?" Pretending to show an interest seemed to be the best way to draw her out.

"He's the only one of my sons who comes to visit me on the data streams," she said with a strange mixture of pride and despair creeping into her voice. Her face stayed blank this time. "We have had many long conversations, especially in the last year. He asked me to please arrange for him to see you alone, once he returns from aiding his brothers."

I hid a frown behind my hand, mind racing. *This doesn't smell right. Should I tell Craze or keep this to myself? And should I meet Sephir, when chances are he's just using his mother to stir up trouble between Craze and me?*

I had to correct myself immediately, as there was already trouble between us. I had no regrets about the sex, but this mark on me? I felt conflicted. He should have known to warn me about it. According to his mother, more casual relationships did exist between members of his race, but Craze had left that bit out.

It occurred to me he was a little selective with the truth sometimes when he spoke to me, and it was more than a bad habit. But I also realized the person he had inherited that trait from was likely sitting next to me right then. And as for the thing with Sephir… *I need to know more. I'll figure out whether to tell Craze about it later.* "I am willing to speak with Sephir. But I won't sneak around behind Craze's back about it."

"Ah, but if you do tell him that Sephir has an interest, he will try to prevent you from going. He's possessive as well as protective, child, just like his father." Those flat green eyes bored into me for a moment, then went back to staring at the view-screen.

"I'll have to think about this. But you can tell Sephir to arrange something." *Though, I might not show up—or if I did, I might not show up alone.*

"Listen to me carefully, child, for I will only say this once. Between you and me, the lot of the Empress Consort is never particularly kind. And the lot of a woman mated to a man of my Lord's or my son's nature…well…" For once, her face contorted in true grief, and I realized then that she wasn't just doing this to interfere with Craze or advocate for Sephir. The matter was personal to her.

Seeing her lose composure shocked me, but the moment she noticed me staring, she withdrew again, face turning masklike and eyes cold and distant.

"I will think hard about everything you have said," I promised. Though considering how my head was whirling right then, it was pretty much a foregone conclusion. This place was filled with intrigues and tragedies. Staying here would mean dealing with such things daily. And Craze seemed to be doing his best to tie me down here, despite any desire of mine to go home.

I don't have quite the same problem she did. I'm crazy about Craze, and I know he feels at least the same. But I know the kind of warning signs I should look for in a man, and being too controlling is one of them. I would just have to wait and see. I knew she had ulterior motives for sowing seeds of doubt in me about Craze…but it had still worked, at least a little. *I'll have to see what kind of man he turns out to be while we're looking for a way to get me home.*

We sat in silence for a few minutes. She seemed to be growing restless as she stared at the screen. "I detect no outsider access of the data systems in the weeks leading to the sabotage. Shutting down city shields and editing sensor reads would require Imperial Family-level access. Whoever hacked the data stream must be extraordinarily talented if they were able to emulate such credentials."

Or the saboteur is a member of the Imperial Family. I opened my mouth to bring this up…and then closed it immediately. Her behavior was so unpredictable, and her motives so hard to read. And she had biases. Lots of them. Better to bring this up to Craze…or maybe even his father. "How long do you think they'll have to be out there?" I worried at her instead, changing the subject.

She seemed to relax a little. "Not long. The battle is surely won soon. We Vixxians have not lost a battle in over a millennium," she stated, face blank but a note of pride in her voice.

"Really?" That was impressive. But it also made the attack make even less sense. The Thezlum raiders must have known just what odds they were up against when they gathered for the fight. And what about this rogue ship that I had overheard Craze and his brother talking about?

"Yes. The Emperor's great-grandfather was a magnificent leader and warrior. No ruler before him could expand the empire's borders so much. He was able to conquer various lesser planets, even with the rudimentary technology available at the time," she explained, her voice taking on the dry tones of a college lecturer.

I listened to her history lesson as attentively as if I were still back at NYU attending a class. She seemed content to rattle on. "His son, however, Hixlux, was not a militarist. But he was one of the greatest minds ever to be born on Vixxia. Utilizing all the resources and work-force made available by his father's battle campaigns, he managed to usher in the dawn a golden age of scientific advancement. During his five-decade reign alone, centuries' worth of progress was accomplished."

I simply nodded. Giving her a chance to be pedantic gave me a break from any more prying into my love life. "That does sound impressive. What has your husband done in his reign?"

"Husband?" Her lips stretched into a hard, thin line as she expressed her confusion at the foreign word.

"Oh, right. Your people don't have marriage. Um…the current emperor," I clarified.

"Ah." Her voice went flatter and colder as she spoke of the man who shared her throne. "Emperor Jilkinio has utilized his resources best of all of his recent line. When he took the throne, Hixlux's legacy was still going strong. Science was steadily making progress, so he focused the efforts of the Science Ministry on military application."

We watched as a large silver Vixxian rocket took off after the largest ship, chasing it through the cloud of smaller fighters. One of the Thezlum carrier craft swept past and opened its maw, disgorging scores of small fliers. The Empress prattled on, her calm narration never wavering despite the carnage on the screen. "The strengthening of our military by improving tactics and equipment, in turn, helped with conquering the two solar systems neighboring Vixxia Prime's. It expanded the empire's reach quite considerably."

War. Conquest. Expansionism. I couldn't fully stomach it. And yet, if the Dragican crime empire was any indication, the Vixxian Empire was the closest thing to civilization that this region of space had. "I see."

"The next step is intergalactic travel, which, after all we have accomplished, shouldn't be much of a challenge. The Dragicans possess the technology, but the seat of their empire is a long way from here—impossible to reach without that very technology. It would be impractical for us to attack them. So, our only option is to conquer the Thezlums, who serve them, and use some of their vessels."

"Empress, what about stripping the faster-than-light drives out of the ship that kidnapped me? Craze says it's still floating out there." Maybe the Emperor could be swayed to allow the expedition if his… mate?…worked on him.

Her face took on a real expression again, a thoughtful frown. "I am surprised that Sephir did not bring this up to me," she murmured then shrugged.

"Craze brought it up as my best chance to get home, so I remembered it. If it is part of your goals to capture this technology anyway, then why not…?" I remembered what Craze had told me. If I wanted to go back to Earth, I would need a spaceship capable of it.

But now that I've become attached to Craze, will I still want to go back when the time comes? And would Craze let me go, or would he try to interfere?

"What's wrong? You look distressed." Her voice, for once, held a hint of compassion. I looked up to meet her gaze—and shuddered, for her eyes were as blank and empty as ever.

"It's nothing," I answered quickly, chilled and wondering once again what was wrong with my hostess. I turned my attention back to the view-screen to distract us both. "Do you know what ship Craze's on?"

"Craze commands the *Solrei*. It is our most advanced vessel. He has piloted it for nearly ten years now. He is still a novice, but it is his duty as the eldest prince, especially since his father has retired from combat." She paused, brow furrowing as she stared at the screen. "Normally, at any rate." She held out a thin finger toward the window, pointing to a sleek-looking spaceship. "The *Solrei* has engaged the enemy leader. With the combination of its technology and my sons' powers, they cannot lose."

Strange how she sounded far more exhausted than proud as she said such things. But then again, as the explosions and volleys of light and missiles lit up the screen, her expression never changed from its placid emptiness. Not so much as a twitch—not even when one of the disabled enemy ships crash-landed in the city around the palace.

I distracted myself by watching the sleek *Solrei* in action and tried to imagine Craze inside of it. I wondered what he was doing. I kept my eyes locked on the vessel as I watched it fire countless volleys, taking down enemy interceptors with ease as it chased after the rogue ship.

A smile appeared on my face as I silently cheered him on and prayed for his safe return. Things might be complicated between us, but he was up there protecting me, his family, and his world, and I couldn't fully distrust someone who did a hero's work.

Then I looked over at the Empress—and saw how her eyes never left the screen. Looking at her blank face, I wondered, *does she pray for her mate's return too? Or does she pray that he never will return at all?*

CHAPTER 13
CRAZE

"Take down that ship!" I barked as I watched the rogue ship start to outpace us. In frustration, I pushed the engines as much as possible. But even so, it was no match for the enemy's vessel. *Definitely not a Thezlum ship. It was just made to look like one. Well, if I can't catch it, I'll have to make sure it isn't around to bother us again.* "Fire all batteries. Now!" I moved to the edge of my seat, locking the targeting sensors on the enemy.

My brothers worked in sync to deploy the last of our missiles, but to my anger, the enemy ship activated a chaff field, confusing the missiles' guidance systems until it managed to outrun them.

I cursed under my breath and slammed my hands down on the control panel. "We lost them." I was disgusted with myself. I couldn't blame my crew, my brothers, or the other ships. I had set out to capture the rogue ship and find out the truth behind the invasion, and I had failed.

"Hey, at least we managed to fight off the Thezlum invasion." Ragar shrugged as if it was no big deal that we had failed in our secondary mission. On a practical level, I could understand his reasoning, but I knew that until we found out the secret behind this attack, we would never know when another was coming.

"But we allowed the main battleship to escape. That is unacceptable," Lysi reprimanded our younger brother for being so foolish.

"Lysi is right. We have failed our empire." I refused to look at my brothers as I stared at the dwindling spark on the view-screen, feeling tense energy snap from the tips of my fingers. I knew I was moments away from losing control if I didn't manage to restrain myself, and so I breathed deeply. I wouldn't humiliate myself again in front of my brothers and crew.

"We could always plan a counterattack," Sephir suggested with a sly grin on his face.

I immediately wondered what he was up to, but I couldn't help but take his words seriously. If we went on the offensive, we could show the Thezlums the wrath of the Vixxian Empire, control when the fight happened and under what terms…and get another chance to discover the secret behind that rogue ship. "Perhaps."

"It would take a while to get to their home-world, but it's not that far beyond our empire's borders," Sephir commented as he looked at his sharp nails, cleaning them out with the point of his dagger. "Perhaps it is time that the frontier was…moved outward."

"Sephir is right. We will launch an attack as soon as possible," I declared as I got up.

"Hold that thought, big brother," Lysi said with a frown as he peered at one of the communications screens at the station next to Gunnery. "According to this report, Father took a division of our warriors to the frontier to intercept a second raiding party."

I froze. "Second raiding party…?" Next to me, Sephir fidgeted slightly in his seat.

"According to this report we're just getting in, they attacked the crippled Thezlum ship and tried to overwhelm the guard we had posted there. Father brought reinforcements. That is all I have so far, but apparently, they were unsuccessful in destroying the ship." Lysi looked up at me with a worried frown.

"So, that is what Father meant about a distraction," I growled. "Of course, they must be desperate to keep their technology out of our hands. It's the only edge that they have."

"I still think you would be better off attacking Thezlum Prime directly." There was a slight edge of annoyance to Sephir's voice, as if my red-eyed brother were angry I had gone from following his "advice" to acting on better information. *So eager to be the one deciding,* I thought in annoyance. *So reluctant to take responsibility for any missions on his own.*

"If you wish to lead a squadron to Thezlum Prime, my brother, you have my leave. But if they were willing to sacrifice scores of their ships and hundreds of their men in a suicidal diversion while they tried to destroy that crippled ship, there must be something there that they are desperate to protect." *Possibly over and above the faster-than-light drive or the transporter.*

Sephir frowned but simply shook his head. "I'm content to follow your lead…for now."

"In that case, I suggest you spend more time doing your job on board and less time questioning me." I looked around at the bridge crew. "Any further objections?" Utter silence filled the space. "Good." I nodded toward the Capitol's vast, shining shape on our view-screen. "Then take us home. I have to discuss this matter with Father as soon as we both return."

With my mind focused on my next mission, I went back to the throne room as soon as we disembarked. Lysi stayed behind to give orders to the flight crew. Sephir almost immediately left for his chambers. *Good riddance,* I couldn't help but think.

I had to get permission from my father to go through with this, but I also knew I wouldn't let him deny me in the face of the cold, hard facts his own scouts had relayed back to us. Resolute, I barged into the throne room, only to find my mother and Misty sitting on the thrones.

My mother sat with her usual machinelike serenity, speaking on some point of Vixxian military history while Misty perched in obvious discomfort on the edge of my father's seat and listened. It wasn't just unusual—it was bizarre, as was my father's absence. Though I had to admit that my little human lover did look quite fetching wrapped in my cloak and seated on a throne.

I stopped, confused. "What is going on here?"

My mother's blank face turned toward me, and when she spoke, her voice held a note of casual amusement. It was as if she had decided to thumb her nose at tradition—or simply hadn't cared enough to give thought to the consequences of her action. "We were waiting for your return. You didn't expect our guest to stand the whole time, did you?"

Misty quickly got up at the end of my mother's statement. "Um, sorry. She told me to sit down," she mumbled, looking down in embarrassment.

"Yes, I did. Am I not Empress?" My mother's suddenly arch tone reminded me far too much of her beloved Sephir.

I just shook my head. "Where is Father?"

"He has not yet returned from the battle at the frontier. They are organizing a much heavier guard for that crippled Thezlum ship. The sub-light-speed jump back home will take a few hours at maximum."

This is not good. Misty came over to me, and I wrapped an arm around her as I leaned against her. I did not want to let on just how much comfort I found in her small body nestled against me and her huge dark eyes staring up at me. But at least my mother's attack of bluntness did not extend to criticizing me about it. "Can you raise him on the data streams?"

"I shall make the attempt." She sat up stiffly again and closed her eyes.

I waited mutely for a response, fighting my impatience. After a few minutes, she looked back up with a small frown. "I cannot seem to raise his flagship," she said, sounding mildly puzzled. "Perhaps they are in transit." The shields had to be strengthened for sub-light travel, and their energies interfered with transmissions.

I bit back a curse. I had been hoping to catch him before he left the wreckage. *I hate duplication of effort.* "Then I will ask you, Mother. I wish to bring a salvage team to the ship and have it towed to the nearest colony world. It needs to be thoroughly examined and stripped of all usable technology."

She was silent as she sat there, motionless as a statue. I waited patiently for her to think it over. I was still wondering why she had invited Misty into my father's seat—and why, besides the disrespect to my father, she had chosen to do so.

Finally, she lifted her head and spoke, her tone dull and exasperated, as if she was indulging a small child instead of approving a crucial mission. "Very well."

I didn't take it personally. My mother's madness had apparently started soon after Sephir and I had been born. She rarely reemerged from the data streams for more than several minutes at a time and was always annoyed when distracted from her addiction. "Thank you, Mother."

Without another word, I started to make my way out of the room. Before I could leave, Misty tugged insistently on my arm. I looked down at her, confused.

"I have to go with you," she said urgently.

My brow furrowed. I wanted to simply refuse her outright and walk on. The journey would be dangerous, as there was a good chance another Thezlum attack would take place on whichever colony world we towed the ship to. "Why?"

She eyed me with an annoyed expression, as if it should be obvious, then pushed aside her hair to expose the flashing disc on her neck. "Look. Maybe you don't think it's a big deal that I've been tagged like a goddamn animal and the Thezlums can now track me anywhere. Not to mention that they can make the disc paralyze me at will, and it's explosive and right over my carotid artery. But it matters to me. You're taking me with you, and we're finding the Thezlums' infirmary and learning how to remove these things safely."

I blinked down at her, stunned and suddenly more than a little embarrassed. It wasn't just because she had taken me to task in public, it was because she was right. I should have been more concerned that the Thezlums could activate—or detonate—her tag at will.

By the hard look on her face, I knew she wouldn't change her mind. Nor would I have, in her situation.

I sighed. "Very well."

She brightened immediately, the look of relief in her eyes so profound that my heart lifted. I was worried about the risks—but she was right. The risks of leaving the disc in were greater.

Besides, in the end, I wanted her to stay with me because she wished to. Not because she was forced to hide out on Vixxia Prime.

"We will take a scout ship to the frontier. It is the fastest model of ship in our arsenal. It doesn't have much firepower, but it can cloak itself, proving very useful to covert missions." I looked her over. "I'll provide you with a jumpsuit. How soon can you be ready?"

"Five minutes after you get me the clothes," she said firmly.

I looked back at her, surprised again by her spirit in the face of disorienting and often dangerous circumstances. "Fine. We both need rest after everything, and the scouter will need to be prepped. We'll leave after that." I glanced at my mother, but she was already sinking back into the data streams, her eyes glazing over.

Shaking my head slightly, I turned my back on the thrones and took Misty's hand. "Let's go."

CHAPTER 14
MISTY

"I had a strange talk with your mother while you were gone," I told Craze, a little surprised I had gotten through to him with my request to go to the Thezlum ship.

Odd how I could see his flaws a lot more now that I had spoken with his mother. His tendency to bull ahead with things without consulting others involved, especially. Maybe I would have been more worried about his possessiveness and overprotectiveness if I didn't want to be with him so badly. But I was still aware that he had these characteristics.

Maybe it's good that he's not starting too high up on a pedestal with me. Sexy, amazing Craze was also stubborn, impulsive Craze, and I preferred to know now rather than having my heart shattered when he jumped off his pedestal eventually.

"Oh?" he asked distractedly as he led us out and down the hall toward the lift. "She does not normally show an interest in our visitors."

I hesitated. *How much should I tell him?* I knew that if we were going to have a prayer of a serious relationship, I should tell him about Sephir's attempt to set up a meeting with me. But I wasn't quite up to that yet. Besides, I had more urgent news. "She commented that whoever shut down the city shields and the orbital sensors had to have Imperial Family-level clearance on the data network."

He stopped in the middle of the hallway and turned to me, blinking. "But that would mean…"

I nodded to him grimly. "Look, maybe she's right and you're facing a particularly talented hacker, but you were the one talking about having a traitor in your midst."

He frowned down at me, his eyes thoughtful, but he didn't address my suspicions. "Come. Don't worry about it right now. We need to get our rest." He led me through the maze of corridors until we arrived in front of the door to his chambers. I tried to memorize the path we took, but it was impossible. I doubted if I would ever be able to find my way around the palace alone without getting hopelessly lost.

I thought he was simply impatient for rest. But when we got back to his room, the first thing he did was take his cloak from me, eyes sweeping over me greedily as he left me in only the flimsy gown. "Hey," I teased him gently. "I thought we were resting."

"We are," he replied, looming over me, his eyes smoldering. "After." When I blinked at him in surprise, he took me by the shoulders and kissed me soundly.

"Craze, I have a question." I gently pushed him away, my hands resting on the sides of his face, making him look at me. His deep blue eyes gazed into my own, making my whole body yearn for him. A startling heat formed between my thighs as I felt my core quiver at the mere sight of him. I bit my lip as I was held in his gaze. *Maybe questions can wait…*

"What is it?" He tilted his head, his long, silver locks falling over his shoulder and brushing against my cheek.

"You said you could lend me some of your powers. How long does that last? Just because I'm insisting on going with you doesn't mean I'm reckless or stupid. If I can get an edge going out there, I want it." As much as I appreciated his ardor, and as much as it stirred up my own, I didn't think I could relax enough to enjoy sex while I was worrying about the journey.

He shrugged, looking a little disappointed that I had put him off for a moment. "It depends. If we practice together enough and are in close enough proximity, you can draw on my power at will. In the meantime, it lasts for perhaps a few days, unless I withdraw it from you or something else happens," he answered plainly. "If you're worried about your safety, why not wait here and let me bring the Thezlum tech you need back to you alone?"

Oops, and he's right back to that. I had better distract him. "Because I'd still be worried sick if it were just you out there. Besides, for all you know, you'd need a team of salvage welders to retrieve whatever device they use to deal with these damn neck tags." I slipped my arms around his neck and snuggled against him flirtatiously. "Anyway, clearly the only way to make sure I have the juice I need to make it through this mission is if you give me another dose."

"You may have a point. On all counts," he rumbled as he started nuzzling my hair. "Are all earthlings as intelligent as you?" He grinned ear-to-ear—then scooped me up and carried me over to the bed.

"Eek!" I let out a laugh and fake-struggled, kicking my legs slightly. Of course, I didn't want to get away…

He tossed me onto his bed playfully, then started taking off the last of his armor. Once the pile of high-tech alloy and animal hide was on the floor, he came back to the bedside, his erect cock pushing out the front of his loincloth.

His hungry, direct manner both frustrated me and turned me on. He had all but ignored my warning about the saboteur in favor of flirtation, which made me worry that he didn't take me seriously. But when he looked at me the way he was doing now, nearly everything but desire drained out of my mind too.

He pounced on me a moment later, making the plush surface of his bed bounce slightly. His hands braced on either side of my shoulders, and his knees straddled my legs. "Did you get more beautiful after I left?" he whispered in my ear, then softly nibbled on my neck. I moaned gently, feeling myself start to shiver. It was easy to set our issues aside when he somehow had turning me on down to an instinct.

"I think you just got hornier," I teased gently.

He raised his head and looked at me, arching an eyebrow. "Hmph. Enough talk for now," he rasped, then leaned down and buried his face in my neck again. His lips traveled down my skin until they lingered on my collarbone, nibbling, and sucking on it slightly. Then he found the pulse point on the side of my neck and sank his teeth in lightly, starting to suck.

Instantly, my hips rose, pressing against his, my body already growing hungry for his. Effortlessly, he untied the laces on my gown and whipped it off my body, leaving me completely naked and exposed. I shivered as I felt the slight breeze in the room. My nipples grew rock-hard in response.

Craze didn't waste a moment as his strong fingers tightened around my nipple, giving it a firm squeeze, and just holding it that way while I whimpered. It didn't hurt…not quite…but it was intense enough that I squirmed and arched my back. He lowered his lips to the other breast, tenderly kissing it all over. Finally, he rolled his lips over his teeth and closed them firmly around the nipple, tugging and lapping at it until I moaned out his name.

"Fuck…you make me feel so good," I gasped out as my hand tangled into his long hair. I could already feel my juices running down my thighs as he continued to toy with my body. His sharp nails slowly trailed along my side. A pleasant tingling ran through me, and I realized his power was starting to flow into me again. I moaned again, the nails of my other hand digging into his shoulder. I didn't know if I wanted his mouth or his cock more.

"You are incredibly intoxicating," Craze murmured as he raised his head from my breast. "I can barely control myself when I'm around you," he admitted, his voice sensual as his hand rested on my hips. He bent to his efforts again, and his lips slowly traveled down my stomach.

"I don't want you to control yourself. I want you to fuck me." My eyes were fierce as I stared up at him, imploring him to use my body any way he'd like.

"So demanding." He chuckled and sat up, kneeling between my legs. I took the opportunity to stare at that god's body of his in good light. I couldn't believe how chiseled his muscles were or what perfect skin he had. It was as if he was designed out of marble. My whole body tensed with sexual anticipation when he finally untied his loincloth and his large cock sprang free. Getting an idea, I licked my lips and I got up, crouching on the bed on my hands and knees.

"Let me return the favor for all the pleasure you gave me at the lake," I cooed as I crawled toward him, pushing him back down on the bed, a naughty look in my eyes as I stared at his erection. My appetite for him was growing with every second. With my hands on his thighs, I slowly spread his legs apart, a grin plastered on my face as I leaned down, kissing his inner thigh. His soft moan pleased me, and I felt my cunt quiver in response, my juices sliding down my legs. "Just lie back and relax."

CHAPTER 15
CRAZE

I watched Misty curiously. I had no idea what she was doing, but her current position excited me. I didn't know what exotic practices humans got up to in bed, but this one looked…promising. I could see a mischievous glint in her eyes as she positioned herself between my legs. My cock throbbed in eagerness, and my balls tightened as she looked my cock over as if considering something. Growing more excited and intrigued by the second, I waited breathlessly for her to make the next move.

Suddenly, she opened her mouth wide and pressed it against the tip of my cock, careful to keep her teeth out of the way. My eyes widened and I groaned in pleasure, feeling the silkiness of her lips caressing my engorged member. The sensations, the air of risk, the sight of her sliding her mouth up and down my shaft… I had used my mouth on all my lovers, but never had one used her mouth on me.

Apparently, I hadn't known what I was missing. My eyes rolled back into my skull, and my toes curled as I felt her take me deeper and deeper into her mouth. Her tongue worked to pleasure the underside of my cock as she slid downward. "Misty!" I called out as she managed to take my entirety into her mouth and throat…and began to suck.

She started to gag slightly on my length, but kept at it nevertheless, bobbing her head up and down with a measured rhythm that made me shudder with pleasure. She had complete control of me right now. She could have stabbed me and I would have taken it, just so long as she kept going.

My hands reached forward, tangling into her hair. I barely resisted the urge to force her head down over me. My hips bucked, and she got the hint and started moving faster. Her hands reached out and fondled my balls, petting them gently and then giving them a light squeeze.

I groaned as I felt them tighten. I was already approaching climax. I didn't want to go off until I had the warm folds of her cunt around my shaft again. Before she could push me over the edge, I took her by the shoulders. "Ahh…stop…stop."

She backed off, looking up at me teasingly. "You like that?" she crooned at me.

I responded with a feral growl as I lunged forward to pin her against the wall at the head of my bed. She gasped and let out a startled little cry, but then wrapped her arms and legs around me, settling her hips over my lap as I thrust home inside of her.

She was already slick with arousal, making my entrance effortless. Aching with the need for release, I rocked my hips back and forth, thrusting into her for all I was worth. She let out a happy cry and started riding me, grinding against me as I thrust into her.

My hands roamed her body, stroking her curves. As I felt my body's tension build, I leaned forward and took her breast into my mouth, sucking on it lovingly. She moaned, head falling back, writhing harder against me.

I continued to pump my cock in and out of her, feeling her smooth walls wrap around me tightly. She moaned out in pleasure, her voice exciting me further as I continued to push us both toward climax.

"Oh fuck, Craze. I'm going to—ahh," Misty moaned at the top of her lungs as her whole body writhed against my own. Her back arched, and her hips pressed down on mine desperately. I gasped for air as I moved my lips to her emblem, kissing it.

Psychic energy flowed through us both. A flash of heat and passion ran through our bodies, making us even more frenzied. My thoughts fragmented, and the next thing I knew, we were both rolling around on the bed, ravaging each other wildly.

Her nails ran all over my body, clawing at my back. Her legs clenched around me, heels braced on the backs of my thighs, trying to pull me deeper inside her. Finally, I pinned her down and held her wrists to the bed, thrusting into her even harder. Her screams echoed throughout the room, bouncing off the walls as she thrashed under me like a woman in a fit. Seconds later, she howled out in ecstasy.

Feeling her folds tighten rhythmically around me during her climax, I grunted, trying to keep back my own—and then felt myself failing. My fingers tightened around her wrists as my eyes locked on her luscious, bouncing breasts. My back arched, and I pounded away roughly, mind blank with lust. As my balls slapped against her supple ass, I felt myself losing all control. Then my muscles locked, and I buried the full length of my cock into her.

I heard my own shouts of joy rise to join hers as ecstasy rolled through me in waves. My seed exploded from me in long spasms. It seemed to go on and on until, finally, I spent myself.

Exhausted, I allowed myself to collapse onto the bed, my breathing heavy and ragged. Misty whimpered and cuddled up against me, burying her face in my chest, overwhelmed. I wrapped my arm tightly around her, pulling her closer. My cock was still buried deep inside of her. Her emblem glowed brightly. I knew that my psychic gift to her would now last quite a while. Nothing would be able to hurt her. If my powers did not ensure it, I would.

I woke up refreshed a few hours later. Misty was still asleep, so after cleansing my body and putting on my garments, I slipped carefully out of the room, making sure not to wake her. Quickly, I traversed the palace toward the armory, looking for equipment fit for a woman of her proportions. Vixxian females tended to be tall and boyish, and their armor would not have room for Misty's fantastic curves. But some of the other races in our empire had more generously proportioned females, and some of them served in the Imperial military.

Finally, I found a nice set of lightweight ceramic armor I thought would fit Misty. Grabbing it, I carried it back to my room, humming.

As I entered, Misty was coming out of the cleansing unit looking refreshed, her hair dripping. I walked over to her side, kissing her cheek gently. "We must get ready for our mission."

She did not complain. "Okay," she answered as she rubbed her hand against her eyes. I gave her a moment to recover from her scrub-down before I helped her put on the armor. It took some struggling, straps had to be loosened in the breastplate, tightened in the bracers. She coiled up her hair to fit it under the helmet and then stood back for me to inspect.

I looked at her with pride. "You look lovely." I pulled her close and kissed her lips, feeling my heart swell.

"Thanks. This all feels a little bit weird, but it's pretty cool." She looked down at herself. "Will this stop Thezlum blaster fire?"

I chuckled and nodded. "Energy weapons, blades, blows. The helmet also has an atmosphere converter in it. Do people on your planet not wear armor?"

"Not like this. At least, not in the last five centuries or so." She went to the tall mirror behind my dressing-curtain and turned around in front of it a few times. "Nice."

"I see." I grabbed her hand. "Come, let's get to the ship."

Misty nodded, following me out the courtyard doors and across the rolling moss lawn to the shipyard. The swift click of her boots on the stone path as she walked beside me was strangely satisfying to my ears. It reminded me of…

Stop that, Craze. You know better. I immediately got very annoyed with myself. There were some things in my past that needed to remain in my past for me to be a good mate to Misty now. What and whom the sound of an armored woman's boots beside me reminded me of was one of those things.

We made our way to the far end of the launch complex, passing all the other ships on our way. They swarmed with flight and repair crewmen of various races, fixing and restocking them all, down to the smallest interceptor. The battle had tapped our resources badly, but I was pleased to see that very few of the launchpads sat empty.

"Has anyone contacted you about their search for the saboteur?" Misty asked me as we walked. She had been thoughtfully quiet for most of the journey, but when she spoke up at last, her voice had a slight edge to it that caught my attention.

I glanced down at her as we walked past the *Solrei*, frowning slightly. She seemed a bit stuck on the subject, and I wondered why. I knew she had nothing to do with the sabotage. I had not left her alone since she had woken up. "I have received no further word. I sent messages to my parents and brothers about the matter, but there has been little response. I suspect they will probably enlist Sephir to assist my mother in the search, but he's far from the most cooperative of men."

She frowned, and she looked for a moment like she was going to say something further, but then she simply nodded resignedly. "I see. Well, at least someone is doing something about it."

"Of course," I said as casually as I could manage. I hadn't really had time to follow up on the messages I had sent, but the bracer with my network connection had not beeped at me. No responses yet.

We reached the small-craft section, walking past interceptors and scout ships, until we stood in front of the smallest one in the entire shipyard. Misty blinked at the tiny craft, barely room for two people and perhaps a week's supplies, lightly armed and simple except for its cloaking device. "Is this really what we are using?" She looked between the ship and its larger companions with a slightly dubious expression as we walked up to it.

I had to grin. It really didn't look like much, barely larger than a one-man interceptor. But it made up for its unimpressive stature in speed and agility. "This is the best ship in our fleet for stealth flights and recon missions," I explained, opening the boarding gate and stepping inside. "Welcome aboard the *Invixis*."

CHAPTER 16
MISTY

I climbed aboard the spaceship, still skeptical about how tiny it was. But I was impressed when I got inside. Everything shone beautifully. The walls were sleek and beige in color. Looking at them, I could see a clear reflection of myself. Beyond the tiny hold sat a two-person cockpit with heavily padded seats facing a huge, curved view-screen and an elaborate bank of controls.

"Close quarters," Craze muttered half apologetically as he bypassed me and sat in the captain's chair. I followed him and sat down in the adjacent seat. Various switches glowed in front of me. I fought the urge to reach forward and flip some of them, not knowing what they would do. "Do not touch anything," he ordered, as if reading my mind.

Oops. Caught. I sat back and placed my hands in my lap, waiting for him to get us airborne. "Do you need any help?"

"No. A single person easily mans this ship. It was designed mainly for solo missions." He leaned forward and turned on the main power with the flip of a glowing blue switch. The spacecraft shook slightly in response as its engines rumbled to life. I held on to my seat and bit the corner of my lip. "Don't be nervous. Everything will be all right," he reassured me immediately, laying a hand on my thigh and giving it a slight squeeze.

I nodded but was still a little unsure. As the ship slowly lifted off the ground, I felt my stomach sink and held on to my seat a tad tighter. Abruptly, the ship shot off into the sky, and I lurched back into my seat. It felt like my heart would slam into my spine.

I could barely breathe as we picked up speed, heading toward the edge of the atmosphere. I had heard of g-forces before, but this was many times beyond anything I had felt in an airplane. I grayed out a little, wheezing, feeling the weight of the world on my chest. When we finally broke through to a starry darkness, the ship leveled out, and I regained my breath.

I leaned forward, my head between my knees as I felt a little queasy. "Holy shit, that was intense."

"Are you okay?" Craze's hand rested on my back as he ran the fingers of his other hand through my hair. "You look sick," he noted as he started to caress my now-clammy cheek.

"Yes… This just wasn't what I expected. It's like being on a plane, but ten times worse." *Deep breaths, there, girl.* The queasiness ebbed away, but that punched-in-the-gut feeling stayed.

"A plane?" He tilted his head in confusion.

"Short for airplane. They're low- to middle-atmosphere-only fliers. Anyway, I'm okay now." I looked out the cockpit shield to find we had left the planet well behind while I had been recovering from our take-off. "Wow. Last time I was looking at this view, it was through a port on the Thezlum ship."

A view-screen on the panel beeped and lit up, showing a diagram of what looked like an asteroid field. I peered out through the cockpit shield and saw it ahead of us, light glinting off some of the larger aster-oids. "Oh boy. Is that dangerous?"

"Oh no. We have this region thoroughly mapped." He closed his eyes and laid his hand on the control panel briefly. I saw sparks fly around his hand, and then he drew it back. "That should do it. This field lies between Vixxia Prime and the frontier. We use it as part of our defense system. I'm actually quite surprised that the Thezlum ships were able to navigate it."

A suspicion immediately crept into my mind—or back in, since it had nagged at me before, when the sabotage had been mentioned. "Craze, I can think of one way they could have gotten that fleet through the field without killing themselves."

"How is that?" He opened his eyes back up and looked at me.

"Whoever it was has access to Vixxia's data streams and enough authorization to get their hands on your map of the asteroid field." My heart sped up a little. *Will he listen this time?*

He sighed and nodded, setting his jaw grimly. "The hacker must be very good indeed."

"You really don't want to consider the other possibility, do you?" I sat back with a sigh. "Craze...look. I hate to be the bearer of bad news, but something more is going on here than just a hacker. Whoever did this not only has access to secret information, they know things that only a member of your court—maybe even your family —could."

He scowled, and for a moment, I thought I had lost him completely with my accusation. But then he sat up, sighing through his nose. "Such as?"

"Such as timing the attack for when the leader of Vixxia's military was preoccupied with his new lover," I replied firmly and sadly. "We weren't exactly discreet."

In fact, it was possible that someone had not only seen us enter the sacred grove that afternoon, but...watched us. The whole idea made me sick to my stomach. My cheeks flamed with embarrassment.

From the dawning horror on Craze's face, the same thought occurred to him. He cursed under his breath, a word that didn't pass the translator. "This is becoming very troubling," he muttered. He closed his eyes again and leaned back in his seat, and I saw his bracer light up, its readouts flickering.

"What are you doing?" I asked a little nervously as the ship made its way into the asteroid field. It steered easily around the tumbling hunks of stone, surprising me. But I stayed nervous. Some of those "hunks of stone" were the size of mountains.

"I'm sending another communication to my mother and father regarding this matter. It's a bit awkward, but I'm afraid that you just made a very good point. The timing of that attack was no coincidence at all."

I sat back in my chair, fuming. The idea that someone had taken advantage of Craze's involvement with me drove me a little crazy. It was almost as if this unknown person had timed it, not just to catch Craze off guard, but to make him look foolish and distractible. And as for me...

God, I probably look ridiculously slutty. I might even look like I was coop-erating with whoever it is to make sure Craze was distracted! "What a mess," I muttered, now even more disgusted and pissed off.

He nodded grimly, and then his expression slowly grew puzzled. "Odd. No return communications. That's the second time." He shook his head. "Father should have been back to the palace hours ago. I do not understand."

"Is there any other way of reaching them?" I hoped it wasn't a stupid question, but the mildly annoyed look he shot me didn't help my confidence.

"We are reliant on the data streams outside of planetary orbit," he said with slightly exaggerated patience.

He's just tense because his father's been out of contact so long, I comforted myself. "Okay. I get it. I just think it's weird too."

He stayed silent, and I got the impression from that and the lights flashing on his bracer that he was continuing his attempts at communi-cation. "Could I be being jammed somehow?" he finally wondered aloud. But then he shook his head and went quiet again.

I tried to distract myself by watching the ship steer us around the asteroids, but that was too stomach-wrenching to deal with after a while. I changed the subject instead. "How is the ship moving by itself?"

He glanced up from staring at a readout on his bracer. "Autopilot."

"Ah," I said as I leaned back in my chair. "What happens once we clear the asteroid field?"

"I double-check our telemetry readings and then engage the sub-light drives. We reach the battle site in roughly three hours."

"I see. What do we do until then?" I needed a distraction from the interstellar traffic jam going on outside the cockpit shield.

"Whatever we'd like." He smiled warmly in my direction, and I caught a faint gleam in his deep blue eyes.

"Anything?" A naughty grin spread across my face as I looked over at Craze, who looked hot as ever even with his magnificent body hidden away in his armor. Without another word, I got up and sat on his lap, wrapping my arms around his neck.

"What are you doing?" he asked, his expression puzzled. Nevertheless, he rested his hands on my hips, pulling me closer until I could feel the slight bulge of his codpiece pressing against my ass. From the little grunt of discomfort he made, his cock was already pushing at the other side of the metal.

"You." With that, I pressed myself forward until our lips met roughly. I darted my tongue into his mouth, teasing his as we began loosening each other's armor.

Our breaths turned ragged as our desire for one another grew rapidly. "Mmm, Craze…" I whispered in his ear. "Keep my mind off those damn asteroids, okay?"

He did not say anything. Instead, his fingers made their way down my body, unlatching the belt of my hip armor to loosen it, then sneaking under my crotch-guard until they found my already wet lips. He caressed up and down the cleft between them, barely entering. I let out a loud moan into his neck, my lips leaving a line of kisses along his skin.

His fingers eventually left off teasing my cunt and approached my ass instead. I arched my back as I felt his hand kneading the cheek of my ass, making me moan again. I wiggled my hips, letting my body call out to him invitingly, but he continued to tease me. His fingers ran along the rim of my hole as it puckered in anticipation.

Instead of penetrating me with one of his fingers, however, he unlatched the entire crotch-piece of my armor, pulling it away and leaving my sex exposed. With his blue eyes shining with excitement, he unfastened his codpiece and tossed it aside, freeing his erection.

He grabbed my hips and hoisted me above his cock. "Naughty, teasing me like this when I should be monitoring. Now you'll have to pay for it…"

I giggled as I realized his intentions. I took a deep breath and relaxed my muscles, allowing him to slowly lower me down on his already rock-hard member. I moaned as I felt his tip probe against my slit and then push inside. Inch by inch, he impaled me on his cock until I felt full to the brim.

My cunt had to stretch to accommodate his throbbing rod as he forced all of himself deep inside of me. I felt his heart pounding in his chest and in his cock, which slid deliciously in and out of my soft, hungry flesh. The slight pain only intensified things.

"Fuck…that feels so good," I grunted as my arms wrapped around him, pulling him even closer. As his fingers tightened around my hips, I leaned forward and kissed him once more.

CHAPTER 17
CRAZE

My whole body came alive as she shimmied around my cock and leaned forward to kiss me. It was like she was imbuing me with her own power instead of the other way around, making me tense with energy. My cock shivered deep inside of her as I moaned out in pleasure, my fingers digging into her hips a little harder.

I wanted to tell her not to go. I wanted to beg her to stay with me once she was free of the tag and could go where she pleased. But future emperors do not beg…so I told her with my body what I could not with my mouth.

I didn't know what poison my poor, mad mother had been pouring into Misty's ear earlier, but I needed to feel connected to her. It was the only thing that drove my demons away and let me just…feel.

Unable to control myself any longer, I started to bounce her on my aching length. Her slick, warm juices coated my erection as I kept on relentlessly. I felt her inner muscles start to tighten around me. As she kept sliding up and down, I rested two fingers on her clit, rubbing it gently. Her breath came now in whimpering gasps, and she writhed over me in ways that drove me crazy.

Wanting more, I started to slam her down on my manhood, our

armor creaking rhythmically with the effort. She yelped then squirmed harder, which only drove me to do it again…and again. Faster and harder with every thrust until the sound of our hips slapping together could be heard echoing through the hold, along with our ecstatic moans.

I sucked desperately on her neck as I continued to bounce her faster and faster. Our frenzy grew and grew, until the pleasure became too much to handle. I groaned in ecstasy as I arched my back, shooting my seed deep inside of her as her fingers dug into my back. My cock was still pulsing when she cried out, and I felt her contractions around me.

We both sighed in happy exhaustion, leaning back together in my chair. I held her tightly in my arms with my cock still buried inside of her, her walls quivering around me in the aftermath of her orgasm. "Wow," she whispered as she kissed my lips one more time.

I WOKE WITH A START AS THE SHIP SHOOK VIOLENTLY. A PROXIMITY ALARM sounded as the overhead lights flashed red at me, warning us of an attack. The *Invixis* jolted to a hard stop, as if it had struck something. Misty and I were flung out of our chair, crashing into the command panel.

"What the hell was that?" Misty asked in breathless shock as she scrambled to her feet and groped for her crotch-piece.

"We're under attack!" I bellowed as I got behind the controls once more and snapped into my crash harness. "Fasten yourself in and hang on!"

She pulled herself back into the seat beside me and hastily snapped her crotch-piece back into place before fastening herself in. I grabbed my own off the floor, suddenly realizing how it would look to rescue crews if I crashed into an asteroid with my dick out.

To my surprise, when I looked back up from fumbling it into place, I saw that we were now just above the orbit for Hexiven, a small, abandoned planet whose colonies had been destroyed years ago in the Great War. *How long were we screwing? How long were we sleeping, for that matter? And how could I have been so stupid?*

But I knew how. I had been thinking with my cock instead of my tactics training, and I had let Misty pull me into sex at the wrong moment. I hadn't engaged the cloaking mechanism before having my fun with Misty, and now we were paying dearly for it as a familiar-looking command ship shot at us.

"It's the rogue ship! How in space did they find us?" Growling, I veered our vessel to the right, dodging another volley of force bolts.

Misty didn't say anything, but I saw her horrified expression as she reached up for the flashing red light on her neck. We both realized it at once. She should have stayed behind, after all. They had followed her tracker's signal.

I knew my small scout ship would not cause any damage if I simply fired at will. So, I had to be very precise if I stood any chance at disabling it. I turned on the cloaking mechanisms, feeling a gentle vibration as the ship became invisible to the naked eye. I quickly peeled away from my current heading and watched as our opponent sent a blind volley of missiles at the spot we had just left.

"I've bought us some time. The cloak should cover your tag's signal as well." Knowing we were now virtually undetectable, I ran a scan of the enemy ship.

I quickly read the results as they came up on my screen. "Thezlum hull structure...Dragican engines...Mersine war missiles..." I ran through the hodgepodge assembly, trying to find some vulnerability that we could target.

The Thezlum raiders and their Mersine allies were notorious for their powerful weapons, but their targeting scanners were subpar. If I managed to position us just below their starboard, it would be nearly impossible for them to shoot at us. "Stay calm. I have a plan."

I was about to move into position when the whole ship shook violently. "What?" A precision shot had just clipped off the end of our left wing—and one of the cloaking generators with it.

"Cloak disabled," an overhead voice announced.

"How did their gunner see through our cloak?" *Psychic powers? But even the Dragicans barely had any ability at all!*

Cursing under my breath, I tried turning on the sub-light engine for a quick getaway—but the damaged ship was taking its sweet time powering up. "Incoming missile," the voice warned. Teeth gritted, I initiated evasive maneuvers, but it wasn't fast enough. Another missile rammed into the side of the ship, sending us spiraling through space as the klaxon wailed and the voice dispassionately reported damages.

When we finally stabilized, I grabbed the steering yoke again and rolled us closer to the planet, then circled back toward the rogue ship. "Just stay calm. I need to focus." Misty obeyed, her face decorated with small beads of nervous sweat as I concentrated on steering the ship toward our one chance of temporary safety.

After a few tense moments, we managed to reach the ship's starboard side, using magnetic landers to latch the *Invixis* to the hull underneath the viewports. I let out a huge sigh and saw Misty relax slightly beside me. She kept her hand clamped over the tag on her neck, as if hiding it from sight could block its signal.

"Are you angry at me?" she asked quietly.

"No." I was, but I knew it was irrational. I was the one who had gone for an offer of sex instead of ensuring our security, and she had not really known better. Meanwhile, the chances of the signal being found at the edge of an asteroid field, with a metal-rich planet nearby, had been astronomically small. As had been the shot that had knocked out our cloak. Whoever was behind this hadn't just bested us temporarily because I had been caught with my pants down. The rogue ship's commander and crew had real talent—and possibly psychic talent as well.

As we waited idly, I watched the rogue ship's cannon pods moving around, trying to lock on us. In less than a minute and to my great relief, they finally halted. "Good. Now they'll be forced to waste time scanning and figuring out why the signal they're looking for is coming from their own ship. If they can see our signal at all and not dismiss our presence as signal echo."

"Will we be able to sneak away?" Misty asked softly as she stared nervously through the cockpit shield.

Before I had time to answer, the system announced an incoming message. I hesitated. Answering it would make us potentially vulnerable to a data-stream hack...or even a psychic attack. But my head spun with questions that demanded answers. *Who does this ship belong to? What rogue is brave, stupid, or suicidal enough to launch an invasion of Vixxia Prime?* There was only one way to find out.

Setting my jaw, I accepted the transmission from the enemy ship, focusing my power to block out any data attacks. Instantly, the main view-screen filled with the image of a shadowy Thezlum bridge, on which stood a single tall figure, dressed in a dark cloak.

"Identify yourself," I commanded.

Slowly, they lifted their head, and my eyes grew wide as I saw a familiar pair of ruby eyes staring back at me. Then the figure let out a familiar mocking laugh, and slim hands folded back the hood to reveal a woman's face framed by shimmering, steel-gray curls.

"Astrid?" I gasped aloud, before I could stop myself. *Oh no. Not her. Not now. She was supposed to have gone back to Dragican! What is she doing here now?*

"Who's Astrid?" Misty's voice was tense as she blurted out the question. A hollow laugh filled our ship as the rogue ship's captain grinned mockingly at my confused mate.

"You know, you Vixxians could really learn a thing or two from all the species you have conquered. Our Mersine allies are really making leaps and bounds in their space-travel technology now that they've fled your space for ours. You don't even need a crew anymore to operate one of their ships," she gloated, her eyes glowing menacingly. "Especially if you have the right gifts."

Gifts? Astrid is barely psychically aware at all. What is she talking about? "You cannot man that vessel by yourself. A ship of that size would need dozens, if not hundreds, of crew members to function properly," I responded in disbelief.

"Really?" A sly grin crept onto Astrid's narrow, pale face as she stepped aside, revealing an empty bridge.

I gawked at the screen. "That's impossible. Where are your medical staff? Your cooks, engineers, and replacement pilots? You cannot be in there by yourself." I was vaguely aware of Misty staring at me accusingly, but I couldn't address that right now. My ex would enjoy it far too much if Misty and I broke into a lover's squabble with her as an audience.

"You really doubt me? After I have single-handedly conquered three planets in Dragican space?" She snorted, tossing her cloak back over her shoulder. The suit of ceramic and metal armor was deep green, chased with the same scarlet as her eyes. It was a Vixxian design, and my eyes narrowed suspiciously. I knew I had not gifted that armor to her. *Who did?*

I had always known her to be brilliant, innovative, and arrogant. Her lawlessness and greed, and her ulterior motives for seducing me, had driven us apart, even before she had chosen to become a space pirate. Now, apparently, she was trying her hand at a new title —warlord.

"Why in space did you attack my home-world?" I asked in disbelief. "And why are you attacking us now?" We hadn't parted on the best of terms, but nothing I had ever said or done to her had warranted a conquest-level attack.

Her lip curled. "I was satisfying the requests of one of my...allies. Someone with a vested interest in Vixxian affairs."

"That's slippery of you. Who?" I cast about in my head, trying to figure out who among us would join forces with a Dragican noble's brat gone rogue.

"That would be telling." She grinned, her sharp teeth showing. Something about that mocking, predatory smile—so unlike the one she had worn back when I had loved her—reminded me uncomfortably of...something. Someone else's face, someone else's smirk. But who? It suddenly seemed terribly important. "But don't you worry, you big, gorgeous lump of pointy-eared man-meat." She pursed her lips in mock-affection. "You'll find out soon enough!"

"I can't tell whether the isolation or all your drinking has done more to drive you mad," I said with a hint of pity in my voice. "You can't possibly be aboard that ship alone." I might have managed to cover all of a ship's station controls by straining my powers to their utmost, but how in space had Astrid done it?

"If you don't believe me, why don't you come inside and see for yourself?" She snickered, her eyes teasing me.

"Don't do it," Misty warned, her voice managing to sound both steely and mildly panicked. "It's a trap. Please don't be foolish, Craze. Just get us out of here!"

I looked at her, half in annoyance and half in acknowledgment. She was right, inexperienced or not.

"I'm waiting," Astrid crooned flirtatiously, broad mockery still coloring her tone. The doors to what I assumed was the hangar bay opened half a ship-length in front of us.

I hesitated, then shook my head. "You're right, Misty. Let's go." It would be hugely risky trying to sneak away, but if we could get to the asteroid field before Astrid could, we could hide there until I could contact help.

"Uh-uh." Astrid waved a finger at us reproachfully. "Let me put it another way since you're being dense as usual." She held up a small gray box. "This is a remote-control box for the kind of slave tags the Thezlum use nowadays. Allow me to demonstrate."

"No!" I shouted, but I was too late. One press of a button, and suddenly Misty convulsed, her eyes rolling back in her head. Her breathing rasped, and it sounded like she was being strangled. "Stop! I swear I'll kill you for this, Astrid! Stop!"

"Say the word, and I will…" she teased as Misty started choking. "Otherwise, your human piece of ass will end up a vegetable in under a minute." She stabbed the button, and Misty groaned incoherently in pain, back arching.

My heart clenched. "Fine. Fine. You win, Astrid. I'll comply. Now, stop torturing her!"

Her pointed eyebrow quirked, but then she shrugged and deactivated the device. Misty collapsed in her chair, shaking and panting. She would recover, but as I glanced over at her, I saw her eyes rolling in terror. I reached out for her hand and squeezed it, keeping it under the view of the communicators.

With no other choice, I disengaged the magnetic landers and steered the *Invixis* forward, entering the vessel's large hangar. I kept looking over at Misty, who stared at me with pained eyes as she slowly recovered. She was bathed in sweat and ashen. I wondered if she was still beating herself up over coming out here while tagged, or whether she wanted to beat me for never mentioning Astrid.

Thinking about it now, it had been a big omission.

My mind raced as I tried to figure out how Astrid could be running that entire ship alone. But I did force myself to look calm for Misty's sake. I reached up and muted the transmission on our end so I could speak to her in private for a moment. "I don't know what Astrid is up to, but I'm going to try to get that control box away from her. It must have a deactivation switch. Once that's done, I'm getting us back to our ship, and we're going to hide out in that asteroid field for a while."

Misty nodded, her drawn face resolute. "Okay."

As the tractor beam caught us and drew us into a space in the hangar, my mind turned to my last memory of Astrid. She had been stealing a Vixxian vessel as I chased her off my home planet—not even an hour after learning of her manipulative plans for me. It had happened five years ago, and anger still coursed through my veins as I remembered. At the time, it felt like she had flown off with my heart. Bitter, trust shattered, I had not touched another woman for years after that. But then along came Misty.

As we landed, I glared at Astrid, still on the screen. "This better not be a trap," I warned.

"Of course not," she answered cheekily.

Nearly growling, I ended the transmission. "Come on. We have to go." I turned to help Misty out of her chair. She moved shakily, but she managed to get her feet under her and walk beside me.

"Be brave," I told her. "Trust me. I'll find a way to get us out of this." But when we made our way down the ramp, I felt my stomach tighten.

I had been all right back on the *Invixis* with Misty by my side and her scent still clinging to me. I had avoided too much wistful thought about the past. I had avoided reminiscing on how much Astrid and I had desired each other, the witty banter, the stunning sex. I wouldn't have traded Misty for a dozen of Astrid, but I still knew what taking too long a trip into those memories would do to me. I didn't want Astrid gaining power over me again.

But the moment I stepped off the ramp and looked her in the eyes, her exotic, spicy scent struck my nostrils again for the first time in years, and I felt my body respond against my will. *Curse it,* I thought and stared back at her stiffly. "Astrid."

"Long time, no see, Craze." She looked at me, then Misty, then back again, her ruby red lips curling into a sinister smile. "Let's you, me, and your new rutting toy have a little chat."

CHAPTER 18
MISTY

"What the hell is all this about?" I challenged the strange woman, doing my best to look fearless and strong. Inside, though, my head was whirling. I was supposed to be impervious thanks to Craze's power. But she had just put me through agony at the touch of a button. Was the power fading—or would the attack have been that much worse if I had not been able to draw on it?

She ignored the question and turned away from me, focusing on Craze instead. "Hmm." She licked her lips and gave him a teasing look. "So. Got a new companion, I see, Craze. Did you put your mark on her the same day you learned her name too?" The Dragican woman's voice dripped with disdain.

Wait, what? I glanced over at Craze, my hand going to the symbol he had branded into my breast without even asking me. *Did he do the same to her?* I saw him staring right at her, a faint look of longing on his face, and my blood slowly came to a boil. *Does he try to keep every single woman he has sex with? Am I not actually special to him at all?*

I should have known. The whole thing had been too fast, too against all odds…too enjoyable. But it still came as a shock. *Of course, this isn't anything special. He just likes fucking aliens, and then he wants to keep us all. His personal Captain Kirk harem. A woman in every spaceport.* My heart sank.

Astrid caught my look and burst out laughing. "Oh, you poor human. This must be such a shock to you. But, guess what?" She unfastened her shoulder armor and tugged her breastplate down slightly on that side—and I caught a gleam of blue. The same double-spiral design as the one on my breast…and it was glowing. "Truth is, he's a big whore. He just likes to mark what he fancies as his territory." Her smile faded, and she shot Craze a look of disgust.

Craze stayed silent, eyes avoiding the both of us, neither defending himself nor me. It made me want to slap him. *And why was her mark glowing while mine remained as flat as paint?*

"Oops, Craze, looks like the piece of ass is starting to figure things out. Won't you be in trouble once she learns the whole truth? That is, if either of you lives that long!" She threw back her head, iron-colored hair tossing around her cloaked shoulders, and laughed at us again. The little gray box of pain stayed in her hand, its switches in easy reach. I stared at it briefly, fighting back the reckless urge to punch her in the face. I needed a proper opening, or I'd end up on the floor in agony again.

I looked between them. My disappointment in Craze raked my heart like claws. He didn't have the nerve to fight back, to defend or comfort me. "What do you have to say for yourself?" I growled at him.

Astrid snorted and tugged her shoulder guard back into place. She needed both hands to refasten her armor, so she clipped the control box to her belt and reached up to work the fasteners.

Seizing the opportunity, I flung myself forward, swinging my leg toward the side of her head, kickboxer style. The move was half opportunistic and half calculated, distract her with the kick, then grab for the control box while Craze used the opening to attack—

Except that he didn't. He just stood there and watched.

Astrid caught my leg with ease, then stepped forward, forcing my leg back until she held my ankle near my head. I wobbled, forced off-balance. "A feisty one. You always did like troublesome women, Craze," she remarked casually. Then she gave me a brutal shove, unbalancing me, and slamming me down onto the metal floor.

I barely avoided knocking my head. *Get up. Craze is being useless. I must fight!* I gritted my teeth and pushed myself back up through the pain—only to have her stab a button on the control box that sent another electric shock through me. I convulsed, panting through my teeth, and then collapsed to the floor again. She let the button go, and the seizure ended, leaving me with every muscle aching.

My head spun, and I struggled to get up. She lunged toward me, about to drive her boot into my side, when Craze finally stepped in to intercept her.

About damn time, I thought, groaning with frustration when I realized I couldn't move yet. So much for grabbing the control box.

For some reason, Craze didn't draw his sword. He didn't invoke his powers. He didn't even hit back. "Astrid, rethink what you are doing," he ordered her as she rained down punch after punch in his direction. She was fast and agile and executed each blow ferociously, but he skillfully dodged them all. "You don't have to live like this. Be a warlord if you want, but quit this vendetta against me and mine. We've ended ours against you!"

"Impossible. You know that conquest and vendetta are in my blood. It's the Dragican way. And it's not just my blood that carries it, either."

"What do you mean by that?" he demanded, blocking one of her fist strikes with his forearm and ducking aside from the next. He still hadn't landed a single strike on her. He was avoiding being hit while *reasoning* with her. It made me want to strangle him. She had just been torturing me! She was responsible for the deaths of possibly thousands of his people! Where were his priorities?

Where the hell were his balls? *Does he somehow care about her more than me…or his people?*

At least his distracting her had bought me some time. I managed to sit up, gasping for air. *Okay. That's a start. Maybe I can get away to recover now that Craze's finally gotten off his ass to help.*

"In time, you will learn for yourself." She rammed her knee into his midsection. He grunted and, incredibly, I heard the metal and ceramic of his breastplate crack.

I managed to get to my knees, my guts still twisted up and my muscles aching from dancing on that damned electronic puppet-string of hers. Astrid lunged at me, but Craze stepped in the way, blocking a boot strike meant for the side of my neck.

He grunted slightly, and then he shoved Astrid back and straightened, shaking out the forearm he had guarded me with. I heard a faint crunch, as if one of his arm bones was setting itself. "Don't torture her because you want to hurt me. Where is your honor?"

"Honor? A Vixxian nobleman wishes to school me on honor? Haven't we had this discussion half a dozen times by now?" Astrid laughed and stalked around us slowly, a predatory grin on her face. "Who are you kidding, Craze? You were born with every damned privilege, and you ride into your future throne on the coattails of conquerors. There is as much innocent blood on the hands of your father and forefathers as on mine or any other Dragican warlord's. Yet you and your father have the gall to call yourselves just protectors of a peaceful empire!"

"I am quite aware of the checkered past of my forefathers and even my father. This ship orbits a world that he bombed into rubble. Do you think I plan to conveniently forget his mistakes instead of learning from them?" He was still trying to reason with her.

She let out a shout of outrage and attacked him again. They battled their way down the corridor between hangared fighters, Craze continuously leading Astrid away from me. But she was clever. She turned and darted toward me threateningly, forcing him to step in and start the process of battling her away from me again.

"You are not capable of learning anything," she hissed at him. "All you do is repeat history. That poor girl over there is proof enough of that. She wears your mark, but she doesn't know what it means or how to use it. You never discussed it with her, and I'm betting you won't be training her to draw power from it either. It's not a gift you gave her. It's a symbol of ownership. It's your very own tracking tag, just like that thing in her neck." She struck out at me again, and this time when he took the blow in my stead, he slid back several feet, grunting in pain.

I stood frozen, staring at him, feeling a vague prickling from the mark on my breast. *Just another symbol of ownership,* my mind echoed.

And yet here he was, getting beaten up to protect me. But why wouldn't he strike back? What was wrong with him?

The one-sided fight raged on, with Astrid's voice rising into a frustrated rant as he kept dodging her blows. "Just because you are the prince of some empire doesn't mean everyone else can live in the lap of luxury. You wouldn't last two days in my shoes." Her voice was venomous as she lashed out at him with incredible speed.

"If you would just tell me what it is that you want, we could end this ridiculous conflict!" The note of pleading in his voice set my teeth on edge. I couldn't figure out what the hell his plan was as I watched. He wasn't trying to restrain her. He wasn't going for the control box for my neck tag. He just kept talking.

"And what if what I want is your severed head mounted on the end of my ship's boarding ram?" Her limbs were a blur as she continued to attack him, her red eyes burning with hate.

In a flash, she grabbed his sword from its sheath, catching him flat-footed. In one quick lunge, she was by my side, holding me against her, the sword pressing against my neck. "One more step and she's dead," Astrid warned.

He froze in place, hands still half lifted toward her, and his fingers spread. "What is this about?"

"I told you. Conquest and revenge. And satisfying a particularly useful pawn of mine." She let out a low laugh and squeezed harder. The blade edge was so sharp that I only realized I had been cut when drops of blood started seeping down my skin. "Which means you out of the way. As for your cute little whore, well…she gets another change of ownership."

"Let me go, you sick bitch—ow!" Now the pressure of the blade was starting to hurt. I froze, wary of getting something vital severed. I could feel perspiration gathering on my forehead as the blade pressed farther into my fragile skin.

"Astrid, don't be foolish. Let her go." Craze's deep blue eyes hardened suddenly, his voice stern as he gave her one final chance to drop the weapon. "I'm warning you." His voice was tense as he looked between the two of us.

The pressure of the blade lessened just slightly. "Warning me, what? That you might not like me anymore if I take off her head?" She let out a bark of laughter. "Forget it. You'll be in love with me until you're dead. The fact that I still draw power from your mark is truth enough of that!"

He stopped dead, expression stunned. "What?"

She laughed. "Oh yes! I've never stopped feeding off you, lover. Once you finally taught me how to draw on your strength, you made a mistake. You told me that I could continue to do so until you stopped loving me. And you never have."

I felt a hot surge of anger rush through me, burning away the fear and giving me clarity. I was pissed at Craze, I was pissed at myself for trusting him, and I was pissed off at this bitch for killing innocents, hurting me, helping those slaver scumbags, and most of all, taking a steaming dump all over my happiness.

She mocked him as he stood there, kept at bay by the blade at my throat. "Every day and every night, whenever you thought of me, whenever you missed me, whenever you thrust into a sexbot and came with my name on your lips, I took a little piece of your power. I took and I took…and now, I'm stronger than you." Her voice had gone high and honeyed, gloating at him, and I saw his eyes narrow.

"That's not possible," he growled, but she just laughed at him again.

I took a deep breath and spoke up, even as my mind started forming a plan. It might be crazy, but… "Listen to him. You don't want to kill me. What did I ever do to you?"

She shrugged. "Not a single thing, kid. This isn't about you. It's not your fault that this walking dick has a past." The blade loosened a little more, the sting of it already fading from my flesh.

I snatched the control box off her belt and used the chunk of metal to shove the sword away from me, before jabbing my elbow backward, slamming it into her chest.

The pain was worth it. She let go of me in shock, stepping back and raising the sword to strike me. I ducked under the blade and quickly dashed over to Craze's side, gripping the control box tightly in my hand. He stepped in front of me. I caught my breath, cradling my aching arm and waiting for him to do something. Anything.

He reached out his hand, sparks of energy flying from his fingertips as he summoned the sword. Strands of lightning shot out and tethered to the weapon. Astrid shrieked as the jolts of energy burned her hand, and she let go of the hilt.

The lightning caught the sword and contracted, bringing it back to his hand. Holding it in a firm grasp, he placed himself in a defensive position as he stood in front of me. "Set down your weapons and step away from our spacecraft this instant," he said, his eyes burning.

"Please, we both know I can just turn around and blow this little skimmer of yours into dust the moment you leave my hangar." Her hand was on the odd-looking firearm on her belt. She had not drawn it thus far, clearly preferring to toy with us. But now, things were getting serious.

"No. You won't do that. You've been shooting to cripple this whole time. You've been trying to capture us. Which means either you want us alive for something, or whoever you're working with does." He pointed his sword at her. "Draw that blaster, and you're going to lose a hand."

"Keep pissing me off, and you're going to be the one to lose something." Astrid laughed—and then suddenly vanished.

Craze cursed, and I looked around in alarm. *Psychic powers? She has some kind of personal cloaking device? Where the hell is she?*

Seconds later, she appeared right in front of Craze, her leg in the air, kicking the sword out of his hand. It clattered to the floor. He ducked a follow-up blow then struck her hard behind her knee, making her yelp in pain and back off a few steps.

I watched, helpless to do anything to keep up with the rapid-fire exchange of blows that followed. Craze's fists left cracks and dents in her armor. Hers mostly struck air now that he had jumped into the fight in earnest.

Suddenly, Astrid focused her attention on me once more. After kicking Craze in the chest, she sprinted in my direction. I panicked for a split second, unarmed and unsure of the power Craze had loaned to me. I snapped out of it and managed to duck at the last possible moment. Her fist dented the bulkhead behind me with a loud clang.

I cringed but forced myself to keep moving. I crouched and swept my leg, kicking her feet out from underneath her. She fell to the floor on her back, cursing something untranslatable. As I was turning to run back to the *Invixis*, the rogue ship lurched to the side suddenly.

I barely managed to protect the control box as I tumbled and slid halfway down the length of the hangar, finally landing painfully on my side. I groaned. The pain lingered this time, leaving me helpless. *Is Craze's power wearing off? Has he cut me off from it, or did his crazy bitch ex interfere somehow?*

I cursed under my breath, knowing I was now vulnerable—and that on top of having to deal with Astrid, something was now wrong with the ship carrying us. I looked around for Craze and found him fending off a flurry of blows as she tried to keep him from focusing long enough to summon his sword. He was striking back, but something still seemed off. He was still holding off from using his full strength, his blows staggering her but not knocking her down.

Damn it, Craze! Your romantic regrets are going to get us killed!

I pushed myself painfully to my feet and prepared to lunge for his sword, planning to shove it into his hand myself. But he held up a hand hastily as he ducked another blow.

"Misty, you have to leave the ship. Get up the ramp and board the *Invixis*. You should be able to activate the autopilot if you concentrate hard enough. I'll come and fetch you once I'm done with her." He glanced in my direction, momentarily losing his focus as Astrid landed a kick to his jaw. "Go!"

I flinched but quickly ran over to the ramp, following his directions, knowing it would do no good to get in his way now that he was finally committed to the fight. I didn't want to leave without him, but I had to trust that he could win this fight and come to join me.

As I got to the top of the ramp, I found to my dismay that the doors were locked shut. I tried to pry them open, but I wasn't strong enough. "Dammit." *Wait. Craze said that if I concentrate...* I put a hand on the door and closed my eyes like I had seen him do. Immediately, I sensed something pulsing inside the door, like a person's heartbeat. Could I influence it? *Open,* I commanded. The door trembled and then slid open a hair. I felt excitement surge through my aching body, and I closed my eyes to try again. But before I could, someone yanked on my hair, pulling me roughly back against an armored body.

"Not so fast. You're coming with me," Astrid's cruel voice hissed in my ear as she pulled me close again, this time, pressing a dagger against my neck. "I'm going to use you as a hostage to get out of here. Then I'll wrap you up like a present for my new pet!"

"What the hell is your problem?" I screamed in frustration, but I was too battered, and what little power I could pull from Craze just wasn't keeping up. I gasped with pain as she cut me a little again, and I struggled to keep my composure. I didn't want to let her know I was terrified. "You call Craze on wanting to own women, and then you pull this shit?"

Astrid snorted. "Hey, I never said that I wasn't an asshole too." The ship shook again, less violently this time, and a far-off klaxon sounded. "Oops. Sounds like the planet's pulling more meteors over from the asteroid field. No wonder this planet was so easy to destroy—all Daddy Emperor had to do was collapse the planetary shield, and the rocks did the rest." She put a hand on the *Invixis's* doors, and they slid open, leaving me steaming with jealousy as she started to drag me inside.

Before she could step through the door, blue sparks crackled around it, and it slammed shut, forcing her to leap out of the way. I struck the inside of her elbow and wrist, breaking her grip on the dagger and sending it spinning down the ramp.

A second later, a huge, black-armored shape leaped to the top of the ramp and knocked her clear off it. I staggered and fell to my knees, then recovered in time to see Craze leap off the ramp, aiming for Astrid's sprawled body on the now slowly tilting hangar floor.

She rolled aside at the last second, clawing for her blaster. But when she sat up and aimed it at him, he held up a hand. Blue sparks flew around her weapon, and the lights on its side went dead.

She all but pouted as she tossed it aside. "That's cheating!"

"Shut up and get away from my ship before I skewer you. We're leaving." His voice had gone flat and hard, that same tone I had heard when we had been racing back to his chambers during the attack.

She lifted her chin and smirked. "Maybe I wouldn't mind if you skewered me again," she crooned, and my blood boiled as I saw him waver.

His obvious uncertainty made Astrid grin smugly. "Face it, Craze. You can't beat me. You're too afraid to kill me, so how do you expect to fight me and win?"

I hissed through my teeth with anger and disgust, knowing deep down it was probably true.

This unbelievable bitch still had a spot in his heart, and if that was true, he would be weak against her.

CHAPTER 19
CRAZE

I bared my teeth as I looked at Astrid, knowing that she was right. Worse, I was failing Misty thanks to my ambivalence. I could feel the weight of her disgust with me—and my disgust with myself.

My mind was muddled, memory and desire, rage and regret, and instinct-level protectiveness toward two very different women. Whatever Astrid might think, I had not given my mark lightly to either woman who bore it just because I had chosen quickly to follow my heart. But my choices and Astrid's had led to all this suffering, and now poor Misty was caught up in it.

"Make your choice, Craze," Astrid purred. "You can keep me off your ship, or you can keep me off your woman." She retrieved her dagger and spun it between her fingers as she stood there. "Let me leave in the *Invixis,* and you may save her life. Block me from going, and I'll shove this knife where you like her best."

"Why, you disgusting little..." The ship shook around us again, knocking Misty off the ramp and sending her to her knees on the floor below. I could see her bleeding slightly from her neck. My power had stopped protecting her.

It's Astrid. She really has been stealing my energy from me! So much that I can't spare any for my mate. And Misty may end up dying because of it.

Rage overcame me as my fists clenched, and my sword glowed blue-white with energy. "You really do ruin everything you touch, Astrid," I growled as I advanced on her. "You'll get neither my mate nor my ship, woman. We leave together. You stay here."

She laughed again, that easy, irritating sound of mockery and recklessness. She strode up to me, gripping the dagger loosely. "Back to this again?"

"No." I jumped forward, plunging my sword deep into Astrid's chest.

Her breastplate shattered under the force of the blow, ribs cracked, and blood flew. She winced, stumbling backward at the blow. "You…" she barely managed to choke out and then coughed, blood from a punctured lung spattering down her chin. "You can't…stop me…"

I stared at her. With the breastplate cracked away I saw her secret. It was not just my sigil still on her breast, but another, half hidden by her shoulder armor and glowing brightly. *No wonder she's so damned powerful. She's drawing from two Vixxian psychics at once!*

Not anymore. As Astrid struggled to pull out the bloodied, steaming blade, I reached a hand out to her. "No more! I renounce you!"

I felt something between us snap, and my spiral mark on her skin suddenly went dark. Astrid yanked the blade free—and then staggered, eyes widening. My sword dropped from her fingers and clattered to the floor. "That…hurts," she mumbled.

Another asteroid slammed into the ship, and more klaxons started going off. "Shield failure," a calm female voice sounded over the intercom system. "Shield failure."

Hastily sheathing my sword, I ran to Misty's side. She looked up at me, surprise in her expression. "My pain's going away."

I sighed with relief. "Then things are as they should be." I helped her up, and together we hurried toward the *Invixis*. "Let's be on our way before she recovers."

"I've got the control box," she panted as she limped along beside me. Her voice was gaining strength as well.

"Good. At least we g—" I skidded to a stop, glimpsing something outside of the hanger viewports. Something dark and rocky—and getting bigger.

I bolted for the far end of the hangar, scooping Misty up to move us both faster. We ran past Astrid, who blinked after us with a dazed look on her face. I ignored her in favor of running like every demon from the depths of space was on our heels.

I had barely cleared the last row of ships when a thunderous crash sounded behind us. The hangar's atmosphere started to rush out past us as alarms screamed.

"Hull breach in hangar bay, atmosphere evacuating," that feminine voice called out calmly again. "Course shifted. Orbit decaying. Please proceed to bridge and abandon ship via pod."

I looked back just once and saw Astrid missing and several of the ships ripped from their moorings and tumbling out into space... including the *Invixis*. The gaping hole where the hangar doors had been grew larger as I watched, chunks of the alloy walls being pulled outward and breaking away.

It took all my strength and determination to get to the far end of the hangar before the emergency bulkhead slammed down behind us. I fell to my knees in relief, barely managing to hang on to Misty. "Give me a minute for my legs to recover," I panted.

"I'm not sure that we have a minute," she replied in a high, worried voice as she got to her feet. Outside a nearby viewport, more hunks of stone tumbled past rapidly. A few moments later, the ship shook again.

"Hull breach in drive section. Thrusters disabled. Orbital decay increasing. Reentry in six minutes."

"All right, perhaps you have a point." I pushed myself up painfully, and we ran for it again, headed down the narrow main corridor toward the bridge. A tiny part of me wondered if Astrid had made it out of the hangar as well, but I couldn't spare enough thought for her right now. I had severed my ties to her.

"So, what's the plan?" Misty was running full-strength beside me now, and now and again, I saw a bluish spark run across her body. *It's working. She can draw on my power now.*

Cold comfort if we couldn't find a way off this dying ship, though.

We finally reached the bridge—only to see Astrid standing

wrapped in her bloody cloak by the bank of escape pods. All had been launched but one, and she was about to climb into it.

"No!" I hurried toward her with Misty in tow—but Astrid just laughed and stepped into the pod, slamming the transparent gate down between us.

"Too late!" she laughed and then started coughing again. "See you around, Craze. I'm off to look after this wound. Good luck surviving reentry!" She winked and just grinned wider as I ran up to the other side of the barrier and started pounding on it.

"You can't leave us here! Astrid!"

She waggled her fingers at me, a mocking good-bye, and then slammed her fist into the launch button. I staggered back as the whole window lit up orange and the last chance to get safely off of the ship rocketed away into space.

Swiftly, I got up, hurrying to get a look at the bridge controls. "Curse it. Controls are fried. There must have been a power surge when the engines were hit." I looked at Misty apologetically. "There's nothing for it. She's left us to ride out landfall."

The bridge shook violently around us as the ship began plummeting at an increasing velocity.

"What do we do now?" Misty asked in desperation as she gazed into my eyes like I had the solution hidden there.

"We move to the center of the ship and brace for impact," I warned her. We hurried out toward the central corridor, while behind us the cockpit shield started to glow red. We found a small room down the hall full of bundled uniforms and towels. I pulled her into my arms, and we huddled together there as the ship started shaking more and more.

"Craze, I have to tell you something," Misty whispered, her body trembling with fright.

I held her closer, my hand moving up and down her arm in an attempt to comfort her. "What is it? Don't be scared."

"If I don't make it…" Misty started, but I quickly silenced her with a passionate kiss. My hands rested on the side of her face as I pulled her body even closer to mine.

"Don't say that. I will protect you. I promise," I tried to reassure her, but a part of me wasn't so certain. At the speed we were going, what would happen once we crashed? Surely the ship would be annihilated. Would Misty be able to survive that?

I shook my head. I didn't want to think about it. I hadn't known Misty that long, but I didn't want to imagine living without her.

"Okay," Misty finally whispered as she rested her head on my chest. I held her close as my mind wandered back to Astrid. What was she doing, leading the attack on Vixxia Prime? Was she out of her mind, or was it another one of her bounties? She had a Vixxian ally—a member of the court, from the elaborate loops of that half-glimpsed sigil. What was their scheme? My body tensed at the thought.

Right now, she was probably floating through space in stasis. It would keep her safe no matter where she went. Escape pods were generally programmed to keep occupants in a deep sleep-like state until they landed. Her life functions would be suspended...except for her stolen healing abilities, which would help sustain her in stasis.

If that was the case, she would recover from my attack within days. I cursed under my breath. I had let her slip through my fingers, and now she was perfectly safe while we were plummeting, very likely to our doom.

"What is it?" Misty asked shakily. She was already sweating. The heat in the ship was increasing as atmospheric friction heated the hull. Looking down, I noticed her chest flutter with her rapid breaths.

"Astrid," I admitted truthfully. "I'm trying to sort out how she's gone from running cons to playing warlord."

Misty lifted her head, looking grateful for any distraction from the ship's uncontrolled landfall. "Who is she?"

"Astrid's an outlaw who currently has the largest bounty in the empire on her head," I explained, looking down at my hands as the ship shook more and more violently with each passing second. Suddenly, the wailing sirens stopped as the systems completely fried. "We were lovers once, before I knew what she was. But she was using me. She's very good at manipulating people."

"What does that mean?" Misty's eyes rolled nervously as the ship shook even harder, and the noises of things falling and breaking sounded from all the other rooms.

"She's a con artist. Someone who infiltrates a government to gain a leader's trust and then betrays them at a critical moment for her own gains. She is also known to be a very skilled warrior. She told me that she was the youngest daughter of a Dragican noble, but as with pretty much everything else she ever told me, I don't know if that's true or not."

"Do you think that all this is revenge for your thwarting her plans?" She sounded slightly comforted by my frank talk about my past with Astrid and at my describing her as a manipulator instead of the love of my life.

An ear-shattering explosion cut off my answer. Suddenly, flames raced down the corridor past our room, shaking the transparent door on its hinges. Then the floor tilted, and the room started to spin.

My hold on Misty tightened as we were bounced about, violently smashing into the floor, walls, and ceiling. I did my best to shield Misty's body with my own, but when she went limp in my arms, I feared the worst.

CHAPTER 20
MISTY

When I woke up, I immediately wished I hadn't, for I felt like hell. My muscles ached. My skin felt singed. My head throbbed and seemed to weigh a ton. I groaned and sat up, only to hit my poor, tender head on something.

"Ow! Oh, hell." Slowly, I opened up my eyes, but everything was dark. I tried to get up but couldn't. Something was pinning me down by the legs. Looking around, I couldn't see a thing, and for a moment, I feared that I might have gone blind from my injuries.

"Craze?" I croaked, but my voice barely rose above a whisper. No answer. Somehow, we had been separated in the crash.

Grunting, I tried to get up again, but shooting pain radiated through my right leg. Something was lodged into it. I reached for it, and my fingers came into contact with a stout metal strut lodged in my flesh, pinning me like a butterfly on a card. I whimpered in pain, trying to push it off me, but it wouldn't move. Panic swelled inside me as I felt my stomach tighten into knots. *What if I die here, helpless and alone?*

"Craze!" I tried calling out once more, but shards of pain ran up my throat, like dry leaves in my airway, and I started coughing. That, in turn, made my head pound and fresh pain run through my impaled leg. I struggled, but the pain was too great.

I found myself on the point of passing out, drifting in and out of consciousness. Time went on slowly, and fear and exhaustion warred within me. Exhaustion—and probably blood loss—was winning.

Just as I was about to pass out, I felt the weight on my legs being lifted. Familiar blue sparks danced along the chunk of metal bulkhead weighing me down. There was a flash of pain as the broken pylon pulled free of my leg, and then the bulkhead lifted aside entirely and I saw a familiar face framed by tangled, blood-streaked silver hair. "There you are," he rasped in an exhausted voice.

I sighed in relief. Craze peered down at me with a concerned expression on his face, then crouched and gently hoisted me into his arms. His damaged armor creaked alarmingly as he hugged me. "Craze. We…we're somehow… We lived, huh?"

"We did." His eyes were watery as he pressed me into his chest. *Probably from crash smoke. It wasn't like a tough guy like Craze would be crying over me.* My heart melted a little despite the pain I was in. I held on to him tightly, even in my weakened state. "I'm so glad I found you," he finally said as he carried me out of the wreckage.

I bit my lip to keep from screaming as the open air hit my wound, making it sting. I dreaded looking at it. I didn't want to witness the damage. "My leg…" I mumbled.

"I see it. You've managed to stop the bleeding on instinct, but you're going to need care soon." Finally, he placed me down on the ground. It felt hard but warm on my back. I looked up and saw a dark sky with clouds the color of ashes. The air stank of sulfur.

"Craze, am I going to be okay?" I asked, a little desperate. He held my hand, giving it a light squeeze before he gently pulled off the shattered plates of my leg armor and peered at my wound. I could tell by the look on his face that he didn't like what he was seeing. "Tell me honestly," I implored, trying to prepare myself for the worst.

"You'll be fine," he said firmly, giving my hand a gentle squeeze. His palms were sweaty, and his fingers shook slightly as he delivered the news. I didn't believe him.

He pulled his cloak off and ripped it into long bandages for my leg. His face was focused, and he didn't speak. That made me even more nervous.

"Where are we?" I asked to change the subject, my voice cracking from my dry throat.

"Shh. You're dehydrated. No more talking, save your strength. We crashed. Not much else matters right now," he muttered. I wanted to ask him for more details, but I stopped when I saw him bending over me to start cleaning the wound.

"This is going to hurt," he warned as he started to pull pieces of shrapnel out of my skin. I cried out in pain, fighting to keep still as he worked, before finally passing out completely.

WHEN I WOKE UP AGAIN, I WAS STRAPPED TO CRAZE'S BACK. MY LEG throbbed feverishly with every jostle as he hiked across the barren landscape. He was walking away from the wreckage. I stared at it; it wasn't even the whole ship. Just a chunk of the inner chambers and the center corridor, lying on its side with the outer bulkhead sheared off, looking like a gigantic broken piece of beehive. I had no idea how I had survived the crash with just a leg injury when it had done *that* to an armored warship.

Looking away, I got a good look at the landscape for the first time. The ground was blasted, melted, and barren, its surface pocked with deep craters. A hot, foul breeze gusted against my face, choking me with its rotten-egg stink. I saw muddy fumaroles bubbling here and there on the ground, giving up yellowish vapors. There wasn't a speck of green foliage or blue water to be found.

I held on to Craze a little tighter as my fears clawed at my chest. Even if we had survived the crash, how could we survive this world?

"You're awake," Craze finally said as he handed me a pale metal canteen with some kind of readout on the side. I took it, and to my relief, there was water inside. I gulped at it greedily, nearly drinking the whole thing before I realized it would be smart to save some for later. I wiped my mouth on the back of my hand and sighed, handing it back.

"The condenser cannot draw much moisture from this atmosphere, but it should provide us with a little water every few hours. It's a good thing I've had it as part of my duty gear for years." He was forcing himself to sound optimistic. I could hear the strain at the bottom of his voice.

"Where are we?" I finally murmured, now that my throat didn't feel like the landscape around us.

"We're on Hexiven. A planet that was destroyed in a war between my father's troops and a religious cult that had colonized it. They decimated it. Made sure nothing was left alive. It's a death trap for anyone who stays here. Without terraformers or a colony bubble, anyway."

"Does that mean we are going to die too?" I asked anxiously. Surveying the area, I saw no sign of resources we could salvage on this vacant planet, and with the ship completely ruined, I didn't see how we were going to get off it anytime soon. "Craze?" I whispered when he didn't answer me. I could feel his body tense up, and he stopped.

"No. We will not die. I will not allow it. I am the Crown Prince of the Vixxian Empire. I will not die on some bombed-out ruin for Astrid's amusement. And I won't let you die either." His voice was firm. After a minute, he started walking again. "I'll find us shelter somewhere, and then you can rest."

"But without any resources, what are we supposed to do? We are going to starve out here." I couldn't keep the panic out of my voice. I was just too tired, too hurt, and too terrified.

"Don't say such things. I will find a way for us to get out of this situation. We will not die on this forsaken planet. I refuse to let that happen." He seemed adamant, but I wasn't so sure. *How can we survive in a barren place like this?*

Before I could ask him anything else, I began to cough. My whole body shuddered with the power of it as I was left gasping for air. The atmosphere suddenly seemed very dense, and I had trouble pulling it into my lungs. The stink of sulfur intensified, burning my throat. It felt like there was an invisible weight on my chest the size of the crash wreckage. "Craze..." I gasped. *Help me.*

"No. Not now." Craze quickly put me down, his eyes full of worry as he examined the side of my neck.

"What...what is it?" Black spots danced in front of my eyes. My lungs burned.

"My power should protect you from impurities in the atmosphere, but you already need a lot of it just to work on healing your leg and replenishing your blood supply. You're not used to drawing on me. You can only pull so much, even now that Astrid's no longer draining me dry." There was a faint note of panic in his voice. "I have to find a way to give you more."

I heard him shout something a second before I collapsed completely, breath stalling in my aching lungs. The black spots grew until they blotted out my sight. Closing my eyes, I felt my lungs closing up and my body rejecting everything about this new world. This was the end. *I'm sorry, Craze.*

CHAPTER 21
CRAZE

As I saw Misty's body rejecting the atmosphere, I felt real, helpless terror for the first time in years. Both times, it had been Astrid's doing. Once, when I had started to suspect that the woman I had thought was the love of my life had been manipulating me all along. Now, by stranding us here, she was choking my new love to death just as surely as if she had put her jeweled fingers around Misty's neck.

I'll kill her for this. But first, I had to make sure that Misty survived this.

My heart pounded painfully hard in my chest as I tried to breathe life into her limp body. My lungs could process out the sulfur, and she started wheezing less as I gave her my secondhand air. *Take my energy, Misty. Take what you need.*

Nothing happened at first. I could sense her drawing on me to keep her body alive, but the flow was weak and she had trouble maintaining it. *I should have taught her how to draw energy properly before we ever left. By the Goddess…was Astrid right about me? Have I thought so much of myself and so little of what Misty needs?*

The realization cut me deeply, shame curdled my guts, and I cradled her to me, mortified and desperate. *I'm sorry. I'm sorry. Just come back to me, and I'll never do it again.*

Abruptly, Misty took in a deep breath, her whole body lurching as she arched her back and her eyes flew wide open. I felt power flow from me cleanly, blue sparks dancing over her skin. I breathed out in relief as I felt my blood flowing through my veins once more. "There. Good girl. Just draw what you need." Grateful, I uttered a soft prayer to the Goddess Silviana. *Perhaps we will get through all this madness alive.*

"What happened?" Misty asked as she sat up, placing her hand on her chest. She looked queasy and scared, but alert. "I was choking."

"Our mating should have transferred my atmospheric adaptation powers to you when you were near me, but you were too inexperienced to draw what you needed. I'll have to fix that when you're feeling better. Meanwhile, we should try to find shelter. The increased amount of sulfur in the air here might mean a storm is coming." I wrapped my arms around her, gently rubbing her shoulders, trying to soothe her after the traumatic experience she had just gone through.

I kissed her lips and pulled her a little closer, glad she was still alive and I hadn't been forced to say good-bye to my lover. The thought of wandering this lonely planet all by myself sent a shudder through my spine. "It's…not the kind of rain you want to be out in."

"Thank you," she whispered, her gaze still rather blank as she blinked, trying to refocus her vision. "Why, what kind of rain is it?"

"Sulfuric acid rain," I said mock-casually, and she rolled her eyes.

"Oh. Great. That's just great." She sighed and sat up gingerly, coughing now and again. "This place just keeps getting more inviting."

I nodded in her direction before helping her up. With my arm around her waist, I inspected her injuries. "Your wounds are getting worse," I commented before I could stop myself. Slowly, I looked down at the discharge that had started oozing from her leg. Apparently, Astrid's ship had been crawling with bacteria from its Thezlum former owners.

"Oh God…" Misty gasped, going ashen again. "I'm going to lose my leg, aren't I?" She stared down at the wound, her eyes horrified, and then gagged and looked away.

"No. I'll get you to help before that happens." I took her hand in mine before tilting her chin slightly, forcing her to look up at me. "I promise." My words were serious, and I was determined to keep my oath. I wouldn't let any further harm come to Misty. Squeezing her hand, I felt a tightening in my chest. I knew I couldn't let her down. She was depending on me.

She gulped, obviously still a bit worried, but nodded nevertheless and forced a small smile. "Okay."

Once I had cleaned the wound as best I could and bandaged it with clean cloth strips, I picked her up and lifted to carry her on my back again. We started off over the rolling, blasted hills as I looked around the vacant landscape for caves or overhangs where we might shelter, along with any source of life.

Unfortunately, everything seemed completely decimated, but I knew I couldn't give up hope. I kept pushing forward, even as my own body wore down from fatigue. I couldn't give up. I had to keep going.

"Craze, maybe you should rest. You must be exhausted." Misty's sweet voice sounded in my ear. I shook my head stubbornly, keeping my eyes locked on the faraway horizon. I couldn't rest until I made sure we were safe.

The dim red disc of the sun, cloaked by layers of smog, was heading toward the horizon. Once the sun went down and the temperature dropped, the rains would start. Even with my powers, we would be blinded and scarred for weeks if we were caught out in them. I kept that in my mind as my legs burned and I gasped in big lungfuls of the reeking air.

Suddenly, my eyes grew large and my heart quickened in my chest as I spotted something strange. The landscape up until this point had been painted in dull hues of reds, blacks, and browns, but in the distance, I saw something green. My heart leaped in hope as I sprinted forward, holding Misty tight to my body, making sure she wouldn't fall off.

As I reached the destination, I gasped. I couldn't believe my eyes. In front of us, covered by a shimmering, terraforming dome, was a large pool. But it wasn't any typical body of water. It had a green tint to it, and at the same time, it was completely see-through. Leaning forward, I could see its stunning, jade-colored bottom lined with perfectly shaped, round rocks. The dome generators were little silver spikes poking from the pale sand that extended several feet from the edge of the water. Incredibly, the sand was streaked in spots with a thin emerald fuzz of moss.

"W-what is it?" Misty breathed as she leaned forward as well. "Why is it green?" She reached experimentally into the dome, which parted for her like a bubble-skin.

"I don't know. But back on Vixxia, it's said that the god Coronus, the almighty ruler of the universe, doesn't like to see any of his creations die. When it happens, it saddens him immensely. When he cries over the death of a planet, a pool of water will appear there that will act as a wellspring of raw life-energy. The same sort of energy that I share with you. My race has searched many planets, looking high and low for such a phenomenon. We believe that it can give someone ever-lasting life." I spoke enthusiastically as I recounted the old lore that had kept me up at night when I was younger.

"Do you think this is it? It smells like apples." Misty smiled as she leaned in through the barrier and sniffed the air.

"That's the moss. It's edible, but it's growing too sparsely here for it to nourish anything larger than a small mammal. What's an apple?" I asked her, finding the word strange. We stepped into the barrier and approached the lake.

"It's a sort of fruit. You eat it. It's good for you," Misty explained. "But you don't think that this is an actual…spiritual phenomenon, do you? Like magic? Or something a god did?"

I smiled faintly as we came to the edge of the lake. I set her down carefully and immediately crouched down to fill the condenser and let it check the water's quality. "I think that someone with knowledge of my world's beliefs has a little squatter terraforming operation here, and I think it may have just saved our lives."

"Is it safe for us to drink or bathe in?" Misty asked warily as she eyed the odd-colored water. Nervously, she bit the corner of her lip. "On my planet, green liquids aren't usually safe. But I'm thirsty as hell, and we have to wash this wound properly."

"Let's see what the condenser says. It's testing the water for conta-minants now." I did my best to speak calmly, but inside, I was still praying. With no medical supplies and with her leg getting worse, I knew we had no other real choice but to give this a try.

Finally, the condenser beeped, and I checked the readout. "All right, then, the water quality is good. It's got an unusually high level of psychic energy. It might have something to do with the algae that is purifying the water."

"Oh. Thank God. I'm going to straight up skinny dip in this stuff." Misty started tearing off the broken bits of her armor impatiently. I reached down to help her, then unwrapped the seeping bandages from her leg. They stuck, and she winced as they were pulled away, but I was gratified to see that at least the leg hadn't gotten any worse since I had wrapped it.

I helped her out of her armor, leaving her only the slightly tattered black body-stocking beneath. I then shed my own shattered armor, knowing it would only weigh me down.

"What do we do if whoever runs this place is hostile?" she fretted slightly as I cut the rest of the cloth away from her wounded leg. I had given her the condenser, and she was eagerly sipping water from it.

"We'll have to take our chances." I tied up my hair with a strip of cloth from my cloak, now down to only my loincloth. I noticed her sneaking peeks at me, and I smiled a little. *She must be feeling a bit better if she can think about sex again.*

Definitely a good sign.

I scooped Misty up and walked toward the water. "Let's go, then. See if your leg doesn't feel better once it's thoroughly washed out." The place might hold unknown hazards, but at least here we couldn't die of dehydration or acid rain.

"Okay. Let's go before I lose my nerve." Her hold around my neck tightened, and I felt her heartbeat quicken against my chest. Holding on to her, I jumped into the pool of water, putting all my faith in Silviana's protection.

CHAPTER 22
MISTY

My whole body surged with energy as we splashed into the cool, apple-scented water. My skin seemed to tighten in response. My heart slowed, and I felt the wound in my leg tingle as if hit with peroxide but without the pain. The aches and itches and faint scorched feeling in my lungs all melted away as the water rushed over me. It felt like I was becoming one with the lake, thoroughly relaxed. I let go of Craze and floated up to the surface of the pond.

I looked down at my leg and saw the pus and brownish old blood flowing away from it in threads that got thinner as I looked. Finally, it stopped altogether, and the faint cloud of wound fluids turned greenish and then vanished, as if devoured by the strange algae that Craze had mentioned.

Why hasn't he come up yet? Treading water, I looked down, only to find my lover floating, suspended in the water. I tilted my head, wondering what he was doing, before I came to the realization that maybe he didn't know how to swim. However, before I could dive down and help him, his eyes opened and he looked up at me. A smile curved his lips, and he darted upward. Seconds later, he broke through the surface.

I gasped upon seeing him. It seemed impossible, but somehow, he had gotten even more handsome. His long, silver hair seemed to sparkle with luster as the wet tendrils framed his face. His skin shone brightly as if he were crafted out of marble. Hesitantly, I reached out, caressing his cheek with trembling fingertips. It seemed like I was dreaming.

"Craze," I murmured in disbelief. How had someone so godlike become even more attractive? *Maybe it's because neither of us has had a bath since we left his chambers, and we've been through a spacecraft crash, tending to nasty wounds, and a filthy walk across this dead planet ever since.* But the glow to his skin and eyes didn't seem like merely the result of a good wash.

As he looked at me, his bright blue eyes grew big and his eyebrows rose. "Misty, you look so beautiful. How are you feeling?"

"Better." I looked down to check my leg, but I immediately got distracted by my reflection. I had expected to look like a battered mess after everything, even once washed off. My skin was flawless. There wasn't a single blemish to be seen. No scars. My lips were full, unchapped, almost glossy-looking with health. A faint greenish shimmer coated me, the algae. I wondered if it was responsible for supercharging our healing powers.

"Did the lake do this?" I murmured breathlessly, looking at Craze.

"I think so," he whispered and moved closer to me. "Whether the gods or the terraformers, someone's given us a miracle." Gently, he wrapped his arms around me, pulling me into a soft embrace that tightened as his breath started to shiver. I could feel a fresh surge of energy run up and down my spine, transfixing me with pleasure as his lips lingered on my neck.

His hot breath on my skin soothed me. I tilted my head back, looking up at clouds now deep red from sunset. I closed my eyes, allowing the sensation of his lips and hands roaming my skin to take over.

I moaned, wrapping my legs around his waist as my fingers ran through his tangled hair. It was soft to the touch, feeling like pure silk, and he rolled his head into my hand like a cat being petted, when I slid my fingers through it. I was about to kiss him, when he leaned his head down, pressing his lips to my collarbone.

Instantly, another moan escaped my lips as I arched my back, tightening my hold on him. His teeth grazed my shoulder, his hand closed over my breast while the other gripped my hip firmly. We should have been watchful. If someone was terraforming this amazing place, they might come back at any moment. But the more he kissed and stroked me, pulling down the body stocking to get at my breasts and belly, the less I could focus on anything besides sensation. With my body now pressed up against his, I felt myself slowly losing control.

Maybe we were stranded on some decimated planet, but at that very moment, it was the least of my concerns. All that mattered was I was with him, and we were alive and well for the moment.

I was about to run my hands down his back when a big, warm raindrop smacked me in the head. I looked up and saw a hideous yellowish mist gathering at the base of the clouds. Huge droplets of greasy-looking rain were tumbling from the clouds, and anywhere they fell outside the dome, the ground started bubbling and smoking. I flinched—but again and again, the rain pattered down on us and the pool and did absolutely nothing.

"What…what is this?" I mumbled, stunned, my arousal ebbing away in the face of this astonishing phenomenon. I looked up—and I saw the rain shimmering briefly on its way through what Craze called the terraforming dome. When it struck the dome, it was like someone was passing it through a powerful filter, and pure water fell on us instead.

"It's processing this planet's water a little at a time," he replied in an astonished tone. "Cleansing the sulfur and other impurities out of it. Probably separating out those chemicals for use elsewhere."

I watched, astounded. As the rain fell, tiny clear filaments rose from the sand, and mushroom caps the size of dimes bloomed. Sparkling spores tumbled from under their caps and drifted low to the ground, catching on the strands of moss. "Living things," I murmured. I looked back at him excitedly. "Could this process revive the whole planet?"

"Maybe. Eventually." There was lingering lust in his eyes as he looked at my lips like he wanted to continue kissing me, but before I could say anything, he was already hoisting himself out of the water. "At this point, I really want to know who is behind this. Maybe they can help us get home." He offered me a hand, looking down at me, his blue eyes fierce with determination. I sighed, knowing our moment of sweet respite was now over.

I placed my hand in his, allowing him to lift me out of the water. He pulled me out with ease, which still surprised me. I wasn't a small girl, and yet he always had such an easy time picking me up. I smiled slightly and held his hand as he looked out at the horizon.

"Once the storm ends and the acid vapor burns off, we need to have another look around, to try to find whoever is tending this place." We both looked around for someplace to shelter from the downpour in the meantime, as welcome as it was now. The temperature would drop fast once the sun was fully down.

We ended up huddled together against one of the short water processing towers, sheltering under its slight overhang. Now and again, it hummed or some of the lights flashed or a spout of warm steam exhaled from the top. That apple smell always intensified when it did that.

I inspected my leg in the last of the light. It was healed, faint green sparkles marking the spots where the flesh had filled in in minutes. The pain was gone, and even those flecks of green brightness were slowly going away now that they were no longer needed.

"I should be able to walk soon," I ventured, running a hand down my leg. I felt a little frustrated that sex had been interrupted, but he was right. As we huddled there, the rain was already turning cold.

"Get some rest first," he replied softly. "We'll explore the surrounding area at first light."

I fell asleep with him watching over me, leaning on his body with one warm, muscular arm around me. I was hungry, I was worried that whoever built this place wasn't friendly, and I still wondered if I would ever see home. But with Craze there, I still felt safe enough to drift off quickly.

CHAPTER 23
CRAZE

We spent the whole day searching the wasteland for miles around the terraforming dome. But in the end, we didn't come across anything else. Besides that little green jewel under its bubble, all that was left on the once thriving planet was rock, rubble, and dust. I was getting tired and could tell that Misty was as well. Her leg had healed without scar, and when we bathed in or drank the water, it gave us energy and vitality…but this place couldn't fill our stomachs. Misty had gone nearly two days without eating. I knew she probably couldn't survive much longer without a proper meal.

This thought propelled me forward in my search, even when I felt like my legs couldn't carry me any longer. Misty was depending on me, and I would be damned if I allowed her to die because of my inability to locate food.

Despite my best efforts, the sun started dipping toward the horizon without our finding a single sign of the inhabitants responsible for the dome and lake. Anger and self-reproach clawed at me as my hands clenched into fists. I didn't know what to do, and I didn't want to think about what would happen if I failed Misty. "My apologies," I muttered finally. "It seems I cannot find any trace of the comings and goings of the lake-tenders."

"Craze, maybe there's another way of going about this than searching." Misty's soft, sweet voice brought me back from my troubled state of mind. I stopped walking and looked at her curiously, my expression softening slightly.

I could see the fatigue in her eyes. If I pushed us too hard on no food, it wouldn't do us any good. "What is your idea?"

"Whoever is tending that terraformed lake must come back every once in a while to check on it. The machines need to be maintained, and even though they're tiny, those little fairy mushrooms and the moss look pretty deliberately grown. The mushrooms show up after the rain stops. Maybe if we wait around there and don't fall asleep, whoever it is will come back." She sounded focused and thoughtful and a lot less scared than she had been the last few days. I couldn't help but feel a bit proud of her.

"That is a very good point," I said quietly as we hiked up a low, slumped hill of melted stone. The evening storm clouds were gathering. Soon acid rain would pour down on everything—except within the dome. I picked up my pace. "Let's get back, and tonight once the mushrooms grow, we'll sit vigil and hope that our unintentional benefactors return." *And that they are friendly.*

The rain started bare minutes after we returned to the shelter of the dome. Bathing in and drinking the waters of the pool kept us alert and energetic, but I was ever aware of Misty's growling stomach and the gnawing in my own belly. She didn't complain. She simply endured, and in doing so, galvanized my desire to save her from this.

I held her as we sheltered together in the shadow of one of the terraforming towers. Eventually, exhausted, she fell asleep in my arms.

I dozed off a while myself and woke to a warm, steamy stillness. The heat of the ground beneath us mixed with the cool rain and created a curtain of fog that slowly boiled away as I watched. I noticed that at the very edge of the dome, a thin rim of living, moss-streaked earth was slowly spreading beyond its protection.

It would take hundreds of years to re-terraform this world, and I have no idea how anyone would survive here until it was done. I suppose they could aquaculture in this small lake, grow edible plants and fish. But aside from the mushrooms and that strange algae, I see no signs of cultivation.

My only guess was that these rogue terraformers were refugees or squatters of some kind, too desperate or broke or both to pick or choose where they put down roots. Whoever they were, I had to admire their determination and their ingenuity. I didn't know whether this facility had been built to take advantage of the tears of a god or of some kind of spectacularly bioengineered algae which radiated vital energy. I suspected the latter, but after meeting Misty, I was starting to believe that anything was possible.

When the mist cleared, the clouds finally blew away and let in the light from a stunning array of stars. I paid little attention to it, busy keeping watch now that the rain and mist were gone and the mushrooms were finishing their growth. Eventually, Misty stirred and lifted her head.

"Mmm," she mumbled, stifling a yawn. "Did I sleep?"

"You did. For a while. The storms cleared away, and the night's crop has grown. We'll have to see if anyone comes to harvest them once they are done." *All the mushrooms vanished by dawn, so either they dried up instantly in sunlight, or they were all harvested before then. I was hoping it was the second.*

Misty got up slowly and stretched the kinks out of her back. The curves of her body gleamed in the starlight, contained only by the ragged, single-legged body stocking. I licked my lips, looking at her hungrily. If only I didn't have to pay attention to other things right now…

"We must find something to keep ourselves awake while we watch," I brought up, stifling a yawn.

"Yeah? Hmm." She looked around and then up and smiled slowly. "I've got it." She walked out onto a patch of sand and moss that was mostly free of mushrooms and stretched out on it.

"C'mon, the sky is so beautiful here. Why don't we lie down together and watch the stars?" Misty offered, giving me an inviting smile.

I didn't know how she managed to keep up such a cheerful mood, but it made me feel a tad bit better. If she could stay hopeful in this sort of situation, then I would do the same. I nodded. "Good."

We lay down together. The sand was soft and fragrant but chilly. I pulled Misty onto my chest, letting her use my body as a warm cushion. My hands rested on the small of her back as I pulled her a little closer, feeling the soft push of her full chest up against my pectorals. I felt my breath hitch in my throat as I kissed her, and again I wished that we could simply spend our time awake together making love. But I could kiss her, couldn't I? There was no harm in that.

My tongue slowly made its way into her mouth as my fingers ran through her hair. I could feel the heat rising between us as our kiss intensified. My heart quickened even more, my hands sliding down her back to squeeze her hips.

Before I could do anything else, she pulled away, looking at me with those bright brown eyes of hers. She smiled at me, her pearly white teeth gleaming. "What is it?" I asked, confused by her reaction.

"Naughty Craze. How am I supposed to watch the stars if we just make out the whole time? Or watch out for visitors, either?"

She had a point. I just wished that she didn't. "Hmph. All right, then," I grumbled. Reluctantly, I pulled her off my body and helped her lie down beside me, pillowing her head on my arm. I could hear her labored breaths as she recovered from our passionate kiss.

"What are we supposed to do?" I asked her, looking up at the stars. It felt so strange to lie there without purpose.

"You just look at the stars." Misty rolled over to rest her head on my chest and looked up at me, eyes twinkling.

"That's it?" I questioned, thinking it was somewhat pointless. I captained the Imperial fleet. I saw stars out of my viewports every day.

"Yep." She sounded excited over it and her warm body snuggled against mine was always pleasant, so I decided not to argue. Instead, I wrapped her in my arms and watched her while she watched the stars. It was a much prettier view anyway.

We stayed there in silence for a few minutes as time seemed to crawl by. I felt myself dozing off before Misty suddenly tensed beside me and let out an excited cry.

"Look!" She pointed up at the sky. I followed her enthusiastic gesture and noticed the burning streak of a meteorite making its way across the horizon. "A shooting star!"

"The meteor?" I peered at it, feeling the hairs on the back of my neck prickle slightly. I couldn't pinpoint what was making me uneasy, but as I watched, another streak of light joined the first before both faded away. The first looked a bit closer than the second.

"It's a shooting star. Isn't it beautiful? Quick. Make a wish before it disappears."

"Why?" I asked. Misty's requests were getting stranger by the minute. Why would anyone wish upon a meteorite? They held no power, aside from the ability to blindly smash things. How could they possibly fulfill a wish?

"Well, on my planet, when you see a shooting star, you make a wish. I don't really know why. It's just something we do." She sounded crestfallen, but then she noticed me staring warily at the horizon. "What is it?"

A handful more of the streaks of light fell over there, lighting up the sky. Then more followed…and more.

"It's another meteor shower, like the ones that destroyed Astrid's spaceship." I sat up, watching it tensely. "It's shifting this direction."

"Will the dome protect us?" she asked worriedly, suddenly clinging to me. I stroked her hair soothingly.

"It should. But it may prevent our unknown hosts from showing up tonight." I set my jaw in frustration as I heard her poor stomach grumble again. At this rate, all the healing water in the world wouldn't help us if we didn't find the terraformers and barter for some food, soon.

CHAPTER 24
MISTY

I must have dozed off for a while. I had trouble feeling bad about it. After all, the constant stress and lack of food had left me exhausted. But when the meteorites started regularly slamming into the hills around us, I woke with a start.

Burning streaks struck the ground all around the dome, kicking up sprays of acrid dust and sudden, hot breezes. I jumped nervously at the boom and crack of their landings, frightened of what would happen when one of them hit us head on.

When I looked back at Craze, he was somehow still fast asleep. He breathed softly and slowly as the thunder of the stones striking earth went on and on, as if he was so used to sleeping in crazy circumstances that the cacophony barely bothered him.

Suddenly, without warning, a chunk of stone the size of a basketball slammed into the dome nearby. It pierced halfway through and got caught, suddenly wrapped in a near transparent gob of energy, which closed on it instantly. Energy rippled outward from the point of impact, the momentum crushing the stone to bits.

As I watched, the force started breaking down the meteorite in such an orderly manner that I could barely believe what I was watching. Rectangular pieces of stone fell from it and stacked up neatly on the ground, chunks of metal in two different shades made their own stacks, and a geode-like crystal formation at its heart was extracted whole and began to be cleaned and polished while it floated there. It was almost as if the shield was…digesting…the meteorite. "Wow, Craze," I finally said. "You're really missing a show."

He let out a grunt. "Just give me a tenth of a cycle," he mumbled and rolled over. A second later, I heard a snore.

Incredible. I'll have to figure out some pranks to play on him while he's sleeping, once we get out of here. He would probably sleep his way through me putting all his hair in giant pink curlers. And taking pictures. The whole idea amused me. But if he was conked out, that left exploring the dome for late-night signs of life to me.

Oh, well. I'll make him pay me back in orgasms later. Sighing, I got up, stretching out my sore body. My shoulders and knee popped, and my leg muscle still felt a little stiff, but that was a lot better that than dealing with an impalement wound and dripping pus to boot.

Looking down, I examined the expanse of thigh that had been grotesquely infected but a day ago. Now, there wasn't even a scar. I was surprised that there had turned out to be substance to Craze's tale about a god's tears. Maybe coincidental substance, but…my leg and I would take it. Despite my disbelief, I was still grateful. *If it weren't for that stroke of luck, I probably wouldn't be alive right now.*

Looking at Craze's sleeping face, I smiled to myself. He was the other reason I was still alive. It was true, I could blame him for my being here. But really, it was the Thezlum raiders' fault, as well as Astrid's. Craze had saved my life several times, even if he had hesitated to kill his ex for me. His determination and will had pushed me forward when I had been about to give up. Even if I didn't love him, I would be grateful.

And I did. I loved this guy awful, like my Italian neighbor used to say about her husband. Flaws and all, he was the reason I was nearly ready to give up New York, Earth, the *Times* and everything. *If we can just survive this.*

As I stood there, I found myself wondering what was going on with the other Earth refugees. Apparently, they had all decided to stay. But somehow, I had never made any effort to contact them and compare notes. Yes, pretty much everything had been going whirl-wind-fast since I had arrived, but I had to wonder at myself for not even thinking about it before now. Had I been that caught up in my romance with Craze that I had not even considered checking in with them before now?

Yeah. I guess I was. I smiled a little, embarrassed, flustered, and a little down on myself. *I'll check in with them when I get back.*

As I stood there, thinking what to do next, I heard something strange in the distance. It was a high-pitched squeaking—like mice or maybe squirrels. I tilted my head in confusion. This planet had seemed so dead up until now.

Curious, I started moving gingerly across the beach, following the sound. Every time I thought I was getting closer, however, I would hear it from another direction. Finally, I stopped, just a little ways off from where I had started, having no more clue about the source of the noise than before. I was getting frustrated.

I stopped and listened as carefully as possible. *There.* Maybe ten feet directly in front of me. It was a musical twittering, almost like bird-song, and very high-pitched at times. I would hear the same call repeated here and there all over the shoreline, echoing to each other, weaving a multipart melody that I quickly realized wasn't at all random. Music, or communication? Both? I squinted, trying to make anything out in the fading light of the meteor shower, but I couldn't spot a thing.

Frowning, I continued walking forward very slowly, but the source of the odd music remained a mystery. There was simply nothing out there. *What the hell is going on?*

Okay, Misty. Chill out and go about this logically. Taking a few calming breaths, I closed my eyes and focused all my attention on listening. The nearest source of that thready music stayed in one place, and I could find where it was if I just followed my ears instead of my eyes. I stepped forward gingerly, toes feeling out the warm sand speckled with bits of vegetation, following the music alone. Once it was excep-tionally loud, I stopped and opened my eyes. *Please let there be some-thing here.*

At first, I felt nothing but confusion and frustration as I looked around. Nothing living seemed to be near me besides the plants, but the music sounded loudly almost right in front of me. Was the singer invisible?

An idea came to me, and I looked…down.

I gasped. All around my feet were tiny creatures, barely the size of mice. They were covered in various colors, shades, and patterns of fur and wore an assortment of jewelry, pocket belts, and bright smocks. Their eyes were enormous, like lemurs' eyes, and a luminous orange-brown. Their faces were flat, similar to those of apes, and bare of fur, but framed by long, fluffy manes.

They wore and carried a variety of tiny tools and what might have been weapons, forged from a silvery metal that glittered with multicolored lights. Their voices rose in an elaborate chorus, and as I listened, my translator chip finally started to process their voices.

"What's this?"

"Who's this?"

"Another Giant!"

"Is it Vixxian?"

"I don't think so!"

"Is it dangerous?"

"It mostly seems confused."

"It's kind of cute!"

I held still, getting my mental bearings as my eyes swept the sands. Dozens of the little creatures hurried around the mushroom fields with small metal backpacks attached to long nozzles. Some aimed the nozzles at the little mushrooms, sucking them up into the backpacks as they hurried by. Others were doing the same to the thin strands of moss.

"Oh, uh, excuse me," I mumbled once I was confident that the translator was working properly. I stepped back, wanting to get away from them. But suddenly, all the nearby ones were pouring forward toward me, tufted tails flowing behind them like banners. Before I could do anything, they surrounded me in a tight circle. "Hey! What is this? Who are you…people?"

Great, just great. I went looking for friendly aliens and wandered into Lilliput.

"Who are you?" A gray-furred member of the group stepped toward me from the circle, its eyes covered with tiny, metal-rimmed lenses that reminded me of old-fashioned swim goggles. I blinked down at it, almost afraid I would squish it if I took a step forward. Then I slowly crouched down, balancing on one knee, bringing myself a little closer to their level. A few of them scattered back nervously as I lowered myself, only to move forward again once I settled.

I couldn't help but smile at the little guy. The more I looked at it, the cuter it got somehow. It even had a tiny, wet pink nose and delicate little ears that looked like mouse ears. "I'm Misty," I answered, managing to avoid squealing about the adorable little beings.

"Of what planet?" several of the creatures asked, in ragged unison.

The chorus startled me a little. "Um…Earth."

"Earth!"

"Did she say Earth?"

"She did!"

"So that's a human?"

"I guess so!"

"I've never seen one!"

Their unexpected chatter caught me off guard. I was instantly reminded of animated movies where animals started talking like people. "Earth!" Their squeals sounded rather excited this time. "Talk to her! Find out everything!"

"Yeah!"

Rapidly, the little gray-haired one, whom I could only assume was some sort of a leader for the group, scurried up my leg, jumped off my hip to my elbow and ran up into my palm. I yelped and nearly flung him off me, but I managed to keep my composure. He sat down, his small, warm fluff of a body reminding me again of a pet's. "I am Chireet, lead scientist for this facility. We have learned much about Earth in our wanderings. Very interesting."

"Yes, interesting," the group chanted, almost as if they were the backing vocals of their leader.

"Primitive, but growing!" He seemed excited, and he pulled out a tiny silver box, waving it slowly in my direction as he apparently took some readings. "Fascinating. I may need to ask for a blood sample."

"Let's...not get ahead of ourselves." I smiled down at them awkwardly. "Um...so who are all of you?"

"We are the Mixims. We recently inhabited this planet after being... displaced...from elsewhere." He puffed out his tiny, gray-furred chest. "This terraforming dome is part of how we survive."

"Oh." This discovery completely shocked me. Had these creatures been here all this time? How had we not come across them sooner? "We've been looking for people but couldn't find anyone. This dome saved our lives. We barely found it before the acid rains started to fall."

More chatter, some of it so rapid that the translator struggled to keep up. "Did you hear that?"

"They almost died!"

"Wait, who is we?"

"More humans!"

"No, the big white snore-beast over there is Vixxian."

I had to stifle a laugh at the last comment. I wondered if Craze would wake up quickly if I called out to him. Not because I was really afraid of the little guys surrounding me, but because he would probably regret not being in on this conversation.

"Where were you all hiding? We didn't see any sign of houses, tents, or anything around here besides the dome." I chewed my lip, glancing over at Craze again. He was still unmoving, a dark shape leaning his back against the water processor, legs stretched in front of him. Just seeing him like that made me want to curl up with him again, but instead, I weighed the options of waking him.

Chireet chittered in amusement. "I do apologize for the confusion. We live underground. When you end up sharing a world with somewhat destructive giants, putting several feet of soil and stone between you and them is...generally a good idea." His whiskers wiggled as he twitched his nose. "That is also why we were cautious in approaching you at first."

My mind raced as I scrunched my brows together. Tiny, subterranean creatures, living hidden from much larger beings. Almost like folk stories of pixies. I wondered if Craze knew about them.

But before I could ask them, my stomach asserted itself with a snarl that made a few Mixims squeak in alarm. "Um...sorry. Do you have any food? My partner and I have been roaming this planet for days. We are starving," I pleaded with them.

"Who is your companion?" a number of them chimed together. I wondered how they had developed the timing to keep doing that. At times, it seemed like I was talking to one being who happened to have several cute, fuzzy bodies.

"Craze. And you're right. He's Vixxian." I looked back at him, wondering suddenly at the fact that he lay so still. Was he faking? Keeping an eye on them?

The Mixims milled excitedly. "Prince Craze is here?"

"Prince Craze is the snore-beast?"

"Let's draw something on his face!"

"Shut up, dummy, that's his girlfriend! You want her to kick you into orbit?"

I stifled a laugh and nodded. "How do you know him?"

Chireet clasped his paws together. "Oh, lucky day. It's a bit of a long story, which I will happily explain on the way. If you can convince Prince Craze to come into the den with us, we will happily feed you. We have more than enough provisions, even for giants." He smiled before he bowed and scurried down my body to join the rest of his people.

I eyed them a little warily, wondering why they were so excited, but then I simply shrugged. In the time I had been away from my home-world, I had experienced things that were a lot weirder. Talking to mice-men didn't even crack the top five. As they followed me, however, I felt a little nervous. I was huge in comparison to them, and I was pretty scared I might step on one of them. It really didn't help that they kept scurrying close to me, nearly getting underfoot several times. Nonetheless, we made it to Craze without a hitch.

The creatures chattered to each other in awestruck voices as they saw the Vixxian prince. "Craze," I said loudly, hoping it would wake him up. He blinked a few times before he sat up and looked at me in a daze, rubbing the sleep out of his eyes. Not faking it after all. I found myself more amused than annoyed at that.

When he saw the Mixims for the first time, Craze jolted upright, pulling out his sword and holding it in a defensive position as he stepped between me and the milling crowd of furry aliens. He did it so quickly that it shocked me. Maybe it didn't matter whether he had been sleeping or not!

I chuckled. "Calm down, Craze. These are the Mixims, and they are friendly. They promised to give us food if we go into their den with them. I'm not really sure what that means, but I don't think we should deny them."

"Misty…" he said in a very wary voice. "Mixims are actually quite dangerous. Perhaps you'd like to come over here with me?"

"Dangerous." I looked behind me at the small crowd of furballs that had trailed after me. *The adorable chinchilla people who communicate by singing and eat fairy mushrooms are dangerous.*

Chireet tittered cutely, and a chorus of giggles rose from his companions. "'Adorable'? Really? You're quite charming, human!"

My jaw dropped. "What in the—?"

Craze winced slightly. "Actually, yes. They're even more powerful psychics than we are, and chief among their powers is telepathy." He held out his free hand to me, and I took it, letting him draw me to his side. He lowered the sword but kept it handy as he looked at them. "I am Prince Craze of the Vixxian Empire, and this is my mate. What is it that you want?"

"I am Chireet, Chief Terraform Engineer of the Royal Engineering Corps. Our crop gatherers discovered the two of you last night. Your mind was shielded as you dreamed. Hers was not. We learned enough of your predicament to bring the information before our Queen for a decision." Chireet seemed completely calm in the face of Craze's potentially violent wariness.

I, on the other hand, looked at these small creatures, which could have harmed us in our sleep and had not. Just as we could have harmed them physically now, but did not. We were short on potential allies and in desperate need. Besides…just because they had the power to cause us a lot of trouble didn't mean they wanted to, or saw reason to. "Wait. Craze, they have been nothing but friendly to me." I decided not to tell him about the suggestion that they use his face as a canvas. "Maybe we should give them a chance."

Craze frowned down at them thoughtfully then slowly put his blade away. "Answer the question, and we'll see."

"Please, Prince Craze, we would love to introduce you to the Queen!" Chireet spoke up as loudly as he could. "She has a proposition for you which I believe will interest you in your current circumstances."

His eyebrows went up. "Can your Queen get us back to Vixxia Prime?"

The whole group broke up into a chittering melody again, singing bits of whatever telepathic conversation was going on between them. "He wants to go home."

"Will he help us go home?"

"Can we trust them to know we are here and not hurt us?"

"I don't want to leave my home again!"

Finally, Chireet nodded, adjusting the goggles on his nose. "It is within the realm of possibility, yes."

Craze gave me an odd expression but eventually sighed and nodded slowly. "Very well. As you wish. We will come to your Queen's audience chamber." He saw as well as I did that we had no other choice but to follow these miniature beings.

Chireet pressed a paw against one of the squat little water towers, a square lit up around his fingers, and the entire side of the tower slid open, revealing the top of a staircase just roomy enough for us to walk down. As they swarmed forward into the staircase, Craze and I held hands and followed them into the unknown.

CHAPTER 25
CRAZE

I had never seen a species quite like the Mixims—not up close anyway. For beings whose dangerous power and inventive genius was whispered about nervously by Imperial fleet veterans, they seemed awfully…cuddly. Perhaps it was because they could afford to be.

I honestly wondered how they could have been driven from their homes, and where and when it had happened. Too many unknowns in this situation. It bothered me. Still, I didn't see Misty and me having any other options for survival if we didn't follow them. I was still wary that this could all be some sort of trap, but there wasn't much I could do but follow this lead.

So I held on tightly to Misty's hand as we descended the staircase. I had to stoop to keep my head from constantly knocking against the arched ceiling. Eventually, we arrived at the bottom, where three tunnels branched off from a central atrium.

"The tunnels are not made for species of your size, but I believe you should fare all right if you crawl," Chireet announced, before the others scurried ahead of us down the central tunnel. Their constant, musical chattering faded away, then went off in different directions.

Eccentric creatures, I thought. I gave Misty a fleeting glance, but she simply shrugged and got on her hands and knees to trail after the gray

Mixim. I hesitated briefly, wary of an attack in close quarters, but I finally caved in and crawled after her, following them down the tunnel.

I had to admit, however, that following Misty's deliciously curvy ass in the tight bodysuit was far from a chore, no matter where we were going. I had to adjust my loincloth as I crawled along, and I found myself glad that my codpiece had been damaged along with the rest of my armor. It would have confined me painfully as I followed those two swaying cheeks through the dark.

"This view is giving me all sorts of ideas," I said in a low, flirtatious voice as I followed her, making her giggle slightly. She twitched her rump at me, and I let out a little groan of lust, barely restraining myself from grabbing a handful in front of our Mixim hosts.

The joking around helped me relax a little bit, but I was still wary. Most of what I knew of the Mixims had been taught to me in history courses by my tutor. It had characterized them as dangerous, unpredictable, and very powerful psychically. Their technology was advanced—but the Mixims themselves were scattered, very rare, and almost unheard-of outside of folk tales. The only thing that all the stories agreed upon was that the Mixims could easily destroy a man's mind if sufficiently angered—but for some reason, they rarely ever did.

It was a tight fit, but we somehow managed to make our way through until the tunnel widened out into a size that allowed us to stand upright again. I stretched, my back popping loudly as I let out a grunt that mixed discomfort and satisfaction. "That's better."

"Very sorry about the long crawl," Chireet twittered politely. "Welcome to our central warren." The last words were said rather grandly, as he gestured around with a tiny paw.

I heard Misty gasp, and I followed Chireet's gesture with my eyes. At my first look at our surroundings, I was completely blown away.

The central warren had been built inside of a sizable natural cave, with delicate white metal walkways running along the walls and crisscrossing on three levels over our heads. Niches dug into the rock and fronted with metal doors and gates served as the various chambers of the warren, but all of it was built around the central plaza we had stepped out into.

The plaza was dominated by a fountain nearly as tall as I was, carved from a single piece of white-gold energy crystal, which glowed softly from within. The emerald-colored water from above ran through the fountain here, the combination shedding bright green light over the walls. Now and again, one of the Mixims would run up to the fountain and lap thirstily at its waters, then scamper off again.

A tiny throne was carved into one side of the fountain, currently unoccupied. "The Queen will arrive shortly," Chireet chittered in a friendly voice, and then he bowed and scampered up to one of the walkways, looking back but once. "Please wait here for a moment."

Misty and I continued staring around in amazement. The walls of the tunnels were covered in advanced technology, far surpassing that of our empire. Tiny view-screens, scurrying robots the size of insects, clouds of nanites digging and constructing and making repairs, and devices I couldn't even identify. The miniature beings seemed hard at work in every crevice of the complicated network of ramps, catwalks, and chambers.

"I thought they were like rodents at first, but that's not how they live. They are like ants or something," Misty murmured.

"Ants?" I looked at her, trying to understand her comment.

"Small insects, they live communally underground. They use pheromones though, not telepathy." She winced slightly. "I hope. At this point, it seems like almost anything is possible."

"Given your experiences of the last few days, I suppose I can see how you'd think that. Though, I doubt that the galaxy is actually heavily inhabited by tiny telepaths." Some sort of automated carrybot the size of my fist rolled past, pushing a cart filled with tiny white-metal ingots. "Look at this place," I breathed as I watched it go by. The whole thing was an incredibly advanced city in miniature, but I could understand her comparing it to an insect hive.

"Technological superiority plus psychic superiority," I muttered as I gazed around. "One wonders why we're not all bowing to tiny conquerors."

I glanced over at Misty, who gave me a concerned look. Reaching over, I grabbed her hand, squeezing it gently. "It's all right, Misty. I do not know why these creatures seem to be so benign compared to the reports, or why they allowed themselves to be displaced from wherever their home-world was, but clearly, these beings are full of surprises. We shall simply have to hope that they keep being pleasant ones."

A trilling chorus rose suddenly from the walls, echoing around the large chamber as every Mixim in sight suddenly joined in the song. "All Hail the Queen, Mother of Pups, Singer of the Creation Song! Bow your heads, for she is here!"

"Creepy," Misty muttered, and I nodded and wrapped an arm around her. The creatures were adorable, their song and voices sweet, but the unnatural chorus seemed strange to the ears of non-telepaths. I supposed that it was perfectly normal for the Mixims.

"Look," I pointed out a moment later. A sedan chair robot walking on jeweled spider-legs crawled down a long corridor and out into the central plaza, then ambled up to the throne. It set itself down, retracted its legs—and then retracted the golden dome it carried, section by section, until the chubby, dainty ball of white fur inside was revealed.

Misty squealed and then clapped her hands over her mouth as the Queen hopped down from the sedan bot and toddled up to her throne. I had to admit, for all my attempts to play the tough and wary guardian in this situation full of unknowns…she was pretty adorable.

She was only a little bigger than her subjects, roughly the size of my head. White as a little cloud, she had a twitchy pink nose, a sweet face and dainty paws with dark golden skin, enormous eyes a few shades lighter than her subjects', and a belly so big with obvious pregnancy that she looked like she had swallowed a melon. Her eyes had pale patches just beneath their pupils, like cataracts. A string of energy crystal beads the size of sand grains wound many times around her furry neck, sparkling like misplaced stars in her fur, and she wore a tiny psi-amplifier coronet that was curved to fit over her fluttery ears.

She settled into the throne with a self-satisfied sigh and peered up at us, ears flicking. Tiny bells tied to her white-tufted tail chimed softly as it flipped a few times before wrapping over one of her forepaws. "Ah," she squeaked. "I have to admit, I never thought that the Crown Prince of the Vixxian Empire would be having an audience with me in my very chamber."

I glanced around briefly, seeing scores of Mixims gathering on the walkways. They squeaked quietly to each other as they watched the exchange. I got the distinct impression that they were excited to have visitors, far more than worried. *Interesting creatures. Are they fearless or foolishly optimistic and trusting? No, they couldn't be the second. They can read minds. They know what most people are.*

I only hoped that when the Mixims had taken the measure of me from Misty's mind, they had found good things. Not only because it would constitute their first impression of me, but because…I very much wanted Misty to think well of me.

"Do you think she can see us? She seems blind," Misty murmured in my ear, trying to keep her voice as low as possible. Even so, the Queen glanced in her direction, her eyes narrowing just a touch. But instead of taking Misty to task, she simply giggled.

"I can see you quite well, my dear. The veils in my eyes help me see in the dark. When we first arrived here, we had to create much of our technology from scratch with only our psi abilities to assist us. Underground, there were usually no lights, and living above-ground in this place was impossible at the time." She flicked her tail again, and her whiskers wiggled.

"Oh, I'm sorry. I didn't know." Misty's lowered eyelids and the slight reddish tinge to her cheeks spoke of her embarrassment.

The Queen just let out another high, amused titter. "I am honored to have such amazing species here before me. First of all, a human from Earth. That budding little fringe planet. I've heard that the Dragicans keep requesting covert raids on your world to capture your females."

"Yes," Misty sighed. "I was kidnapped a few days ago, along with three others. Craze and his crew rescued us." She turned a warm smile on me, and I nodded.

"It is tragic, but if you make enough allies here, you will find that it benefits your whole race. After all, the Dragicans will not dare continue their predations on a protected world." Her whiskers twitched as she peered up at me thoughtfully, and then she turned her strange little wrinkle-nosed smile back on Misty. "Not many races outside of the Dragican home system can boast about meeting one of your kind." She sniffled slightly in Misty's direction. "What do you think of this part of the galaxy so far?"

Misty took a deep breath, her smile going a touch awkward. "Well, Your Majesty, it's…the weirdest damn thing that's ever happened to me. It started out awful. But I met Craze this way, so even with all the drama and risk, I…um…I wouldn't trade it."

"Aww." The Queen tilted her head, eyelashes fluttering and her little paws clasped like a squirrel begging for a nut. "I heard humans were an affectionate species. That is just adorable." She caught herself and cleared her tiny throat. "Welcome to my warren. It's not much, but it is improving by the day."

"Um, well, thank you, Your Majesty. It's…well, after wandering the wastes so long, this place pretty much looks like heaven. Especially if there's food." She gave the tiny round Queen a hopeful look.

"Oh yes. Of course." She squinted her eyes briefly, and the crystal in the psi-amplifier sparkled. "We'll put together something for you within a few minutes. It's only a matter of finding big enough bowls." Another little laugh. "I never thought I would meet members of the giant races that are actually friendly." She turned her gaze to me. "And the Vixxian Crown Prince. How lucky could I be?" She let out a tinkling laugh.

I frowned, feeling something brush against my mental shields. The "watched" feeling of being read by a telepath washed over me briefly and then withdrew. It left me unnerved and a touch scandalized, but I decided not to mention it unless it kept happening. A peek to ensure my trustworthiness, I would allow. Constant eavesdropping on my thoughts would leave me forced to take action.

"Thank you for your kindness, Your Highness," I said, bowing down to her. Misty followed my lead, quickly bowing down by my side. The Queen's smile widened slightly.

"You flatter me. Though it seems you don't know much of our race's true history." Her voice had gone slow and thoughtful, as if she was processing whatever she had seen in my thoughts. "So, what brings you here? No one besides us has visited this planet in years. That is in part why we chose it."

"I apologize for our unintentional intrusion," I said earnestly enough. "Our presence here is not by our will. We were deliberately stranded here."

She fluttered her pale eyelashes. "I don't understand. Someone dropped you off here?"

"We crashed here in a spaceship that had been caught in the meteor storm. We were on our way to the frontier on a salvage mission when we were intercepted by the space rogue Astrid—"

The Queen's tail suddenly stood out like a brush, and she chittered angrily. "Astrid? That filthy Dragican plunderer of planets?"

I sighed. There would always be a part of me that would want to leap to Astrid's defense. It had grown smaller and weaker with each fresh realization of her villainy, and then starved even more when my love for Misty had started growing to overshadow it. Claiming that Astrid "wasn't that bad" to excuse my previously horrible taste in women wouldn't do anyone any good at all. "The same," I said simply.

High-pitched chattering and angry little barks erupted all over the cavern. The Queen's tail lashed angrily. "What did she do this time? We had hoped never to see her around our space again!"

"Astrid attacked Vixxia with a rogue fleet of Thezlum raiders. She managed to escape, and meanwhile, another attack formation went after a captured Thezlum vessel that we had under guard near the frontier. Once she fled, I arranged for us to take a stealth ship out to the area. But she was waiting for us."

"An ambush. Strange that she knew exactly when and where to lie in wait for you," she pointed out with more shrewdness than her appearance led me to expect. But then again, pretty and fluffy didn't necessarily mean stupid. *Look at Misty.*

"There is a strong suspicion that we have a traitor among us." If only I knew who it was. I had my suspicions here and there, a slightly cagey vizier, my oily and power-hungry twin, even perhaps my mother...whose loyalty had come into question once already, a long time ago. "Finding them is first on my list for when we return home."

"I see," the fluffy little Queen mused, whiskers wiggling. "When it comes to returning home, we could perhaps make a deal," she chirruped. "But once we do so, you will be in our debt. And when you take the throne, we will collect."

I hesitated, suddenly wary. "What is it that you are asking for exactly?"

A chorus of twitters and squeaks erupted from one end of the chamber. We all turned to see a line of robots, similarly designed to the sedan bot but larger and plainer, walking toward us down one of the lower ramps. "Ah, here is food for us all. Let's fill your stomachs before I fill your ears with negotiation terms."

"Very well," I said a little reluctantly, watching her as she leaned forward when the first robot approached her. It walked up to her, turned sideways, and straightened its legs so that it became a makeshift table before her. The dome retracted, revealing a salad of mushrooms and mosses.

It wasn't the most appetizing thing I had ever seen, but after days without food, I found my mouth watering. Misty and I sat down on the floor, and the two other serverbots walked up to us and deployed as well.

The rich scent of the cooked mixture rose to my nose, and Misty and I exchanged surprised glances. The Queen had already dug in and was holding a mushroom cap between her little paws, nibbling daintily at its rim.

"Eat carefully," I advised Misty as I turned to her. "Not everything in their diet may agree with u—" I paused and blinked, frowning at her slightly. "Oh."

She looked up at me guiltily, a quarter of her tray's contents gone and her mouth stuffed full. She swallowed. "Um...oops?"

"Well...never mind, then," I said with my eyebrows up. If she ended up vomiting or hallucinating, at least I knew I could heal her.

She giggled a little and kept eating, though a bit more slowly. I glanced at her once in a while, forcing myself to eat slower still, even as the first few tough but savory bites woke my hunger in earnest.

The whole time, I kept half an eye on the Queen, who had business with us but had made me wait on bringing up exactly what it was. She might not even have intended the delay, but my trust in new people was shaky right now, and I felt a little tense as I slowly filled my stomach.

"I'm afraid we still don't have much to work with here when it comes to varying our diets. Until our bioprocessors come fully on-line, we can't reconfigure organic materials at will, and so we end up breeding endless flavors of mushrooms." She sounded so bored of mushrooms at that moment that I bit back a compliment aimed at the food in a fit of decorum.

"It's fine," Misty said to fill the silence. "I haven't eaten in days, so, you know, mushrooms are good with me."

"Well, an empty stomach makes everything taste good." From the way she mechanically nibbled at her meal, however, it seemed the Queen might have preferred to go hungry had she not been eating for…it looked like at least half a dozen.

Once I was satisfied that my system could handle the contents of my platter, I ate with gusto. Misty was already looking disappointedly at her empty server as it wandered off. *Poor thing,* I thought. At least she would sleep well tonight on a full stomach.

Finally, I sat back with a sigh and wrapped an arm around Misty, who already looked better for having had a proper meal. "So," I brought up again somewhat pointedly to the Queen, "how may I be of help to you, in return for your assistance getting home?"

"My price for our assistance is twofold. One is information, which we will ask for before we help you return to Vixxia Prime. If you two are willing to help my scientists learn more about your species, we will gladly help you in any way we can." She offered this calmly, all-business, her white-centered eyes staring directly at us. "Once you have returned home, and upon your ascent to the throne, I will call in the second half of my debt." She sat back from her empty platter, which started walking off.

"What…form…will this second half take?" I asked very carefully.

"We wish the assistance of the Vixxian Emperor in regaining our ancestral home," she replied very simply.

It seemed a harmless enough thing to promise, but I felt another surge of wariness. I could certainly sympathize with her people's desire to return to their homeland, but I had no idea where that homeland was or how much help even an emperor could be in the matter—unless the land in question was within the empire, of course. I suddenly wished that I knew more about the Mixims than a few eerie children's fables.

Misty looked at me, and I nodded. We didn't have any other choice but to do as the Queen asked. I turned back to her, praying that I was making the right call. "Of course, Your Highness."

CHAPTER 26
MISTY

"What do you think about the Mixims? I find them rather cute," I murmured sleepily as I rolled on top of Craze. We were in a freshly dug food-storage chamber since it was one of the few unused rooms that was large enough for us to sleep in. Overall, the small species had been very hospitable, but they clearly weren't used to having "giants" like us as guests. Still, the round, dirt-floored room was clean, dry, and had fresh air that didn't smell like rotten eggs, so I was happy enough. Especially now that my stomach was full.

"I think they are quite generous," Craze said as his lips made their way to the hollow of my neck and his hands ran up and down my sides, stroking and squeezing me gently before settling more firmly on the globes of my ass.

He tangled his legs with mine and smiled up at me lazily, his long silver hair splayed out beside his head. "It is not the royal suite at the Capitol, but it serves its purpose and gives us privacy." He leaned up and buried his face in the trailing strands of my hair, letting it flow over his closed eyes. The whole time, he took in deep breaths of my scent. He did that sometimes, just...smelling me with the enthusiasm of an animal. It was sexy...if a little weird.

"Do you think they'll be able to help us get back home?" I asked, tilting my head. As I did, he took the chance to kiss me again, his lips lingering against my jawline. I giggled at his teasing before placing my hands on his chest and pushing him down. "Seriously. This is nice and all, but I like your planet much better." I couldn't quite keep the sarcasm out of my voice, and I worried a little. The Mixims' little flower-petal ears were very sensitive.

"I do too." Craze was smiling way too much, and I relaxed after a moment, distracted by his happy look. "I also noticed how you called Vixxia Prime 'home.'" His deep blue eyes searched my face, and the hope in them made my cheeks heat up and my smile get a little wobbly.

"I did, didn't I?" I replied hesitantly, but I did manage to smile. *Really, is the idea of staying with him so bad—if we can somehow get through all of this craziness?*

"Yes. It gives me hope that perhaps you will stay, now that the tracker will soon be disabled." He glanced at the other side of my neck, the side he never kissed, where that damned tag still lay under my skin. I couldn't even feel it, but I knew it was there, and sometimes I scratched on sheer instinct, angry at the invasion of my body.

I brushed my fingertips over the spot. "The control box got damaged in the crash. I managed to keep hold of it, but I'll need to find out if the Mixims can repair it."

"Better yet, perhaps we should ask them if they have the means to destroy it without damaging you. Their technology is impressive." He gently tugged my hand away from it and squeezed my fingertips then brought them to his lips. "I do not understand why our stories caution against them so."

I nodded slowly, frowning. "Neither do I. I mean, yes, if they're powerful psychics, they wouldn't need to grow very large to succeed as an intelligent race. But if they were so awful, they would be doing the conquering, instead of ending up as a diaspora."

"Diaspora?" He cocked his head and then went back to nuzzling my hair.

"A scattered people. Some are driven off their lands. Some are kidnapped as slaves and taken far away. Some have their homes destroyed, or so many of their members that they can no longer form an independent society." Despite the serious subject, my voice was silky with relaxation and desire as I ran my fingertips over his chest. A deep warmth had settled into my belly, and I felt his lazy caresses stoking it slowly.

"There are many worlds who wouldn't think twice about taking in a miniature race, especially one that is benign and has amazing technology to trade with. They require little land and resources, they tend to be less expansionist and violent, and these beings…well, they thrive through cooperation." His eyelids lowered, pale lashes barely hiding the gleam of his eyes. I felt his erection stir against my belly. "It is my hope that they can extend that to us just as readily."

"I think they will, if you make good on your end. They got screwed over really badly fairly recently by some local race. I don't know which one, but I know it would make any race wary." I nuzzled his warm, stubbled cheek, smiling a little. His face was usually clean-shaven, so closely that I had wondered if he was even capable of growing a beard. I knew he would rid himself of it as soon as he got home and had a chance to, but for now, I like the scruffiness.

"I will keep that in mind," he said slowly and then went right back to petting his long fingers up and down my spine. I arched a little against them, all but purring. "I just hope I can get a tight timeline out of them quickly. I don't want to think about what might be happening back home in our absence." His muscles tightened, and I ran my palms over his shoulders soothingly.

"Well, they did mention they were going to calibrate their transporter for larger passengers," I reminded him. I hoped the Mixims would keep their promises, but given all the technological prowess they boasted, I wasn't really worried about their ability to do so. "Apparently, it's a bit on the experimental side." *I really hope they don't try to beam us up and we both end up part of the asteroid belt.*

He frowned thoughtfully as his fingers slid through my hair hypnotically. "I can't believe they figured out long-distance teleportation. Our scientists have tried to solve it for generations but have always come up short." He seemed fascinated—and a little jealous. "With technology like that, the Mixims won't even need spaceships.

They won't even have to maintain a fleet, just…national borders from afar." The potential for this technology made his eyes light up.

I was less impressed. Not because I wasn't grateful to be going back to Vixxia Prime, but because Craze's mind seemed to have immediately jumped to its combat applications. I definitely needed to distract my lover before that kind of talk totally killed the mood.

Fortunately, I had just the thing. "Well, they are incredibly smart, apparently. We just have to trust them. But until then…" Grinning, I leaned forward and kissed him, letting my lips dance over his. His mouth was hot on mine as I held on to his hands, my fingers tangling with his. I squeezed his hands slightly as the kiss intensified, my tongue slipping into his mouth delicately, then retreating and making room for his. One of my hands let go of his and slid down his body to start untying his loincloth. When I heard his excited grunt, I smiled to myself, feeling his growing erection press against my thigh.

Before I could say anything, he flipped us over, pushing me into the floor. I could feel the soft dirt pressed up against my back. The smell of living earth mixed with our scent and turned me on further as he bent over me. "Craze," I moaned quietly, wrapping my arms around his neck and my legs around his waist, pulling him closer. Only the ragged body stocking I still wore lay between our skins as his throbbing cock slid against my thigh.

"Mm, you're really turned on tonight." Maybe because the last few times, we had been interrupted—once before orgasm and once in the afterglow. It was a frustrating track record, and I could completely understand his ardor. I needed to feel his body on mine, his tongue on my skin, and his hot breath in my ear as he thrust into me. These thoughts pushed me on as I lifted my hips up to him.

"So are you," he mused, seeing the lust in my eyes. My cheeks burned at his comment and I looked away, but he gently pushed my head up to look at him. "You want me." He smirked as he made the observation.

"So bad," I whispered, slipping out of the sleeves of my body stocking and pushing the fabric down so that it barely covered my breasts. He let out a contented rumble and bent to push the fabric down farther with his lips, then ran his tongue along them hungrily.

I finished untying his loincloth and unwrapped it from his hips, taking out his now hard cock. I started to rub his smooth shaft as it stabbed into my belly, stroking it softly and then with more urgency. A loud grunt emerged from his lips as he bucked his hips, eyeing me fiercely. "Come and get me," I taunted.

Craze didn't hesitate as he sat up and peeled down the body stocking in one rough motion, tossing it to the side. Moments later, he pulled me onto his lap. I gasped and wrapped my legs around him, rubbing my belly against his erection as his lips latched on to my breast. I moaned, arching my back and shivering with excitement. I gripped his powerful biceps as I tried to compose myself, my heart beating so fast that it made me dizzy. But as his tongue flicked over my nipple, I tensed and started to whimper and squirm, instantly thrown into a sexual frenzy.

He continued to suck my nipple, his teeth nipping delicately at it for a moment before he pulled away. "Your breasts are so lovely," he murmured as he slowly leaned me back and ran his fingertips along my body. He lingered near my navel as I shuddered, my ragged breaths causing my bosom to heave up and down. His eyes locked on the motion as a devilish grin appeared on his face.

My eyes widened slightly as I saw that look on his face. "What… what?" I mumbled a second before he pounced.

In a flash, he had his knees on my arms, pinning me down to the soft dirt. I looked up at him, trying to figure out what he was up to, when I felt his large hands start kneading my breasts again. He pinched my nipples between his thumb and forefinger, firmly rolling them in between. I arched my head back and let out a full-throated groan, nails digging into the dirt as I struggled for breath.

This seemed to please him as he squeezed my breasts even harder, pressing them together. I watched, my whole body tingling from the breast play, my eyebrows lifting. It was only when he slid the tip of his cock against my soft flesh that I figured out what he had in mind.

"Naughty…" I moaned, seeing him slip his swollen head between my breasts. He grunted in ecstasy as I bit my bottom lip. Slowly, he started to fuck the cleft between my boobs, making them bounce and jiggle with each jerk of his hips. He started slow, feeling out how much room he had to play. Then he threw himself into rough thrusting, quickly picking up speed until the friction turned his cock rock-hard.

I could already see a soft trickle of pre-come making its way out of his engorged tip. *Is he already near orgasm?* The thought alone heightened my arousal as I bucked my hips and tried to find some way to please my neglected cunt. There wasn't even a draft to tease me. Watching him use my breasts like that, hearing his voice turn into grunts and shouts of pleasure, it turned me on—but it couldn't satisfy me.

I whimpered as Craze continued to fuck my breasts harder and harder, forcing them around his shivering, swollen cock. "Please, Craze... I need you."

He looked down at me. Our eyes locked together, and I felt a jolt of excitement running up my spine as I noticed the wild, lustful look in his gorgeous eyes.

I'm in for it, I realized and licked my lips. I couldn't wait.

CHAPTER 27
CRAZE

As I looked into Misty's beautiful eyes and heard her soft plea, I couldn't control myself. A sexual jolt of energy possessed me as I jumped off her. She whimpered softly as my eyes clouded over with lust. Moments later, with my heart pounding a mile a minute, I pinned her down, my hands at her wrists and my mouth soldered to the glowing symbol that I had branded on her breast. I positioned myself impatiently and thrust my hips hard, ramming my full length inside of her. She gasped and dug her nails into my back, pulling me closer. "Ah...good..." she barely managed to gasp out and then started rolling her hips up to meet me.

Her tight, slick walls wrapped around me, making me shout shamelessly with pleasure as I drew back and sank my cock deep into her again. I raised my head to look at her panting under me, her eyelids fluttering and her lips parted. Reaching a hand between us to stimulate her, I started kissing her hungrily as I thrust my hips, going as fast and as hard as I could.

She didn't seem to mind that she was lying on bare earth, or maybe she didn't even notice. She rolled her head back and forth, hips pumping in response to my thrusts, her breasts bouncing, her nails clutching at my back. It took all my waning focus to keep my fingers moving against her clit as I drove myself toward my climax.

My body was moving almost on reflex now as I pounded away at her. Each thrust brought me closer. I felt my balls gather tight to my body as our bellies smacked together. The room swam in my vision, and I closed my eyes, my breath coming in harsh grunts. I had but moments before my climax.

Eager to make her go over the edge before me, I flicked my tongue over one of her nipples once more. My fingers teased her engorged clit, rubbing it and teasing it until she was moaning loud enough that her voice went hoarse. I fucked her harder, our bodies sliding together with ease as our sweat and her juices mixed on her skin. I kept at her, never easing off, making her writhe rhythmically underneath me.

Then, just when I thought I couldn't hold back any longer, I felt her body tensing up. She held her breath and arched her back, her head tilting back, exposing her neck. "Fuck," she gasped, her wet cunt quivering as it tightened delightfully around me. I grunted, my fingers digging into her flesh even further. "I'm coming!" she cried out as I gave one final thrust with all of my might, ramming into her, balls deep, my tip caressing her inner walls.

Her fingers dug into the dirt floor as her whole body shook with orgasm. I could feel her cunt quivering with pleasure. As she tightened even more and started clenching rhythmically, I lost all control, spewing my load inside of her. My voice came bellowing out of me, and even letting out that long, immodest cry felt like paradise.

Groaning, we collapsed together, completely exhausted. "Wow," Misty murmured, panting up at me with her eyes soft with satisfaction. "That was amazing."

I chuckled and pulled her closer. I was just glad we were still alive to have moments like this. If we had kept wandering the surface of this planet, we would have perished, whether from hunger, acid rain, or meteors falling on our heads. Now, however, we had stumbled upon the Mixims. Within a few days, we would hopefully be back on Vixxia Prime, safe and sound. And soon after, I would have my fleet behind me and my boot so far up Astrid's ass she'd think I had invented a new kink just for her. With that thought in mind, I wrapped my arms around Misty's shoulders, pulling her just a bit closer before kissing the top of her head.

Misty smiled sleepily at me, making my heart melt. There was a deep sheen on her ebony skin, as if we had bathed in the spring again. I gently ran my fingertips across her luscious curves, feeling my excitement grow once more. But before I could do anything about it, I heard the soft, even sound of Misty's breathing. When I looked down, she was already fast asleep. I smiled and kissed her forehead one more time before settling in and finally surrendering to sleep myself.

WHEN I AWOKE, CHIREET WAS STANDING CASUALLY ON MY CHEST, HIS TAIL looped over one arm. My eyes widened and my breath caught in my throat. I almost flung him away before realizing what was going on. "Chireet, don't do that. You startled me," I scolded, finally letting out my inhaled breath. *How long exactly had he been standing there using me as a stage? I wonder if Mixims developed from felines.*

"My apologies, Prince Craze, but the Queen would like to speak with you." He adjusted his goggles briefly and then jumped down and scurried off before I could even give him an answer. I stared after him and shook my head slowly, not sure if he was that way from personal eccentricity or as some trait of his odd, telepathic race.

Sighing, I got up and looked down, only to find Misty still fast asleep. I wanted to let her sleep a little longer, but I didn't think it was wise to keep the Queen waiting, so I leaned down and gently shook her awake. "Misty," I whispered softly, pushing a few strands of her hair behind her ear. I smiled down at her, drinking her in, beautiful cheeks, flawless skin, and kissable lips. She was a goddess.

She grumbled and sighed a bit, but she eventually opened her eyes and looked up at me. "Unh. Time to get up?" She sat up and gave me a curious look, then glanced around. "What is it?" she yawned, bringing a hand to her mouth.

"The Queen wants to see us. Chireet was just here, but he didn't mention why," I explained, tying on my loincloth, straightening my hair, and doing what I could to make myself presentable. "He's always dashing off somewhere. It's like talking to an intelligent tree-hopper who has had too much sugar."

I watched her stretch before she finally got up to get dressed, her slim muscles flexing under her silky skin. Then she went to pick up her discarded body stocking and pull it on. I helped her into it, a smile on my face as I smelled our mixed scents on her skin. I could still feel the way her inner muscles had flexed around my cock as her climax had touched off my own. It was a feeling I would never tire of. I knew that now, and I knew as well that I needed her to stay in my life.

"Chireet is a strange one. But I like him. He seems nice. Kind of nerdy and eccentric, but nice," Misty said, more to herself than to me. I nodded and grabbed her hand, guiding her back toward the towering cavern that held the Queen's throne.

As we stepped into the room, we saw the Queen perched on her little crystal throne, gold dust brushed into her fur today, nibbling on a bit of fried mushroom with a bored manner. Two of her subjects were rubbing her dainty little feet. She sighed, squirming uncomfortably, as if as tired of her enormous pregnancy as she was of eating fungi.

We walked up and bowed in front of her, giving her our respect. "Ah, Misty and Craze. Always a pleasure," she greeted us with a friendly smile. "Please, sit."

"You wanted to see us, Your Majesty?" I asked, my voice steady and firm as I addressed the tiny royal. I never quite let my guard down around her, and I didn't want to show weakness. Cute and benign as she seemed, she could read our every thought, and I knew she had been less than specific about the price of her help. Especially that bit about regaining her homeland. *Where even is the Mixim homeland?*

"Yes. It seems our scientists have successfully calibrated the transporter. Once they conduct a basic examination and take some blood, as we discussed yesterday, you may leave whenever you wish."

My heart stopped for a moment when I heard her words. "That quickly?" When the Mixims had promised to send us back to Vixxia, I had been skeptical. But now I felt a dash of pure hope in my heart. "Do you have any experience with teleporting the larger races?" I asked in my most cautious tone.

"Yes. And I would like you to know that if you ever need help, we

Mixims will gladly be of assistance." Her whiskers wiggled again. "The one who aids us in regaining our homeland will have a friend for the life of his society." She tilted her head. "Of course, we will ask that you leave some token of your promise, if at all possible. Something that you value personally."

I bowed my head and nodded, grateful to have an ally of such potential. "I'm honored."

"The scientists are eager to get started. Their laboratory is a short crawl down that far corridor. I'll send the serving trays with your breakfast so they can get started without your having to sit there with empty stomachs. You can decide what to leave as a token while you are there." Her pale-pupiled eyes twinkled briefly, and then she waved us off toward the tunnel.

"Ouch," Misty grumped slightly a few minutes later. We both sat down in the middle of the laboratory floor, another domed, dug-out room, this one with walls lined with more devices I couldn't identify.

Several Mixims were clambering over us both, waving instruments and taking notes on tiny tablets. One had just taken Misty's blood with a tiny needle and was now examining it using a computer barely larger than my fist. "Um, Doctor?" she asked one of them as he hopped past.

The Mixim she addressed had black-and-white stripes running down his back and had a habit of humming squeakily to himself. "Yes?" he chirped distractedly.

"I was wondering if you could deactivate and remove this tracking disc I have under the skin of my neck. We can't tamper with it as there's an explosive charge connected to my artery, and the control box was damaged in the crash. The Thezlums can find me and kill me with it wherever I go." She looked at the little creature pleadingly.

He tugged thoughtfully at the tuft of fur at the tip of his tail. "That is a problem, yes indeed. Fortunately, we've run across Thezlum and Dragican technology several times. Let me have a look." He hopped up onto her shoulder as I watched and peered at the blinking disc.

"Unpleasant device. I believe I'll have the nanites handle this." He chattered instructions at two of his assistants, and one of them scrambled up one of the miniature ramps to a niche, returning with a tiny silver capsule. The other tapped symbols on a minuscule tablet, peering at Misty now and again.

"Is this safe?" I asked, wanting to make certain. I only had one Misty, after all.

"Absolutely safe, yes. We will be dismantling the device to a very small scale and removing it through her pores." He accepted the capsule from his assistant and bounded back to Misty's shoulder again. "Are you ready, my dear?"

"As ready as I'm going to be." She shrugged nervously.

He popped the tablet open, and an oily silver mass poured out of it and dropped onto Misty's shoulder. We both stiffened—but the mercury-like droplet rolled up the skin of her neck toward the flashing red light, swept over it until a silver circle covered it, and then sank into her skin and vanished from sight.

"Wow, this feels…weird." Misty was clearly struggling to keep her hand down and not poke at her neck. "Kind of tingly and itchy."

As I watched, the red light suddenly went out and did not come back on again. I held my breath…but nothing happened. The outline of the disc beneath her skin started to soften and shrink. Moments later, bits of silver started to dot the side of her neck, and then began running together to form the droplet again. It was nearly twice its original size now, thanks to the burden of the broken-down tracking disc.

Misty sat up and put her hand to her neck as the animated droplet rolled down her skin and ran back to its capsule home. The doctor smiled in satisfaction and closed the capsule again. "And there we go. A good meal for the nanites, and no more problem for you."

"I'm free of it?" She blinked and then let out a joyous little laugh and hugged me. "Thank you, Doctor," she said as the Mixim hopped down.

"A small matter. I am glad to be of help."

We were all smiles as we submitted to the last of the tests. Once again, we owed the Mixims, and this time, they had asked for nothing in return. I had to make certain that they knew just how much I valued this new alliance, and I had just the token of good faith to do the job.

Before we went to the teleportation chamber, I returned to the

Queen with Misty. "Majesty, I have the token that you requested, and I would like to present it to you."

"Interesting!" she chittered and waved a tiny paw. "Please come forward and present it."

Slowly, I pulled my sword from my belt and walked up to the Queen, laying it at the foot of her tiny throne, my head still bowed. "In the name of all Vixxians, I present you with my sword, Exredilan."

CHAPTER 28
MISTY

I was surprised when Craze gave up his sword. I knew how much it meant to him and how monumental this moment was if he was willing to part with it. Was it gratitude for our lives? For the alliance? For setting me free of that horrible Thezlum tracker? All of them? I didn't know. But given how often he showed the sword off or used it in battle, I knew it had to be one of his most prized possessions.

I stood there and watched as the Queen hopped down from her throne and stood on the hilt, a warm expression on her face. "The Mixims graciously accept your gift. Let it stand as a pledge for our new alliance, until such time as all promises are kept." Her voice was soft and level, a touch more formal than usual.

She stood there with her eyes closed, statue-like, making me wonder if she was using her powers, and for what. Then she opened her eyes again, which pierced me despite the vague, blind look their white pupils gave them. "If you would follow Chireet, he will bring you to the transporter." She closed her eyes once more.

Before I could question her odd behavior, Craze grabbed my hand. "Let's go."

I nodded and started walking with him, eager to get somewhere

where we didn't have to crawl through tunnels to avoid a horrible outside environment.

By our feet, the tiny Chireet skittered along, his small body impossibly fast. When it came time to crawl, he took the lead, and Craze insisted on bringing up the rear again. I had my suspicions as to why, and I giggled as I made my way along the tunnel. I couldn't tell if he was more of a boob man or an ass man, but he was certainly into every bit of me, and that was good enough.

Soon, we emerged into a large chamber carved from the bedrock. All around us, Mixims in a variety of coat colors worked away on advanced machines with glowing screens and arrays of tiny switches. I had no idea what any of the machines were and could not even begin to understand how the Mixims were capable of achieving this level of technology. Maybe it was easier to invent things when you could join your minds cooperatively with others. Certainly, it must cut down on misunderstandings.

"Right this way." Chireet's voice broke through my train of thought as he led us to the back of the room. There, a group of scientists wore proud looks on their faces as they stood waiting for us. They all wore matching blue jumpsuits to protect their fur, and one or two held tools that included what looked like a little bitty silver monkey wrench. There were small splotches of black on their clothes that kind of looked like grease stains. I tilted my head and chuckled to myself. They looked like the universe's cutest mechanics.

"Ah! Twyll, it looks like you and your team have been hard at work. Are we ready to go?" Chireet was a bit tiny to look so officious, and I had to stifle another giggle. I wasn't going to miss this godforsaken planet, but I was definitely going to miss these little guys. I hoped we would see them again.

"We have finished calibrating the transporter. It will bring you both to Vixxia Prime. In order to ensure accuracy, however, we had to forfeit speed, so it will take a few hours to get there," one of the mechanic-looking Mixims chirped. He had gray-brown fur and chubby cheeks, and the jumpsuit strained slightly over his round little belly.

"A few hours? What are we supposed to do during that time? Will there be problems if we move around?" I asked them. I had no idea what teleportation was like. Would we still be in a solid state, or would we be decomposed into billions of tiny particles, only to be reconstructed at our destination? From what I remembered of my kidnapping, that was how the Thezlum tech did it. I wasn't looking forward to experiencing anything like that ever again.

"You are free to do as you please. We have perfected solid-state transportation, so you will be in full control of your bodies." He responded to my question with a dignified voice. "We have reading-tablets to pass the time, but I don't think we have any that are big enough for you."

"Oh…okay." *Well, I don't have to go through being ripped apart on the molecular level. I guess that's a blessing.* I glanced over at Craze, still unconvinced.

"How does it work?" Craze asked.

"We start the machine like so." Together, the crew scurried around the back wall, twisting knobs and pulling down levers. A series of whining noises came from the back wall as if the devices connected to it were warming up. The one section of wall that was not crowded with circuitry was smooth metal. It slid up suddenly, and I crouched to see a chamber roughly large enough for a small car to sit in. The walls were white, and a faintly glowing silver disc was set into the floor, taking up most of its space.

Suddenly, a spark of light emerged from the middle of the disc. It was purple-white and grew quickly, dancing upward in the center of the circle. It looked like living lightning. Finally, it ran in a writhing column from floor to ceiling. Now and again within its arc, I caught glimpses of a dim green space beyond. It crackled after a moment, and I could faintly smell the green scent of the grove where Craze had first made love to me.

I took a step back, apprehensive of what I was getting myself into. "Okay. What now?"

"Now, you two simply step through," Chireet announced, as if it was obvious and this was a normal thing that he did every day. *Except that he absolutely did call this technology "experimental." That was a thing. I heard him.*

I gulped in fear. My heart was racing as I pictured myself walking through the energy field and burning to a crisp—or getting ripped apart and not put back together again. The longer I thought about it, the more choked up I got.

It became harder and harder to breathe as a strange feeling swept through my body, making me sweat and causing my fingers to jitter. *Oh, crap, is this a panic attack? I've certainly overdosed on adrenaline enough lately. Maybe this has kind of been too much for me.*

Craze, on the other hand, looked completely confident as he grabbed my hand. "It will be all right, my darling." He gave my hand a firm squeeze before he took a step forward toward the machine. His face was frozen in a stoic expression as he stared at the transporter. In his eyes was a hint of amazement as he seemed to take in every detail. No doubt he wanted to relay as much of this experience as he could to his own people. The Mixims might not want to share their technology with the Vixxians, but at least now he could go back and tell his scientists that such an advance was actually possible.

"Come," he said, looking over his shoulder at me. I gulped again but nodded, taking a shaky step forward. While we continued to hold hands, he stepped into the transporter and disappeared. All I could see of him was his hand still holding on to mine. *Please don't let it fall off or something.* But the hand squeezed mine gently, clearly still attached to him. Putting all my faith into the Mixims' cleverness, I closed my eyes and stepped into the transporter.

When I opened them once more, I gasped in amazement. We stood in a bright white space that was completely featureless. There was absolutely nothing around us. We were standing, and I felt solidity beneath me. Yet when I looked down, there was nothing under our feet. Adding to the surreal experience, I felt my stomach lurching around, like I was being spun around in some sort of centrifuge. "What's going on?" I asked, tightening my hold on Craze. I was terrified to let him go.

"I believe this is the inside of the transporter," he responded after a moment's observation. "Though, apparently, that definition is a little bit…relative."

My eyes kept straining to fix on anything, even the hint of a horizon, only to slide off into endless blank whiteness, adding to my sense of vertigo. "It's empty."

"Indeed." His voice sounded distracted despite his firm grip on me.

I glared at him. We were in the middle of nowhere, literally, and all he had to say was "Indeed"? *Come on, man. I'm freaking out. Say something comforting!* "This is really not normal."

"No, it isn't. Not even by my standards." He finally caught on. "Are you all right?"

"I've got vertigo. It feels like I'm falling in multiple directions at once." I hung on to his arm, gaining at least some sense of stability from it. "Isn't it messing with you too?"

"Not so much. But I am used to sub-light travel, which can be somewhat…jarring." He looked around. "I think this is where we wait for the few hours they talked about," he mused, spinning around, trying to find some distinguishing feature. "You are right. This is disorienting."

"Well, what do we do in the meantime?" I asked, finally spending a lot of time with my eyes closed to keep them from straining to find things that weren't there.

"There's only one thing we can do." He chuckled and pulled me close, then scooped me off the ground entirely.

I let out a nervous little laugh and hugged him, wrapping my legs around his waist. A moment later, his lips were caressing mine passionately. He took my breath away as we maintained the kiss for well over a minute, his tongue tangling with mine and his breath hot on my cheek.

When he finally broke away, I could feel my heart pounding and my skin tingling. My cunt suddenly ached with need for him. I pressed my body against his and ran my hands up and down his back. "That's nice."

He grinned and gently kissed my neck as he gave my ass a firm squeeze. I wanted him to keep going, to touch me all over, but we had no idea how closely the Mixims were monitoring us in transit. Instead, he just held me in this embrace like he never wanted to let me go.

We clung together for a while, and finally, he lifted his head from my shoulder and looked at me. His expression was very serious, but his eyes were bright with hope. "I must ask you something while we return," he said quietly.

I smiled and nodded up at him, thinking at once that I knew what he would ask. And I wasn't wrong.

"I don't understand this custom of marriage which you spoke of a few days ago. I do not know if the commitment is entirely the same as you are used to. But...I want you to stay with me. Here." He swallowed and glanced away very briefly, before the boldness returned to his eyes. "Be mine, and when the time comes, rule beside me. Vixxian blood is compatible with many races. It has been done before, when the ruler sees fit. You would be...welcome, I think. Even my mother likes you enough to speak in person."

I blinked up at him slowly, my head spinning a bit more now. "You want to make this...permanent." My hand slipped up to the mark on my breast, thinking of every crazy thing we had been through together, and how, no matter what, my feelings for him only grew.

"Yes," he replied, and I couldn't help but smile.

"Okay," I murmured finally, still a little uncertain, but knowing chances like this—not to mention guys like this—just didn't come by very often. Whatever risks or politics or weirdness were involved, I didn't want a future without him in it. "I'll stay."

He hugged me tighter, burying his nose in my hair. I gently laid my head on his chest and closed my eyes, just trying to enjoy the chance to hold each other quietly for a while. *Well, I guess I'm committed now. I hope his family likes me.*

CHAPTER 29
CRAZE

We floated through space together in a tight embrace. My heart beat hard with my happiness and excitement. I had never expected to be able to win her under such insane circumstances, but the bond was true, and now I no longer had to dread the day of her leaving.

Time seemed to vanish as I listened to her soft heartbeat, my ear against her chest as I nestled my head on her ample breasts. It was a soothing sound, and I felt myself drowsing in and out of consciousness even though the dazzling white light shone brightly through my eyelids.

Suddenly, a warm sensation wrapped around my entire body, like a cocoon of heated air. I started sweating. It grew hotter and hotter, as if we were trapped in an oven. For a moment, I worried that the Mixims had miscalculated—or even perhaps had decided to play a particularly cruel parting joke. I quickly shoved the thought aside. *No. This will pass.*

But it didn't, and the temperature kept rising to an almost unbearable level, making my heart beat fast and sweat pour off my body. I pressed Misty even closer to my chest, wanting to comfort her and make her feel safe even though I didn't know myself if we would survive the next five minutes.

"Craze, what's going on?" Misty's voice had a high note of panic in it.

"I don't know," I ran my fingers through her hair. "It's all right. We're going to be fine," I murmured in her ear, hoping it would calm her down. "The Mixims won't let us down."

I hope.

She let out a little cry as everything suddenly went black. "Shh," I murmured and held her close. As I caressed her hair, a bright light twinkled into existence far off, like a star. It grew bigger and brighter until we were both forced to look away.

An ear-shattering squeal shot through my ears, leaving them ringing. A deep thrum rattled my bones, and a second later it felt as if we passed through a thick, cool membrane. The light vanished, and we tumbled onto something soft and moist. Looking down, I was amazed to find a stretch of thick Vixxian moss beneath me.

"Ah!" I gasped out, delighted. "We're home! Misty—"

"Something's wrong," she said in a shaky voice, and I hurriedly looked up.

I gasped. We were at Silviana's Center, but the whole area looked… sick. The trees sagged and were slowly shedding their leaves, the moss had yellow patches, and worst of all, most of the once deep silver water had now condensed into a clotted black sludge. A few inches of healthy water remained, and there I saw the glowfish and other inhabitants of the sacred lake thrashing as they struggled to stay alive.

"Someone has defiled Silviana's Center. Only a few things could disable it like this. Normally, the psychic energies here are strong… unless certain types of catastrophe have happened." My heart sank and my anger grew. What had caused this? "Come on. We must get to the bottom of this."

Misty looked disoriented as she rubbed her temples. "Just give me a minute. That left me feeling pretty sick."

I looked back at her impatiently, but she was ashen and her eyes had a sunken look. "Of course. Here. Let me share my energy with you."

This time, the energy flowed cleanly between us, and I saw the light return to her eyes as she sighed with relief. "Thank you," she murmured. Then she lifted her chin, giving me a determined look. "Okay. I'm ready. Let's go see what's up."

I took her hand, and we hurried out of the grove toward the nearest palace entrance. The rolling moss lawn was all but deserted, and though there was a crowd in the plaza, they were strangely quiet and subdued. I noticed glints of red light flashing among them and peered in that direction, but I couldn't make out the source.

I was too distracted right now to worry about it. My mind was reeling with all the possible scenarios for why the Center was dying, but they all came down to one conclusion.

Astrid. I knew she was behind this. She had to be. She had already tried it once just a few days ago. She had tried to kill Misty and me as well. Who else would be capable of completely decimating Vixxia Prime like this? I clenched my fists together. *She will pay for this. Pay dearly.*

"What is it?" Misty whispered beside me as we hurried toward the double door that led into the lower ring.

"I don't know yet, but we must keep moving." A knot of servants was headed our way along the same path, likely on their way to join the others on the plaza. Their manner was subdued as well, and as they drew near, I saw a flash of red.

"Oh God," Misty mumbled in horror. "Craze—"

"I see them." My voice was grim and full of rage. Every last one of the servants had a round red light flashing in the sides of their necks. Every last one had been tagged with a Thezlum tracker.

One of the servants turned her head slightly to look at us as we walked past. Her eyes fixed on my face and widened, and for a moment, I thought she would start pleading with me. But then her lips trembled, and a look of pure terror crossed her face. Turning away from me, she hurried to catch up with the others.

"So Astrid circled back to attack the Capitol again as soon as she thought we were dead." Misty kept her voice low, looking around warily. She was panting just a touch as she hurried along beside me, but so far, I was impressed. She was keeping up, even with legs a foot shorter than mine.

"That seems to be the case. I'm not seeing any Thezlums, but for all

I know, they're all inside." I suddenly, fervently wished that I had my sword. The alliance with the Mixims had been worth it, but I felt naked without the blade at my hip.

"What's the plan?" She jumped slightly as a green harper-bird landed in a fruit tree nearby, then sighed when she saw what had made the noise. Sighing, she waited for me to open the door's palm-lock, then walked inside with me.

"Get back to my chambers, get proper clothes and weapons from my personal arsenal, and then go looking for Astrid." I managed to keep my voice low as well, but restraining my steps to keep my boots quiet on the stone floor drove me a little crazy. I wanted to storm my way through the palace with an army on my heels. But I had no army, my people had been enslaved, and my only friend now besides Misty and possibly the Mixims was stealth. So, quiet and restrained it was.

The hall looked deserted, which only unnerved me further. Where was the court? Dead? Enslaved locally? Sent off to the Dragicans to be sold? *How did all of this happen in only a few days?* "We only have one option," I said, more to myself than to Misty.

"Which is?" Her eyebrows were pulled together, and her eyes flicked nervously toward every little noise. She was scared, still functioning, but very, very frightened.

"We have to go to the throne room. She'll be there. I'm sure of it. She very likely has my parents hostage." My voice was harsh as I tried to push the other possibility out of my mind—something which always made the sacred lake go black for a while. The death of an emperor.

Did Father ever make it back from the frontier? Or was he ambushed, just as we were? My skin prickled as the possibility that he was gone flashed through my mind. And with Father gone, there would be little left to anchor Mother to reality outside the data streams anymore...

I pictured Astrid in my mind, her bright red eyes, and her steel-colored locks. That manic laugh. *I should have killed her when I had the chance.* I felt disgusted with myself for letting nostalgia, and hope for the good I had once seen in her, stay my hand. "She must die. No half measures this time. She must be stamped out."

"Wait, don't you think we should, I don't know, maybe think this through before we just storm the throne room? It's obvious that something terrible happened here, and if we just barge in there, we put ourselves at risk," Misty tried to reason with me, but I wasn't listening. I couldn't even process her words. All I could think about was getting to Astrid and making her pay for what she had done. Then, I would look for what was left of my family.

"We can't waste any time." Before Misty could protest, I grabbed her wrist and pulled her faster down the hall. We were close to my chambers now. I couldn't wait to get my hands on a weapon.

As I quickened my pace, I began to wonder where my brothers were. Surely, they would have been able to stop Astrid if not interfered with in some way. But then again...when I had vanished, they might have gone looking for me. And Astrid might have ambushed them as well. A sickening feeling grew in my stomach as I thought about my family and what might have become of them. *Gods grant that I am wrong.*

"Craze, I really don't think this is such a good idea." Misty looked apprehensive, but she continued to follow me faithfully nonetheless. I knew I was putting us in danger with my now less-than-subtle headlong rush, but I couldn't make my heart or my feet slow down. I barged around the curve of the hallway and saw the door to my chambers unguarded. We were in luck.

I got the door open—and nearly ran straight into Sephir, who was stepping toward the other side. He looked up, and his eyes widened in shock. "Craze! My beloved brother—you're alive!" And he opened his arms.

I was so relieved to see one of my brothers alive—even if he was an asshole—that I started stepping forward just as Misty gasped suddenly.

"Don't let him touch you!" she cried out.

I paused a split second, confused. And in that moment, he stepped forward and drove something fine and sharp into the artery at the side of my neck.

"How very inconvenient." He finished his sentence as all the strength left my limbs. "Still, it does mean that I get to kill you in person. How lovely."

I fell to the floor in sections, my knees hitting first, then my palms, and finally the rest of me, my whole body feeling heavy and numb. Finally, all I could do was keep my eyes open as I lay there, my cheek pressing against the cold flagstone floor.

"You bastard!" Misty yelled, but her cry cut off in a squeak of shock as her feet scuffed against the floor. I couldn't turn my head any more to see what was happening to her. "Let me go!"

"Little bitch is a handful," Astrid's voice grumbled.

"Well, use the tranquilizer. That's what it's there for." His voice dripped sarcasm, but there was a note of affection in it that made me sick to hear.

"Fine." I heard Misty yelp and then the soft thump of her collapsing. "There, much better."

"Good. Now, don't damage her. I may have a use for her later." My brother stepped into my line of vision and smirked down at me, twiddling a long, black syringe in his gloved fingers. "You always were too trusting, my brother. So much so that I thought more than once of using you as a patsy when I finally sent that waste of an emperor to his grave." A gleam came to his crimson eyes. "But then my new associate here suggested a better way."

Waste of an…? The surge of adrenaline from my outrage helped me find my voice, choked and hesitant but still full of fury. "He is your father!"

"He is not my father!" Sephir hissed, iron-colored hair storming around his head as he rounded on me. Then he lifted his head. "My father is Dragican. Mother's little secret. At least, until your father found out and had him killed." He grinned widely at my confused look. "Oh, I know, they never told you, little brother. I was the first-born. *Me.* But because my blood was not the sitting emperor's, they passed me over and gave the crown to you!" His look of fury melted into a wobbly, gloating smile. "Which is why I've seen fit to correct things."

"You… Father…"

The traitor. The one who gave Astrid and her forces the map to the asteroid field and sent them information on our defenses. The one who deactivated the city shields, while making sure that our own held so that his coward's hide wouldn't be bruised. The one who put the second sigil on Astrid. It was Sephir all along. "What did you do, Sephir? Where is the Emperor? Where…is our mother? Our brothers? What did you do?"

My horrified shout echoed down the hallway, and Sephir's mocking laughter followed it.

"Not so high and mighty now, are you, little brother?" Sephir squatted down and grabbed hold of my hair, forcing me to look at him.

Astrid came over and wrapped an arm around him, while his hand snaked around to rest familiarly on her hip. Seeing them together, the red eyes, the steel-colored hair, and the sharp features only proved the truth of what Sephir had said. There was Dragican blood in him, and he was as treacherous as all the rest of them.

I wanted to spit in his face, but my mouth went slack, and my eyelids started to weigh more and more. Nodding in satisfaction, he allowed my head to drop and looked over his shoulder at someone. "Take them down to the dungeon."

CHAPTER 30
MISTY

When I woke, my head throbbed and my vision was so blurred that all I could see were vague blobs. The last thing I remembered was Craze's brother standing there with that evil look on his face, while Astrid had yanked me backward by the hair and jammed a syringe into my neck.

I hadn't wanted to believe that one of Craze's siblings would be capable of double-crossing him. But then, when I had seen Sephir walking out of his room, I remembered how he had used his mother to try to gain a secret meeting with me. And suddenly, things had all clicked into place in my head.

If only they had done so in time to warn Craze.

As I sat up, I could feel some sort of restraints around my forearms, binding my arms together from wrists to elbows. My shoulders already ached from being forced into that position. Not to mention, having my arms bound back like that made my boobs jut out so blatantly that it embarrassed me. I had no doubt that it had been Sephir's idea.

I groaned and tried to stand up, but the same kind of device was wrapped around my knees and ankles. I could sit, I could perhaps kneel with my head far forward, and I could lie on my side. That was it.

"Craze?" I called out, looking around and blinking as my vision slowly cleared. I was in a small cell. The bars in front of me were made of the same light purple metal as the cuffs. I figured it would be impossible to escape without help. "Craze?" I called out again, crawling over to the bars and looking out.

Outside the bars stretched a long hallway lined with other cells. They seemed empty, all was silent. At that moment, I felt all alone. My heartbeat quickened as I started struggling against my bonds. I had to get out of here and figure out what had happened to Craze. There was no telling what his crazy brother and crazier ex could do to him.

"Craze!" I called out, voice cracking. I could feel my throat closing as I went into panic mode. *No.* I couldn't let myself have a panic attack. Not now. I had to keep a level head and remain calm if I stood any chance of getting out of this situation. I took in deep, controlled breaths and closed my eyes, focusing on dealing with the crazy situation that I found myself in.

Abruptly, I heard a faint but familiar groan somewhere nearby. I crawled toward the right-hand wall. "Craze?" I asked in a hushed whisper.

"Misty?" Came his voice from the next cell over. He sounded confused and disoriented.

I sighed in relief. At least he was alive. "What happened?"

"I don't know. They knocked me out as well." His voice was strained. I heard another grunt and what sounded like him sitting up and propping himself against the wall. "All I know is that I have one less brother." There was venom in his voice.

I cringed and tried to think of something to say. "I can't really blame you. I realized that he was the traitor after he went to hug you. It was a lot of little things adding up, but that he's never affectionate and he seems to hate you made him suspicious."

"I always had a hard time trusting him, but I never thought he would actually do something like this. I should have known better when he dropped out of the army. He always wanted the throne, and he never much cared about the effects of his actions on the rest of us." His tone had gone bitter, but at least his voice was gaining strength.

Before I could say anything, a massive door creaked open loudly down the hall, followed by heavy footsteps. A few moments later, Astrid walked up to our cells, the cloth-of-gold cloak that the Empress had worn draped over her armor. Her red-painted lips curved in a mocking smile. "We meet again," she purred, staring in at us, her arms crossed over her chest. "I bet you wish you had killed me back on my ship, Craze, instead of trying *reason* like an idealistic fool." Her smirk widened. "Well, it's too late now."

"You filthy scavenger. What did you do to my mother?" Craze's voice shook with rage, and I stared out at Astrid, wishing I had the power to set her on fire with anger alone.

"Oh, me? Nothing. No one had to do a thing to her once your father was out of the way. She took care of all of that for us." She let out a low laugh at his mute reaction. "Anyway, if I were you, I'd really be more worried about myself."

I watched her as she stepped out of sight, moving toward Craze's cell. I heard the clank and rattle of the cell door being opened and then a brief struggle and his muffled curses. More laughter from Astrid. "Oh, we locked a psychic damper onto your head as well, darling. Don't even think of breaking your limbs to get free. Even if you had the leverage, you wouldn't be able to heal yourself after. And you can't take the damper off with two broken arms!"

Seconds later, he groaned in pain. "What are you doing to him?" I demanded, dragging myself to the front of my cage. "Don't hurt him!"

"Too late." I heard a heavy thump and then a dragging sound. Astrid reemerged, pulling Craze's unconscious body along by the back of his sword belt. He wore the same lower-limb manacles that I did, and a band of dull gray metal had been bolted around his head. A trio of lights set into it by his temple shone red, occasionally flickering.

"Craze!" My voice broke, but as she started laughing again, I fixed her with a stare that momentarily shocked her into silence. "We're going to kill you for this. If Craze doesn't do it, I will." Of course, I had no idea how…but I would damn well find a way or die trying.

"I think you have that all backward, human." She pulled him a little closer to my cell. "Do you have any last words for your lover?"

"What do you mean?" I kept my head up and my voice angry, but deep inside, I was suddenly terrified.

"Well, this is the last time you'll ever see him. Emperor Sephir has ordered me to execute him." Her voice gloated as her eyes bored into mine, craving a reaction I couldn't help, and gleaming in satisfaction when she got it.

"Execute?" I cried out, feeling myself growing faint. No. She couldn't kill Craze. He was invincible. *This can't be happening.*

"Don't worry. I'll come back for you soon enough." With that, she dragged him away.

All I could do was crouch there at the bars and gasp for breath as I heard the heavy door close with a thud behind them.

CHAPTER 31
MISTY

I fell apart as soon as I knew Astrid was out of earshot. Tears streamed down my face as I sobbed in fear and helpless anger. *Not Craze. Not him. This can't be how things turn out after everything we have been through together.*

It seemed like my stomach would stay forever fixed in an excruciating knot of rage and grief. This was worse than mere captivity and impending death. Knowing that Astrid would likely torture Craze before murdering him only made things worse.

But slowly, slowly, the grief and helplessness started burning away as my anger grew. *If she kills him, I won't have anything left to lose. And that makes me very dangerous. I'm going to make Astrid regret ever being born.*

Strengthened by my rage, I renewed my efforts to try to get up. It was hard to gain balance with my arms pinned behind my back, but after a few minutes of struggle, I managed to get into a standing position.

I looked around my prison, searching for anything that might help me. I had no idea how to get free of the manacles, or escape the cell if I did, but I had to try.

I was still looking around when I heard a sound that made me freeze, a conversation starting up faintly down the hall, in the direction that Astrid had gone. It sounded calm and friendly, but I couldn't figure out who the two male voices belonged to or what was going on.

Suddenly, the conversation cut off in a startled yelp and a heavy thud, and I heard the door creak open. I tensed as quick footsteps approached the front of my cell. Then a tall, broad-shouldered figure in a gray cloak stepped into view on the other side of the bars. I nearly screamed, but I managed to keep silent as he pressed his finger to his lips, urging me to stay quiet.

He folded back his hood partway, and I recognized him at once, Ragar, one of Craze's younger brothers. He winked at me and produced a spike-shaped tool, which lit up when he gripped it. "I'll have you out in a minute," he rasped softly, and I felt my heart lift out of hell.

"She knocked Craze out and dragged him off," I whispered urgently as he worked on the door lock. "We have to rescue him. They mean to execute him!"

"I know," he said distractedly. "And that's why, once we get you out of there, we're going to stop them." He looked up and gave me a hard smile.

"Please tell me you've got a spare gun or something, then." *Hell yeah. Now, we're talking. I'm going to make good on that promise I made Astrid, and then we're going to make things right around here.*

He grinned—and pushed the door open. "Yeah, we can arrange something for you." Moments later, he managed to free me of my restraints. In my enthusiasm, I jumped up, but my legs were asleep and I toppled forward. Before I could face-plant into the ground, however, he caught me. "Easy," he whispered and helped me up.

Once I could walk more or less steadily, he led me down the corridor to the door at the far end. The cages were mostly empty—but recently, they had been stuffed full. Empty food bowls and random belongings had been left behind by a small crowd in every cell. I saw a child's doll among them and shook my head. *Monsters.*

In the cell nearest the exit door, I saw a guard knocked out cold, tied and gagged. He had one of the flashing lights on his neck. *It's easy for Sephir and Astrid to command loyalty when they can blow open the arteries of anyone who displeases them.*

Outside, the guard post was deserted, the hallway strangely dark. I was about to ask Ragar what was going on when a deep male voice spoke from a shadowed doorway. "Is the girl injured?"

"No," Ragar laughed. "As soon as I had her loose, she asked me for a weapon."

The unseen figure chuckled. Then the shadows seemed to draw aside like a curtain, and they contracted inward into the shape of a man. Another man crouched next to him, scarred, pale hair tousled, and twin knives at his hips. I recognized them as Craze's other brothers—angry-eyed and armed, except for the dark one, whose expression couldn't be seen.

"What are you doing here?" I asked, my voice hushed.

"Sephir was the one who convinced my father to fight in the last battle. He sabotaged the *Meleri*, Father's ship, and the *Oburos*, my own. We never got off the launchpad, thanks to my technicians discovering the sabotage. But by the time we found out, the *Meleri* had activated its sub-light drives and was out of contact." Ragar looked grim. The others nodded.

"The shield monitors were altered to provide false information that shields were at full strength, when they were actually set to ten percent power and would crumble after a few shots. They may have done something to the *Invixis* as well. That was our guess when you vanished."

"The cloaking device malfunctioned. Astrid was able to lock her weapons onto us and cripple us even while they were supposedly operating." I looked around at them, a little proud that I had figured that one out.

Lysi, the wild one, looked disgusted. "Same trick, different system." He coughed into his fist and picked up Ragar's story. "I was aboard Father's ship when Astrid's rogue ship attacked. She started taking us to pieces within a few shots, and we had to abandon ship. But before we could get Father safely away, she hit the bridge straight on with a pair of missiles. It's only luck that the two of us did not die with my father and the bridge crew."

That poor old guy. His poor sons. And his poor Empress, drowning her sorrows in the data streams until it killed her. "So, what do we do?"

"We save our brother," Lysi stated, his white hair falling into his eyes as he bared his teeth in a vicious smile.

"Good." I turned back to Ragar. "Where's my gun?"

He chuckled and shook his head. "All right, then." He reached to the small of his back and pulled out a small, silver weapon that looked like a cross between a pistol and a hair dryer. "Sonic disruptor. Turns living tissue into soup. That red button arms it. It lights up when it's ready. Don't arm until we run into hostiles, and be careful where you point it."

"Got it." I took the small but very heavy weapon and held it pointed muzzle-down as we started down the hall.

CHAPTER 32
CRAZE

The last thing I remembered as I slowly awakened was Astrid jamming a stunner into the base of my spine and giving me a jolt that had felt like a starship landing on me. I blinked and looked around one of the old interrogation rooms Father had ordered sealed when I was a boy. The stone floor was tilted toward a central drain, which was rimmed with rusty marks from old blood. I lay in a heap just a few feet away, still unable to move. When the numbness retreated some and I could finally lift my head, I saw Astrid standing over me with a grin on her face.

"Why are you doing this?" I demanded, head throbbing. I was disgusted and frustrated with my helplessness…though it was starting to go away, I realized as I managed to wiggle the tips of my fingers.

"You know full well why," she hissed as she pulled me up by my hair, standing me up in front of her.

"If you had just swallowed the bait like a good oaf and not looked too deeply into my reasons for marrying you, you could have gotten out of this with your life. But you just had to go be righteous about it all. So, now, you'll die, and I'll become empress anyway. And as for that human you've been mating with? Once we've reimplanted her with a locator tag, she'll spend the rest of her life as Sephir's toy."

My mind went blank with rage, and I lunged toward her, growling —only to have her step aside and easily kick my bound calves out from under me. I landed heavily on my side, and she came back to crouch over me.

"So you were trying to move on, huh?" Her sharp nail made its way under my chin, forcing it upward as her cold lips pressed against my neck. I could feel my skin crawl at the forced intimacy. It was hard to believe that at one point in my life this woman had made my heart race. Now, however, all she managed to do was disgust me.

"Get your hands off me," I growled. "We're well away from the point where you could turn me on."

"Well, isn't that a shame. Really, I can't believe you'd want to be faithful to some little shrimp from a backward planet that hasn't even unified its government yet!" She scoffed and let my hair go, but she stayed too close, staring down at me.

"You know nothing about her. And far less about me than you thought." I stared up at her—and then shuddered as she responded by leaning down and running her sharp-nailed hands up and down my thighs.

"I'm sure that once you're gone, your earthling won't much mind being Sephir's toy," she taunted me, her red eyes gleaming.

I shook my head, baring my teeth in anger. "Misty would never take pleasure in captivity or in being touched by such a man." Behind my back, I flexed my hands, feeling the strength starting to flow back into them. Promising. But I had a long way to go before I could defend myself against her increasingly uncomfortable attentions.

"Are you sure? She isn't a saint, you know. All women have needs. And at the end of the day, a cock is a cock." Astrid kept on petting my thighs, her voice going disconcertingly low and sweet. "In fact, she agreed to a quiet little one-on-one meeting with Sephir, not even a day after you brought her here."

I blinked at her, stunned by the whole idea—but then shook my head. "Even if that is true, I trust her far more than I have ever trusted you." Even back when I was young and stupid and had mistaken intense lust and mind games for true love. At one time, I would have killed for Astrid. But I would die for Misty.

"Nonsense. You're nowhere near over me. If you were, I wouldn't have been able to tap your powers for years after you chased me off-planet. You never stopped thinking about me, and you know it." She ran her hands over my hips and belly, her fingertips getting closer and closer to the clasp of my pants.

"Don't you dare," I hissed, glaring at her. As recently as a few days ago, her touch would have brought on a painful and embarrassing erection. But now, I could have been dead below the waist. All her caresses did was stoke my nausea. On the other hand, the extra adrenaline was quickly bringing life back to my limbs.

"Or else what?" she challenged. "You couldn't kill me on my ship. You mean to tell me you could do so now? Face it, you still have feelings for me. Just admit it, and I'll give you one last good fuck before I behead you at the foot of your father's throne."

I spat on the floor. "The only thing I want to shove into your body is a blade."

For a split second, I thought I saw her look almost…hurt. But then she laughed and tossed her head. "One last fight, instead of one last fuck? Tempting. But I'm not sure you're up to it right now."

"Try me," I challenged. I pushed myself up as she stepped back in surprise, allowing my large frame to tower over her, dominating the space around me. I rolled my broad shoulders and raised my head, hoping it would intimidate her. Under it all, my legs were still feeling wobbly, so I had to lock my knees to steady them. "That meteor storm interrupted our last fight. Let's finish this."

"So if I unbind you, and we fight and I win, I get to fuck you a last time. But what happens if you win? Not that it's going to happen." She lifted an eyebrow, her eyes reflecting a manic light within them.

"If I win, I kill you," I promised, eager to fight, to make her pay for the crimes she had committed.

"Hmm." She grinned, her lips twisting cruelly. "A battle to the death, then. Because, believe me, no matter who wins, you're not getting out of here alive."

I didn't hesitate. "So be it." If I had to, I would die in battle before I let her use my body and betray Misty.

I thought back to the time when Astrid and I had been courting.

She had asked me for help learning to fight. I had agreed playfully, foolishly assuming that she had known nothing. She had bested me many times since then. I didn't know if it was natural talent, or if, like me, she had trained from a young age and had simply been toying with me.

This time, though, the woman who had my heart was in my mind. I had to save her, my world, my people, and whatever was left of my family. Astrid was not going to get in my way.

"Excellent." She stepped forward, undoing my manacles and pulling them loose. Her eyes swept over me teasingly before she stepped back. "There you are, then."

I rubbed my wrists and widened my stance, staring at her. "Weapons?"

Astrid laughed as she drew out a pair of curved swords from back sheaths. She tossed one of them to me and grinned. "I hope you're ready." With that statement, she lunged at me, her eyes suddenly wild.

I just managed to roll out of the way. The circulation was still coming back into my limbs. I kept my grip on the sword, but just barely. Painfully tingling and even more painfully slowly, I threw myself aside again as the sword descended.

"Oh, come now, Craze, is this your best?" She pressed the attack, backing me toward the far wall of the small chamber. "I'll be riding you to slaughter in minutes at this rate."

Furious, disgusted, I lashed out, taking her by surprise. I backed her off with a flurry of sword blows and kicks, blocking her return blows or ducking aside from them. "Not a chance!" I shouted, swinging the curved blade with all my strength.

The blow knocked her blade aside and streaked toward her head. She barely ducked aside in time, and I heard her let out a small cry of surprise. She skittered back, almost stumbling, and her free hand went to her cheek. A thin line of blood trickled down her porcelain skin from the long cut I had made. "Why, you stupid oaf! My face!"

She leaped into battle with me again, and we started trading blows in earnest, fighting back and forth through the room. The clangs and grunts of effort and her occasional startled curse were loud enough that I feared they would bring the guards—but I couldn't think about that now. All I could focus on was besting her.

I was starting to back her into a corner when the door burst open, and four figures came running in. I looked up quickly—and smiled with relief when I saw my three loyal brothers and my beloved Misty, all unharmed, all of them with drawn weapons that they quickly pointed at Astrid.

She pouted at yet another interruption, petulant as a child. "This is so disappointing," she grumbled. Before any of us could reach her, she touched a control box on her belt and vanished again. I cursed under my breath, reprimanding myself for letting her escape for the third time. I couldn't keep letting her win.

But now, I had something much better to think about. Shoving the sword into my belt, I turned to look at Misty and my brothers, smiling in relief. "There you are! I thought I had lost the lot of you. What's happened in my absence?"

"It's a long story," Misty said as she crossed the room quickly to throw herself into my arms. The moment her tears of relief touched my chest, I felt my heart finally lift with hope.

"Tell me everything," I replied, looking around at my brothers as I held her.

CHAPTER 33
MISTY

A huge wave of relief washed over me when I wrapped my arms around Craze. While everything had seemed so hopeless, I had not allowed myself to feel just how frightened I had been. But now, clinging to him, I shivered uncontrollably.

I could smell his musk and see the thin layer of sweat on his body. "What happened? I thought you were dead. I was so scared," I murmured into his neck. I was so happy he was okay.

"Astrid was planning to execute me in front of whatever is left of the court, but I easily tricked her into one last fight. I'm fine," he assured me, running his long, nimble fingers through my hair. I relaxed some in his arms, but I still felt jumpy. With Sephir and Astrid on the loose, we weren't safe.

Ragar stepped forward, approaching his older brother. "I'm sorry to interrupt your little lovefest, but we still have two murdering wannabe tyrants to take care of."

Craze nodded grimly, but he didn't let me go. "How did they get control?"

"Force of numbers. They came in with a ton of Thezlums, some Dragicans and Mersines, and a bunch of mercenaries. Rounded everyone up in waves, threw them in the dungeons for processing.

They've put those explosive trackers on everyone in the city, including all of our guards. They'll have to fight against us if we go in too conspicuously, or Sephir will kill them at the touch of a button. I saw him do it." Ragar rubbed his face, grief and anger in his eyes.

"He's right. We have to take down Sephir before he completely destroys our planet's ecosystem. The sacred lake has nearly dried up," Nemesch pointed out. "The rest of the land will quickly follow suit if a usurper takes the throne."

"What do you suggest we do?" Craze asked Lysi, who wore a serious expression for once.

He looked up, the scars on his cheeks gleaming. "We go after Sephir. There's no other way." Lysi's words were emotionless. I wondered how many of these men grieved the loss of their brother, and how many simply wanted to kill him for the betrayal. Craze seemed to feel both ways.

Craze nodded. "So be it." He didn't even seem to hesitate. "I always knew he was the least trustworthy of us, but I never thought he would be capable of such treachery." Craze looked disgusted as he folded his arms over his chest. I moved to his side, my arm wrapping around his waist. I felt his tense body relax slightly as he settled an arm across my shoulders.

I felt a little guilty as I thought back to the secret meeting Sephir had tried to arrange between the two of us. "I tried to ignore how much of an asshole he seemed to be because he's your brother. But…" I hesitated. The brothers all glanced at me, and I felt my cheeks heat up. "He did a few things that should have made me more suspicious than they did. He even wanted me to meet him alone, though at the time I didn't realize just how creepy that was."

"I'll beat him a few times before I kill him just for that," Craze growled, but there was a strange note of relief in his voice.

"Anyway, hindsight is always keener." I didn't like seeing him beat himself up over something that would have been hard to avoid in any case. "Let's go before those two cause any more harm," I offered, letting go of Craze and giving him the most confident smile I could muster.

He gave me a slight smile and then leaned down, kissing the top of my head. "Stay close," he warned, before straightening himself out and eyeing his younger brothers. "I have no doubt we'll be able to take down Sephir. He was never very strong, but with Astrid by his side, they're a force to be reckoned with. She is an unprecedented warrior and will stop at nothing to get what she wants. More importantly, she isn't afraid to fight dirty. Remember that if you find yourself face-to-face with her." Craze's voice was level. "Worse, we have our own army forced to fight against us."

"I don't want to kill any of our boys," Ragar protested.

"I won't," Lysi said flatly.

"We may have to," Nemesch pointed out with a voice full of regret.

"Wait," I spoke up. "These discs have a stun function. Craze, you can control machines sometimes, right? Why not tell the discs to knock the guards out?"

Craze exchanged surprised glances with his brothers, then turned to me. "It would be risky. If I make a mistake, they could die. But since I don't have an army of those nanites handy, perhaps I should try it."

Ragar looked confused. "Nanites?"

"It's a long story, my brother." Craze gave him a tight smile. "I'll need a weapon that is better than this package-opener I took from Astrid."

"Where's yours?" Ragar asked, noticing Craze's empty scabbard. He shrugged after a moment and unlimbered the single blade he wore tucked on his back amid a trio of rifles.

"With a good friend," Craze responded, accepting it before turning and leading us down the hall.

CHAPTER 34
CRAZE

We managed to make it to the armory, which was guarded by four of our men. I decided to try the trick Misty had suggested, reaching out to the tiny computers embedded in the discs. I sent a mental command —and after a short delay, all four convulsed suddenly and collapsed. I walked over and checked the nearest one's pulse. Alive, just unconscious. *Perfect.*

We entered, and I immediately started searching the racks lining the walls, looking for a good replacement for Exredilan. I frowned, growing increasingly frustrated as I made my way down the wall. How was I supposed to go against one of the most dangerous criminals in the galaxy with subpar weaponry?

Finally, I settled for a red-hilted sword, lined with the same energy crystals that were used in psi-amplifiers. Using such blades seemed like a crutch to me as I had always relied on my own power. But if I was supposed to knock out an army of our men without harming them, I could use the edge.

I grabbed the sword, feeling my hand tingle as the stones' faint glow brightened in contact with my aura. "Are we ready?" I asked, looking around at my brothers and Misty.

"Yes," Lysi answered for all of them as he stepped forward, tucking another throwing knife into the bandolier across his bare, scarred chest. I nodded and then guided us out of the armory.

We moved down the hall toward the lift tube. Now and again we would run into guards, and I would make them fall asleep with my powers. Each time, I blessed Misty in my mind, because each guard that fell asleep was one fewer that I had to kill.

None of them got a chance to radio in before I took them out. It seemed almost too easy. Maybe it was all some kind of trap. "Think Sephir's lying in wait for us?"

"Astrid will have run right to him," Ragar replied in a low voice. "Chances are that between here and the throne room, we'll run into something big."

I reconsidered barging into the throne room for a moment, but I didn't see any other option. We had to act quickly or the planet would perish. Once the coronation was done and the throne and crown taken by a usurper, it would be the beginning of the end for Vixxia Prime. And Sephir, who believed in nothing of the old legends, wouldn't have accepted that truth even if I had shoved his head into the lake's black sludge. *Anything for power. I can't believe he even let our mother waste away and die.*

As we finally reached the hallway leading to the throne room, we instantly saw trouble ahead. There were no guards in the area, but the passage was blocked by a deep red force field. I cursed under my breath. "This is Astrid's doing." No doubt she had fortified the throne room in anticipation of our arrival. "She probably has every entrance and window covered with these."

"What is that?" Ragar whispered.

"It looks like a regular force field, but knowing Astrid, there has to be something more to it." I reached out to the energy field, trying to shunt it aside, and let out a grunt as pain stabbed through my temple. "Seems to be hardened against psionics."

As we spoke, Nemesch stepped forward. "Allow me to try something." Slowly, he reached into his pocket and pulled out three small white balls. He rolled them between his fingers thoughtfully for a moment. Then he threw one of them at the barrier. On contact, it fizzled and disappeared. He threw another. The same thing happened.

The final one actually exploded with a small *pop*. He stayed there a moment, observing the force field before stepping back. "We can't get through."

"What do you mean, we can't get through?" I demanded grumpily. There had to be a way. I wasn't about to turn back now. I knew Sephir was on the other side of this wall. I would be damned if I allowed him to continue his reign of terror.

"The barrier protects against Vixxians, psychic energy, and any weapon or ammunition with the Imperial brand. The first sphere contained Vixxian blood. The second, a charged power crystal. Lastly, a speck of Imperial gold." As he finished his statement, he stared at Misty thoughtfully. "Actually, let me be more specific. *We* can't get through."

I stared back at him. "What do you suggest we do, then?"

"We could try to lure them out," Lysi suggested. "Sephir's ego is so huge that he can't tolerate any taunting or insults."

"I don't think that'll work either," Nemesch stated. "Astrid is obviously the one running the show here. She has woven her web around Sephir and is using him as a puppet emperor. So she wouldn't let him just come out and get himself killed."

Misty sighed and spoke up. "Let me go through it. If there's a device to deactivate it on the other side, I'll need instructions. But if this thing is calibrated to hurt members of specific races, well... humans are rare. It probably won't affect me."

I looked between her and the force field. I could see the projector right next to the closed double doors leading to the throne room. If she could make it that twenty feet and turn the field off, we could go in and deal with Sephir and Astrid. But she would be doing it alone, and we couldn't even cover her with projectile weapons. "I'm really not sure about this." I would have to force myself to let her do it, and I was not certain I could manage it.

"She's our best hope," Nemesch murmured, and after a few moment's reluctance, I nodded. I had faith in her, but limited-entry force fields disintegrated anything banned from entering. I just hoped I was making the right decision.

CHAPTER 35
MISTY

I approached the force field with my stomach twisting with apprehension. Craze gave voice to my fears in a much steadier tone than I would have managed. "Can we make certain that she can pass through safely?"

Nemesch shrugged. "Of course. A strand of your hair should work." Before I could protest, he snipped a short lock of my hair off with a sharp blade I could barely see and made his way over to the force field again. He tossed the small handful of strands at the red wall of energy, and it simply fell through. "As I thought," the walking shadow mused. "It won't have any effect on you. Which could mean one of two things. Either Astrid forgot about you or couldn't calibrate this thing for an unknown race, or she is purposely trying to lure you inside."

I nodded, realizing what this could mean.

"It could well be a trap." Craze scowled and shook his head. "We should find another way."

I shook my head, holding my ground. "I have to do this. It's the only shot we have, and I want to help your planet. It's *my* planet now too." I squared my shoulders and held Craze's gaze. "Give me a stun weapon I can carry through. I'll go through, deactivate the field and run back. I'll be as careful as I can. But if any soldiers of yours come out, I don't want to have to kill them."

"Fine," he grumbled. The frown on his face made it clear he wasn't happy with this plan, but it wasn't like we had any other choice. "But if anything happens, I'm coming after you, barrier or not."

I simply nodded. The look of determination on his face told me I wouldn't be able to convince him otherwise. I kissed him hard, trying to assure him that everything would be okay. With my hands on his cheeks, I gently rubbed my thumb against his skin, trying to soothe him. But his whole body was tense, and I knew he would remain that way until this was all over. I couldn't blame him.

"Listen carefully." Lysi broke our moment as he placed a hand on my shoulder. "I'm giving you this handheld stunner. It's effective through armor, but you have to be within three feet. I'm hoping you don't have to use it, but better to have it and not need it than need it and not have it."

I nodded, accepting the weapon, which looked like a cross between a medieval dagger and a big carving fork. It had a thick hilt with a textured grip and a set of flickering LED lights on its crosspiece. The two-pronged business end was pale and constantly blurred, making me wary of it at once.

"That might work, but it could just as easily get her killed," Nemesch pointed out, his voice monotone as ever. I shivered at the mention of my own death.

Craze turned to me, swallowing. He placed his hands on my shoulders and leaned down, his face getting closer to mine.

My heartbeat quickened even more as our lips came together in a passionate kiss. It felt like we were saying good-bye. I didn't want to think about leaving Craze, but at that moment, I didn't know if I would ever see him again. I wrapped my arms around him tightly, getting as close to him as I could without risking touching him with that nasty knife. I bit my lip, knowing that I couldn't cry. Not now. I pulled away, bracing myself for what I was about to do. "I'm ready."

CHAPTER 36
CRAZE

I watched Misty move forward with Lysi's stunner in her hand. I had seen that force field disintegrate matter, and the fact that Misty could pass through it without a hitch just made me worry. It had to be a trap. And yet, what other choice did we have but to hope Astrid had somehow overlooked my human lover?

Misty looked back at me once as she stepped in front of the force field. We locked eyes, then I held my breath as she turned her gaze back to the door and took the final step forward. The red wave of energy washed over her body, but nothing happened. I let out a sigh of relief.

Misty hurried over to the control panel. She reached for it eagerly, and I tensed, ready to join my brother in a charge to close the gap. She had almost reached it when the double doors banged open, and Sephir lunged for her.

"Look out!" I shouted, and she whirled around, bringing the stunner up. He backed off immediately, Father's Imperial robes flapping around his legs ridiculously. In his hand was a control box for the slave tags, and he stabbed its button, then gaped in astonishment as he stared at her.

"You should be in agony!" Sephir's voice cracked. "What's wrong with this thing?"

"Surprise," Misty snapped. She feinted a throat strike with the stunner, then jammed her knee up into his crotch-piece as hard as she could when he ducked the strike.

He wheezed with agony and fell to his knees, armor clanking against the floor. She bolted for the control box, determined—only to barely duck in time as a blue energy beam seared the wall beside her.

"Don't move," Sephir hissed, pointing a small beam pistol at her as he gasped for air and clutched his crotch. "You're my hostage now. And believe me, you'll pay for your insolence later."

I ran up to the barrier, shaking off Ragar's attempt to restrain me. "Let her go, traitor!"

"And give up my newest toy? I don't think so." Sephir stood up and stalked over to her slowly, gloating. "Unless you want to come here and do something about it." He looked over at me and made a come-hither motion with his fingers, challenging me to defy the barrier.

My eyes met Misty's, and then I focused all my power on amplifying my healing. I gritted my teeth and bolted through the force field before I could talk myself out of it. Searing pain engulfed my body, and for a few moments, I was left breathless. My vision blurred, and I could feel the strength leaving my muscles, but through the sheer power of will, I managed to stay upright. Momentum carried me through the rest of the way, and I was able to fight through the pain just long enough to tackle Sephir.

I pinned him to the ground, my rage strengthening me as I slammed his head into the stone floor. He gasped with pain, but his needlelike nails dug into the skin of my wrists, forcing me to draw back or risk severed tendons. He scuttled away from me, gaining his feet. His lips were still frozen in a smirk, but the mask had slipped, and I saw the fear in his eyes.

"Did you really think that we would let you get away with murdering our parents and stealing the throne?" I stalked after him, closing the gashes in my wrists as I did. I was vaguely aware of Misty edging toward the control box.

He couldn't cover both of us with one pistol and he knew it, so instead, he trained it on her. "One more step, and I blow a hole in her."

Misty froze. I paused and then tilted my head slowly, staring at him, letting every bit of my rage burn in my eyes. "And then what?" I demanded.

He stared at me. "And then she dies, and you're alone again."

My mouth worked. I couldn't let him see how much his threat horrified me, so I forced myself to relax and look casual. I even smirked. "Let's turn this around. If you so much as fart in her direction, I will spend days in killing you, instead of a few seconds."

His eyes widened. The pistol wavered away from Misty, swinging around to point at me. "Then I had better not w-waste any more time with you."

Misty yet out a yell and drove the stunner into his shoulder before he could finish aiming. Blue-white light arced. He gasped, and the shot went wide by a few feet, vanishing harmlessly into the force field before he could stumble out of her range. A second later, a throwing knife shattered his bracer and went deep into his forearm. I looked up, Lysi grinning madly as he reached for another blade.

Even with my body still repairing the damage from going through that force field, I managed to summon the strength to charge Sephir. His breastplate cracked as I slammed my shoulder into him, driving him back. The pistol spun from his grip as his wounded arm went slack. Roaring, I picked him up and threw him against the wall, more plates of his ceramic armor shattering on impact.

Sephir had never been much of a fighter, and I could see the fear in his eyes as he pulled himself painfully to his feet. Before I could do anything further, he turned and dashed through the doors into the throne room.

Misty ran over to the force field generator and lifted the shield on the power switch, then flipped it. The red field shimmered once then vanished. I sighed with relief as my brothers ran to join us.

"Are you all right?" Misty whispered. I nodded. We clasped hands briefly.

"Let's go. There are no other exits from the throne room. He's trapped." My voice was flat. Killing even a half brother was a grim business, but this one deserved it—the world and justice both needed his death.

I drew my sword, and I led the way as we went in through the doors. What lay beyond was a scene so mad that even I hesitated as soon as I saw it. Beside me, Misty gasped in horror.

The room was crowded with uniformed soldiers, each one with a flashing red light on his neck and an expression of reluctance, horror, and helpless anger. They all trained their rifles on us at once, while on the dais behind them, Sephir clambered up my father's empty throne and lounged in it, laughing at me.

But it was the occupant of the other throne that made me stare in shock, for it wasn't Astrid. My mother still sat there, head engulfed by the data-stream helmet, her cloth-of-gold robe hanging off her gaunt, gray body. Truly stiff as a doll now, she sat bolt upright, blue-white sparks of psychic energy dancing occasionally around her head. She looked like a corpse that had been left in the desert a week, dried up and leathery-skinned, but now and again, her body still twitched.

"What is this?" I breathed. My brothers skidded to a stop beside and behind me, shouting in horror. "What have you done, Sephir?"

"I told you, she did it to herself." He tilted his head indolently toward our mother. "She has been trying to upload her consciousness into the data streams nonstop for three days now. She told me that only her husband was keeping her here. She even thanked me for giving her the opportunity to escape." He laughed lightly. "Of course, her consciousness will fragment anyway when her body dies, but who knows? Perhaps she'll actually succeed for a while."

I shifted my stare from her to him, my blood boiling. "I'm going to kill you."

He snorted. "Problem with that, little brother. You see, to get to me, you'll have to kill your way through all of your soldiers, including your own starship crew. Who I'm currently forcing to do my bidding thanks to the use of those lovely Thezlum tracker tags." He pulled the control box from his pocket and waved it at me mockingly. "Any last words to them before I order your execution?"

"Yes, just one last order," I said, and I looked around at the pale, miserable-looking men in front of me. I focused my powers as best I could around the remnants of my pain and said, "Sleep."

All of the neck tags flashed at once in rapid succession, and the soldiers went limp, dropping their rifles and collapsing to the floor in a chorus of sighs. They almost sounded relieved.

Sephir stared around at them in horror and then looked up at me. I walked toward him, sword drawn, half blind with rage as I strode past the fallen soldiers.

"Now, what was this about an execution?" I growled as I stepped up onto the dais.

His eyes bugged out slightly. "I...I..."

"You turned our mother into a puppet. You weren't satisfied with just killing her. You let her go crazy and slowly start killing herself— after you and your whore murdered her husband!" I started climbing the throne stairs as Sephir suddenly realized that he had trapped himself. In desperation, he leaped down—only to find himself surrounded by my brothers and a very angry Misty.

"Tell us where Astrid got to," I warned him as he cringed. I walked back down the steps toward him, sword trembling just slightly in my grip. "Do so, and things will go easier on you."

"I-I-I... She said that she would be right back..." he stammered. Then horror slowly dawned on his face. Just in that moment, far off at the royal airfield, a single rocket engine roared to life.

I laughed at him. "Looks like she's abandoning you just like she abandoned me. Did you really think you were special to her?"

He stared at me, face contorting in a succession of emotions: shock, horror, betrayal, cowardly fear...and finally, irrational rage. Shouting incoherently, he drew his pistol again and pointed it at Misty.

I struck twice before he could wiggle his finger.

Sephir blinked in surprise when his hand fell off, the pistol clattering to the floor harmlessly with it. He took one step...and then pitched forward, falling to his knees. His head tumbled off at the neat incision I had made, and his body fell forward as his head rolled away.

There was a rustling noise nearby as Misty got up and ran over. Avoiding the corpse, she threw herself at me and wrapped her arms around my waist as tightly as she could. As she laid her head on my chest, I relaxed a little and dropped the bloodied blade atop my half brother's body.

I started stroking her hair as I focused my powers on healing myself. Regret and relief mixed in me. I had been protecting her. I had been protecting my people, my whole planet. As I wrapped my arms around her and looked down into her warm brown eyes, I knew I had done the right thing. I had lost a brother but regained an empire.

CHAPTER 37
MISTY

Craze and I held each other as he recovered from the fight with Sephir. I refused to look down at the corpse by my feet as I buried my head into my lover's chest. I could hear his heartbeat, which was slowing as he caught his breath.

"Craze?" I looked up at him worriedly.

It took him a minute, but he eventually looked down at me. "Yes?"

"Are you okay?" I whispered, clinging on to him a little tighter. He felt wobbly on his feet, and I heard his breath rattle a little in his lungs. I didn't know what exactly going through that force field had done to him, but apparently, he was a lot less recovered from it than he had let on.

"I will be," he rasped in response, then turned somewhat painfully to address his brothers.

"Astrid is still on the loose," Craze announced. "She's stolen one of our ships, and with Mother in such a state, we can't shut it down remotely using the data streams."

"We'll go after her," Ragar declared, looking determined. "You are still healing, and someone must restore order here. The slaver tags must be dealt with to make certain Astrid can't murder our people from afar. The people must have a leader ready to keep them calm and give them hope. And…" His gaze crept toward the old empress, her body now completely atrophied like some kind of cyborg mummy.

Craze looked ready to argue, but I laid a hand on his arm and shook my head slightly when he glanced down at me. He might be too proud to admit the degree of his injuries to his brothers, but I wasn't going to let him face off with Astrid until he was well enough to fight her.

He nodded then and looked at his brothers. "Go. Take my ship." He eyed Ragar. "Bring her back in one piece, or I'll kick your ass."

He laughed, and so did Lysi. Nemesch was still staring moodily at the bodies on the dais, Sephir's, in pieces, and his mother's, still technically alive. If you could call it that. I felt a stab of sympathy for him, but I found I could look at neither body without shuddering.

Once the brothers had left, Craze took me in his arms again. "Are you okay?" he whispered, resting his hand on my cheek, caressing it gently.

I nodded and smiled slightly at his affectionate touch. I nuzzled into his hand and looked into those beautiful blue eyes of his. Gingerly, I rose on my tippy-toes and kissed his soft lips, letting my own linger on his. Even after all the drama and chaos we had experienced together, it still felt deliciously right to kiss the alien prince. "I'll be fine. But what about you?"

His smile looked a little wobbly, and I saw sweat beading on his pale forehead. "I ran through that barrier, and now I'm feeling the aftereffects. It's like all the energy has been drained from my body," he explained, his breathing labored.

My eyes grew big at his response. "You need to rest, then," I whispered, horrified at the prospect of my invincible prince collapsing again.

"I will, but I have to take care of a few matters first." Going over to his brother's corpse, he retrieved the control box and examined it. Laying his hand over it, he closed his eyes. Blue sparks danced around the box, and suddenly, every red light in the room winked out. "That should deactivate them."

The soldiers started stirring, a few of them groaning and pushing up to their knees, looking around in confusion. Then they saw Sephir's body and Craze standing there, and a ragged cheer went up.

Craze gave them a triumphant smile as he stood with his arm around me. "The tyrant has been overthrown, but Astrid is still at large. I want my starship crew and the Second Division to the spaceport immediately. Everyone else, I want word spread that they are free, any prisoners released, and any torture victims or wounded brought to the infirmaries. Is that clear?"

Shouts of affirmation answered, and a few of them cried out, "Hail the new Emperor of Vixxia!"

He smiled and waved at them, but I saw how quickly the color was draining from his cheeks. I walked very close to him as he stepped down off the dais and walked out. "Someone take care of that rubbish!" he called, regarding the corpse of his brother. It horrified me for a moment, but then I understood. Sephir had murdered, had enslaved, had betrayed everyone and nearly destroyed the planet out of sheer ego. He deserved nothing better.

"What about your mother?" I asked him very gently as we walked out.

He paused and looked back slowly at the stiff figure on the throne. "Once I have rested, I will try to free her. If I do it now, I risk being trapped in the data streams myself." He turned back around and started walking again, and I swallowed, understanding this grim truth as well. From his tone, he did not believe that his mother could be saved. But he would try anyway.

The moment he was out the door and we were out of sight of his men, he stumbled and would've fallen forward if it wasn't for me catching him. "Whoa, hey. Careful there, babe." Even though he was quite heavy, I managed to support him with his arm around my shoulders. Slowly, I navigated my way through the palace, trying to find the way back to his old room while he limped along semiconscious beside me. Finally, we arrived at the right door.

I opened it, and we all but fell inside. I managed to get Craze over to the bed just as he closed his eyes and seemed to give up in his battle with fatigue. His knees buckled, and I caught him again and lowered him to the mattress. Gently, I pulled off his boots and pulled his legs up onto the bed, then gripped his hand.

It seemed limp and lifeless, and for a moment, I feared he was dead. My heart stopped beating. I quickly leaned down and laid my head against his chest, listening for his heartbeat. To my great relief, I felt the soft brush of his breath stirring the hairs on the top of my head. He was still alive.

CHAPTER 38
CRAZE

I awoke with only a fading headache to remind me of the agony of going through that force field. I knew I should be counting myself lucky, but as healing hangovers went, this one was gigantic. I sat up and looked around my bedroom. I couldn't remember how I had gotten there, but from the lovely fresh-scrubbed scent by my side, I could guess who had helped. Rubbing my temples, I looked down to see Misty fast asleep next to me. I smiled and leaned down, kissing her head ever so softly so as to not wake her. "Thank you, my darling."

I spent a moment staring at her and running my fingers across the ebony skin of her back, remembering all she had done for this planet, and for me. She had nearly given up her life in order to save Vixxia Prime. A sense of pride washed over me. *She'll make a perfect empress.*

Eventually, I got up and looked out one of the bubble-windows that overlooked the courtyard. To my great relief, color was starting to return to the grove surrounding the lake. The purple leaves had stopped falling, and I saw a frosting of lighter, brighter purple within the foliage, where new leaves were forming to replace those lost.

After writing Misty a quick note promising to return, I showered and dressed, then left the room and slowly walked down the empty halls. The courtyard windows revealed that the lawn and plaza were crowded with people, some celebrating, and some crying with relief. I smiled with pride to see them again. *Free. My people are free again.*

Grinning, I went out to meet them, accepting their cheers graciously and reassuring them where I could. Soon enough, my brothers would return—hopefully, with Astrid's head.

Once the crowd settled down a little, I made my way to the grove and walked through it toward Silviana's Center. Hesitantly, I walked out of the trees to the lakeshore, wondering what I would see once I looked into the water.

I closed my eyes and moved forward until water lapped against the toes of my boots. Taking a steadying breath, I opened my eyes and looked down. I sighed in relief, seeing the silver water filling the lake up to its natural brim. Silviana was once again pleased with us. The disaster had been averted. *And not a moment too soon.*

Now I would have to undo all the damage caused by my brother's actions. It would be hard work, but I knew I could handle it, especially with Misty by my side.

I braced myself after that, for the next leg of my journey would be the hardest. Getting up, I took a deep breath and turned to go to the throne room.

Mother was still there, sitting stiffly in her seat, her eyes closed, her face sunken against her skull. I felt my emotions storming around inside of me as I climbed the stairs to get a closer look at her. She did not seem to be moving anymore, though every once in a while, a bluish spark of her power would circle her head.

"Mother," I said softly, drawing close. I smelled no decay, but I couldn't hear her breathing either. "Why didn't you tell me? Is this why you grieved so much? Why you didn't want to deal with people? Why you lost yourself in the data streams? Did you fall in love with someone else, but Father would not let you go?"

Sephir had always been her favorite, the son of her unknown lover. And I had killed him in front of her. Yet, without his poisonous influence, I might have saved her, even once Father was dead. "I'm sorry, Mother," I said quietly.

"I am pledged with Misty now. She will bear your grandchildren. I had hoped…you would be around to see them." My stomach clenched.

I had been totally unaware that there had ever been strife between my parents. But then again, nobody decided to hook themselves up to the data streams for most or all of their time unless they were trying to escape from something. "But you didn't want to be here, did you?"

The data screens all jumped at once, flickering violently, while static burst briefly from the speakers. I blinked and looked around at them then back at her. "Mother?"

I heard a sound like a sigh, and I reached for her bony hand. But no sooner did I touch it than it crumbled, and her whole body followed. Her braids slithered free of the spherical helmet and dropped to the floor. Her shape fell away into gray dust, and her robe fell emptily to the ground. Her body was gone, but I suspected her consciousness was now connected to the data streams. She was nowhere and, most likely, everywhere.

Some of the dust must have gotten in my eyes. I wiped wetness off my cheeks impatiently as I walked out.

AFTER A FEW MORE STOPS, I MADE MY WAY BACK TO THE BEDROOM. MISTY was still fast asleep when I arrived. There was a gentle smile on her face as she rolled over and hugged my pillow. Just the sight of her lifted some of the weight that had sat on my heart since I had said good-bye to my mother.

I sat down on the edge of the bed and gently caressed Misty's cheek before leaning down and kissing her forehead. She started to stir and wake up at my touch, her eyes fluttering until they finally opened. "Hi," she mumbled sleepily, that muzzy smile curving her lips.

When we locked eyes, I leaned down and kissed her lips, harder than I had ever kissed her before. My lips pressed into hers until I thought they would meld together. She stiffened slightly, but she seemed to sense the yearning behind the kiss. One of her hands slid up through my hair, and she kissed back, softly at first, but soon just as fiercely as I.

My hands slid under her short, fuzzy sleeping-gown, caressing her hungrily and then lifting it off over her head. I hastily stripped out of my trousers and tunic, kicking off my boots and crawling onto the bed in my loincloth. Then I went right back to kissing her. Soon enough, I was on top of her, my body entwined with hers as the kiss intensified.

My heartbeat quickened, and my grasp on her tightened as her tongue slipped into my mouth. I quickly adapted, my own tongue toying with hers until we were both breathless and she pulled away, a sparkling sheen in her eyes. "Thank you," I said to her softly.

"What for?" Misty asked, a grin on her face as she slid her hands up my chest.

"For your willingness to sacrifice everything in order to save my planet," I whispered, softly kissing her neck. My tongue gently trailed over her skin, teasing her.

"Anyone would have done it," Misty responded, as modest as ever. "You can keep doing that."

"That's not true," I pressed. "Most people are far more self-interested. Including me, sometimes."

"Well, whatever. I just did what I thought was right." She shrugged. "Besides, a lot of it I did for you, and that made it an easy decision."

I chuckled and hugged her tightly. "I love you." The words escaped my lips before I could stop myself. She blinked in shock, and I glanced away briefly, the tips of my ears prickling. "You're what I've always wanted in a woman. You're brave. Affectionate. Strong. Faithful. And you care about people. I'll be proud to call you my Empress."

Before I could continue, she wrapped her arms around my neck and pulled me toward her, our lips joining once again. She kissed me hard, and I smiled into the kiss, pulling her a little closer. I knew I would never want another woman in my life.

"I love you too," Misty whispered when she finally pulled away. Our eyes locked, and my grief and my losses melted away. The only thing that existed in my world now was her.

CHAPTER 39
MISTY

I couldn't believe we were finally safe again. Safe, triumphant, and in love. I shivered, already turned on, and my fingers slid over his back. He pressed his lips against my collarbone then lower, running his mouth over the sigil. He traced his tongue over it, kissing it softly as his sharp teeth nipped at my skin hard enough to put an edge on my pleasure.

I arched my back and presented myself to him as his roaming hands and lips stoked a fire inside me. In response, he grabbed my thighs, his fingers digging into my flesh. I moaned out as he wrapped my legs around his waist, pulling me hard against his body. I knew where this was going, and I couldn't hold back my surging excitement.

"Craze," I whispered, bending forward to press my lips to his neck, kissing his skin. I sucked hard, marking him, as he panted and groaned. I smiled and leaned back to look at him, wondering what he would do.

He seized me and leaned forward, locking his lips around one of my nipples, sucking on it as his expert tongue flicked over the hardening nub. My mind reeled and I shivered in anticipation, knowing that each time I was with Craze, it brought forth something new and exciting.

But as I felt him turn slow and steady, I got impatient. I couldn't hold myself back. "Craze," I said, pushing aside shyness. "Roll over, huh? Let me drive for a while."

His eyebrows went up. "Drive…? All right, never mind, just demonstrate, and I'll figure it out." He rolled over obediently and smiled up at me as I climbed over him.

Eagerly, I pressed my hands to his wrists, mock-pinning him to the bed. He raised an eyebrow in my direction but did nothing to defy my newfound dominance.

I placed his hands above his head, and then let go of his wrists. "Stay there. Don't move, or I'll punish you by stopping." I winked at him, and he grinned in response, nodding his head. From the enormous erection now poking against my thigh through his loincloth, he was enthusiastically on board with this.

I untied his loincloth and unwrapped it from his hips, tossing it aside and freeing his swollen cock. I licked my lips and leaned down, my hot breath caressing his length. I hovered over it for a moment, teasing him, then started stroking. My fingertips danced over his flesh, making him shiver in delight. I could sense his excitement as he waited for me to make the next move.

I slowly got up, balancing on the bed and swinging my hips a little, giving him a bit of a show. He drank in the sight, his eyes burning like blue embers. I knew he was dying to pull me down and ravish me. But at the same time, the curious glint in his eyes told me he was eager to find out what was going to happen if he followed orders.

I ran my hands down my body, my fingertips sliding slowly toward my already aching pussy. I allowed my fingers to glide over my clit, rubbing it just a bit so they could get nice and wet with my juices. Bending over, I wiggled my ass a tad, making sure he was mesmerized by it. While he was distracted, I presented my fingers to his lips. "Do you like what you taste?" I tilted my head and offered him a warm smile.

He hesitated for a moment, but then he licked my fingers clean. A low growl rumbled in his throat, almost like a tiger purring. His poor cock had gone almost purple and jumped a little with the rapid beat of his heart.

I smiled back and then sat up on my knees, turning around and positioning my pussy over his head. "Meal time, sweetheart." I lowered myself, shimmying lightly against his face until he leaned up and started kissing me eagerly.

He didn't hesitate this time as his tongue reached out, lapping at my folds. I moaned loudly and lay down on his body, my breasts pressing into his stomach as I came face-to-face with his huge cock. I grabbed it, squeezing it and starting to stroke.

His hands gripped my ass as he forced his face deeper and deeper into my cunt, feasting on me while making little guttural sounds of delight. It was hard to tear my focus away from the pleasure, but I wanted to reciprocate. He gasped as I kissed his cock. There was already a small drop of pre-come on his tip, and I greedily licked it up. I licked my lips in delight before I wrapped them around his cock head and started taking him in.

My tongue searched every inch of him, making its way under his foreskin and teasing him until he was moaning into my folds. The sound of his moans caused a slight vibration that enhanced his greedy licking, making my whole body shudder.

I gripped his thighs hard as I slowly started to slide my head down his cock, inch by inch until his tip hit the back of my throat. I held back my gag reflex and forced him even farther down, then swallowed against him a few times. He jolted as if stabbed and let out a breathless shout.

As his licking sped up, I couldn't resist moaning. With his cock forced down my throat, he could feel my moans reverberating through his throbbing shaft. When my voice rose in pleasure, his followed it. I squeezed and stroked his balls as I sucked him off, leaving him shuddering violently under me. Once I felt that I was running out of air, I pulled back just enough to take a deep breath through my nose before returning to deep-throating him as hard as I could.

He all but screamed into my cunt, his hips rolling reflexively, and then lashed his tongue against me with renewed fury. I grinned and went even faster, determined to give him the best sixty-nine of his life.

CHAPTER 40
CRAZE

Once again, Misty was showing me something new and exciting, turning me into a wild animal that feasted on her as she feasted on me. I kept lapping at her juices as fast as I could. She tasted so good…and meanwhile, her sweet little mouth was only driving me wilder.

I felt myself slowly losing control as my fingers dug into the supple flesh of her ass. I shivered in delight, trying to hold back my impending orgasm. But it was quickly overcoming me, my balls tightening and my muscles going rigid. I desperately swirled my tongue over her clit, trying to take her with me. She wailed against my skin, and her hips jerked rhythmically. As I felt a rush of her juices spill over my face, I lost all control.

I spewed my load into her hot mouth, and she sucked up every drop, tonguing and kissing me until the last spasm had passed. Exhausted, I lay back, completely blown away.

After a few moments, she got off me and lay by my side. She wiped her mouth clean, revealing an impossibly bright smile on her face as she kissed my shoulder. "How was that?" she asked.

"Amazing," I kissed her head and pulled her closer, rubbing her arms as I lay there, staring at the ceiling.

The grief and rage over Sephir's betrayal and necessary death, my parents' deaths, and Astrid's escape had ebbed away, as if they belonged to my dreams, and my bed and the circle of Misty's arms were my waking reality.

"Are you all right?" she asked me softly.

"I will be," I told her, and then I pulled her gently against me as I settled in to rest awhile.

TWO WEEKS HAD PASSED, AND VIXXIA PRIME HAD ALMOST THOROUGHLY recovered from its abortive coup. The wounded had been healed, the dead, buried, and those who had lost their homes or belongings had been relocated and compensated. The human refugees had been freed from their trackers, and despite all the chaos, had still chosen to stay. A hopeful sign. I did not like the idea of Misty never seeing her people again.

The last of the tracking discs had been removed from the necks of my people by the Mixims, who were slowly becoming a common sight as their delegates roamed the halls and courtyard of the palace. The Queen herself could not yet visit, not wanting to risk teleportation when her litter was due so soon. As thanks for all her help, I made sure to send the Mixims home with gift baskets of fruit, nuts, and other delicacies—and not a single mushroom among them.

Just one thing bothered me. My brothers had yet to return from their mission to find Astrid, and I had become increasingly worried about their well-being. I had confidence in their ability to take her down in a fair fight, but Astrid cheated. At least now she had no foolish Vixxian men to draw strength from.

I had been waiting for my brothers to come back for the coronation ceremony, but Ragar had finally sent a message asking me to proceed in their absence. The empire needed a sitting leader, and we were already postponing our parents' memorial service until my brothers' return. There was no point postponing the coronation as well. Still, I regretted that none of my family would be there to see me take the throne.

The Capitol was abuzz with excitement as people decorated, baked, and gossiped in preparation for the ceremony and the celebrations to follow. Meanwhile, I was being dressed in the traditional garments, a long, gold and green robe with my crest embroidered on it and my armor underneath.

Misty too was being outfitted, against her mild protests. I looked over as various maids milled around her, fitting and adjusting her clothes. I could see the uncomfortable look on her face as she met my gaze, her large eyes pleading for rescue.

Poor thing just isn't used to being fussed over. I chuckled and moved forward, dismissing the maids. "You look lovely." Her dress, which matched my robes, hugged her body to perfection. The low cut showed off the emblem I had burned into her skin the first time we had made love. I smiled and leaned down, gently kissing it, sending a shiver of pleasure through her body.

"Thank you," she finally said, keeping her eyes glued to the ground.

"Are you nervous?" I asked.

She shook her head and puffed out her chest in an attempt to appear confident, but she ended up looking bosomy and nervous instead of just nervous.

I smiled at her efforts, about to tease her affectionately, when one of the younger cadets barged into the room with a worried expression on his face. "My Emperor! An urgent message!"

"What is it?" I held out my hand, and he pressed the message crystal into it, his own hand shaking a little. At once, I found myself on edge.

"Your brothers, my Emperor. They've sent out a distress signal."

He stammered slightly, then forced himself to go on. "The message came in two minutes ago."

"Wait in the hall for my reply," I said distractedly, staring at the crystal. He turned and hurried out.

Misty made her way over to me, looking at the crystal in my hand. "What's going on?"

"My brothers. They might be in trouble," I explained as I concentrated on activating the device. A second later, it vibrated, and my brother Ragar's voice spoke from it urgently.

"Craze! We have found her, but she managed to badly damage our ship! We're going down." Ragar's voice was suddenly drowned out by a cacophony of klaxons and crashing sounds that were all too familiar. I winced.

Moments later, the crystal spat out a ragged chorus of male screams and curses—and then complete silence. I held my breath, praying to hear anything else.

What came next, however, was the furthest thing from comforting, Astrid's maniacal laughter.

Her voice crooned mockingly at me. "Craze, I know you're listening to this. I want you to know that I'm not done with you just yet. I'll stop at nothing until you and everything you love has crashed and burned. I've already killed all of your brothers. Now, all that's left is that little earthling of yours, and then…you're mine.

"See you soon, my prince."

CHAPTER 41
CRAZE

"Call off the coronation. This instant. Tell the others it is postponed until my return." The messenger nodded as I spoke. "And send my backup flight crew to prepare the *Oburos* for an emergency launch. Move!" I didn't know if Astrid had lied about killing my brothers, but I couldn't risk abandoning them if there was a chance that they were still alive. No. My brothers needed me, and I would be damned if I allowed them to perish at Astrid's hands.

Once the youth ran out, I turned to Misty. "I'm going after her and ending this, once and for all. She has caused too much harm for me to allow her crimes to go unpunished," I growled and tossed off my coronation robe. At this point, I felt like I didn't deserve it until I finally put an end to Astrid and rescued—or avenged—my brothers and crew.

"Craze, please consider what you're doing. Astrid is a criminal freaking mastermind. You can't just go after her while you're emotional. You have to have a plan." Misty tried to reason with me as she struggled out of her own gown and reached for the tunic and trousers she had walked in wearing.

"We can plan on the way. There's not a second to lose." I grabbed my own clothes and started pulling them on.

She sighed. "Fine. But I'm going with you. Don't you dare think of leaving me here waiting and worrying."

I looked up at her, jaw working. I wanted to leave her here where it was safe, but I had already learned that with Astrid around, "safety" was a myth. "Very well."

I made my way out of the palace into the courtyard, sweeping past workers who looked after me with a puzzled expression. I could hear their hushed whispers as they tried to figure out what was going on. The coronation had been planned to begin in a few hours, but here I was, rushing out of the palace with the soon-to-be Empress chasing after me. I could only hope that my functionaries could keep things in order in my absence.

We reached the Imperial shipyard and headed for Ragar's ship, which was being outfitted and checked over by a small swarm of busy crewmen and mechanics. As we walked, I gritted my teeth as I racked my mind for options. There had to be something I could do to help me get rid of Astrid.

"So what's the plan?" Misty asked, a tiny edge to her voice that made my back teeth hurt. She knew I still didn't have one beyond the basic and instinctive.

"Go to the transmission location. Find her ship, blow it out of space, then search the area for the *Solrei's* wreckage and, hopefully, my brothers." My face was stoic. "I'm sorry, Misty, but I must do this. I have no other choice."

"You could go with backup. Or send soldiers in your place—a whole fleet of them. You simply can't go alone. If you leave now, you leave this entire nation without a ruler or proper direction. They'll be defenseless, and you know that." Misty's voice pleaded, but there was real strength behind it.

I stopped. In a way, she was right. If Astrid decided to use the distress signal as a way to lure me off the planet, then my people would be vulnerable without a leader to guide them and organize a defense. Still, I couldn't just wait around and let Astrid come to me. I had to get to her before she caused any more harm. Rank and file soldiers, she would outsmart and kill like insects. This was my fight.

And I also had to think of my brothers, who might still be alive, but whose chances would diminish the more I dawdled.

But that didn't mean I had to play into Astrid's hands.

I sighed and stopped, turning around. "How do you suggest we proceed, then?" I rested my hands on her wide hips, giving them a slight squeeze.

She lifted her chin, galvanized by my finally stopping to listen. "We ask for help."

"Who would be able to come here on such short notice?" I questioned, running through a mental list of all the Vixxian Empire's allies. None of them had combat superiority over us or weapons technology better than ours. All they could offer us was increased numbers. *Tempting, but I need more.*

Misty's full lips curled up into a smile as she leaned in close as if she was just about to tell me a monumental secret. "The Mixims," she whispered ever so softly.

My eyebrows rose. "But the Mixims are pacifists. That's why they haven't reconquered their home-world. How are they going to help us take down the fiercest criminal in the galaxy?"

"Trust me." Misty smirked almost cockily. "I know how to make the Mixims her worst nightmare."

CHAPTER 42
MISTY

"The Mixims have advanced technology, don't they?" I asked Craze.

He frowned. "Yes, but I don't see how that is going to help us right now."

Ugh, now you're just being dense. "Are you kidding me?" I looked at him. "If they can build such a sophisticated transport device as the one that got us home, what's stopping them from outfitting one of these ships with the technology needed to take down Astrid?"

"Hmm…you may have a point," he admitted. "Very well, go ahead and contact them. Meanwhile, I'll give some directions to my military leaders and court functionaries." With that, he turned and strode back toward the palace entrance.

I sighed in relief, glad I had managed to talk him out of blindly running after Astrid. At least now he could go after her with some sort of an advantage, instead of running headlong into another of her traps.

Hurrying over to the plaza, I looked around until I saw a familiar cluster of fuzzy shapes gathered atop one of the plaza tables. They were all working on a single berry tart they had sliced into tiny pieces, chirping to each other between enthusiastic nibbling sessions.

I ran up, puffing hard. "Hey, guys."

"Hi, Misty!" a brown-and-black spotted one chirped back. I had never seen her before, but when dealing with a telepathic semi-hive-mind, unexpected recognition seemed to be par for the course.

I smiled. "Look, I need a big favor. We need the Queen's help, and I need your help getting out the message."

Four purple-smeared muzzles turned my direction, and little paws put down slices of tart. "Oh no," a black one squeaked. "Is someone in trouble?"

"Craze's brothers. Astrid attacked them, and we need help rescuing them." I gave them a pleading look.

The spotted one stood up and hopped over to the edge of the table, peering up at me. "I'll send it. Go ahead."

I took a deep breath. It was weird talking into a person like I would have a phone. "Craze and I were about to be coronated, but we received a disturbing distress signal from Craze's siblings. They had gone after Astrid but were attacked during their mission, and we fear they might have ended up space-wrecked like we were, dead, or captured. We need to rescue them if possible and defeat Astrid."

The spotted Mixim's eyelids fluttered, and then she spoke up. The cadence of her words had changed, reminding me of the Queen's. "You don't have technological superiority over her with your remaining ships."

"Yes, Your Majesty." I bowed my head. "That's why we need your help. With our leading ship now destroyed, we lack the means to hunt her down."

"Oh dear, that's terrible. I'll send help right away." She waved a paw. "Chireet will lead the mechanics' team. Expect them in three hours." I thanked her, and the Mixim shook her head and blinked as the telepathic contact apparently broke.

"Thanks, guys. I owe you one. I'll let you know what happens when we go looking." For the umpteenth time, I fought the urge to pet one of them and hurried away, headed the direction Craze had gone.

When I walked into the throne room, I found Craze, sitting on his soon-to-be throne, looking irritated. "Did you contact them?" he asked me, a serious look in his eyes. His posture was ramrod straight, eerily reminiscent of his late mother.

"Yes. They should arrive here in three hours. Chireet is coming with some of his people." I offered him a smile, hoping it would ease his troubled mind, but his lips pressed into a hard line. "It'll all work out," I said soothingly as I approached, but he just scowled.

"I hate sitting around waiting when my brothers could be dying out there." He gave me a glance that was almost apologetic. "It's nothing against you or the Mixims."

"Oh, I know." I kept my tone comforting. "I wish I could just fly out there and save them right now myself. But I don't have that kind of power. Neither do you, not yet. But the Mixims can give us the edge we need."

I climbed up the stairs, and Craze sighed and gathered me onto his lap, burying his nose in my hair. I noticed that he had piled several furs and thick cushions over that uncomfortable seat, and I smiled a little. *Good on him. I refuse to sit on a throne that destroys my ass. Only my man gets to do that.*

"She has to die this time," he murmured into my hair. "She's taken far too much from us both already."

I sighed and laid my cheek on his shoulder. "I know."

THREE HOURS LATER, WE STOOD ON THE LAUNCHPAD AT THE BASE OF THE *Oburos*, waiting. Craze had grown impatient, pacing back and forth as crewmen rushed past with the last of the ship's supplies.

"So where are they?" Craze grumbled. "I have waited more than long enough!" Just as he finished speaking, a bright light erupted in front of us. I closed my eyes, shielding my face with my arm.

A loud, whining noise echoed, making me cringe, and then suddenly, everything went silent. I slowly opened my eyes. In front of us on the tarmac stood hundreds of the little Mixims, looking up at us with their huge russet eyes. Chireet stood in the forefront with his tiny goggles gleaming, looking rather satisfied with himself.

He stepped forward and bowed to us. "At your service." He gestured, and a group of Mixims skittered forward, carrying the weight of Exredilan. It looked different somehow. It was shinier, and its hilt was outfitted with new ruby-colored gems that glowed faintly.

"What's this?" Craze questioned, grabbing his faithful sword, which almost immediately tethered to his hand with jumping blue sparks. "Hmm. It's gotten easier to run energy through the blade."

"We were told you're going after Astrid, so we made some modifications to your sword. We did our best to improve it without changing its energy signature. We did slightly adjust the molecular composition of the metal alloy, however. You'll find the blade lighter and sharper. It will cut through any armor you set it against, including starship bulkhead," Chireet explained as Craze blinked rapidly at him in surprise. "I have plans for retrofitting your ship with some of our enhancement systems. It should take roughly an hour."

Craze blinked some more, swallowed, and then said simply, "Oh."

I walked up behind my man, resting my hand on his shoulder and leaning my lips to his ear. "I told you so."

The Mixims giggled.

CHAPTER 43
CRAZE

It was agonizing to watch the Mixims working on the *Oburos*. Time seemed to drag as they scurried over the vessel. They made progress astonishingly fast, lasering pathways for new circuitry, adding a new console to the weapons section, and swarming in and out of the engine room. It just wasn't fast enough for me. All I wanted was to get out there and go after Astrid.

Misty walked up behind me, carrying a flute of nutrient drink that I took and downed gratefully. There had been no time to eat with all the messages I was taking in and sending out. My head buzzed with data-stream traffic, distracting me. Nothing like weathering my first crisis as emperor before I was even properly coronated. At least my time in the military had taught me to delegate. "When will they be done?" I questioned her.

"Soon. Don't rush them. They're doing the best they can. They have already installed the new drives down in the engine room and upgraded all your crystals. And it's only been half an hour," she reminded me.

"Yes, while that may be true, for every minute we're delayed…" I shook my head. She had heard it all before. No point in another repeat.

She laid a comforting hand on my arm. "I know. But this is our only shot of getting anywhere near her. Also, the new engines will make up for every bit of the lost time, from what the Mixims have been telling me."

I sucked air and stared at her. Suddenly, the reality of the situation got through to me. The long view was that our new allies had provided us with a technological edge well beyond the Dragicans' faster-than-light engines and matter transporters. And it had cost us nothing but good faith, some information, and a promise.

I would have my vengeance and rescue my brothers if I could. But there was a life for my people beyond that personal mission, and it had just gotten a lot brighter. And the fact that my scheming half brother and vicious ex had unintentionally arranged our first meeting with these new allies was a revenge in itself. *Sephir would go mad with rage if he knew. And Astrid is in for a really unpleasant surprise.*

Misty smiled and nodded. She was about to say something else, when Chireet scurried toward us.

She crouched down to give him a perch on her hand. "What is it, Chireet?" I crowded in beside her to listen.

He flitted his tail proudly. "We have completed the ship. It's now outfitted with some of our best defensive technology. Slipstream engines. Trans-phasic weaponry. Ablative hull armor. Everything you could hope to have when going after someone as insidious as Astrid." He produced a small data crystal, which I gingerly took between my thumb and forefinger.

"Thank you." I held out my other hand for the little creature to shake. "Are you going back to your home planet?"

"No. I'll be accompanying you, along with half my team, in case there are any problems with your new ship. I don't expect any, but it isn't as if we have time to explain the new additions to your repair team," he piped up.

I nodded and smiled. "Very well." We were finally in business.

"So, I command the ship normally?" I looked down at my control panel, which looked no different than the standard Vixxian technology, aside from a few new buttons and one slightly small screen.

Chireet nodded from his perch atop the console. "Precisely. Your computing technology is actually pretty advanced. We just streamlined it and boosted its power. Have a look."

I closed my eyes and laid my hand on the panel in front of me, sensing the energy streams of the ship. The new circuitry burned white-hot in my mind. I explored it, finding the rest of the ship's systems sluggish by comparison.

Satisfied, I opened my eyes. "What kind of a crew complement will I need to fly it?" I questioned. I wanted to keep my full crew, but I was curious as to how much automation had been built in.

"Ah, that's something I wanted to discuss. One of the technologies we installed is an assistive AI. It was something that Astrid stole from us a few years back, creating the bad blood between us."

I nodded, eyes widening slightly. *So that was how she could fly the rogue ship on her own.* "So you have given the *Oburos* a mind." I looked around. *You know what? Ragar isn't getting this baby back. I told him not to mess up my ship, after all...*

"A rudimentary mind, though it will develop over time. It will allow you to command the ship entirely on your own or working with a copilot. We would recommend having someone with you over the solo option. It's always safer," he explained.

I nodded, looking over in Misty's direction. "I have my copilot right here." I pulled her near me and kissed the top of her head. Some of the Mixims awwwed, and one or two let out little squees. For some reason, this made Misty blush. I just thought it was cute. But she was cuter.

"Very well. Just a few last particles of information, and we can be on our way." Chireet went through a few bits and pieces on handling the slipstream engines, which sounded fairly straightforward. I nodded in response, making a few mental notes.

"Are we ready for lift-off, then?" I asked, eager to go after Astrid.

"Yes, Emperor," he answered quickly. He chittered to the other Mixims, who scrambled up the walls into little seating niches they had made for themselves. Restraints extended across their fuzzy bellies, and they settled in, chattering to each other quietly.

"Fantastic." I cracked my knuckles and glanced over at Misty, who sat down in the seat next to me, a determined look on her face. I grinned to myself, knowing this woman would forever stay by my side, not only as my copilot but as my Empress as well. And who knew? I had never found out if that terraforming center had been built around a blessed spring or made by technology. But the possibility of being immortal gave "forever" a whole new weight.

I would take it. And her.

On Chireet's mark, we switched on all systems, and the ship hummed to life. I smiled to myself at the low thrum of the new engines cycling up beneath us. Never before had a Vixxian ship sounded or felt this powerful. I looked at Chireet with an appreciative smile. He waved from his niche, and I turned back to the controls as our vessel slowly lifted off the ground. Once we cleared the height of the palace and ground control signaled that the flight path was clear, I triggered the new engines, and we dashed into the sky.

CHAPTER 44
MISTY

The retrofitted *Oburos* proved itself again and again as soon as our impulse system got us clear of the atmosphere. We arrived in the same sector that the distress call had come from within minutes of activating the slipstream engines. With the Mixims' new sensor arrays installed, we were able to find Astrid relatively quickly by tracing the radiation signature from her beloved Mersine missiles.

When I looked at Craze, I could see he was tense, as his hand wrapped white-knuckled around the hilt of his sword. I had to admit that I was a bit nervous myself. At least this time we would be fighting Astrid while safe inside a giant, high-tech ship instead of face-to-face.

"Approaching target," the system warned us in a chirpy little Mixim voice.

The corner of Craze's eye twitched. "Image and data to main screen."

I looked over at our forward observation screen to see a small ship floating through space. I thought back to the last time we had engaged Astrid. Her ship had been much larger. Maybe she was finally running out of resources. Or maybe something else was going on.

The hairs on the back of my neck prickled, and I frowned. What was this feeling? Craze knew what he was doing. All I had to do was watch and cheer him on.

"Target locked." Craze's voice was a terse rasp as he held his finger over the trigger. His muscles were tense as he waited for the systems to give him the okay to fire at will. "All weapons on standby."

Wait, why isn't she responding to the target lock? Her sensors would read it just like ours would. Shouldn't she be shifting course or aiming weapons or raising shields? I opened my mouth to speak up—but the new weapons array lit up green, and Craze shouted, "Fire main battery!"

An arc of purple light fired from each corner of the main view-screen and streaked toward the small vessel. A split second later, there was nothing left of it but a rapidly expanding cloud of debris.

Silence filled the bridge as Craze and I stared at the screen. Had we done it? Had we finally put an end to Astrid? It all felt a little too easy. "Craze...something's off."

He glanced at me and nodded once. "*Oburos*, give me a full sensor sweep of surrounding space out to ten thousand ship-lengths. Intensify scan for potential cloaking fields."

"Confirmed," squeaked the AI adorably.

"I'm really going to need that voice recalibrated," Craze grumbled in a pained tone, while I stifled a giggle.

"What?" chirped Chireet completely innocently.

"Oh, nothing," I said, forcing myself to sound serious while Craze coughed into his fist next to me.

"Multiple ship-to-ship transport sleds incoming!" the AI squeaked urgently. "Too many small targets to lock!"

"What in the—" Craze snapped. "Display on main screen!"

There were dozens of them, glittering bright things like arrows headed straight toward us. The lead ones smashed into the shields and exploded—but they just kept coming, pounding away at the rippling field of energy. Finally, it couldn't rebuild itself fast enough, and a few slipped through. As they did, Craze glimpsed something that made his blue eyes widen. "Are those things equipped with breaching drills?"

"Hull breach! Intruder is aboard!" the AI screeched.

Craze turned to look at his tiny crew. "I want a lock on her location and direction, and if she came with company."

"Yes, Emperor!" The Mixims tapped at tiny panels set into their niches, but before they could finish their search, a loud explosion sounded below us.

"Several hull breaches on the lower decks!" Chireet called out. "Trying to seal them now." Then his whiskers and ears drooped in dismay as he consulted his panel. "The intruder is coming up to the bridge. She is alone, but very heavily armed."

"Curse her. I've had enough of her tricks." Craze got up quickly, drawing his sword. "*Oburos*, full stop, focus on rebuilding shields and containing the hull breaches. Mixims, get cover." There was a skittering noise as scores of furry crewmen ran and hid. "Misty—"

Suddenly the bridge doors exploded inward in a hail of shrapnel, forcing us to duck for cover behind the consoles. Astrid stood on the other side of the ruined doorway, holding Ragar's favorite rail gun, a wild look in her red eyes.

"Fancy new weapons system you've got here," she gloated as she stepped through the breach. "Thanks for demonstrating on my decoy ship. I'll definitely have to keep this ship, once it repairs itself."

"Stop hiding behind that rifle and draw your sword, you cowardly whore," Craze growled. "You'll pay for what you have done to my loved ones."

"No," Astrid hissed, lowering the rail gun slightly. "You will pay, again, for what you did to my pride when you exposed me to your family!" She aimed the rail gun at him—just as an emergency bulkhead slammed down in place of the door, nearly crushing her.

The rail gun skittered across the floor as Astrid threw herself aside, ending up practically at my feet. I hastily grabbed it and ducked back into cover, looking it over to try to figure out how it operated.

"Damn!" Astrid tossed her head and drew out a long, curved sword that gleamed red, like forge-heated steel. "Fine. You want to cross blades, Craze? I've already killed three Vixxian princes today. I think it's about time I scratch the last one off my list." She curled up her lip—and then launched herself toward Craze.

Craze blocked the downstroke of her sword with the flat of his, striking red and blue sparks. Then he waded in, lashing out at her again and again. His sharp face was taut with focus, and his eyes burned with growing rage. He unleashed a dizzying array of attacks with sword, elbows, and feet, but she blurred with speed as she dodged each one effortlessly.

Back and forth across the bridge, they fought. Craze constantly forced her to dodge instead of attacking, but then he couldn't land a blow. They were moving so fast that I couldn't get a clear shot either. "Damn it!" I yelled in frustration as I kept trying.

"What is it, Misty?" Chireet squeaked as he poked his head out from beneath the control panel.

"They're too evenly matched. He can't use his enhanced sword on her if he can't touch her!" I couldn't keep the frustration out of my voice.

"Then we will assist," the Mixim said calmly. His whiskers wiggled, and then I saw a few golden sparks dance around his head as he closed his eyes.

Astrid let out a yelp and stumbled suddenly, slowing down. Her eyes tracked around wildly. "What is that?" she snapped, barely dodging Craze's next blow. "Who's in my head?" She flailed around on pure instinct, swinging her sword. Craze ducked it and counter-struck, and this time, his sword caught her cloak as she spun away.

The would-be conqueror's eyes were full of terror now, and she looked everywhere, as if her surroundings were suddenly horribly unfamiliar. Her voice rose to a scream. "What is this? What happened? Why is everything so big?"

My eyes widened at the sheer panic in her voice. *Okay. Maybe the singing telepathic chinchilla-folk are a little scary, after all.*

Craze took advantage of her confusion, pressing the attack—and now, suddenly, she was barely fending him off. Her eyes rolled around in shock, her vision so apparently distorted that ultimately, she closed her eyes and started fighting blind. That gave her back some of her advantage…but not enough. Soon, he had her backed into a corner, her burning sword raised only to parry frantically.

The superior alloy of his reworked blade bit deep into her own— and suddenly shattered it. Astrid shrieked as red-hot metal pelted her face and arms. She fell backward, half-blinded and bleeding.

Craze stood over her, his face cold. "You're done, Astrid."

"Wait, wait—you can't kill me!" She held up her hands, simpering desperately. "If you kill me, you'll never find out where your brothers are!"

"She doesn't know herself!" Chireet piped up from the safety of my lap.

Craze's eyebrow lifted at the telepath's words. "Oh, really?"

Astrid's smile died. "Oh, shit."

Without a hint of hesitation, he drove his sword right through her throat.

CHAPTER 45
CRAZE

Astrid's eyes grew wide as she looked down at my sword, now protruding from beneath her chin. The flesh around the blade was searing, but she was still standing. Disgusted, I put one of my boots between her breasts and shoved her off my blade. Blood spattered the floor, and she choked once then collapsed. The mad light winked out in her eyes.

"Clean up this mess and blast it out an airlock," I snarled, walking away from her twitching corpse. Servos whirred as a small army of plate-sized robots emerged from the walls and scuttled over to follow my order. I didn't watch.

A sense of relief washed over me when I realized I would never see Astrid again. She would no longer threaten those I loved. I would always blame myself for ever trusting her, but not as self-torture. Merely as a warning, for myself and my sons, that women could be predators too.

I sheathed my sword once it burned itself clean of her blood, and I walked heavily back to my chair, settling into it painfully. *"Oburos, status report."*

The chirpy voice spoke up much more calmly. "Shields back at seventy-five percent and rising. Hull integrity will be restored in twelve minutes. All systems are on-line. Zero casualties."

"Good news at last." I spoke up. "We resume the search for my brothers in fifteen minutes. Meanwhile, continue long-range sensor sweeps." If I could not save them, I at least wanted to give their bodies a proper burial—something that, thanks to Astrid and Sephir, my parents could not have.

I held hands with Misty as we waited. Every minute was crawling by again. As much of a relief as it was to be rid of both Sephir and Astrid, I wanted my brothers back.

"I have something," Chireet squeaked about eight minutes in, trying to get our attention.

I looked over at his niche. "What is it?"

"We have picked up a handful of very weak homing beacons from ship escape pods in this sector. It seems that at least some of the crew escaped Astrid's attack. We are scanning for their identities now." Chireet wiggled with excitement.

I blinked at him in astonishment. "But you said yourself that my ship must have been destroyed. There's no trace of it in the sector."

"The *Solrei* may have been destroyed in battle, but apparently, all three of your brothers managed to get to the escape pods before the ship crashed." He beamed at me, and Misty squeezed my hand and smiled.

"Where are they?" I demanded.

"We've already established a course. They landed on a wandering asteroid, not far from the planet Jujix," he explained cheerily.

I nodded and settled back in my chair with an enormous sigh of relief. I couldn't believe it. It seemed that I was going home with my brothers, after all.

Sure enough, we found the escape pods scattered around the surface of the asteroid, which was just big enough to generate a respectable gravity field. Instructing the *Oburos* to scan for any drifting pods we had missed, we got them on board as quick as we could.

"Ugh, nothing like a stasis hangover to finish my day," Ragar grumbled as he sipped a cup of hot spiced wine. "Nice job finding us. Still pissed that we had to abandon ship, but she loaded up that stolen attack ship with bombs and rammed us."

Lysi yawned, stretching his scarred limbs, expression as casual as if he'd just gone down for a nap for a few hours. "At least you got your rail gun back."

Ragar perked up and patted it. "Yeah, I was pretty pissed off when that bitch took off with it."

Nemesch, wounded, was visible, most of his power occupied with healing his shattered arm. He ran his hand back through his short, pale blond hair and sighed. "Our parents are avenged and our empire safe. I'll be happy to see home again." He checked his chronometer. "I may even get back in time for my…'date' with Linda tonight."

Misty gaped. "Wait…you're dating one of the other human refugees?"

I blinked at him. "And you didn't tell us?"

Nemesch smiled quietly. "Actually, it looks like all three of the other surviving human refugees are interested in seeing Vixxian men. Two are dating, one is looking. I didn't want to bring it up, for between Ragar's lover, your pledge with Misty, and this, I thought Lysi might get jealous."

"Of course, I'm jealous," Lysi growled, folding his arms sulkily. "Now I'm the only brother who hasn't gotten laid in over a year!"

Ragar laughed. "Well, maybe if you took a bath once in a while—"

"Shut up!"

I chuckled and patted Lysi's shoulder soothingly, grateful to have all of my brothers by my side once again. "Relax, our luck will rub off." I looked over at Nemesch. "Are you well enough to get food with us down in the mess hall?"

He nodded. "The cast has hardened, and I have use of the other arm. I'll be fine." We all got up and walked out of the infirmary into the ship's main corridor.

Outside, small robots swarmed along the floor, carrying bits of equipment and materials for the many small repairs still needed after the battle. Here and there, Mixims scrambled along, singly or in small groups, chattering to each other in their chirpy, singsong language.

Ragar paused, eyebrows rising rapidly. "Uh…"

"What the drakk?" Lysi watched one of the tiny engineers ride past on the back of a spiderbot, waving.

"The crew is looking…rather small and fuzzy today," Nemesch commented as he blinked around at the Mixims. I realized suddenly that none of the three had been present when I had introduced our new allies to our people.

Ragar walked over and took me by the shoulders, looking at me earnestly. As I blinked at him, he rumbled, "Look, I'm not mad or anything, but I just need to know. Exactly what drugs did you give us when you brought us out of stasis?"

The soft choking sound I heard next was Misty doing everything in her power not to laugh.

Once our stomachs were full and Nemesch's arm was healed enough that the shadows were starting to blur out his features again, we returned to the bridge. I settled into my seat and looked over at the group of Mixims repairing the last few bits of damage around the bridge. "Chireet?"

"Yes, Emperor?" He looked up from where he was consulting a tiny data tablet.

"Come here a moment." I held out my hand, and obediently, he bounced over and jumped into it. I brought him closer to my face. "I just wanted to thank you for all that you and your people have done to assist Vixxia. We're forever grateful. Please convey that to your Queen as well."

He beamed, whiskers wiggling. "Oh! No need to thank us. We're eager to help. You two have helped us learn so much about your species. We only ask one last thing in return for our services." His expression grew more serious. "And since you are to be coronated soon, it is time for us to collect on what you owe."

I looked at him skeptically. I didn't quite like the sound of this suddenly. I had no idea what he was going to ask for. But I would hear him out, I owed the Mixims too much not to. "And that is?"

"Do you remember when the Queen spoke to you about regaining the home-world we were pushed off of? Well…that home-world is what you now call Vixxia Prime." He watched as my jaw dropped in shock. "Yes. Though we have called other worlds home for many years after our scattering, your world was once our world."

"And you want it back?" *What have I done? I can't keep an oath that will leave my people homeless!*

"Oh, no, no, no." He waved a paw dismissively. "What we ask is that you allow us to gradually relocate to Vixxia Prime, where we can all live together."

He went on as I gave an internal sigh of relief. "The resources on Hexiven are sparse, and even with the teleporter for bringing in supplies, we won't be able to thrive there for much longer. We're aware that your people have mostly spread out into your off-world colonies, and currently, only about a third of the planet's area is populated. We would gladly take another third which is less hospitable to Vixxians. The warrens of our ancestors are largely in what is now deep wilderness."

I thought of this, now realizing why my ancestors had character-ized Mixims as wicked and dangerous. We had beaten them in a land war and driven them into space, all the while fearing their powers. Perhaps, with time and effort, I could start to heal the breach between our two peoples. "For all that you have done for us, what's mine is now yours. Of course, we'll discuss it further once we're back, but I'm sure we can accommodate you." I smiled at the little creature. "And tell the Queen she's always welcome at the palace."

Chireet beamed at the news. "Oh, wonderful," he piped excitedly. "The Queen will love to hear this." I nodded and smiled down at him. He jumped off my hand and ran off to join the rest of his people.

I looked at Misty and grabbed her hand, squeezing it tightly. She smiled and squeezed back. "We did it," she whispered.

I looked at our observation screen as we made our way back to Vixxia Prime. "Indeed, we did, Misty. Indeed, we did." I couldn't stop smiling at my success. After everything we had been through, we were finally free to start our new, happy life together.

As the weeks went by, everything returned to normal in the capital. Nemesch healed up and went on his date—and several more after it. Ragar and Lysi still squabbled at every opportunity, and as for Misty, she was thriving. She had made friends with Linda and the other two human refugees, and she and I were happily building a life together.

My mother's ashes were buried in the family crypt in the double vault meant for her and my father. They were memorialized. Sephir was not. And as for Astrid, she was nothing but a legend now, and that would fade with time.

The Vixxians were getting along nicely with the Mixims, who were slowly settling in the eastern end of one of the larger continents. In such a short amount of time, they had managed to create a small settlement called Greenwell. It was already bustling with trade, research, and construction in preparation for the rest of their population to relocate.

The only problem was that no Vixxian could enter that city without the fear of destroying a building or two with a single misstep. Fortunately, the little creatures were not shy about bringing their goods and technology to the Vixxian capital.

"What are you doing?" Misty walked up beside me at the bubble-window, where I had been standing thoughtfully for over a minute.

"Watching the Mixims installing the new teleportation center near the launchpads. Chireet claims it will be done within ten days. It's impressive that they can accomplish it so quickly." I tore my eyes away from the new spire rising near the rockets and smiled down at her.

She smiled and stepped closer to me, running her hands up my arms. "Well, they are full of surprises. But you know what else will be impressive?"

"What?" I tilted my head.

"My Emperor, when he's crowned tomorrow." Misty kissed my lips gently, wrapping her arms around my neck.

I smiled, instantly grabbing her by the hips and pulling her closer. "Not as impressive as my beautiful Empress. You will be the envy of the entire galaxy," I murmured into her hair, smelling its fresh scent.

Each day, it seemed like she was growing even more beautiful. Though, it was possible that I was biased.

"I can't wait," Misty whispered, her hand tightening around my own.

"Would you like to see your dress? The seamstresses have finally finished altering it."

I couldn't wait to see the look on her face when she saw it.

She smiled and nodded. "Absolutely."

I grabbed her hand and pulled her down the hall. Along the way to the seamstress's chambers, we passed the kitchen. A cacophony of sound emerged as frantic workers rushed about, trying to finish making all the pastries needed for the grand celebration. I stole us a couple of berry tarts and ducked out again. We strolled along, enjoying our stolen snacks.

Finally, we reached the chambers at the far end of the palace, where I opened a door. In the middle of the round room with its cutting tables and bolts of cloth hung a magnificent red dress on a display dummy. It was detailed with gold trimming all around and featured a stiff, gold-embroidered collar. Around its waist was a belt made of jewels, which sparkled in the light. Attached to the collar was a large, beaded necklace carved from energy crystals, a family heirloom that had once belonged to my grandmother.

"Do you like it?" I asked her softly as she walked in, staring at it. Her eyes were very wide, and I smiled, waiting for her to get her voice back.

"It's amazing," she breathed finally and turned to me for a kiss. "So are you."

CHAPTER 46
MISTY

The dress was completely breathtaking. Slowly, my fingers ran along the fabric, which was silky but had a metallic sheen. It looked expensive enough to pay for a small island somewhere, and I dreaded what might happen if I ate in it. But impractical as hell or not, I knew I would actually feel like an empress when the seamstresses sewed me into it.

To think that at one point in my life, I had been a simple earthling, no different from anybody else on the planet. Now, I was about to become Empress of Vixxia. "Why is it red?" I asked, remembering how the first dress had been green.

"We're also celebrating putting an end to Astrid's evil legacy. Red is the color of victory," Craze explained.

I nodded, glad that the woman who had caused us so much trouble was finally out of the picture. "Well, it's amazing. Thank you," I whispered, walking up to him.

He took me into his arms, a smile spreading across his face. "Don't thank me yet. Thank me once you have a crown on your head."

THE BRIGHT SOUND OF AN ALIEN PROCESSIONAL ECHOED THROUGH THE AIR as the Imperial orchestra played in their stands at the back of the throne room. I smiled, my heartbeat mimicking the tempo of the music. It felt like it would thump out of my chest at any moment. Seconds seemed to drag on longer and longer as Craze walked down the aisle with me.

He was adorned in his own red robe and cloak, chased with gold and layered over his armor. It looked amazing on his tall, broad-shouldered body, causing me to bite my lip to restrain my desire. *Man. How did I land such a handsome man?*

Finally, we reached the edge of the dais. He turned to me, holding out his hand. "My Empress."

With my fingers trembling, I managed to reach my hand up and brush it against his. He took it firmly, the crowd cheering as we ascended the dais.

Confidently, he led me toward the twin thrones, which had been stripped of their electronics and decorated with flowers. There was a wide smile on his face before he guided me to the Empress's throne, where he eased me into the cushion. Moments later, he placed a crown carved from energy crystals on my head. It felt a little strange at first, but as the whole community of Vixxians and Mixims cheered together, I felt accepted into a new family.

Leaning down, Craze kissed me on the lips before taking his own crown from the high priestess and setting it on his head. As he ascended the throne, his brothers started to whistle and howl. Outside the windows, the sky lit up with brightly colored fireworks.

I admired them in a daze. It seemed like it was all going by so fast, and there wasn't enough time to capture everything and commit it to memory. But I would gladly try.

That night, the whole capital danced until midnight, and we danced with them.

With my head against Craze's chest, I could hear his heartbeat. It had its own steady rhythm, but anytime I touched him, it would quicken for a moment before settling down again. As time went on, it seemed like we were the only two people who existed, locked in a lover's embrace. Outside this small bubble of time, the fate of the empire rested on our shoulders. But tonight, our duties could wait.

Eventually, we grew too impatient for each other. As the celebration raged on into the morning, we retreated into Craze's chambers for some badly needed privacy.

The seamstresses were celebrating, so Craze obliged me by drawing out a small, whisper-sharp knife and delicately cutting the threads that bound me into my coronation gown. My chest heaved as he freed my breasts from the confines of the tight bodice and ran his hands over them. A few more cut seams, and he pulled it away entirely, leaving me nude from the waist up.

He set aside the gown bodice and cut the hip seams of the skirt, then stepped back. "Strip."

I had no sexy lingerie to wear under what had essentially been my wedding dress as well, so I had decided to surprise him in another way. I stood there and shimmied out of the skirt, rolling my hips until the fabric slid off and he saw I was nude and freshly trimmed underneath.

Craze's eyes widened, and he hastily threw off his cloak and robes and started unfastening the plates of his armor. Ceremonial finery was a bitch to get off, apparently, and I made a mental note of trying to influence local fashions toward the slightly easier to get into and out of. *Because this is just a little ridiculous.*

I laughed as I moved into his embrace. He threw aside the last of his clothes and pulled me against his pounding heart. Then he leaned back just enough to bring his mouth down on mine.

We kissed as the fireworks went off, and his cock slid against my belly as his hands started to roam over my skin. I trailed my hands over him as well, cupping and kneading his ass, running nails down his thighs, and finally taking his cock in hand and using it like a leash to lead him to bed. He followed behind me, chuckling at my audacity.

We fell on the bed together, kissing and snuggling and laughing a little as we tangled up in the bedclothes trying to get under them. Our crowns glowed softly on the bedside table, and now and again, a splash of colored light spilled in the bubble-windows from outside. In the multicolored dimness, we tangled our bodies together as he sank down over me.

I heard his groan in my ear as he entered, my body already slick and ready for him after hours of dancing and kisses and hand-holding…and anticipating right now.

I arched my back against the mattress, and he bent down to take one of my nipples in his mouth. He sucked it greedily as he pumped his hips against me, and I whimpered and thrashed, lifting my body to his with each thrust of his hips and pull of his mouth.

My voice had gone from soft sighs and giggles to rising moans, his cock pushing them out of me over and over as he thrust and thrust. I looked up and saw a huge splash of purple and gold dart across the domed white ceiling as my flesh started to tighten around his surging shaft.

He sped up, the soft slap of our bellies together muffled only a little by the fluffy blankets as his grunts grew more guttural and desperate by the second. I dug my nails into his shoulders and struggled to keep my breath as his thrusts roughened, pushing my hips deep into the mattress. He was starting to tremble.

His hand slid between us, gently rubbing my clit even as his thrusts grew more violent. I wailed. The precipice I had been inching toward suddenly rushed up at me, and I went rigid, back arched as every thrust of his cock felt better than the last.

Finally, he bored down on me hard and threw his head back. The pressure and his long, musical groan pushed me over, and I sobbed joyously. My cunt clenched around him again as his seed rushed hot into me. We clutched each other tightly until finally, the last spasm ended and we collapsed to the mattress.

We lay there after, catching our breaths. I curled on my side against him, my head pillowed on his shoulder and his hand stroking up and down my back. "I am glad that you stayed," he murmured into my hair as I dozed lightly in his arms. "I would not wish to imagine my life without you, crown or no crown."

"I'm glad too," I whispered, marveling that all those horrible strokes of luck we had both endured had somehow managed to end like this. "Never thought I would be glad that I got abducted." It was true. In their own way, those kidnapping Thezlums had done me a huge service by bringing me into Craze's path. Not that I would have ever thanked them for it.

I had never imagined I would become some sort of alien royalty the night I had jogged through Central Park. But now, I didn't regret a thing. I knew there was a bright future ahead of me, one where Craze would always be by my side. Together, we would lead this empire like no other rulers before us.

I smiled as I drifted off to sleep.

RAEVU

CHAPTER 1
RAEVU

I held the data screen in both hands, staring down at it in disbelief. I scanned the missive twice before its contents sank in—the experiment had reached stage two.

The Earth primitives have finally come through for the Juhlian people. I was starting to think that the benefits of our trade agreement were all one-sided.

With a deep breath, I composed my expression and made sure my hands were steady before looking up at my deputy prime minister. "J'da," I addressed him.

"Yes, my lord?" He was tall and spindly, with spidery fingers and a long, intelligent face. His milky blue eyes glanced up at me mildly. Despite all the drawbacks of being born a eunuch, his ability to remain dispassionately calm in emotional situations made him invaluable.

It was difficult not to distract myself by reading that message again. It actually worked. Fifty years of searching for a biologically and sexually compatible intelligent species. Six years of negotiations with the humans once we found them, and ten years of sending them technology and trade goods while they paid us back with empty promises. Finally, they were able to make good. I wanted to crow in triumph, but J'da was waiting for his answer.

I met his gaze. "Ready the fastest cruiser. That message came from Earth—we've reached stage two. We leave at first light." I got up from my command chair, straightening my cloak.

"Of course, my lord." He bowed as I passed him, already reaching for his communications pad as he straightened.

I stalked away from him, heading for my chambers to rest and pack. I was confident that everything would be ready at dawn. J'da was stunningly competent, and he knew just how important this mission was—important enough that I had to deal with it myself.

THE HYPERTUNNEL'S TERMINUS SPAT US OUT JUST OUTSIDE EARTH'S ORBIT, the vast metal and ceramic ring flashing with a million multicolored lights before the milky vortex inside of it collapsed. A few of my crewmen sighed with relief; hyperspace travel had its risks, even with a stable terminus to link to.

I ordered, "Send hails to Earth command."

My communications officer, Kymptar, nodded and coded in the commands on his holo-console with thick, black-nailed fingers. As the connection request went out, we gazed down at the blue-green ball below, with its satellite layer shimmering all around it.

The view-screen flickered, and a human communications officer appeared, sitting at a desk, her bland expression balanced by an enormous pair of velvety brown eyes.

She gazed at me briefly, a mix of confusion and lust in her eyes before her expression turned neutral. "Envoy ship, we have received your hail with registration information. May I help you?" she requested.

I cut to the chase, "The ambassador, please. He'll know why I'm calling."

She nodded and tapped on her own screen. "Patching you through to the ambassador."

The screen fuzzed for a moment, and then a burly but weak-chinned older human man appeared on the screen. His skin was pinkish, he wore a poorly knotted tie of dusty burgundy that clashed with his coloring, and his bald spot had widened since our last video call. He offered a saccharine smile.

"Good morning, Your Majesty Raevumon," Ambassador Reynauld spoke in a clipped tone.

It was nearing sunset, but I ignored that. "Good morning. I got your missive about the compatibility project. I want to know about the experiment results. In detail."

"We looked for the qualifications your ministers and scientists specified, performed the tests as requested, and injected the five finalists with the DNA samples provided."

Somehow, his voice always sounded oily to me, as if he were trying to slip through the conversation without telling me the whole truth.

I scowled at him. "Only five finalists? Do you realize the straits my planet is in, Ambassador? Fewer women are born on Juhl with every generation. Without women to breed with from a compatible race, the Juhlian people will all die out. We need more than five human women to help our situation."

The ambassador held up a hand. "There were only five that fit all of the criteria your scientists provided, sir." His voice was placating.

Months of searching, and yet the best the humans had was a tiny pool of potentials?

We stared at each other, and I finally sighed and shook my head. There was no choice but to work with what we had. "Five will be a start. I will get our scientists to work on recalculating and adapting our growth plan."

Reynauld winced. "I'm sorry, please allow me to clarify. There were five, Your Majesty. There aren't five anymore. There is one."

I blinked at him. "I don't think I am hearing you correctly." I turned toward Kymptar and barked at him to look at the translator circuits, certain there was a loose connection somewhere.

As my communications officer scrambled to make sure all components were working properly, Reynauld blathered on as if he hadn't heard me. I scowled but listened, hoping I wasn't missing anything in translation. "There were complications with four of the finalists after we injected them with the DNA as your scientists instructed." The ambassador's small green eyes flicked nervously back and forth as he explained. "Two were immediately violently ill. One, unfortunately, died as a result of some allergic reaction to a spore or virus in the samples. Two had only mild physiological reactions, and we had high hopes for both. Unfortunately, Jane Cleveland, one of the two finalists, started hallucinating violently. She did not respond to medication or implant therapy, and she ended up committing suicide." He must have caught sight of my expression and added hastily, "For which we are very sorry. The psychologists should have seen that inclination in the genetic or psychological screening but somehow failed to do so. So, that means we have…one fully viable candidate." He stared at me, throat working.

With a patience that would have pleasantly surprised my father, I shifted my stance, head up and hands clasped behind my back. My voice stayed calm. "Ambassador Reynauld, our agreement was for an exchange of technology and science for women—plural, as in multiples of them, not a singular woman—who could help us rebuild our race, voluntarily. We have held up our end for almost a decade. And now that we have finally reached Phase Two, you present us with only one viable woman?"

"I… On behalf of Earth's science team, I deeply apologize," he started. I shook my head, and his mouth snapped shut.

"One woman will not help us rebuild my people. One compatible human woman will not bring us the stability and fertility our race needs to survive. Our agreement will not be considered met with only one woman to exchange." I could feel my temper rising.

"Of course, we will continue our genetic screenings of volunteers for as long as is required to find others as needed." He waved his chubby hands at the screen in a placating way, and I growled under my breath in annoyance.

From one side of the room, I heard my first officer T'ral clear his throat. *Curse it.* I took a deep, cleansing breath. Shouting at the Earth Ambassador would get me nowhere. "Tell me about the remaining candidate," I invited.

"We are unsure about our final subject's results," Reynauld spoke hesitantly.

I turned so T'ral could see the growing impatience on my face. He remained, as always, impassive, his black eyes emotionless. I huffed and turned back, imitating T'ral's expression. "What's the complication?"

"She has grown moderately ill—fever, chills, fatigue, nausea. If she were not perfectly healthy before the injection, we'd say she had the flu." Then, at a mumbling interruption behind him, Reynauld cleared his throat. "Influenza. It's a disease that is typically viral in nature, and usually, the symptoms are treatable, but in this case…"

I'd had enough. "Reynauld, I know what the flu is. We have something similar on my planet. You already admitted that your samples were not properly sterilized. She must have picked up the virus that way. We can cure it easily. Tell me more about the female. Is she otherwise well?"

His eyes shifted again. "Not…entirely."

I rubbed my hands over my face. I was tired of dealing with this slippery fool of a man. T'ral came and stood just behind and to one side of me to offer his silent support. I crossed my arms over my chest and waited, one eyebrow lifting.

"Um…Your Majesty, this was completely unexpected. This last woman has developed a series of welts in an unusual configuration. Almost like a symbol."

"A symbol?" That was bizarre. "Do you have an image available?"

"I-I— The latest data has not yet been transmitted from the medical unit." He was getting more nervous by the second, and I quickly realized that the humans, after making us wait so long, had almost completely botched their end of things.

And we're relying on them to save our race?

A muscle jumped in my jawline as I fought a scowl. I rubbed my hand across my smooth jaw to ease the tic. "How long until we pass quarantine and can make landfall?"

"Two days after your arrival." The ambassador sank down in his seat.

Primitives.

"It seems then that you have a small reprieve. I want all the current data on the project, especially anything that you have on the survivor…what is her name?"

"Eva Knight, Your Highness." He took a shivery breath, blinking too often. I had scared him. Perhaps that would prove motivating, or perhaps he was simply the hapless messenger of an entire incompetent system. Either way, I had little sympathy.

"I want every bit of information about her sent as soon as it is available. From now on, as long as we are within transmission range, I want you to send copies of all reports about all candidates, living and deceased, to my ship immediately, so we can review the information." I saw all the pink leave his face. "Is this in any way unclear?"

"No, Your Highness. I will get you the data as soon as possible."

"Good." A hand tightened on my shoulder. I twisted around and met the blank look T'ral was pointedly giving me.

I sighed. Pasting on a small, professional smile, I turned back to the view-screen. "Thank you for your cooperation."

The ambassador nodded and swallowed, and the screen went black. I puffed out a sigh and slumped in the command chair. "Are all Earthlings this painfully incompetent?"

"No," my second replied solemnly. "But bureaucrats move on their own timetables throughout the galaxy. Might I remind you of that shipment of data cubes we were forced to wait for over a year?"

I rolled my eyes again and bit back a sarcastic remark as I levered myself out of the command chair. "I don't judge our people as perfect, T'ral, but this is getting ridiculous."

The corner of his lipless mouth tugged up. "Yes, it is, but losing your temper won't do anything but give the ambassador digestive trouble."

I snorted. "I'm taking a break. Contact me as soon as they make their next data delivery."

"I shall." He went back to his station to continue monitoring our orbit.

I brushed past him on the way and headed to the tube lift. Maybe a workout with Baelon would put me back into a more charitable frame of mind before I dealt with the human again.

I stepped into the lift. "Once you receive the reports and review them with the science team, I want to go over the documents myself. We'll need to review the genetic profile of this 'Eva' and any others who pass the screening, to see if the exchange will be a viable one. We need results." The lift doors swished shut before T'ral could reply.

CHAPTER 2
RAEVU

Baelon, my arms-master, could see the sort of mood I was in the moment I walked into his practice chamber. His eyebrows rose almost to his shaved hairline, and the corner of his mouth twitched with knowing amusement. "Trouble with the human bureaucrats again?"

"Foolishness from top to bottom. They found only five candidates that made their way through the full screening, and four of them died. The fifth one suddenly fell ill and has some kind of disfigurement." I shook my head as I removed my cloak of office and went to the wall to grab a practice staff.

"Are they continuing in their efforts?" He took up a practice staff as well and activated it, the repulsor fields shimmering to life around each end.

I activated mine, nodding. "I'm also having them send details on the survivor. If she is tough enough to survive that botched inoculation, she might be exactly what we need." It was the only bit of hope in this whole mess.

Baelon had taught me everything I knew. We had practiced together since I was small, and doing it again was like slipping on a favorite pair of boots. He put me through a series of exercises, then opened the sparring match with a surprise attack—and we were off, swiping, clashing, and dodging our way around the chamber. The fears of our people and the annoyances of dealing with the human government faded to a small part of my mind.

We switched weapons after the first several minutes, tossing aside the deactivated staves and snatching paired swords off the rack. I circled him with practice blades ready, watching his tall, lean form for the shifts in stance that would tell where his next movement would come from.

There! My trainer twirled his twin swords over his head, and they spun with deadly precision toward my head and midsection. With a resounding clang, my blades met and repelled his attack.

Without letting him consider his next move, I twisted and wrapped my advancing leg around the one he was using for stability. I jerked my knee toward myself, and he fell backward onto the practice mat.

Before he could roll to a standing position, I threw one blade into his path on one side. I heard its thunk as it stuck into the practice mats solidly, and I threw the other one to Baelon's other side. Even as it impacted the practice mat, I swiped his swords from his grasp and held one to his throat.

To my satisfaction, Baelon was breathing as hard as I was at our exercise. "I yield, King Raevumon," he said wryly, an amused twinkle in his eye.

I held out my hand to give him additional leverage to stand. With a grunt, he rose to stand beside me. Our hands still clasped between our chests, I grinned at him. "I can count on my hands the number of times you've said that to me, Uncle."

"I must start looking for a replacement arms-master when we return home. Obviously, I am growing slow and soft." His eyes twinkled.

I laughed. "I replace you, Uncle, only after the ceremony devoting your ashes to the gods."

"Gods willing, after many seasons, nephew." Baelon released my hand and swiped his forearm across his brow, wiping away sweat. "Good workout, sire. But I sense you are still agitated. Did you want to talk about this Earth matter further?"

His question immediately brought the human ambassador and his oily, placating manner back to the forefront of my mind. An attack of restlessness took me again, and I strode to the edge of the practice mat and flung the sword in my hand down with a clatter.

"Humans! Whose idea was this anyway? I do not care to deal with this Reynauld fellow any more than I have to, Uncle. But even if he were replaced, I would still be dealing with incompetence." I turned and paced to the other end of the mat.

"We have gotten further with our human allies than with any other species," my uncle reminded me gently, but it didn't help.

"I foresee excuse after excuse of why they cannot supply us with fully viable mating candidates, while they continue to beg for our technology." I ran my hand over my smooth scalp.

"I thought that they finally had a viable candidate, however." He tugged his short, pointed russet beard.

"Uncle, that's not sufficient. You know the dire straits we are in. We need hundreds of compatible human women to help us rebuild our race, not just this one Reynauld has said may be viable." I continued to pace, trying to run through my frustrated energy.

"And your own science officers have been of little help still, I take it?" He pulled a bottle of Klaata juice from a chilling unit and tossed it over to me.

I caught it in midair and flipped the port open, swallowing half the minty green liquid down. "The scientists' experiments with test tubes have not worked consistently enough. We still end up with only males with very limited genetic diversity. We need females of outside lineages in order to flourish as a people. I just cannot believe that this farce is the closest we have come to succeeding!"

Baelon let me rant; this was a routine we'd worked out over the years. He stood at rest, letting the waves of my frustration crash about him without effect. He knew that as soon as I dealt with the excess rage, I would find the resolve to go solve the problem that was enraging me.

It only took a few minutes this time. I finally caught my breath as he watched, and he tilted his head. "You have gotten far closer to finding a solution than your father ever did. Perhaps you should not give up on the humans quite yet."

I nodded, my pride and determination overcoming my frustration. "I will solve this, Uncle. Our world's genetic problems end during my reign. I will be known for it."

A moment after my vow, the chamber doors crashed open. We looked up quickly. T'ral stood there with a data screen in hand, his normally impassive face ashen. "Sire, Earth has sent the first data broadcast. I have something here that you need to see."

With a cocked eyebrow, I held out my hand. T'ral stepped forward and gave the screen to me. I exchanged a look with Baelon before looking down at the screen. Neither one of us had ever seen T'ral so disturbed.

Stranger still, there was nothing visible on the screen but a picture of a nude human female. Not a bad-looking one, either. Her curly hair was a jet black, and her skin was a warm sienna hue. She was small of stature but generously curved, her hips wide and her waist narrow. This picture was of just her back, so I saw no details of her face and found myself wishing that I could. "She's not bad, for a human. What's the problem?"

T'ral coughed softly. "Just…look, sire."

Suddenly something riveted my attention. The subtle mark on her shoulder blade and up her neck. It was about the same height and width as my splayed hand and just slightly darker than the surrounding skin. I would have thought it was a tattoo, except that it appeared slightly raised, like a welt.

My eyes traced the shape again, its familiarity shocking me. This wasn't possible.

"Who sent this design to them?" I demanded immediately.

"No one, sire," T'ral replied, sounding tired and a touch baffled.

My anger at the humans came roaring back. "Impossible. There is some trickery going on. Is this the 'rash' that fool spoke of? Someone will pay for this insult. If this female was in on this hoax, she will pay dearly. If she was not, then the person who has marked her thusly will pay with his life. The humans aren't even supposed to know about this symbol."

Baelon moved to my side and looked over my shoulder at the screen. His imperturbable smile vanished, and he blanched. "Can you zoom in on the marking?" he inquired. "Is this an image enhancement trick?"

T'ral was already shaking his head in the negative. "I considered all of these things, sire. I have my most trusted people scanning through all the transmissions to and from Earth from our first contact with them a decade and a half ago. In none of those transmissions is this design seen or described. Nor is any human aware of the significance of finding it on a female. That aspect of our reproductive cycle is not in any histories or culture abstracts we provided to the humans. There is no way they could have known." He licked his lips a bit nervously, and I just nodded at him to go on, speechless with anger still.

He took a steadying breath. "Once I started that research, I also had someone check to see if there had been tampering with the image. As far as we can tell, the photograph is a true one. The motif on her skin is real. We will not know more until we can examine her ourselves in three days' time."

"Impossible." I refused to believe that this could be anything but a sham. I continued studying the picture. Analyzing the shape of the emblem on the female's neck and shoulder, I shook my head. It was even in the exact spot a marriage mark would be. It was positioned perfectly on her right shoulder blade and up her neck, in just the place a spouse's hand would rest if she were standing at his right side and he had set a loving hand upon her. There was no way that a "rash" from a genetic inoculation could have spontaneously formed in the exact right shape and location.

I turned to T'ral, seething. "Check through the records once more. Go through them yourself if need be. See if it was on the hem of a formal uniform or on a medal or document the humans might have spied."

He held up a hand. "Sire, we looked. This design isn't used for anything like that. According to our law books, due to its symbolism, especially on a female, it is illegal to use it outside of its usual context. It certainly wouldn't show up on any formally approved designs or documents. Only a direct print from the Royal Seal by a member of your lineage can be used, never its mere image."

I stared at him, chest heaving. *Then how did it get on the back of a human volunteer for our breeding program?*

T'ral seemed to have the answers to any questions I could come up with before I could think of them. This, of course, was his job and what made him so critical in his position. Yet every time he came back at me with facts, he frustrated my urge to deny the whole thing.

My hands were growing sore, and I realized I had been gripping the data screen quite tightly. I looked up from it and scowled. "T'ral, we need to figure this out. Find out how my family crest wound up on a human female's neck, marking her as my life mate!" I threw the data screen across the training room where it shattered into pieces.

CHAPTER 3
EVA

I need another blanket, dammit.

I wriggled and drew up my knees to my stomach to try to hold in my heat, but it was no use. I just got colder and colder.

Worse, I was still feeling sick. I sneezed, the inside of my nostrils itching and hurting and my ears stuffy. *I'm fucking miserable. Why the hell did I agree to this shit?*

I wished I was back home. Ivy would know how to make me feel better. She'd probably heat broth in a cup I could wrap my hands around and give me an extra blanket to hold in the added warmth. We would talk as I started feeling better, and I would quickly know that things were all right.

I could feel the tears begin to fill my eyes and then trickle down my cheeks. I blinked them away angrily. Joining the program had been my idea. *I can do this.*

I pulled the one puny blanket tighter across my shoulders. It rubbed on the still tender mark, making me wince. The faint irritation reminded me why I couldn't go back home.

I had been chosen.

I was it…the last surviving test subject to go through the program without quitting.

The others had already washed out and gone home, according to my medical monitor, Dr. Ostrov. I envied them, even as determined as I was to hang in there where they hadn't.

I had given my word that I would go through with this, and I never went back on my word. Even more importantly, I was doing this for Ivy and her kids—Trevor, Mark, Josephine, and little Jaylynn. They had taken me in and treated me like family when I hadn't been able to stay at the Children's Ward any longer.

It was my turn to take care of them. That was the promise I had made myself.

Participating in an off-world genetic surrogacy program had made me into a guinea pig now getting over a damn alien flu, but it paid very well.

Ivy had been against this idea, but I had talked her into it. The fifty thousand credit sign-on bonus had helped sway her, especially after it had freed her from the mortgage on her housing pod.

Now, the kids were going to a real school instead of dialing in on a third-rate computer, and Ivy could go back to her job full time. Her letters these days were full of hope, and she was happy to admit how wrong she had been.

I couldn't disappoint her now. I didn't care what I had to go through.

We had seen the advertisement in the posts on the vid screens in the square. Ivy had mocked the Peace Opportunity Program when we'd read the fine print about the "dying alien race" and "advanced technology." But something about it had tugged at my heartstrings.

Afterward, I couldn't let the idea go. I kept imagining how awful that would be. *So few children that the whole race was dying out? Only one female born in every two thousand births? Having advanced technology that still couldn't fix the situation?*

How helpless they must feel.

I knew I might not be able to help, but the five thousand credits the program had offered just to let them try to see if my DNA was compatible with the alien DNA had seemed like a godsend. *There was no way I will be accepted*, I had thought. All they would do was test me, say I was incompatible, give me my credits, and send me home. Or so I had thought.

Ivy had worried so much when I had gotten my offer letter from the program, announcing that my genes were theoretically compatible with those of the mysterious aliens. I had been pretty scared, but after thinking about it, I had decided to go for it.

Ivy and I wrote to each other as much as we could on the monitored communications system. I always did my best to reassure her that I was doing fine. But the truth was, the experiments were grueling and sometimes very painful.

The retrovirus therapy they had used to bridge the genetic gap between humans and aliens had all sorts of weird effects on me. Fevers, light sensitivity, hallucinations, and finally, this damn flu or whatever it was. It sure felt like the worst flu I had ever had.

My muscles and joints were stiff and ached. Shifting to my other side to face the wall was torturous. Of course, the shapeless hospital gown-thing they'd given me to wear got twisted under my curvy hips. I pushed myself up and caught sight of the skin on my arms. Now I really wanted to cry. My beautiful skin. Usually the color of the specialty hot caramels we'd save up credits for during the holiday season, it was now ashy and pale, with a sallow look. At least that painful all-over rash was gone, aside from the welts running down the side of my neck and my shoulder blade.

My head pounded with pain. I was stronger than yesterday, at least, and I thought I might be able to get up and deal with it without calling the nurse. I hated feeling helpless.

While up on one hip, I glanced around my assigned cubicle for a cup for water. *Nothing.* Once again, whoever handled room supplies had forgotten something. I'd have to get a handful of water from the sink in the lavatory.

Groaning in pain, I rolled to the edge of the cot and placed my feet on the cold tile. It was a very good thing that I was wearing socks. My feet still ached as the chill radiated through them. I stood to my full height of five foot one and immediately slumped just a bit. I was much too tired and achy to walk with my usual attention to posture and attempt to flatten my tummy. A shuffling walk was all I could manage. But at least I was walking again.

Whatever they'd done to me was still hurting like hell. At times like this, I felt like I'd been so wrong to go through with this. I comforted myself that at least my family would do better from now on, no matter what happened to me.

The advert had called for healthy females between the ages of eighteen and thirty. It had asked for "clean, healthy, of sound mind, literate" and a whole host of other things including "being able to bear children without having been pregnant on previous occasions." It had struck us as no weirder than some ovum donor programs I had considered before. It was just that the beneficiaries in this case weren't human.

I'd bathed and taken great care with my appearance the day we had gone for my test. My thick, curly fluffs of black hair had been tamed with oil and conditioner, and I'd pulled it back off my face to draw attention to my almond-shaped eyes. Ivy had found me a dress of deep blue that accented my generous curves. It had given me a touch more confidence to arrive dressed up, and I would wonder later if the choice had affected their decision.

Ivy had walked me to the Medical Ward, where the line to sign up had stretched all the way around the block. The queue had moved quickly, though, as only one in ten women had been let through the gates.

The gate personnel had turned away the elderly ladies, the coughing or crutch-wielding, the ones with babes at breast or at hand, and the pregnant ones. They had refused entry to prepubescent girls, no matter what their mothers had said to try to get them in, and the tears of the desperate girls had not swayed them.

The guards at the gate were unyielding in their decision. They would take one glance at the woman walking toward them and, in an instant, decide whether she met the criteria or not. When my time had come, I had hugged Ivy quickly and strode for the entry, sure in my knowledge that I met all the prerequisites.

Sure enough, checkpoint one had let me through with a smile. Checkpoint two had required a brief pause at a table, where I had been made to place my hand on a scanner and speak my name in order to confirm my identity. They then had handed me a small screen device. I had to read the information on the screen and answer some questions about what I had read—proof that I was literate. Many women had been turned back then. Even on Earth itself, literacy had dropped like a stone since the public schools had closed.

The third checkpoint had been a mental health screening by a psychiatrist. The doctor's signature had been required for the credits to be transferred. I had sighed in relief after he'd signed the screen, sending the credits winging into Ivy's bank account, one less thing to worry about.

A month later, the offer letter welcoming me to the program had come, shocking us both.

According to the letter, only five of us had qualified for the program. I had wondered at that. *Five? How could five women help a race of people that needed thousands?*

All the more reason for me to tough it out once the pain had begun, and it had. Medical screenings, blood tests, and physical exams. They had checked my heart, my breathing, my skin, my eyes, my hearing, my breasts, my womb, and my vagina. Nothing had been left un-probed. It had been painful and humiliating, but I had never complained.

And when they had finished, instead of getting back my lovely dress, I had been given my current outfit, which was changed for an identical one every morning. It consisted of a long, shapeless pale blue gown that stretched just a bit across my breasts and hips, and an actually nice, cozy pair of socks. The lack of a bra had given me backaches for a while, but then I had gotten sick and had spent most of my time lying down.

Now, I was finally recovering—and I was also, officially, the last woman standing. I leaned against the lavatory sink to catch my breath. *Crap, this is humiliating.* It felt like most of my muscle tone was gone.

On a daily basis, I had walked most everywhere I needed to go for my life in New Atlanta, only occasionally catching the tram. I had considered myself in pretty good shape. Good enough that a ten-foot hobble should not have exhausted me.

If whatever they had injected me with had made me this sick, no wonder they didn't want those who had already felt ill; this stuff would've killed them. Maybe that was why they had kept the five of us isolated from each other, to prevent cross-contamination with any of those screwed-up alien diseases.

It's too bad, though. The loneliness was the worst part of all of this. If it weren't for the letters from home, I think I would have gone a little crazy. I turned on the water and slurped down a few cupped handfuls quickly, taking the edge off my headache.

Maybe a hot shower would help ease some of my aches and chills. Certainly couldn't hurt. I reached into the tiny shower closet and turned on the water. Steam immediately began billowing around me. I breathed it in, enjoying the idea of the water pounding on my skin. I shut the water off and got ready for my shower.

Back when I had lived in the Children's Ward as a kid, showers had been rationed. We had gotten one every other day as wards of the state, on a timer that had stopped the water after five minutes.

While I had been living with Ivy and the kids in her living pod, the water shortages had started, and I had truly learned what rationing meant. In her small living quarters, we had gotten a full shower of seven minutes once a week, and we had made do with cleansing-pad sponge baths every other day, no matter what.

As a current "guest" of the Medical Ward, I could take a shower several times a day if I wanted to and had the ability. But after everything I had been through, I considered that idea so wasteful that I would never allow myself the indulgence. So, I had gone back to five-minute showers, shutting off the water to lather up.

Now that the damn fever had broken last night, the doctors were eager to get me back on my feet, but it would be a while before I was anything close to camera-ready. I wanted to try to be at my best when the Peace Opportunity Ambassadors came to call. Cleaning off the sweat of my illness seemed like a pretty good first step.

I heard noises out in the main room while I bathed, but I ignored them. I knew that while I was in the shower, my gown and socks would be whisked away and replaced with fresh ones, as would the sheets on my bed and that short, inadequate blanket, which they never added to no matter how often I asked.

I knew the doctors were always watching me. I had understood that from the beginning, and I had figured I'd better get used to it. I knew I'd signed up to be a lab rat.

Not many knew anything about this alien race. They were the first who had made direct contact with us. But I knew that the treaty was important. It had already netted Earth several technological break-throughs, including the use of hyperspace tubes. But our new friends had been very tight-lipped about a lot of aspects of their world and culture.

The doctors had told me that some of the aliens had joined the observation group that monitored me 24/7 through the surveillance system. I didn't even get privacy in the bath. *I can feel their eyes on me even now.*

Shit. I hate this part. Stripping with a damn audience. Somehow, it always seemed so much more intimate than either washing or dressing again, or maybe it was that I had to get used to it every time. I looked longingly at the streaming, steaming water, and kicked off my socks.

Suddenly, I felt new eyes upon me—a strong, distinct sensation that made me feel more self-conscious. I straightened up and glanced out the bathroom door into the cubicle, but it did not seem that anyone had entered beyond a bland-faced attendant stripping the bed. She wasn't even looking my way.

"Hello?" My voice creaked and cracked like a teenager's. I could still feel those eyes on me, so I looked up to where I knew there was a camera in a corner of the lavatory ceiling.

I stared at the camera, whose blind gaze had taken on a strange sort of life. I didn't know how I knew, but someone was watching me through it. Someone…special…

My stomach did a quick flip, and my breath became shallow as a totally unexpected flood of desire washed over me.

If the program was successful, I was told I would be paired with the alien who was my genetic match. And depending on how well I got along with the alien, they might request a traditional mating with me. Otherwise, they would ask to harvest some of my ova, which they could use for in vitro fertilization.

I didn't know how I knew, but I was absolutely certain as to who was watching me. It was the alien I'd been matched with. And the whole idea of his staring at me as I undressed made my toes curl from lust.

I wanted him. I wanted him to see me, to touch me, to possess me. Whoever he was, somehow, he had already captured my interest, sight unseen.

Without taking my eyes away from the camera, I faced the lens squarely and moved my hands to the fastenings at the shoulder of my gown. Slowly, I untied the lacing. I pushed the cloth to one side to expose my shoulder and let the sleeve slide down one arm. I repeated the process on the other side while holding the gown in place across my large breasts. All at once, I released the gown and let it slide down my body and fall into a pile onto the floor.

Tilting my head back and thrusting my chin up slightly, I ran my hands down my naked body. I trailed them from my shoulders down to my breasts, where my dusky-hued nipples were hard and sensitive. I cupped my heavy breasts briefly and then continued smoothing my hands down my ribs and over my belly to where my thighs met, the delta of my sex, and the soft tangle of curls. I stood there for a moment, letting my mystery partner look, then with a deliberate movement, I reached behind me and turned the water back on. I slowly stepped backward into the shower and under the cascading water.

I kept one hand covering my mound and trailed the other back up my body to my breast. I let the water pour over my body for a moment while I rolled one responsive, aching nipple between my fingers and slipped one finger of the other hand between the folds of my sex.

My lips parted, and a moan escaped me. I was much wetter than I had expected to be. Still staring at the camera, I brought the finger, now covered with evidence of my arousal, up to my lips and placed it in my mouth.

At the very same moment, I slammed the curtain to the shower closed. My alien had had enough of a show, and he could damn well come and talk to me before he saw anything else.

CHAPTER 4
RAEVU

The woman from the image haunted me every moment of the two days it took for us to get through quarantine. T'ral had his best people looking into how my life mate could possibly be a human woman, but their research had turned up no results so far. I didn't know whether this Eva had stuck in my mind because of the shock of seeing the mark on her, or because we truly were meant for each other. Either way, I had to know more about her.

Too bad I had to go through that shifty, incompetent ambassador to do so.

I faced the main communication screen directly. I'd spent time with humans before. The lower ranks were easily impressed and easily overwhelmed by appearances. From our greater height and muscle mass, to our weaponry and armor, to the hairlessness of our fertile males, we were exotic to humans, and thus both exciting and a little frightening.

To placate the humans, we all wore human-styled clothing. I had my uncle Baelon and an elite squad of handpicked soldiers, who had all trained with me, dressed in identical black outfits, similar to Earth military uniforms.

On our planet, uniforms were unnecessary. Individual countries had been unified under our rule, so we only battled against dangerous beasts or aliens from other planets. But humans seemed to have a respect for extreme conformity in clothing, so we had chosen to take advantage.

As for T'ral and me, our uniforms were business suits. Pants, jackets, and shirts, in somber shades of gray and black—paired with bold but useless strips of cloth the humans called "ties." The tailor we had seen on Earth on our last visit had called them "power suits." I didn't feel any particular power resting in the suit, but it would serve well to help us blend in a bit when walking around Earth-side buildings and markets.

Kymptar signaled that the transmission was ready to come through, and I nodded to let him know to go ahead. Immediately, Reynauld's face appeared larger than life on the huge screen. I suspected he was using a tight close-up to try to appear intimidating and hide his fidgeting hands.

But that close up, his nose looked like a massive, pasty mountain, and his eyes squinted into slits to focus on us through the view-screen. After a murmured comment behind me, several of the squad chuckled. I fought down a smirk, keeping my face composed.

I motioned to Kymptar to attempt to zoom out so that Reynauld's face wasn't looming over the lot of us and asked, "What news?"

Reynauld looked as nervous as he had sounded on the communication two days earlier. Of course, he was looking at a conference chamber full of soldiers in their prime and the two most powerful males of a planet. I brushed that thought aside and waited.

He blotted perspiration off his balding head with a handkerchief and pulled at his collar. Two telltale signs of discomfort my father and uncle never would have allowed me, and I'd never allow from one of my soldiers or other underlings. "Your Majesty Raevumon, we look forward to seeing you this evening."

Dryly, I replied, "The miracles of modern advancements in your quarantine procedures ever astound us." It had taken twenty times as long as a bioscan back home, but we had held back on that technology upon discovering that Earth was suffering so many…setbacks. "Now, please, an update on the female?"

He cleared his throat and pulled a data pad in front of him to read from. "Her condition is stable. No changes. She still has flu-like symptoms, although we've tested her for the flu and it's come up negative. We're not sure how to treat the symptoms since it isn't actually the flu. What we've tried so far just isn't working." He scrolled through information on his pad. "All other vital signs are fine and normal. The female subject…"

I started slightly when he said "subject." Yes, I had been calling her the female, to differentiate her from a woman of my race, but I certainly didn't like her to be referred to as a subject. We did not understand why yet, but the mark on her indicated she was to be my life mate. It still didn't sit well with me, but given that I had never expected to have a mate outside of a laboratory auto-womb, I wanted to give this experiment a chance. If there was any possibility that she was mine, I needed to make certain she was not mistreated.

Reynauld continued, "…is handling isolation fairly well. Her appetite is meager, but she could stand to lose a few pounds anyway." One nostril quirked in a brief expression of disdain that really annoyed me.

"Stop. What did you just say? Isolation? Losing weight?" My back stiffened. *What are they doing to my mate?*

"Well, yes." Reynauld blinked his eyes at the communication screen. "Due to the unknown nature of the flu-like symptoms and the strange rash on her neck and shoulder, we thought it best to keep her quarantined. And, as she is nauseous, the doctors put her on a bland diet. She just isn't eating a whole lot of the food. Not to worry, though, Your Majesty, she is under constant video surveillance, so we will know at once if there is any real problem."

I couldn't believe my ears. "You have her under constant camera observation, with no privacy?"

Behind me, I heard T'ral and Baelon exchange a few hurried words. Baelon muttered an order to one of the soldiers, who hastened off to do his bidding.

The ambassador breezed on, not seeming to notice my increasing anger. He talked about treating one of his own people like a laboratory animal as casually as if it were something that happened every day.

"Oh, yes. Doctors and scientists are watching her every move. They do so in day and night shifts. If they believe they've missed something, they just have to rewind the recordings and review past data.

"I'll open the live feed right now for you." Reynauld turned back to his screen and tapped a few buttons. His image was replaced with that of a sterile hospital room and an empty bed. There was no window, no images on the walls, and the flat-screen monitor in one wall was dark and lifeless. The only furniture sitting beside the bed was a nightstand and a very uncomfortable looking chair.

"It looks like a prison cell," I observed with an edge to my voice. Out of sight of the communicator, I clenched a fist hard.

"Hmm. Maybe she's in the bathroom," Reynauld's voice came through loud and clear over the live-stream. He did not seem to have noticed my comment or to have a problem with the analogy if he had. The display on the screen flipped to one of a woman in a small bathing chamber, and I felt the ship surge beneath my feet. We were now breaking out of orbit and preparing much more hastily than usual for landfall. I'd instructed Baelon and T'ral to get me to the heathen planet Earth to collect my life mate as soon as possible—*our safety be damned.* My female needed me.

With rapt attention, I watched as the female stooped over slightly and kicked off her foot coverings. I was overcome by a need to see her face. My wish was granted after a moment as she straightened up and glanced about the room, as if she could sense me watching her.

"Hello?" Her voice was scratchy but still low and sweet, and her face stunning, surrounded by a cloud of black hair. Her skin was the color of the honey trees back home, and her eyes a dark, rich-soil brown. Over plump lips sat a broad, adorably shaped nose that turned up slightly at the end. Her cheeks were high and flushed with color at the moment.

I wanted her to look at me…to see me to know that I was watching. Abruptly, she glanced up at where the camera must have been placed. Our eyes held. It was as if we had eye contact even through the camera connection. I couldn't look away, even if I had wanted to.

She faced the camera squarely and moved her hands to the fastenings at the tops of her covering. Enticingly, she untied the lacing while my eyes slowly widened, and then she pushed the garment off her shoulders.

My breath turned shallow. A flood of desire washed over me. I licked my lips, mouth suddenly dry. The covering was now held in place across her breasts by one arm, then she moved her arm to her side and the covering puddled onto the floor.

Baelon barked a command. I heard all my soldiers, T'ral, and Kymptar turn and face away from the communication screen. None would look at the bare body of the woman who had the mark of my mate upon her.

My jaw dropped. She was beautiful—flawless dark skin, large breasts, and generous hips. I wanted to run my hands over her skin and feel how soft it was.

Almost as if she could hear me, she began to run her hands down her naked body, from her shoulders to her breasts, where perfect nipples were already pebbled. She cupped her breasts, and I could almost feel their delicious weight in my own hands.

She smoothed her hands over her ribs and across her belly to where her thighs met. The movement pushed her breasts together and caused her to arch her back slightly. My shaft stirred in response to her gesture of invitation.

At the juncture of her thighs was a tangle of curls that she covered teasingly with one hand. Slowly, my temptress straightened and stepped backward into the shower and under the streaming water.

I caught my breath at the sight of the water making her skin glisten. She trailed one hand back up her body to a breast. To my surprise, she rolled one responsive nipple between the fingers of one hand and slipped one finger of the other hand between the folds of her sex. Her plump lips parted, and I heard a moan escape.

My own breath emptied my lungs in a burst, and my arousal could no longer be hidden. My erection strained the fabric at the front of my trousers as I temporarily lost the ability to blink. She brought a finger, now shimmering with evidence of her passion, up to her lips and placed it in her mouth, and then she snapped the curtain to the shower closed. I'd been concentrating so much on the one finger I hadn't seen her other hand move. *She's beautiful and amazing.* I blinked my eyes a few times and cleared my throat.

Reynauld's oily voice came over the intercom. "Well, that was unusual. I can assure you, Your Majesty, she has never done that before and never will again. We will take steps to let her know that such behavior is unseemly." His face replaced the live video feed.

Immediately, my lust was quenched, and my anger flared. "No, you absolutely will not."

He blinked several times and peered at me. "Beg pardon?"

"Ambassador Reynauld, you need to remember that this female is under the protection of our agreement. There are several things I expect to be taken care of before we arrive at your Medical Ward in…" I paused briefly to be updated on our ETA.

T'ral filled in for me, "Four of their hours, sire." T'ral and Baelon had gotten the captain to halve our expected arrival time. If I hadn't been so angry, I would have been impressed.

"Four hours. In the meantime, my adviser, T'ral, will be sending a docket of our expectations regarding her treatment, and they will be carried out." I locked eyes with the ambassador, whose gaze wavered, and he nodded mutely.

I went on, "To begin with, she will have new accommodations that are worthy of habitation by an intelligent being, not a prison cubicle." I stared at him coldly. "And no more isolation."

"I'm sorry, Your Highness, I don't understand the problem. She has been treated just like the other subjects of the program—"

"Well, no wonder she's sick and the others are dead. Whose idea was it to treat the women we are seeking as compatible mates worse than we treat murderers? Or have such poor quality controls on your experiments?" My voice was rising.

"Your Majesty, I assure you that we have done as much as we can within budget limitations—" He was probably nervous about the possibility of losing the treaty and, with it, any chance at the rest of our technology. If that happened on his watch, I could only imagine the trouble he'd be in, and he would most definitely deserve it.

I folded my arms, scowling. "That 'rash' on her back is part of our heritage. That symbol marks the life mate of the royal heir. This 'female subject' of yours will be my queen. Treat her as such, and get the damned cameras off of her."

Leaving Reynauld gaping like a fish, I stormed from the room and to my quarters. I needed to change clothes and return to the training room. Too many emotions were roiling through me. Baelon and blade practice would help me work them off.

But what I really wanted as I walked away was to storm the Medical Ward and rescue my mate from the humans. Not just because of my disgust with any regime that would treat medical patients in such a fashion, but because I had told the truth. Now that I had accepted it, I knew. *She is mine,* and I would not allow the humans to continue harming her.

CHAPTER 5
EVA

A flurry of noise woke me from a sound sleep. A skinny blond nurse was bustling about my room. After two weeks of not seeing a single soul but an attendant who never spoke to or looked at me, I stared at her in wonder.

I wasn't sure why she was here. All my vital signs had been taken by sensory equipment placed about the room. When they needed to draw blood, they spoke over an intercom, and I slipped my arm into a hole in the wall where invisible, but gentle, hands manipulated a port in my hand to get what they needed for their many tests.

Now to see a person—a real person—delighted me. I sat up on my cot carefully. "Hi."

"Oh, good! You're awake." With a cheerful, no-nonsense manner, the nurse smiled at me. "My name is Tammy. Let's get you dressed."

"Dressed?" My voice cracked since I hadn't used it in a bit. I cleared my throat and tried again. "I am dressed."

The smile widened slightly, and her voice warmed a little. "No, dear, in street clothes. You don't need to be in the clinic gown anymore. They're removing you from quarantine, so it's time for better accommodations for you."

I set my feet on the cold tile floor and used the edge of the bed to help me stand. As soon as she saw how wobbly I was, Tammy came over to help me. She had a small bag with her. I looked at it curiously.

"New clothes." She grinned at me and gave me a conspirator's wink. "They're a gift."

"Gift?" I was bewildered. *Who would give me new clothes?* I spoke up hastily, "The clothes I came in were fine. Clean, well-fitting, and quite pretty. I need them back, please. Can you find them? Blue dress? Black flats? Plain underthings, but all I had, so…"

"Not anymore, honey!" She laughed and set the bag on my bed.

"I still want them back." I reached for the lacing on my hospital gown, loosening it. "You know how it is when you have a nice outfit for the first time in a while, right?"

She nodded, seeming to get it immediately. "Okay, I'll look into it for you."

I eyed Tammy as she walked into the bathroom to give me privacy to change, a little wary of her sincerity after the cold, impersonal treatment I had gotten for months. But she seemed nice, so once she shut the curtain, I turned my attention to the unexpected gift.

Out of the bag, I pulled a dress, shoes, bra, and panties—all in silk, even matching shoes. Everything was color-coordinated in shades of rose, pink, and cream, with little touches of green, reminding me of a flower.

The bra and panties matched. I'd never owned matching lingerie that wasn't stark white, but these were a deep ivory color with sage green embroidery around the edges. I stripped down and tried them on. Both the bra and the panties fit perfectly; apparently, the full-body medical scan they had given me more than once doubled as a pretty good clothes-fitting guesser.

Over underwear, I pulled on a cream dress that fitted close to my breasts and skimmed my waist, but then widened across my hips and swung freely about my knees. The pumps had just enough of a heel to have me feeling feminine without having to worry about my balance.

After I was dressed, I called for Tammy, who came out saying, "Now about your hair…"

I got very worried. There was no way a blond government nurse was also experienced with the particulars of African-American hair styling. I liked my natural curls just the way they were, fluffy and not straightened.

But Tammy pleasantly surprised me again by pulling a rose-and-green scarf and some black rubber bands out of the bag, along with a wide-toothed comb and soft-bristled brush. "I didn't know how you like to wear your hair, so I thought I'd bring you some gear and options."

Oh, honey, where the hell have you been this whole time? I was completely amazed. *Was Tammy new, or was she just the nurse in charge of quarantine discharge?* I guessed the latter—she seemed completely at ease in the weird little cubicle.

Her little bag even held a desktop mirror and some makeup. We decided on a braid, but I held on to the silk scarf, tying it around my throat as a decoration. She helped me add some eyeliner and mascara, and even had some scented moisturizer for my dry skin. A few minutes later, I was finally ready to leave this place I'd called home for ten weeks.

Tammy guided me down corridor after corridor. The first few were obviously hospital-like in nature. After a few twists and turns, we came to a set of utilitarian hallways that seemed familiar.

When I heard the sound of children at play, I recognized that we were right outside the section of the Children's Ward where I had grown up. I frowned, wondering what we were doing here.

With just a few more turns, we came to an amazing architectural lobby hall with luxury chairs, beautiful carpets, multiple corner pendants at varying heights, sculptural side tables, and rock-crystal overhead chandeliers. It was full of decorations of exotic design— reliefs and sculptures of some strange multicolored metal, which I immediately knew came from the aliens. A fountain was shaped like a narrow-towered castle, and terrariums were filled with odd, wildly colored plants. I stared at wonder after wonder.

I was raised this close to luxury?

It seemed that the cafeteria shared the kitchens of the Children's Ward with the complex workers and its guests. After passing the cafeteria, we went down the hallway behind the kitchen area and straight into the opulence of the guest suites.

Rich fabrics, multihued crystal lights, and more gleaming statues greeted my every glance. I tried not to let my mouth drop open, but I felt like a tourist on her first visit to the big city. Tammy took me straight past the elevator bank, bypassing a check-in desk. I guessed I was expected.

We went down a short stretch of corridor where Tammy led us into a stretch of floor-to-ceiling windows. From my spot, I could see straight down a long street and into the heart of New Atlanta. I should have felt relief, finally getting a chance to see outside, but as I stared at the city spread out beneath us, it looked…desolate. The city covered all the land in metal and concrete. It was an ugly grey area with no trees or grass.

So many people.

So much excess.

So much…of everything except green.

It's so damn sad.

The glorious, sparkling glass and metal gleamed at me through the windows, with only the swarms of people giving it any hint of life.

"Come on," called Tammy, coaxing me away from the windows. "Just a bit farther."

We turned down a short hallway to a set of double doors. After using a keycard for entry, she pushed open the doors, and I smelled food on the warm air that wafted out.

I was ushered into an apartment that easily could have fit four of Ivy's flat in the front room alone. Directly in front of me was a sitting area with a chaise longue, a couch, and two posh chairs covered in deep sea-green fabric. To my left, beyond an alcove with a smaller couch in front of a monitor, was a set of gold-inlaid double doors. To my right, a dining table with enough chairs for eight people was set with several covered dishes.

Tammy's smile vanished, and she once again became no-nonsense. "Through those doors is your private bedroom and bath. No one will go in there without your express permission, although it has already been stocked with other clothing and necessities for you. There's a small kitchenette beyond the dining table. The other side of the alcove is a restroom for visitors. Here's the intercom unit—" she pointed to a device on the wall above the small couch "—in case you need anything at all. If you want to go out into the city, there's a car available for you."

I stood there numbly, taking in the place and everything she was telling me. The contrast with what I had gotten used to in the Medical Ward left me wondering what part of the experiments this was. *Something psychological? Maybe a moral ethics test? Is this where they are stashing me for a news crew, so they can pretend they didn't have me in solitary in that damn cubicle for months?*

"Where are the cameras?" I interrupted, looking around.

"What do you mean?" Tammy looked genuinely confused.

"The cameras? Where are they located? I'm not seeing the little lenses like I could in my cubicle or the bathroom." I checked around again and shook my head.

Tammy laughed a bit nervously, "Oh! Don't be silly! There aren't any cameras in here. Why would anyone be watching you?"

Suddenly she didn't seem that trustworthy anymore. I looked at her a bit dubiously as her chuckle trickled off. She blinked several times and took a deep breath. "So anyway. Where was I?"

"There's a car available," I prompted after a long pause. I kept eye contact with her now, which seemed to make her nervous. I knew she was aware of what I had gone through, the isolation, the tests, the sickness, and the constant monitoring. But after a moment, I offered a tiny, flat smile. Maybe she was being monitored herself, even now.

"Oh right, the car. Just use the intercom to schedule rides." She brightened considerably and went on with her instructions. "And if there's anyone you would like to see, call to Geoffrey, and he'll arrange it immediately."

My mind ignored the unfamiliar name and latched on to another detail. "Like, to see? As in visitors? I can have visitors?" My heart soared. Maybe I could see Ivy and the kids. Make sure they were all right. Let them know that, in spite of all this craziness, I was too.

"I'm sure. Geoffrey can also arrange for any books or other reading material you'd like. The monitor over there is voice-activated, so you just have to request a show or a channel, and it'll get rolling for you." It sounded like she had given this speech before.

"I'd like to see my family, then, please." I wanted so much to surprise Ivy and the kids. Maybe see if they could stay overnight with me in this luxurious place, until it was decided whether I was going off-planet or not.

"You'll have time to make those arrangements as soon as we're done here," she replied patiently. "For now, I'm sure you're hungry. There's food in the dishes on the table. Enjoy!"

Enjoy? The whole situation was so bizarre that, this time, I fixed her with a very suspect stare. *Why had they gone from treating me like a lab rat to treating me like a pampered guest?*

Her smile started to crumble and then firmed again, and she lifted her chin. "Well, I'd better get back to the medical wing. Thank you for being such a great patient to work with." With a wide smile, Tammy left the room and closed the doors quietly behind her.

Wow. Okay. I don't know what's changed, but I guess I should take advantage of it while I can. But still, I felt wary. I crossed my arms under my breasts, hugging my waist.

Slowly, I walked around the sitting area and over to the large picture windows that made up one entire wall of the apartment. I could see out over the whole Government Center and into the city beyond—an even better view than from the huge windows outside the cafeteria.

Again, the entire landscape looked both majestic and sterile. The Center was pristine. It was our government building, hospital, school, public housing, and civic center all in one place. It glittered and gleamed coldly, threw sharp flashes of light off corners and windows, and bustled with movement as people went about their business.

New Atlanta beyond provided a sharp contrast. What movement there was seemed furtive and skulking in the dingy streets. A haze hung sluggishly over all the buildings, which hunkered down against each other in various states of disrepair.

Way off in the distance, I could just barely make out the edge of the city. Beyond it lay a faint green strip. The beginnings of Landover, the designated suburban zone, where those who could afford it lived in clean housing away from the poverty of the city.

Ivy's living pod had been moved to a better neighborhood once she had paid off her mortgage. Its new location was two-thirds of the way up one of the housing towers, well above the smog layer. We had thought of that little place as paradise, even after they had started cutting our water rations. But it had simply been a marginally better neighborhood in a slum that ran from the Center to the city outskirts.

Shaking off another wave of sadness, I turned away and went to check out my breakfast. I needed to calm down before I reached out to Ivy, and I had to figure out what to tell her.

Besides, the smell had me starving. It had been a long time since I had eaten food that actually smelled and tasted like food, instead of the pale, starchy paste that had become my staple during my illness.

I lifted up the platters' covers and peeked beneath to see the offerings. *Oh my God. There is so much food.* Pancakes and waffles, sausage, bacon, fried chicken, crepes, fruit salad, melon slices, and toast with what I guessed might actually be real butter, a goddamn feast. More than enough for me, Ivy, and her kids for this meal and possibly another, depending on how hungry they were.

I wondered at the promise of guests and glanced at the intercom. It occurred to me that I had no idea who Geoffrey was. Maybe he was the attendant on the other side of the intercom. *Should I try it?* I shrugged my shoulder. *What the hell? They could just tell me no.*

For a centerpiece, the table had a basket of fruit. I reached out and plucked a handful of grapes off the bunch and took them with me over to the intercom, munching on a few to take the edge off.

Taking a deep breath and with a firm grasp on my most assertive voice, I pressed the buzzer. Immediately, a rich, cultured male voice responded. "Hello, Ms. Knight, this is Geoffrey. How may I help you?"

"Geoffrey. Nurse Tammy told me I could have visitors, and I could go out into the city. Is this possible?" I felt my stomach do a little flip of apprehension and excitement. I had missed my family so much.

"Of course, ma'am."

"I would like a car brought around. I want to go collect my adoptive family and bring them back here to eat with me." I couldn't stand the idea of stuffing my belly while Ivy and those sweet kids tried filling their bellies with ration packets and a lot of water.

"Very good, ma'am. May I suggest, however, that as you've been ill, I contact Mrs. Fuller instead, and I'll send a car for her and her children? Just bring them to you? That way the food is fresher and your energy levels stay up, ma'am." His voice was precise, calm, reasonable, and without a touch of Tammy's shiftiness.

I blinked in surprise. *Who is this man? And how did he know about Ivy and her kids?* This man knew so much about me without my telling him anything. I glanced about the room again to see if I could spot where the cameras might be. *In the light fixtures? Part of the artwork on the walls? The mirrors? Or the window frames?*

Wait, calm down. This guy was assigned to me. He's part of the staff. He must have access to my medical data. I was being paranoid after my ordeal, and I shook my head at myself. "All right, Geoffrey," I acquiesced. "That'll be fine."

"Very good, ma'am. We'll prepare enough food for company for lunch, then. If you'll let me know when you're finished with your breakfast, I'll have someone come and clear it away."

"Um. Okay, I can do that." I hesitated. "Can I ask a favor?"

"I beg your pardon, ma'am?" He sounded very curious, as if the request were novel. "Please elaborate."

"There are a lot of kids at the Children's Ward who won't get a chance to eat food like this very often. Can I donate what I don't use?" I knew it was a weird request, but it was the only way I'd feel like I could settle my conscience about the rich meal. It just didn't feel right to eat so much otherwise.

"I will inquire after the matter with the kitchen staff. It should not be a problem, provided none of the children have prohibitive allergies." He sounded so smooth and calm that he reminded me somehow of talking to a teaching artificial intelligence system.

"Good. I will let you know when I'm finished." I went back to the table, my mouth starting to water.

"Thank you, ma'am." And the voice was gone.

I stood for a moment, still a little confused by the experience, and then sank down onto a plush chair. I opened several of the platters to see my selections. The options nearly overwhelmed me. In the end, I took a little bit of everything and felt like I was having a feast day. Scrambled eggs, we ate often enough, if the reconstituted powder counted anyway, but not real biscuits, much less real gravy. The bacon and sausage tasted divine. The two things I enjoyed the most were the coffee and the fresh fruit. When we bought our fruit, it was usually very close to being overripe. These grapes and bananas were perfect.

I saved some of those, as well as the apples, pears, and oranges for later. They were the kids' favorites. The coffee was heavenly. Long after I was finished eating, I sat and sipped at multiple cups of the heady brew, rich and aromatic—real stuff, without the greasy aftertaste of synthetics. This coffee tasted like it had been ground from real beans, just like Ivy's Christmas gift last year. I just sat and enjoyed.

A loud chime sounded throughout the room. I jumped, startled. "What was that?"

To my surprise, Geoffrey's voice immediately answered over the intercom, "Ms. Knight, that is your doorbell. Ambassador Reynauld is here to see you. May I send him up?"

I feel myself tense up and set aside my cup. "Who is Ambassador Reynauld? I don't know this person."

"Ambassador Reynauld is one of the Peace Opportunity Program Ambassadors, ma'am. He is one of the maintainers of the agreement between the Juhlians and Earth."

Juhlians. Finally, someone gave me the name for the race of aliens. When I'd first arrived here, my briefing on the aliens had been very short. "Oh." I paused. "Well, send him in, please, Geoffrey."

"Yes, ma'am. He'll be up directly." The connection silenced.

I wasn't sure what to do with myself. *Should I sit and be relaxed when he came in? Or answer the door attentively? Should I be aloof or bubbly? How should I treat this man who had helped to change my whole future for better or worse?*

I finally sat on the chaise longue, arranged my dress about me, and draped my arm across its back. I felt terribly awkward and pretentious. I gave a slight chuckle at myself and decided dramatic presentation was not quite my style. At the knock on the double doors, I stood, caught my balance, and took a step in that direction.

"I've got it, ma'am," came Geoffrey's voice. I heard the lock click, and I blinked in confusion.

"Who are you, Geoffrey?" I demanded.

"I am a computer interface, ma'am. I control the systems in your room, and also the auto-car assigned to you." His voice sounded stunningly human, except for its serenity, which suddenly made me sense.

"So, you aren't a person, a concierge waiting behind some desk?" I asked, quite bewildered.

"No, ma'am. Unless you want to think of me as your personal concierge. I am here for you and you alone." I could hear feet walking down the hall toward my suite.

This was too fascinating to brush aside yet. "What can you do?"

"I am connected with the system that encompasses the entire Center. I can control the doors and contact the staff of the building. I can control the communications within the building and the services, such as plumbing, room service, maintenance, communication…"

Wow. If a hacker ever took control of Geoffrey, they could throw the whole complex into utter chaos. "Okay. Thank you."

I needed to wrap my head around this Geoffrey concept. I had my own personal computer porter. I didn't even know what to do about that.

"Shall I let the ambassador through the inner door now, ma'am?" asked Geoffrey. "Otherwise he will be waiting."

Distractedly, I replied, "Yes. Please, Geoffrey."

The double doors swung open as if by magic. A short, balding, sweating man in a rumpled suit came scuttling toward me, his nose leading by almost an inch. I tried not to back away, but it was difficult. Something about him seemed kind of creepy.

"Hello, Eva. May I call you Eva?" He didn't wait for an actual answer. "Good. My name is Reynauld. You may call me Ambassador or just Reynauld. One of the two," he laughed, his voice thin and nervous.

Reynauld had two bland-looking male underlings with pads in hand accompanying him. They were industriously tapping and poking at their screens.

Before he got to me, I sat back down at the dining table, putting it between the two of us. The man was barely as tall as me, and his whole face and neck seemed covered in nervous sweat, but harmless-looking or not, I instinctively avoided letting him get too near.

"Am I interrupting anything?" asked Reynauld. "I thought I heard voices." His voice was blandly polite, but his little eyes searched my face closely.

I smiled primly as I picked up my mug. "I was speaking with Geoffrey."

"Oh, yes. It's here for your convenience. Whatever you might like, please let it know. It is supposed to make sure you get it." Reynauld rubbed his hands together. "Now, on to more important matters." He smiled unnervingly, and it didn't reflect in his eyes. "Your fiancé will be here in a matter of hours."

I just stared up at him as he stood across the table from me, not taking a seat. "Fiancé?" *Wait one goddamn minute. I was supposed to meet these alien guys and talk the whole thing over. How did we go from that to, boom, I'm engaged to some alien I've never met?*

"Yes, you shall be married to the ruler of Juhl. That's whom our Peace Opportunity is centered around. Hopefully, you can produce offspring for their sitting king, and the success will buy us more time to—umm, improve relations between our two people."

"Contract? Alien king? None of what you just said makes sense," I said.

Geoffrey's rich voice chimed in. "Ma'am? Sir? I have an incoming transmission from the Juhlian ship. King Raevu would like to speak with you. Do you have a moment?"

I felt terribly overwhelmed and confused. *Who are these people?* I knew I had signed up to help the Peace Opportunity Program and apparently, the Juhlian people. But suddenly, nothing made sense, and I just wanted to lie down and sleep again, alone. I needed time to process all this confusing shit.

Reynauld replied on our behalf. "Yes, Geoffrey. Connect us."

I crossed my arms, giving him a dirty look, but the asshole didn't seem to notice.

The wall in front of the low couch faded, blurred, and transformed into a projection screen. On that monitor, I saw several men. They were all handsome in an exotic way and definitely fit, but one in particular caught my eye. He was in a business suit similar to Reynauld's, but much better fitting. He was quite striking, even among the other gigantic men.

I let my eyes roam over him while he and Reynauld spoke. He seemed very tall. His suit was well-fitted and classically suited to his muscular physique. He was broad-shouldered and slim-hipped, and my eyes traveled up his body to his face. He was fascinating, and I couldn't look away from him.

His skin was a deep blue. He was completely hairless, either naturally or through shaving. The mix of his bald head, powerful body, and strong features seemed dangerous and enticing all at the same time. He had brow ridges that were dominant and expressive—over eyes as golden as a cat's. I suddenly wanted to run my fingers across his ears and over his scalp. *Could it be as smooth as it looked?*

Behind him, I saw movement and heads bending toward each other. They were chatting together about us. I smiled to myself, more than a little relieved by that very human behavior. Only, their words were not quite audible, yet I could understand a word here or there.

How is that possible? This was an alien language. I was human. I had never had contact with this language or culture before. *I couldn't understand their words, could I?*

I sat quietly, watching and listening, trying to learn as much as I could. From Reynauld and this enticing male, I was hearing an argument of sorts, the meaning of which grew clearer as I started to understand more of the alien language.

They were tossing terms back and forth, the delivery of something, a bad experiment, death and sickness, and agreements being dishonorably broken. As for the muttering behind the really hot alien male, I heard at least two different sorts of opinions.

One seemed to think I was a "beauty" who would "help them grow" and "give them hope." And the other was disparaging, "ugly" and "fruitless" were the kindest words they had for me. I couldn't tell which words were coming from which gathered heads. But I did notice one thing, their leader, the man in the suit, snarled back over his shoulder whenever anyone said anything negative about me, and the belittling voices quickly went silent.

Suddenly, the man defending me locked eyes with me. I felt an electric warmth run through me again, and I remembered the feeling of being watched, back in the bathroom. *This is him,* I realized suddenly, my cheeks going warm even as I felt myself start to get turned on. The person I put on that little show for.

"How do you say your name?" His voice was deep and almost gravelly. He smiled faintly for a moment, and I crossed my legs, suddenly very glad that I was sitting down.

"Eva. Long 'ee' at the beginning and soft ah sound at the end," I replied, trying to keep my voice calm.

"Interesting." He looked at me thoughtfully. "Your name means 'dawn' or 'hope' in the language of my ancestors."

"I know…" I said. But I didn't know where that knowledge came from. "What is your name?"

"Raevumon, but most just call me Raevu." His mouth twitched at one corner. I had to wonder if he was pulling my leg or not. He was devastatingly attractive, but his nickname sounded a little…silly.

"Raevumon. It's a very nice name. I'm glad to meet you," I said politely as I nodded a quick greeting. I didn't stand. I still didn't trust my legs to hold me up just yet.

"I look forward to meeting you in person, Eva. We'll be there in less than four of your hours." That deep, smooth voice sent a small shiver down my neck and back. The gleam in his eye reminded me again of the little performance I had put on for him the day before, and the shiver turned into a long shudder of need.

Holy shit. What is going on with me? My toes were curling in my shoes.

"Ma'am, alarm! Alarm!" Geoffrey's voice broke in, tinged with urgency, and I looked around, startled.

A loud rumble sounded from the hallway. I could smell smoke filling the chamber as a cloud of dust rolled in and swelled through the room. The four of us immediately started coughing as the noxious waves hit us.

On the screen, I could hear Raevu barking orders at his men and underlings. I continued to cough and blink my eyes against the roiling smoke. Through the now open doors, I saw several figures in black rush into the chamber. One of them held up a small device and pressed a control. Immediately, Geoffrey's alarm bell and voice stopped sounding. That couldn't be a good sign.

The smoke was making me very weak. I heard someone yell, "You won't take our women, alien. We won't let you. They're ours, you fucking freaks."

Rough hands picked me up, tossing me over a shoulder. I kicked and made contact with a sensitive spot, if the man's curse was any indication. *Good. You fucker!*

I lashed out, scratching his skin with my nails and trying to get the mask off his head. Surely, the cameras were recording, and they'd be able to identify him. I felt the rubber mask and filter slide off his face and heard him swear. I fought being carried and manhandled, but the smoke burned weirdly in my lungs, and I quickly grew weaker. I continued struggling before everything went black.

CHAPTER 6
RAEVU

And now, on top of everything else, the humans have allowed my mate to be kidnapped from right under their noses!

I could sense the warriors around me feeling just as agitated as I was. With more control than I thought I had, I held calm and kept myself still. We stood at the top of the ramp, waiting for the signal that we had finally landed and could lower the doors and descend.

I was not looking forward to speaking with Ambassador Reynauld in person. That squat, bumbling idiot had made a mess of everything so far. I made a note to have T'ral review the treaty and find a way to get Reynauld replaced. He had been in the suite when Eva had been taken, and he had done nothing to protect her. He was less than a man in my eyes. He was a coward.

I felt my anger rising again and went through some breathing exercises to calm myself down. In a moment, I would have to deal with humans who were unused to Juhlian tempers. It wouldn't do to scare the fools to death when I needed their help to recover Eva.

I also would be calling a friend from our transport vehicle. Ken had been a minor state official on my very first visit to this planet. His job had been to show me, the Juhlian heir, around, to make sure I had fun, and to keep me out of trouble. He'd done his job well, unlike the idiotic ambassador. After that, Ken and I had formed an instant friendship. I'd heard he'd moved up a few steps on the bureaucratic ladder, and I was tired of going through official channels. The humans had already botched everything. It was time to start calling in favors and dropping names.

I felt the almost indiscernible thump of the airlock regulating. The hiss of the opening doors cued us to move forward into the sunlight. I'd had the captain open the viewport screens before coming to a full stop, so our eyes would be accustomed to the yellow light from the sun when we emerged. We strode out as a unit.

A group of humans waited for us. The one in front was not Reynauld. *Good. I will not deal with that one any longer. Inept fool.*

This man was almost as tall as my warriors and me and easily as broad. He also wore a "power suit" as crisp and tailored as my own. He held out a hand in greeting. Remembering T'ral's advice and our previous journeys here, I clasped it with my own and shook it once.

"Derek Willoughby, sire, at your service. I'm here to take you straight to the president." He fell into step beside me. I heard a grumble or two from my warriors about how close he was standing. *Could he be a threat?* I stopped walking.

Willoughby turned to look back at me. "Sire? President Maeda is waiting."

My eyebrow rose. "He is a president and will be replaced. I am a king and irreplaceable. He can wait on me. I haven't seen your President Maeda in quite some time. I have been dealing with your Peace Opportunity Program Ambassadors for months. Why is your planetary president finally getting involved now?"

Willoughby had the grace to look a bit discomfited. "We believed we had placed the breeding program in the most capable hands, sire. Reynauld was given extremely good references. He had the scientific background to handle executing administration of the Peace Opportunity Breeding Program, and he understood the science behind it as well. Unfortunately, we were wrong to trust him with this program, as both he and the medical director in charge are now being investigated for mismanagement."

I stared at him. "Now that Eva has been kidnapped right out of his hands?"

"Yes." He lowered his gaze slightly, and then looked back up at me firmly, his manner remaining calm and polite. "All of the details have been brought to our attention, and we have every intention of getting Ms. Knight back safely."

"I do not plan on sitting through endless meetings, Willoughby, while your bureaucrats debate what actions to take. My warriors and I will be taking action immediately. Take me to Eva's quarters, so we can start tracking her. Maeda can meet us there." I started walking again, heading toward the limousine Willoughby had motioned to when we started out.

There were a number of vehicles in the motorcade. I stopped several feet away and gave a hand signal to Baelon. Our squad separated on cue, each warrior heading for a different vehicle.

"What are they doing?" Willoughby asked me.

"Inspecting," I retorted.

"Inspecting for what? These vehicles have been thoroughly searched and vetted by our mechanics and security personnel." Willoughby seemed more confused than anything.

I snapped, "And now they will have been thoroughly searched and inspected by my security personnel. So far, Earth's government has done little to earn my trust—and an appalling lot to lose it. So I'm sure you understand when I say that we will take no more chances."

Willoughby swallowed and then nodded slowly, seeming to understand that I would not tolerate any further problems.

I moved forward again at Baelon's all-clear. I knew Baelon's search would be thorough and complete. Willoughby lengthened his stride to beat me to the door and open it for me.

I was surprised President Ken Maeda himself was already seated inside the vehicle. He was on the shorter side, like the ambassador, but slender and fit. His hair was a mix of black and silver, interestingly with more silver in it than the last time we'd met.

He gave me a small, polite smile and inclined his head. "I figured that's what you'd want to do. Take action. So, that is what we will do," he said dryly.

I relaxed slightly. "Ah! Your presence here saves me from making a call to you. I grow tired of the embassy channels. They have made a mess of things. I had already decided to go straight to the man in charge—you. This will be dealt with today, Ken."

~

I REINTRODUCED MAEDA TO BAELON AND T'RAL. ALL OF US HAD actually previously met Ken before he had been elected to his current position of planetary president. I hadn't been aware of just how much of a promotion my friend had achieved, so he had managed to surprise me pleasantly despite the tense circumstances.

The ride to the local Center didn't take very long. Baelon, T'ral, Maeda, Willoughby, and I used that time to discuss Eva's abduction.

"We've reviewed the hallway footage of the attack, sire." Willoughby put in. "No group has claimed responsibility as of yet or asked for ransom for Ms. Knight. Of course, it has only been a few hours since she was taken, but sometimes terrorists move quickly with their demands. We were hoping to have more information by the time you arrived."

"That's what I was hoping as well. My warriors are also trained trackers. We will find her," I stated. I would accept no other outcome.

Maeda broke in with his quiet, yet firm, voice, "There are a few restrictions we will have to place upon you and your warriors while you are here, Raevu. You can't have free rein to dispose of these radicals any way you desire. I won't have innocent citizens endangered."

My eyes narrowed. "This female bears my family crest, Ken. She will be my life mate and my queen. These 'radicals' have not kidnapped some ordinary woman off the street. They will be dealt with accordingly," I insisted.

Maeda nodded. "Yes, but if you go for a full-force extraction, she and innocent civilians might get hurt or killed. I don't believe her captors see her as anything other than a pawn in their game against the government and your race. Expendable. I'm not sure if it would be better to keep them in the dark, or to let them know the true value of their hostage."

I exchanged stares with my two most trusted advisers. We had discussed this same idea in the time before landing. "We believe they should not be informed of her importance as of yet. Let us…what do you say? 'Play our cards close to our vest' and use our information as the secret weapon it can be."

Maeda nodded in agreement. "Absolutely. That's the answer we were hoping you'd give." The fleet pulled up smoothly to the entrance of the Center's ambassadorial guest quarters. Grand columns held up an entryway, and several doormen moved as one to start opening car doors. My warriors were out of the vehicles and surrounding my limousine before the doormen could get close. We stepped out, and the men surrounded us, escorting us inside the building.

After just a few short corridors and turns, we came to the rubble that I was informed was once the entryway to Eva's quarters. A security detail stood at the entrance of the hallway that led up to the suite, but they moved aside silently when they saw us and stepped back into place on guard after our passage.

My warriors fanned out, making their way over bricks and shattered paneling littering the floor. In our tongue, they quietly shared information of what they saw, keeping only with the facts at hand.

I stepped into the room and looked around myself. I knew T'ral and Baelon were accumulating the data and would come to conclusions we would discuss when the survey was complete.

In the middle of the conversation area, a silk scarf patterned in green and pink caught my eye under a small side table. When Eva had asked my name, this scarf had been at her throat.

I bent over and picked it up. A whiff of scent drifted to me. I breathed deeply. I couldn't identify it, but somehow, I knew it was hers. Now, I had her scent.

Four of my men moved back out into the building. I knew they were going to canvass the Center's nearby entrances and exits. They would interview any people they saw, no matter the person's rank, to discern if the person had been a witness or not and bring that information back with them when their task was finished. Knowing the job was in the best possible hands, I asked sharply, "Ken, why was her room right off a public-access plaza? Surely, a visiting diplomat receives quarters more secure than this."

"That's a good question. One we need answered. We put too many details under Reynauld's authority," Maeda replied. "He's in custody, as are his assistants. Anyone involved in the Peace Opportunity Program is under surveillance." He coughed into his fist. "The device they used to deactivate the security system makes it clear that they had help from the inside."

Brusquely, Baelon inquired, "You, the president's aide. You never answered my king's question. Why did you step into this matter now and not before?" T'ral cleared his throat. "No, T'ral. I want to know. I won't ask it in a more polite manner."

I glanced over to see T'ral shake his head.

Willoughby answered, "Reynauld called our office in a panic after the attack. He was in over his head. When I reviewed the communications and records of the program, it was obvious that when he interviewed for the job, he faked several of his references and commendations. I've taken over. The program will now fall under the oversight of my office."

"And who are you?" Baelon continued just as bluntly.

"I'm President Maeda's secretary of state. We'll be coordinating with the Department of Security, and we can get resources from the Defense and Justice if need be to ensure a smooth recovery of Ms. Knight." Willoughby's answer was slick and well-prepared. I had no doubt that he and Maeda had rehearsed it on the way over to meet us.

Baelon continued his interrogation. As these were questions I wanted answers to as well, I let him continue. I liked Ken, but these mistakes were simply unforgivable. "What department was over the Peace Program? The Department of Ineptitude?"

Willoughby's calm response was a stark contrast to Baelon's heat. "The Department of Science and Advancement, sir. Your Majesty, if I may?" He turned to me.

"Yes?" I answered.

"How did your government decide which DNA to send to us to use for the experiment? How did you know it would work?"

"We sent mine," I answered. "The royal lineage is the most genetically pure, with little degradation."

He blinked at me slowly, then removed his spectacles and polished them before replacing them on his face. "It makes sense that you would send the best sample. However, if a human were inoculated with your personal DNA and survived, that would mean that she has a compatible biology to your own."

And that explained the mark. If she weren't my life mate, it would have killed her like the others. It helped my confusion to draw these connections, but I hated the idea of the setback costing lives. Mixing our genes with humanity was a huge gamble. And we didn't yet know if it would work.

I took a deep breath and offered the two humans more honesty than I had before now. "Our Council hasn't approved this treaty yet. The Council will not agree to this exchange on a planet-wide scale if it isn't feasible. There was only one way to proceed with the biological trials."

They both blinked back at me in surprise and said nothing, so I went on, "The treaty is actually just between your planet and my family. I couldn't ask someone else in my family to send DNA for an experiment, so I had them send mine. If it works, then I have proof for our council to go planet-wide."

"Is that why the crest appeared on her skin? Would some other family crest have appeared if other DNA had been sent?" Baelon sounded curious.

T'ral answered, "No. Traditionally, the crest appears on the life mate's skin after the bonding ceremony, which is a blood exchange. The DNA we sent had no blood traces. We double-checked the samples before we left. Also, historically, no other families have ever had life mates with visible skin markings—only the royal family."

"Perhaps the exposure to your DNA was enough," Willoughby ventured.

Baelon was still skeptical. "So even with a personal treaty with the royalty of another planet, you assigned an incompetent man to the task?"

"Baelon, enough," T'ral interrupted.

I stayed quiet, just lifting an eyebrow. I wanted them to work out their dispute without my intervention.

"No, T'ral, I'm not sure it is enough," Maeda interjected. "He has a point. We let Reynauld have too much slack, and Ms. Knight and the other volunteers paid for our mistake. We won't make a mistake like that again. You have ambassadorial quarters waiting for you here in the Center. I'll be staying next door until this matter is resolved."

"Sir…" Willoughby began.

"No, Derek, we need a show of solidarity with the Juhlians. We need to show our citizens that we fully support this peace initiative. I feel we have not done so prior to now. By giving the assignment to an underqualified individual, we did not show our people how important it was to us. They must think we're not endorsing this treaty, when, in fact, we need it. Get the two topmost floors. We'll reserve the highest one for Raevu and myself, and the one just beneath for his warriors and our security detail. If we need more space than that, continue taking over whole floors as a safeguard."

"Yes, sir," Willoughby conceded. "I'll make it happen." He turned and left the room, speaking into his communication device as he went.

Maeda turned to me, "Now what, Raevu?"

I smiled slightly, finally getting the sense that something around here was being done properly. "I'm impressed, Ken."

"It's time. Policy stands, but we need to uphold it and reinforce it. This is a start."

Maeda and I watched my warriors converge on T'ral. He pulled up a data screen and began compiling information. One by one, the four that had spread out through the Center came back and added their details to the rest of the gathered intelligence.

T'ral's fingers flew across the screen. Baelon pulled out his own data screen and watched the data organizing itself within the display. I waited for their conclusions.

A chime rang through the room. My warriors went on guard and moved into defensive positions around me. A rich but strangely emotionless male voice sounded over the intercom.

"Mr. President, Your Majesty, there is an incoming transmission. I am attempting to track its source, but it is encrypted. I will send all information to Lord T'ral's data communicator as I receive and decode it."

"Who was that?" I barked, wary.

"Thank you, Geoffrey. Hold the transmission for a moment, please," Maeda said as he turned a mild expression on me. "Geoffrey is a computer interface we assigned to Ms. Knight. Unfortunately, Reynauld did not think to put a communication chip in her lapel so Geoffrey could track her and reassure her of our progress."

"Geoffrey, who is calling?" I asked.

"Unknown, sire. As it is encrypted and coming to Ms. Knight's suite, I'm assuming it could be her kidnappers. May I patch it through? I will continue to collect information as it relays."

Willoughby started to protest, but Maeda held up a hand, and I ordered, "Yes, Geoffrey, patch it through."

The monitor flashed to life on the wall, and we all turned to face the screen.

The focus of the picture was a man dressed completely in black, including a black mask. He couldn't disguise his eyes, though. They had a wild, gleeful gleam in them, almost crazed.

Immediately, my rage burst from the tight hold I'd had it under, and I spat out at him, "I know your face from when she pulled your mask off. The mask does you no good."

He snatched off his mask and sneered at us through the communicator. "That's fine. I don't care if a blue alien freak knows who I am." His voice was a high wheeze, as if his throat had been damaged.

His ashy, blond hair and pale skin appeared washed out against the black turtleneck he had on. "We're the Humans for Humanity League, and you won't be taking any human women from this planet," he declared in a righteous fury.

"Is that so?" I replied, unimpressed.

"Yes! Every woman you attempt to kidnap we will free from your alien clutches. We will shut down the 'Peace Program,' which is nothing but human trafficking, and we will liberate our women to live happy lives where they belong. Here on Earth with human males!" He shook his skinny fists at the screen.

President Maeda cut into his tirade, "Where is Eva Knight?"

"Ah, Mr. President, finally we get the recognition we deserve." The terrorist's scratchy tenor voice was grating on my nerves, and all I wanted to do was leap through the screen and strangle him. But I held still and silent, waiting for his answer.

He smirked. "She's fine. She's right here with me." He stepped to one side to reveal a figure sitting in a chair behind him. No, not sitting, at least not voluntarily. Tied to it and struggling against her bonds. My anger flared anew. Eva didn't look hurt, but her eyes held so much anger it made me want to rip off the man's head.

He scuttled over to where she wrestled against her restraints. Now that he was next to her, the microphone clipped to his collar picked up her voice, and we could hear how she yelled against the gag in her mouth.

"Trust me. She has plenty of human fire to give to a human male." He reached out a hand, cupped her breast, and gave it a squeeze. She bucked in protest to the touch, rage in her eyes. I took an involuntary step forward. *How dare he touch her?*

The pervert's lips twisted, wet and trembling. "She likes my touch. See how she arches into it?"

What I could see was Eva's jawline firm in threat as she grew very still. My guess was that her thoughts were very similar to my own...*I'll kill you.*

"She, like all human women, craves the touch of a man. A human man's touch." The man took his hand away and slipped it under the top front of her dress. "Human women's nipples grow nice and hard when a man tweaks them a bit. Give them a nice little pinch, and they're perfect—"

Just then, Eva struck. The man had leaned over a bit to watch himself play with her breast. She slammed her head forward and into his face. Blood immediately gushed from his nose and lip. My rage at her being mauled shifted slightly at her fighting spirit. I hoped she'd broken his nose.

His hands flew to his face, and blood drizzled out from between his fingers. For a few moments, all the man did was choke and stagger back as his eyes and nose both streamed blood.

"You crazy bitch!" Striding forward again, the kidnapper back-handed her across the face with enough force to knock her chair over to the floor.

I growled and stepped closer to the screen. T'ral and Baelon were hurriedly exchanging words behind me, but I only had attention for the woman on the screen. Her gag must have been knocked loose by the blow and the fall because she spat it out and started to speak in a low, controlled voice. "You fucking bastard. Touch me again, and I'll kill you. Do you hear me?" She licked her lips and turned her head to wipe her mouth on her shoulder. A smear of blood was left behind. "Untie me now, you nasty son of a bitch. You didn't rescue me. You took me hostage!"

"Cunt! You'll regret that. You broke my nose!" He held a rag to his face and turned back to the communicator. "These are our terms: she gets released when the alien freaks have left our planet and have promised not to return ever again. That's all. They go away, she goes home." And the screen went black.

"We need to track down her captors and rescue her at once!" I pivoted on my heel to see what my advisers had come up with. I hoped it was a plan of action that ended with me killing that human idiot with my bare hands. No other outcome would satisfy me...or the anger that boiled inside.

CHAPTER 7
EVA

The first thing I noticed when I woke up after being kidnapped was the pain in my head. Sharp and throbbing, it felt like an illness coming on. My thirst intensified it, but I focused first on the stinging radiating outward from the center of my forehead. I lifted my hand to investigate the spot for a bump or abrasion. To my surprise, I felt both hands coming toward my head. My hands were bound together. My eyes flew open. Everything was still dark, but this time, it was because the lights were off. I used my tied hands to push myself to a seated position.

I had no idea where I could possibly be. All around me were vague shapes and looming shadows. *Fuck. How was I going to get out of here? Who the hell were these crazy bastards, and what did they want from me?*

As if responding to a cue, a door clicked open then a harsh light flashed on overhead. It took a moment and some blinking to be able to adjust my eyes to the light.

Three men dressed in black walked toward me. The one in front was tall, moderately built, with almost white hair, pale gray eyes, and ashy skin. There was nothing remarkable about him except, perhaps, his lack of remarkable features.

The second man was shorter and rather pudgy, with dark brown hair and cold black eyes. The third stayed back from the others. He acted unsure of the men. He was tall and gangly, balding, and seemed nervous as he kept scanning the room, not letting his eyes rest on any one thing for too long.

I noticed that he kept watching the other men when he thought they weren't looking. Almost as if he didn't quite trust them.

"Good, you're awake," the man in front spoke with a rough, nasally tenor voice. It grated on my nerves. "We've liberated you from your captors. You're free."

"Captors?" I croaked. Talking made me cough. It hurt, and I was appalled at how feeble my voice and cough sounded. I cleared my throat and tried for more oomph. "You're the ones who have me tied up. You're my captors. Set me free." I held up my tied hands awkwardly.

"Oh no, lady. We can't have you running from here to the authorities. They'd just hand you over to those alien freaks. We're holding on to you for your own good, until those alien creatures are off our planet, never to be heard from again." He shifted his weight, leering at me.

"I was being monitored medically when you grabbed me. For all I know, I could be contagious or something. Or you could be denying treatment I need to survive. Certainly, you're not helping me one bit by tying me up." I struggled against the ropes that bound my wrists and calves, but I couldn't budge them.

He shook his head with a smirk. "You were in the Center's ambassadorial guest quarters, not put up in some random hotel. You're important somehow." His smirk dropped into a frown as he peered at me mockingly. "You don't look it. You look average and frumpy."

I bristled under his scrutiny. *Average and frumpy*? But I knew nothing would be gained by trying to reason with an ignorant asshole like him. I turned to the short one. "Surely you see the ridiculousness of this whole—"

"Shut it, bitch," He cut me off before I could even get started with my plea. "You have some sort of alien mark on you. Dashon should just go ahead and kill you now. You're probably already contaminated flesh, tainted by the aliens."

"Wow," I hissed, "both of you clearly need a psych intervention."

Shit. It seemed the coldness in his eyes reached as far as his heart. I promised myself to avoid being alone with him if at all possible. The first guy was crazy, and this one was full of bitter hatred.

I turned to the third. I licked my lips again and spoke softly, "May I go to the restroom?"

He glanced uncertainly at the other two men and then moved toward me.

"Cleve? Really?" the cold one protested. "Don't coddle the bitch."

The one called Cleve continued toward me. His voice was low and gentle. "I'm not coddling her. She's a human female we're rescuing from the aliens. She's not to blame for any of this." Cleve looked up at the cold one and scowled. "It was supposed to be a rescue, not a hostage taking. Did you forget that?"

The hateful one stared hard at him, face pulled down into an almost comically huge frown, but Cleve just stared back at him implacably and kept moving, until the other looked away and started sulking.

Cleve stopped in front of me. "I'll take you to the bathroom, miss."

"Go ahead, Cleve, take her," Crazy spat.

I muttered to the nutcase, "You're definitely a big fucking hero of the human race. Not." He just tittered as Cleve crouched to untie my ankles.

"Don't listen to him. We really did intend to rescue you," Cleve said, but that just got laughter from the other two.

"Oh, for fuck's sake. Give her a communication unit and the controller to the monitor so she can watch her favorite shows too." Cold threw up his hands and rolled his eyes theatrically. "Who cares if she's not even entirely human anymore. She's not dangerous or anything like that."

"Shut up already. We really were supposed to be there to free her, no matter how fucked up your morals are, you bitter prick." Cleve held my arm and helped me to my unsteady feet. I desperately wanted to ask for something for my pounding head, but I figured that'd be a mistake in front of the other two men.

He helped me walk to the doorway and down a short hall to a tiny, dingy bathroom. I needed his support much more than I wanted to.

There, he released me and told me he'd wait for me outside. I held my tied hands out toward him.

"No." He spared an anxious glance down the hall. "I'd better not. I'm sorry. Do your best." He turned his back to me.

Trying to figure out how this was going to work, I closed the door. There was no lock. As I walked over to the toilet, I shot a glance about the room. Only about five feet square, it had no windows, no cabinets, and nothing I could arm myself with.

I reached down and hitched up the hem of my dress, noting the smears and small tears on it. No wonder I felt so bruised. On top of the whatever-flu symptoms I had, I'd been tossed around like a bag of rice. *Seriously, some rescuers these fuckers are!* I'd take fifteen "hostile alien abductions" by Raevu over another minute with these asswipes.

Clumsily, I tucked one side of my dress under my armpit and reached for the other. It received the same treatment, then I scooped my thumb under the top edge of my panties, pushing them down while wriggling my hips back and forth in an awkward motion. I wasn't sure if I was going to be fast enough, but just in time, the fabric slid over the curves of my butt to my thighs. I sat down with a sigh of relief. *Phew. I'm sure that freak outside would enjoy it if he found out I peed my panties.*

I had to figure out a way out of here. I didn't care where I was. Surely, I could simply report myself to any authorities, and they'd get me back to the Center. I'd just have to keep my eyes open for an opportunity. I wouldn't let the aches and pains slow me down, either.

I cleaned up and reversed my wriggle process to try to get my panties all the way up. That done, I hesitated in coming back out. I figured this was the only privacy I was going to get, so I paced back and forth trying to think of options. Knowing none of my resources, I came up empty. *Fuck.*

I opened the door to interrupt Cleve in mid-knock. He looked up, startled, and then gave me a humorless smile. "Oh. Good. You need to get back to the room."

"Could I have a glass of water? And maybe something for this headache? I think they tossed me around a bit and bumped my head against something. It sure hurts." This was the only one of the men whose sympathies I might gain. I needed to work him.

Without glancing over, he nodded briskly. "I'll be bringing you food shortly. I'll have it then."

He escorted me back to the storage room where I'd started out, and then left me. I was pleased to note I hadn't needed to lean on him to get back to the room. I surveyed the hallway as we progressed. Other than it looking remarkably like the corridors of the Children's Ward, I couldn't see any maps, windows, or exit signs. Maybe it was underground.

Cold and Crazy Man each gave a flourish over a straight-backed chair, "Your throne, Queen of the Aliens."

I didn't trust his intentions, but I sat anyway. It was better than the floor. Cleve tied my legs back to the chair, and my waist as well, but let me keep my bound hands in front of me to eat. As he did so, I noticed he left a lot more wiggle room than whoever had tied me up before.

Once he was done, the only sane one of the three turned and left, presumably to get my food and water. Being alone with the other two men made me so uneasy that I barely kept myself from shouting after him. Left alone with Crazy and Cold, I watched their every move.

They went and stood by a tower of boxes and exchanged words. I didn't catch much, although I strained to hear what I could. To cover my spying on them, I slumped down in the chair and picked at the folds of my skirt.

Cold was only worried about identification and getting out of here. Crazy had some kind of agenda. He wanted the aliens to leave without any human women and never return. He'd repeated that several times.

I kept playing with the fabric of my dress and looked around the space. Stacks of boxes, bins, and tubs filled the room. There were haphazard pathways through the mounds, but I couldn't determine any sort of organization. *Great, it's a damn maze, and I bet they know their way around.*

Cleve chose that moment to return with a tray in his hands. The tray looked just like a hospital meal tray I got at the Medical Ward. He pushed up a crate in front of my chair and set the tray on top of it.

True to his word, there was a full glass of water and a bottle for refilling. A covered plate sat in the middle of the tray. Next to the water, a very small plastic bowl held two white capsules. I looked at them, and then looked at him curiously.

He jerked his head toward the pills. "For your head. I'll take the tray back in fifteen minutes. Eat up." Cleve moved over to join the other two men.

Immediately, he was assailed with comments about "futility" and "wasted time" from Cold and more propaganda from Crazy. They were both pathetically broken, irrational people, so much so that I wondered how they had conned Cleve into putting up with them. It was so messed up that I would have found it hilarious if I weren't at the mercy of these wackos.

With a roll of my eyes, I lifted the cover from the plate. Plain, typical clinic fare greeted me. Green beans, mashed potatoes with watery, bright-yellow margarine, baked chicken—all quite tasteless and needing seasoning.

This really did remind me of Center institution food—the stuff I had gotten used to, growing up in the Children's Ward, and later, staying in the Medical Ward. A notion struck me, and I ate slowly, taking in every detail I could from my environment. *How far did they actually take me?*

I finished my meal and took the pain relievers. Hopefully, between the food and the capsules, my headache would go away. Well, my physical headache. The psychological headaches of Crazy and Cold were staring at me again, and a couple of pills wouldn't make them go away.

In a belligerent tone, I snapped at them, "What?" I wasn't going to be polite to men who wouldn't untie me to pee or to eat.

"We have to contact your keepers to let them know our terms," Crazy said. "I'm just not real sure what to do with you until then." He stalked over to where I sat.

"Give her to me," Cold said, in such a disgustingly gleeful voice that I would have shot him in a second to keep his creepy ass away from me. "We can make an example of her."

"What the fuck is wrong with you?" I snarled defiantly at the socio-pathic little shit. "Do have a problem with all women or just me?"

"Only those with tainted blood!" Cold spat with all the blind vehemence of a racist.

"Do you think my sister had tainted blood?" Cleve's voice was very calm, and for a moment, even colder than his associate's.

Cold hesitated, some of the color leaving his face as he switched from bully to coward for a split second. "No, of course not. I-I won't speak badly of the dead."

"A real prince among men," I scoffed, and he shot me a hateful look that should have terrified me, but I refused to cower.

Cleve stepped over and took up the tray. He pushed my makeshift table back to its place amongst the other crates. "I say just let her sit quietly in the background while you live-stream. It'll show that she's alive and unharmed, Dashon." His jaw was set, as if he was resisting the urge to yell at them more, then he left the room.

Crazy's real name must be Dashon. I filed that away for future reference.

Crazy meanwhile started ranting at me again. "Really, you should be grateful. We rescued you from being taken away from Earth by aliens to be part of a breeding program. You have no idea what they're like in private. Those aliens probably killed all their own women. What do you think they will do to you?"

"They didn't force me. It was voluntary, and, actually, I got paid to be part of this experiment and the Peace Program." I found myself using my most patronizing tone, but I figured they deserved it. "You kidnapped me. You are my captors. And you need to let me go!"

Cold bustled up to me, shoving his face level with mine. "Shut your damn mouth, bitch! Answer only if we ask you a question, and we haven't. Disgusting. Getting paid to be with aliens. You're their filthy whore, that's what you are."

"How dare you?" I acted without thinking, lunging at him in a rage, throwing my whole weight against the ropes. They creaked and started slipping a little, letting me stand partway. I slammed my tied hands across his face, catching his cheek with my nails at the same time. He howled with pain.

I hit him again as I yelled at him, "You watch your mouth! What's your problem with me...with women? You can't get a date, so you want to blame aliens for stealing us all? There were only five of us, and none of us would have fucked you even if you were the last man on earth!" As I readied my arms to swing back for a third blow, I was caught around the waist from behind. The one I called Crazy grabbed the back of my chair and hauled me backward. I kicked and used my elbows to try to hit his ribs, but I smacked my upper arm into the chairback instead. He tried to get his hand around my throat, I bit down hard on the webbing, and he yelled and stumbled back from me in shock.

"You fucking tramp!" Cold came at me purple-faced, with fire in his eyes. I must have hit a nerve or several.

Just as Cold got within arm's reach of me, he swung his arm back to hit me. I kicked free of the loosened ropes on one side and slammed the toe of my shoe right into his groin. He stopped, bent over, and clutched his balls. Not bothering to kick free of the ropes around my other leg, I threw my roped-together arms around his neck and lifted myself out of my chair slightly to slam him in the balls again. He let out a high whine of pain and went limp. I used my free leg to keep kicking him as he fell at my feet, until his eyes showed nothing but whites.

Crazy recovered and grabbed my shoulders, slamming me down into the chair hard enough to knock the wind out of me. I sat dazed just long enough for him to get extra bits of cord and tie my ankles tightly to the chair legs. I caught my breath as he was looping cord through my elbows and around the chairback. I wasn't going to be able to move.

"Son of a bitch!" I yelled. "Untie me. Let me go." I renewed my struggles. "Bastard. I hope you fry. I'm going to the authorities as soon as I'm out of here, and they'll waive the trial and shoot you. I know you'll fry in hell."

"Enough!" Crazy shoved a gag into my mouth and tied it around my head. "I don't want to hear any more of your shit, lady."

Cleve walked in on the chaos and blinked, taking in all the details. He must have been able to piece it together to his satisfaction because he didn't ask questions. "C'mon, Al," he said to the collapsed asshole, who was slowly recovering on the floor. "Let's get you some ice for your nuts before you have to go put on your uniform and clock in at the station." He looked at Crazy seriously. "Dashon, don't hurt her. That's not what we agreed on when we planned this. Let's just get this done, and let her go." He once again helped a limping person from the room, but this time, I watched in satisfaction at the slow progress they made. I hoped Cold spent the rest of the day puking his guts out.

"Ugh, what a Boy Scout." Crazy rolled his eyes and addressed me, that smirk still frozen on his face, "Okay, Miss Foul-Mouth, we're going to go ahead and let those government fucks and their alien buddies know what we want. Then we'll decide what to do about you."

I stared at him coldly, unable to speak intelligibly with the damned gag shoved between my teeth.

"After that stunt, Al's going to be even more determined to kill you than he was before, just so you know. Maybe you should be nicer to him." Crazy walked over to a stack of crates just across from where I was sitting and placed a portable monitor on top of it. He tapped a few controls on its screen and then stood waiting. After pulling his black mask back over his head, he put his hands behind his back and rocked back and forth on his heels, humming some tuneless melody.

Nicer to him? Sure, I won't. I watched him closely, but I kept pulling at my bonds, hoping to find a weak spot. I couldn't see what was on the screen, but I could hear Geoffrey's voice loud and clear through the unit. "Transmission commencing."

Before Crazy could even start talking, I heard a voice that made a part of me melt, even while it gave me strength. I couldn't even begin to figure out why Raevu's voice affected me so much. I shook the feeling away and focused only on escaping my bonds.

"The mask does you no good," Raevu's commanding voice barked.

Crazy snatched off his mask and sneered at the communicator. What followed was less a hostage negotiation as a furious butting of heads between Crazy and Raevu. Crazy was outmatched by a lot. Literally, the only advantage he had was the gun to my head. I seriously doubted it would be enough to force Raevu and his people to leave the planet. Raevu's disgusted response reassured me he would find me, and when he did, these fuckers' heads would roll, and I would be free.

Meanwhile, I was tied up so tight, I was immobilized and mute. As far as I was concerned, Raevu couldn't get here fast enough.

Crazy, eyes watering still and nostrils rimmed with blood, punched a control on his wristband to shut down the communication and snapped, "Just stay there for now. Maybe Cleve will help you in a minute.

"Fucking cunt. Al's right. We may just 'release' you the way he wants us to. That'll show everyone we mean business." He stared at me, and then smirked and pulled out a knife. I froze for a moment, but all he did was slide the blade between the gag strap and my cheek, cutting the band with a swift jerk of his wrist.

I spat out the gag and stared at him, sick of wasting words on someone this bullheaded and crazy. But right now, words were about my only weapon. "If you let me go and run, you might be able to get away before he finds you and cuts your hands and dick off for groping me." I caught a flicker of fear burning through the crazy in his eyes, and then his face collapsed into a petulant scowl.

"We should kill you just to spite him." He stomped out of the room and left me tied to the chair.

I took deep calming breaths to rid myself of the anger and try to clear my head. I was alone. This was my best opportunity to escape, but first, I had to get myself untied.

CHAPTER 8
EVA

Crazy might have tied me to the chair extra tightly, but he hadn't stopped to fix Cleve's work before stomping out. The rope around my hands and forearms was definitely loose—so loose that I wondered if he wasn't intentionally giving me the chance to escape. I twisted and finally snaked one hand free of the mass of ropes around my wrist.

My shoulder popped painfully as I twisted it and my arm until I could pull it free of the loop around my elbow. Shaking the loose ropes off my other arm, I rubbed the burns my efforts had made on my wrists. Having my hands free made it easy enough to shimmy out of the straps tying my arms to the chair, and from there, it was short work to free my feet. I slipped off my heels so I could move as silently as possible.

I wouldn't be able to skirt any cameras in the corridors, but if I was where I thought I was, the lunatic men didn't have access to those camera feeds anyway. I just needed to be quiet enough to get away from them. I had wondered why they had access to the Center's systems, let alone their secure inner corridors. Now I had a strong suspicion about it. If I was right, I wouldn't have to run far to be free.

I took the bottle of water Cleve had left for me, figuring it'd be a good resource both for thirst and as a weight if I needed extra power behind a punch. I crept to the door, cracked it open, and peeked both ways down the hall. *All clear. That's weird.* But it only strengthened my suspicions that Cleve might be trying to help me without risking a confrontation with his unstable companions. *Who was he?* He seemed so normal compared to his partners. *What drama had driven him to join up with terrorists?*

Whatever. If he was deliberately looking the other way on his guard shift while I took off, I had to take advantage. I could wonder about his motives when I was safe.

Moving as quickly as I could, I chose to go away from the bathroom. The corridor ended in blind corners either way I went, so I had to get around a bend as soon as possible. I knew there was a possibility I'd walk straight into one of the three men during my escape, but I wouldn't be me if I didn't try.

It felt like an eternity passed before I made it past the four doors that led down to the corner. Once around the corner, I looked for an exit sign or another turn or juncture. I figured the more corners between my captors and me, the better.

Four random twists later, I finally spotted an exit sign. It looked like a beacon of hope to me. I knew that right now I was running on an adrenaline high and would soon be crashing, so I had to get to somewhere safe, fast.

I had begun passing people about two corridors back. I had hidden from them at first, but soon I realized they barely paid any attention to me. I still didn't know where I was, so I didn't call out to any of them for help.

When I spotted an odd look or two thrown my way, I realized I was still carrying my shoes, and my face and hair were torn up. I stopped briefly to slip on my shoes and smooth my hair. Nothing I could do about the split lip but keep my head down when I passed people. So I did, praying none of them was in league with the men who had kidnapped me.

The exit door truly felt like liberation as I walked through it—and caught sight of a familiar plaza. *I was right!* I'd never left the Center.

Those men had hidden me in a storeroom in the Center basement. I knew exactly where I was.

I walked straight into a crowd and attempted to blend in. Now no one would give my roughed-up face a second glance. I needed to decide where to go and how to hide. I couldn't go to Ivy's flat. The radicals probably knew I lived there, and it would be watched and searched.

I was a bit concerned about Cleve's comment to Cold Al about putting on "his uniform" and clocking in "at the station." Could Cold Al be a police officer or Center security? If he was, this would be very difficult. I couldn't turn myself over to the authorities. I might just be handing myself back to my kidnappers. And the remarks about "being determined to kill you" and "releasing you the way he wants to" scared the shit out of me.

No, I couldn't go to the authorities. I'd have to be strategic. For now, though, I needed to get somewhere safe, *but where was safe?*

Two places immediately came to mind, Gino's and Laura's. Gino's was a restaurant. A little hole-in-the-wall family place that only stayed in business because the neighborhood locals loved it so much. I helped out waiting tables for Gino if his daughter, Val, needed extra hands or had waitstaff call in sick. I'd never officially worked there, so my name wasn't on any of the payrolls. That was good. I was not officially associated with it, so no one would look for me there.

I took stock of my surroundings and changed directions to head to Gino's. On foot, I'd be getting there right before closing. Perfect timing. Calling Laura would be my next step.

Laura was just my age. She would have volunteered for the experiment if it hadn't been for Amber, her daughter by a teenage crush. Said teenage crush didn't want anything to do with fathering a child, so Laura was on her own. Amber was the most sweet-natured child I'd ever met, always smiling and happy. Her "dad" was missing out, but Laura was blessed.

I was too. Laura was wonderful, the best friend I could ever hope for. We joked periodically that if either of us decided to be interested in women, we'd turn to one another. I loved them both dearly. Next to Ivy and the kids, they were the closest I had to family.

Just in case cameras were tracing me, I slipped into the alley behind Gino's place. I skulked down the alley, keeping to the shadows. At the rear delivery door, I paused and listened to make out if anything unusual was going on. All I could hear was the normal bustle and hubbub of a restaurant near closing time. I stepped in and appraised the activities throughout the large room.

Tall, big-eared Franco was desperately trying to make sure all of his desserts looked perfect before the waitstaff grabbed them and toted them out to tables. Black-haired twins Dmitri and Alfonse were cleaning their knives and other utensils, taking advantage of a lull up front. Waitstaff and busboys were frantically scuttling in and out through the constantly moving service doors. *Normality.* I sighed with relief and leaned back against the door.

"Eva!" a huge bass voice boomed my name. All activity in the kitchen paused as the workers looked up to see if their boss was upset or pleased. He had come through from the dining area and spotted me immediately, an Italian giant with a flamboyant mustache and dancing brown eyes. For a large man, he could move very quickly. In just a couple of steps, he'd crossed the entire kitchen and swept me up in a bear hug. I put my arms around Gino's beefy neck and let him twirl me around, tears of relief gathering in my eyes.

I always felt twelve years old again within Gino's hugs and very safe. Kitchen noises resumed as if they'd never stopped. Gino set me down and took my face in his meaty hands, cradling it like a wounded baby bird.

His brows drew together. "Who did this to you? I will kill him!"

I'd forgotten about my bloody lip and bruised face in my relief at having made it to my goal. "It's a long story, Gino. Can I go sit in the office to tell you? And I need to call Laura. May I use your communicator?"

"Of course. You know you can." Gino turned his six-foot-six frame and lumbered toward his office with me in tow. He was wearing his usual uniform, black dress pants and a white shirt with a tie—askew, of course. And, as he couldn't resist putting his hands into every dish that left his kitchen, he had an apron on over his clothes. I smiled at his back.

At his low-pitched request, Dmitri nodded and began putting a plate together, I assumed for me. *Thank God, real food after that institution crap.*

We walked into the office just off the kitchen. His eldest daughter, Val, looked up from her ledgers and blinked a bit blearily at me, then she leaped up, eyes widening at my appearance.

Almost as tall as her father, but willowy where he was brawny, Val had an enormous, frizzy head of brown hair. Her hug was just as emotional as her father's had been.

"Eva! We've been so worried. Did you know you're on the communications net? All over the posts and the vids? President Maeda is going to hold a press conference about you in just a little while. President Maeda, Eva! Are you okay? What happened to your face? They're saying you were abducted. Ivy is frantic." Her questions and comments kept tumbling one on top of the other at me. I finally put up my hands in protest.

"Stop! Whoa, Val!" I shook my head. "I don't know what's going on. I just need to contact Laura right now. She'll contact Ivy for me. I can't do it. The people who took me may be monitoring her communications." If they were cops, they could do so easily.

"Who will find you? Sweetheart, do you know who took you?"

I was starting to get my headache back. "I just need to make this call, and I'll tell you everything I know."

"Val." Gino's bass broke through Val's answering flurry of words. "Let the girl be. She needs to use the comm."

"Oh. Yes, of course." Val moved out of my way.

Dmitri knocked on the door just then and popped through with plates heaped high with noodles covered in rich sauces and cheese. A piece of crusty bread was stuck on the side of each plate. The smells had my mouth immediately watering. He winked at me as he put the plates down on the desk, and he backed out of the room without a word.

"You'll eat after your call," Gino grumbled. "Your color is off. You need garlic! We'll get you right again. Now call Laura."

I smiled my gratitude and tapped the code that would connect me with Laura's apartment. Instead of Laura, a small, cheerful face answered. "Hello?" Her pale pink complexion flushed with pleasure when she saw who I was. "Eva! There you are! I'll get Mama!" Short, brown pigtails stuck out at odd, random angles all over her head and bobbed a bit as she turned and ran away from the communicator screen.

Almost instantly, she came back into view holding the hand of her mother. Same pale pink skin, same deep walnut hair, but very different eyes. Amber's were the color of the sky on a clear day, bright, vivid blue. Laura's were deep gray, the color of thunderheads right before a storm. Laura plunked herself down in front of the communication console and pulled Amber into her lap.

"It is you. I was worried Amber was telling stories. Oh, thank God." Laura's soft voice was a pleasure to hear again.

I cut to the chase right away. "Yes, it's me. I need your help."

"Anything, just name it. What happened to your face? What bastard hit you? I'll kill him!" I could almost see lightning flash in those gray eyes as Laura got herself worked up on my behalf. For a moment, I imagined her, Gino, and his family wiping the grin off Crazy's face for good.

"I'm good. I'm okay," I soothed. "Can you send Amber to Ivy's for some clothes for me? And then bring them here? I'm at Gino's."

She gave me a puzzled frown. "Just come here."

"I can't. I don't want to be on the streets. I don't want to be seen."

"Where is your imagination? Be a delivery person. Dress in one of Gino's staff uniforms, fix your hair, put some makeup on those bruises and bring me and my baby some supper!"

I laughed. Laura was just the person I needed to call. She always had an idea at hand. "I'll talk to Gino. That just might work. If not, we'll call you back."

"Okay. I'll tell Ivy you're all right, then get you clothes and stuff, and come back home to wait for you. I'm glad you're okay, honey. I was so worried." She hugged her daughter, both of them smiling, Laura with relief.

I drew a deep breath and gave them my most reassuring look. "I'm okay. Love you."

"Love you too. Bye." Laura clicked off the communication screen.

I turned to Gino. "What do you think? Do you need a new delivery person? For just one delivery?"

He patted his ample belly with one hand and nodded his head. "I think we can make that work."

CHAPTER 9
RAEVU

I lay on my bed, exhausted but unable to sleep. We'd had nothing but frustrations all day. Even training with Baelon hadn't helped calm or center me.

After the communication with the kidnappers, we'd held a brief meeting to discuss options. Knowing that charging out of the room and ripping apart every blond man I saw wouldn't be an option T'ral and Baelon would entertain, I refrained from mentioning it. But I knew they saw my hands flexing throughout the discussion as I imagined doing just that to the bastard who had dared touch my Eva.

T'ral had the idea of tracking the kidnappers through the corridors by way of the camera feeds. It was a brilliant idea, but there weren't cameras in every hallway, especially not on the maintenance levels.

Geoffrey managed to piece together a trail of sorts through the Center, but it ended with three men, one of them a blond, carrying duffel bags out of a maintenance area door, getting into identical nondescript vehicles, and speeding off in three separate directions. He had lost them after they'd made a couple of turns in New Atlanta's crowded streets.

To Baelon's disappointment, I'd punched a wall at that point. I'd imagined it was the face of the human who had hit Eva, and it felt good. The discomfort of stinging knuckles was of no account and easily dismissed.

Just remembering it now made me roll over in the bed and punch my pillow to make it fold into the shape I wanted. *Damn! Where is Eva?* The thought of that man touching her again nearly had me up and out of bed, but I closed my eyes and recited a mantra for calm.

If I didn't get any sleep, I would be no good to Eva when she needed me tomorrow. That couldn't happen. I forced myself to imitate a sleeper's breathing and relax every muscle, chasing sleep with deep determination. We'd start our search again. And I would find her. Until then…I dreamed of her.

I found her sleeping on her back in a small bed in a dingy room that resembled both the medical cube I had seen her in and the room the captives had live-streamed her in. As I approached her silently, her eyes flew open, and she stared up at me in curiosity. I saw no fear in her eyes, just question. "How did you get here?" she whispered.

I knelt down beside the bed and reached out to cup her face in my hand. Her skin was silky smooth as she rubbed her cheek into my palm and smiled.

"Are you real? Or a dream?" she asked me in her throaty voice.

"Both," I answered.

"Both?" she laughed, and my heart leaped in my chest at hearing amusement from her instead of pain or fear. "How can you be both? If you're a dream, this isn't happening, and I can have my wicked way with you. If you're real, then I need to wait to get to know you better. I've saved myself for this long, what's a little more time?"

"Saved yourself? What do you mean by 'saved yourself'?" I asked as I stroked my fingers around the curve of her face and down her neck to her neckline. Her skin felt smooth and soft. I could even smell her, fresh and clean. She must have just bathed. Eva's curly hair was piled on top of her head, forming a pouf of ringlets. My eyes drank in the sight of her.

Her tiny hands reached up and touched my face, mimicking my gestures on her body. "I've never had sex. I've waited and saved my virginity for someone I wanted to share my body with, but I guess that's out now that I've volunteered for the program. I suppose I'll have several mates, technically, if you harvest my eggs." Her hands were on my shoulders now, exploring the muscles in my arms as I used a finger to trace back and forth along her neckline.

I was dumbfounded at the idea that she's been saving herself for me without even realizing it. It struck me to the heart, and I let her go on instead of trusting myself to speak.

"I know what happens during sex, but I've never experienced it myself." She looked me directly in the eyes. "I want to experience it with you. I've never wanted a man before, but I want you."

My heart felt like it was going to beat its way right out of my chest.

She leaned toward me, and I became aware of the shadow falling between her breasts inside the neckline of her nightgown. "You saw me in the shower, didn't you? I could feel your eyes. Your beautiful golden eyes." She took her hands and smoothed them over my scalp and around my ears. "Just as smooth as it looks. No hair at all." Her light touch skimming over my head and ears sent a shiver along my spine. Her boldness and how she made me feel had me speechless.

She sat up in the bed. "I don't know who you are, Raevu, but you're constantly in my thoughts, and now you're in my dreams." She reached up to her neckline and untied the little bow of pink ribbon nestled between her large, lush breasts.

My mouth went dry as she pushed the straps off of her shoulders, displaying her full breasts. Now I was speechless for another reason entirely.

She lay back again. "Touch me, Raevu." Even as I stared at her breasts, her nipples hardened and puckered as if anticipating my caress.

I slid into the small bed beside her. My large body pressed up against her soft curves. I looked into her deep black eyes and cupped my hand around one breast. Her heated skin was warm under my palm. Her pebbled nipple begged for my mouth, so I had to oblige. I bent my body and lapped at the small nub, then drew the whole thing into my mouth with one gentle suckle. She gasped and arched her back, which pushed her breast against my face. I traced my tongue around her dusky areola and kneaded her breast under my fingertips.

My manhood sprang to attention. I pressed its throbbing length into her hip and drew on her nipple a bit harder.

Her moan of pleasure delighted me. With my free hand, I took hold of her wrist and guided her hand down to the pulsing shaft begging for her touch. When she made eye contact with me to ask permission to touch, I flicked my tongue across that sensitive nipple and grasped her other breast. Her tiny hands encircled my hard cock. I had never been so glad I slept without clothes on as I was at that moment.

I gently squeezed her breasts. She squeezed my shaft. I flicked my tongue across her nipple. She flicked her thumb across my tip, eliciting a gasp of indrawn air from me and a chuckle of pure, wicked pleasure from her.

With her nipple in my mouth, I kept sucking on it, drawing it in and out, running my tongue around and around, but I took the palm of my hand and ran it across her soft belly, down to her hip and inward toward her center. I placed my hand at the apex of her thighs and began to dip my finger between the folds of her sex, just as she had done in her previous provocative show. Her sweet scent intensified, and I knew she was getting wet for me. I pushed my finger into her womanhood, all the way to the base of her sex and then curled my finger back up to the little bud at the top, and I stopped for a moment. I removed my mouth from her breast and looked into her eyes. They were half closed with pleasure, and her lips were parted, her breath coming in shallow pants. I pressed my lips down on hers, tasting her mouth with my own. At the same time, I began moving my finger in small, slow circles around her most sensitive place.

Her hips bucked, and she moaned into my kiss. I sped up my circling. Her stroking of my shaft was gaining momentum as well. I wanted to mount her…making her mine, and then, suddenly, we heard a female's voice. "Eva, I don't think anyone knows you're here." The woman paused. "Oh. Um…wow. Sorry, Eva. Looks like I'm interrupting a great dream…"

"Laura!" Eva's voice gasped, and my arms were suddenly empty.

I sat bolt upright in my guest quarters' bed and looked around me. I wasn't in a small, dingy room with a luscious, curvy woman moaning beneath my touch. I was in a high-ceilinged, airy room, lying in a huge, spacious bed with an aching shaft and empty arms.

What just happened? My extremely hard cock thought it had been the best dream ever, but I wasn't so sure about the "dream" part. Some of it had been just too real.

I flopped back onto that generous bed and thought back about the dream. *What about it had been real? What about it wasn't?*

My cock throbbed insistently. I reached down and gripped it in my right hand with a firm squeeze, and I began an age-old rhythm of strokes. I wished it were Eva's hands instead of my own providing the pressure and the movement.

With the vision of her luscious breasts in my mind and her taste on my tongue, I came and released some of the built-up tension in my body.

Ugh. Curse it. I couldn't go on like this much longer. We had to find my life mate and soon. I needed her.

CHAPTER 10
EVA

"Well, why won't you tell me about this 'dream' you had?" Laura's tone insisted. "Because it looked really hot!"

I swallowed hard. "Laura, quit it. I already told you. It was some kind of erotic dream. I don't know where it came from." But she was right…it was smoking hot.

Laura smiled as she scrambled the eggs in a battered aluminum bowl. "There's nothing wrong with—" She shot a glance at Jaylynn and spelled out, "m-a-s-t-u-r-b-a-t-i-n-g. In fact, should be every woman's best friend." She turned around and slid the eggs into the hot skillet, which hissed and popped.

I rolled my eyes. "I know that." I continued trying to braid Jaylynn's hair into some semblance of order. "Hold still, little miss! What did you do? Take scissors to your hair as soon as I left?" Laura and I had already managed to get Amber's hair into a set of matching ponytails for school today, but Jaylynn, as usual, was being stubborn, even if unintentionally. She crossed her deep brown arms and gave us a rebellious look.

"I don't want to go! I want to stay here with you, Eva. You're going to leave again, aren't you? I need you." Big crocodile tears brimmed in her deep mahogany eyes. They were almost my undoing.

Laura, as usual, rescued me. "Wouldn't today be a great 'Apple for the Teacher Day'? And lookie there! I happen to have one green apple and one red apple. Who gets which apple?"

She made the choice between green or red sound so…vital and exciting. I could predict which girl would take which apple. Red was Amber's favorite color, and green was Jaylynn's. No argument and no fuss later, they each had an apple to take to their teacher. The interlude had also given Jaylynn a chance to sit still long enough for me to whisk her coarse hair into a simple braid. I was glad Ivy had brought her over the night before when they brought my clothes, but a five-year-old could be difficult to negotiate with.

I loved that Amber and Jaylynn were best friends. It truly had made life much easier to deal with for me and for Laura. The girls ate their scrambled eggs and toast and chattered happily until it was time to leave the apartment to catch the transit for school. Right as she hit the door, Jaylynn stopped, turned around, and ran back to me. She threw her arms around me and said, "Don't go, Eva. Don't leave us forever. I love you." Then she just as abruptly turned and ran away.

When Laura came back from escorting them to the transit station, I hadn't moved and had tears in my eyes.

"Oh, honey." She put her pale, slender arms about my shoulders. "It'll be okay. We all knew this was life-changing when you wanted to sign up for it. We talked about it for a while, but we agreed you wouldn't be happy unless you tried."

I wiped my eyes and went back to inspecting my split lip. "What?"

"Gino, me, Val, and Ivy. We talked about it when you brought it up. But we discussed it and figured you needed to do this for you."

"You all sat down and talked about me?" I had a hard time wrapping my mind around that little tidbit. I didn't like the idea of them sitting around worrying about me.

"Well, of course. Just like you and I did when Trevor ran away, and we didn't want to tell Ivy."

"I'm not a child," I said indignantly.

"Of course not. But that doesn't mean we don't love you just the same, and want what's best for you." Laura hugged me hard. All I could smell was the lavender shampoo she used. "Eva, I love you.

You're my best friend. But I think this decision is what'll make you the happiest." She pushed away and looked me directly in the eye. "Now, we need to figure out how to get you back to the Program without those wackos getting the chance to grab you again, especially if this Raevu alien makes you very…erotic-dream-having happy." With another laugh, she kissed my heated cheek and went to refresh her coffee.

What were the odds she'd walk in on the first erotic dream I had in my life? And it had been a strong one. My whole body tingled at the feeling of his mouth on my nipple and his hand stroking me. My whole center still ached with the need he'd created.

I closed my eyes and pictured him moving toward me again—his blue skin glistening in the moonlight as he stormed across the room. The warmth of his body pressed against mine in that too-small bed of Laura's. Raevu's gold eyes seeming to pierce into me just before he plunged into a kiss that made my lips quiver as I relived the experience.

I reached my hand up and traced my bottom lip with my finger. *Was it my imagination, or did my lip feel swollen from his kisses? Damn. It had felt so real.*

"How do I get back safely, Laura? I don't know if I can trust the authorities."

Laura tidied up her kitchen and wiped down her counters. The whole time she had on her thinking face. She always did her best thinking while she was cleaning. "I'm not sure, Eva. If this Cold guy is a cop or something like that, going to the local precinct is suicide. But the Juhlians are here for you. You can't just stay here. You promised yourself to them." She continued to clean her kitchen even after it was spotless. "What would I do? What would I do?" With her eyes closed, she wiped the same spot on her counter three times. I smiled at her distraction as she went on. "I would do the unexpected. Shout from the rooftops, holler in the streets. Draw as much attention as possible so the bad guys couldn't sweep me under the rug."

Laura dropped her towel and grabbed my hands. "That's it. After last night's press conference with President Maeda talking about how much we need this treaty, you need to show up in a public place like the broadcast station. Somewhere on camera so no one can hide you or sweep you away." Her eyes were aflame and excited with her idea. "We need to sneak you to the broadcast station and get you on camera!"

CHAPTER 11
RAEVU

"Who is Laura?" I asked T'ral as I stepped into our suite's common space. It was stuffed with examples of our people's art, displayed without any knowledge of the proper method to do so, like precious jewels thrown haphazardly.

"What is a Laura?" Baelon interjected.

"I had a dream last night of Eva. Someone named 'Laura' interrupted it and caused me to awake. Who is 'Laura' to Eva?" I demanded.

"Well, if you're insisting… Though, it was a dream, sire." T'ral consulted his data screen. "There is a Laura Evans. She is a human female and friend to Eva Knight. She has a daughter—age five and same age as Ivy Thompson's youngest child. Otherwise, there is no connection. They did not attend the same schools. Never employed by the same companies."

T'ral continued to study his data screen. "No, no connection other than age, gender, and the age of this child they each live with."

Baelon scowled. "This is the problem with eunuchs. You don't see emotional connections. There could easily be a connection between this female and Raevu's just through the fact that Raevu's female has taken care of the children."

T'ral gave Baelon a flat stare. "I can see emotional connections just fine. I am merely not enslaved by them."

I shook my head in warning at Baelon. He was obviously in a hostile mood today. "Let's not take our tension over this situation out on each other."

"Of course not, sire." Baelon turned back to the monitor where he had been flipping through entertainment and news broadcasts. He stopped abruptly on one and sat up attentively. "That is us!"

T'ral and I turned to see what he was looking at. A photograph of us with President Maeda at yesterday's press conference was up on the screen. Splashed across one corner was the title "Found!" in big, bold letters. The image switched to a close-up of a human male.

"Turn on the sound, Baelon," I ordered.

"Exclusive! Ms. Knight has expressed her desire to stay here at the CNR Broadcast Station until the Peace Opportunity Program Ambassadors can collect her. Her tale is one of amazing courage and cleverness."

The camera zoomed out to show the male sitting in a chair facing a woman with rich brown skin and black hair. *Eva!* I pivoted, stepping toward the door just as someone knocked on it. Derek Willoughby and Ken Maeda were standing outside my suite.

"Eva is on the television. I'm going to get her." I started to push past them.

"Wait, Raevu, please," Ken said.

I scowled at him. "There will be no waiting, Ken. She needs my help. I have to go to her now."

"Yes, we will get her, but you are the king of your planet and indispensable. We can't trust that this Humans for Humanity League or some other terrorist group will not to try to attack. Send warriors you trust to collect her. Derek here will take them to the broadcast station." His voice was terribly reasonable, making me bristle slightly.

I began to growl my dissent, but T'ral answered before I could,

"Sire. That is a very good idea. Baelon and your men should go to ensure her safety. Your first meeting with your life mate should not be broadcasted to the entire planet. It should be a private moment between you two." His smile was perfectly polite and reasonable.

I hated that he was right and did not appreciate the position T'ral had just placed me in by agreeing with Ken's sensible strategy. T'ral forced me to think beyond my desires of the moment...to run out to claim Eva.

Baelon was already moving. "Let's go," he barked at Willoughby. Willoughby spun on his heel, and they left the suite.

I kept the news broadcast playing on the monitor. The reporter asked Eva why she had volunteered for the program, what her experience with it was, how she was treated when she was kidnapped. She deftly managed not to give him very many clear answers. In listening to her responses, I heard nothing new and nothing that could be said or used against her.

It seemed that she had snuck away from her captors, but I didn't believe it was that simple. Her kidnappers would not have left her alone unless they were confident they could recapture her. I wondered if they had attached some kind of tracking unit on to her. No. Eva was smart. Even if they had, it would be reckless for them to kidnap her while she was in public and on television.

"This is live, isn't it?" I asked when there was a commotion on the screen. Startled cries could be heard off-camera. The reporter and Eva glanced around, probably to see what was causing the disturbance, and both sprang to their feet.

I moved closer to the monitor, as if I could throw myself between Eva and any danger coming her way. The terrorists must have dared a public assault on her. Baelon and my men strode into view. They dwarfed all the men around them, and except for her luscious curves, Eva almost looked like a child next to their brawn. They moved right up to her, ignoring a brunette yelling at Baelon to back away and leave Eva alone.

When they reached Eva, my warriors knelt, bowing their head. Quite clearly, I heard Baelon say, "My queen. We've come to escort you home safely."

"Queen? Laura, is this some kind of joke?" I could tell by Eva's voice that she was puzzled. I had gone from tense to fighting a smile as I saw her stunned expression.

The brunette, I assumed, Laura, looked just as confused. "Not mine, Eva."

Baelon and my men stood in a smooth motion. They placed themselves strategically around Eva and began scanning the room for possible threats. I nodded in satisfaction at their efficiency.

"Raevu sent me, my lady." Baelon remained very formal and stiff. The two women exchanged glances. Willoughby then appeared on the scene, trying to calm station personnel for their abrupt arrival.

I ordered, "T'ral, contact the ship. We leave for home at first light tomorrow." My life mate was safe and in our custody. We were going home.

CHAPTER 12
EVA

"No!" I said as firmly as my tired voice would allow. "We are not leaving right away. That is not happening." My fatigue was creeping back, and my headache had returned with a vengeance. "I am absolutely sick of strange men trying to grab me and drag me places." My ordeal had ended in total anticlimax, but I had been right about one thing, Cold was a Center security man. We knew that now because the crazed son of a bitch had actually tried to get into the broadcast station with his duty gun. One suspicious call to Center security quickly exposed Cold as not being there on Center business, and he was now in custody, along with his partners in crime, after he'd snitched on their location. It wasn't the humiliating, painful punishment they deserved, but it would land them behind bars, and I would take that justice.

Baelon turned to face me squarely. "My lady, the king, who also happens to be your life mate, has decided that we need to leave right away for your safety. Therefore, we will leave for our home as soon as possible."

"No, we won't. I'm sick. I just had to rescue myself from a kidnapping because neither you nor Center security could manage it. And I'm not taking orders from anyone until I see my family and get some damn sleep." I reached up with my hands and rubbed my temples as he stared at me awkwardly.

I had been able to ignore my flu-like symptoms while adrenaline had been pumping through my body, but now that I felt safe from my abductors, every symptom clamored to be noticed.

"It is tactically ill-advised for us to stay, given the terrorists who are still after you have not been captured." He tried to reason, my defiance deflating some of his arrogance.

I glared at him. "I'm saying that I still have free will. I am not your property or your king's. You will respect my rights. Including my right to quit this contract and walk away from all of you if you keep calling me to heel like a fucking dog." I'd had enough and was completely at my limit. I was emotionally and physically exhausted. I locked eyes with the alien until he looked away.

"Well, you have spirit, Eva. I will give you that." The huge man sighed, sounding strangely wistful. "But ultimately, it's the king's decision."

I snorted. "If you go today, you will be leaving without me. Unless I'm dragged kicking and screaming onto that ship, we will not be leaving for several days." As he opened his mouth to speak once again, I continued, "Baelon, you and I are not going to agree on this. I will speak to Raevu, the king and, according to you, my 'life mate' myself. He and I will have to come to some sort of compromise. If we are life mates, and I'm not terribly sure I believe all that, we'll be compromising for the rest of our lives. We may as well start now." I sighed and leaned back in the vehicle seat.

My tired mind whirled with too much information. *This mark, the one that had suddenly appeared on my skin after I'd been injected with the alien DNA, was supposed to prove that I was the "soul mate" of their king?* That type of shit only happened in fairy tales. *Ridiculous.* This mark has become a liability.

But on the other hand, I did sign up to help the Juhlian people, and in whatever capacity necessary. My word was my bond, and I would help them, but I needed time to rest. "Honestly, I don't know why you would want to push me into space travel when I'm sick."

The last comment seemed to shame him into silence because he was quiet for the rest of the drive.

"We are here, my lady," Baelon finally said with a small smile. He opened the car door and climbed out, then reached back in to give me a hand.

I was appalled to discover I needed the assistance. Once out of the vehicle, I stood still for a moment until my head stopped swimming. He remained by my side, watching me carefully, seeming to realize that even with my strong will, I really was sick as hell right now. I nodded to Baelon to show I was ready, and we proceeded into the Center's guest quarters. When I'd last been here, I'd been housed in a suite on the ground floor. Now, I didn't know where they were taking me. All I knew was that I'd get there swiftly enough with this escort. People in the halls parted for us like a school of fish before sharks.

The Juhlian warriors that Raevu had sent to fetch me from the broadcast station were all huge males. Well over six feet tall, broad in the shoulders, ribs, and hips, they made all the human males we passed seem almost scrawny and lanky in comparison. And their skin fascinated me. It was blue, almost like a blueberry. They wore military uniforms and seemed to radiate an aura of "you don't want to mess with me." I tried to imagine a large army of such intimidating warriors and couldn't.

They had fallen into a formation around me, which meant I was surrounded by a mobile wall of muscles. I was quite sure that if even one of these males had been with me, the Humans for Humanity League never would have been able to take me. With all of the Juhlian warriors at hand, I felt as secure as a baby in its mother's arms. But I still looked around nervously, painfully aware that if one of the terrorists who had taken me worked for the Center, they all could. I wondered what their story was, especially Cleve.

Cleve, who, from the way they had talked, probably had a sister who was part of the program—a test subject, like me. Something terrible must have happened to her. And from my experience with the program, I had no doubt that the government had covered it up. Now, I wondered if the other subjects had really quit or had never left the lab alive.

Silently, we marched through the lobby and to the elevators. Inside, and away from prying eyes, I let myself lean on Baelon for the ride up to the top floor. He offered his arm stoically, no longer seeming frustrated with me.

I let my mind drift to Raevu. My dream the night before had been so erotic and sensual. Just thinking about it, I shivered deliciously. Raevu, in my dream, had been so gentle and attentive when he had come to me in my bed. He'd aroused me with his kisses and knowledgeable strokes against my body.

My eyes fluttered closed, just remembering the feel of his hot blue skin under my hands. I'd never touched a man like that in my entire life, yet, with him, I'd been bold. I'd shown no hesitation when I had invited him to join me in bed and touch me. And, oh…the way his mouth had burned trails down my neck to my nipples was just so unreal. I swallowed hard, recalling how I took his large, rock-hard cock into my hand, stroking it while he touched me intimately.

My eyes snapped open.

In my dream, he seemed so patient and gentle. I hoped he was just as open-minded in reality because I couldn't leave Earth right now. I needed rest. Time to adjust to my new future that would apparently be forged on his planet. He had to understand there were things I'd need to finish before I could leave my home…Earth…for good.

We stepped off the elevator, stopping briefly while two of the warriors checked for danger before one knocked on the suite's door. He didn't wait for an answer but opened it and did a quick scan inside before motioning us forward.

Once we were in the suite, I stared in amazement. It was ten times the size of my suite downstairs. The alien warriors relaxed their vigil, fanning out behind me.

Now, I could easily look around the space. My attention zeroed in on one figure who had risen from a conference table and was moving in my direction…toward me.

It was Raevu.

He was taller even than Baelon and just as powerfully built as every one of the Juhlian warriors he'd sent to fetch me. His blue skin contrasted against the business suit he wore. But it was his aura that made me stare; he was the poster child for an alpha male and bore an air of command.

I swallowed hard. This would our first in-person meeting.

His gold eyes locked on to me as he strode like a deadly, sleek but glorious panther.

Nothing about the alien was soft. His eyes were hard and glinted in his angular face. The jawline I'd caressed in my dream was firm and fixed. The alien in my dream I felt I'd known and trusted. This man was a stranger that looked menacing and unyielding.

He reached for me. I stepped back, right into the wall that was Baelon's chest.

Raevu stopped abruptly, within arm's reach, and examined me quizzically. "Eva? You look just as you did in my dream."

My eyes widened. *How did he know about the dream?*

"Are you well?" he inquired.

His voice resonated deep within my belly. I swallowed and held my head high. "Yes, I am…mostly. Baelon says you have plans to leave Earth immediately?"

Raevu folded his muscular arms in front of him, studying me. "Yes. The mismanagement within the program has endangered your life, and all of your kidnappers have not been captured. For your security and safety, I want you in an environment that I control. Juhl is the safest place for you. Second safest is our ship."

An enormous sneeze exploded out of me. The antihistamine I'd snorted at Laura's was wearing off, and the ruckus I'd made startled the Juhlians. I shook my head. "Raevu, we can't leave right away."

His eyebrow lifted imperiously. "Why not?"

I lifted my chin. "For one, I am very sick, probably contagious. I'm also injured and exhausted from the kidnapping. And I need some damn rest before I am whisked off anywhere. Next, the only clothes I have are the ones I am wearing, and if everyone on your planet is male and tall, there's nothing that will fit me. And last but not least, I have loved ones here I need to say good-bye to if I am leaving Earth forever." At the last point, my voice cracked a bit, with tears welling up in my eyes.

Damnit! Do not cry, Eva.

I blinked furiously, still holding up my chin stubbornly and refusing to let my tears fall. I didn't know this commanding and flinty alien, and all my fears of the unknown bubbled up inside me, threatening to emotionally overwhelm me. *What the fuck was going on with me? I'm never this emotional or insecure.*

"Leave us," Raevu barked. Immediately, all but Baelon and one other left the room. "Baelon, T'ral, you as well." This was spoken less harshly but with just as much command.

Out of the corner of my eye, I saw the other figure leave, but the wall against my back hadn't budged. *Come on, Baelon, don't be an asshole. Raevu and I need to hash this shit out in private.*

Raevu broke eye contact with me and glared over my head at him. I could feel the rumble of Baelon's deep drawl through his chest against my back. "Begging your pardon, nephew, but I am now Queen's Guard. I will do only what I think best for her or what she orders me to do. She is trembling, so I know she is not comfortable in your presence right now."

I shut my eyes in mortification. *Shit. Betrayed by my own weakness and, it seems, my staunchest supporter…Baelon.*

Raevu frowned but stepped to one side, waving his arm toward a chair. "By all means, let's make her comfortable."

His dry tone did nothing to ease my discomfort. Baelon nudged me a bit to get me moving and chuckled at the glare I threw over my shoulder at him. I wasn't sure how knowing him for an hour made me feel at ease in his company. But I did know that the big male across from me, Raevu, made me decidedly nervous. This was the most intense case of pre-date jitters ever.

I lowered myself onto the couch in the seating area. Raevu settled his bulk into a chair that had been made for someone of much smaller dimensions. He didn't seem worried about its creaking under him as he leaned back and crossed one ankle over his knee. Baelon moved to another part of the room, and I heard the clink of glassware from that direction.

I refused to let my symptoms render me weak in any way. Instead of resting, I spoke up. "I have some questions for you." Maybe if we spoke for a while, I could find some glimmer of the male I'd seen on the live-stream and the gentle one from my dream, instead of the hard, unemotional blue alien sitting across from me.

Raevu nodded. "As do I, for you. For one, who gave you that mark that you bear on your body?"

My hand flew to the welted area where my right shoulder met my neck. Of all the questions he might have had for me, this one surprised me. "Gave me? No one gave me this damn mark. It appeared out of nowhere after the experiments began."

His feet thumped as they hit the floor. He leaned forward and put his elbows on his knees. "Are you sure? Is it a burn? A tattoo?" His tone was piercing, as were his bright gold eyes. Now, I was starting to get offended by his tone.

"Don't you think that I would know if someone burned or tattooed me?" My eyes narrowed. "Let's get one thing straight. I do not lie. So, what I said is true. No one fucking touched me. This is not a burn or scar from a cut or heat, and it certainly isn't a fucking rash." My voice got louder with each sentence. "Whatever experiments were done resulted in disfiguring my neck and shoulder with this damn port-wine looking birthmark. Besides, what the hell business is it of yours where it came from anyway?"

Baelon chose that moment to hand me a glass of water. I thanked him as I took it, but I continued to scowl at Raevu. There was no way in hell that I was going to be bullied by the likes of him. Baelon handed Raevu what looked like a strange purple-colored beer and kept another for himself.

Raevu's voice remained calm. "What I'm asking you is important, Eva. Very important."

Now, I was intrigued by the worried expression on his face. *What the hell is going on?*

"Is it as important as the fact that one day I was part of this alien science experiment and the next I was brought here and told I was your fiancée?" His eye twitched at my last statement. I was onto something, so I continued my interrogation. "Is it as important as the fact that I thought, when I signed up for this program, that I would be one of dozens, if not hundreds, from around the planet—only to find out later that I'm one of five?" His eyes narrowed. I pushed on. "Hmmm…

maybe I'm the only one who survived, but perhaps you can shed some light on my theory. Am I the only survivor of this alien experiment?" I looked between the two of them, and I stilled at the expression of dismay on Baelon's face.

Holy shit! I'm the only survivor.

I went on, "Truth be told, when I signed up for the Peace Opportunity Program and went through all the screenings and let myself be injected with whatever mad scientist concoction they put inside me, I suspected I'd end up being treated like some kind of soldier or lab rat for the rest of my life. I certainly wasn't expecting to be told I was now engaged to a king of an alien planet. A king? For fuck's sake, that type of fairy-tale shit only happens in movies." I ran out of steam and took a big gulp of my water then clasped the glass as if it was a life preserver.

Belligerently, I glowered at Raevu, who was staring at me like I had two heads. This was certainly not the male I'd offered myself to so freely the night before in my dream. Maybe I was looking for some Prince Charming to sweep me off my feet, whisking me off to happily ever after. It was a stupid dream. This was balls-to-the-wall reality, and this fucker was not interested in anything but saving his people using any means necessary…me.

Angry and utterly disappointed, I fought to stay stoic as overwhelming emotions threatened to sweep me away in a fit of hysterical crying. *Pull up your big girl panties, Eva. You knew full well what you were signing up for.* I felt like an idiot. The dream had given me hope for something more…a relationship that was less cold and clinical with Raevu. It had shown me what I'd desired most…true chemistry and romance with him.

His voice was infuriatingly calm when he uttered, "I agree. A fated mating doesn't happen. Soul mates—I believe humans call it—is something from a children's story." He paused. "That aside, do you know what the mark on your body is?"

My energy was spent, and I was done with this alien. For that's just what he was, an asshole alien who didn't believe the word of a woman. *Seems like males are males, no matter what planet they originate from.* I leaned forward and placed my glass on the low table between us. I mimicked his posture, feet solidly on the floor and slightly apart, elbows on knees, tilting forward. I spoke in my lowest, calmest tones. "I've answered your damn question once. So, if you're going to continue to ask me the same question over and over again, it's going to be a long night—for you. I'm out of here." As gracefully and steadily as I could, I rose to my feet. Before either male could move, I spoke again, praying to be answered, "Geoffrey?"

My personal computer concierge answered immediately, "Yes, madam?"

"Would you open the door to my room, please? I'm exhausted and need to lie down." It had definitely reached the point of a need. My legs were so wobbly I feared I would collapse to the floor.

Immediately, a door nearest the windows swung open. "Thank you, Geoffrey." I tried to sweep gracefully from the room, but I began to stumble before I could make it across the space. Baelon caught my elbow and walked me the rest of the way to my door. My cheeks burned with embarrassment, but I didn't pull my arm from his grip.

"Eva," Raevu called from his seat.

I paused, shaking harder. I was starting to hurt, and it was putting me in a fouler mood. "Yes?" I snapped.

"In my dream, you said that because you were part of the program, you believed you'd have many mates. This is wrong. You will only have one mate. Me." His eyes were glowing again, his desire smoldering toward me as he looked me over.

I stared back at him, using the last of my resolve. "Maybe if you earn it, I'll be interested. But as of right now, you're not doing a very good job of showing that you deserve me." I turned to smile my gratitude at Baelon for his help.

"Well played, my queen." Baelon winked at me, seeming amused by my standing up to Raevu.

Without another word, I simply withdrew into my cavernously large bedroom, locking the door behind me.

CHAPTER 13
RAEVU

I drank down my qua in one long swallow as Eva made her grand exit, and I cursed under my breath. I hadn't gotten the answers I needed, and we were stuck here waiting on her for at least another day.

There was no doubt in my mind that I should have been thinking more of her physical and emotional welfare, instead of doing nothing. The fact that I didn't did not sit well with me, but when I was around her, I had trouble thinking logically. All common sense escaped me in her presence…and my baser urges pressed to the forefront, with strong urges to claim and mate her in the most animalistic manner.

She's mine. My life mate…to hold, touch, stroke, and claim.

I sat there, bewildered. But for the life of me…I didn't understand how our interaction had gone so wrong, so fast.

Before she strode through the door, I had been replaying the dream in my head and her sweet words of encouragement and enjoyment at my touch. Yet, once she was actually in front of me, all I felt and heard from her was resistance to me.

Were all human women this complicated and stubborn?

All she seemed to want to do was stay here on Earth and tend to her wounds and illness, when I had the most state-of-the-art medical treatment on my ship. *And why was she so resistant to leaving her fellow humans? Didn't she know that they could visit her on my planet? It is my duty and privilege as her life mate to make her happy. Why didn't she understand that?*

Had I made a mistake in thinking she was my mate? Was the mark just some bizarre coincidence?

No. It couldn't be. The pull toward her was too strong. I'd never experienced it before, but I knew it was the mating call my people talked about for centuries. It wasn't just her beauty that attracted me, but it was her strong personality that drew me to her like a moth to a flame.

Baelon came back over and sat in her vacated spot. He gave me a long, steady look and reached out to hand me his glass over the low table. I took it and knocked back its contents.

It didn't help fast enough. I shoved to my feet and started pacing the floor, then shucked my jacket and tossed it over the back of a couch. "I don't understand. I didn't ask anything inappropriate. I need to know how and from whom she got the mark."

Baelon nodded slowly, stood, took both our glasses, and went to refill them. His silence spoke volumes. He was disappointed.

"What, Uncle? You obviously have an opinion. And what the Kyrpa was that 'Queen's Guard' business? Since when do we have a 'Queen's Guard'?"

He turned and walked back over to me and handed me another glass of the dark-flavored qua. "You, my king, are a fool." Baelon's words were quiet and emphatic.

My eyes narrowed. "What do you mean? I said nothing wrong."

"No, you didn't. But in your desire to get information, you completely forgot what the female has gone through in just the last few days. Her illness. Her exhaustion. The trauma of her time as an experimental subject, and the trauma of being kidnapped, tied, and beaten. Even just how her life has changed in the last few weeks." He shook his head sadly. "If my Amira were still alive, she would slap me if I ever made demands of her when she was that worn out."

I eyed him. "I have a whole planet at stake here, Baelon. All of my people are at risk. I thought this experiment, this genetic trade, could help ensure our prosperity as a people. But instead of dozens of females, we end up with one. And she somehow bears our family crest? Marking her as my life mate? How is that possible?"

"I'm your uncle and your arms master, not a scientist. How can I presume to guess? Call T'ral back in. Maybe he has more answers."

I rubbed my hands over my smooth head and said aloud, "Geoffrey, would you tell T'ral to come back in here?" In exasperation, I unbuttoned my cuffs and rolled up my shirtsleeves. But even as I expressed exasperation with my uncle, I felt a tug of worry. *Had I really made that much of an ass of myself with my future mate?*

The ever-present voice replied at once, "Of course, Your Majesty."

Within moments, a door leading off into another part of the suite opened and closed, and T'ral entered. Here were two of my most trusted advisers, military and political. Between the three of us, surely, we could come up with some answers on what to do about Eva.

He must have seen our glasses arranged on the table in front of us, for he paused briefly at the bar area to fill a pitcher of qua and grab a third glass. As he sat down on the couch next to Baelon, he asked, "What have you discovered?"

"Nothing," I said dryly, "except that Baelon here has formed a Queen's Guard for the soon-to-be queen. Our lady claims not to know how the mark got on her skin. It just appeared, according to her. And —" I held out my glass for a refill "—Baelon believes I am a fool."

T'ral unbuttoned his suit jacket and leaned back on the couch. "Well, all of that could be true."

"Thank you for your support of your monarch, T'ral." My tone got even drier.

The corner of T'ral's mouth actually twitched in annoyance. "Raevu, a Queen's Guard is actually a good idea. We know that, here on Earth, there are already factions that do not want a treaty between humans and our people. It was fine when we were trading goods and services, but when we wanted to include genetics in the mix...the opposition reared its head. She must be protected at all costs."

"Don't you think I know this?" I barked.

They both stared at me with doubt written all over their faces. I huffed in annoyance.

T'ral spoke on, with the manner of a scholar giving a lecture. "So, as far as the mark goes, according to our history, it appears when the life mate to the king comes of age. According to archives, the mark on the female is accompanied by weakness or sickness, which can only be remedied by a mating ceremony between the king and his life mate under the Sopu tree, when it is in bloom."

"But that doesn't explain how a human can be an alien's mate," I stated.

"This is not a clear-cut answer. But in the past, the king's female was always a distant relation, so there was a trace of the king's family's DNA in the female's system. The only answer I can extrapolate from this current situation is that since it was your DNA sent for the experiment, and Eva is of age, that once she was exposed to your family DNA, her genetic material accepted you as a viable match, hence the mark indicating that she's your life mate. But that's just my speculation. There is no precedence for what happened between you and Eva." He shrugged. "My theory is that if we continue with this program, exposing more of our people's DNA to the human females, then we should expect to have more life mate matches. Now, whether that results in saving our race from extinction, well, that's a whole other story."

Baelon and I both looked at him in surprise.

"How did you find this information? You had several clerks looking into it when we left, and they'd had no luck as of last word," I countered.

T'ral loosened his tie, muttering something about human males liking nooses around their necks, and smiled ruefully. "They were focused on scientific logic and deemed the human females as inconsequential to this matter. That was their first mistake. I knew the humans were the key to unlocking this mystery, so I started there first. One thing the humans have done extremely well is create 'search engines' that sort through information for you. For all of our advances in other areas, this is their genius. I dumped our histories into Geoffrey's data system, and within a very short time, he had used what he called keywords to find the information we sought. And two words kept popping up every time, 'female choice.'"

I frowned. "Explain."

"It's strange, really. It is a form of mate choice, when females in certain species use physical or chemical mechanisms to control a male's success of inseminating them. Namely by selecting whether sperm are successful in fertilizing their eggs or not. I believe with the introduction of your DNA to Eva's body, this is exactly what happened. Female choice. She selected you as her life mate." T'ral sipped his qua. "Shocking, I know, but my clerks had to read through each document. And due to the sensitive nature of the situation, I was limited in telling them exactly what to look for. Geoffrey just had to skim, and we have no worries about his allegiance or whether he'll make a judgment against us. I am going to make a request of President Maeda, sire, that we be allowed to take Geoffrey with us when we leave."

Baelon shook his head. "Eunuchs! Always wanting new toys!"

T'ral looked at him flatly.

"Not today, you two. I need my advisers, not an additional headache." I interrupted their usual derisive banter before it could even begin. I rubbed my temple and forehead with my free hand, as a headache had begun to form. I set down the qua and picked up Eva's water glass. I couldn't believe it. Eva chose me, and she didn't even know it.

"Raevu," Baelon inquired, "what ails you?"

"Nothing. I am fine," I replied. It was probably just my immune system destroying some alien bacterium. "What else did Geoffrey's search discover?"

T'ral was looking at me curiously. "He discovered that, in many cases, the mating ceremony could not take place immediately. At one time, it was several years between the time the queen-to-be came of age and the king returned from war. The people couldn't have a sick queen-to-be for an indeterminate amount of time, so a solution of sorts was discovered."

"Of sorts?" Baelon scoffed. "What is this 'of sorts'?"

"The solution is an elixir, but it doesn't completely remove all of the symptoms, it eases them. It does have two side effects, according to the archives. One, that when her monthly cycle is upon her, the remedy will have no effect at all, and all symptoms will return." At this point, T'ral began looking decidedly uncomfortable.

"That sounds perfectly miserable," Baelon commented. Of all of us, he would know, having actually lived with a woman at length.

I agreed wholeheartedly. "And the second?"

T'ral took a drink from his qua and cleared his throat.

"Well?" I demanded, "What is it?"

"While taking the elixir, she will be extremely sensitive and highly suggestible to contact of a personal nature." T'ral coughed into his fist.

As one, Baelon and I sat back and let this information sink in. T'ral had cloaked it in formal language, so we had to decipher it. A wide grin spread across my face when I finally understood.

"You're saying she's going to want me to mate with her…often. I think I can handle that."

"It's a bit more, sire. She's going to want you to mate with her, but in the past, the urge has made females at times paranoid or angry or even fearful. As she is human, we have no idea how the side effects might manifest…" T'ral leaned forward so I could see the earnestness on his face. "She will need to be watched over by only your most trusted."

"I have already sworn to that duty," Baelon said indignantly.

"I trust Baelon implicitly. And I will be with her. Between us, we can handle the side effects." I smiled again. "She may not be ready to allow me to mate with her. But surely, I can touch her intimately to ease some of her warring emotions. I look forward to it."

"Perhaps, Raevu, we should discuss this with her present?" Baelon was most definitely her champion. I winced, imagining Eva's reaction to this conversation in her current mood.

To my surprise, T'ral agreed. Usually, they seemed to disagree just to be able to argue.

"No, not now." I rubbed my aching neck and shoulder muscles. "She's bathing, and after that, she needs rest."

"How do you know that, sire?" T'ral asked.

"I don't know. Wait…" I thought a moment. Surely it was impossible. "I can sense her. Not her body, but her. How is this even feasible?"

T'ral and Baelon exchanged wide-eyed looks, and then both shook their heads at me. "I don't know, sire," T'ral said. "I will look into it. What exactly are you sensing, and when did it start?"

"I can feel the headache, the muscle aches, and the upset stomach. I can almost feel the water of the bath against my skin, but more, I can tell she's bathing because the heat from the water gives her pleasure. She's relaxing, not feeling as frustrated." I felt like I was straining to hear, but with my whole body instead of just my ears. It was undeniable. "How can I feel what she is feeling? And why now? Why not when the mark first appeared?" We seemed to have answered a couple of questions about Eva and her condition, only to end up with more questions to answer than when we had started. Surely, we would find these answers when we got back to our own planet.

I slumped back in my chair and continued rubbing my ghost headache with my fingertips. It may have been Eva's actual pain, but it felt real to me. I waved dismissal to my two advisers, who immediately stood.

T'ral said, "One other thing the histories repeated, sire."

I looked up and was sure this was not going to be something I wanted to hear.

He continued, "She cannot be breached by you or anyone or anything else until the mating ceremony. She must remain pure... whole. Once the ceremony is completed under the Sopu tree, then she is yours to mate."

Baelon interjected, "Nephew, if you're sensing what she's going through, including the side effects, and add in what you're feeling already, that'll make for some pretty intense moments. You will have to hold yourself aloof from them."

"Baelon, my uncle," I assured him, "I am a king and a warrior. I can handle this. We will hold our meeting first thing in the morning, when Eva and President Maeda can join us."

Both nodded, and I gave them their marching orders, "T'ral, you may make your request for Geoffrey then, if you can figure out how to get him to work with our computer systems. Baelon, as you cannot be on duty for your queen-to-be at all hours of the day and night, I need you to set up a duty roster for your select few that will be rotating the duties with you. We may need to make adjustments when she begins taking the elixir."

They nodded their agreement with this plan and went to their own rooms. I put my feet up on the low table and considered all the things Eva said she wanted, and how to supply them.

CHAPTER 14
EVA

I needed to freshen up, and the bathroom in my section of the suite was glorious. The whole space was done in some kind of iridescent, pale stuff that looked like a mix of mother-of-pearl and opal. It was like walking into a gigantic jewel, almost enough to jolt me out of my anger and frustration at being so very wrong about Raevu. *Almost.*

How could someone so hot be so arrogant and thick-headed?

I knew that looks and smarts didn't always go hand in hand, but he and I had spoken a couple of times. He hadn't seemed stubborn then. Yet talking to him directly had reminded me of trying to break through a brick wall by repeatedly banging my head against it…it was painful.

I took a long soak in the enormous, pearly tub, enjoying the way it loosened me up and distressed me. Meanwhile, I mulled over how to get through to Raevu. It seemed we would be spending a lot of time together, and we needed to get along.

Besides, things were quickly getting weird, and we would have to work together to deal with it. I still couldn't process that we'd actually shared a dream. *How else could he have known about the "many mates" statement?* I'd never even shared that fear with Laura or Ivy. I'd only ever voiced that worry to him in my…our…dream.

And then there was my body's traitorous reaction to him. I was attracted to him, and my desire kindled the moment I saw him. I took a deep breath and forced myself to set my frustrated desires aside while I cleaned myself then brushed out my thick hair. I was still thinking about him when I wrapped myself in a spa robe from the linen closet and left the bathroom.

I was still weak, so, occasionally, I used the backs of the furniture to help my balance. Reaching the bedroom door, I sighed at the lovely view of the bed covered in a white and gold damask duvet, flanked by nightstands that each held a regal-looking lamp.

Against the wall was a monitor screen and an extremely comfortable-looking deep brown chair with an ottoman. Why there would be a chair facing the bed, I had no idea, but I knew I would soon be on very good terms with that chair if I didn't start feeling better.

The other door that led off from the room granted entry to a closet as large as the bedroom Trevor and Mark shared in Ivy's apartment. I stared around at all the outfits, bewildered.

"Geoffrey?" I asked.

"Yes, ma'am?" his rich voice answered, as I knew it would.

"Why are there already clothes in this closet?" They were my size, but so diverse in style, color, and coverage that it confused me further.

"They're your clothes, ma'am," he responded. "They were moved up here from the other suite after King Raevu took up residence."

Vaguely, I remembered someone telling me about clothing. *The ambassador?* No, the nurse who had guided me to the suite. She had said I had clothing waiting for me. I'd never imagined so many clothes, though. Within the closet was a three-drawer chest, and it was filled. The top drawer held numerous set of lingerie—all of them matching. Pajamas and nighties, comfy and sexy, filled the second drawer, and the bottom drawer held socks and scarves. There was quite a variety of clothing hanging from the hangers: dresses, pants, skirts, blue jeans, jackets, and sweaters. There were shoes of all types on the shelves, and tucked into a corner was a set of luggage to pack it all away when necessary. I was speechless. I trailed my fingers along the edges of the garments' sleeves to feel all the different textures. I shook my head in amazement.

It was time to give one of those pajama sets a test drive. I grabbed a teal silk set and then threw off my robe, pausing to have a look at myself in the mirror. I was surprised that neither my illness nor my injuries showed much.

I turned away from the mirror and looked back over my shoulder at the mark that no longer smarted when I poked at it. It didn't look inflamed anymore, but the slightly raised and darker-pigmented pattern was still clearly visible.

I couldn't believe Raevu thought the mark meant that I belonged to him. I chose who I wanted…not him. And the way I saw it, he had to seriously step up his game to redeem himself in my eyes. His high-handed treatment of me was deplorable and enraged me. But there was the undeniable fact that I wanted him more than any other man. Just thinking about him sent a surge of lust zinging through my body.

My urge to have him was strangely strong. Desire to give myself to him in the most hedonistic manner was shocking. The image of both of us naked, with me riding him, flittered through my head. His muscular arms wrapped around my waist as his thick cock surged forcefully into my throbbing cunt. The slapping sound of skin against skin. His moan. My sigh of pleasure. The vision bloomed, becoming more vivid as I trailed my fingertips down my neck and over the full, round globes of each breast to my nipples. They were already hard, and I circled them with my fingers a few times and continued down my body.

I imagined Raevu's thick fingers joining mine to caress me, and as my fingers slid across my pussy, I shuddered. I tucked my finger between my slick folds and began to make gentle circles. With my other hand, I massaged a heavy, full breast. My pleasure grew, and my circles quickened. My hips jerked. I began to gently pull and pinch at each nipple in turn. No longer circling, now hard flicks back and forth had a coil of tension building until, with a moan, my orgasm shook through me. I withdrew my hands, sleepily forcing myself to pull on my pajamas. It was time for a well-earned nap.

I just couldn't shake the wish that Raevu would join me.

CHAPTER 15
RAEVU

Once I realized I could feel what Eva was feeling, I had a very hard time getting any rest that evening. I felt her sensual pleasure in the bath, the comfort she took in the soft robe against her skin, her shocked gratitude at all the clothes she had to choose from in the drawers, and her sexual release as she pleasured herself.

I was already naked between the sheets of my bed, and it was no great leap of imagination to picture her beside me. Instantly, I was aroused and rock hard. After she came, I sensed she went to sleep, but my body demanded her attention.

Groaning, I took myself in hand and caressed my shaft. I hadn't had to satiate myself this often since I was a youngling with little control over my sexual urges. I closed my eyes and pictured Eva in bed as her sienna skin glistened with sweat and she writhed under my rapt attention. Her nipples tightening and begging for my fingers to pluck and rub them, her sweet moans of pleasure as I devoured her lips. My hand started to stroke faster up and down the length of my shaft.

One day soon. She will be mine.

I would have her in my bed and she would straddle my hips, and the pressure I felt would be the warmth of her womanhood surrounding my cock. The strokes I'd feel would be her body rising and falling on my shaft while I licked and suckled at her breasts. She would quicken her pace as she got closer to her climax, pumping her hips up and down as I thrust up into her tight sheath. And then, when she felt the exquisite pleasure of wild release coursing through her body, I'd feel the waves of orgasm tighten her innermost walls, and I'd release my seed into her womb.

I hissed as my essence spilled over my hands.

"This is unbearable," I groaned, rolling off the bed, getting to my feet. Storming over into the bathroom, I turned on the shower, letting the water run cold. I needed to get my mating ceremony over with as quickly as possible and Eva in my arms. And whatever I had to do to get my queen-to-be to agree to this, I would do.

CHAPTER 16
EVA

I dressed indulgently after my nap. I had a smile on my face after the first good sleep I'd had in…I didn't even know how long. I wore a knee-length black leather sheath dress that hugged my curves, and I paired my attire with black stilettos. After I fixed my minimal makeup and ran my fingers through my hair, I went out to join the males in the main room.

Stepping through the doorway that joined my smaller suite to the larger one, I skirted to a stop. The men in the room stood as a gesture of manners when I walked in, but my attention focused entirely on Raevu.

My breath caught slightly as we locked eyes. I didn't know how, but I sensed his urgent desire and need to touch me, and a tingle of pleasure swept down my body.

Enough, Eva. Get your mind off him and sex.

I pasted a smile on my face and turned to the other men in the room. "Good morning, gentlemen. I hope you slept well." I walked toward Baelon, the male in the room I'd known the longest, which wasn't saying much.

He stepped over to a chair next to Raevu and pulled it out for me. I moved toward it and took my seat. Baelon then proceeded to plunk a little bit of every food selection on the table onto my plate. I didn't recognize half the dishes, so I didn't protest at getting a sampler.

"Eva," Raevu began, drawing my eyes to him, "this is President Ken Maeda. Maeda, this is Eva Knight, my betrothed."

Hearing it spoken such a formal and official manner startled and bothered me. I had never actually agreed to marry anyone. I forced a smile anyway. "Hello, President Maeda, it's nice to meet you."

He replied, "Eva. Please, call me Ken."

I'm now on a first-name basis with the president? Damn. I've come a long way in a short span of time.

I couldn't believe that the man who sat in the Ivory Office on the Humanity Space Station was now sitting at the same table as me.

I pinched back the urge to relish this total fangirl moment. When I glanced up, I thought for a moment I saw Raevu frowning at me, but even as I focused on him, his face grew calm. Then he looked over at the male called T'ral, who was speaking. "...should be ready to leave within the week, barring incidents. A channel shall be kept open between our two worlds so that any communication about the progress of our genetic trade shall be considered priority one..."

I interrupted him. "It may be possible to leave within the week, but it seems that I need to remind you that it depends on how soon my requests are taken care of. I've made it clear there are several things that have to be taken care of before I'll be going anywhere." I set my knife and fork down resolutely. I had to make sure what I wanted and needed was seen to even before my physical needs were satisfied.

"Yes, Eva," Raevu agreed. "And all of your requests shall be handled expediently." His voice was sultry, as always, but also calming and soothing. I narrowed my eyes, suspicious of his motives.

"So, you agree to all my terms?" I asked archly.

"Within my power to do so, yes," he agreed.

"What does that mean?" I asked.

"It means that there may be things I cannot make happen during the time frame we have to work within. I will make as much happen as I can, and we will set other things into motion. All of your concerns, needs, wants, and desires will be listened to, considered, and, hopefully, relieved." His voice seemed to pluck at strings deep within me, and I felt a tingle of need begin under my belly.

He continued, "There are several things that need to be taken care of as swiftly as possible, and we need your input on them."

I was astounded. He was actually listening and seeking my opinion. *Much better.* Maybe his surly attitude yesterday was from lack of sleep. I nodded in agreement and twirled my fork in the air as if to give them permission to carry on.

As I ate, they spoke of supplies for the length of the trip. It would take the equivalent of three Earth months in warp space to get to the Juhlian solar system, and another two Earth weeks before we could disembark on the planet itself.

They spoke of duty rosters and rations, reminding me that they were a military people in nature. And they spoke of a ceremony that would be held on the Juhlian planet when that three and a half months had ended, a mating ceremony between Raevu and myself.

At that point, I interjected, "Mating ceremony? Is this like a wedding?"

The Juhlian men looked confused for a moment, but T'ral came to the rescue. "In fact, my lady, yes. It would be considered similar to a wedding of Earth origin, but Juhlians mate for life. There is no desertion of the vows. There are more informal unions, but for a Juhlian king and his life mate, nothing less than the mating ceremony under the Sopu tree will suffice."

"And we are hoping that our—" I searched for the right words "—union will bear fruit?"

"Fruit?" Baelon looked completely confused. "No, we want children. Preferably girls."

President Maeda and I were the only ones who chuckled at Baelon's confusion. "Baelon, I'm sorry. I don't think the translator units handle metaphors very well," I said. "In this case, 'fruit' means children."

He understood immediately and nodded, chuckling a little.

Damn. Well, I guess I should figure out what to do about potential kids now.

I looked over at Raevu and T'ral. "You have physicians on Juhl who are practiced at delivering babies?" It seemed ridiculous that they wouldn't, but according to the literature on their genetic crisis, naturally born babies were incredibly rare.

All of the males nodded, but T'ral answered, "Of course, my lady. We have what you would call obstetricians on our world. Physicians and scientists expert in pregnancy and fertility."

I replied, "But these doctors are expert in Juhlian anatomy and fertility, not human. I think we should see if there's a human obstetrician, preferably one with expertise in fertility, who's willing to go with us," I proposed. I didn't want to be thousands of light-years from a doctor who understood how my body worked when I did get pregnant and had questions or, God forbid, problems.

"Quite a reasonable request," Raevu stated. "What other tasks would you like to see done before we depart?"

His easy acquiescence after yesterday's misunderstanding pleasantly surprised me. I had come into the room expecting to have to fight for everything I wanted. I began to go over the list I'd made in my head as I'd gotten dressed earlier. "I discovered that the clothes issue isn't an issue at all, as I now have a complete wardrobe. A good night's sleep helped me feel worlds better, but I still feel fatigue, chills, and aches. I'd like those symptoms treated before traveling. Also, I have some personal items to collect from Ivy's apartment, and I have some shopping to do. There are some supplies I'll need to get until I can figure out if the Juhlian equivalent is sufficient for me or not."

All the males at the table just stared at me silently. I couldn't tell if I was making valid points or if I'd numbed them into speechlessness. This last part was the most difficult. I swallowed before continuing, but I held my head high. "And, if my new home will be Juhl, I'll need to say good-bye to Ivy and her kids, Laura and Amber, and a couple of other people I care about." Finished, I took my coffee cup and sipped the now-tepid brew.

The males all sat in their silence for a moment more.

Raevu was the first to speak. "I believe that most of that can be handled promptly."

Baelon interrupted, "My lady, if I may ask, if you didn't think you'd be making your home on Juhl, where did you think your home would be? You did understand you were signing up to see if you could be compatible to breed with a male of our race, did you not?"

"Yes." I frowned as I thought this through. "My briefing left out many details. It wasn't clear to me whether I would be going myself or simply donating ova. I knew I needed to help the people of Juhl. I knew I needed to sign up and pass all the screenings. If asked, and no one did, I think I would have said that the women who passed would all live together in barracks-type housing, be a type of soldier for the cause, and we'd get furloughs and visits home. Honestly, I didn't think about the 'breeding' part. I thought I was an experiment, so I guess I believed I'd be artificially inseminated. I never thought past the experiment part of it."

President Maeda coughed quietly. "It seems that I must apologize again for the severe mismanagement of this project. Who are the names you mentioned, Ms. Knight?"

"Ivy gave me a place to stay after I couldn't stay at the Children's Ward any longer. I'd been her babysitter for a few years, so she knew me." I spotted T'ral's open mouth and guessed at his question. "People can hire from the Children's Ward for a small fee for certain jobs like babysitting, yard work, or trash cleanup. We don't get the funds, but we get out of the Center for a while and get to meet people. I was good at babysitting, and Ivy couldn't afford regular child care."

T'ral nodded and sat back.

I continued, "Ivy's husband passed away when she was pregnant with Jaylynn, her youngest daughter. That's when I started helping out. She has four children, Trevor, Mark, Josephine, and Jaylynn. They're all under twelve years old. My friend Laura has a daughter, Amber, who is the same age as Jaylynn. None of us is related, but they're the closest I have to family."

Now T'ral spoke up. "These supplies you need, my lady? Can you make a list? And possibly calculate how much of each you'd desire for some set amount of time?"

I nodded. "Sure."

Maeda smiled. "Raevu, we stand by our trade agreement. You will send an official ambassador here to establish an embassy. We can then start making regular trading missions between our two planets. We can exchange more than information: trade goods, livestock, plants, medicines, and, of course, genetics, if more women than Ms. Knight are compatible and amenable to the exchange. So, you won't need to stock up on quite so much as you might believe."

The President turned to me. "I'm hoping you, Ms. Knight, will agree to temporary ambassadorial status until we can get someone appointed and moved to Juhl."

The whole conversation was beginning to make my head swim. "Of course, Mr. President, sir." *Me? An ambassador? Wow.*

T'ral said, "We can put out notices for doctors interested in applying for the position. And—" he turned his attention toward Raevu. "Sire, the needed elixir has been made ready and is on board our ship."

That caught my attention, and I opened my mouth to ask about this "elixir," but what Baelon said next distracted me.

Baelon cocked an eyebrow at him. "And what of Geoffrey?"

T'ral smiled smugly back at Baelon. "We get to take him with us. Thank you, Mr. President."

President Maeda dipped his head in acknowledgment. "Actually, you're doing me a favor. The computer programmer in charge of keeping up Geoffrey's maintenance has been clamoring for something to do, a new challenge to oversee. Adapting Geoffrey to your technologies was a challenge he couldn't resist. He's packed and ready to go whenever you are."

I was quite pleased to be able to "keep" Geoffrey. He'd been more than helpful so far; he'd been a godsend.

I had about used up my energy for the morning. My head was pounding. I pulled the soft white cardigan I'd draped around me closer about my body. I could feel the chills and aches creeping back into my muscles, and I was reminded that I hadn't had my painkillers since getting up. I took a couple of mouthfuls of water and tried to focus back on the conversation around me.

Raevu stood up abruptly. I followed him with my eyes.

"Excuse us. I believe Ms. Knight may be feeling unwell, and I need to speak with her a moment." He walked over to my chair and helped me push it back from the table.

As I stood, he placed a hand on my elbow. I could feel the electricity in his touch even through the layer of clothing between us. He kept a sturdy hold on me as he walked me back to my sitting room.

I lowered myself into one of the chairs. Not as comfortable as the brown chair across from my bed, which I was already fantasizing about, but it would do until I could get back into my room.

"Please sit," I requested of him. "You're very tall, especially from this angle." I hoped my tone came across as calm and not cranky.

"First, I'd like to apologize for the overbearing manner in which I asked about your mark yesterday evening. Its origins are important, but I believe you when you say that you know no one explicitly put it there." Amazed that a king would apologize, I nodded my acceptance. "Secondly, I need to speak with you about this illness of yours."

His voice, as usual, sent a shiver of need down my spine. It settled deep in my belly.

"Yes? What about it? I'm usually quite healthy. I've never had flu symptoms this long. But I'm sure I'll get over it quickly enough now with rest and fluids."

"No, I'm afraid you won't." His golden eyes stared into mine. "The mark and the illness are connected. The mark appears on the royal heir's life mate when she comes of age. With it comes illness of sorts, fatigue, chills, upset stomach."

Troubled, I began making a list of questions in my head, but I nodded for him to continue.

"The illness remains until the mating ceremony is completed between the two life mates. There is an elixir that will help ease the symptoms, but it has side effects."

"That's why suddenly I'm your betrothed?" He nodded. "And why I'm no longer part of the Peace Opportunity Program?" He nodded again. "What is this mark?" I demanded.

"It is the royal family crest. If there is more than one possible heir to the throne, it appears on the rightful one's chest. If the royal heir has not mated by a certain age, when his life mate comes of age, it appears on his life mate in precisely that spot, according to our histories."

I nodded slowly, my eyes widened.

"Some heirs and kings have refused to take a mate until the crest has appeared on their special one, their life mate. Some have not worried about it. So many of our kings had taken mates before a crest appeared, so we had almost forgotten about this tradition. For the last several generations, the number of females has diminished, so there were fewer to choose from. They all seemed to have chosen well." He quirked a half smile at me.

With my fingertips, I traced the mark on my neck and shoulder. I stood and went to a mirror, pulling my clothes aside to study it. It was an intricate pattern of loops that were raised up out of my skin. It was also slightly darker in color than the skin around it, like a tattoo.

"How did I get it?" I asked.

Raevu came up behind me and studied my reflection over my head.

"It's not definitive. We do know that it was my DNA you were injected with, and you are already of age as you are over the age of twenty-four years on your planet. We are life mates." His eyes looked hotly into mine. "I think we can both appreciate the benefits of that."

I blushed slightly at his reminder of our shared dream, but I refused to look away. "What is this elixir? Can I start taking it now?"

Raevu shook his head. "It's made from the Sopu nut, the same tree under which our ceremony must take place. It's on our ship. As soon as we are underway, you may begin taking it."

"Why do I have to wait?" I spat out. "Is this how you convince me to leave immediately? 'You'll stay sick until we go?' That's pathetic! I can't believe you'd use my illness against me like that!" I began to storm off, intending to find something to throw at him, when he clasped my arm.

"No," he said simply. I stared daggers at him. He sighed. "We cannot give you the medicine until we are underway as the side effects are slightly unpredictable. We'll need you in a secure place where we have easy access to more of it, your protected quarters, and only those most trusted by me and you."

I looked coldly and pointedly at his hand on my arm. He removed it. I refused to acknowledge how my skin tingled where he'd touched me.

"Please, Eva. Yes, I want to get you home. To our home." I could hear the earnestness in his voice. "But not for selfish reasons. The last thing on my mind when we started this program was my own life mate. I looked only to the continuation of my people. But now, seeing you? You, my life mate, are constantly on my mind. I want you well, happy, and safe. I want to help make sure you are all three. There's only so much of that I can do until we have the mating ceremony." He lowered his head slightly. "And if you are on the medication and you are kidnapped again and kept from me, it could be disastrous. Trust me, there is no other ulterior motive."

My demeanor must have softened. He reached a hand toward me, stroking the back of his fingers down my cheek. I let him.

"Your skin is as soft as it was in my dream of you. You are so much lovelier, though, in person." He stepped closer to me. I could feel the heat of his body through his suit. Unconsciously, I leaned toward his warmth.

He turned his hand over and cupped my cheek. The whole side of my face fit in his large hand. I turned my head, slightly brushing my lips against his palm. He smelled…deliciously male. I could smell the soap he used; there were lingering traces of lemon, orange, and patchouli. But underneath those surface smells was warmth. I didn't try to explain to myself how a smell was warm. I just breathed him in.

He tilted my face up toward his and leaned down. His lips brushed across mine once, then once again.

"So soft," he murmured.

He pressed his lips firmly to mine and slid his hand around to the back of my neck. I kissed him back, and I couldn't explain why, but it felt…right.

His other hand moved to the small of my back, pulling me into the hardness of his body. This alien was the epitome of virile.

I moaned. He took advantage of my slightly opened mouth and traced his tongue along the edges of my lips. When I cautiously skimmed my tongue against his, he pulled me in tighter and plundered my mouth with his tongue. His kiss was demanding, forceful. Swept along, I returned his passionate kiss.

Suddenly, he pulled back from my lips but held me close in his arms, for a long moment just staring into my eyes before he eased away.

Tracing one thumb across my bottom lip, he said, "We will take this slow. Besides, there's only so much we can do until we have the mating ceremony." His voice was husky and deep.

I nodded shakily. "I understand. I'll be ready to leave within the week."

CHAPTER 17
RAEVU

Despite her and my best efforts, Eva was not ready to leave by week's end. I couldn't really blame her. I felt her pain and fatigue acutely, but although she moved more slowly as the days progressed, she refused to show any signs of weakness, and she pushed on. She was doing her best, even though I suspected she didn't entirely trust me yet.

I did manage to get her to lie down a couple of times a day, usually after meals. When we were alone, she freely shared bits about her past, and sometimes our bonding time turned into moments of us kissing and caressing each other. But I refrained from going any further, which was starting to drive me mad.

I wondered what she would be like once the elixir had taken hold. Part of me was filled with dread at the temptation I would have to resist.

Maeda and I hammered out the duties and requirements we had of ambassadors, after which he and I both interviewed several candidates he thought had potential as ambassadors for Earth on Juhl. We finally agreed on one, who accepted the appointment. It would take almost a full Earth year before he and his family could make the trip to Juhl, however, so Eva would have to be well-versed in the responsibilities of her role as temporary ambassador, but she seemed more than willing.

While I held T'ral in meeting after meeting with me, I called my Seneschal down from our ship to handle Eva's affairs. M'kir was quite small for a Juhlian, but he was still taller than Eva. He was second only to T'ral in keeping details and figures straight in his head, but M'kir was in charge of our household's daily routines.

I felt Eva's frustration when she butted heads with him day after day. He questioned her every decision, not because he thought her unintelligent, but in order to place that decision in its proper position within all the other details organized in his head. If he'd not been born a eunuch, he would've made an excellent war strategist. As it was, even his highly organized mind couldn't get Eva ready to leave before the week was out. She just wasn't well enough, and we kept running into complications.

M'kir quickly obtained the supplies that Eva desired to bring with her and even calculated a rough estimate of how much she would need before a trade ship could bring more. He also thought to ask her about her favorite foods and delicacies, so he could lay in a supply of those things as well.

He went to something called a nursery where he picked up some plants she described as pleasing, as well as a large variety of seeds to test in our soil. After each accounting, I shook my head in wonder at the ideas that hadn't occurred to me.

I watched and felt her sorrow and pain when we took her to collect her things and say her good-byes to her adoptive family. There in front of those small, crying children, she extracted my vow that transmission packets could be sent from her to them and vice versa with recordings of their images. Her manipulation of me both irritated and pleased me greatly. There was no fear in her of me or my stature, which was as it should be as she was to be my queen.

M'kir began the selection process of a fertility specialist. Many who applied he crossed off the list as he said they were "more interested in getting off planet than in taking care of your lady." Maeda had his men look more carefully at those doctors' private doings. Once Maeda had it narrowed down to three, he had them come to our suite for an interview with Eva. Her selection was a Theodore Mackelroy, whose manner seemed a bit abrupt to me, but his history and ideas were quite sound. Eva felt pleased because she felt he'd be honest with her and not "sugarcoat" anything she needed to be told. He would be able to come in with the first trade ship, in about six Earth months, which would be roughly three months after we arrived home and had our ceremony.

Finally, it appeared everything was in order. Our bags were packed, and we headed to the shuttle to our ship. I was more than ready to go home.

CHAPTER 18
EVA

I'd never been so nervous in my life. Raevu had agreed for us to leave first thing after breakfast, when I had the most energy, but I could feel my usual drive being drained away by anxiety of the unknown.

I'd never even been on an airplane. *How would I manage a shuttle to a spacecraft?* I'd never been more than ten miles away from the Center. *How could I live hundreds of light-years from Earth?*

We stepped out of the car and into the bright sunlight. M'kir had told me that the Juhlian sun was much hotter and more blue than Earth's yellow Sol. I lifted my face up to its cheerful rays and whispered a good-bye to it as well.

All the Juhlians and the little, skinny man who was Geoffrey's creator hustled to get on board. I walked at a steady pace. Each breath I took in was deep and slow. I let the air out unhurriedly. I kept my gaze moving, trying to ignore the headache gnawing at the back of my eyes.

The clouds moving across the bright blue sky fascinated me. *Had I ever paid this much attention or appreciated their intricate shapes and shades?*

I heard birds trill and chirp, dogs bark, and wondered to myself what kind of animals I would find on Juhl. I'd never asked. It seemed like a strange omission, not to think of animals before. I would miss birds, cats, and small dogs. I always enjoyed other peoples' pets.

Despite my hard life here, I would miss Earth.

We reached the shuttle's stairwell. Resolutely, I gripped the handrail and marched up the steps. At the top, I took one last look around. I felt my eyes well with tears that I refused to shed. I turned and ducked into the shuttle's cabin.

After he made sure the buckles on my seat were fastened securely, as they hadn't been made for someone of my small size, Raevu took my hand and kissed my palm. His gold eyes stared into mine. Without a word, he moved to his own seat to pilot the shuttle. It was time. I was leaving this world and journeying to my new home, and I wondered if I would ever see my family or friends again.

CHAPTER 19
EVA

After climbing out of the transport shuttle and into the larger starship, I received a brief walking tour of the areas I'd be allowed in during our journey. We first went directly to the bridge, where Raevu introduced me to the captain of the ship, who had called me his "Queen" with a graceful bow.

We strode through Baelon's gymnasium arena on our way to the handily close medical clinic, where I met my physician for the trip, Willem. He also greeted me with a bow and a smile—and my first dose of my medicine. From there, Raevu directed me to our adjoining chambers, which were every bit as opulent as the grandest room in the Center. For him, it seemed normal, but I spent a good ten minutes running my fingers across furniture and fixtures to feel the variety of textures while T'ral, Raevu, and Baelon talked.

My translator unit shifted each word to its English equivalent, but I could still hear the words and phrases that they spoke underneath the translation. Slowly, bits of it were starting to make sense to me. Just individual words and a few short terms, but it was getting easier.

One of these days, I thought I might turn off the translator and surprise them. Surprise…him.

Raevu suddenly looked up, puzzled, and came over to me. "How are you feeling?" he asked.

I paused in my exploration of a velvety soft plant in one of the terrariums. I leaned over it to look at its underside. It was certainly a plant of some kind, but as the whole thing was bright purple, I couldn't tell if I was handling a petal or a leaf.

"Eva," Raevu interrupted my investigation, "quit fondling the Karitsan plant for a moment." I looked up into his eyes quizzically. "How are you feeling?"

"Oh. Um. Fine." I assessed myself for the symptoms that had plagued me for months now. "Good, actually. Normal, even." I smiled with relief. "I hadn't even noticed the symptoms fading away. How wonderful!"

Raevu still looked a bit puzzled. "But I can't sense your—" He broke off suddenly.

"Sense my what?" I asked.

"Your fatigue in the way you hold yourself, my queen," T'ral spoke over Raevu's shoulder. "The elixir must be doing its job well. It's blocking those releases of exhaustion that had us all so concerned for you. We're all quite glad we're on the ship where you can safely take the treatment without concerns for the side effects."

They still hadn't told me what exactly these "side effects" were, or why they had wanted to contain me aboard the ship before I started taking it. I contemplated asking straight out when Raevu reached for my fingers that still held the thick, almost woolly petal and took them in his powerful hand. "So soft." He murmured as he rubbed my fingers between his own, much like I had the leaves. He smiled into my eyes, drew my hand to the crook of his elbow, and led me to a settee in the middle of the chambers. "But don't overdo it on your first day. Which part of the ship would you like to see next?"

EVERY DAY OF OUR JOURNEY THROUGH THE STARS, I'D ADMINISTER MY elixir, which the medic called Sopulir, myself. I refused to take up a physician's valuable time with something as trivial as what amounted to me using an inhaler. My friend Laura's daughter, Amber, had asthma, so I knew how to use an inhaler. It was easy. Someone hovering over me would've just pissed me the hell off anyway. And I couldn't figure out why I was still so moody.

Quickly, I developed a routine. I preferred taking the Sopulir in the mornings, as it seemed to give me an energy boost right away. I could always tell when it had worn off, as soon after my evening meal I'd begin feeling like a worn-out dishrag. And each night, I dropped into a deep, exhausted, dreamless sleep.

And since we were traveling through hyperspace to reach my new home, day and night quickly became arbitrary terms. My schedule aligned with Raevu's, and we spent a great deal of time together.

It was intriguing that I got to see him in several new capacities, which was a good thing since we were to be married when we reached his home world.

It had been fascinating to watch Raevu work. Over breakfast, he would review screen after screen of data with T'ral. I could almost see his mind piecing the information together. His decisions and orders seemed reasonable and were always given with confidence and authority. After dealing with the planetary transmissions, he shared something remarkably similar to coffee with the ship's captain, then we'd walk the ship. On a space cruiser with over four hundred crewmen, he knew everyone by name. Our "State of the Ship" walk, as I called it, was followed by an hour's workout with Baelon for me, two hours for Raevu. Baelon, as training master, was teaching me self-defense, and I got to use Raevu as my training dummy. None of my strikes landed unless he let them, but I learned a lot.

After I was finished, I watched Baelon and the rest of my Guard take turns trying to knock Raevu down. The only one who ever managed it was Baelon, and he was sweating and breathing hard by the end of the exercise.

Strangely, watching all the finely formed, half-naked males hack and hit at each other while throwing taunting names and good-natured insults seemed to turn me on, which was weird because I'd always considered myself a one-man woman. But like clockwork, I'd leave the gym every day with a flush in my cheeks and a scorching need to fuck burning deep in my belly. A want that Raevu couldn't satisfy until the stupid ceremony with that damn tree happened.

Not in a million years would I have thought I'd be the one in our relationship wanting to get the sex party started sooner rather than later. But waiting was a small sacrifice in the grand scheme of our future together. When I thought about all the sacrifices that had been made in the name of the continuation of Raevu's people: Raevu leaving his home world under the care of people he trusted and sweeping halfway across the galaxy to come and fetch me; him engaging in a genetic experiment without the support of his planetary council, and using his own wealth and resources to fund it; and when he'd discovered that the experiment had entwined his destiny with that of a human—me—he had simply accepted it and me. All of the circumstances and sacrifices he made were pretty impressive.

Every day, Baelon kept training me in self-defense. The patterns and moves he taught me reminded me of Earth's tai chi that I'd seen people performing in the parks or on the videos back home. I knew that none of them expected me to have to defend myself, especially since I had a Queen's Guard made up of five of the most elite of Raevu's warriors, including Baelon. But with my recent kidnapping on Earth, they didn't want to take any chances with my safety.

And still, every day, I was tired, achy, and sweaty after the practices. Today, like every other day on the ship, I was taking a long, bubbly soak in the small swimming pool that the Juhlians called a bathtub. My shoulders popped painfully as I scrubbed them, and I winced, but I felt proud too. I was glad I was getting the opportunity to learn how to protect myself. I wanted to prove that I was tough enough to do it. Everyone's overprotective behavior was frankly getting quite annoying.

I am strong and self-sufficient, thank you very much! I nodded my head in satisfaction.

"What are you smug about?" a deep, sultry voice interrupted my musing.

I squawked in surprised indignation, and my eyes flew open. Sitting up, I tried to cover my breasts and hide my sex at the same time. It didn't work very well, *damn my huge breasts.*

"What the hell are you doing in here?" I asked Raevu. "Can't you see I'm bathing? Get out!"

"I made plenty of noise coming in. Didn't you hear my footsteps?"

"Obviously not or I wouldn't have been startled. Now, get out!"

"I need to tell you something." His handsome, smirking face was just crying out to have a sudsy sponge flung at it. I narrowed my eyes at him.

"What?" I snapped. "And why couldn't it wait until I got out of the bathtub?"

His gold eyes began to glow with desire. I looked down at myself to see just how much of my skin was revealed to him. Almost all. I barely had my nipples covered with my hands, and my knees were drawn up as far as I could get them. And he still had plenty to stare at and did, with an infuriating smile. I was about ready to say, "Fuck it," and give him a taunting peep show.

"It couldn't wait because you take long baths and then usually go directly to bed for a while. T'ral had a missive from home he says has vital information. I want you there when we discuss it." He continued staring hungrily at me while he spoke. In haughty response, I looked him up and down as well. As always, I found no flaws, and, also as usual, heat flared up deep in my cunt.

Damn. I wanted him badly.

His body was divine. His muscles flexed as he moved and drew my attention whenever he walked into the room. His skin was smooth and hairless, and I wanted to feel it under my fingers.

And I loved the way he looked at me, as if he wanted to devour me alive.

But right now, business was getting in the way as much as necessity. I sighed. "Fine. I'll get dressed and be right there." When he still didn't move, I glared at him. "What? I am not getting out of this tub until you leave. Go, Raevu! Now!"

He turned then and made his way out the door. I watched him go and enjoyed the sight he made as his shirt and pants clung to his muscled back and tight butt as he moved. *Damn. The man was poetry in motion.*

Not until he was completely out of the room did I stand and reach for a drying cloth. I muttered to myself the whole time I got dressed about him being a tease. After dressing, I sailed out of my assigned queen's quarters and into the main living area of the suite that belonged to Raevu aboard ship. I curled into my favorite chair and stifled a yawn, settling down to wait for them.

Daily after lunch, I sat through culture and language lessons. The language was coming to me more and more easily. I didn't know how. As a matter of fact, we spoke only in Juhlian Standard now. I was still relying heavily on the translator, but less and less each day. The only English I ever spoke was in cuss words or when I got very tired or upset.

I'd seen pictures of their planet, learned about their gods, their sentient trees, and their war-filled history. I didn't think I'd pass a major exam on any of it, but I could hold my own in a conversation.

Raevu lounged on a couch-like bench, waiting as well. Baelon stretched out on a similar one across the way. He threw me a wink when I looked his way and shrugged when I gave him a questioning look.

T'ral bustled in. He held a small data screen in his hand and reviewed the information on it as Raevu asked, "Okay, what's this about?"

T'ral answered, "Two things. They may be interrelated. Death threats to the soon-to-be queen."

I froze. *What the fuck? I'm helping these idiots repopulate their race! How can some of them not want that to happen?*

Baelon sat up. "No one will harm my queen." I felt the threat coming from his voice.

"That's a given," Raevu hissed. "T'ral, what is the other?"

T'ral set down his handheld screen and looked directly at Raevu. "Acidi."

"Oh, *Kyrpa!*" Raevu sat up, the Juhlian obscenity spat out loudly. He rolled his eyes and rested his hands on his knees. "What now?"

Now I was intrigued. Death threats against me didn't even cause him a blink, but whatever "Acidi" was had him cussing.

"What is Acidi, and how is it a threat?" I asked. "I thought I knew most of the words of your language, but I don't recognize that one."

Baelon said wryly, "That, my queen, is because Acidi is a who and not a what. She is a jalkavaima and fancies herself above any others."

My mind struggled with what the translator spat out. "She's a public concubine? I don't understand."

T'ral explained, "We have few females. A hundred and fifty years ago, our people realized that changes had to be made. Marriages weren't forbidden, but females were encouraged to become jalkavaimas. They are honored in our society. A class in and of themselves. Mothers to us all. Marriages became less and less common. Males fill out applications to try to become fathers. If their applications are accepted, they interview with the local jalkavaima Grand Mother, and then interview with several available jalkavaimas until they feel there is compatibility. Those two will stay together until the child is born. The child, usually a male, of course, lives with its father. The jalkavaima can choose to stay until the child is aged one year or leave right after its birth. And the process starts anew. How much contact the jalkavaima has with her offspring is completely up to her. I, for example, see my mother once or twice a year. I know several males who have never met their mothers."

Baelon interrupted, "And if I didn't visit my mother at least once or twice a week, she'd string me up on a pole and make me dance."

"That all makes sense, but who is Acidi?" I asked. "And why is there a problem with her?"

Baelon and T'ral both looked toward Raevu, who again cursed. "Acidi was assigned to me," he gritted out.

I blinked. "I'm sorry. What do you mean?"

He let out a deep, frustrated sigh. "There is always a jalkavaima assigned to the king or royal heir when he comes of age. It is to ensure the continuation of the line. I was quite young and foolish when I chose Acidi. I chose for looks and didn't do much interviewing. She is smart but far too ambitious. Manipulative, aggressive, and ruthless. The Grand Mother warned me against it, but I didn't listen. Honestly, I didn't care. She was beautiful, and I figured I wouldn't be around her much except in bed."

Oh, what kind of bullshit drama have I been dragged into here?

"What the fuck, Raevu?" I spat. "Why did you come get me if you had a baby momma right there? Do you have a whole batch of little boys running around already?"

I hated useless, no-account men who neglected to tell women they were interested in that they had a family. The more baby mommas a guy had, the stronger the guarantee that he would leave you ruined and pregnant as well.

I seriously wanted to punch him in the throat. He had spent this whole time talking about how I was his life mate, and I was his, and we would be together forever. But the whole time, this situation with Acidi had been waiting at home to cause problems, and he had known it.

He held up a placating hand. "No. It doesn't work that way. We were to have no relationship beyond what it took to produce an heir. She was not with child when I left Juhl. I am done with her and have been for a while now. I came to get you because you are the hope of my people." Then he nearly growled, his eyes alight, "And my life mate."

I was so done with this bullshit.

"I can't be the hope of your people. I am only one measly human female," I snarled back, "and I will not join some other woman in your bed if I am your life mate."

He marched over to me. "Acidi has no place anywhere near my bed or my throne. But as for you...." He leaned down, face level with my own, and growled out, "That mark on you is my mark. You are my life mate. We will be joined. You will be in my bed. Accept it."

I looked back at him coldly. "You keep talking to me like I'm your goddamned slave, and I'll rip your cock off. You got that, 'life mate'?"

He gaped for a moment, blinking at me, and then backed off. He turned to T'ral. "What does she want?"

"My king, she announces her pregnancy, and that it is a girl."

What the fuck?

"Not with child, huh?" I spat at Raevu. "You damned liar."

He gave me a shocked look, and for a moment, I thought maybe he hadn't known himself, but I caught myself at once. *That look from him wasn't shock. It's the panicked look of a cowardly asshole male who's been caught in one of his damn lies.*

"Holy hell…" I said. "Are you fucking kidding me right now? I made this trip to live on a strange world with a strange man, and I left my loved ones for what?" I stood up. "I want to go home. Turn this fucking ship around, and take me the hell home. Pronto."

T'ral blinked. "Miss Eva, I assure you that this is a misunderstanding."

I shook my head. Tears were welling in my eyes. I didn't even want to consider why I was feeling so emotional about this, but I wouldn't let those tears spill even if it killed me.

Baelon began to step closer to me, protection written all over him.

Raevu shot him a killing glance, and he stopped moving. Then Raevu did something even stupider. He tried to intimidate me again. Leaning close, he said intensely, "You bear the sigil. The mating ceremony is the only thing that will remove the feelings of ill health from your body. Obviously, the gods want us together. You will stay."

"As your prisoner, then, you selfish asshole?" I snapped. "Because I will never go anywhere with you willingly!"

He blinked sharply as if I had slapped him, but instead of answering, he turned back to T'ral. "What Acidi claims is impossible. She was not with child when we departed."

T'ral shrugged. "In the missive, she says she just didn't want to say anything until she was positive. That when you left, there was still doubt, and she wanted to know the gender before she announced it."

"Fuck this noise," I hissed. "I've heard enough. The wedding is officially off." Without waiting for an answer, I stood, turned, and left the room.

"We'll finish this, Eva," Raevu called after me.

"Go fuck yourself, Raevu," I snarled.

If we hadn't been on a starship transport, I would have enjoyed slamming the door behind me. The soft whoosh of it closing just didn't have the same emotional impact I wanted to impart.

Once I was alone, I started sobbing. It hurt like fuck that another woman was pregnant with his child, but what was worse was his nonchalant attitude toward me. I didn't care if the experiments made me want him. I'd peel the fucking symbol right off my skin before I'll let him force me to be his mate.

My emotions were all over the place. Deep down, I feared that I was out of control, that the drug or something else was unbalancing me. But either way, Raevu was definitely being a controlling ass. I locked my door and then shoved a heavy couch in front of it. I didn't want to see or deal with any of them anymore.

CHAPTER 20
RAEVU

This is completely mad. What is Acidi doing?

I shouldn't have said anything to her about the experiment before I left. But I thought I was doing the more gentlemanly thing by telling her myself that our contract was over. I should've just kept my mouth shut and had the Grand Mother recall her.

And now Eva, who had already endured too much, had her trust broken by the whole mess with Acidi. Perhaps I should have expected it. But Eva's anger at me, her refusal of what the gods had decreed, and her complete rejection of me when I had asserted the truth of the matter was unreasonable.

I threw my glass across the room in frustration. It shattered into a barrage of crystal slivers.

Baelon, without opening his eyes from his reclined position, asked, "Frustrated, nephew?"

"Keep quiet, Baelon," I replied flatly. "You're absolutely no help."

"I told you not to choose Acidi, and I warned you Eva was in a delicate state and shouldn't be pushed. That was my help," he replied, and then he pushed himself to a sitting position and stood, eyes locked with mine the whole time. "And instead of listening, you chose Acidi, fucked her, ignored her instability and greed and all the warnings you were given, then started the program, told her what was going on, and left the planet. Adding to the chaos, you accepted Eva as your life mate without telling her about Acidi." His eyes narrowed in actual disgust now as he stared at me. "And finally, you proceeded to respond to Eva being understandably upset and wanting to leave by acting like a complete beast. What did you hope to accomplish by telling her that she no longer has any choice, that you're going to force her to stay here and essentially fuck her whether she wants it or not? Because from where I was sitting, it sounded to me like a kidnap and rape threat."

"What?" I blinked in shock, amazed he would accuse me of such a thing when all I had been doing was asserting my claim on my rightful mate.

"You heard me. Do you think she suddenly got violently angry because she has a problem with authority? You do not tell or even imply to a woman that you will force her to stay with you or force her into your bed. What is wrong with you that I even have to tell you this?" He kept staring back at me, no matter how hard I glared.

He pointed a thick finger at me. "You're the author of these problems. You can't expect women to simply submit to you and have no thoughts of their own about the situations you drag them into."

Slowly, a trickle of doubt worked its way through my rage. "That wasn't my intention," I protested slowly.

Baelon steepled his fingers. "Oh? Really? Well, how did you mean it? Because I had to sit here and listen to it, and it sounded very much like you intend to force her if you cannot win her. Which, at this rate, you're thoroughly failing to do."

I heard a choking sound from T'ral, but his face was impassive when I turned to look. *Had he been laughing at me?*

"I am not going to hurt her," I snapped. "We all know that the medicine is just making her unreasonable." I couldn't understand why my heart was suddenly beating so fast or where this creeping sense of unease came from.

"The medicine is making her more emotionally sensitive, but it's not unreasonable to protest against the prospect of being held against her will. Let alone mated against her will." My uncle wouldn't stop staring into my eyes. I had the sudden impression that I had become a kid again and was being sternly reprimanded.

I bristled at the thought. "Whose side are you on?"

"Oh, I'm on your side, even when you're being a great bombastic idiot about things. But I am also on Eva's side. It is, after all, my job to keep that lovely thing in there safe from the likes of Acidi and any others who might harm her." Baelon looked serious. "Now, what will you do about Acidi?"

"Get the physicians to test her to see if the child is mine," I barked.

Baelon's eyes narrowed. "Which they can't do until after the child is born."

"We'll proceed with the life mate ceremony," I hissed. My blood was starting to boil with frustration.

"What if Eva won't cooperate?" Baelon countered. "Especially after the mess you just made of things?"

"*Hitto Soikoon*, Baelon!" I swore. "You're my adviser. Give me answers and advice," I burst out. "Quit coming up with obstacles."

He smirked. "I'm just making sure you think your options over thoroughly and face facts about the consequences of your actions."

I glared at him, but there came that doubt again as I remembered the outrage, disgust, and hurt in Eva's eyes. *Didn't she know that I would never take her against her will?*

T'ral spoke up, "My king, I believe we should take a wait-and-see attitude here. Without many invasive tests, we cannot know whether or not Acidi is telling the truth. And, in our culture, that path is taboo as she is jalkavaima. Provided that we can get past these…setbacks, we should proceed as planned with the mating ceremony. We can then make a treaty presentation to the council and plan to allow our warriors to marry human women if the women so agree. I believe there are human women who would become jalkavaimas to get out of their current situations, and jalkavaimas who would marry and become full-time wives or mothers to their partners if it were allowed. It just hasn't been an option in many years." He frowned and looked up at me. "But about Acidi—"

"Enough!" I barked. "I will deal with Acidi tomorrow. She has no control over me or mine. Quit fretting like old women."

Baelon frowned. "Like you've ever met an old woman." He stood and turned to face me. "And if the Grand Mother hears you say that, my next several visits will be nightmares."

I snorted. The Grand Mother doted on Baelon. Of her many sons, he was her first and her favorite. "As T'ral is the only one with any good advice, I will be listening to him. We shall just proceed," I commented.

Baelon didn't seem the least quelled by the flat looks I was giving him. He stared back at me placidly, but I could see a hint of disgust in his eyes. It surprised me. We had always had a good relationship. *Could I actually be in the wrong, as he had asserted, in my treatment of Eva?*

I couldn't think about it right now. "T'ral," I continued, "send a reply. Grant Acidi an audience late in the day when we arrive. Request the Grand Mother to join us. Baelon, you will consider these threats against Eva. Keep a guard near her at all times."

Both males nodded once and left the room.

What a ridiculous disaster, I thought as I dropped onto a couch. I'd been less and less inclined to visit Acidi's bed in the last several months before this last trip to Earth. As a matter of fact, I couldn't even remember the last time I had joined with her. It simply hadn't been that remarkable.

Of the five females the Grand Mother had suggested I interview, Acidi had been the loveliest. I hadn't actually interviewed any. Just chosen based upon the holofile in the data screen. The Grand Mother had frowned at that decision and told me in no uncertain terms that I needed to interview them, but I'd refused and stubbornly stuck by my choice.

Poor decision, that. I rubbed my hands over my scalp. Acidi had played mind games, demanded constant gifts and attention, and lain like a stone during sex, pushing away my hands when I tried to please her. It was as if she would never ever give up control, even long enough to have an orgasm. Nor was Acidi's presence in my life the only mistake I got to look forward to paying for. The look on Eva's face as she'd left the room haunted me. I wished, not for the first time, that I could still feel what she was feeling.

Briefly, back on Earth, I'd been able to sense her emotions. Once we'd gotten on board and she'd started taking her daily elixir to relieve her flu-like symptoms, that connection was lost.

Now, it felt like another connection had been severed between us. Her look had been so closed. So empty. I couldn't tell if she was angry, hurt, or…what.

Her emotions typically could be read plain as day on her face. I could easily tell if she was happy or angry, but not this time. It seemed that the moment I had made the mistake of demanding submission, she had walled off her heart from me.

Baelon had left his glass of qua on the low table. I reached for it and downed its contents in one gulp. I reached for the pitcher that had been left behind and swore viciously. *Empty.* As I crossed the stateroom to refill my glass from the bar, I remembered a moment just the previous day when Eva's face had been tender and laughing and teasing.

Each day before our evening meal, Eva and I spent a couple of hours together. We ended up teaching one another the games we liked to play. She liked games of chance, cards particularly. I'd had plenty of practice with those during my time on Earth with Ken. She could bluff me every time.

I preferred games of strategy. I tried to teach her to play a game called Shakki Mestari. It was very similar to Earth's chess, but it had two levels of boards. When my piispa piece had placed her koninsga into jeopardy for the fourth time, she'd laughed.

"Can't we play checkers?" she'd asked as she had placed a hand on my arm. "I seem to be terrible at this. I don't get how the second board does anything but benefit you and terrify me."

That simple touch had sent an electric shock through my entire body. Multiple times, I'd caught her moving backward on the game board. I was almost sure she was doing it on purpose.

I'd waited and watched her carefully to see if signs of the Sopulir's extrasensitizing side effect would take her over and she would suddenly become desirous and in need of my touch, but that never seemed to happen—or if it did, she was hiding it well.

Her flu-like symptoms had abated as promised, but exhaustion set in by the end of every day aboard ship. I was terribly disappointed. I had been looking forward to that particular potential side effect of the medicine. We'd figured that her human DNA must have negated that notable effect. *Or were my actions and words driving her away somehow? Could Baelon be right?* I thought I was being a decisive warrior and king, but...

I sighed, reminiscing. When I'd asked what "checkers" was, Eva had attempted to explain. Geoffrey managed to get the matter printer to fashion what Eva called an acceptable board, and she taught me the game.

She'd leaned over the board to jump three of my men in a row. Eva had looked up into my face, laughing as she had scooped my pieces up and blew me a kiss mockingly. She had been so very close to me, I had imagined I could feel the kiss breezing my way.

Our eyes had locked, and the moment had seemed to stop. She had been so very close. A bare tilt of my body had brought our faces in line. I had brushed her warm, parted lips with my own. Once. Twice then, pressing my lips to hers, I'd taken what I hadn't even attempted to take since we'd left her planet. A kiss. A simple one, or so it had seemed.

But when I had broken the contact and backed off, it had taken a moment or two for her large, dark eyes to flutter open. She had breathed in deeply even as I had. I couldn't have said I had been unaffected. Before either one of us had been able to move or speak, T'ral had appeared in the doorway to announce that our evening meal was ready. I had thought I saw disappointment in Eva's eyes. I knew there had been disappointment in my heart.

I rubbed the bridge of my nose, trying to ignore the headache forming. I wanted that easy laugh and electrifying touch again. She seemed to soak up T'ral's lessons in language and history as if she were somehow just remembering them instead of learning them anew.

And watching her move through the patterns Baelon was teaching her for self-defense? Well, it was a good thing she used me as a practice dummy or certain parts of my anatomy would be embarrassing me on a daily basis. She was beauty and grace, so intent, concentrating on Baelon's words and motions.

My mistakes with Acidi would not take this away from me. There was no way that baby was mine. We had carefully checked to make sure Acidi wasn't pregnant before I'd left Juhl. Of course, possibly Acidi didn't realize that. She did have scientific training and a brother who worked in the fertility labs, now that I thought about it. That was an avenue I would need T'ral to look into more carefully. Her brother.

Acidi was excellent at grand scenes, and it was just like her to stage one knowing that I was bringing home a bride. A human queen. And she would have to know, as transmissions had been sent back and forth to prepare for the ceremonies.

Histories had been referenced and cross-referenced. The Grand Mother had been consulted. And Acidi most certainly had her share of informants and spies throughout the entire palace since she'd lived there for so many seasons. That was definitely another thing T'ral would have to look into, Acidi's web of people that fed her information she had no right to.

We had to work fast. It was our last day in space. We'd be home in mere hours, and now Eva wouldn't talk to me.

I had a vague plan forming on how I could relieve some of Eva's isolation and hopefully regain her favor. But I would need to send off some transmissions to Earth before it could come to completion.

Perhaps Baelon had been right, and Eva had taken my show of dominance as something hostile. I would have to convince her that it was simply the natural dominance of my people. We were warriors, conquerors, alphas that took, not asked. I was an alien that had a lot to learn about the human female. But in time, and through her patience with me, everything would have to work out the way I wanted it to. I was the king, and I would make sure it happened just that way.

CHAPTER 21
EVA

I offered only a perfunctory "Good Morning" when I joined the males at the morning meal. I didn't want to speak to any of them, not even Baelon. I hadn't slept well last night since I had told Raevu to pretty much go fuck himself. After that, too many thoughts and emotions had spent the night vying for attention in my brain.

I ate in silence and let the masculine voices wash over me. I knew why I was pissed at Raevu, for treating me like a slave who had no choice but to follow his orders. But it was the whole mess with Acidi that really pushed me over the edge.

Why am I feeling so betrayed?

When I'd signed up for the Program, I'd never thought I'd find the love of my life, get married, and live happily ever after. From all of the fucked-up men I had met in my life, I knew Prince Charming didn't fucking exist. So, I'd figured I'd be part of a group of women trying to help the Juhlian people. Truth be told, this was no different from the description of the jalkavaimas. But I hadn't known about them. I hadn't thought about being added to an existing pool of women.

And, for the last several weeks, the whole life mate idea had been explained, reinforced, and focused on so much that I had forgotten completely about being willing to be the partner to several different

Juhlian males. To discover that Raevu had a long-term partner he'd actively been trying to get pregnant was…disconcerting.

Was I bothered because she could so easily be me? Or was I bothered because she had a baby by Raevu and had gotten to sleep with him, while I have been forced to wait?

The food I ate passed my lips without my notice. I was trying to decide if I was angry or just hollow inside. I had been extremely angry last night, but mostly about the whole trying to hide a baby from me thing. *After all, I can't get angry at the fact that he's had a previous girl-friend, right?*

It was at moments like this that I wished Laura and Ivy were here with me. Women I could talk to and who would understand.

The males all rose from the table, and I followed their cue. I trailed along in silence as we made our way to the transport bay. We climbed aboard what I had dubbed the "ship-to-shore" ferry on our trip upward.

I settled into the same seat I had occupied on the outbound trip from Earth and remained quiet. Baelon sat beside me. He made sure my restraining straps were properly fastened, gave me a nod of satisfaction, and promptly closed his eyes and ignored me for the rest of the voyage. He seemed to understand that I needed to be left alone.

I ran through all sorts of conversations in my head. Some with Laura, some with Ivy, even one or two with this Acidi person I'd never met. I truly needed something to think about other than the parallels between her life and the one I'd signed up for and the worry that I might no longer be necessary.

Damn, that will piss me off if it turns out to be true.

I had gone through so damned much to help out these aliens, and the idea that I would get tossed aside after everything made my stomach hurt.

Screw it.

If Raevu was going to be a dick and try to force his will on me, maybe Acidi could have him. Maybe I could live with Baelon. I liked him pretty well. Except, I really thought Ivy would like him even more.

With hardly any turbulence, we burst into the atmosphere and through the cloud cover. At just the same moment, the wall next to me became transparent. I gasped and focused entirely on the landscape unfolding below and around us.

All I could see was green. Green leaves, vines, and trees. Juhl's landscape dripped with emerald vegetation. Even the sun seemed to shine down greenish rays of light.

I was sure my jaw dropped open. The trees towered over everything. Vines draped like streamers from branch to branch. Huge, fern-like plants waved gently in the soft breezes.

All the plant life hid the buildings. I had to search for them. And then I realized how far away from the trees we were—and how big the trees actually were. Structures nestled in amongst the roots of the trees, and in many cases, were built into the roots themselves. I could even see tiers of buildings built into the sides of the trees, as if they were cliff faces.

We skimmed along over the tops of those behemoths of nature. I kept my face plastered to the sight unfolding before me. Flying creatures, brightly striped and bat-winged, darted through the air. Some of them seemed to have riders on their backs.

Far below, I thought I glimpsed a lumbering animal on a track, but we jetted past too quickly for me to be sure. Our passing hardly seemed to stir the mammoth branches, and when I looked farther down the horizon line, I saw several skimmers similar to ours zipping high above and between the branches like a swarm of insects.

Gently, we sailed to a stop on a platform built near the top of one particularly majestic tree. Baelon helped me unbuckle, and we walked outside.

I felt surrounded by jeweled light. Everything seemed to have a green cast to it. Even the Juhlians, whose skin had been mostly blue on Earth, were now definitely green, with some brown shadings for depth.

I held up my own arm to see how it had changed in color. My skin tone seemed to have deepened, but its undertones were still quite warm.

I wandered to the edge of the platform to look out into the branches. Everywhere, I saw light and movement. This Juhlian city lived in the trees. I could hear music playing in the distance. An unfamiliar animal brayed. I stepped closer to the edge, fascinated. Suddenly, a brawny arm wrapped around my waist and yanked me back against a solid, male chest. The whole world literally spun around. By the time I got my bearings, I had been turned completely away from the city and was several long strides back toward the transports.

"Let me go, Raevu!" I drove my heel back against his calf as hard as I could, and he grunted.

"What the *Kyrpa* do you think you're doing?" Raevu demanded. "Trying to kill yourself? I know you're upset, but that is no way to handle things. Good gods, woman. Do you have any idea how dangerous that was?"

I stared up over my shoulder at him in disbelief. "What the hell are you talking about?" The heat pouring off his body was easy to feel through the gossamer dress I had chosen that morning. But strangely enough, he was shaking as if I had managed to genuinely frighten him by endangering myself.

Am I that important to him? Is he just a bloody fool about showing it?

It was definitely a possibility. I wouldn't let it distract me, though, from the fact that he was currently hauling me around like a sack of meal. "Raevu! Put me down!"

He did, quite gently in contrast to his voice, next to Baelon, whom he glared at. "You're supposed to be watching her. Keep her safe from her own foolishness as well!"

"Wait just a minute here. Baelon is not my keeper—"

"He most certainly is. He appointed himself the captain of the Queen's Guard. You will be queen. He and these other warriors are to protect you from anything and everything, including your own reckless behavior." Raevu turned then and stormed into a small vehicle sitting in a hollow on the other side of the landing stage.

I looked at Baelon in bewilderment. He bowed his head toward me and spoke in a low tone, "The Tovari tree we're on is over one hundred of your stories high, my queen. There is no railing on this landing pad. One more step and you could have fallen. If Raevu had rushed, he possibly could have convinced the tree itself to catch you, but they move slowly, and you would have been very badly hurt by the impact with branches by the time it could have reacted. Please stay away from the edges. It is quite dangerous."

Holy shit! I could have died.

I stared at him with an open mouth. "Over one hundred…stories high?" *A tree could grow that big?* And from what I could see, most of the trees in this area were about that height. The city I was from on Earth was large, but none of our buildings was taller than the fifty-five-story Center. I had never stood this far above the ground.

"My queen, if you would come this way please?" Baelon waved his arm toward the smaller transport Raevu had just entered. I looked back toward the rim I had walked toward earlier. Two of the warriors who were part of my Guard were now between me and the rim of the platform. *Oh, for fuck's sake, I'm not a toddler. Now, I understood the danger.*

We walked over to the vehicle and climbed in. Raevu sprawled in one of the bench seats lined up against the walls. I sat on one directly opposite him. Once we were all seated, the giant elevator pad the vehicle rested on began to lower us into the depths of the green.

I considered Raevu, and now I was conflicted because he was obviously concerned about my safety.

How can this man make me feel so many contradictory emotions at the same moment over the same issue? It was so fucking frustrating. *Does he have any idea of the impression he's making on me, or does he just not care? Maybe it was the obstacle of the differences between our races making this so difficult. If it was, then this was a culture clash on a mammoth scale.*

Not wanting to wallow in my problems right now, I focused on my journey. I wished there were windows so I could watch our progress downward, or for an indicator of some kind so I could see how far up we were and where we were stopping.

My imagination was going crazy with the idea that they lived in the trees. I braced myself for what I might see. *Will it be like a log cabin? All woodsy and heavy-looking? Will it look like something out of a jungle story? Or maybe something out of a fantasy novel?* My mind raced with all the possibilities.

At some signal I couldn't discern, all the males stood at once. We must have come to a stop. The silent door revealed my new home to me.

It was magnificent, like a cathedral. We stepped out onto a flattened area, wide and smooth and polished to a mirror shine. The tree's bark pattern could easily be seen through the gloss. "I was expecting to see the concentric rings that tell a tree's age and history."

Confused, Baelon asked, "What do you mean? Why wouldn't you see the bark of the tree? We're still outside of it."

"Well, yes, but we're within the perimeter of the tree's circumference. Didn't your ancestors have to cut into the tree to build your palace?" I asked.

Now Baelon looked slightly horrified. "No! We live in a symbiotic relationship with our trees. These are the Tovari trees. Our partner trees. They provide us shelter and protection. We take care of them and provide them entertainment. They are sentient trees. They can move slowly and control their growth. If we ask for a certain room or addition, if it is feasible, they will make it happen. If it is not possible in that place, another tree might be able to do it more readily, or there might be dead wood we need to prune from them that we could use for building materials. They cannot take care of their parasites or dead wood, so we must do it for them. The city planner and the tree together design the space, and their vision ends up being the final project. This antechamber was created by my four times great-grandfather—and this tree, of course."

I looked around in amazement, walking around the enormous space. The floor beneath me stretched out for several transport lengths. The walls and ceiling appeared to be branches that were lined up next to each other and met in a peaked arch far above our heads. Light peeked through the branches. It was just as beautiful as any stained-glass church picture I'd seen in the libraries on Earth.

"Eva?" Raevu called from up ahead. His voice was so much gentler that I stopped ignoring him and turned to him. "We must continue." He beckoned from some stairs at the far end of the hall. Large double doors faced him. They were embossed with what looked very much like the sigil on my neck. My hand flew to my neck when I recognized the likeness.

"Yes. It is the same," Raevu said.

I didn't reply, simply nodding.

The doors opened soundlessly. We stepped through into a much smaller and darker room but no less grand. This space was lit up with dozens of floating balls of iridescent light that bobbed ever so slightly and seemed to be unattached to anything at all. The walls and floor were the same highly polished bark as the antechamber, throwing reflected light all over the area.

Toward the end of this room, I could see a stand with two wooden thrones on it. *This was a throne room!* The thrones appeared to have grown right up out of the floor, which was a distinct possibility now that I thought about it. And then I noticed the silent and still figure standing just to one side of the thrones. Slightly in shadow, the form was tall and lean. It made no movement, only waited. When Raevu saw where my gaze lingered, he looked that same way. His expression hardened.

"Acidi." I heard none of the sultry qualities I usually did in his voice. Now I heard cold shards of ice. This woman was not his old flame. He loathed her, and he was furious at her unexpected presence.

This is Acidi? My eyes narrowed. *Why would she be here, now?*

It seemed Raevu and I were in accord in our thinking, "Why are you here? I have not yet granted you an audience," he clipped out.

"My king." Acidi dipped into an almost impossibly graceful curtsy then glided forward. "I needed to speak with you on a private matter of great urgency." She stopped several feet away and looked me up and down. "I can come back when you are alone and timing is more…convenient."

Her voice was silk and temptation. I could see nothing of her figure, for she was cloaked, but now that she was close to us, I could see her face. She was beautiful.

She was almost as tall as Raevu. Long and lean, that much I could tell. Her skin was a light blue shade and her hair a dark moss. None of the male Juhlians I'd seen so far had hair, but this female certainly did. Her tresses were piled upon her head in an elaborate style that must have taken someone quite some time to create.

Her face was every jealous woman's nightmare. It was flawless. She had high cheekbones and full lips, large, tilted eyes and perfectly arched eyebrows, an aristocratic nose, and what looked like the hint of a dimple. I decided I would have hated her on principle even if she weren't an awful person.

"Acidi, you know that you may not come here until you are invited. Why did the Grand Mother let you come?"

Raevu stepped closer to me, moving just a little bit in front of me as if to shield me from her with his body. *Does he feel I need protection against Acidi?*

Please.

If she flinched in a manner that was even a little aggressive, I'd go batshit crazy on her ass.

I held my chin just a bit higher and looked at her in challenge.

"She agreed that you needed to be aware of certain changes, my king," Acidi's voice dripped with saccharine sincerity.

"Surely these things could have been set up in a meeting or council with a representative who is better trusted than yourself. I would happily have come to the Grand Mother's office if need be." Raevu sounded as if his patience was growing short.

"There is some news, my king, so momentous that it cannot wait." At that statement, Acidi took her hands and threw her cloak over her shoulders. She revealed a long, slender figure. Small and perky breasts high on her body. Legs that would make a supermodel envious, and a very pregnant belly.

I didn't know what reaction Acidi had hoped for. Whatever it was, she didn't get it. Raevu didn't move, nor did his stony expression change even one iota. When he spoke again, his voice had grown even colder. "When I left for Earth, you were not pregnant, Acidi. Not with my child. We had medically confirmed that, remember? And in case I need to remind you, even if you somehow preserved my seed and got yourself pregnant, it only means that our contract is at an end. Return to the Grand Mother. I will call for you when I wish to speak to you."

"My king…" Acidi started, just a hint of doubt entering her expression. Her big reveal had not gone as planned, no real reaction, not from me or from Raevu. *Is she delusional or something, thinking that a pregnant belly he already knew about would shock him when he saw it in the flesh?*

Raevu silenced her with a glare. She dipped another curtsy and slipped from the room, shooting me a nasty look as she went. Raevu waited until she was completely gone to turn to me. "My apologies, Eva. Her presence was unexpected and unwelcome. T'ral will make sure everyone knows she is not to enter or remain in the palace without the Grand Mother at her side."

I could tell he was uncomfortable with the entire situation. And from my experience with him, I knew that he didn't apologize much. Frankly, I had to give him credit for the attempt. I graciously nodded my head in acceptance of his apology, but I made a mental note to find out just how far along this creepy bitch was supposed to be in her pregnancy. Something about her whole dramatic reveal felt too contrived.

But, if she wasn't pregnant when Raevu left, how can she be so very round now? She looked ready to pop—at six months pregnant, maximum.

Behind the thrones, a door opened and closed. Raevu turned to the sound and again placed his body between me and the unknown person. A moment later, three males walked around the dais.

"There you are!" Raevu barked. "I was wondering why the three of you weren't here waiting in the throne room."

"My king," the one in front spoke with a slightly high voice, "false messages were sent to us. We were told to meet you on the northwest platform. As soon as T'ral sent us an inquiry asking why we weren't waiting here, we realized we'd been misled."

I looked around at T'ral and Baelon. They were speaking in hushed tones to one another. I wondered who had the power and knowledge to send false messages. *Was it Acidi?* If it was, then that was a really bad sign. *Should she have that kind of influence at the palace?*

Baelon looked over at us. "We'll find out what happened, Raevu."

A hard glint flashed in Raevu's eyes, and he nodded, as if fully trusting these two advisers to get to the bottom of it. He cleared his throat before saying, "Eva, I'd like to introduce you to the men who've been running things while we've been away." Placing a hand against my lower back, he ushered me forward.

"Certainly," I replied. I still kind of wanted to punch him for the mess he had been making of things, but I decided the best thing to do with Acidi lurking around was to act like the ambassador Maeda had asked me to be. I stepped forward a little to greet them.

All of them were shorter than Raevu and Baelon, but taller than me. T'ral had informed me that, although dwarf Juhlians existed, everyone else was taller than me by far.

Mikkel, the high-voiced one, was Raevu's Secretary General, or third-in-command when it came to warriors. He had the same warrior build as all the other burly men I'd seen, brawny shoulders and muscular arms, a blocky torso leading into beefy thighs. His greeting was short and cordial.

For Seneschal, Raevu had A'dam. He governed and took care of Raevu's household. Day-to-day matters like menus and cleaning, to major party planning, fell under his purview. His build was significantly leaner than Mikkel, and he exuded energy and inquisitiveness. M'kir was his assistant.

The third male fascinated me. I'd not seen a plump Juhlian yet, and this one was Friar Tuck-sized. His skin was also the darkest I'd seen, a deep, moss-green color and almost black eyes. I seemed to be just as compelling to him. His scrutiny didn't make me uncomfortable, but seemed full of curiosity.

Raevu introduced him as Brother Etsija; he was the assigned priest to the palace and spoke on behalf of the priesthood and the trees. *So, he's the Lorax,* I thought, managing to keep a straight face.

The priest stepped forward and held out a hand. "May I…?" And he motioned to my neck. I nodded consent. His hand gently touched the marking where my shoulder met my neck. Immediately, I felt a buzzing course through me. I looked up at Raevu to see his eyes widen in amazement, and then he smiled reassuringly, so I relaxed and turned back to the pudgy priest who had now removed his hand.

The priest's smile was radiant. "She is the one. We will prepare her now. The mating ceremony need not be delayed."

Wait—whoa—hold on a second! After an exchange of glances, I realized Raevu and I were both confused. I happened to speak first, "What do you mean?" I was still sorting out whether I could deal with Raevu's brusqueness and bossiness long term.

The priest smiled. "We may hold the ceremony with the setting of the sun this evening."

Raevu arched a brow, "Today?"

"Yes. In four hours' time, you two will be joined as life mates." The priest stared at me. "Eva, you are the one. Please come with me now." He held out his hand again, but this time, in order to take mine.

I opened my mouth to protest, remembering Raevu's flat statement that he would fuck me, that he was going to keep me forever, and I had better just get used to it. I didn't want to, not with a man with his abrasive attitude. "Whoa, time-out. Doesn't free will factor into this?" *As in, mine?*

"The priests are the ones in charge of it all. They decide when." Raevu seemed more startled than anything else. All his earlier anger seemed to have drained from him with the priest's actions and words. His voice dropped to where only I could hear it. "Your mark glowed, Eva. It lit up from within when he touched it. It was spectacular and amazing," Raevu said. He lifted a hand, and with a knuckle, traced down my cheek. He didn't seem to notice how I held perfectly still. "Let's have our ceremony."

I wasn't sure I wanted to, despite the fact that I had come this far and all eyes were on me. I contemplated my predicament. One, I had no other way of getting rid of this illness. Two, in my gut, I suspected that Acidi was trying to manipulate Raevu. And three, I would be damned if I stepped aside, letting her railroad him with a baby that possibly wasn't even his.

He watched my face as I mulled over the situation. I ignored the pressure on me and thought hard about what I wanted and would make me happy, and the most important facts kept pushing to the forefront. I had committed myself to help this planet's people. I had suffered all sorts of indignities, risks, pains, and troubles just to get here...from the experiments to being kidnapped. I had endured all of this to do right by the Juhlians. *Am I going to back down now that it's time to deliver on Earth's end of the bargain?*

I didn't know what to think about Raevu's belief that the gods had meant for us to be together. I didn't know whether there could be much of a future for us if we couldn't live together equally and peacefully. But I could at least do the right thing by him and the Juhlians… give them hope for the continuation of their race.

I could give him a child, as promised. I could even go through with this weird ceremony so the child would be legitimate and entitled to his or her royal birthright. I didn't know about staying on this planet forever or if I wanted to be Raevu's queen. The possibility of all of those things would be determined if our relationship could get better. But a deal was a deal, and I would damn well do what I came here to do…see if I could help their race survive.

I glared at Raevu. If he thought he was going to control my life because I was giving him a baby, I'd be a divorcée and on my way back to Earth in a flash.

Nodding once, I turned to take the priest's hand and was led away into the green shadows.

CHAPTER 22
RAEVU

Three hours had passed, and I stood with those I considered family in the grotto of the Sopu tree. Baelon, T'ral, and I had taken the time to bathe and dress in our finest clothing. I smiled to myself at the picture they both made, but I knew they did it more for Eva than for me. The woman had already captured my men's loyalty and respect.

As shoes were not allowed in the grotto, our feet were bare. I could feel the warm soil under the soles of my feet. I wiggled my toes a bit in anticipation. *Finally, a life mate of my very own.*

I scanned the area, wondering where Eva was. This was a relatively small space in the very middle of the palace, directly between the palace's more public areas and those reserved for the royal family. The floor had been covered with dirt, and rocks had been brought in. The Tovari tree had outdone itself on the beauty of the setting for its little cousin. The ceiling, glossy and shining, arched over us in a perfect dome. The rocks had been placed to form stepping-stones leading to a deep pool.

In the middle of the chamber was the Sopu tree, widespread roots buried deep into the water and the earth and joined with the Tovari tree itself. Its silver trunk gleamed in the light that filtered through the Tovari's branches. Its leaves were broad, and branches filled the room.

It was just beginning to bloom. Tiny white flowers hung in clusters at the end of each branch. Their fragrance, a heady honey smell, filled the chamber.

One of the priests entered from the other side, leaf-patterned robes rustling.

"We are almost ready for you, my king." His voice was low and musical. "We shall bring your lady out in just a few minutes. Do you know anything about the mating ceremony?"

"Only what I have read in the histories," I replied.

The priest's reply was dry. "That is all any of us know. There has not been a mating ceremony held in over three hundred seasons. Thank the gods that the trees know what to do. We just have to make sure the two of you are in the right spots and are both willing participants."

He smiled. "So far, she…is." I noticed his slight hesitation, but I was filled with too much bliss to stop and examine it, staying quiet as he continued. "My presence here is to make sure that you are as well."

Absolutely. Let's get on with it. Bring me my mate! "Aye. I am a willing participant."

"You do hereby attest that you are taking on a life mate of your own free will? You vow to cleave only unto her until death?" he asked.

"Aye. I do this of my own free will. I will be faithful to her until death."

He smiled again and gave a brief nod. "I will go summon her. She is a lovely woman, this human. She has a luminous spirit." His steps echoed as he backed out of the chamber.

We waited. The only sound in the grotto was that of the water being stirred by slowly moving roots. I kept my eyes focused on the door the priest had gone through. *What is taking so long?*

After what seemed like forever, he returned, escorting Eva proudly.

My eyes widened. She glowed.

She had bathed and changed her clothing. She radiated calm and health as she hadn't since I had met her. I looked at her, and it took all of my willpower just to keep control of my senses not go to her right then.

She was dressed in a white gown. The material was very thin, almost sheer but not quite. It was long in the front and back but open on each side, held together with several slim bows running from just beneath her arms down to her hips. The neckline was cut wide, exposing most of her shoulders so that her mark could easily be seen. She was wearing nothing else.

The priest led her across the stepping-stones to a spot directly under the Sopu tree and within touching distance of its trunk. He beckoned to me. I followed those same steps and stood on the stone he indicated, which faced her.

She looked up at me, her eyes calm and thoughtful. The priest had me place my right hand directly upon the sigil on her neck. Eva had to place her left hand atop that. We both then put our other hands on the trunk of the Sopu tree.

The priest stepped back and away. At first, nothing happened. I was beginning to wonder if this was all there was to it when there was a surge of power from the two trees. As it radiated up through my bare feet, I could feel the vibrations from the Tovari tree. Even more powerful, through my hand shot a surge of power from the Sopu tree. It felt both tingly, like electricity, and soothing, like a warm bath, at the same time. It was flowing into both of us from the tree and swirling through us and through our joined hands over her sigil, which had begun to glow with an inner light, and then crossed back through our arms into the trees.

For that brief moment, we were one with each other and one with the trees that sustained so much of our life.

We both laughed. I was astounded at the feeling, and I felt Eva relax. Baelon and T'ral were clapping their hands, broad grins on each of their faces. The three priests stood there with large smiles creasing their cheeks as well. One of them stepped forward. "You are now bonded one to the other, to Juhl, and blessed by the trees. Truly life mates. Now the bond needs to be consummated within this chamber. You will be given privacy for a full turn of the day. Sometime during that time period, rinse in the pool. Thoughts for your comfort have been provided as well." He bowed slightly. "My king. My queen." The priests turned and left the room.

Baelon and T'ral stood for just a moment, showing honor to the union, then voiced their congratulations before leaving the chamber. Baelon paused long enough to command the guards just outside the door, "They need their privacy. See that no one disturbs them." He turned and smiled before walking away. The guards secured the chamber doors behind them.

Now, Eva and I were alone with no restrictions placed upon us. *Finally.*

I dropped my hand from the tree, placing it firmly around her, pulling her forcefully up against my body. She grew very still and intense before her hands trailed up my arms and reached around my neck. Her lips met mine. So soft, so sweet.

There was no hesitation from either of us. I ran my fingers up into her hair, cupping the back of her head and pulling her even closer. I could feel the heat of her body through the sheer clothing she wore. My cock responded instantly, growing hard and throbbing with desire for her.

Finally, the moment we'd been waiting for. The moment we could indulge in each other as we'd only dreamed. I deepened our kiss, my tongue stroking and probing, exploring her mouth. Her tongue joined willingly in the dance. I let my hands travel down her back and hips, cupping her butt cheeks in my hands. I squeezed them, pulling her even closer.

Her breasts pressed firmly into my chest. Her nipples were hard and responsive. She began exploring my neck and shoulder muscles with her hands. I wanted to lay her down and look at her more thoroughly. I pushed my hips, grinding up against her soft body, and broke the kiss to glance down at her.

The thought of her sliding down onto her knees made my cock throb a little harder. I wanted to plunge into her, taking her right then and there. With a slow, deep breath, I backed away slightly. She moaned just a bit as if in disappointment. She was killing me. I took both her hands in one of mine and went to explore the rest of the chamber.

"Where are we going? I thought we had to stay here," she protested, sounding confused.

"We're staying in the chamber, but I want to do this right."

A teasing note entered her voice. "Do this right? Sounds promising."

I turned back to her, pulling her close in for a kiss then I trailed kisses down her jawline and neck while I spoke. "This is your first time. Our first time. I am not going to toss you down onto the dirt. I want to make this special for you because you mean everything to me." I traced my tongue lightly along the line where her dress and skin met across her breasts. *Gods, her skin tastes so good.* I felt her shiver.

We continued around the broad trunk of the Sopu. Sure enough, on the other side, spread out between two wide-spaced roots, was a bed of sorts. Blankets had been laid out on a grassy area, with an inviting pile of cushions on them. It was perfect.

I gently tugged Eva to the middle of the space. I dropped to my knees in front of her. This put her delectable breasts easily in reach. I wrapped my arms around her full hips and pulled her in tight against my body. I felt surrounded and comforted by her. I'd never wanted a female like I wanted her right now, and my shaft throbbed with need.

Her thin white slip of a dress revealed more than it covered. I placed my mouth over one straining nipple and slid my hands slowly up and down her sides, unraveling the delicate ties that held the dress together.

She tilted into the pressure as I tugged on her nipple, sliding my hands under the edges of the material and onto her warm, silky skin. She gasped at my touch, and her little sounds and movements were making me harder than I'd ever been in my life. I needed her…and soon. But I would not rush this. I wanted her to enjoy our union and know that I'd worship and respect her as my mate forever.

Releasing her nipples, I gently drew her down to her knees in front of me. She hesitated a moment but then complied. With a swift motion, I whisked the thin dress up and over her head, tossing it away.

I stopped and took a good look at her. She was perfection. Her dark skin glowed on her large, round breasts with perky nipples, and I ached to touch them again. And there, nestled between her curvy thighs, was the darkly tufted treasure that would hold me soon.

I must have paused too long in my staring at her, for she spoke. "Is something wrong?" Her voice came cautiously.

"No," I answered immediately. "Everything is right and perfect." I stood up quickly, pulling off my own tunic and leggings and letting her look her fill. It pleased me to see her stare at my body, before reaching my shaft, examining it with wide eyes.

She gulped and then looked back up into my eyes and smiled. "Well…you are huge, but I'll make it work."

I chuckled at her sassiness before I picked her up, carrying her over to the bed, laying her back and covering her body with my own. I wanted to touch her everywhere all at once. She continued to gasp and squirm as my mouth and hands roamed freely across her skin. I could feel her heating up underneath me, arching to meet my touches, gripping the covers with her fingers.

I reached between her legs and brushed my fingers across her soft black curls. She shivered, and her eyes widened. I slipped one thick, probing finger between her tight, swollen folds and was greeted by silky wetness as she let out a moan of pleasure.

Her body arched, her head turning with eyes closing in anticipation. Under the tip of my finger, her sensitive bud was all mine now. I gently flicked my fingertip across it and was rewarded with another groan that I swallowed with a hard kiss.

"Raevu," she moaned when I broke the kiss and let her speak.

"Yes?" I replied with my lips on her neck and my finger stroking back and forth.

"I need you…" Her murmur made my heart pound faster.

Her body was begging for my touch, her hips lifting to meet my probing fingers. Her hands reached up, attempting to draw me in, but I wanted this to last.

Grabbing her wrists with my free hand, I smiled and pulled them up above her head. She gasped, her eyes rolling closed. Her body continued to rock against me, begging for me to make her mine. I felt my cock throb even harder as I watched her body thrash in ecstasy.

Finally, I couldn't wait any longer either. Releasing her hands, I reached down, resting one hand on her hip while easing the tip of my manhood into the folds of her wetness. Gently pushing her hips down, I thrust in a little and felt her tense slightly.

"Shh. I'll go slow." I remained still, nibbling at her full bottom lip.

Little by little, her body relaxed again. And inch by inch, I eased my rod into her hot, tight core.

My hands began their wandering over her silken flesh. I again turned my attention to her beckoning breasts, and then she started to move. Gradually, tentatively, she shifted her hips, then rolled them, lifting them toward me. I drew myself back and plunged forward again, feeling my shaft grow harder and more sensitive with each slow stroke. In tune, our rhythm escalated into a sensual dance. Her hips met each of my thrusts hungrily. Loud moans escaped her lips.

Our breathing quickened. The smell of the Sopu blossoms mixing with the sweet, musky scent of Eva filled my lungs. Suddenly, the walls of Eva's sheath clenched tightly around me.

She cried out, "Raevu!" and I felt her nails dig into my skin as she thrashed against me. She began pulsing and throbbing in waves around my length. My life mate was beautiful and glorious, and I couldn't hold back anymore. With a final thrust, I emptied my hot seed into her welcoming womb. This was an experience I wanted to savor and remember for the rest my life with Eva.

When I regained my awareness, she was lying drowsily under me. I kissed each of her heavy eyelids gently. She reached a languorous hand up to my cheek, cupping it tenderly. With a slight, mischievous smile, she spoke softly. "Wow. Let's do that again."

I pulled away with a chuckle. "Oh, we will, my mate." I wrapped my arms about her, drawing her into the cradle of my chest. "Every day until death do us part."

CHAPTER 23
EVA

"I need something to do, A'dam," I protested. "I cannot and will not just sit around all day staring at the walls of my rooms." It was difficult keeping the frustration out of my voice. After all, my restrictions were not on A'dam's orders, but Raevu's.

"My queen, anything you wish to learn to do, I can get a teacher for you. Weaving of tapestries, painting, creating of mosaics or pottery, I can have an instructor of any of those here for you within the hour."

With a very unladylike groan, I rolled my eyes. "Those are my only choices? What if I want to learn about the animals and plants of my new home? What if I want to go out and see the city and meet my people? What about my self-defense classes? I'm good for more than idle hobbies!"

I didn't know why I was asking. I knew the answer. After weeks of searching, Raevu and his people had not discovered the source of the threats on my life.

I was on "palace arrest" until the threats ceased or the culprits were caught. If what I wanted could be brought to me, I could have it. If not, too bad. Even Baelon and the rest of my Guards were unmovable on that. The palace Tovari tree was the safest place for me, as the tree itself would stand as a kind of backup sentinel and a messenger for Raevu if something were to threaten me.

The gilded-cage treatment didn't just annoy me. It was creating fresh tension between Raevu and me as he went back into overprotective mode. We had worked hard on building our relationship for weeks after our joining, and we had actually been starting to get closer when more death threats rolled in. I understood his concern for my safety and I sure didn't have a death wish, but I needed to do more with my time than sit around waiting for them to capture the culprit or culprits of the threats to my life.

Especially since back home, I could go anywhere and do anything. I had friends to talk to. I didn't have one job, but several, where I could see people and learn new things all the time.

I desperately sought something interesting to keep myself occupied and from slitting my wrists out of sheer boredom. Besides, when the boredom lasted too long, I began thinking about Acidi and my lingering, gnawing doubts about my new relationship.

On the day after our arrival, due to Brother Etsija's announcement that I was "the one" and our subsequent hasty and enjoyable mating ceremony, Acidi and her claims had become the furthest things from my mind, especially when Raevu told me about their mate choice theory. I still couldn't believe that my DNA had more than likely chosen him as the viable mate. The concept empowered me, even more when I'd seen how Raevu worked hard to prove to me that he sincerely wanted to earn his place as my chosen mate. His commitment to making our mating work went a long way in cementing our relationship. It was a beautiful harmony between us, and it had mostly stayed that way. But when I grew bored, thoughts about Acidi crept in. Insidiously. And then I'd start to worry about her persistent maneuvering to break up my happy life.

Any questions about her latest ploys I directed to Raevu, and he didn't ignore my inquiries—more like he deflected any detailed response by saying she was being handled. I didn't know what "handled" meant. All I knew for sure was that her regular updates about her pregnancy indicated that it was proceeding at a normal pace, which meant she should be in her last month.

Within the next few weeks, Raevu would be a father. At least, according to Acidi. Raevu had doubts about that, but I didn't see how the baby could be anyone else's.

The local Grand Mother, who also happened to be Baelon's biological mother and one of the many leaders of the jalkavaima Grand Mothers on the planet, kept Raevu apprised of Acidi's actions and progress.

The Grand Mother even had come to visit me once. She was tall, lean, and imposing, and I certainly never wanted to be on her bad side. I had minded my p's and q's with her during my audience, and every sight, sound, and smell of that visit seemed imprinted on my brain.

But visits like that were too few and far between, and now, sitting with A'dam in my guesting chamber, I was so bored I was ready to scream.

Suddenly, an idea hit me.

"A'dam, I want a perfumer, a lotion maker, and a candlemaker. Surely we can start integrating some of Earth's flowers and scents into Juhl's market."

Maybe it was my imagination, but A'dam looked a bit relieved. "Very good, my queen," he said, turning to leave.

I held up a hand. "A'dam. Wait."

He paused mid-step.

"I also want to speak to an historian about the decline of female births."

After a moment's hesitation, he nodded. "Yes, my queen."

"Also send a message to Medic Willem to please come see me. I haven't been feeling well lately." It was nothing compared to the sickness that had gnawed at me before Raevu and I had joined, but it was still a little troubling.

He didn't seem to look relieved anymore, but he simply bowed his head. "Of course, my queen."

"And would you tell Brother Etsija that I am out of the Sopu flower incense again? I like to have it burning in my room." *Oh lord. I sound more than a little spoiled. I needed to find a worthwhile hobby or cause…fast.*

"Certainly, my queen." His footsteps slowly faded away.

Shit. My two best friends would have laughed at me if they could see me like this. Fussing over perfumes and incense while I spent my days in utter idleness.

Tears did begin to well up at the thought of them. *Damn.* I missed Ivy and Laura and all the kids so much that it was painful. Before I could say anything more to A'dam, I whirled around and paced over to one of the round, greenish-lensed windows.

The vivid green of the leaves and branches swayed in front of me, but I didn't focus on them. Everything had gotten so damn complicated since I had come here. It wasn't just about sorting out how—and if—Raevu and I could work as a couple long term. Joining with him had provided some relief from my symptoms. The sex then and since had been fabulous. I was fairly happy with the pairing, even if Raevu's ego and tendency to shove his foot in his mouth sometimes caused problems.

It was me that I couldn't live with. In fact, I couldn't stand myself lately. I was weepy and moody. I was bored easily. I just seemed to feel uncomfortable in my own skin. My clothes were of the softest and finest fabrics, but they chafed against my breasts and made them tender and sore.

I think I had watched every form of entertainment the Juhlians had available on the video screens. Disinterested, I nodded off midway through most of them. The only time I ever seemed to have energy was when Raevu came to our bed each night.

Now, that thought made me smile. He set my whole body on fire with just one look or touch. I craved him inside of me all of the time. Just standing here thinking about his hands and mouth and tongue on me caused my nipples to tighten and the sensitive folds between my legs to grow wet with want.

Two months ago, the night of our bonding ceremony, when I'd woken under the Sopu tree in Raevu's arms, I'd been a little sore from first-time sex, but his attentions had swiftly made me forget that discomfort.

The dip in the pool, which had started innocently enough but had quickly turned erotic and sensual, had completely alleviated any twinge of tenderness I'd felt.

Raevu seemed to know exactly where and how to touch me. In

return, I'd grown to know Raevu's body quite intimately. I licked my lips in anticipation. Raevu had said he had a surprise for us tonight. He'd told me to lay out several scarves. I could tell he had something special planned, and my body hummed in anticipation.

Damn. I can't wait.

Just as I was considering relieving my urges with my fingers, the door chime sounded to my sitting room. "Open the door, Geoffrey," I called to our electronic "butler."

"Willem!" I called out as my visitor stepped inside. I'd seen him about two weeks before. He came by periodically to check on me. It was always nice to see a familiar face.

Not like there were very many familiar faces for me on Juhl so far. I knew maybe ten men, including Raevu and all the members of my Guard. No women. I needed somehow to meet some.

Willem smiled as he paced toward me. I turned from my spot at the window and moved to greet him. "My queen, you look radiant."

"Bonding under the Sopu tree must have agreed with me. The flu symptoms stopped almost immediately. Since then, I've generally been the picture of health." My stomach gurgled slightly, and I forced a smile.

"Until recently, I hear." The doctor dug into his medical bag for a scanner to take my vital signs.

"Yes, which I don't understand. Nothing has changed. Not my diet or sleep cycle or exercise. Baelon comes to the palace training room daily for my pattern practice. A'dam has the chef well trained on my favorite foods, both Juhlian and from home."

Since I had laid aside my translator completely over a month ago, we spoke in Juhlian while the scanner whirred, clicked, and beeped, lights flashing.

"What is that smell, my queen?" he asked as we waited for the results of his tests.

"I've grown quite fond of the fragrance of the Sopu tree's elixir. When I no longer had to breathe in the medicine, I inquired about filling my rooms with scent. Brother Estija keeps me supplied with blossoms and leaves, which I simmer in water around my quarters. It relaxes me, gives me energy and a feeling of well-being, and, well…"

As he was my physician, I felt I could tell him the rest even though I'd never shared such personal information with anyone else. "The smell seems to influence Raevu as well. He becomes quite amorous."

I could feel my cheeks heating up at the memory of some of our sweaty and rigorous activities, on a nightly basis. It was no wonder I slept so soundly each night.

Willem's mouth quirked to one side, and I flushed hotter, thinking of the scarves laid out on my bed in the next room. "My queen, I think I know what's different about you."

"Really? That was easy. What is it?" I leaned forward, curiosity overtaking me.

"You're pregnant." He turned the scanner so I could see the screen. "Here, where the heart rate is showing? It shows multiple beats, and the hCG level in your blood is significantly higher than it has been in the past."

My heart raced. *Pregnant?* "But you didn't take a blood sample. How could you know that?" My mind reeled with all the possibilities, but suddenly all of my current symptoms made sense. I was feeling almost exactly what Ivy had felt during her last pregnancy with Jaylynn: nausea in the mornings, fatigue, and breast tenderness. And then it hit me, since Raevu and I had our bonding ceremony and started making love every night, I hadn't had a period, which I'd just concluded was due to my body adjusting to alien life. I must have gotten pregnant almost immediately. My legs wobbled, and I had to sit down.

His eyes twinkled as he explained. "My instruments are extremely sensitive. I have them programmed for human body analysis, and they look for anything out of the norm. It seems you have several readings beyond the 'norm' for an individual human female, although you are well within the norms for an expecting female." He gave a slight bow with his whole body. "May I be the first to extend my congratulations, my queen?"

I shifted on the lounge and covered my lower belly protectively with my hands. *Holy shit.* I knew I was expected to try to get pregnant as quickly as possible, but this was beyond all my expectations. Since I was human and Raevu was Juhlian, I had thought there would be complications we'd have to endure to get our bodies in sync to procreate. Instead, we'd hit the ball out of the park on almost our first time up to bat.

"Are you sure, Willem?" I asked. I needed that reassurance before I allowed myself to be happy over the news.

"Absolutely, my queen."

Excitement made me feel giddy. "I'll tell Raevu tonight." *Damn. I was going to be a mother.* I smiled a bit wickedly. *And my sexy alien would soon be a father…*

CHAPTER 24
EVA

A light chime sounded, alerting me that there was a visitor at the door.

"Are you expecting someone, my queen?" Willem asked politely as he packed away his medical scanner. "I can make myself scarce."

"No, Willem, please stay. You're one of the few people I know here," I assured him, "I always enjoy your visits, and now I have several questions for you." I raised my voice slightly. "Geoffrey?"

His soft voice replied to me, "Yes, madam?"

"Who's at the door? Am I expecting them?" With everything going on, I had to be cautious. "I believe her name is Linnea, madam. She is a historian of some renown." The computer concierge that had been my almost constant companion since I'd been removed from the clinical side of the Peace Opportunity Program had also become my electronic secretary and appointment keeper.

"Linnea?" Willem inquired. "My queen, did you send for an historian?"

"Do you know her? I'm a little nervous to be meeting a female Juhlian," I admitted. "I've only met the Grand Mother, and she was a bit intimidating."

Willem smiled. "I believe you will like Linnea, my queen."

I smoothed the soft fabrics that draped lightly about my curves and reached up to make sure my curls were all in place, or as much as they could be in their natural abandon. I had to laugh a bit at how ridiculously nervous I felt to be meeting a female, but there were so very few of them on Juhl. I felt like I was meeting a celebrity or luminary of some kind. In a sense, I guess I was.

Since my arrival here on Juhl nine weeks previously, I'd only ever seen two females…the local—and supreme—Grand Mother and Acidi.

With Willem giving this Linnea a positive reference, I was hopeful we'd get along well. So far, no one had said anything positive about Acidi except that she was beautiful—which I saw with my own eyes—and quite smart. I always wondered how dangerous she really was.

I shook my head, determined to stay in this moment. Willem was here and had just given me the very best news. For now, I'd keep it close to my heart until the perfect moment to share it with Raevu later. I wasn't terribly sure what my feelings for him were, but he had a right to hear this before anyone else did.

"Please let her in, Geoffrey," I requested.

"Willowy" was the first word that popped into my head when the lady walked in. Tall, long, and lean, of course, as most of the people I'd seen on Juhl were, she had straight, pale green hair past her hips, and she exuded energy and curiosity. She began talking almost as soon as she was through the door.

"Hello! I'm Linnea. I heard you wanted a historian, and I volunteered." She took both my hands in hers and searched my face with her eyes. She seemed familiar, but I couldn't place my finger on why. "And, Willem," she continued, without stopping her study of me, "she is just as lovely as you described."

Startled, I glanced over at Willem, who just smiled serenely at me.

"Please," I said, remembering my manners and finding my voice, "have a seat."

"Absolutely. And don't be formal with me, Eva. May I call you Eva? I feel like I know you already. Between Willem and Father's stories of you, I've gotten a pretty good picture."

"Okay, wait. Stop." I shook my head, trying to wrap my mind around the implications of what she was saying. "Who's been telling you stories about me? Willem?" I sat down on the comfortable lounge next to Linnea, who was still holding one of my hands, and glanced over at Willem archly.

He smiled, unfazed. "Linnea and I are in a contract together at the moment. It started just before we left to go get you. We'd like to make it permanent. I think, with your news today, the council will allow more Earth females to come here, and Linnea can leave the jalkavaimas and bond with me."

Linnea's hold on my hand tightened. "You're pregnant? Really? Already?" Her jade green skin paled, then flushed. "I am so happy for you." Tears welled up in her eyes. "So quickly! That's so much more than we could have hoped, but Brother Etsija did say you were 'the one.' Father says you're well matched with Raevu." She released my hand, finally, to swipe at tears she wouldn't let fall from her gray-green eyes.

"Father? Do I know him?" I felt a little lost.

"Yes." Linnea gave a teary smile. "Baelon is my father."

"Oh, he just must have not brought it up." No wonder she looked a little familiar.

"They aren't supposed to. We have an unusual relationship. My great-grandmother was the previous Grand Mother. Like her, the current one, my father's mother, she wants progress and change. She wants families again. She encourages the jalkavaimas to stay with their progeny until the child is two or three and can have memories of her, but tradition is hard to break. That's how I came about." Linnea leaned back against Willem, who'd moved over to be near her when she'd become upset.

I nodded, interested to learn more about this strange society of women. "What happened?"

Linnea started rambling, all overexcited intellectual mixed with happy daughter. "Mother stayed with Father until my brother was nearing his third birthday, and she discovered she was expecting me. So, she stayed longer. I got to stay with Father until I was five years old, which is unheard of, and I get to see him anytime I wish. Most jalkavaimas don't even know who their fathers are, it's buried in the records somewhere. I suppose so that preference can't be given to males who already have female offspring. Historically, though, that might be wise, to try to continue breeding with males who have proven themselves to be able to sire female babies."

"Now, she's talking history," Willem chuckled, "and you'll never get her to stop." The look in his eyes belied his light words. It was obvious he was trying to distract her.

"Are your children with their fathers, then?" I inquired. "How old are they?"

"Willem is my fourth contract" —tears welled up again— "and I have no children. Since he's a medic, we're trying some fertilization techniques. We have high hopes."

I flushed, mortified. *A woman in her profession who was infertile?* I felt so bad. Here in this faltering culture where being a female meant that your imperative was to bear children, and yet to be unable to bear children? What could she possibly be going through? I'd really stuck my foot in it. "I'm so sorry."

"Don't be, my queen," Willem said softly as he let his large hand run gently over Linnea's shoulder. "We've been friends for a very long time, and we thought we'd give this a try. We also just discovered that we have deeper feelings for each other. Your news is wonderful and comes at the perfect time. If we can get more human women to come here, the pressure to bear as many children as possible is removed from the Juhlian females, and more research can be focused on fertility." He kissed the back of her head.

"At any rate, my fertility isn't why I am here." Linnea cleared her throat and straightened her back. "My message from A'dam said you wanted to know more about when we first noticed the decline in female births?"

"Yes," I replied. "I am sure your historians and researchers have looked into it. I just thought maybe, with some fresh eyes and ears on it…" I trailed off. Surely, these people had thought of everything I could possibly come up with. In the last couple hundred years, the number of female births had declined until now it was only one in roughly two thousand. Females born now were immediately placed into their own rank in this society. They became jalkavaima, and men applied for and interviewed with them in order to attempt to become fathers.

The jalkavaima contract was a sacred one, and she held much of the power. So far as the relationship with the child and father went, the jalkavaima could stay with the male as long as she pleased: until the child's birth, up to the child's first birthday, or could have even less contact, having the child delivered to its father after its birth. If the child was a girl, the father gave up all rights. She belonged to her mother and the local Grand Mother of the jalkavaimas and would be raised in their company.

"No, Eva," Willem interjected. "I agree with you. We study what's been tried before with our history. We haven't looked at it with someone else's history."

Linnea spoke next. "The first census records where there are definitely fewer females than males in the populace are from about forty generations ago at the end of the Hattennen Dynasty."

I interrupted Linnea's obvious lecture mode. "What we need is what happened before all of that. This is surely a cause-and-effect type of situation. What happened a few generations before then? Something that would have to have been planet-wide or that started small but became planet-wide since it affected your entire populace."

"Oh, of course." Linnea seemed to think hard about my question and was having a difficult time coming up with an immediate answer. It would have surprised me if she had. They'd been dealing with this situation for generations; I couldn't solve it in an afternoon.

Suddenly, Raevu burst through the door, and my heart did its now customary little bump and flutter when I saw him. "Willem, there you are. It's happening. Grab your bag."

Without asking questions, Willem did just that. I stared after him, gaping slightly, annoyed as hell that my big announcement was being one-upped by something else.

Linnea and I made eye contact and stood up. Whatever was going on, neither of us was going to be left out. We followed the men out the door.

CHAPTER 25
RAEVU

From the moment we'd gotten back to Juhl from picking up Eva, Acidi's pregnancy had been bothering me.

What disturbed me was that before leaving Juhl for Earth, I'd decided it was time for our contract to be over and had Willem come over and subtly run some scans. Acidi had not been pregnant, and with great haste, I'd spoken to the Grand Mother to have her recall Acidi.

Later, to my shock, I'd gotten the news from Earth that one of the women who had volunteered for the Peace Opportunity Program appeared to be a viable option. While I was gone to fetch my life mate, Acidi had been recalled to the jalkavaima complex, and it was then that she had quite conveniently discovered she was pregnant—and with a girl, no less.

It all seemed much too contrived to me, too convenient. I didn't know how she could have done it, but somehow Acidi had engineered this pregnancy situation.

And now she was in labor, a full two months early. This disturbed me as well. Ten weeks was a long time in the gestational period. It was a lot of growth and development this baby would be missing out on, and I hoped Willem could stop or slow down the labor.

After the labor news was relayed to me, I was also informed that Acidi didn't want anyone but her own doctor and her brother in the room, but I wasn't going to give her an option in this demand. I was pulling rank on this one and had notified the Grand Mother and located my most trusted medic. They would be in that delivery room with Acidi.

We reached the quarters where Acidi had been housed in the jalka-vaima complex since her recall. I noted absently that her taste in decorating hadn't changed—bright, clashing colors, lots of metallic glints from statuettes, and baubles scattered haphazardly about the room. It looked like an Earth magpie's nest.

Eva's taste ran more to the deep colors, and I'd noticed that if she said she liked something somewhere in the palace, it'd find its way to her rooms. I don't think she ever requested or demanded, but she had a winning way with people that made them want to please her. If she said she liked something, A'dam or one of her Guard spoke softly to a passing servant, and that thing—be it tapestry or statue or ornament—appeared in her quarters.

I knew she had no idea that the painting she'd admired and that now hung over her chaise had been done by my three times great-grandfather, or that the small female statuette that now held a place of honor in the center of her guesting chamber was fashioned in the like-ness of my mother.

Even the sentient Tovari tree seemed to have fallen for her. The light in Eva's quarters always seemed softer and greener than it did in other places. The tree itself was filtering out our harsher light and warmer temperatures to keep her comfortable.

It troubled me that my life mate had been out of sorts lately. I wondered if it was due to the fact that she was on palace arrest thanks to the death threats. But even confined to her quarters, she still had an impact on my people. Any functionaries left the palace Tovari tree with stories of her. Brother Estijen sang her praises to anyone he ran into, and her Guard took turns going out into the community to talk about her and keep an ear out for further threats against her person.

The threats were becoming fewer and farther between as more males met her and realized what her coming to Juhl meant for us. A way to revitalize our female numbers, a means to overcome possible extinction as a race, a queen in name and also in office. *And what did that mean to me? A life mate.* So much meaning was wrapped up in just two small words.

Willem went directly to the room where the muffled screeches and crashes were coming from within Acidi's quarters. I assumed it was her bedroom because I'd never been to these quarters. In the past, my nights with Acidi had been just like her personality…planned, systematic, and filled with a show of no emotions.

Eva's instinctive passion and spontaneous gestures of affection toward me both touched and distracted me. Like now, when I should have been thinking of the child Acidi said was ours. Instead, I was always thinking about Eva.

A guttural bellow interrupted my reverie. "Get out!" Acidi's usually modulated and temperate voice sounded distorted. "Aaromon and my doctor are the only ones who should be in here. Get out!" Another crash resounded throughout the space.

The Grand Mother herself strolled out of the back room just as Eva and Linnea rushed through the front door.

"What are you doing here?" I queried to Eva. One of her Guards stepped through right behind her, and I saw two more take up stations outside the apartment's doorway. Immediately, part of me relaxed because I knew Eva had been safe the whole time she'd been on her way here.

"What's going on?" Eva's voice never failed to send an electric charge through me.

"Acidi's baby is on its way," I replied.

"Hello, my dear," the Grand Mother said as Linnea rushed over to kiss her cheek.

"Hello." Linnea smiled at her grandmother and stood at her side.

The Grand Mother announced to us all, "Acidi seems to be having a perfectly natural term birth. We'll see in just a little bit if my suspicions are correct."

We waited a bit longer as the moans and cries from inside the chamber grew closer together and more frenzied. We heard one long, anguished shriek wherein Eva stood closer to me, and I thought I saw her place her hand protectively over her belly, but surely, I was mistaken.

Suddenly, there was silence. I saw Linnea holding her mother's hand, and I began to reach for Eva's without thinking, when a shriek of outrage sounded from the next room.

"Impossible! What is that? Take it away! It's not what I created! Aaromon, what did you do?" Unintelligible squawks and screeches followed from the back room, but once Willem entered our room with a small bundle, we paid no mind to the noises from the rest of the suite.

Willem walked sedately into the room from the back, holding a small, swaddled form in his arms. All of our attention centered on the squirming blue bundle he held so tightly. Eva stepped forward first.

"What is it, Willem?" She held her arms out to take his burden from him.

"It's a girl. Acidi didn't lie about that. She appears to be full term, which should be impossible. We've started some DNA tests that Raevu has requested, and she's healthy otherwise, but..." His voice trailed off.

I'd walked over to see the tiny bundle in Eva's arms, strangely touched by the picture she made holding a baby.

"But?" I asked. My hand cupped the infant's entire head; it was so small and delicate.

"She has a birth defect. A clubfoot. Acidi is denying her now," Willem said with a shrug.

Eva looked up at him, outrage evident on her face. "For a clubfoot? Trevor had that when he was born. It's nothing. Completely correctable." She held the babe closer to her chest. "This baby is innocent. She can't help how she's born. She is beautiful and perfect, damn it. Why is Acidi so hateful?"

"Oh, dear, we've all been wondering that for years." The Grand Mother smiled and shook her head.

Looking down at the small figure cradled in Eva's arms, I had to agree. This tiny creature was perfect. No one in his or her right mind would reject her, birth defect or not.

Eva smiled at the babe in her arms. The picture they made together struck me deep in my gut. I wanted to gather them both up, keeping them just as they were forever.

The silence we created as we watched Eva smile down at the babe in her arms shattered as we began to hear words shrieked from the next room. "It's a monster! What did you do? Aaromon, I trusted you. This was the plan…but the baby is imperfect. Now I'll never be queen."

Eva glanced over at me at that last statement, and I shook my head ruefully. Acidi would never have been queen, just as my mother and grandmother and great-grandmother had never been queens. They were jalkavaima, and they retained that status even after bearing royal babies. Even though my mother had been special, as she had remained in the palace for a couple of years after I'd been born, she'd died when I was two years of age. Where Acidi had gotten the idea she'd ever be queen was a mystery. Maybe her mind had finally gone. I shrugged at the question in Eva's eyes and asked if I could take her adorable burden from her.

Gently, she transferred the squirming bundle into my arms. Now it was Eva's turn to stroke her hand over the small head. "Where will she go?" she asked softly.

The Grand Mother answered, "We may place her in a jalkavaima nursery nearby or somewhere else around the planet. When I get back to my office, I'll see who has the most personnel at the moment."

Her no-nonsense tone offended me. "If she is mine, she will stay nearby," I said in a low voice.

"Females aren't under the regular rules, Raevu," the Grand Mother replied dryly. "We may do with them as we please if the mother doesn't want them."

Eva gasped, "She will go nowhere. If she is Raevu's, then she will stay right here. As a matter of fact, she will stay with me in the palace Tovari tree." Eva whirled and faced Willem. "How long will the DNA tests take?"

Her ferocity seemed to take Willem aback. I smiled down at the infant in my arms. If Eva was this fierce in defense of an unrelated infant, then her own would be in the safest of hands.

"Just a couple of hours. Not long, my queen." He gestured to the infant. "They're already started. We don't usually question the paternity of our babies. DNA tests aren't run terribly frequently here."

Eva made a face at Willem and turned back to the bundle in my arms.

"Trevor, Ivy's oldest son, had a clubfoot when he was born." She gently stroked her knuckle down the baby's soft green cheek. "Ivy told me that she and her husband were so scared, but the surgery was commonplace and an easy correction. I'd never have guessed Trevor had been born that way by the time I came into the picture. He played soccer and football and ran track. He was just an ordinary boy. Having a clubfoot is nothing. What's wrong with Acidi that she thinks this makes her baby a monster?"

Linnea and the Grand Mother exchanged looks. "Acidi's always been vain," Linnea remarked.

I snorted. "That's putting it mildly," I commented, still holding the small, soft infant in my arms.

"Egocentric, immodest, conceited…" The Grand Mother smiled benignly at me. "I could go on."

"Please don't," I interrupted. "I think Eva gets your point."

Willem interjected, "She doesn't want this baby. It's defective in her eyes." And there he paused. "Although I will tell you it's full term. My scans have shown this. This baby isn't two months early as we thought. It's fully developed, and the only way it could be fully developed is if she had been four months pregnant before we left to go to Earth." He shook his head. "She certainly wasn't four months along when we left."

I nodded. The baby wasn't mine, and the tests would confirm it.

"As I suspected," the Grand Mother stated. "Acidi's pregnancy wasn't natural. There's information missing from her files that I suspect has to do with her fertility. We're struggling more and more with that. A solution must be found soon."

The Grand Mother held out her arms imperiously for the baby.

"No," I said, "Not until we get the DNA results."

Eva chimed in. "We're taking her home with us. She's ours." She looked up and smiled at me before saying," And her name is Hope."

CHAPTER 26
EVA

I hadn't heard from Ivy or Laura lately. I needed to tell them about my pregnancy and talk with them about it. So far, the only people who knew were Willem and Linnea. Probably A'dam knew as well, but so far as I could tell, A'dam knew everything.

Ivy had taken me in as family, and Laura was my closest friend. It almost physically pained me that I hadn't been able to tell them about this newest development in my life. This was certainly an aspect of the situation I hadn't thought of when I'd originally signed up for the Peace Opportunity Program. I had known I'd be away from them, surely, but I didn't ever think we'd be without contact.

I don't think I'd ever even thought I'd leave Earth. These past several months had been beyond my wildest dreams. Ivy and Laura would understand if I could just talk to them. I knew the first thing they'd tell me to do would be to tell Raevu about the pregnancy.

I still hadn't managed to confess to Raevu that he and I were expecting. I kept thinking of everything that could possibly go wrong. Maybe this was a false positive. Maybe this was a strange reaction to stress my body was taking.

Maybe… Honestly, maybe I was just nervous about telling him. Would my usefulness be over once it was known I was pregnant? *Was I just a baby-maker to him?* If only I could get in touch with Ivy or Laura. They'd help me talk through this.

My days were filled with Hope. I refused any kind of help with her. I was her mother. She was my child. Every evening, I'd fall into my bed, exhausted, and immediately go to sleep. My nights were also filled with Raevu, and most nights, I'd awaken to the delicious sensations of his hands running over my skin. He'd slip into our bed and start his sensual worship of my body. I'd wake thrumming with need, nipples pebbled from his plucking, a pool of moisture at the juncture of my thighs aching for him to thrust himself inside. And being pregnant seemed to make everything more sensitive; there was a heightened awareness of my body. And Raevu seemed to know exactly what to do and where to touch me until I was on the verge of begging for him to fuck me hard.

Even now, the memory of last night, when his large hands cupped my generous breasts, rolling my nipples between his fingers and tongue, made a shiver run through me. Damn…the way his muscular body had looked all stretched out beside me, while his hand had stroked down my body and across my belly to my center. And then he'd parted my lower lips with his fingers and found the sensitive bud of my clit throbbing in anticipation of his touch. He'd placed one finger on each side of that little nub and began slow up-and-down strokes. My hips had rocked with his strokes, meeting his hand, making it easier for him to reach and begin to enter my core with just the knuckle of one finger, teasing me with light sensation.

Wanting to touch as well as be touched, I'd grasped his erection, gratified to hear the small moan he emitted as I began to stroke him up and down, while my other hand I had smoothed over his bald head, arching my back to get my nipple closer to his mouth. Our movements grew faster, deeper, and more urgent with each stroke of a hand. A tremor had shot through me, once, twice. I had suddenly needed more and deeper.

I had stopped our play, and he had let me nudge him onto his back. Swiftly, I had thrown one leg over his torso and straddled his hips. Placing one hand on either side of his head, I had arched my back and settled downward until I could feel the pressure of his manhood poised at my entrance.

Slowly, I had sheathed him with my body. He had filled me, stretching me with his girth as I sat back until hips met hips and he was completely embedded within me. With a couple of quick flicks of my tongue over his lips, I had settled back again. Up and down, forward and back, I had rocked our bodies together. His hands had gripped my hips and aided my rhythm.

I had pushed myself hard, driving us faster and faster, feeling the tension build and curl inside me. I remembered feeling it twisting, tightening, and spiraling deep in my center. I had shuddered with the force of the orgasm that surged through me. I had felt myself clenching around Raevu's shaft. The extra pressure must have sent him over the edge of control too, because he had grabbed me, and without breaking our joining, rolled us over. With a couple of deep plunges, he had shuddered and expelled his hot seed inside me. With a deep sigh, he had settled on top of me, his weight comfortable and warm. Within moments, with him still cushioned between my legs and on my breasts, I had fallen asleep.

Hope cried, shaking me awake. She'd miraculously slept through the night since we'd brought her home. Willem's DNA testing had proven that Raevu was indeed her father, but that Acidi wasn't her biological mother. Once Raevu and Willem knew that, they'd pieced together what Acidi had done. Aaromon, her brother, confirmed their thoughts after a few questions.

Acidi had scientific research training. Aaromon was a medic in the labs the Juhlians had set up to try to discover ways to produce more girl babies. Hope was actually a test-tube baby.

When Acidi had first gotten hints that Raevu was growing tired of her, she'd redoubled her efforts for a while to get pregnant. After one such effort, she'd "harvested" some of his sperm for use in their labs. She had discovered that, like Linnea, she couldn't produce viable eggs. So, they'd stolen some from the labs and set about to create a child for Raevu and her.

Their timing was a bit off, and Acidi had some difficulties with her hormones being out of whack since it wasn't a natural pregnancy.

Because of this, there had not been quite enough room for Hope to develop properly in utero, resulting in a completely nongenetically based clubfoot.

Everyone was horrified at what she'd done, and Raevu and I were furious. There was no question of Acidi ever seeing the baby again now. I wouldn't allow it. The Grand Mother wouldn't either. She'd sent Acidi to another jalkavaima complex on a completely different continent. There, she would be part of a scientific research team studying birds or something. Aaromon, since he had succeeded in ensuring a healthy female baby, was put to work under strict supervision and told to replicate his findings faithfully—if he wanted to avoid exile.

Hope's biological mother was unknown, but the baby officially had been given to me to raise. Now I never had an opportunity to get bored or restless. I spent every waking moment with the little girl who had captured my heart.

Just days after her birth, she'd had surgery to repair her clubfoot. Seeing her leg in its tiny, flexible cast always broke my heart just a little and made me want to curse at Acidi. I still didn't know how she had thought she could leverage this poor baby to force Raevu to become life mates with her. But like much that she did, her motives were not just mysterious—they seemed irrational to the point of insanity.

How any mother could carry life under her heart for any length of time and then deny the child when born out of anything but necessity was completely beyond me. I didn't understand it at all.

But I felt that Hope was like me, when my parents had abandoned me, throwing me away for no damn reason. I knew the Grand Mother meant well when she'd planned to take her, and Hope would have had a better life than I did growing up in the Children's Ward. But she never would have had a real mom or a real dad. And I realized now that that was the worst part for me growing up.

I vowed to give Hope what I never had. A mother who stuck around, protecting and loving her.

When Hope was napping, I took care of other business. I'd met briefly with perfumers and candlemakers who seemed enthused about adding Earth scents to their repertoires. Anything resinous, green, or floral attracted them.

I had A'dam send a message packet to President Maeda on Earth. With my current ambassadorial status, I had a great deal of leeway in requests I could make. I asked for plants and seeds that produced the scents in question, and I asked Maeda if a botanist would be interested in making the trip.

We began, over transmission packets, to negotiate trade in the form of restaurants, entertainment, and market stalls, and, most importantly of all, families that might want to immigrate to Juhl. I figured that if families with girls in them were here, then nature could take its own course and the population could expand through the regular interactions between our people. Even if not all were genetically compatible now, the project would eventually find a solution.

Raevu would still have to meet with his council about arranging for a large influx of just human women as brides or jalkavaima. But to convince them, he'd need to know our mating experiment was a success. A complete success, unlike the disaster I had barely survived back on Earth.

That thought discomfited me. I was an experiment. *Did Raevu still see me that way?* I knew I'd started out in his mind as "the female" and even "his female," *but was I still?* I traced a hand lightly over the sigil that forever marked me as his. *How do I really feel about him now?*

I smiled because there was no doubt in my mind that I loved my sexy alien mate. Yes, he was domineering, brusque, bad-tempered, and impulsive. But he was also brave, caring, nurturing, funny, protective, charismatic, intelligent, and fucking spectacular in bed. And despite our ups and down together, I wanted to stay with him…forever.

I sat down abruptly in the nearest chair, and tears came to my eyes. Furiously, I blinked them away. *I am independent and self-sufficient, dammit! And I love Raevu.* I wanted to stay with him, build a life with him, and have lots of babies. And somehow, those things didn't really feel like they were in opposition anymore.

Seeing the camaraderie between him and his most trusted advisers, T'ral and Baelon, while we were on Earth, and watching them interact had been interesting. When Raevu's old friend, Ken Maeda, the president of my planet, had been added into the mix, everything had shifted to fascinating… They were extraordinary men doing ordinary things. Connecting and working together just like I'd seen cooks and chefs work with Gino at his restaurant when I'd taken shifts there to pull in extra money.

And when we'd gotten on board the ship and I saw in action how the respect had flowed back and forth between Raevu and his people, I knew then that he genuinely cared for their well-being, and they cared right back for his. I had seen that even more profoundly when we arrived on Juhl. Raevu's people could absolutely count on him to lay down his life for them.

Yes, I also saw his arrogance and stubbornness—and how hard I would sometimes have to work to get him to communicate his thoughts and intentions with me clearly, without him being an asshole. But I knew now it was just him to keep things close to his chest and not share them like I thought he should, but it was because he'd never had a mate to share that part of him. Several of our arguments could have been completely avoided if he'd just told me why we were doing something a certain way, instead of assuming that I automatically understood his rationale. Raevu had his faults, and so did I. We both weren't perfect, but no one was. What was important was that he was considerate of me and respected my thinking. He'd taken to talking with me of policy and government just before our evening meal every night. And he was so passionate in his lovemaking and could set my whole body aflame with just a look. And then it was how tender I'd seen him be with Hope. He was so large, but his hands couldn't be gentler in his handling of her like a precious package.

I swiped at the tears on my face from all of the love I felt for both Raevu and Hope. But I had to get my shit together; Linnea would be here any moment now for another history lesson. She couldn't see me when I was this emotional mess.

I grinned. Damn. I loved Raevu, and I wanted to stay and make a family here and build a life. By God, I hoped I'd read all the signs right and he'd love me back.

CHAPTER 27
RAEVU

I hoped Eva liked her surprise. Keeping it a secret had been difficult. I'd been almost bursting with it for weeks now.

Thank goodness for Hope. Eva and I could discuss Hope, and I could set aside thoughts about the secret and manage to once again avoid blurting it out. Well, the moment of truth was at hand. I'd find out now how she felt about surprises and secrets.

I'd picked a moment when I knew Linnea was with her, thinking that if I had someone I knew well there, the moment would be less awkward for me. I glanced around to make sure all was in order, as best it could be anyway. The excitement was palpable. I asked Geoffrey to open the door to Eva's suite of rooms, and I let myself and our newly arrived guests through.

Bodies seemed to tumble through the doorway and spill into the room. Happy cries of Eva's name sounded over and over as each person clamored for her attention. I couldn't even find her in the bedlam I'd helped to create.

And then I did. She was a light of calm amidst the bubbling sea surrounding her. Tears streamed down her smiling face as she struggled to hug five boisterous, wiggly Earth children at once.

Her deep brown eyes linked with mine, she mouthed "thank you," and turned her full attention back to the demands of her very own multitude. I went to stand by Linnea, who had backed out of the path of the stampede when the children had rushed for Eva.

"Are these the little ones you talked of?" she asked, wide-eyed. "Ivy's kids? Laura's Amber?"

I nodded and grinned briefly, proud to see the results of my planning and secret-keeping. "Who else could it be?"

Linnea shook her head slightly. "Yes, how silly of me. How long are they here to visit?"

"They are not visiting." I leaned against the wall and continued to observe the happy chaos. "They're here to live."

"That's the sweetest thing I've ever heard." Linnea patted my arm. "Does Eva know that?"

I had to fight down another grin. "Not yet, but she will."

She beamed. "Oh, I see. Where are their mothers?"

"T'ral and Baelon are bringing them down. We thought it'd be fun for the kids to get their hellos out of the way first. The adults are taking a more scenic route past their new quarters."

Eva had managed to get the children all settled where they could each be touching her. She had the two boys snuggled up against each hip beside her on her chaise, the older girl leaning on her back with two little arms wrapped tightly around her neck, and the two younger girls of light and shadow leaning against each knee.

She had just managed to convince the boys that her tears were happy ones. Finally, when T'ral and Baelon arrived with Ivy and Laura, I noticed the disgruntled looks on Baelon's and Laura's faces. I wondered what was wrong, but it couldn't have been terribly important because T'ral and Ivy just looked amused.

Eva stood up and rushed over to Ivy's open arms. Ivy pushed Eva back to arm's length and looked her up and down and said, "It worked? So quickly? You're pregnant."

I blinked very slowly, pushing off from the wall as I stared between them. *What?*

Eva's startled gaze flew to me. "I haven't had a chance to tell Raevu yet."

I stood there in shock. She stared back, a guilty, worried look on her face. I blinked, and a slow grin spread across my face. I walked over to Eva, feeling the need to touch her. I reached down and trailed two fingers down her cheek. "You're pregnant?"

She straightened her shoulders, lifted her chin, and nodded.

"Since when?"

"I found out the day Hope was born." Her eyes shifted around in embarrassment at the admission.

"But that was almost three weeks ago," I said. "Why didn't you tell me?"

"I meant to. I planned it out, but then I'd fall asleep before you got to bed, or then we'd be busy…with other things. And what if I miscarried? Or what if it had been a false positive due to stress and exhaustion? We've been through so much lately. I wanted to make sure I was pregnant before I said anything to you."

I wanted to interrupt her with more questions, but I saw she was struggling to explain, and I forced myself to nod in acknowledgment and keep listening.

"I kept waiting to talk to Ivy or Laura about my doubts and concerns, but I couldn't get in touch with them. Now I know why." Eva shrugged her shoulders. "It's kind of ironic. I had decided today that I wasn't going to wait any longer. I was going to make sure to tell you tonight. I swear. But Ivy kind of spoiled that surprise." Eva laughed and brushed away a tear.

I was filled with emotion. I could have been very angry at her for hiding the truth, but I was coming to learn that some things were more important than the satisfaction of my expectations. Eva was more important.

I bent and wrapped my arms about Eva and swept her off her feet into a giddy turn. Since her face was conveniently close to mine, I kissed her softly. "Pregnant. That's the best news I've ever heard."

I carefully set her back on her feet. She was quickly swept away into Laura's arms for a hug of hello and congratulations.

Baelon walked over and slapped me forcefully on the back. "Good job, nephew. Now, quit staring at her and let's go tell everyone. Let's see if the boys want to come with us."

I looked back at my life mate briefly, and then went on with my uncle. I had two children and my new life mate that I loved more than life. I had been truly blessed by the gods.

CHAPTER 28
EVA

I adjusted Jaylynn's arms around little Hope so that Hope's head was supported more securely. "She's kind of green, Eva. Why is she green?" Amber asked as she patted the moss-colored down on Hope's head.

I laughed, even as Laura hissed for her daughter to mind her manners. "Haven't you noticed, Amber? Everyone here, except for the group of us, is either blue or green."

"She's beautiful," Jaylynn murmured. "My very favorite shade of green."

"Every green is your favorite shade of green," Amber protested to her friend. "But why? Why is everyone blue or green?"

"I really don't know, honey. Does it matter? They're blue or green. You're white. And I'm black. It's just another color."

"No, it doesn't matter." Amber continued stroking the velvet. "I'd just like to know why."

"Eva," Ivy's daughter Josephine called from where she'd been talking with Linnea. "When is your baby due?"

"In the season the Juhlians call Kavat," I replied. "We'd say early spring, I think."

Amber walked up to me and tugged the edge of my shawl. "Hugs?"

I picked up Amber and twirled her around. I couldn't believe my family was here with me—and staying. "I don't understand how you got here!" I cried.

"On a spaceship," Amber giggled as she was spun.

Laura rolled her eyes at that. "Yes, honey, that's exactly what Eva's asking." Laura seemed restless; she kept wandering the room and touching the knickknacks and ornaments scattered throughout. "We didn't really have all that much to stay on earth for. Ivy and the kids don't have any other family. I'm on my own with Amber. We both had pretty meaningless jobs."

Ivy nodded and spoke up. "Raevu sent a messenger packet and offered us free room and board, and education for the kids. How could we lose? Move somewhere exotic where you can live for free in a palace near your best friend, or stay in a tiny living cube and work a job you barely tolerate just to pay the bills. Not a difficult choice." Her eyes twinkled.

"Besides, I'm now a certified nurse-midwife, and I can help you with your pregnancy." Laura smiled. "And Ivy is a teacher and can teach all of our kids."

"Mama," Jaylynn called. "Can we have this baby when Eva has her own?"

I shook my head at that, though the kids' immediate attachment to Hope made me smile. "No, Jaylynn, I'm not giving up Hope. She's mine."

Amber's eyes grew round, "But she isn't yours. Your baby is in your belly. Will you still want her when you have your own?"

"Of course I will," I objected. "She's a beautiful, innocent baby. I consider her my own now. She'll be my oldest child just like Trevor is the oldest or, if your mommy ever has any more children, you'll be the oldest. Ivy loves all her children, and your mommy will always love you. And I will always love Hope, no matter how many of my own kids I have."

I was kind of glad that Baelon, Raevu, and T'ral had taken Trevor and Mark with them on a tour. Those two boys needed more male figures in their lives. "How are Gino and Val?" I asked.

Ivy answered, "Their restaurant is moving—as in, here. They will be one of the first Earth restaurants to open up here on Juhl. Some man named Willoughby asked them if they'd be interested. They said of course! And half the staff wants to come along as well."

"I think Raevu has to propose it all to the Council, but, Eva, the plans you've proposed to him about immigration here make sense," Laura concurred.

I arched a brow. "Raevu knows about all of my immigration proposals?"

"Of course he does," Linnea laughed. "Raevu reads every message packet before it leaves. He's seen the suggestions you've made in your ambassadorial capacity to your president, and he loves them. Willem has mentioned them a couple of times when he's come home."

Extra hormones must have been flooding through me, and I got teary-eyed for the third time today. Typically, I wasn't even a crying type of chick.

Laura smiled at me. "Eva, it's obvious that Raevu is as head over heels for you as you are for him. Just watching the chemistry between you two lets me know everything… You two are definitely in love with each other. And I couldn't be happier for you. You deserve happiness." She winked at me. "By the way, what is that wonderful smell?"

"What smell?" I asked, bewildered.

"She means the Sopu tree," Linnea said. "Isn't it marvelous? Relaxing and delightful at the same time. I've taken to simmering it in pots around our quarters as well. Makes Willem very affectionate." She blushed lightly under her pale green skin.

"Is that included in the messenger packets?" I wondered. "I think this fragrance would sell marvelously well on Earth. I need to ask Brother Estijen about supply and demand. I doubt they would let any of their sentient trees be exported, but they probably shed plenty of foliage that isn't being used."

I paused and then winced slightly. "Speaking of supply, Linnea, did all the information get supplied to Geoffrey?" We weren't getting anywhere in our historical search for answers going solely off Linnea's memory of learned events from four hundred years earlier. We had been forced to utilize another resource, Geoffrey, my computer concierge, who could filter through data and information in a fraction of the time it might take a person. He could identify the patterns we might not be able to see.

"It should all be uploaded by tomorrow morning. I wish the two computer systems were a bit more compatible and could just dump data back and forth. Data entry is tedious," Linnea complained, "but, as we have ten men working on it, almost all of our history books and files are in his system now."

"Good! We can start feeding him search parameters tomorrow. Who knew research was so exciting?" I pulled Josephine in for a hug, so glad I had my family surrounding me once more.

CHAPTER 29
RAEVU

Things were looking up. There hadn't been a single death threat in weeks. The Council had been surprised and thrilled to hear of Eva's pregnancy so soon into our union, and they had passed an immigration bill allowing unwed Earth females to join jalkavaima complexes if they so desired—after getting a clean bill of health, of course.

The immigration bill also had a stipulation that jalkavaimas of either race could settle on a more permanent relationship if both the male and female were in accord with this.

When we passed the bill and coordinating treaty on to Ken Maeda and Earth, the response was overwhelming. Thousands of women were willing to become jalkavaimas to get off the overcrowded Earth. Some were willing to do it for just a couple of years until they could get established—or find a mate. Other human females, like Eva, were doing it only to help out our population. Many women were willing to have in vitro fertilization and have babies, but they didn't want to formally become jalkavaimas.

The outpouring of support and generosity from the Earth women was remarkable to me. But I still had to take precautions. I was sure there would be some just like Acidi, opportunists and manipulators.

Provisos were placed into both bill and treaty that allowed for a zero-tolerance of criminal activity or suspected manipulation of information. A trial of peers made up of Grand Mothers, jalkavaimas—both human and Juhlian—and a few males would be held for those thought to be abusing the system, and those found guilty would be deported back to their former situations.

Eva, Maeda, T'ral, and I discussed the wording for the treaty quite carefully. *Gods, Eva is fierce now!* She had transformed into a confident, passionate proponent for both humans and my race.

Less than a week after I surprised Eva with her friends and adopted family, Willem and Linnea announced her pregnancy. Linnea claimed it was the Sopu fragrance that had turned the tides for them. Scientists were now working with the Sopu, suspecting that the sacred tree had an effect on Juhlian fertility, perhaps human fertility as well.

With the fear for Eva's safety diminished, we decided she could move out and about amongst the community, if her Guard were vigilant. She took little Hope with her everywhere she went, and often took Amber, Jaylynn, or some or all of the other children as well. The sound of children's laughter hadn't been heard in these boughs in centuries, and now they rang with it.

It had a strong effect on my people. It offered optimism. Every man among us, be it warrior or eunuch, seemed to walk around with a smile on his face.

I was in such an optimistic mood that my guard had relaxed some. Fortunately, I had others looking after me. I was waiting for Eva to return with the children when I suddenly felt the Tovari tree's disquiet.

"What is it, my friend?" I asked a bit distractedly. A fresh message packet had come in, and I was reading of the dispatch of Eva's doctors to come to Juhl earlier than expected. She'd be thrilled with that news.

The uneasiness grew more pronounced, cutting through my bliss. I couldn't shake it off or ignore it. I set down the data screen on the desk and walked over to the great trunk of the tree. I placed my hands squarely on the bark and asked again, "What is it? Show me." I closed my eyes and concentrated on listening.

My anxiety grew. I could hear Hope crying and the little girls calling Eva's name. I saw flashes of our quarters and the apartments of

Ivy and Laura, all places where Eva would ordinarily be, burst into and out of my vision. In none of the pictures was Eva.

"She's not there?" I asked. My heart started to pound with fear. Dread grew, and I wasn't sure now if it was strictly from the tree or if it was mine. *Where could Eva have gone?* I thanked the tree for its message and rushed to our quarters. When I got there, I found Laura giving orders like a battlefield general.

"Mark, stop pacing and go sit down. Josephine, get me a cool washrag. Geoffrey, have you located Raevu, Willem, or Baelon yet? Trevor, go get the baby, please. You know how to change a diaper?" She was kneeling at the side of one of Eva's Guard, who was blinking furiously.

Rage and alarm filled me. "What happened?" I barked.

"Raevu, thank god you're here! We can't find Eva. Ivy and Delan were knocked out cold. I have Jaylynn and Amber looking after Ivy, and Eva's guard only just came to. He's got a knot on his head the size of a baseball. I need Willem!"

"Where is Baelon?" I demanded, trying to make order out of the chaos at hand.

"Geoffrey's trying to find out, but his communication channels are screwed up, and he isn't able to reach anyone outside of these apartments. We've tried getting in contact with you and him with no luck. Frankly, I don't know how you showed up just now, but thankfully, you did."

Josephine scurried back up with a wet washing cloth. "Momma won't wake up, Laura." For all her strong voice, she had tears running down her cheeks.

"Help Delan hold this gently right here, baby. I'll go check on her."

As Laura pushed herself up to standing and moved to the next room, I moved to Delan's side.

"Soldier, report!" I barked.

"My king!" His eyes struggled to focus, and he winced. "It was Aaromon and Acidi. No idea how they got past Acidi's ban. They must have bribed someone. They approached the group we were in and claimed they just wanted to see the baby. I didn't want to let them in, but my queen…" He stopped and closed his eyes.

"Eva probably pitied Acidi, as her pregnancy has made her more emotional and kind," I finished for him. *Curse it. I couldn't even be angry at Eva for giving Acidi the benefit of the doubt.*

"Yes," he continued haltingly, "she invited them to come closer, along with the rest of the group. Eva went to go get the baby. I couldn't keep all of them in my sight at the same time. Acidi followed my queen, and Aaromon stayed here. I heard a thump and cry from the next room and moved to see what it was, then I just felt pain."

"Lie back down, Delan. Willem will be here soon." I helped ease him back into a reclining position. "Geoffrey?"

"Sire, my wires and circuits are scrambled beyond these quarters. There is some kind of blocker keeping me from contacting anyone outside these rooms."

I hurried to the doorway. There, I saw Ivy slumped down on the floor, one little girl at each wrist, silent and grave, as little girls should never be.

Laura stood up from her inspection. "No knots or hits. They must have given her a drug someway. I just don't see how."

Mark was sitting with a dazed expression. Trevor walked in with Hope cradled in his arms. She gurgled and smiled happily at him. He walked over to Laura and handed over his charge, then went and sat at his mother's head and stroked her hair. His face was just as serious. Looking at him, I felt my rage bubble up dangerously.

No child should go through this, and neither should my mate. *I'll kill Acidi this time.*

Willem and Linnea charged through the doorway and nearly ran into me. Willem hurried over to Ivy's side and shooed the girls away from their vigil. He talked as he inspected, and his scanner beeped and clicked.

"Delan has a serious concussion. I've contacted the medical branch to come and get him. I've sent a message to Baelon, and he's on the way up. As for the young lady, this is a knockout drug, a strong one. Probably not hazardous, but she's going to be out for a while. Look for a syringe." This last statement was directed at Linnea, who nodded and immediately started canvassing the room.

"How did you know to come here?" I asked.

"Linnea knew. She said something about the tree being agitated."

"Yes," I said, "the tree told me. I'm hoping the tree can help me find Eva. Help Ivy."

Linnea swooped down on a small object halfway across the room. It was a mini tranquilizer syringe used on animals in labs.

"It's just a tincture of Mellin sap. She'd have to drown in it for it to kill her. The brother's doing, I suspect. He's not completely callous. In short, she'll be fine." He gave the children a reassuring smile, and all five relaxed visibly, that terrible graveness going away. "She's going to sleep for a couple more hours. I'll get some saline into her, maybe that will flush it out of her system faster." He typed some instructions on his data screen to the medical branch.

I went over to the tree trunk again. "Okay, friend. Everyone here is safe. Help me find Eva." I placed my hands on the trunk and even leaned my cheek against the bark. I'd never been this scared in my life. I loved Eva and my life with her in it.

I adored seeing her smile and play with Hope. And the absolute love shining from her as she cradled that little one in her arms to feed her always made me smile. I didn't know when her opinion had become so vital to me; I only knew that before I made a critical deci-sion, I wanted her take on the situation—to know how she'd put those same pieces together. I wanted to touch her constantly, have her near me. I found myself reaching for her in the night to pull her up against me.

I loved her.

All this I sent into the tree. It sent me one image back—the landing platform, high above us.

CHAPTER 30
EVA

"What the hell are you doing, Acidi? Stop this shit at once," I used my most commanding voice on her as I fought against her grip on me. "You're fucking nuts. Kidnapping or even killing me won't get you anything." I was calm. I had to be in order to get out of this predicament alive.

"Shut up, human. Your words mean nothing to me." Her long fingers dug into my arm as she dragged me out into the middle of the landing platform. I dug in my heels and leaned back, resisting as much as I could, but she was far stronger than I was.

"This is ridiculous." I turned my head, realizing that saying anything to the crazy bitch was a waste of time. I would have to look for an opportunity to break free of her instead. "Delan and Ivy are okay, aren't they? Aaroman?" I asked.

The small—for a Juhlian—man glanced nervously at me. He gulped, eyes shifting fearfully between his sister and me, as if he was too intimidated by her to do anything at all unless she ordered it. His brow furrowed, and he finally spoke up. "Acidi, why are we here? I can't fly a skimmer. We've always had a servant to do that for us." His voice was whiny and high-pitched. He held himself carefully out of Acidi's reach. And from the long scratches down his cheek, I could guess why. *How long has he lived in terror of his nutty sister?* I felt a faint bit of sympathy for him.

"Raevu will come for his human. We're waiting. He just needs to see the two of us together. And he'll know then that I'm his queen." Acidi's voice scraped against my nerves. "Human, your mark is false. Mine is real, earned, deserved, and endured."

Thinking back on the weeks of illness, testing, and complete lack of privacy I'd had to undergo because of the mark on my neck, I wanted to laugh in her face. But there was no arguing with crazy. And Acidi certainly looked the part of an insane asylum patient. Her eyes were wide and frantic. Her lips quivered as if she didn't know whether to smile or cry. Holy fuck! Acidi had lost her shit. It seemed her failing to blackmail Raevu into taking her as his queen seemed to have pushed her into crazy land.

My eyes narrowed on her. The last time I'd seen her, she'd been all grace and poise, even very pregnant. Dressed to impress, she'd been the very picture of a beautiful Juhlian woman, and I'd felt remarkably inadequate next to her.

Now…I felt like the belle of the ball in comparison to her. Acidi looked like a hot mess. Her hair was bedraggled, as if someone had taken a random pair of scissors to it. Her clothes were disheveled and stained. There were tears and holes in odd places, and… *What the fuck?* Acidi had on only one shoe. She couldn't seem to modulate her voice anymore either. She went from whisper to shriek almost mid-word, and her eyes kept flitting back and forth. I wasn't sure what she was seeing.

Maybe she was drunk. It would explain her completely reckless theatrics.

I said evenly, "Aaromon, this insane bitch sister of yours is about to get the both of you killed for treason. I know the law. They'll exile you from the planet without the benefit of a spacecraft. Is that what you want? The chance to burn up on reentry for someone whose crackpot plan was never going to work in the first place?"

And then I felt it…rage, determination, alpha power. We all seemed to sense it when Raevu stepped out onto the platform with us.

Aaromon moaned. Acidi stood up a bit straighter, and her eyes focused on Raevu. I tried jerking my arm out of her grip, but she just tightened her hold until my bones felt like they were grinding together.

"See this foreign whore, Raevu? She can't be your queen. She isn't Juhlian. You chose me. I am yours. I have the mark. It's mine by right and by trial." She reached up to where her dress rested on her shoulder and ripped at it. There, where her neck met her shoulder, was the royal sigil. Sort of. It looked like a child had drawn it there in crayon, but much redder and angrier. It even looked…wet in places. I gasped in horror when I realized what it was. The mark was cut into her skin, roughly and haphazardly.

Had she used a knife?

Acidi had completely lost her mind. She glanced over at me at the small sound I made, but then she just glared at Raevu and shook me hard.

"Hers is false. Did you find out how it got there? Who did she bribe to carve it on her to fool you? Or did her human masters do it for her?" Acidi used her free hand to slap me hard across the face, spitting out an unfamiliar curse.

All right, that's it. Time to put into practice what I had learned.

Instead of pulling against her, I moved toward her, placing my hands on her ribs and shoving with all my might. She didn't let me go; she dragged me down on top of her. Our impact with the platform jarred her hand loose from my arm, and I immediately rolled away from her. Acidi shrieked in outrage and turned into a whirling dervish of elbows and knees, not even bothering to stand up fully. I received two sharp jabs to my side and a hard blow to my thigh before I realized she was aiming for my belly.

My baby! She's trying to harm my baby.

"Raevu!" I cried out.

"Eva! Stop moving!" Raevu snapped.

I froze where I was and curled into a ball to protect my belly. Acidi had followed me for the first couple of rolls, but then I felt her lifted away from me.

Cautiously, I uncurled to see where I was. I was less than a foot away from the edge of the platform. She had been trying to force me over it, baby and all. Remembering Baelon's description of it being over a hundred Earth stories high, I began inching myself away from the side.

I heard Acidi screaming curses at Raevu, but I couldn't take my eyes away from that precarious rim. When I felt I was far enough away, I slowly sat up and then dragged myself to my feet. My ribs and leg hurt, but I had felt a lot worse, and she hadn't touched my belly.

I looked around at the scene in front of me. Aaromon was squatting down by the lifts, holding his head and moaning about wanting to go home. Acidi stood nose-to-nose with Raevu, spewing out nonsense about being his queen, until she spotted me standing there, safe and almost unhurt.

She screeched, "No! You have to die!" With her arms outstretched to claw at me, she ran toward me, just out of Raevu's reach.

"Eva!" he yelled. "Move!"

I spun out of Acidi's way at the last second, and the much larger woman freight-trained right past me. I stumbled, stomach flipping at being close to the edge again, only to be caught in Raevu's arms and gathered close to him.

Acidi didn't have time to stop herself; she went right over the side. Her shriek faded away until we couldn't hear it anymore. "She's gone," her brother sobbed, bringing trembling hands to his face. "She's gone. I'm free."

A wave of dizziness took me over again as my life mate carried me away from the ledge. All I could hear was him repeating, "It's okay. I've got you, love. I love you, Eva. You're safe."

CHAPTER 31
EVA

They found Acidi's body two-thirds of the way down the tree, hanging like a ripped flag from a spur of new growth that had impaled her through her heart. I had trouble seeing her like that, but I felt at peace with it. Perhaps it was because she had already been on her way out, like a rabid animal.

The tree could have caught her. It had instead grown that spur. It chilled me a little to think about a tree deciding to make itself a weapon, but Raevu had just said quietly that she had been judged by a higher power than himself.

Aaromon surrendered immediately, and Raevu had very nearly called for his execution, for his treachery had placed us all at risk this time. But I spoke up. I had to, and I asked very pointedly what Aaromon had meant when he had thanked the gods for freeing him from his sister.

The story he told in return chilled us both to the bone. Acidi and he were barely a year apart and had been raised together before the pair had been suddenly orphaned. Acidi was taken in by the Grand Mother for her training, and her brother had been on his own.

Acidi had bullied, blackmailed, manipulated, and terrorized her shy, sickly, but brilliant brother from the time they were very small. If he did not constantly supply what she wanted, she had many humiliating secrets to spill about his fondness for men. Acidi then ensured that he had even more torrid things to hide by blackmailing him into more crimes in servitude to her.

She had woven a web around the timid scientist, breaking him down for years until he had completely become her puppet just to survive. Only upon understanding this did Raevu decide to show some leniency, but it was very conditional.

Aaromon agreed to give us the names of everyone who had accepted a bribe or offered information within our staff and guard. He promised as well to submit all scientific data related to the fertility experiments he had conducted, and he asked if he would be expected to train his successor before being sentenced to death.

Raevu had instead ordered the man hospitalized until his mind could recover from his years of emotional abuse and a proper mental assessment could be made of him. The little scientist had wept anew when taken away by the Guards, shocked by what may have been the first taste of mercy he had ever had in his life.

Finally, feeling worn and bedraggled, Raevu and I trudged back into our quarters, hand in hand. The scene that met our eyes when he pushed open the doors amazed me.

Willem and Linnea stood next to the windows, cradling Hope and giving her a bottle. Baelon had both Laura and Amber enfolded in his arms and was quite soundly kissing Laura.

Ivy was propped up on pillows on the couch, blinking sleepily over a cup of coffee and occasionally yawning like she had just gotten up from a nap. Her four kids were scattered about the room, obviously busied with tasks an adult had just given them. Trevor looked up as soon as he heard the door open, smiled a big Trevor-grin at me, and waved.

I didn't see my poor guard, who had gotten a nasty crack on the head, but from the general atmosphere, I didn't get the impression we had lost anyone.

"Well…" Raevu's sultry, rich voice sent a shiver through me. "Geoffrey, is there a room in this suite where my queen and I can get a little privacy?"

"I know of one," I answered before Geoffrey's computer voice could reply, and I tugged Raevu toward our bedroom.

CHAPTER 32
EVA

Brother Estijen had his hands full. I didn't feel the least bit sorry for him. He'd volunteered for this duty. I rubbed my hands over the ripples of my distended belly and spoke softly, "Quiet, Eavon, you'll be out here with your sisters soon enough."

The little guy wasn't even born yet, but he already took after his father. He was strong, had really big feet, and didn't know when to quit his fussing. "Ugh! Eavon, stop kicking my bladder!" His frequent kicks and nights of no sleep were definitely some of the hazards of having a house full of kids.

Raevu was ridiculously happy about having a son given how common they were on Juhl. He loved his beautiful daughters, but he had wanted a boy. Now, we just had to wait for the little guy to arrive any day now.

I smoothed my hands over my belly. The fabric of the deep blue dress—an exact copy of the dress that Ivy had found for me to wear that day I vied for entry into the Peace Opportunity Program—felt silky. The garment was a sweet reminder of Earth and how different my life was now. I smiled, remembering when I'd told Raevu about the dress and how much I missed it. He'd immediately contacted the Peace Program officials, demanding that they find the garment. When they couldn't locate it, he'd done the next best thing. With Ivy's design help, he found someone on Earth to make an exact replica—with alterations to accommodate my pregnant belly—of the dress. Tears came to my eyes just remembering the night he'd surprised me with the dress as a gift. The gesture was sweet and unexpected...just like my alien life mate.

My thoughts snapped back to the present. Brother Estijen was trying to teach our four-year-old twins, Flora and Willow, and five-year-old Hope how to plant a Sopu seedling in the pocket the Tovari tree had created for it. They sometimes giggled and got distracted, but he quickly redirected their attention back to the task at hand.

I wasn't startled when I felt Raevu drape his arm around my shoulder, letting his hand rest on the sigil that marked me as his life mate. A thrill, as always, ran through me when he made that casual motion. "Hello, love. So, how many trees does this make?"

I tilted my head back to look at him. "In the palace community, or in general?"

"Both." He kissed my forehead.

I laughed. "I don't know the count for 'in general,' and you know it. Once Geoffrey, Linnea, and I figured out it was the Tree Blight that had killed so many Sopu trees, which, in turn, affected your female birth rates, it became easy to convince people to plant the seedlings. After all, even if we were wrong, they're beautiful trees and give off a wonderful fragrance." I leaned into his side. "But this makes number thirty-seven in the palace community."

Raevu's eyes glowed yellow for a moment, shooting sparks of desire through me. "You weren't wrong. At last count, in the areas where Sopu trees are planted and flourishing, female births are increasing. Between bringing human women here to give us a boost and planting our trees, you saved us, my queen. You saved me." He leaned down and kissed me.

His lips lingered on mine before our daughters spotted him. "Daddy! Daddy! Come help us plant trees."

He gave them a mock frown. "Don't you see me kissing Mommy?"

"You're always kissing her," Willow said, then giggled.

He kissed my nose. "To be continued, my Eva," he promised before walking over to his precious, beautiful daughters.

I watched his big frame crouching down as Willow jumped onto his back, and he laughed.

I smiled, filled with love for my family.

It had taken a lot of work and many leaps of faith to get here. But now, I knew for certain that it had all been worth it...for love, hope, and my alien life mate, Raevu.

SEKKOL

CHAPTER 1
KEIRA

The walk from the office to the subway station felt like torture. Heading home wasn't something I was too thrilled about since my parents' death. I inherited the apartment we all shared, and the ghosts of their existence haunted me. Still, selling it felt wrong.

"Hey, Keira," a voice said, breaking me out of my trance just as I came down the stairs.

I hadn't seen the two girls approach until they spoke. "Oh, hi, Monica."

She looked at the other blond girl to her left, and they shared a telepathic message. It seemed they either had not decided what to say or they had some trouble deciding if they should. I just stood there, looking between the two, getting more annoyed by the second.

Finally, Monica said, "So Stacy and I were wondering if you would like to go to TAO with us tonight? They have a club and all."

She said, "Stacy and I," but I could tell the wondering was all her. "I think I'll pass. Thanks for the invite, though." I smiled.

"Okay, well, if you change your mind, you know how to reach me," she said as she turned and walked away.

There was an awkwardness about them, and I stood there for a while longer, watching them walk away with their heads huddled together.

"I told you she wouldn't come," Stacy whispered, but not low enough. "She never goes anywhere."

"I just feel sorry for her," Monica replied and then looked back at me, the smile returning to her face when she saw I was looking. She nudged Stacy, and then the two of them disappeared outside.

Hey, they weren't wrong. I hardly ever did anything. In fact, I thought of myself as socially awkward. The only place I knew I fit in was the PTSD meetings I went to every week. My parents died five years ago, and I'd been going every week for the past two years. It didn't make for much of a social life, but at least I had somewhere to go when the thoughts stormed my mind. I felt completely and utterly alone except for those days.

I sighed then, swiped my card through the slot, and pressed through the turnstile. I headed down another flight of steps to await the train that would take me home, where I'd be even more intimate with the depression I felt creeping upward.

As I was standing there, wallowing in my self-pity, I got the sinking feeling someone was watching me. I turned to look and made eye contact with the man standing at the other end of the car. He was staring straight at me.

He was wearing a white T-shirt, blue jeans, and a scowl that was partially hidden beneath his thick facial hair. His black, beady eyes cut through the other passengers and made a home with mine. I shivered and turned away. This was not the usual look I was used to getting. It actually looked like one I would get from someone who was about to do something crazy.

My heart started racing, and I grew uncomfortable standing there. When I looked back, he was gone, but I was much too paranoid to rest easy. And I had no intentions of getting off at my station, just in case he was still there and would follow me home.

I should have gone to my meeting. I was definitely regretting that decision now.

Hopping off at Canal Street, I decided to walk the rest of the way home. But as soon as I was off the train, I got that same creepy feeling;

someone was watching me. Glancing over the crowd, I didn't see anyone who stood out. It was the usual marching of pedestrians, their faces either overly blank or equally animated.

Adjusting the bag on my shoulder so I could reach in to grab a smoke, I suddenly felt something sharp poke me in the side. I shrieked and turned, wondering what I possibly could have rubbed up against that would hurt that much.

"Not another sound," a gruff voice said from behind me.

I managed to crane my neck to see the face, but he grabbed on to my hair and yanked it back. My scalp felt like it moved back an inch when he jerked me, and instantly, my temples started throbbing. I twisted my body, all the while wondering how no one was witnessing any of this. "What are—"

I didn't get to say anything more. The hand came down on my neck, and I felt a searing pain shoot up my spine and I grew dizzy. I tried to maneuver my body, just to see who was holding on to me, but I couldn't make out the face. Nor could I see anyone close by. How convenient for me. The way he held me, any passerby would think we knew each other.

A black sedan drove up just then. The windows slowly rolled down, and a voice came from inside. It was not attached to any face that I could see. "Is this another one?"

"Sure is," the gruff voice replied. "Jonas will like this one."

"Okay, put her in and hurry," the voice shot back.

The next thing I knew, I was being shoved into the back of the car, where I met the face behind the voice. He gripped my shoulder and twisted me around in the same moment he snapped something over my wrists.

"You're a pretty one," he said and pulled on one of my curls. "Kind of plump, but they will like you just fine." His breath smelled like stale alcohol.

"What are you doing? Please let me go," I pleaded, but my words only fell on deaf ears in the same instant I became aware of the gun in his hand. The tears I hadn't acknowledged before started racing down my face.

"Don't worry. You will like it there. It's nice I hear," he said and reached for a black pillowcase.

I tried to pull away, but it had already become clear I was being kidnapped. "Where are you taking me?" He unfolded the cloth and leaned closer. "My boyfriend is expecting me home. He will know I'm missing." I held my hands out defensively while I grasped at straws.

"You have no boyfriend, no friends, no life. You should thank me," he said and lifted the bag.

I wanted to scream, but my eyes lingered on the .38 revolver resting on the seat. I wasn't ready to die yet. I looked back outside, for perhaps the last time I would see that place. My eyes widened when I recognized the man from the train. He glared at me just as the black pillowcase came down over my face, and the world I knew disappeared behind my temporary satin prison.

CHAPTER 2
KEIRA

"Make a left at the next intersection," I heard a voice command. The car made a sharp swing left, and I slid down the leather seat.

I had seen the movie *Taken*, and I tried to use the same skills Liam Neeson had employed to track where he was being taken. But my head was foggy, and I could not conjure a complete picture of anything by the time the car made two more turns.

"Please don't do this," I whimpered, even though I had no reason to believe he would listen.

It seemed like he knew things about me, so he knew no one would come looking. I was royally screwed, and I could only hope I didn't wind up like Neeson's daughter in the movie.

I spent most of my time watching movies like *Taken* and *Hostel*, where tourists were kidnapped and made into sex slaves or to play survival games for the wealthy. Was that what this was? Had I been kidnapped for someone else's pleasure? I could hardly believe my luck.

He made no reply, but just then, the car came to a stop. There was a sliding sound when a gate opened, and the car eased inside and rolled to a stop. Then I felt a hand on me as I was yanked from the back seat. I wriggled, but the hands holding mine were much too strong.

"Let go of me!" I screamed and wrestled with the man. I figured things were already bad, and I might as well go down swinging.

"Whoa, we got ourselves a fighter." He grabbed the pillowcase off my face.

I spat at him then, and when he slapped me, I came face-to-face with another man on my left side. My cheek throbbed, but I continued struggling.

"Fuck, man," he shouted angrily as he wiped his face on his shirt.

"Put her with the others," the other man from the car said.

There are more? I wondered as I was hauled to a large container at the back of what seemed to be an old warehouse.

The man reached into his pocket and pulled out a bunch of keys. He fingered through them until he found the one he was looking for. When he opened the lock and pushed the metal door upward, I saw a few people already waiting inside. They seemed to be chained together, and some started shouting as soon as they saw the lights.

"Get us out of here," one woman pleaded.

With tears in my eyes, I turned to the man and started begging again. "You don't have to do this, please." I was already beginning to feel weak and that my pleas were not meeting any fertile ground.

"I know," he replied as he stepped closer to me. He was American, and I couldn't understand why he would do something like this to his own people. "But I want to." He sneered and then shoved me inside with the others. "Be ready to move tomorrow," he said to someone else as the doors started to close again.

I was trapped in the endless night with the others.

At first, I wasn't sure what to do, whether to sit, stand, or rally support for an escape. The latter seemed improbable, but still, instincts would permit no other thought at that moment. I backed into a corner, slid to the floor, and refused to cry anymore. It was useless anyhow. Instead, I sought to try to make sense of what was happening to me and where I was going.

Why the fuck hadn't I gone to the PTSD meeting? *Dammit.*

"Miss?" someone to my right said. I didn't reply; I wasn't sure how many misses were present in our metal cave. "You, the one they just brought in." The voice persisted.

"You talking to me?" I asked the darkness and turned to where the sound was coming from.

"Yes," it replied. "Do you know what's happening?"

I paused for a few seconds and then rested my head on my knees that were pulled up under me. "No," was all that came from me. I wanted to say more, but what? I only had speculations, and that wasn't something anyone needed in this dire situation.

The voice started whimpering now, until it turned into full-blown wailing.

"Look, we're all in this shit together," another woman barked. "Makes no sense crying and annoying the rest of us."

"Got that right," another said. "Besides, I can tell you what's happening. I heard something about slaves, so brace for it."

"How can you be so cold?" the whimpering voice asked.

My eyes were shifting back and forth, trying to keep up with the voices racing each other around the space. But the word slave had caught my attention fully. "What do you mean, slave? Like plantation slavery?" I realized I must have sounded naïve, but nothing else came to mind.

"No...well, maybe," the voice replied in an irritated manner. "I'm thinking they meant sex slaves, but it could be both."

I didn't know why she sounded so comfortable with that, but I wasn't going to ask. "Well, at least we aren't going to die right away." I sighed and rested my head on my knees again. It made no sense closing my eyes; the darkness that overcame me with my eyes open was equivalent to trying to shut my mind off.

The woman started crying again and did so for what seemed a considerable time.

I'm not sure when I fell asleep, but I was awakened to a slow rocking motion, and I perked up as I realized we were being moved.

My heart fluttered in my chest, and suddenly, I heard a loud banging noise as the other people in the container started making a ruckus. I remained on the floor, determined not to waste my energy. I would save my plans for escape for a later time, when it made sense.

After a while, the shaking and rocking began to make me nauseated. I closed my eyes and rested my head against the tin wall, hoping to quell the surge in my stomach as if it had been pulverized. Unable to hold it in any longer, everything that remained in my stomach from lunch—pasta, chicken cubes, wine sauce, broccoli florets, and mushrooms—all squished together, coming out in one sour mess. I cringed and shivered as some got into my nose.

"Did you have to do that?" someone asked when they heard me gushing.

"I'm sorry. Maybe I'll be more sensitive the next time I'm being kidnapped," I snapped sarcastically, just before another wave hit me. I hurled again, and I could see, even in the darkness and through my mind's eye, the others backing away from me, and I could smell the foul stench that would travel with us to our destination. I wiped my hand across my mouth and then squeezed my stomach that felt like it had constricted.

Eventually, the rocking stopped, and my fear returned. It was deathly silent. I managed to stand as I pressed my ear against the metal wall to discern any distinguishable sound. There was nothing but silence for so long, it converted all the paranoia and anxiety swirling in the container into a giant cosmic bubble. All it took was one wail, and soon, the noise was unbearable.

Eventually, we could hear murmuring outside, and then the container rocked, almost tipping us over. We fell on top of each other, gripping and clawing as we tried to hold on to something. Then it leveled again, hit the ground with a thud, and it was over.

When the door rolled upward, I realized it was night and we were in a forest of some sort. But where? We all stood there, wanting to run but not daring to move. Just then, there was the faint sound of an engine that quickly grew louder. I saw a Jeep come to a stop about a hundred feet from where we were. I stepped forward, and as I did, there was a booming sound.

"Take one more step, and you die," a voice said through the trees. It seemed to dominate the entire space.

I tried to squint and see but found it hard to determine the source, so I remained still. Afraid even to breathe, I held up my hands in defeat. Based on the movies I'd seen, we were probably in Bulgaria or

Amsterdam or some other European country, but I couldn't be sure since I couldn't see anything.

A man appeared from the side of the container and motioned for us to move forward. When we were all standing on the ground, they forced us into a single file as we moved forward in the dim light. I stumbled a few times as the men with machine guns escorted us to a huge metal vessel some yards away. It wasn't an airplane or anything I'd ever seen before.

"Step up. One at a time for your language translator," the man at the front of the line commanded.

Shocked, I stared at him for long seconds. *Language translator?*

"Move," he hissed at me.

My back straightened at his tone. Eyes narrowing, I studied the platform that extended to the ground that we were expected to climb to enter the vessel. My heart started pounding in my chest, and I could barely feel my legs as they moved. I couldn't make out anything in the vessel before I entered, but as I got to the door, I saw other men standing inside around a huge digital screen, gesturing animatedly while emitting strange high-pitched sounds with their mouth. They seemed to be communicating with each other in what must have been their native tongue.

I was so distracted by their bizarre interaction that I didn't notice the man to my left who reached across and yanked me to him before jabbing me in the neck with the small silver device clutched in his hand.

I felt a stinging sensation in my neck, and my hand flew there instinctively. I looked at him, still in shock, as I checked to see if there was any blood. There was none, but my neck throbbed. He pointed animatedly at my neck while annoying clicking sounds burst from his mouth.

"What?" I asked. "I can't understand you."

The man frowned and the clicking sounds that he was making with his mouth got louder and faster. I blinked when suddenly I could understand bits and pieces of his words.

He snapped, "There's a glitch with the language translator."

My mouth flopped open before snapping shut. "I can understand you," I croaked.

He nodded his head. "The translator implanted in your neck automatically interprets any language spoken to you. It also converts your English to the native tongue of the person conversing with you."

"Native tongue?" I asked quickly. "I don't understand what…"

"Move along now," he urged before moving to the next female.

Inside, to the right of the screen, were several glass chambers that seemed to be filled with smoke or vapor. Apparently, that was the direction I was supposed to take, and my legs started moving.

"We only have twenty-seven this time around," I heard one of the men by the screen say.

"That should be enough," the other replied. "We will get more next time."

"But will this be enough? The demand for them is greater than it used to be. They keep wanting more, and…" He stopped speaking when he saw me looking, and when he turned his back, I lost wind of anything else being said.

I trained my eyes to see their faces, and it was then I noticed there was something off about their features. Their eyes appeared to be twice the diameter of human eyes, and they were spaced farther apart. They also had longer necks but wore long, black coats, so it was hard to see much, and I was moving farther away at the same time. I walked down the long stretch and joined the other women who stood trembling there.

Now that I was still, I looked back at the path I had just taken. There were three men standing around the screen, pointing at numbers and coordinates dancing around that made me dizzy. Other than that, there was not much of anything else by way of seating. Just then, as if to satisfy my curiosity, one of the men tapped something on his arm, and three seats descended, still attached to the roof by coiled wiring. Wasting no time, I followed the other women and scrambled to take a seat. When we were all inside, the men directed their attention at us, and the seats floated down the passage.

"Welcome," one of them said coolly. "If you please, we ask that you enter the pods as they open. You will be provided with oxygen for the journey."

"Journey to where?" The words sprang out before I could control them.

"To Jupiter," he replied, and then the seats drifted upward. They remained there like gods as they watched us from their lofty perches.

It was then I realized they were either from some remote part of Europe or they weren't human at all. When they spoke, their lips moved differently than the words they were actually saying.

"Ju—" And then it all made sense. What they were saying before, the sting on my neck, why their lips moved funny, and now…Jupiter? Earlier, I thought my worst fear was I'd be a prostitute in Bulgaria; now it was slowly becoming apparent we were being taken off Earth.

I stepped forward and instantly felt a shock wave pass right through me. My eyes bulged, and I was held in place by some magnetic force.

"I wouldn't do that if I were you," one of the men said.

The pods opened then, and we were ushered inside, each in our own domain. It was cold, and I rubbed my arms in a bid to generate some amount of heat. There was a flashing light above that was red before, but when the door to the pod slid shut, it turned green. Metal bars shot out from hidden orifices and wrapped themselves around my ankles and waist. Then the pod tilted backward, and I was lying on my back. I started to feel woozy—trapped in a box with no air. Then slowly, the vapor lifted, and I could feel the oxygen returning. I gasped as I sucked in a lungful.

Not long after, there was a loud, hissing sound, and the vessel started shaking. My eyes began to feel heavy, and I realized it wasn't just oxygen coming through the spores overhead. I tried to fight the urge, but it was useless, and before I could gather a logical thought, my world went black.

CHAPTER 3
SEKKOL

The planet Jupiter was what Earth would look like a millennium in the future. Though it had a medieval appearance, with stone walls and wooden enclosures dominating the landscape, the metropolitan areas seemed to be made solely of steel and glass. Both the air and the land —which was flat and mostly made of compressed claylike matter except where the urban life met the rolling hills and valleys of green— were buzzing with hovercrafts, space scooters, and what looked like oversized bullets.

There were five main cities: Anon, Castor, Xenon, Jordan, and Bulova, and several districts situated within each. There was just one prison, located on the outskirts of civilization, and which was kept grossly underpopulated because capital punishment was still practiced. Those who wound up there were clearly not the worst in society; the worst were already dead.

The people on this planet resembled the humans, if only slightly. They were taller, on average, by at least two feet, and though they aged similarly from infancy to adulthood, they lived up to a millennium. They were slender, with pale skin that looked like the sky on a clear summer's day, and had piercing black eyes on flat faces. They all wore their hair long, both males and females, and at some point, it became difficult to tell who was who or how old they were.

At present, a large throng of them was gathered in the town square, awaiting the execution of a man who had become something of a perpetual disturbance in society. Stealing, fighting, and committing other illegal acts, the Tribunal had decided the prison population no longer served as adequate punishment. The man was displayed before the swelling crowd, wearing white overalls and a look of fright. Next to him was a large cylindrical chamber that was empty at the moment but would be filled with his pulverized body parts in a few minutes.

"That's one of our guys," Brom said to me with a grin.

And by that, he meant someone we had captured a few weeks back, smack dab in the middle of his fifth assault. "I'd say it's about time they fry his ass," I replied. It was the one thing that made my job as an enforcer worthwhile, ridding the streets of unwanted criminal acts. Not even the slightest act against the law was tolerated, and my team was there to make sure no one escaped.

There was a loud beeping sound as the alarm was triggered, signaling the last moments of the man who seemed ready to run. He looked about wildly as two other men in white jumpsuits joined him there. His legs had been chained to the flooring, and one of the men stooped to release them. He started pressing backward when the other opened the chamber, but his movement was slowed.

"I would love for him to escape now," Gideon, one of the other members of my four-man squad, interjected. "My fingers are itching to put him down."

"Easy, Gideon," I told him. "He isn't worth the hassle."

"I'll tell you what's not worth the hassle: going downtown to watch Jonas offload his can of human slaves again," Thorax, the final man, added.

"It is a must," I declared and eyed the men authoritatively. "There is no point in questioning it."

There was silence after I spoke, as all eyes faced front, watching the man being pushed into the chamber. He resisted all the way, and when he was inside and the door closed, he started banging on the fiberglass enclosure. His voice was muffled, but it didn't matter. One of the men went to the column to the far right, and they placed goggles over their eyes simultaneously. There was a reverent hush, as all stood in anticipation of the execution. The executioner pressed the button, there was a blinding light, and then it was over. When the light faded, the man was no more.

I checked the device on my arm and saw it read fifteen minutes past three. "It should be there by now," I told my men. "Let's clear this crowd and move out."

Not a word was uttered as they instantly started clearing the street. Some of the people seemed solemn, perhaps feeling sorry for the man. Others walked away expressing their contentment at the justice that was meted out. In short order, life had been restored, as if someone had not just died.

We headed to the hovercraft we used to get around, especially when it was just us. I hopped on, and Brom took his place next to me. Gideon and Thorax shared the other, and we sailed off through the now empty street. We arrived at the port just as the vessel was coming in, and Jonas instantly shuffled over when he saw me arrive. He was a snake and a crook, the way he handled his business, but he had broken no laws. He knew I was just waiting for him to slip once.

He hurried over to the landing gate and stood by the chute for the pods to emerge. His eyes kept returning to mine, like he had something planned that I was interfering with. Then there was a whooshing sound as the first pod came down. He opened the port and received the first of this shipment. It was a dazed-looking human, hair of gold and eyes that seemed frightened, not unlike the others who had come before.

I didn't plan to stare at each individual entry but turned instead to the eager onlookers slowly forming a circle. "Get back!" I shouted and gripped my device strapped to my side. I bore down on them, but they made no attempt to get any closer, and I held them in place with my eyes.

Suddenly, I felt a tap on my shoulder, and I whirled around, my weapon already discharged.

"Whoa," Brom said and held his hands in the air. "Just telling you they are done."

"Already?" I looked around him to discern the truth for myself. Then I reattached my weapon and gave the small crowd one final flash of my eyes before walking off again.

"Not many today," Brom informed me.

He was right. Usually, there were more than the…*nine, ten, eleven…* I had begun to count through the lot when I spotted her. She had skin that looked like the earth, and her hair had these strange knots in it that bounced on her shoulders when she walked. Her eyes were searching the crowd, probably for some means of escape, when they found mine.

Suddenly, my world grew still, and all the noise around me died. I felt like I was suddenly jumping from a cliff into a green and grassy meadow…with her. My heart fluttered within my chest, and I gripped it to stop it from leaping right out. I could see nothing else, hear nothing else, feel nothing else. There was only her, and instantly, I had an urge to protect her and make her mine.

It was then I knew I was in trouble.

CHAPTER 4
KEIRA

What is this place?

My head turned this way and that as we were shoved between the growing throng of...aliens. That was the only word that came to mind when I saw the creatures staring back at me curiously. Almost as if they were inspecting us.

They had eyes black as coal that were stuck on faces that seemed human, except for their skin. It had a bluish hue to it and was sort of beautiful as it shimmered in the sun. I might've had a better appreciation for it were I not shackled to a group of people I didn't know and being taken to a place unfamiliar to me and everyone else on Earth. For it had become clear I was no longer on my home planet.

My eyes were roaming the sea of faces when they stopped on one of them. He was taller than the average human, and still, he seemed a foot above the rest. He seemed to be calling to me, though he didn't move. His long black hair, the parts I could see, hung from under a hat, and he resembled a mercenary of sorts. It seemed as if I knew him from somewhere, except there was nowhere I could have seen him before. It felt strange, and before I could make sense of it, the woman behind me shoved me along.

"Where are we?" she asked.

"Not Earth," I replied as our feet dragged on the ground. It was then that I glanced down and saw it was red and looked like clay. Which was good. At least it wasn't dusty. The sun bearing down on my already sensitive skin was making me itch, and there was no way for me to scratch it. I felt like a stranger in my own body.

"This way," the man who had freed us said. He must've been the Jonas person I kept hearing about. My head felt heavy on my shoulders, and I could only assume it was caused by whatever was pumped into my lungs that made me unconscious for the trip.

Still, as groggy as I was, I couldn't help but admire this new world. The buildings were made of some form of metal and glass and were shaped like pyramids, oblong, and some even seemed to be sloping at odd angles. It was like an abstract painting, and when I looked up, I ducked when I saw some flying objects whooshing past. By the time we exited the compound, I saw that was how the people got around. I was in a futuristic world, being sentenced to a backward way of living, my new life as a slave.

Just then, there was some sort of commotion as a group of men, one of whom I had noticed before, stormed through the procession of our strange admirers.

"Jonas, where are you taking them?" he asked gruffly.

Jonas took his hat off and held it in front of him, which didn't seem sensible, as the sun now hit him directly in his eyes. He blinked rapidly to counter the effect. "I-I'm taking them to the tank," he told the man.

"Aren't you supposed to be taking them to the park to be sold?" he asked. His legs were apart, his hands behind him. He never once took his eyes off the man, and I could tell just from this encounter that he was a man who was generally feared.

"Well, yes," he replied nervously. "But, Sekkol, sir, it is rather late, and I am afraid there won't be enough buyers at this late stage. Better to keep them until morning." Jonas was slightly rotund, and he kept shifting on his legs as he spoke. He wiped his face now to rid it of the sweat beads that were racing downward.

He stepped back and nodded as if his approval were law. Jonas smiled slightly, bowed, and hurriedly covered his head once more. He took his place before us, and we started moving again.

I still had my eyes on the strange man, and just then, his eyes caught mine. I quickly averted my gaze in case he should make an example of me for staring too hard.

"Move along," Sekkol urged us, and I held my head straight, though I had the odd sensation he was still watching me. I tried to ignore it, but something caused me to turn around again. This time, I caught him just standing there with a perplexed look on his face. He seemed to be reconciling something in his mind, but before he could make sense of it, his friend came up behind him. They seemed to be a squad in the police force, and he was obviously the leader.

His crony pulled him away, and he reluctantly moved off. His eyes never once left mine until he was walking away. And then I collided with the woman in front of me. They had stopped, and I hadn't noticed.

"Hey, watch it," she replied as she shrugged her shoulder to rid herself of me.

"Sorry," I replied and straightened up. I recognized the voice as the woman who had spoken of sex slaves on the container, and I craned my neck to get a glimpse of her face. She was my height, with red hair that was a tangled mess, and she kept squinting. It might be wrong to harbor clichés, but she seemed like a drug addict. It was then her comment in the container made sense. She was hardened and always prepared for the worst because that was all she had ever gotten.

"What's the deal?" she asked, anger taking hold of her. She nudged me with her elbow when she caught me staring, or maybe it was because I was closest to her and served as the most available avenue of relieving stress.

"Hey!" I fired back and did the same in retaliation. "Don't take this out on me." Tempers were flaring, and it was evident our situation wasn't getting any better.

"Take it easy," Jonas said and hurried to where we were. "There will be time for that later."

"What are you going to do with us? I want to go back home!" I shouted. The next thing I felt was his hand on my cheek and then the intense pain as it pulsated. I rubbed it to get some measure of relief and then lunged at the man. Someone pulled me back, but I didn't care anymore. At that point, I felt like death was a better escape from this nightmare.

Jonas, who was a puny pug before, was now barking like a Rottweiler as he stood before me, surveying me and sneering. "I like you," he said and gave me a toothy smile. He reached out and cupped my face with his hand. "I think I'll get a pretty piece of jewel for you." And then he walked off.

The woman in front of me turned to me and shook her head. "Don't draw unnecessary attention to yourself," she told me.

"Kind of hard," I replied and rubbed my cheek again. I could tell when my fingers found a lumpy surface that it was swollen. "We are the show."

She shrugged, acknowledging the truth of my statement, and we continued marching on. We were led past what I presumed was the square, receiving winks, nods, and the occasional tugs from the inhabitants we passed on the street. It kind of reminded me of an alternative Manhattan. We eventually got to a huge building made of stone. It seemed like it had been carved out of a giant rock, like the home of the King of Gondor situated in the universe of Middle Earth in *The Lord of the Rings*. A dark tunnel loomed ahead, and we tripped along until we got to what seemed like a cave within a bigger cave. Once inside, the chains that had held us together were pulled off. Even without them, I felt more the prisoner.

Jonas handed one of the natives a key, and after he had stuck it into the huge keyhole, he hauled the partition back, and we were ushered inside like cattle. I stumbled, and then almost instantly, I broke free of the pack and was back at the iron fencing.

"Please. Let us out!" I screamed, already forgetting the punishment I had received a few minutes before.

There was no response from Jonas as all the men walked out, leaving us in the dungeon. I moved away from the bars and to the wall, where I slid to the cold earth, realizing then it was all stone. I looked at the rest of the humans who had come over with me. Their faces were bland, and they resembled brainwashed subjects in an experiment. I saw the woman who had been whimpering the entire time. Her eyes were red and puffy, and she seemed spent.

Some time elapsed between when we were shoved inside and when I heard voices down the passageway.

"Hey, we're hungry!" I yelled, hoping to grab someone's attention. "Hey." Some of the others joined me until there was a growing commotion surrounding me.

An angry-faced native approached. I could tell his flesh had turned a deeper shade of blue. "What?" he barked.

"Food," I told him. "We would like some food."

He snarled and then looked at the rest of us. "Jonas!" he bellowed.

The man I had grown too acquainted with returned, and he muttered something to him. He looked back at me and then at the others. He waved us off and walked away again. The guard chased after him and grabbed him by the shoulder. He said something that stilled him, and Jonas nodded. I supposed he must have understood that to have us die from hunger would not be a financially sound decision.

He returned a few minutes later with a platter of what I could only assume were edible things. He slid it under the metal bar at the bottom, and even though we didn't know what it was, we knew one thing for sure: it was food. We scampered to the tray, much to the amusement of the guard, and as the juice from the fruit trickled down my chin, I looked up and wiped it off.

Yep. Life on Jupiter. Better get used to it. And then I lowered my head again and ate some more.

CHAPTER 5
SEKKOL

I couldn't control how I felt, or whom I felt it for. And I couldn't understand how, when I had never harbored any affections for the humans, I would have imprinted on one. Especially when it was forbidden. Her eyes haunted my sleep that night, and in the morning, her ghost shadowed me. If it were something I could dispel, I would have readily done so, and I cursed my stupid nature for this obscenity. She consumed not just my mind, but she was manipulating the rise and fall of my manhood that pulsated each time her face flitted into view.

The bed seemed rather big now, and I resented even its sturdy structure as I slipped from under the covers and walked to the opening in the wall. The sun rose on the other side of the building, and before me lay the Great Pike—the ancient structure that still housed Magnus. He had remained the supreme ruler of Jupiter for over 284 years, and I doubted he would die anytime soon. Which was just fine with me.

If he never died, then I would have no need to assume leadership of Jupiter. I was his only son and heir to the throne, but I preferred living on the perimeter of the Great Pike rather than in it. But this morning, I had an appointment with him I could not escape, and I dreaded that he would look within me and find the secret I needed to hide.

I sighed, looked down, and saw Brom was already outdoors, as he usually was. The other enforcers were on the eastern side of my house but close enough to the Great Pike in the event any unfortunate incident happened. I washed up and slipped into my clothes, strapped on my boots, and threw the black coat around me. My hair fell down my back, and I often wore it loose, an easy convenience for me.

By the time I slipped into the great hall, Magnus saw me. "Sekkol," he called to me. He was still wearing his robe, his graying hair splayed across his shoulders, giving him an air of stateliness. We met in the middle and hugged briefly. Despite living so close, we hardly saw each other.

"So you wanted to see me?" I asked.

He kept his hand on my shoulder as we walked toward the dining hall. It was hard not to notice it would be light out soon, and that meant Jonas would be selling her.

"Can't a man ask to see his son every now and again?" he inquired. "Dory, make that two cups," he told the cook when she hurried past us with a pot of brew. My father still loved a hot cup of malt in the mornings, but I preferred juice. I remained quiet on the matter to indulge him. "So how is it going with Commander Styx and the rest of your men? I don't know why you didn't take the post as Lord Commander when it was offered."

"Let's not get into that again, Father," I told him. "I am perfectly fine with having my own elite squad." Furthermore, it gave me more privileges than being the commander, and with fewer eyes on me. I figured I had enough attention as the son of the Supreme Ruler. And enough constraints, too.

It was just us sitting at the long glass table that was made for at least forty people. All the way through breakfast, I kept my eyes averted. But even that was too obvious for my father.

"There is something different about you," he told me. When I looked up, he was squinting at me, and I could feel his eyes searching me. Then they twinkled, and he laughed. "You've imprinted on someone, haven't you?"

And suddenly, I felt like the veil I was hiding under was yanked away and I was standing bare before him. Still, my only defense was denial. "Impri—no… No, no, no." I protested too much and then grew uneasy in my chair.

"I can tell," he said and sipped on his brew that was likely cold by now. "And I want to meet her."

"There is…will be no her," I argued.

"You know it isn't something you can contest, Sekkol. Besides, it is time you assume your place here. I am growing weary of this government."

"I think I am more comfortable in the streets, where the action is."

"You don't belong there. Leave that to Styx and those other boys. You are more than that, Sekkol."

And so went every other conversation we had had the last half-dozen times I had been there, and as always, I opted for a hasty exit. I stood, and the chair scraped the floor when I did. "I've got to get going," I said and went around to shake his hand.

He held on to it for a while longer than I anticipated. "Sekkol, I want to meet her. She is our legacy." Then he let go and returned to eating his meal, and I was forgotten.

I walked back down the long hall, and when I got outside, I saw the sun was just peeping over the hills. It was already warm, and I skipped down the steps, my hands deep in the pockets of my coat. I turned my head to the south, where I would find her. What was happening to her now?

Stop it. I slapped my palms to my temples as if that would rid me of her image.

I was still wearing a scowl when I got back home. The sun was over the hill now and slowly taking over the darkness on the landscape. The sounds of spacecrafts, children chattering outdoors, and the regular bantering of the people slowly took over from the silence of the night. But nothing in my head was still.

I paced the floor, even while contemplating the implications of being with a human. I wasn't allowed to be with her, and it didn't make sense to reason with the logic of our culture. I knew full well the penalty for transgressing any law. What I couldn't come to terms with was how much impact this recognition of her had.

My head was swimming as I wrestled with the conflict of my predicament, and though I knew what would happen, I couldn't stop my feet from moving. I wanted to see her again. Maybe if I did, one more time, I could make it stop. And then I'd be free.

I walked back to the door and headed out in a hurry. I was barely down the walk when I ran into Commander Styx.

"The Tribunal will be assembling before the Great Pike shortly," he told me and grabbed my arm.

I looked down at it and then yanked myself free. "You should be able to handle that, Commander," I replied sarcastically. Then I attempted to move off, but he stepped into my path.

"I am your commander, and you should do as I say," he growled like the animal he was.

I made two steps that drew me even closer to him. He was about a foot shorter than I was, so in this position, I towered above him. "Remember your station, sir," I mocked. "Get the men and handle the Tribunal. I have somewhere else to be." And then I walked off.

Ever since he had been appointed the role, and I in a lesser one, he had made every attempt to belittle me and talk down to me from his position of power. But I was above him still, and I only yielded when it suited me. It did not suit me then.

I found the hovercraft and hopped on, and within minutes, I was cruising toward town.

CHAPTER 6
KEIRA

My sleep was disturbed by loud noises and voices surrounding me like a fog. I blinked and waited a few seconds for my eyes to once again adjust to the darkness of the cave. It was strange to me how a place like this, a dungeon, could coexist in the world I had seen outside. It was out of place, and I couldn't imagine there were many such as this.

"Get up," Jonas was saying to us.

I sprang to my feet, finding energy I didn't realize I had, and rushed to him, babbling so fast I was sure he could not understand me.

He grinned and gripped my arms. "Keep calm, feisty one," he told me. "You will be sold soon enough. Come on." He abruptly ended what little conversation we just shared and diverted his attention to the sluggish movement of the others, who were not quite eager to be made a spectacle of.

Needless to say, it was out of our control, and like the cattle we were, we were chained once more and led to what was called the marketplace. I hadn't showered in days, and the camisole I wore was now stained with sweat, tears, and dirt. I could feel it clinging to me, and as the first rays of the sun grew warm on my skin, new sweat beads began to form, soon to mingle with others that had just been resurrected.

We all stood, like ducks in a row, on an iron grid in the center of a steel platform. We were separated now, no longer units in the same chain gang, but still heavily guarded.

I couldn't help thinking this was it, and I saw my new life stretched before me, beyond the people gathered there, already clamoring and making demands. I knew without a doubt that my future was bleak, and by the looks of things, not only were we going to be sold, but we were also going to be made into a public spectacle at an auction.

I had never been to an actual auction before. Nor did I think I would eventually become a part of the show.

Jonas stepped up and began making a speech to the crowd. It seemed to elevate their spirits, for soon they were hooting and wailing and seemed impatient. I tried not to look at their faces just in case I attracted anyone in particular.

Instead, my mind was transported to the comfort of my bed and my PTSD group, who I was sure were not surprised at my absence and who wouldn't notice if I didn't show up again. Then I remembered the almost empty desk in the corner of the office where I spent most of my days, cooped up in a cubicle as if hiding, though visible to everyone. My memories flashed before me one at a time, and I was stuck in time in a desperate bid to escape the present.

My thoughts were disturbed when I saw the whimpering girl pulled to the front of the group. "For this petite thing, she will make a great domestic helper." Jonas began. "Nice firm skin, not too bad to look at, and very strong, too." He listed the personal attributes of the woman, and the crowd mumbled while he did. "Bidding starts at two copper pieces." The noise erupted as his voice increased and sped up as he pointed from one person to another. At the end of it, no one was willing to spend more than seven copper pieces for her. I wondered what I was worth.

The name of the buyer was logged in a digital device Jonas had, and the girl was taken off the platform, kicking and screaming all the way.

And so it was for the fourth, fifth, and sixth woman, all the women, until it was my turn. I could not see where the familiar faces from the container had gone, even though I tried to. I stood there feeling like filth as Jonas started pointing to different parts of my body, motioning to my hair, and demonstrating my skin, in a tell-all show of my usefulness to the next man who wanted to buy me.

As with every other woman before me, the bidding started at two copper pieces. I blinked rapidly and then closed my eyes, not wanting to see the man to whom I would belong in another couple minutes. But the minutes dragged on too long; the last I heard, I was up to one silver piece. I assumed the scale of their monetary system consisted largely of metals and jewels. I wondered what their highest unit of currency was —anything to distract me from my current state. And then the noise abated as the buyers discussed my current price.

"Come on," Jonas urged. "Who says one silver and one copper piece for this dark-skinned wonder?" There was silence, and the last bidder waited anxiously, ready to pay his silver piece for my life.

"Two gold pieces," someone from the middle of the crowd shouted, and all heads turned to see who in their right mind would do something so ludicrous, having the gall to pay two entire gold pieces for a slave. The man looked as ordinary as the rest, and I assumed he would be no less of a slave master than the others.

"Anyone for three gold pieces?" Jonas asked, but no one seemed willing to go above that. When no one responded, he declared, "Sold," and documented the sale. I was taken off the stage, and it was then I discovered where the others before me were taken.

I was marshaled into a large room that seemed to be made of glass behind the platform and hidden from the public view. The others were quiet, and I was the same as I joined them. When the auction was over, Jonas came to us, and one by one, our new owners made their payments and received their rewards. The whimpering girl looked back at us for the last time as a tear rolled down her face. I would never see them again. Not unless I was lucky, and it was evident I did not fall into that category.

When it was my turn, I nervously watched the glass door for my new owner to enter. He didn't seem half as bad when he did, but he hardly looked at me. He gripped my arm and tugged me outside just before slinging me into the second seat on the flying thing.

"Are we going to your house?" I asked him. I was trying to strike up a conversation; maybe if he liked me, he would be kind to me.

"No," was all he said and continued along.

He got to a large structure made of stone and mirrors, or so it appeared to me. It was quaint and, in another sense, rather exotic-looking. He hovered toward the back of the house and then hopped out. He handed me a large coat with a hat and instructed me to cover up with it. Was he hiding me? That was the first thought that came to mind when I observed him and noticed his limited conversation.

He tapped the clear rectangular screen outside the door, and it beeped and then slid open. He directed me inside, and I heard a click as it closed behind me. When I turned around, he was gone. I raced to the door and then stopped when I realized I had no clue how to open it. There were buttons, levers, and strange markings that meant nothing to me, and when I touched one, a loud alarm went off. I covered my ears and looked around wildly, thankful it only did so once.

It was evident I was alone, so I wandered around the house, taking note of my new abode. Or, at least, I thought that was what it was. I felt like I was in a science lab; almost everything was made of either steel or glass-like material, despite the older-model exterior. It was a fusion of old and new that came together beautifully, and I, for the first time since I had arrived at this wretched place, was in awe.

I wasn't sure how much time had passed since I'd gotten there, but I was growing impatient and overly anxious. I walked to the window and looked out, seeing far and wide the general layout of the city. Just then, I heard a sliding sound, and when I turned around, I saw him, the man from the compound I had noticed when I'd just arrived.

He walked over to me, his presence looming over mine. He didn't have a smile, but a sour temperament and a confused look about him. My hands gripped the window's edge and pressed downward. He stood before me, and his eyes flashed dark and wicked. I tried to pull my eyes away, but it seemed he had some power over me that prevented my movement. He searched me with his eyes, his nose now turned up and his glare disapproving, and I grew conscious of his disdain.

I tried to push him away, but he grabbed my hand and wheeled me around so my back was now pressing against his large frame. The hairs on the back of my neck stood on end when he lowered his head, and his breath frightened even them.

"You're mine," he whispered and then let go of me rather forcefully.

I stumbled before catching my balance just shy of him. I thought I had seen a look of admiration when I first saw him in the streets, but now I realized I must have been wrong. As I stood there looking at his back, I hated him, and I didn't even know him.

I was still seething with rage when he grabbed me and led me into an all-white chamber.

CHAPTER 7
KEIRA

Just a few days ago, I had been walking home from work, listlessly at best, and drifting into another lonely night that would precede yet another mundane day. I didn't even know other planets with active lives existed until I was kidnapped, not by any alien, but by other humans. The anger in me grew to enormous proportions when I thought of the days that had ensued, the brutality, the inhumane conditions that had greeted me upon arrival, and of my being auctioned off like cattle. I hadn't been sure what to expect after that, but the once-admiring face of one of the aliens had now turned its sunny side down, and I was greeted with only a scowl.

He stood there looking at me, and I made every attempt to match his countenance. But I found it didn't take much effort.

"What now?" I asked him.

"Go into the chamber," he told me.

"The… What the hell is a chamber?" I asked as my face contorted. I had no intentions of being vaporized or some other shit I wasn't sure about. He came over, and I looked into his face, observing piercing black eyes and skin that was sort of bluish. It was hypnotic, and for a second, it distracted me from the hold he had on my hand as he tugged me into the room.

"There," he told me. "Now, I have to go. Sari will tell you what to do."

"Sari? Who the fuck is Sari?" I shouted after him, but his long black hair that fell to the middle of his back, swishing across the bodysuit he wore, was all I saw before he disappeared outside.

I started to move off, but the door slid shut before I got to it. "What the…?" I asked myself as I pressed my hands on the glass and looked upward for a way out. "Hey!" I shouted, but I soon found it was useless.

Now what?

I sighed and folded my arms as I walked around the room, not knowing what I was supposed to do. There was nothing there but a white cushioned stool of sorts and metal railings bordering the plain white room. There was a vent in the center of the eastern wall, too high for me to reach. Too bad. I looked around and, remembering the door that wasn't there before, started tracing my hands along the wall. It was smooth, almost like plastic, but I found nothing. I was growing more frustrated, and I stomped and yelled to no one in particular but the room and myself.

"Hello. I am Sari. How may I assist?"

The voice was that of a woman, and I jumped, looking around wildly for the one who had spoken. "Who is that?"

"I'm Sari. How may I assist?"

The voice echoed in the room and seemed to be coming from no distinct place. But it was automated, so I assumed it was electronic and resonating from hidden speakers.

"Sari, how do I get out of here?" I thought I might at least try.

"My sensors detect a high bacteria count. Please proceed to the cleansing pod."

"Cleansing pod? Just get me out of here!" I shouted to the machine or robot or whatever the hell it was.

Suddenly, another glass door slid open, but I saw nothing there but white. I walked closer to it, ever cautious and expecting anything. I stuck my head inside while my hands remained firmly glued to the wall to my left.

"Please step into the center of the pod."

"Step? Hell no," I said and moved back. I wasn't sure what this "Sari" was about to do, and I wasn't feeling experimental.

"Please step into the middle of the pod to avoid alternate decontamination."

I hurried to the door and started banging on it. I slid my hands along every crack I could find, but there was nothing there that would allow me to open it. Frustrated, and with my heart hammering in my chest, I pressed my back against the wall and prepared for the worst.

My life flashed before me—the small cubicle I had occupied in my downtown Manhattan office, my apartment in Brooklyn where I spent almost every hour not spent at work, my PTSD group meeting that had been the remainder of my life and had become a vital necessity. I didn't have much of an active social life, and at that moment, I felt sad I might disappear from the face of the earth, or this planet anyway, and I could quite easily be forgotten.

"Alternate decontamination will begin in five…four…three…"

My heart roared in my chest and echoed in my ears as my chest heaved. When Sari got to "one," I closed my eyes and pressed my hands into the wall. There was a loud beeping sound before I felt something wet on me. It was landing on my skin in sheets, and I dared open my eyes. It was water. I looked up and saw it coming down from the ceiling, and though I was scared before, I calmed, and slowly my breathing resumed normalcy.

"You could have just said that!" I shouted to the walls and wiped my hands down my face. "Alternate decontamination."

It had been days since I had taken a shower, and I welcomed the feel of the water on my skin. My clothes were slowly getting drenched, but I didn't care. It was at that moment I thought I'd return to the "cleansing pod" for additional "decontamination." I smiled at the idiocy I had just displayed and then looked around, wondering if anyone might have been privy to my shame.

No matter. The deed was already done.

I hastily stripped off my clothes, even as the water saturated my head of black curls now resting limply on my shoulders. It was raining indoors, and I smiled at the thought as I stepped into the unit.

Instantly, the water outside stopped, and it started raining inside the unit instead.

I stood there for a considerable amount of time, allowing the water to wash away the feel of the man's hand on me as he had dragged me to this house right after he'd bought me at the auction. I hadn't been sure where I was going, but I'd known the purpose for which I was brought to that house. Apparently, the women of Earth were abducted for the main goal of being slaves to the people of this planet. I didn't plan on making it easy.

I was still splashing water on my face and raking my scalp of the unwelcomed dirt when the water stopped abruptly.

"Decontamination complete," came Sari's voice again.

"Damn," I said as I stepped outside the pod. "You people really need to learn some decency," I muttered as I stood there hugging myself and wearing a blank expression on my face, wondering what to do next. The water from my hair kept running down my skin and through small openings in the floor I hadn't noticed earlier.

"Sa-Sari?" I called and shrugged. "What do I wear?" Might as well give it a try. At the moment, she was my best friend.

"Proceed to the linen chamber while I scan for your measurements," she instructed, and once more, an opening appeared in the wall.

"It would be so easy to hide someone here," I observed aloud.

"The walls are two feet thick and have a depth of three feet into the ground, surrounded by tungsten metal. Not large enough to fit anyone."

"Well…thank you for that tidbit," I replied, amused she had felt the need to respond.

"What's a tidbit?"

"Never mind," I told her as I went to the chamber, this time, less bashful than my first attempt with the cleansing pod. I stood in a small, cramped space as an object, similar to a laser, moved toward me and scanned my body. I staggered when I felt the ground move underneath me as the stand started revolving.

"Scan complete. Please wait for your suit."

After a few minutes and me dripping all over the floor, a pulley rolled out, and a neatly folded piece of cloth rested on it. I took it, and the pulley rolled back, and I stepped back into the larger room.

I still needed to dry off, so I went back to the pod and moved my hand around until I actually found a button. I pressed it, and out rolled another lever, this time, bearing what appeared to be towels. I took one and began drying my already wrinkling skin before stepping into the all-white bodysuit. It fit perfectly, like it had been made for me.

My stomach, as if acknowledging my body was now clean and I needed to tend to other urgent matters, began to growl. I pressed my palm there and looked around the room. "Sari, where can I get some food?"

"Right this way," was her response as the glass door that had held me prisoner slid open. I looked around and noticed everything was very white; it seemed they took cleanliness very seriously. There was a white sectional in the center of the room and a few more cushioned stools handsomely placed around. There was a table in front of the sectional with a glass vase on top. It was filled with the most beautiful white wisteria flowers.

There was a large screen positioned in the wall, which had a blank screen. The carpeting was plush, perhaps what mink felt like, and I sank my toes into it as I enjoyed the feel. The home was lovely. But no matter. This wasn't a place I wanted to be in, and I would find a way back to mine, even if only to the miserable existence I was drifting through, content in the fact that it was misery of my creation and not instead an imposition.

Sari led me to the kitchen, which, like every other room I'd seen so far, had everything hidden from view, neatly tucked away inside the walls. Or beneath me. A screen came to life as I stood there, and several meal options slid across the screen like a menu you would see at a fast food restaurant. My eyes barely got a chance to register the first set when others came into view, until I just named one of them I saw. After I did, the screen went black, and a few minutes passed before an opening emerged in the kitchen wall above the counter and a glass of some sort of juice came out. I took it, sniffed, and then cocked my head to the side.

"Well, the house hasn't killed me yet," I said and placed the glass to my lips. It wasn't bad either, and in short order, the glass was empty. Another five minutes had passed before the entire meal rolled out, and without thinking, I stood there and gobbled it down, barely noticing the taste.

When I was full, I left the plate on the countertop before returning to the other section of my all-white prison. My day was spent between growing increasingly bored and returning to Sari for distraction.

"Sari, what is this place?" I asked her.

"This is the Planet Jupiter. It has a population of 7,857,000 in five main cities."

"How do I leave?"

"The doors."

I started laughing at her reply but stopped when I began to feel guilty for the act. I wasn't supposed to be laughing in a place like this. I decided to make my questions more specific.

"How do I get back to Earth?" I asked and waited for another sardonic reply.

"That matter will have to be referred to Sekkol, master of this house."

Right. So that's what his name is. Interesting. I sat there in silence for a long time, anxious for the return of this Sekkol. When evening came and I saw the door slide open, I stood, ready to meet him.

CHAPTER 8
SEKKOL

I leaned against the door after it clicked shut and closed my eyes as I tried to brace myself. Immediately, her image flashed across my mind. The soft, dark curls that bounced on her shoulders seemed to spring with every step she took. Her skin was darker than mine and the others I had seen before. It resembled the sands of the desert of Epoch.

I remembered the frightened look she'd had when she first stepped off the vessel. She had just arrived from Earth with the newest batch of humans who would be sold as slaves. Her eyes were bright and seemed to dazzle even more than the sun, and she had staggered, unable to walk fully upright because of the shackles around her. Despite the filthy clothing she wore, she had been like a mirage, cool, inviting, and unexpected, and when I had tried to blink it back into extinction, I had felt the sting of recognition. I had unwittingly imprinted on her, and she was now mine, even though she didn't know it. Only that was now my folly, for unions with the humans were forbidden by law.

I clenched my fists as I opened my eyes and shoved off to join Brom. He was waiting for me at the bottom of the steps with a questioning look on his face. Though I was his secondary commander, we were more friends than the other two members making up our four-member team.

"Do you think that was a good idea?" Brom asked as I got to him, referring to the fact that I had bought the human at the auction, with his help, for two gold pieces. It was even more than they were commonly sold for, but I had to ensure I would not be outbid.

I clenched my jaw and checked the weapon attached to my waist. "It had to be done," was all I said. He didn't persist with the questioning. We were friends, but I was also his superior as the son and heir of Lord Magnus, Supreme Ruler of Jupiter. "Where are Gideon and Thorax?"

"Commander Styx has them over at the Great Pike," he replied as we got to the hovercraft.

I grimaced as I looked at the building where my father and the members of the Tribunal resided. He, of course, wanted to meet the woman, the human I could not introduce, and Jupiter's potential legacy. And I didn't even know her name.

"What's going on there?" I asked him.

"Tribunal making an announcement," Brom replied and looked at me strangely. "Commander Styx said he mentioned it to you before. Are you okay, Sekkol?" he asked.

I had forgotten our earlier encounter, but then, I always tried to forget everything having to do with the commander. At present, I'd rather be guarding the prison than be in his company. The man was cold, harsh, calculating, and brutal and carried a long-standing grudge against me.

"Right," I said and hopped onto the hovercraft. "I thought that was over," I added, making a measly attempt at covering my emotional tracks. This was not like me, and just the idea that she would be there when I returned home unnerved me.

"I think it is. I saw one of the members of the council just now. Also, I checked while I was waiting, and the command log shows some activity taking place in Centry," he added.

Centry was one of the districts in Anon, and it had been quite busy lately with petty criminal activity. Brom had a look on his face like he had something else to say but was nervous, because he kept shifting from one leg to the other.

"What is it?" I asked when I couldn't ignore it any longer.

"If Lord Magnus finds out about the human, he will—"

"It is none of your concern, Brom," I said through gritted teeth. "Just let it go." I held his eyes with my own and forced him to back down, and his arms came up in surrender. "As far as Lord Magnus is concerned, she is my slave, and that's still allowed."

Brom only nodded as he hopped onto the hovercraft behind me. I tapped the screen where the disturbance in Centry popped up, and a microimage appeared, revealing a small gathering of sorts.

"Here we go again," I muttered and tapped the Action Confirmed button before kicking the hovercraft into motion. "Brom, get Gideon and Thorax over there as well," I told him without looking behind.

"Of course," he replied as he tapped the passenger screen and sent the instructions. "It says they are already at the location."

"Good," I replied and whizzed down the street, appreciating the roar of the wind in my ears as it slapped at my face.

It didn't take us long to get there, and the craft hovered above the heads of the gathering that was already swelling.

"Wonder what it is today," Brom said as I lowered the scooter and he hopped off.

"Let's go find out," I replied.

We were frequently in Centry, making raids and disarming militant rebels, albeit few in number but ever constant. It was one of the only districts where violence was largely practiced still, and the one that gave my men too much pleasure visiting. At present, it proved to be a most welcomed distraction.

As with so many days before, there was a brawl developing. There was a man standing in the middle of the crowd wielding a dagger in his hand, seemingly trying to stave off an attack from the throng. Some men were pressing forward, trying to get close to the man to disarm him, but he moved too quickly and in constant revolutions, so it seemed impossible to get to that point.

"Back off," he was heard saying. "I didn't do anything to that woman." His eyes were red and wild, and his long hair flew all around each time he turned.

"Just let me get my hands on you," another man shouted as he tried to press forward. He instantly jumped back when the wild-eyed man lunged at him.

"What's going on here?" I asked as I pushed through the crowd. A few faces turned to mine, and then a path opened.

The man with the dagger shrank before me. "Master Sekkol, these men accuse me of assaulting a woman, but I didn't do it," he told me. His hands were still guarded, and his eyes continued to roam the crowd. "I never done it," he repeated.

"Where is the woman?" I asked him.

"She isn't here," the man hurried to say. "That's what I'm saying. I didn't do anything, so there is no one to be here."

"Here she is," a voice said from the back as I felt something brush against me and saw a woman stumble past. She fell onto the surface of the street, and the people at the brim of the crowd receded.

She looked around and then scurried away from the man and closer to me.

"Has this man done anything to you?" I asked her. She nodded and then whimpered, her hands folding before her defensively.

I looked back at the man, who was shaking his head profusely. "I never done it," he repeated.

"What did he do?" I asked the woman next to me. I noticed how she was determined to stay away from him, even though it meant being closer to me.

"He forced himself on me," she replied, and her quivering had become visible.

"No, no, no," the man denied. But it had become evident to me he had, in fact, done something, and a punishment was now warranted. I had not yet determined what kind to mete out when I saw Commander Styx approaching. I gritted my teeth and sank my feet into the earth. Brom stepped closer to me in a show of support, as he was prone to do.

"What is the crime?" Styx asked as he stepped into the ring that had formed around us.

"Rape," I replied while shooting daggers at him with my eyes. "But I have it covered."

"Do you?" he asked, intent on challenging me.

"I do," I told him. My legs were apart, and I bore the same military stance Brom had displayed earlier. There was a slight wind, and my hair fluttered on my shoulders and tickled my neck.

"And what have you decided?" he asked me. It wasn't unusual for him to display his arrogance in public, but I was not in the mood to entertain him today.

"I'll take him in and have him fried," I told our commander. That was a process that would have him chained by his hands and feet and left in a chamber, heat radiating through him until his color turned.

"Oh," Styx replied and walked over to the man. "He is going to get *fried*." He said that with such disdain I wanted to fry *him* instead. Or worse.

I folded my hands behind me as Gideon and Thorax came into view and stood close by. "That's what I said."

"Now that's not the Sekkol I know," he said as if in sermon to the crowd. "The Sekkol that we know would want nothing but disintegration for the slightest vagrancy," he said.

Though detestable, the audience nodded and then jerked when I flashed a warning look at them. But Styx wasn't doing that to show me up. No. He had a point he was itching to make, and so I waited for it.

"I don't think he should be fried for rape. What say you?" he asked the crowd now. They chanted, fists pumping in the air and echoing Styx's suggestion.

I couldn't argue with his logic just because my head was messed up. I stood there, teeth gritted, as he went over to the man, produced his conical laser, and lifted his hand in the air. The man cried out, using his hands as a shield against the blue light that disappeared inside him when Styx brought his hand down. The first sign of the man's death was the blood that fell, like an anvil, onto the ground. And then he crumpled to the floor. Styx shielded his laser once more and stood before me.

"You are getting weak, Sekkol," he said, taunting me as he always did. But it had nothing to do with the lifeless body lying in the street only a few feet from where we stood. "I don't know what she ever saw in you."

And there it was. He had been carrying a longtime grudge against me because I had refused his sister's advances. He knew his position held no sway over me, but he used every opportunity he could find to undermine me. At the moment, his sister was the fuel he desperately needed.

"Maybe you need to retire to the Great Pike and let the real men handle the street work," Styx continued and came before me, his shadow blocking out the sun.

But I would not be intimidated. I took two steps and stopped him in his path. "Commander," I said through clenched teeth. "You have a body in the street that needs removing." I stared him down until he backed away.

"Someone get rid of that," he said angrily as he backed away and tore through the already thinning circle of onlookers.

A drone appeared after a few minutes, and the remains of the man were shoveled inside before it buzzed off. I gathered my men after that, as we had separated the throng of onlookers. Commander Styx had already disappeared, though his presence had not been needed at all. We got back to the hovercraft, and I scanned the log for any other active duty we had been assigned. There were several.

I could feel the anger, the confusion, and the frustration swimming around in my head like a whirlpool, and I was growing dizzy from its effects.

The hovercraft lifted from the ground and moved slowly before it increased in speed. Just as I exited the space, I saw Commander Styx eyeing me from his vehicle. He was angry—that much was clear—but there was something else in his eyes, like he too could see through me. I quickly turned away, even though I was growing more anxious inside as I thought about what awaited me at home.

CHAPTER 9
SEKKOL

As soon as I got to the door, it slid open, and the trusted voice of my automated companion greeted me.

"Welcome home, Master Sekkol."

But she wasn't the only one. Before I could take note of where the woman was, she found me.

"What the fuck kind of place is this?" she asked angrily.

Her language was unfamiliar, and I didn't recognize the "fuck" word that she spoke. I stood there looking at her, a perplexed expression on my face.

"Is this how you treat people? Lock them away all day while you go about your business? Just let me go!" she shouted as she charged at me.

I grabbed her by the arm, braking her steps, which only caused her to crash into me.

"Let me go!" she cried as she lashed out at me with the other hand.

I used both my arms now to hold her in place as she flailed about.

"Stop," I barked, and she jumped at the sound of my voice. But only for a second. "Are the rest of your people this defiant?" I asked her as I moved away from the door. Her feet dragged behind her as I pulled her to one of the stools.

"Defiant?" she spat at me and then brushed her loose curls from her face. "You kidnapped me. For God knows what. And I'm not supposed to be defiant?"

"You are very angry," I told her as I tried to analyze her face. Her skin color had grown lighter in her cheeks, and the white in her eyes now displayed red lines. "Is this how the women of Earth look when they are angry?" They were strange to me, and though I did not understand why I had imprinted, she made me curious.

"Look, *Master* Sekkol," she said as she prepared to stand again, "it's clear this isn't going to work, so I would appreciate if you would just send me back to Earth." She folded her hands in front of her, and I watched as her chest heaved. As angry as she was, she seemed even more beautiful to me.

When she rose, I held her and pressed my lips to hers. I felt her stiffen, and then she pulled back. Her eyes widened in horror as her hand came down on my face, leaving a stinging sensation.

"Don't you fucking touch me again," she told me and backed away.

By this time, my patience had worn thin, and I felt the fire rise within me to match hers. "You dare touch me?" I bellowed. She cringed and almost fell from the stool as I moved in her direction. I reached out and caught her hand before she did. "I am master of this house, and you are mine. You will do as you are commanded," I told her as I brought her back to a sitting position.

She pushed my hand away and stood. She had so much fire in her, and I was not used to this amount of intolerance.

"The hell I will," she shot back. She folded her arms before her as she challenged me.

I was not in the mood for another round of animosity. I walked away and headed to the bedroom. I knew there was nowhere for her to go.

"Hey, don't walk away from me, alien!" she shouted after me. "I'm talking to you."

"Be quiet, or I will find something else to do with you," I snarled.

It had been a long day, and I had not anticipated this degree of defiance. Plus, I was always of the belief that when one imprinted, the other would feel attraction, too, on some level. It seemed whatever I was feeling, I was alone in it. I looked back at her standing there in the center of the room.

"Now, if you don't mind, I need to cleanse myself," I told her and walked down the narrow hallway that led to my room.

Only the bed was visible, everything else neatly tucked away. I fell on it, facedown, and allowed the dreadful day I'd had to suffocate into nothingness. The weariness rested on me now like dead weight, and my body felt limp as I remained there. Soon, I removed all my clothing and hit the section of the wall only I knew. An opening formed, and I discarded my garments there before stepping inside.

The water came on, strong and forceful, as it beat down on me. But of everything, it had been the kindest thing to me all day. The faces of my father, of her, and of Commander Styx danced across my mind, and I slapped my hands to my temples to rid my memory of their influence. I stood there and let the water run over me, hopefully washing away my troubles.

I had just stepped from the pod and was gathering a sleep suit when I heard her again through the walls.

"Hey!" she shouted and started banging on the door. "Where do I sleep?" I did not respond. "Where do I sleep?"

I pretended as if I didn't hear her and stayed inside a while longer. I thought I'd punish her, if even a little, for her earlier insubordination. Soon, her voice died down, and the house became still. I didn't even know if she had eaten, but I saw she had clothes. For that, I could thank Sari. Which meant she might have eaten, too. But I wasn't sure, and it gnawed at me that she might be feeling some discomfort.

I groaned and got up, stepping into the hallway and down to the sitting room. "There is a..." I began to say but stopped when I didn't see her anywhere. I panicked and looked around for her for a few seconds, until I saw her draped over a chair in the library, the only other room that was visibly open. I stood there for a few seconds, wondering why she had chosen that room to fall asleep in and not the sitting room.

Her face was peaceful now as she slept, and I walked over to her so I could get a better look. Her breathing was normal, not as short as before, and I watched the slow rise and fall of her chest. Her hands twitched as she sat there, her head now rolling to the side. I went over and propped it up, feeling the softness of her curls. I closed my fist around a clump of her hair and felt the silky strands, though a little rougher than mine. Her eyes fluttered as if to open, and I remained still, lest I woke the sleeping beast.

I lowered myself then and gently scooped her up into my arms. She was a plump little thing, and her flesh was soft to the touch. My hands sank into her like she was made of cotton. She stirred for a second as I stood there, admiring her face in the dim lighting. Then I started walking to the only other available room I had, one she could not have found on her own. When I got to the bed, I rested her there, and she moaned when I did.

I found that I understood why I had imprinted on her now that she was asleep, and I admired the smoothness of her skin and fantasized about her touch. But I didn't realize how difficult it would be to deal with the human when she was awake. Her eyes fluttered open once more, only halfway and still heavy with sleep.

I leaned in and whispered into her ear, "What is your name?" There was no sound at first, and I repeated the question.

"Keira," she replied, barely loud enough for me to hear, and then she fell back into a deep slumber, from which she would not awaken soon.

I leaned in and kissed the top of her hair, and despite everything that swam around in my head and how wrong everything seemed, at that moment, it was real and it was right. "My Keira," I whispered before I stood and walked out of the room.

It was a long night after that. I twisted and turned as I tried to reconcile, in my own mind, the events of the last few days. Nothing made sense. Sleep was slow in coming, and when it did, relief did not accompany it. I jumped out of it, breaking out in a sweat and breathing hard not long after I had closed my eyes. I punched the bed, frustration embracing me too intimately, and swung my legs around to the side. I stood and went out of the room and found the window of the sitting room. I remained there while the soft light of the moon danced over my chest, and the cool air brought me solace.

Behind me, I could hear her approaching. I turned to see her standing at the edge of the room, a picture of shock. Her eyes dipped low and then back to my face before she hurried off and disappeared again into the room. It wasn't until after she had gone that I remembered I was naked.

CHAPTER 10
KEIRA

After I saw him standing there, I found it difficult to fall asleep again. He was naked, and his back was turned to me. The moonlight had been streaming through the window and bouncing off his rigid frame. His skin was glistening, and I found it challenging not to admire the way his muscles contoured, making hills and valleys that beckoned me. I was immobilized as I stood there as if in a trance. And then he turned, and my heart thumped in my chest. I couldn't see his face clearly; the light obscured the image, and I only saw its shadow. I fled then, my embarrassment with me. But I had already seen him, and the image had fully registered in my mind.

Sleep slowly made its way back to me, and when I drifted off again into peaceful slumber, he followed me. I jumped up what I thought was not long after, but when I went into the sitting room, the sun was already high in the sky. I peeked around every corner I was aware of, but it seemed he had already gone.

"This is ridiculous," I declared as I rested my hands on my hips. I went to the door and tried to pry it open, but it only activated Sari instead.

"Please refrain from undue pressure to the doors."

"How else am I supposed to go out?" I asked, but this time, she chose to remain silent. I couldn't see any buttons or a pad or lever, even though I searched high and low. "Come on," I muttered and then went to the bathroom, or whatever they called it.

And so began my long and dreary day in my prison home.

By the time he returned, I was fuming with rage. "This is not going to work," I said as soon as he stepped into the room. He had blood on his clothes, or what I thought it to be, and his face wore a scowl. I was only now noticing how flat his face was, like that of an Asian.

"*What* isn't going to work?" His voice sounded slow, deliberate, and almost dangerous. His eyes flashed, and he slowly pulled a cylindrical object from his waist.

My movement stilled as my eyes followed his hand, and my words got caught in my throat. "This," I replied, suddenly frightened of what he might do. I stepped back a little, but even that wasn't far enough from him. He stood there, looking at me and forcing my explanation. "I had a life back home, and being here is disrupting that. Just send me back," I told him as I slowly regained my courage.

"We will have this discussion no longer," he said as he began to move away. "You will remain here until I decide otherwise." And then he was gone.

It was useless. I came to the realization that my current strategy would get me nowhere. I needed a different approach. I went back to the sectional and sank into the soft, leather-like cushioned seating.

I was staring at the door when the thought came to me that I didn't know how the door opened manually. By all indications, Sari recognized him when he came home. If I was at the door when he came home, then I could easily slip through and make a run for it. The thing was, I wasn't sure what time he would be home. And where would I run? I didn't know, but I didn't want to remain here, not like this. So for the rest of the evening, I was quiet, and I noticed when he went for dinner that night how he observed me.

I couldn't figure him out, even though I looked. His face was always stern, and whenever I tried to approach him, he would grow even more aggressive, like I was invading his space. I'd had it.

The next morning, I rose early. I had not yet seen him leave, but I knew it had to be early since he was always gone when I got up. I was already dressed and in the library by the time he emerged. I kept my head low and waited as he got tea or something from the kitchen. Then he walked off. My heart raced as I slowly crept from the room. His back was turned, and I was thankful for the carpeting that made being stealthy easy.

I tiptoed to the sectional and ducked just in case he turned. When I peered over the edge, he was standing at the door. He hit a spot on the wall, and a transparent monitor appeared, displaying images. It had the face of a tablet, and I looked closely as he tapped something on the screen. He shifted to the left, and I buried my head again. By the time I looked up, he was gone.

"Here goes nothing." I raced to the door while looking around and wondering if Sari had cameras. I felt around the spot for the button and was relieved when the screen appeared. "Thank you, Lord," I said ecstatically and scanned the surface. There was no keypad, just instructions, and I was surprised when I saw the *open* button. I tapped the screen, and sure enough, the door slid open. With no further thought, I dashed outside…and straight into Sekkol's hands. My heart pounded while he held on to me, disapproval shining in his eyes.

"You must think I'm stupid," he said as he gripped my arm and led me back inside.

"Stop. You're hurting my arm," I cried, and I stumbled when we were inside and he finally let me go. I rubbed the spot that throbbed now.

"You will learn," he began as he moved toward me, "that I always get what I want. Right now, you are mine, and I want you. You are going nowhere, human." He grabbed me and pulled me to him. I slammed into his hard chest as his hand flattened me to him. His smell was overpowering, and I grew dizzy from the effect.

"Don't…touch…me," I said as I gritted my teeth and tried to squirm from his hand. But he was too strong, and before I knew what was happening, his lips were on mine again. "No," I mumbled against him, trying to push him away, but he was determined to show me his prowess. At that moment, I realized I did not possess the skills to stop him. I remained tense as his lips crushed mine.

It was then I discovered my purpose to him: I was to be his bitch.

The thought angered me for a couple seconds, until I thought I could use that to my advantage. He had his guard up because of the way I acted, so changing it might make him less skeptical and provide me with an exit.

So I stopped fighting as hard, just enough to put on a show. I pulled against him still, but my lips never responded. It was hard to believe this alien was trying to have sex with me, and I closed my eyes as the idea repulsed me. I kept them closed while his lips dominated mine and his hands explored my body. I cringed when he grabbed my hair and tugged it, and when he pulled back, I opened my eyes. Where I had seen fury before, there was now an intense need burning there, and I shivered as I looked at him.

"Take off your clothes," he told me as he released me.

I stood there, militant and unmoved. "I'm not giving you anything. If you want it, you can take them off yourself."

I hadn't realized how fragile the fabric was until I heard it ripping as he tore it from me. The first tug came down below my left breast, and I gasped as my hand automatically shot up and covered it. I folded my body, but he gripped my shoulder and pressed me backward as he yanked the rest of my clothes off.

It wasn't until I stood bare before him that I abandoned the idea of giving in to him. "No, I can't do this," I said and started backing off. I wiped the smears of him off my lips and turned. I pressed my hand against my chest as it heaved.

He came up behind me and wrapped his arms around me. "You will," he told me, and my eyes closed again. He squeezed my breasts, one at a time, and his hands ran over my body as if he were trying to memorize it. He inhaled sharply, and his lips descended on my neck. Shivers ran down my spine as I stood there like a robot. He grabbed a handful of my hair and whipped my head around, bringing my lips to meet his once again.

I gasped when he made a sweeping motion that took me off my feet. Soon, I was lying completely beneath him. His breathing intensi-fied as he kissed me again. My heart rate quickened.

I got confused when felt my cunt quiver with want. I jumped, and he looked up at me with curious eyes. He began to move his fingers slowly, as if trying to recapture my reaction, until I could feel my womanhood growing wet.

Shit! The voice in my head cried out, telling me to stop, but some parts of me didn't want to. It was a thin line I was straddling between playing a game and losing complete control. Right now, I was tipping to his side. "No," I hissed. "I don't want this."

He stared at me perplexed. "You do not want me?"

The noise inside me grew louder and came out in soft pants at first, and when he paused to lay himself bare before me, I choked. My eyes glued to his elongated member that waved from side to side in anticipation. It was every bit like the ones I had seen before, except for the color. It seemed transparent, almost plastic, and I could see blue lines crisscrossing it like border lines on a map. It pulsated visibly.

"No. I do not," I answered.

He stared at me as if he doubted the truth of my statement but he rolled away. Now lying on his back with his breath coming out in loud pants as if trying to calm himself.

Shit. Shit. Shit. I squeezed my legs together as I tried to feel nothing. Despite the situation, I did find him attractive.

This is not happening. I tried to convince myself otherwise. His presence overwhelmed my senses, my thoughts, and me, and for an instant, I forgot the plan I was hatching as I fought the urge to touch him. My eyes closed again. I heard him move and my eyes popped open. I watched him walk away while commanding Sari to lock up. Then he left, and I was alone.

I fell back against the plush carpeting, still feeling traces of him against my lips.

CHAPTER 11
KEIRA

I wasn't sure how much longer I could play this game. It had been two weeks, and we'd barely been civil toward one another. I had been outdoors twice, always accompanied by someone of his choosing. But never with him. I wondered about that and finally decided I would broach the subject one afternoon.

"So…" I began when I saw him walk in. "Are you afraid to be seen in public with me?" I asked. I was on a chrome stool next to the counter separating the kitchen from the sitting room.

"What do you mean?" he asked, his brows knitting once more.

"I have not been outside with you. I'm starting to feel a little perturbed about it," I replied. "Is there something that I should know?"

He frowned.

I huffed. Fuck it…I would just get to the point. "On Earth…I have people who are worried about me." It was a lie, but I thought I could appeal to his sensitive side.

"They will learn to adapt without you," he replied. "And to answer your original question, I am not seen in public with you because that is not how we do it here. Here, the women stay home."

I scowled. "And do all alien men take human lovers?" I asked curiously. I had seen the lustful stares he gave me when he thought I wasn't paying attention.

"I do not understand," he replied.

It was frustrating to talk to him sometimes. We were speaking the same language, made possible by the language translator still implanted in my neck, but communication barriers between us were still mounted high.

He gave me a blank stare, and a weird look came upon his face. He seemed to be battling something inside, and he moved away without answering.

I ran to him and held on to his arm. "No, you are not doing that this time, Sekkol," I said.

He looked down at my hand on his arm and then into my eyes. "I have work to do," he told me before brushing my hand off.

I ran around to his front and pressed my hand against his chest. "Surely you can take one minute to answer me."

"If you want to talk, I can have someone sent up. Otherwise, Sari can answer any question you may have," he said firmly and tried to move again.

I would not be deterred. "No, I want to talk to *you*. Sari cannot answer the questions I have, like why you try so hard not to be seen with me. You allow me to leave with an escort, but it is always away from you. And when I mention sex, like I did just now, your face changes and you get quiet. What's the big deal?"

His lips thinned to a slit in his face, and his bluish hue grew almost purple. "You ask too many questions, human," he replied. "What you see is nothing. Now, I need to go."

I didn't budge, but it wasn't hard for him to step around me. He departed, and I was left with a nagging feeling within me. There was something he wasn't telling me, but rather than remain inside, I decided I'd go out. Without telling him. I was tired of playing the slave girl. I waited until I thought he had gone before opening the door and going out.

"You should not be going out alone," a voice came from behind me at about midway down the flight of metal stairs. I looked back and saw a man coming toward me. He was a little shorter than Sekkol, with a jovial demeanor and the face of my only friend. He wore a silver body-suit and had a belt of gadgets around his waist. His black hair was pulled to his nape, and the smile, which showed perfect rows of white teeth, came next. I had first seen him when he had bought me at the auction—for Sekkol, of course—but he had grown to be the only friend I had.

"Hi," I replied as he got to me. "I just wanted to take a walk."

"That's all? You weren't thinking of escaping again?" He had apparently heard of my last attempts.

"Nah," I replied and started off again as he followed me. "Where would I go?" I asked him. And it stung me as the words I had refused to accept hung from my lips.

"That's right," he replied. "It's not easy getting off a place like Jupiter. It has never happened before. No earthling has ever escaped," he added for good measure.

"Has anyone ever tried?" I wanted to know.

"All the time."

"And what happened?" I stopped to survey his face and judge his response.

"They got fried," he told me.

"Fried?" I asked.

"Yes," he answered. "They go into a chamber and face direct heat until their skin burns off."

My eyes popped wide when he explained, and I shrank under his gaze. "That's a harsh penalty," I replied eventually and started walking again.

"It encourages subordination and cooperation," he explained. "We take great pride here in our legal system."

"So is that what you do? You and Sekkol?" I asked him.

We got to the bottom of the steps, and I watched as hover-crafts lifted off and whizzed overhead. The buildings were scattered in odd shapes, a pyramid-looking one here, a diamond-shaped one there, some flat, others set at an angle, but everything coming together into a handsome abstract masterpiece. Some other locals eyed me as I walked past, and I noticed a few humans along the streets paved with a claylike matter. It seemed to be the same throughout Anon, the city of which I was now a resident.

"Yes, we are Enforcers," he told me. "A little above the regular patrol guards."

"So Sekkol is just a glorified policeman," I said and gave a mocking laugh. "I am the slave of a fucking cop."

"You speak strangely sometimes," he replied. "And Sekkol isn't just a regular guard, even though an Enforcer. He is the—"

"Well, well, well," a man said as he stepped into view. "Brom."

"Commander," Brom responded and made a slight bow.

The man had a harsh exterior, with a face that could easily be made of stone. He looked nothing like Sekkol nor my companion, Brom. He had beady eyes on a head that seemed like a boulder, squished and dented around the edges. His frame was large, and it gave him the appearance of a mountain. His hair was white and thin and fluttered in the breeze, as did the bronze coat he wore.

"I didn't know you had a slave," he said as he eyed me.

"I'm no slave," I retorted, already taking offense at the word.

"Oh?" he asked and stepped closer to me. "What would that make you, then?"

"I am a companion," I told him.

"Whose?" the man asked and straightened his shoulders. He had a wicked look about him, and more than anyone else, he frightened me. But I had come to believe that Sekkol would protect me. I hoped.

"Sek—"

"She is mine." Brom jumped in. "I got her from that last shipment Jonas brought in from Earth."

"Hmm," he grunted and then looked around. "Don't you already have one?" he asked Brom.

And why had Brom told him I belonged to him and not Sekkol?

"Is there a law against two?" Brom asked and stepped between the commander and me.

"No," he replied and pushed the man away. "But there is one concerning defiance and conspiracy to the same."

"There is no conspiracy, Commander. She is mine, and we were just walking—"

"Slaves don't take a walk with their owners," he barked as I jumped and looked back in the direction of home. I had no other name for it.

His eyes narrowed as he looked back at me. "There is something about you," he said. "Something familiar."

"I-I don't know what…"

"Silence, human!" he shouted.

"I will not be told—" The next thing I felt was his hand on my face and the burning sensation that followed. The fury swelled in me, and I raised my hand in retaliation. I was getting tired of being slapped by these fucking aliens.

"No," Brom said and grabbed my hand before I could strike the man.

"A troublemaker," the asshole said and laughed. But it was not an amused one. "I think we might have to teach this one a lesson."

"Commander, please allow me to take her home. I apologize for any unintended insult, but I will see to it that she is duly punished," Brom assured as he gripped my wrist even tighter and held it to his side.

The commander grunted and came to stand before me. He tilted my face upward and growled, "See to it that she is kept trained, Brom."

"Yes, Commander," he replied. And then the man walked away.

"Why did you tell him…?" I began, but Brom's face had grown sour.

"You do not understand how things are here, human," he told me as he gripped my hand and led me back the way we had come. "From now on, you keep a low profile. You do not want the commander knowing to whom you really belong." He looked around him wildly now as he led me back, and I was more frightened than I had ever been. I could feel my cheek throbbing, and with the other hand, I touched the spot, the same spot Jonas, the black-market dealer, had struck me when I first arrived.

"What's so special about Sekkol? What would have happened if he had known I belonged… That I was his…?" I paused when I couldn't find a description adequate enough.

Brom stopped in his tracks and grabbed my arm, shaking me as he did. "Because Sekkol is no ordinary man. Because he imprinted on you and because he was not supposed to."

He spoke, but I understood nothing he said. What did he mean, he imprinted on me? And why wasn't he supposed to? Why had he?

"I don't understand," I finally had the chance to say. "Imprint?"

"Let's just go." He scoffed as he all but carted me off. Brom stopped and checked his surroundings once more for a few minutes when we neared the steps to Sekkol's house. "Stay indoors," he warned me as he led me up the steps.

I was at the door and about to enter when I heard a sound behind me. Brom wheeled around and drew a cylindrical device from his waist.

"I knew something was wrong with that story," the commander said as he materialized into view. "Something about it being your companion. I thought to myself, *Now, why would it refer to itself as a companion if it wasn't treated as one?* And why were you so nervous? Now I know," he said as he chuckled and then laughed heartily.

What is so funny? What is he saying? I stood there, not knowing what to say or do, realizing now that there was too much I didn't know.

"Guards." He whistled, and two men bounded up the steps. "Take this human away," he told them.

"What?" I asked in surprise as I realized what he was saying now. "No!" I ran behind Brom, hoping for his defense again. He just stood there, looking ahead and unable to defy his superior.

The men got to me, and each took one of my arms. They were leading me down the stairs as I kicked and screamed against muscles I knew I could not fight.

"Brom!" I yelled to him. He had a sympathetic look about him, but he was powerless. "No. Stop!" I screamed as I drew the attention of some of the locals.

Sekkol's hovercraft appeared just as we got to the bottom of the steps.

"Well, what do we have here?" the commander taunted as he stood before him.

He must be able to save me.

"What are you doing, Commander?" he asked.

"I think it is clear. Getting rid of your human *companion*," he growled with emphasis and turned to look at me. Sekkol gulped and made a move toward me. "I wouldn't do that if I were you," the man said and dared Sekkol to defy him. Sekkol stood there without a word. "And to think, you gave up my sister…to be with a human?" he spat.

"This is none of your concern, Commander," he replied. "Release her to me, and I will deal with her."

"None of my concern?" the commander asked. "You know the laws, *Master Sekkol*," he sneered. "Better than anyone. I wonder what Lord Magnus will have to say about this." He grinned.

What is going on? Who is Lord Magnus? Who is Sekkol?

"Sekkol," I begged as I stretched my hand out to him. I pleaded with him with my eyes, but the commander seemed to have all the cards.

The guards tugged at my arms and yanked me away. The last thing I saw before I was tossed into the hovercraft with the two guards was Sekkol and Brom standing together, unable to save me the second time around.

CHAPTER 12
KEIRA

I bounced around in the hovercraft as it took off and sped to my doom. Panic swelled within me as I tried to stand. The vehicle made a sharp turn, and I rolled to the other side, knocking my head against the hard plastic interior. It reminded me of the vessel that transported me to this hellhole of a planet, and for the first time in years, I missed the silence of my former life.

I would probably be sitting at my desk now, poring over numbers or writing a report for my finance manager. Celeste, the redhead in the cubicle in front of me, would be drinking coffee and chatting on her phone, right before the supervisor showed up and the mad scrambling began as she scratched at the papers on her desk in pretend labor. She would smile at him and flirt, and he would adjust his glasses and give her a warning before walking off. And as soon as he disappeared, she would hit the redial button.

"I can't believe this shit is happening," I muttered as I braced myself against the walls and finally stood when the machine leveled.

I traced my hands along the interior of the craft that was different than the one Sekkol and Brom usually rode around on. This was like a space car or truck because it had a storage unit at the back and thick black glass separating me from the driver. The ones Brom and Sekkol rode resembled flying motorcycles.

I hobbled over to the glass and began pounding. "Hey, let me out. Let me out." My palms were growing red the more I banged, but not once did the window roll down or the driver reveal himself. "No," I whispered as I slid back to the ground, the glass now to my back. "No!" I screamed as I felt the tears beginning to trickle down my cheeks. "Not again."

A few weeks ago, I was chained to a set of humans, fresh from being kidnapped from Earth. I didn't even know life in this place existed, but I was a fast believer.

I had thought Sekkol strange and cruel at first and was irritated at how he expected me to bend to his every will. But there was also a side of him that intrigued me. My curiosity was even further piqued when I was taken by his commander, a cold and cruel alien man who seemed to have a sinister agenda, and by how Sekkol had tried to defend me.

Now here I was, trapped in the commander's vehicle and being taken to God knows where. I wasn't even sure if Sekkol would be able to save me this time or why I had been taken from him. As far as I understood, slaves were allowed. But there seemed to be something different about him, and I might not even get the chance to figure it out.

I was still ruminating when the hovercraft stopped. My eyes popped open, and I got to my feet. The door opened, and the sun reflected on my face and blocked my vision. My hands fell over my eyes to form a shield before my pupils adjusted, and I saw the evil commander again.

"Get it out of there," he said to someone I couldn't see just yet.

Two other aliens appeared shortly after, hopped into the hovercraft, and grabbed my hands.

"No. Let me go!" I shouted and struggled against them, kicking and flailing my arms as I did. Their grip on me tightened as they dragged me outside.

The commander was standing there wearing a mean expression and scowling, and he seemed to be surveying me. "Bring her to me," his voice boomed.

I was hauled to the place he stood, with the other aliens on either side of me. I looked into the harsh face of the man, and I saw no trace of humanity there. Or whatever it was called here. He reached out and squeezed my cheek, and I cringed and turned my head away as I felt his bony fingers pinching my skin. He gripped my chin and brought my head back around, forcing my eyes to his.

"It is such a weird-looking thing. Bring it inside," he told the men and walked off.

The aliens led me to a building that was made of glass and shaped like a diamond. The steps leading up to it were constructed from steel, and it was hard not to notice how resounding my steps were, how they echoed with each one I took, like they were signaling my impending doom. When we got to the top, the doors opened, much like they had at Sekkol's house when the automated system recognized the owner. My heart started fluttering as realization hit me that he had brought me home. I was to be the evil commander's slave.

"Let go of me!" I started shouting this time, adamant that I would not be put through the same fate twice.

"The thing has quite a mouth on it," the commander said and turned to me as the door closed. Then he took the same cylindrical device I had seen Sekkol with before and brought it to my face. "If you don't keep quiet, I will personally drive this through you."

"Do it," I cried as I lunged at him. I could feel the rage swelling within me, and I no longer cared about the consequences of my words. I'd had enough, and I was ready to die. "Just fucking do it!" I screamed at him.

"What is going on out…? Oh…" A woman's voice came from behind him, before she materialized into view. He looked around and turned to face the woman. "What is that?" she asked and placed her hands on her hips.

She was of the same race as he was, with the stony face and wispy hair. But she was slightly more attractive than he was, perhaps because of her feminine appearance. Her face was flat and not as dented as his, and her hair was pulled back at her nape. Her skin was white, not the beautiful bluish color as Sekkol's skin, but more like ash.

"I thought you said you would never bring an earthling here," she said to him.

"No worries, sister," he said and turned to me. "It is not mine."

"Then why did you bring it here? I will not have our home contaminated by filthy earthlings. Such ugly creatures if you ask me," she huffed and turned her round nose up at me, showing her pointed chin.

"Are you kidding me?" I asked. "I'm the ugly one?"

"Oh," she replied in surprise. "It dares speak to me?"

"Look, I don't know who you are or why I'm here, but since I'm not wanted, how about sending me back to Earth? Then everyone will be happy. How about that?"

"If it were up to me, you would never have come here, but the others wanted it, and Lord Magnus didn't have what it took to deny them." She was wearing a dress, the first I had seen since I arrived, and it swished and wrapped around her ankles as she came toward me. "There is something queer about this one," she said as she got closer, and her eyes narrowed as she inspected me. "Where did you get it?"

"From Sekkol," the commander replied as his eyes grew icier.

She looked over at him, an odd expression on her face as they shared a surprised glance. Then she turned back to me, and this time, instead of just looking, she circled me, too.

"What's going on? Why can't I just go back to Sekkol? Who are you people?" I wanted to know as I turned about to keep tabs on her. I couldn't even believe the words that were coming out of my mouth concerning Sekkol, but I could see he was my only ally.

"Sekkol? You belonged to Sekkol?" she asked.

I may not have had many boyfriends in the past, but the sound of jealousy was uncanny in her voice. "What's it to you?" I asked.

"Please leave us," the commander told his men, who had been forgotten during the banter, and they nodded and went back outside.

I rubbed my arms where they had held me and looked back at the woman.

"Did he…? Is she…? Was… Did he consort with her?" she finally managed to ask her brother. She had started asking me but then diverted to him, apparently after she decided the question would serve him better.

"I found her in the streets with Brom, one of his Enforcers. She mentioned she was Brom's companion, but there was something wrong about it, so I watched them. When they left the streets, they went to Sekkol's house. I can only assume *he* is her actual *companion* and that Brom was covering for him."

"But isn't that treason?" she asked as her eyes widened.

"Once Lord Magnus hears about this, things won't look so good for Jupiter's heir," the commander sneered.

"Maybe Lord Magnus doesn't have to know," the woman answered as a devious look crept on to her face. She lifted her hand and touched my hair. I pulled back and slapped her hand away.

"Don't touch me," I told her.

"Feisty, too," she replied and laughed. Her voice screeched and reverberated in the room, and she gripped my neck in her long and cold fingers. I jumped when she did as my heart sped up and my breathing got short. "You, my dear, will bring me that which I have desired the most." I could smell her breath, ripe and tangy, causing me to grow nauseated as she held me there. I lifted my right hand to press her back, but the commander was right there to catch it and bring it to my side forcefully.

"What do you speak of, Nala?" he asked as he tried to keep my hands in place. "How can she help?"

"Sekkol refused me before, but if he agrees to marry me, then no one need know of his treason," she said and grinned. "He will have to do what I want or suffer the wrath of the Tribunal. Either way, I win," she declared and let my face go with such force I felt a sharp pain in my neck.

"That's your plan?" I asked, already fearing if he agreed to marry her, my demise would be certain. "And what if he doesn't? I can see why he never married you before," I jeered and then coughed; my neck had not yet recovered from her hold on me.

She took two steps and slapped me hard in the face. "Mind your tongue, earthling," she spat.

My neck twisted when her hand came down on my face, and without thinking, I grabbed her throat and started squeezing. The next thing I felt was a sharp pain across my back as I was hit from behind.

Before I could collect myself, I felt another blow that sent me sprawling on the floor. I turned my head to the side and saw the commander standing over me with the same cylindrical device he had reached for earlier.

The woman came over and kicked me in the side, and the pain shot through me as I curled into the fetal position to ward off any further assault.

"You won't be so lucky the next time, earthling," she sneered. "Now remove it, Jared, before I do it myself," she threatened and then stormed off.

"It won't work," I pressed, even as the commander dragged me from the ground. "He will never marry you."

As if I knew. But I wanted them to believe that desperately and find no further use for me. Yet I didn't have a say in the matter, and before I could utter another word, I felt his hand come down on my neck, and I grew dizzy as the floor rose to meet me.

CHAPTER 13
SEKKOL

The last time I went to the Great Pike, it was by invitation to have breakfast with my father. This time, I was summoned. The building was just a few structures over and situated too closely to my own home, yet the walk there felt like an arduous one. I sighed as I recalled the way Keira had been plucked from my grasp, in much the same manner as she had fallen into it. She was mine, whether I wanted to admit it or not—and even worse, whether it was even allowed. I wished it weren't. Otherwise, I would not be on this journey now to whatever demise my father had planned for me, for all of Jupiter knew that to lie with a human was completely forbidden. It was even worse for me, being of royal lineage.

My father was required to follow the very laws he and our family had instituted, even if it meant he had to create another heir after I was gone. A thousand images flashed before my eyes as I trudged up the walkway and climbed the steps to meet him. But his face did not reflect what I thought it would. What greeted me instead was a huge smile and a pat on the shoulder.

"Why did you not bring her to me sooner?" he asked as he led me into the great hall.

"What?" I asked, truly confused as to what he was speaking about.

"I knew you had imprinted on someone. I, for one, thought it would have been a woman from Anon, but we all know we can't choose who we imprint on. So a woman from Bulova is fairly acceptable."

"A what?" I asked again, this time, his meaning truly lost on me.

"Don't be so shy, Sekkol. I know you had meant to keep her secret from me, but—"

"Oh, my Sekkol." Nala interrupted as she swished into the hall, her hands outstretched as she flew into my arms. I stood there with my arms still at my sides and completely taken aback by what was happening.

"I will leave you two alone," Lord Magnus said and backed away. "You can join me in the banquet chamber when you are through." He beamed and then disappeared through the same doors Nala had just come through.

As soon as he was gone, I threw her from me. "What is the meaning of this?" I thundered.

"Now, now, Sekkol, is that any way to treat your future queen?" she asked as she batted her lashes at me. She repulsed me, and my stomach turned just by being that close to her.

"I don't know what you have concocted in that deceitful mind of yours, but you need to stay away from me." I grabbed her wrist as she was holding it up to touch me and then tossed her hand back to her side. "I don't know why you told my father such a lie, but I will correct all of this misunderstanding now." I started walking away when I heard her footsteps, slow and deliberate behind me.

"You will do no such thing," she said.

It was not customary for her to be speaking to me like this, and I was not in the frame of mind to tolerate it. "What did you say?" I turned and asked her.

"You won't want to tell your father about this wedding not happening, not if you don't want him to find out about your human." She was playing coyly with her fingers, as if what she had just said was not enough to warrant disintegration.

"What have you done with her?" I asked as I took two steps back to her.

"Nothing…yet," she teased. "And I won't do anything to her as long as you do as I ask. I will be your queen, or she dies. And maybe you, too."

"Nala, I swear if any harm comes to her, no one will be able to tell the difference between your body and the sands of the desert," I gritted out through my teeth. "Where is she?"

"She is safe," she replied as she continued playing games with me she could not win. Though, in my current predicament, victory was not in view.

I reached out and grabbed her by the shoulders, sinking my fingers so deep into her collar she buckled under the pressure. "I am not going to marry you. I will never marry you. Not even if my father agrees again." I pierced her eyes with my own until hers grew glossy before I released the pressure on her. Then I let her go and walked off, heading to the steps instead of the banquet chamber.

It was not the first time Nala Styx had tried to ensnare me. Years ago, and before I had the sense to know better, I had been in her company when a group of mutual friends had decided to sneak into the desert for an unapproved party. I had overly imbibed, and Nala had taken advantage of it. The next thing I knew, I was being told by her brother, though he wasn't the commander at the time, that I had lain with her and she was bearing my child. A wedding was arranged, even though I had not imprinted on her. But as was our custom, it was the right thing to do. That was until I found out there was no such child. I chased her away then, and her brother had tried to counsel my father against my actions. Now she was here, thirty years later, rehashing the same plot. I would not be so deceived again.

"Your father is expecting you for lunch," she shouted after me.

"Tell him I lost my appetite," I shouted back and bounded down the stairs. I got to the hovercraft in my parking bay much faster than it had taken me to get to the Great Pike.

My father lived there, with the members of the Tribunal, and he desperately wanted an heir to take his place, an heir who came with a wife. Any wife.

I was just mounting the hovercraft when I saw Brom and Gideon approaching. Brom gave me a curious stare, and I knew he was wondering about my meeting with my father.

"Sekkol, Commander Styx—" Gideon started saying.

"I will hear nothing of Styx at the moment," I interjected. "Brom, he has the human girl, and I need to get her back. Come."

"What human girl? What are you talking about?" Gideon asked.

Only Brom had been privy to my actions, but right now, the Enforcers needed to be kept up to speed. I would need all the help I could get rescuing Keira from Styx. And I had no doubts she was holed up in his dungeon beneath his diamond home.

"There is a human girl that belongs to me. She was taken by Styx, and now we need to get her back before my father gains knowledge of her," I told the men.

This time, they both looked at me in horror. "But…sir, Sekkol, we can't just go to Commander Styx's home and retrieve her," Brom stuttered.

"What will your father say when he finds out you have a human?" Gideon asked.

"Which is why we need to get her out right away," I told them.

"And then what?" Gideon pressed. "What will you do with her if you can't take her home?"

I paused, the answer not yet known to me. "I don't know," I admitted. "But she can't remain there with me."

Maybe there was something in my voice when I spoke, but after I did, Gideon, who had already imprinted on a woman from Anon, saw the same in me. "You imprinted on her," his voice drawled.

I sighed and turned my back to them. "I do not understand why, nor did I know it was even possible, but yes, I imprinted on her. I can feel her fear, I can imagine the fright in her eyes, and I can see her cowering under him as he strikes her down. She cannot remain there."

"But, Sekkol, won't the guards come for you if you go for her?" Brom asked.

"They might," I replied. I could feel the weight of Jupiter resting on my shoulders, but nothing else was clearer to me at that moment than the need to free her. "It is a chance I will have to take."

"Sekkol, I completely understand what it means to imprint on someone, and I will help you in any way I can," Gideon added. "Maybe she would be safe if you get her to the desert of Epoch. I have family there who would help hide her until you decide what to do."

I stood there with my back turned, looking at my home. If I took her, I might not see it for a long time. And there was no guarantee I would be with her.

I heaved an exasperated sigh and turned to the men. "Let's do it," I told them and hopped onto my hovercraft.

CHAPTER 14
KEIRA

I didn't realize how easy it was to sweat inside a diamond; it was ironic to me, given its cool appearance. I was being held in a room downstairs, a padded room that reminded me of mental health hospitals. I was sitting on the ground with my back against the wall and wiping the sweat beads off as they popped up on my face. I had just begun fanning my face with my hands when the door opened and Nala stormed in.

"Get up, Earth woman," she commanded, though she did not wait for me to do so. She came over, grabbed me by the hair, and tugged me off my ass.

I grabbed her hand and squeezed into it, forcing her to release me. Her eyes were inflamed, and she flung daggers at me, twisting her body as she prepared to slap me.

Not this time. I held up my other hand and blocked her blow and then shoved her backward. She stumbled, and by the time she regained her balance, I was on top of her. But she was stronger than I had anticipated; she pressed into my shoulder, and I fell on my ass. I felt her hand cover my face as her bony fingers searched for my eyes. She was filled with fury and rage, and she snarled, like she had cornered her prey.

"Get off me," I cried and twisted my body.

Her hands still gripped my face, and I clawed at her until I was able to pry her hands away. I felt the fear creeping inside me that I could die right there, and Sekkol's image flashed before my eyes. I panicked even more when I acknowledged, in my moment of near death, it was the face of the alien cop that appeared to me.

She stopped then, backed off, and stood, panting and heaving as she wiped the telltale signs of her rage from her lips. "He would have you and not me?" she asked in wonderment.

"What's the big deal?" I asked as I got to my feet. "Get someone else. I've seen plenty of other aliens around." I was bent over, my hands resting on my knees, breathing hard like I had just crossed the finish line after running a marathon.

"You don't get it, Earth woman. Sekkol is heir to Lord Magnus, ruler of Jupiter. If he takes me as his wife, then I…"

"Will be queen," I said for her. And it was then I understood.

"Yes," she replied. "I would be queen."

"But doesn't Sekkol work for your…the commander?" I asked. There were still a few things that had not come together just yet.

"Sekkol works for no one but himself," she spat and wiped her mouth again. "Jared is the commander, but only because Sekkol didn't want the office."

I started laughing when I saw the full picture, despite the burning sensation on my face where she had scratched me. The commander disliked Sekkol simply because he was not his better, and Sekkol was clearly refusing the commander's sister as his wife. And he had chosen a human instead.

"I don't understand why you laugh," she said. "Whether he chooses me or not, you die." And with that, she hit a panel in the wall and withdrew a conical device. She pointed it at me and sneered. "Let's see who laughs now."

"Wait!" I shouted and held my hands up. "What if I talk to him?" I shrugged my shoulder, hoping to appeal to her logic. I could see why she would never catch his eye, and I didn't plan on dying just to soothe a jealous alien's ego. She stood there watching me and waiting for the explanation. "Sekkol doesn't want to marry me, so he is still fair game."

"What does that mean, fair game?" she asked, squinting her eyes. "He has never been hunted."

"It means he is still available because he and I are nothing. So if I could just get the chance to talk to him and plead your case, then maybe he would agree to this marriage proposal you speak of."

"Do you take me for a fool?" the woman asked as she bore down on me. "I was just at the Great Pike, telling his father that he had imprinted on me, thinking that would have made a difference. Do you know what he did?"

No, of course, I don't know what he did. And what is this imprinting thing?

"He walked away," she snarled. "And that's because of you. I will not have my future in ruins because of one earthling woman."

She brought her hand up, the device high in the air, and her eyes glowed red as she brought it back down. I dodged and swung to my left, and it hit the ground and charred it. I staggered, the blood rushing to my ears and my eyes scouring the room for something, anything, that would act as a defense. There was nothing, but I was not going down without a fight.

She charged into me, and just as we got entangled and my hands found her thinning wisps of hair, the door opened and the commander walked in.

"What is going on?" he shouted, immediately rushing to pull us apart.

I was heaving, and my hair was askew. I slapped the pieces away that dangled before my eyes. "Get this psycho away from me," I answered while keeping my eyes on her.

"Nala, what is the matter? I thought you went over to the Great Pike to see Lord Magnus."

"I did," she snarled again. "Sekkol came and all but spat in my face."

"I don't understand. Didn't you tell Lord Magnus he had imprinted?"

"I did. He summoned Sekkol, and when he came and got wind of the story, he stormed out without even a word to his father."

"Hmm," the commander growled and looked at me as if I were to be blamed for that, too.

"I have a solution," I quipped, and they both stared at me like I was rude to speak. I had been getting that a lot since I'd arrived on this planet. I had the feeling they thought their kind was better than the humans, but their behavior had shown them to be lesser beings. "Just send me the fuck home. I want to go back to Earth, and then you and she and Sekkol can work out your problems. I won't be a part of it any longer."

The commander walked over to me and gripped me by the face. I held on to his hand, but my strength was no match to his. "Do you think Sekkol would allow that? He bought you for a reason, and if we were to send you…" He paused and turned to his sister, a sinister look clouding his face. "Then again, that may not be such a bad idea. We can take her back to Jonas so she can be sold again."

"No. No!" I shouted as I remembered all too well the horror of the cave when I had arrived. Jonas had been the one to receive us when we got to Jupiter, and we were chained and held like criminals, barely fed, and allowed little sleep. "Don't send me back there."

"Oh, the poor little thing doesn't want to go back," Nala drawled as she sashayed over, smoothing her hair to the back of her head as she did. "We will send you back, and if Sekkol tries to take you, Lord Magnus will hear of his treason."

"I don't understand," I pleaded. These two were like gutter rats, scavenging off the nobles in a bid to climb the social ladder, and I was fast learning they had no conscience to appeal to. But I had to try. "What is this treason?" Maybe if I kept them talking long enough, it would give Sekkol, or Brom, enough time to figure out I was being held here. She did say she had mentioned me to Sekkol, so I could only hope he would risk saving me. He was my only hope now.

"Sekkol isn't supposed to be with an earthling," Nala explained. "None of us is, but he is held especially accountable, being the heir to Lord Magnus. I couldn't imagine being the subject of an Earth queen," she said with such disdain it contorted her features.

"All the more reason to send me home," I told them. "I'll be gone, and Sekkol will be with you, or whomever."

"If he wants you, he will have you, and I can't have that," she replied. "Come, Jared, let's take her to Jonas before Sekkol figures out she is here."

The commander pushed me toward the door, and I stubbed my toe when I missed the first step. I grabbed onto the metal handrail while Nala pushed me on the back, urging me on. I didn't want to think about the life I would meet if I wound up being the slave to someone like the commander and his maniac of a sister. Maybe Brom would be a better master. I certainly had been living it up being at Sekkol's house.

But if he knew the trouble he would get into by having me there, why did he buy me at the auction? Why did he keep me at his home? What did he really want with me?

The questions ran amok in my mind, but I was hurled back to reality when we got to the landing and I fell to the ground.

"Nala, get the hovercraft around to the front," the commander told her, and she hurried off. I reluctantly rose to my feet, not certain which fate was worse: remaining with them—the devil I knew—or with another owner who potentially could be worse.

I didn't get the chance to decide. He came over and sank his talons into my shoulder, and I let out a screech when I felt them piercing my flesh. I could feel the spot burning now, and I glanced over just in time to see fresh blood begin to appear. I staggered to the door with him as he hit the panel and the opening appeared. He shoved me through, and we waited for Nala to return.

I could hardly face my impending doom, and I stood there, remembering my parents and the crash and the solitude of a life that had followed. For a fleeting moment, I thought it might have been better if I had died with them, for I had experienced no quality of life since they had gone. And now to die in a strange way, in a strange place, was sort of an anticlimax.

I was still brooding when I saw the hovercraft come around the side of the building and felt the commander's hold on me tighten. He started down the steps, pulling me behind him, and I tripped a few times before I got to the bottom. He brought me around to his front as the hovercraft settled lower, and for the first time since I had arrived on Jupiter, I felt relief when I saw it was Sekkol.

CHAPTER 15
SEKKOL

It seemed we got to the commander's home just in time to see him pulling Keira outside. I hit the descend button just a few yards from where he stood and then hopped off. Brom and Gideon did the same, and we stood before him now, blocking his path.

"Don't even think about it," I said as I moved closer to him. He had been reaching inside his waist to retrieve his communication device.

"Sekkol, stand down," the commander growled and bared his teeth like an animal.

"I will not let you take her," I replied. "She is mine." I could feel the blood rushing inside of me, driving me to madness. I could hardly believe anything that was happening, and I knew very well the consequences of my actions. But I felt my choice had been stripped from me, and I was only left with the desire to protect her at the expense of my existence.

"You know that if…*when* Lord Magnus hears about this, he will have no choice but to punish you, his only son, for this act of treason," he said, perhaps as a way of intimidating me, for he now wore an evil grin that was slowly spreading all the way across his face.

"I won't say it again," I said and pulled my device from my waist. "Hand her over to me."

"Or what?" he barked and then looked to his right when Nala's hovercraft came into view. He pulled Keira back and wrapped his arm around her neck as she struggled against his weight. She pleaded with me with her eyes, and something inside me cried out.

I was not about to watch him take her away, nor did I have any intentions of facing my father and his wretched Tribunal either. I stepped closer, and my blue laser shot out and aimed at his head. I saw Brom and Gideon come up on either side of me, their weapons already raised, too.

"Back down, Enforcers," Styx barked and staggered back as he went closer to Nala, who was poised at the edge of the craft, baring her teeth. "I am your commander, and you must obey me."

I saw them glance at me for a brief second before turning back to their commander. I saw him look at Nala, and then, as if in silent communication, he grabbed Keira and hoisted her where Nala was supposed to grab her into the hovercraft and take her away.

"Brom, get her!" I shouted as I started running toward Styx. The commander tossed Keira, who landed halfway onto the craft. She dangled by her legs as it prepared to move away. Brom was just in time to block Nala from moving. He settled beneath Keira and pulled her back down and onto his hovercraft. I realized she was not in as much danger anymore and fully focused my attention on the commander.

He had backed away and had his device to his lips now. He stashed it just as I turned around, but I knew that meant we didn't have much time to make our escape before the armed guards were upon us.

"Gideon," I called, and the man raced with me to the hovercraft. Styx was wearing a scowl and watching the skies, and I knew it was time to go. "Come on," I told them as I joined Gideon on his hover-craft. I urged Brom forward as we took up the rear, all the while watching for any signs of an attack.

It wasn't until we were halfway across the city that we saw a few black specks in the distance.

"Here they come," Gideon said.

"Make the switch," I told Brom, and he slowed so we could pull up alongside him. He stood and hopped onto the craft while I took my place before Keira. I looked behind and noticed what seemed like the entire fleet of guards chasing us.

"Sekkol, do we engage them?" Gideon asked.

"Fire at will," I told them and armed my craft as I responded. They would not relent, and neither would we.

Brom looked back while Gideon controlled the wheels and aimed at the nearing vessels. The fast-approaching hovercrafts whizzed between and around the buildings as they tried to escape getting hit.

I felt Keira's hold on me tighten as I swerved and faced my craft around. I started firing at my attackers, the same men I had been working with not so long ago, and watched as some of them lost control and collided into the sides of the glass buildings. One burst into flames and bounced and rolled along the sides until it crashed into the street below.

"Sekkol, we cannot defeat them all like this," Brom said over the communications device. "I need to create a diversion and get you away from the city."

I looked back at them and instantly swerved, a laser narrowly escaping me. It hit the glass to my right and sent shards flying. I heard when Keira cried out, and I glanced around to see her clutching her arm. "Okay," I said to Brom. "I will lead them into a loop close to the tunnels, and you go around. I will lose them on the other side, and you can take it from there."

"Copy that," Brom replied.

"Hold on," I told her, hinting at the fact that she could not cling to her arm any longer, despite how hurt she was.

She clutched me around the middle as I lowered my head and shot forward. The buildings were a blur as we hurtled past, and I was acutely aware of her fright as she dug into me and buried her head against my back. The tunnels were coming up close, and I looked behind for a fleeting moment, long enough to see Brom and Gideon a little way back and farther above. They were firing at the oncoming vessels still and spinning around and sideways as they dodged the lasers being fired at them.

I got to the tunnels and hit a button on my hovercraft. An entrance opened, and I popped inside, and it closed around me as I did. I slowed the gear and waited as I tried to detect Brom and Gideon. Their signals were visible and moving fast as I saw them fly past the hidden door. I slowly restarted the engine and cruised through the narrow tunnel, the lighting barely bright enough to see.

Keira was still flattened to my back, and her fingers seemed to have merged with the fabric of my clothing. I could feel her heart beating rapidly against my own skin.

"Are you all right?" I asked her as I got to the other end and shut the engine down. Styx could easily read my signal from his main control; I needed to get another hovercraft.

"Hmm," she groaned and didn't attempt to move.

"We need to go," I told her as I slowly pried her hands away. I hopped off and helped her down. She wobbled as she walked, the fire I had come to expect from her temporarily banked. "This is a little secret place I keep that I've never had a use for before now." I held her hand as I led her along, very conscious of the softness of it.

"Why are you doing this?" She tugged on my arm, pulling me to a stop.

"This is not the time," I replied and attempted to walk off again.

"No!" she cried. "This is exactly the time."

I stopped, held my head down, and sighed. "I promise I will answer your questions, but right now, we need to go," I said to her. I looked at her, the fright and panic still remarkably visible on her face, but she didn't persist. For once. I turned again, and this time, she followed me silently. *Humans are such complicated things.*

I got to a door and searched for the panel along the wall. The screen shot out, and I traced my fingers on it as I made a pattern. Then there was a whooshing sound as mist escaped from beneath, just after the door cracked open. I pressed my hand against the wall and pushed it to the side. I stepped in and looked back at her, ushering her inside just before the doors slid shut again.

"Welcome, Master Sekkol."

"I don't have much time, Sari," I told my automated companion and instantly started combing the place for what I needed. "I need food and medical supplies. And is the hovercraft suited for travel?"

"The hovercraft is fully functional, sir. What kind of supplies are needed?"

"Anything that can last me a few days away from home," I replied and went to the back of the room where I could find the pod containing the hovercraft I kept in case of an emergency. I had never used it before.

"You have everything here that can last you several months."

"I can't stay here, Sari. My father knows of this place," I said and looked back to Keira. She was standing there in awe, or perhaps fright still, her hand clamped over the spot where she had suffered a bruise earlier. Her hair was a tangled mess, and she turned about in confusion as Sari spoke. There was much I needed to tell Keira, but I didn't think eternity was long enough to explain.

"Very well, sir. Proceed to the bay area where you will find all you need. And, sir?"

"Yes, Sari," I answered her.

"Please be safe. My sensors detect elevated levels of endorphins."

I smiled after she spoke. At least she didn't detect any injuries. "Thanks, Sari," I replied and went to the section of the room she had indicated. Soon enough, the wall opened, and a trolley rolled out containing food items, water, and medical supplies. "Help me with these," I told Keira as I began to lift them off the trolley.

She slowly came over and started to help, and we quickly gathered the things and brought them to the hovercraft. I opened the storage unit, hastily packed them inside, and then lifted her onto the seat.

"Sari, open the door," I told her and jumped into the driver's seat. The door eased open, and I tapped the screen to fire up the engine. Slowly, it purred to life, sputtered, and whirred for a few seconds, and then the lights came on. The hovercraft buzzed beneath us, and I guided it to the door.

"Sari, seal the room," I commanded.

"Request confirmed. Powering down."

The craft just barely made it out before the doors sealed shut behind us. I cruised to the other end of the tunnel and edged the craft above it on the other side. There was no battle in the sky any longer or any craft hovering above.

"Where are you going?" she asked me.

"To the desert of Epoch," I answered her. "We should be safe there for a while." I was not capable of truthfully replying to any further questions; they were all answers I did not know and longed to be enlightened about. I had never been away from my home, not for an extended period of time. And I did not know for how long I would be gone. Only one thing had been made clear: I needed to go. *We* needed to go.

She said nothing else as she wrapped her arms around me, and I guided the hovercraft out of the city. We traversed the city of Anon and then crossed over into Bulova, from where the commander and his family originated. The lands were mostly made of jagged stones and rough sands; I did not expect to encounter many life-forms during the daytime. However, I kept the vessel high enough to remain undetected as we jetted past the prison on the outskirts of civilization before we entered the barren lands of the desert.

We had ridden for a considerable time before I saw the mountain I had envisioned. It was made of granite and would serve as adequate shelter and protection from the glaring sun. An opening appeared on the far side of it, and I easily guided the craft inside. Keira remained on the hovercraft while I looked around and secured the place. When I returned, she was already on the ground and tracing her hands along the smooth walls that were cool to the touch.

"This is beautiful," she said and sounded almost as if in a trance. I wondered if the heat had made her delirious, and I stepped closer to have a look at her. She turned away and hugged herself as she backed into the wall. I paused in my stride, and being aware of her protective stance, I hopped onto the hovercraft again and positioned it at the entrance of the cave, where it would act as some sort of shield and also be ready for sudden flight.

Then I fell against the wall of the cave and slid to the floor in exhaustion. I hadn't even realized how tired I was until that moment. I closed my eyes for a few seconds, and when I opened them again, she was standing before me.

"Thank you...for coming for me," she said and sat next to me.

And for the first time, I saw her smile, and my face mirrored hers.

CHAPTER 16
SEKKOL

I wasn't aware I had fallen asleep or for how long. But when I opened my eyes again, her head was resting on my shoulder and she was deep in slumber, too. I could hear her breathing, and it came out sounding like a gentle wind. The rest of my hand that she was resting on was cramping, but I didn't want to move it and disturb her. So I remained still while it grew numb, until she turned and her head rolled onto my lap. She flew up then, her large brown eyes searching the space until they landed on me. She made a start and sat upright, seemingly conscious of being too close to me. She hugged herself and pulled her legs under her, appearing every bit the frightened animal.

"What time is it?" she asked.

I looked outside and saw the sun had already kissed the mountaintop and was slowly making its descent west. "Late in the evening," I replied and rested my head against the granite wall.

"So..." she drawled as she searched for something to say. "What now?" She yawned and rubbed the sleep from her eyes.

I sat there looking at her, marveling at her beauty and innocence, and I could see nothing wrong in what I had done. I reached out and took one of her black curls in my hand, coiling it around my finger. I was staring at the black loop when she turned, and without thinking, I leaned in and kissed her. This time, she didn't pull back. She remained still while I ran my tongue over her lips and then slipped it in her mouth. Her lips were warm and soft, not as cold and wet as the women I'd known. And with her smell, she reeled me in, ensnaring me with her delicious aroma, and I found it hard to maintain control.

I twisted my body and used my left hand to cup her face as I got lost in her kiss. When her mouth moved in response to mine, my heartbeat quickened. My hand slid down her arm, and I jumped when I heard her yelp. Then I noticed the bruise from the glass that had reddened her skin, and I leaned forward and kissed the spot. When I looked up, she was smiling, and I smoothed my hand over her face and pulled her back to me.

Our lips collided, and where there was abrasion before, there was now the welcome softness of her lips and the patient touch of her hand as it fell on my own. My hands moved to her sides, and I gripped her flesh through the thin fabric of the suit she wore. She moved against me, and I could feel the heat transferring between us. With our lips still locked, I traced my hand over the swelling on her chest and then clenched my fingers, covering it within my palms. Her breasts were firm yet soft and seemed to melt under my touch. I felt her move then, and her breathing got ragged as I opened and closed my palms around her breasts.

I unfastened the clasps to her suit that began at her throat and watched as they popped open right to her chest. I glided my hands inside and quivered when I felt her warmth seeping through me. I lowered my head and caught her in my mouth and suckled her breast. I had never been with a human before her, and something about the experience was exquisite. Her skin was beautiful and strangely different from everything else I'd seen on Jupiter or among the other humans I'd noticed before. It was similar to the others who had skin that looked like the sand when the sun caught it, but different still. Hers resembled what the desert would look like at sunset or if the sands got wet, a deeper shade of what was already beautiful.

She was moving under me now, making funny sounds and gripping my hair. I wondered if that was a natural human reaction, and though it felt painful at first, I didn't make a sound. She pressed my head down onto her breast even more, as if begging me to continue, and I circled my tongue around the peak and sucked the dark areas around it. She was trembling as I released the other and did the same.

She was intoxicating to me, and the blood rushed to my head the longer I played with her. I checked upward for her reaction, and seeing that her eyes were closed and her head tilted back, I slid the rest of her clothes to the cave floor. I stood and took my clothing off as well and made a bed with them before guiding her onto them. Her eyes moved over me, and she bit her lips. Something about the act sent shivers down my back, and I felt my member grow in response.

I knelt next to her, admiring how her body curved. I ran my hand along the contours of her figure and began kissing from her neck to the patch of curls that beckoned me. Even the curls there were soft, and I ran my fingers through them, feeling the hardened nub that lay in the middle. I rubbed it with my thumb and watched as her legs moved and she began making sounds again.

She touched my hand and arched her back, and I could hold it in no longer. The pain from my erection was growing, and I needed some release. I parted her legs and gazed at the soft pink opening that invited me in. I answered the call and guided my manhood into her tight entrance. I quaked as I felt her walls close in on me, and I sank my nails into her hips as she cried out.

I stopped, thinking I had hurt her.

"No," she told me as she clawed at my chest. "Don't stop."

My mind registered her request deeper than her words, and in an instant, I was driving in and out of her like mad. Her body was warm all over, and the longer I remained in her, the more I realized that was the heart of the furnace. She burned hot there, and my body responded in ways I never thought possible. I stroked hard and fast now, responding to her cries and pleas to continue, and I could feel myself growing dizzy from it. Then she locked her legs around me, forcing me even deeper within her, and I, feeling the sensation rushing to the tip of my manhood, pulled back so I could preserve the emotion a little while longer.

She lay there looking at me like I had done something wrong. Then she looked down at my erection and smiled when she realized I was not done like she had possibly thought. She turned on the ground so she was on her hands and knees, and I could still see her entrance from that angle.

I rose and touched her posterior and watched as her upper body lowered as she waited for me. I inserted myself into her once more and lost control when I heard her cries begin again. I pumped into her, hard and fast, marveling at this new way, this human way, of consummation.

Her body rocked as she matched my motions, and she began slamming herself into me. I remained still and watched her, and when I could no longer do so, I gripped her around the middle and buried myself within her. All of me. She took me in and charred me with her heat, and when I felt hot liquid washing over me and felt her tremble in its wake, my own body recreated her actions and the liquid rushed up to the surface once more. My cries were deafening as it burst from me, and I emptied myself into her. I did not have the strength this time to hold back, and when it was done and my legs started to tremble, I collapsed onto the floor of the cave and welcomed the cool feeling it brought.

She remained on the clothing while I tried to regain the proper usage of my lungs. When I looked over, she was still breathing hard and surveying me. Then she got up, got dressed once more, and handed me my clothes so I could do the same.

"Not bad for an alien," she said as she sat on the ground once more.

"You don't have to keep calling me that, human," I replied and smiled. I tugged on the rest of my suit and sat across from her in the cave as I waited for my body to adjust to its normal temperature.

"Fair enough," she replied, brushing a few strands of her hair from her face. She looked toward the mouth of the cave for a considerable time, until she turned back to me. "Why did you risk so much for me?"

And then it was my turn to gaze into the nothingness outside the cave. I wasn't sure I had an answer for that, and I thought I should begin with my bare honesty. "I don't know," I eventually told her.

"Is it true?" She continued, "You aren't supposed to be with a human?"

"Where did you hear that?" I was curious as to how she had come by that knowledge when she had been in my presence for the majority of the time she had been on Jupiter.

"Nala said something like that… That it is treasonous for your kind to take on a human as a mate or companion or whatever you call it," she replied. "And then I keep hearing this word 'imprinting.' What is that?" It wasn't just her eyes; her entire face questioned me as she knitted her brows and stared into my eyes as she waited for clarity she hoped I could provide.

I heaved an exasperated sigh and then stared at the cave floor. "It is true," I finally managed to say. "We can take you as slaves, but not as partners."

"And…?" she prompted after I spoke.

"What?" I asked, not sure what she wanted me to say or do.

"That imprinting thing… What's that about?" she asked me again.

"Here, with my people, we imprint. We meet one person whom our soul connects with, and that person takes you over and you spend the rest of your life with them. Usually, it happens only once, and we have no control over it." I got up then and went over to the hovercraft as I tried to make sense of it still.

"Oh," she replied. "And you… But if you have no control, how can they punish you for it?" She got up then, too, and walked over to me. "Back home, we were able to choose anyone and for any length of time. Some people believe in true love and love at first sight, but not me. I haven't had many boyfriends, but still, if I wanted to have one, then—"

"This is not Earth!" I shouted at her. "We don't get to choose." I was growing impatient with her questions, and I no longer wanted to continue the conversation. Everything that was happening was strange to me, and I didn't need her in my head confusing things anymore.

"Fine." She huffed and stomped off to the spot she was sitting in before.

That was just fine with me. I started rummaging in the storage unit for the medical supplies and some water. "You need to get a wrap for that arm," I told her.

"I'll live," she shot back.

I was finding it hard to believe the females of Earth were always this mouthy, and I wondered how the males would have handled it. I shook my head and tossed a bottle of water to her. She caught it instinctively and then pouted at me.

"At least have the sense to hydrate," I said, and she placed it at her side, ever the rebel. I was looking through the contents when I paused; I thought I had heard a noise.

"You know, if this is the way you intend to treat me, then—"

"Shh." I interrupted her.

"Don't tell me to shh," she retaliated.

"Stop and listen!" I shouted, and then she obeyed. Her eyes lifted upward as she too listened.

"What is that?" she asked.

I wasn't sure, but it sounded like an incoming vessel. Who could have known about this place? I fished around inside the craft, pulled out my laser, and crept to the mouth of the cave. "Stay there," I told her when I saw her advancing, too.

I got to the entrance and pressed my back against the wall. The sound was getting closer, and I thought I might have a better chance of defending myself if I were on the hovercraft rather than trapped in the cave.

"Get on," I whispered to her and motioned to the hovercraft. She crept to it and got into the passenger seat. I was just hurrying back to it when the vessel outside came within view, and I saw it was Gideon.

"Gideon?" I called and then looked back protectively at Keira.

"Sekkol," he said, and the sound of relief was evident. He got the craft closer to the cave and hopped off. "I've been looking all over for you."

"Why?" I asked. "What's the matter?"

"Why didn't you go to my family?" Gideon asked.

"I thought about it, but I didn't want to involve anyone else. What is the problem? I know you didn't come all this way to check on my well-being." I could tell something was eating at him, and I needed him to assuage all the fear that was slowly building up inside me.

"It's Brom," he began.

"What about Brom?" I asked right away, eager for the news.

"We got hit after you entered the tunnel. Commander Styx picked him up, and now they have declared they will disintegrate him for aiding in your treason unless you return to answer to the charges." His gray eyes beamed at me, but they offered no respite.

"So my father knows of this?" I asked in defeat. I knew he would in a matter of time, just not quite so soon and before I knew how to handle things.

"Yes, the commander has informed him of everything, including the harm to the other guards who were chasing us," Gideon said. "Brom told me not to come and to tell you to stay away. But...I thought you should know," he hastened to add.

"You were right to come, Gideon," I assured and patted the man on the back. "Even if I didn't go back, they wouldn't stop searching, and Brom would have died in vain." I folded my arms behind me and stared out at the sky that was slowly turning black.

By this time, Keira had come up behind me and overheard the conversation. Her brown eyes widened in horror when she realized the gravity of the situation.

"Can they do that?" she asked. "To Brom?"

"They have done it for less," I told her.

"But they don't have to know," she pleaded and flew before me. "Sekkol, I can always tell them I was your slave. They don't have to know anything else."

"And what would happen to you?" I asked her. "They would have you fried or disintegrated, too. Or worse, sold to the people of Bulova."

"But you have power, don't you?" she pressed. "You must make them understand."

"It is no use, human!" I thundered as the weight of the situation pressed upon me. Then I sighed and looked at her, already regretting that I was falling back on my promise not to call her that. "Keira, it is much more complicated than that."

There was a long and uncomfortable silence after that, and I watched as the tears formed in her eyes just before she turned away.

"What are you going to do?" Gideon asked, his voice low and rife with sympathy.

I touched her arm, but she shrugged me off. I could hardly blame her. Our futures hung in the balance, and I was as much a victim of it as she was. But the choice had already been taken from me, and though she pleaded with me with her eyes, there was only one thing that could be done.

"I have to go back," I said and then turned away from her as I looked toward the city of Anon, the city I had known as my home for over ninety years, and that would likely be my ruin.

CHAPTER 17
SEKKOL

Everything over the last couple of weeks was a blur. It felt like only hours since I had seen her walking through the crowd of humans that had just arrived on Jupiter. I had felt an instant connection, and despite the stringent laws banning any mating with the humans, I had been unable to withstand the pull. Now, I had been forced to make the desert my refuge, until I was told Brom had been captured and would be killed unless I returned to face my punishment.

The wind slapped against my face as the hovercraft glided over the sandy plain. The sun was barely visible, its yellow light creeping over the dark land and racing to Anon even faster than me, but the heat it brought with it was already seeping under my clothes. My skin felt clammy, but that was the least of my problems. The noise in my head was getting louder the closer I got, and it didn't make matters any better that she was right there, clinging to my middle.

"Sekkol, this doesn't make any sense," she said.

She just didn't understand. Our laws on Jupiter were final and irrevocable. There was no fighting it. I would be found guilty of transgressing them, even though this was my first offense. But my people, including me, had never shown great tolerance for rebellion, and we punished severely for the slightest offense.

"Keira, I have no choice," I told her. "This situation has nothing to do with Brom. I can't leave him there to suffer the consequences of my actions."

"But maybe you can find another way to get him out of there without turning yourself in." She continued. "Maybe your friend can—"

"It is no use!" I shouted at her. "It is done."

"It is not done," she retaliated, as she was prone to do. She had proven herself a formidable rebel, always challenging my every word ever since the day we first spoke. But it was that defiance that kept me interested in her, though it was beginning to annoy me now.

"She may have a point." Gideon's voice came through the speaker on my hovercraft. It was a feature we often used when we went on patrol, to make communication easier. I had forgotten it was still active until I heard his voice and realized he had been listening in.

No one had known what Keira meant to me until Gideon had figured it out when the commander had come to take her away. He had been instrumental in our escape, which had lasted but a short time.

"What point?" I asked as I gritted my teeth. The wind stirred and caused the sand to gently lift from the desert floor as it swirled around us.

"If you go back, there is no guarantee they will even release Brom. You could wind up signing a death sentence for him, for her, and yourself," Gideon said.

He was right. I could not, under any circumstances, guarantee what would happen when I got back, except Keira would be taken away and I would still be accosted.

I slowed the hovercraft, a million thoughts coursing through my mind. I couldn't stay in the cave forever, nor could I go back home. My father, even as the Supreme Ruler of Jupiter, and I, his heir, would be powerless to stop any action deemed necessary by the Tribunal, the tripartite membership that determined the fate of the guilty brought before it. Any action he wrought against their decision would compromise the very foundations of the legal system generations before had instituted. There was no scenario where I didn't qualify as being guilty.

"I may have a solution," Gideon suggested after my prolonged silence. His cruiser was bobbing next to mine, and he waited for me to acknowledge what he had said before he continued.

"What would that be?" I asked and heaved an exasperated sigh. I was tired, bone-deep tired, and there was no rest lingering on the horizon.

"Like I told you before, I have family near here. I could take her to them so at least she could be safe. I don't think Lord Magnus will allow his only son to be disintegrated for one indiscretion. They won't even be able to prove what they are accusing you of unless you show up with the evidence," he said as he pleaded with me. One would assume, just by listening, that it was his neck on the line.

"What he says is true," she said from behind me as she leaned sideways to get a look at my face. "If I go back, that's it. They will take me to God knows where. So, short of killing me yourself, I agree with him."

I had to admit the feasibility of Gideon's suggestion. No one knew for certain what she was doing at my house or what she meant to me. Except my father. He had been able to detect it from the very beginning. But how would I be able to look at him now and deny her importance to me? Still, I couldn't very well turn up with her; I would lose her.

"Take me to your family," I said to Gideon and watched as he nodded and turned his hovercraft around.

We passed the cave that had acted as our temporary home and continued in a westerly direction until we were able to see the small community Gideon mentioned. It was a few miles south of Castor, one of the five major cities on Jupiter, and would not be a place they might think to look. I hoped. I couldn't deny the level of anxiety I was feeling. It was something completely unfamiliar to me. And I still had not found a permanent solution. I had a pretty good idea what the scene would resemble when I walked into Anon, and I was not prepared for it. This would be the first time I was caught on the erring side of the law.

"This is it," Gideon said as we dipped and flew past the cluster of houses. They were different from the ones in Anon, and instead of the glass and metal that dominated my home, this community was predominantly hard plastic. This type of material was best suited to the heat and cold that was associated with living in the desert.

Gideon stopped at a door on a cluster of attached homes, the only thing making it distinguishable from the other doors being a circular insignia molded into the plastic. The other doors I could see had different shapes and symbols, representing the different families. He hopped off and pounded on the door a few times, while we waited for someone to answer.

I felt Keira's hands tighten around me, and I could feel the fear emanating from her, with my body acting like a conductor for it. But instead of passing through me, it remained inside, and my body made her fear its own. I absorbed her trepidation, and like magic, I felt her breathing subdue like a calm had come over her.

The effects of imprinting were new to me, and I had no idea what it did to a person. I knew I had to protect her, but some of the other things came on suddenly and strangely, and I could never tell what would happen next. Except it would be something that drove my behavior and controlled my emotions. I would do anything for her, could *only* do anything for her, for my heart and my mind would allow nothing else. She consumed me, and like fire burning through me, charring everything in its wake, it devoured me.

My hand moved involuntarily and touched her hand that was still wrapped around my middle. I felt her fingers twitch then lock around mine, and I warmed on the inside as I embraced this feeling that was so novel to me. Having her close gave me some level of strength, some sort of masculine prowess I hoped would last for the time I needed it. I reluctantly untangled her fingers from my own and jumped from the hovercraft before helping her down. She stood next to me as we waited for someone to answer Gideon's knocking.

The door opened, and a woman stood in the entrance.

"Mother," Gideon said and pulled her into an embrace. She returned the act, her eyes riveted on us even as she did.

"Son, what are you doing here?" she asked as she pulled away.

"I need your help," he told her and looked back at us. "Would you mind if we came inside?"

"Sure, sure," she said as she stood aside.

The woman remained at the door as we passed, her eyes mainly on Keira. She closed it after Gideon, and we stood, like children, as we waited for the verdict. She would, after all, need to give her permission.

"What's the matter?" she asked as she indicated the blue-green cushioned slats used for seating in the center of the room.

The home was a colorful one, not like the white interior of mine. The walls were a soft shade of yellow and gave the room a welcomed level of warmth and hospitality. It was a handsome place, and I wondered then if all the other homes were this aesthetically pleasing.

"This is Sekkol—" Gideon started.

"I know who he is," she said, stopping Gideon. "I recognized him the minute I saw him. You've been doing a good job with those vagrants who keep trying to defile the system."

"Thank you," I replied, even though I wasn't sure if I deserved her praise at the moment.

"My son has the greatest amount of respect for you." She beamed. "Can I get you anything to drink?" she asked without missing a beat.

"That won't be necessary," I told her. "I have to leave soon."

"But you just got here," she said. I got the impression she didn't have company often and was grateful for the little she was getting now.

"Mother, I have a favor to ask of you." Gideon intervened. "This is Keira, and she belongs to Sekkol."

"She is lovely," the woman said, like what Gideon said had not registered. She smiled at Keira, who smiled back and already seemed at home.

"She is, but that's the problem. Sekkol has imprinted on her, and according to the laws…"

"That's not allowed," she finished softly as she finally understood. Her eyes bulged, and her hand went to her mouth in shock.

"Exactly," Gideon said. "But she can't go back to Anon with him, or they will sell her…or worse."

"I don't mean to inconvenience you, my lady," I added, feeling the need to explain the circumstances, rather than fully leaning on Gideon. "I need a place for her to stay until this can be resolved. Gideon mentioned you might be able to keep her here until such a time presents itself."

"Why, of course." The woman beamed and rubbed her hands together with glee. Her black eyes twinkled, and her bluish face glowed. "I mean no disrespect, Master Sekkol, but I always thought that was a stupid law anyway. One does not have control over whom they imprint on. I wonder if things may be different now that it has happened to you."

And by that, she implied they might change the laws because of my station on Jupiter. I was not inclined to believe so at the moment. For years, it had made sense to me, perhaps because I didn't know it was possible for different species to imprint on each other.

"Thank you for your generosity," I said to her and turned to leave. "I don't mean to be rude, but I have to get back now."

Gideon nodded at his mother and followed me to the door.

I looked back at Keira as she stood there watching us, and before I could even think, she rushed across the room and flung her arms around my neck. I was taken aback at first, and then I wrapped my arms around her. I could feel her heart beating rapidly against my chest, and all I could think about was keeping her safe, right there in this embrace. My mind returned to the moment in the cave when we had last made love, and right then, my body started to respond as my member began twitching. My fingers dug into her through the thin fabric, and I felt her breath warming my neck.

I looked behind her now and saw Gideon's mother watching us too intently, and then I remembered where I was. I slowly released my hold on Keira, but then her lips came up and gently brushed against my cheek. My skin burned with need at the spot, and I knew I had to get away or I would take her right there.

"Be careful," she whispered so low only I could hear.

I brushed her hair back, nodded, and followed after Gideon. When I looked back, Keira was just standing there with a frightened look on her face. I wanted to take her with me, but I knew, under the present circumstances, I would only be making things harder for us. She would be safer here. And I kept telling that to myself all the way back to Anon.

I still had no idea how to get Brom free without replacing him. But even if I did, the greater problem still remained. How would I finally be able to be with her the way my soul pressed for?

The thought rested on my mind as heavy as lead and plagued me all the way back home, even as I entered the city gates and saw the smile that slowly broke on the commander's lips.

CHAPTER 18
KEIRA

I stood there staring at his back until he disappeared outside and the door closed after him. I clasped my hands before me, not knowing what to expect or how to feel.

The woman turned to me then, and her eyes swept my body. I felt my skin itching right at my nape, where they had injected the microchip when I was first brought to Jupiter. I rubbed the spot and then twitched when I felt the area begin to burn. I instantly moved my hand away, fearing I might dislocate it and lose my ability to speak with Sekkol or anyone else.

"Maybe we should get you cleaned up," the woman said.

I could not deny that invitation. I too clearly remembered the way the cruel commander had held me right before Sekkol had rescued me. And having slept overnight in a cave had me feeling filthier than ever before.

"That would be nice," I said and smiled at her. "I'm Keira, by the way," I said and extended my hand to her. She looked at it like she had no idea what to do with it.

"Geneva," she said as she eventually copied me.

Her hand felt extra warm, and I could easily understand that, based on the location of her home. She was strangely beautiful, too, with an upright posture, her head held high, and her black and silver hair flowing down her back.

"Come with me," she instructed, and she led me to another area of the house.

It seemed a lot bigger than it did on the outside, and as I followed her, I took notice of the bright colors that made up the space. There was seating in the room, a bluish-green set of cushions, and as I passed, I touched it and realized it was a lot softer than it appeared. My eyes wandered around the room, taking in the walls painted yellow, the colorful accessories strategically placed, the large painting of what appeared to be a sunflower on the accent wall, and the glass-encased shower stall. This was nothing like Sekkol's home, which was predominantly white and voice-activated. This seemed homier.

The woman led me to the shower, and I removed my clothes before stepping in. As soon as I did, the water powered on, frightening me, and I jumped. I looked around and saw no buttons and assumed it was sensor based. Typical. I closed my eyes and allowed the water to rid me of the evidence of my night in the cave.

"Do you need help?" Geneva asked from the other side of the glass.

I paused then and wiped the water from my face. I hadn't realized until then that she was still there. "No, that's fine. Thanks," I replied.

"Are you sure?" she asked, like it was odd for a woman, or anyone for that matter, to shower by herself. I still wasn't familiar with all of Jupiter's customs, and I was beginning to see it wasn't as general as I had first thought.

"All right, then," she said after I assured her I was fine.

I listened until I heard a clicking sound, and I peeked out and saw she had left the room.

She was a pleasant-looking woman and gave me an idea of what the grandmothers in fairy-tale stories must look like.

I slid the door shut once more and splashed water onto my face. It was warm and inviting, and with my eyes closed, I was transported to Sekkol's home and his shower. I could still feel his hands on my skin and his large member as it squeezed into me, and suddenly, my heart began to flutter. I paused and stood there in the shower, allowing the water to work more than my hands, and watched as my chest heaved.

It wasn't clear to me what would happen to him when he returned or why it felt he had made a sacrifice for me.

I was still lost in thought when I heard voices on the other side of the wall. My eyes flew open, and I tried to listen, but with the water running, it was impossible. I quietly slid the door open and stepped out onto the cool tiles, and as soon as I did, the water automatically powered off.

"I have to get one of these when I go back home," I said and then started turning around. "Now what to wear?"

Just then, as if she'd read my mind, Geneva entered with a dress draped over her arm. She seemed oblivious to the fact that I was naked and came right up to me with the clothing. I looked around and wondered how she'd known I was done, but something in me told me I didn't want to know. I shuddered as I thought she had been able to see me all along.

"This should be able to fit you," she said as she held it out to me.

I took it from her and held it up at my front. "It's lovely. Thank you," I told her as I immediately slipped into it. The fabric felt light and soft and caressed my skin as I was enveloped in what felt like a cloud.

She stood there looking at me, pleased at her handiwork. "Used to be one of my favorites," she said and walked off again. "Come with me."

I followed her back into the room, where I saw the source of the voice I'd heard earlier. It was a man, the spitting image of Gideon, though slightly shorter. His hair was black, too, and braided; the neatly styled hair fell over his shoulder and stopped at his midsection. His black eyes searched my face, but he remained still as I followed Geneva. My first instinct told me he was probably Gideon's brother.

"Hmm," he grunted and then set what appeared to be a blade against the wall. "So you belong to Sekkol?"

"I don't belong to anyone," I answered and then sat on the seating. I was still not comfortable with the reference. It felt like I had no say in the matter.

He began to laugh, and his voice echoed in the room. "I heard over in Anon that Sekkol was wanted, but I didn't realize it was on account of a human," he said.

"This is not a joke, Roan," the woman said.

"It really isn't," Roan agreed. Then he looked back at me.

"I don't understand," I confessed. They kept saying I was his like I had no control over it, and worse, that he didn't either. "Can't he just go and be with someone else?"

Roan smiled, his two perfect rows of white teeth glistening under the soft, yellow light that filled the room. He got up and walked over to me and touched my damp hair, swirling one of the strands around his long index finger. I dipped and let the strand uncurl from his finger. My heartbeat started increasing in intensity, for I was in the home of strangers, on a strange planet, and unsure of what they would likely do.

"You *don't* understand, do you?" he asked. "It seems on Earth things are different."

"Yes," I said and backed away from him. I smoothed my hair and tucked it behind my ears. "I've heard of this imprinting thing, but—"

"Oh, you have, have you?" he asked.

"Roan, leave the girl be." Geneva intervened. "She has been through enough."

"*She* has been through enough?" he asked and shook the house again with his laughter. "From what I've heard, Sekkol is the one going through a lot while she remains safely here."

"You say that like you care," Geneva added. "I remember not so long ago, you and Master Sekkol were involved in a battle when you decided it was a good idea to challenge his authority."

"He *was* being condescending," Roan answered. "But I have nothing against him. I'm just saying she isn't the one paying for what's happening to him. As a matter of fact, I think she should be right there, too, not hiding here. Is that what the people of Earth do?" He challenged me. "Do you just let others fight your battles for you?"

I had enough. "Fuck off. No one is fighting anything for me!" I shouted at him.

He looked at me strangely after I spoke, but he didn't seem rattled by my rising temper. "Then what do you call this?" he asked. He seemed to be angry with me for something I was yet to discover.

"I didn't tell him to go back," I said. "As a matter of fact, all I wanted was to get off this planet and go back home."

Roan's face contorted into a disgusted look, and he stood and took up his weapon once more. I flinched and shrank before him as he came over to me. My eyes remained on the metal as it dangled before me.

"Maybe he should have sent you back," he spat. "He may have imprinted on you, but you don't deserve him." And then he walked away, leaving me feeling inadequate. He slammed the door, and his mother jumped when the sound bounced off the walls.

She was overly quiet after that, and I felt the need to press. I was missing something, and I needed answers. There was too much I didn't understand.

"Why was he angry with me?" I asked. She held her head down and toyed with her fingers and then heaved a sigh. "What is it?"

"You speak so rashly against something that is held sacred here," she began and then got up. "I'm going to get dinner. Something hot should do you some good." She went toward what I believed to be the kitchen, so I followed her.

"Geneva, I really appreciate your generosity, but there's something I need more than food right now," I told her. "From the minute I was taken to Sekkol, I've felt like I was in the way. Why is everyone angry at me?"

"You are very impatient," she said. "And not very knowledgeable either. I have never understood humans." She sucked in a deep breath, like she was about to say a lot. "My son is angry at you because you are openly rejecting an imprint."

"I don't even know what that means," I told her.

"Here on Jupiter, each person is given only one chance at love. Just one. Usually, it is the man who imprints on a woman. At that moment, when he recognizes her, their souls connect. After that point, he can love no other or be with any other unless he is willing to risk living an unhappy life. The love never goes unrequited," she explained and turned to look at me for apparent effect, or to get an idea of what I was feeling. "Even if the woman doesn't understand right away."

"But none of this is my fault," I replied.

"Neither is it his," she added. "Imprinting on you can only lead to negative consequences for Master Sekkol. By rejecting him, you may have condemned him twice."

The weight of what she just said rested heavily on me, and I slouched under its influence. It was now very clear we were both victims of the same laws, though he had chosen to bear the brunt of it.

"But he didn't return to Anon because of me. He went back to save Brom," I said, hoping to rid myself of some of the blame.

Geneva smiled and then leaned over to take my hand in hers. They were warm and soft, and I looked down at them, still marveling at how surreal my current existence was.

"Think about it," she said. "Why was Brom captured in the first place?"

She was right. Brom had been the one helping me all along, helping us, before he was taken. Sekkol's decision to go back was a noble one, though he was forced. His purchasing me had set in motion a series of things that were knocked over by that first domino.

"He isn't just out there fighting to save Brom," she continued.

"So what am I supposed to do?" I asked.

"He is out there fighting for love. Maybe you should do the same for him," she said and then rose once more.

"How?" I asked. "I don't know this place. I don't belong here."

"I don't know how to answer that." She stopped without turning around.

I didn't either, so she kept walking, and suddenly I was hungry. But this time, it was for more than food, as my heart started searching for ways to save him. My love life back on Earth was nonexistent. Though it was something I desired, it just didn't take root. It was odd that love had found me on a strange planet and with the most unlikely of persons.

"As far as people go," the woman said, "he is not such a bad choice."

Then I was left alone with my thoughts, which were making more noise than Roan had earlier. But it was now that I finally understood.

They were slaves to love and whomever it chose for them, and Sekkol was going to be punished for it. Jupiter was, after all, a cruel place.

I sighed and went after Gideon's mother, only now starting to feel the rumbling of my stomach. I was starving, and if I was going to go to war, I'd need ammunition.

CHAPTER 19
SEKKOL

"So what now?" Gideon asked as we crossed the city line.

"Same plan as before. We get Brom," I replied and then circled overhead. "Where do they have him?"

"I'm afraid that won't be so easy, especially since Commander Styx saw you enter the city," Gideon replied.

"It will be. They want me," I replied and then shot forward and settled my hovercraft before Commander Styx. "Where is he?" I asked the commander.

He grinned, but he gave me no answer. "Take him in," he said to the men gathered around him.

"You will do no such thing," I snarled and glared at them. They froze in their steps, unsure of what to do next.

"Go!" Commander Styx barked, but none dared move against me. He looked over his shoulder at them, and then his eyes turned to me and were now as red as blood. "I gave you a command," he said to them.

I watched as they looked amongst themselves and shuffled about until two of them stepped from the group and advanced toward me.

I pulled my weapon from its sheath and held it at my side. "I will not refrain from using this," I warned them. I was not intent on having a verbal battle or an optical showdown with Commander Styx. I owed him no allegiance, and he would not deter me now. The men knew the level of my seriousness and would come no closer. "I am going to speak with my father."

"But that's exactly where my men would be taking you," Styx replied.

"That is not necessary," I said and lifted the hovercraft once more. "I know where to find him."

I could feel his eyes staring holes in my back, but that was nothing new. The two of us were not friends, nor were we ever on polite terms; he hated me as I hated him, and as the days went by, I discovered new heights to that emotion. I represented something he could never be. I was to be the next ruler of Jupiter, and it bothered him tremendously that I kept rejecting something he so desperately wanted.

That desire for power was spread along the branches of the family tree, as his sister Nala had tried on more than one occasion to get me to wed her. She had deceived me once into thinking she was carrying my child and only lately had tried to blackmail me into marrying her yet again by holding my secret love for Keira as ransom. Styx had taken my rejection of her personally, and he was desperate to find a way to get rid of me. Keira provided him with the perfect weapon.

"Sekkol, is that you?" Thorax's voice came over the device on my hovercraft. He was the last of the four-man squad I headed and was presumably concerned about my current affairs.

"Yes, Thorax," I replied.

"Why did you come back?" he asked, his voice more of a reprimand now than concern. Gideon had apparently briefed him.

"I couldn't let Brom suffer for my actions," I said.

"He wouldn't be suffering your consequences. He was willing to die for his own," Thorax said.

"It was all on my account," I told him. "Where is he?"

"They have him over at the Great Pike," he explained. "They figured that's where you would go." There was a long pause as the hovercraft glided toward my doom. "What do you suppose will happen now?" he asked.

We were usually the ones meting out punishment to guilty parties.

It was strange for them to see me in this position, and I knew it troubled them.

"Don't worry about me," I assured, speaking to both him and Gideon. "I will get Brom. Then you can go back to your regular duties like none of this happened."

"Except it did," Gideon said, and I caught his gaze as I turned to my right.

Just then, I saw the outline of the Great Pike, and I was not obliged to have either of them caught in a trap. I handpicked the Enforcers; it would give the commander great pleasure to make his own squad and be the all-powerful ruler of the guards.

"This is where you stop," I said to them as I approached the steps. "I appreciate all your help, but I have to do this alone." They were about to argue, but I held up my hands and commanded their silence. They nodded and turned their hovercrafts around. I watched until they were a distance away before I leveled the hovercraft and hopped off.

As soon as I entered the large doors that led down the long passageway, I felt two hands clamp down on my arms, on either side. I saw they were two of the royal guards posted there, who had clearly been given instructions to take me in at first sight. I struggled against them, but they were trained arms, and I was caught unaware.

"Sekkol, you have been found in contempt of law twenty-eight, subsection four, which states that any and all association with humans that exceed their role as—" one of the guards started reciting.

"I know what it says," I spat. "Take me to my father!" I shouted as I writhed.

"The Tribunal requires your presence," the guard said this time as they pulled me along.

"Let me go to my father!" I shouted even louder, my voice filling the passageway.

A door opened on the right a few steps away, and my father came out. "Release him," he told the guards.

They nodded, pulled their hands back, and locked them behind their backs. Then they retreated and resumed their position at the door.

"Come," he said to me and went back into the room.

I shrugged my shoulder and straightened my clothes before I followed after him. Entering the room, I closed the door behind me.

"Sit," he commanded, and I looked at him oddly as he spoke to me in a tone I was unfamiliar with. He remained standing as I obeyed him, and he locked his fingers behind him. He was staring at the monitor on the wall, and I only now realized it displayed my childhood days, each one flitting by as he relived them again. Then he stopped on one, where I was just being taught how to ride the hovercraft.

"Do you remember this day?" he asked. "I had dreamt so long of that moment, when you would become a man and I would teach you these things. You were such a fast learner." I didn't respond, and I heard him sigh loudly.

"Father, there is something I have to say." I began and then stood.

"No, there is not." He stopped me. "When I felt you had imprinted, I was excited you would finally take your place here. To find out you imprinted on a human…" He trailed off and then turned to look at me. The disappointment in his eyes was profound, and for the first time in a long time, I felt I was the one who had done something wrong. Except I didn't.

"Father, how could I have known that was even possible?" I asked. "And how can I possibly go back from this?"

"There have only been speculations." He began again. "I saw the change in your appearance some time ago, and I recognized it immediately as evidence that you had imprinted, but you denied it then. You need only deny it once more to the Tribunal and be done with this."

Be done with this? I felt as if I were a child again; I always did when I was in his overbearing presence. "How can I do such a thing? You know I will never be able to imprint again." What he was saying made no sense and was not something I was remotely willing to consider.

"No matter," he said. "You can just choose a woman to be with, and she can bear you heirs. You cannot be with this human. No human has ever assumed leadership of Jupiter."

"Then I won't be ruler of Jupiter. We can live a simple life—"

"My son will not live a simple life just because of one human!" he barked. "You will do as I ask."

I stood there listening to him preside over my life, and it was at that moment the decision was made for me.

"You've always taught me to be strong and to stand up for my beliefs, never to cower and never to back down. Jupiter demands a leader it can respect, not a coward who hides behind the laws when it suits him, but one who is bold enough to stand even against it. I cannot deny her, nor will I settle for anyone else."

"Sekkol, this is insane," my father pleaded.

"I have made my decision," I told him.

"Then I am afraid there is nothing I can do," he said and then he walked out. After he did, the guards showed up, ready to take me away.

All the way to Anon, I had thought seeing my father would have made things different for me. After all, he was Lord Magnus, Supreme Ruler, who had the power to overturn any decision made by the Tribunal or any other court. This outcome was not what I had in mind. My only consolation was seeing Brom being led to the door as I was taken in the opposite direction.

CHAPTER 20
KEIRA

It felt odd waking up in a strange place. My eyes fluttered, and I wiped the sleep from them with the back of my hand before stirring under the covers. Instantly, my mind found Sekkol, and I wondered at the outcome of his return to Anon.

The customs on Jupiter were still strange to me, but I had to acknowledge their nobility and respect for their system. I sucked in a deep breath and slid from under the satin fabric. My body felt rested, but my mind remained tormented as I staggered to the bathroom Geneva had introduced me to last night.

She had given me my own accommodations, which proved to be even more comfortable than my apartment on Earth. Still, I missed the leather sofa bed with the quilted throw that I fell asleep under almost every night while watching TV; the dark curtains at the windows, securing me from the world; the kitchen that was mostly devoid of life and all activity, displaying neat rows of pots and pans which fit nicely with the other decorative items that never got used; and the ice cream and leftover pizza that would likely be rotten by now. This place, this world, was nothing like the one I knew, but it was fast becoming the only reality I had.

Ever since I arrived here, I'd been trying to find a way to get back to Earth, which included playing the helpless victim to the alien who had taken me and made me "his." I lost that game the minute I started enjoying his company, though I fought hard to hide the budding emotions. Now, and perhaps because of Roan's reaction to my words or his mother's explanation of what imprinting does to a person, I had grown more sympathetic. Now, I wanted to know more, to be a part of this, and to feel things the way they did. But most of all, I wanted to do it with Sekkol.

"How did you rest?" Geneva asked as soon as I emerged from the room.

"Okay, I guess," I replied as I tried to stifle a yawn. "Did Gideon come back?" He was my only link to any development with Sekkol.

"No, he did not," Geneva replied and rested the cup she'd been sipping from in the palm of her other hand. The act itself seemed so proper she could have easily been the queen at Buckingham Palace. She sat in an upright posture, her hair smoothed back and her countenance dignified. It was hard not to be impressed by her appearance.

"Oh," I said, and my gaze wandered to the walls and then to the plant before she arrested my attention again.

"I know you are concerned," she said, "despite your words. But I'm sure he is fine."

"How can you be certain?" I asked and then stood. I could feel my chest heaving at the same moment I wondered at the strange feelings suddenly overwhelming me. I clamped my hand onto my chest that had started to feel constricted, and my breathing began to come out in short gasps.

"Are you all right?" Geneva asked as she sprang to her feet and set the cup on the side table.

"Yes," I said and then bent over, grabbing my knees in the act for support. "I'm not sure," I finally admitted. I felt almost faint, and immediately, I recognized the feelings as the same ones that had overcome me after my parents' accident. I was having an anxiety attack.

I went back to the cushioned seating and sat down, and she sat next to me, worry easing itself into her posture.

"Would you like some water? Or air?" she asked, touching my hand.

I could feel my heart thudding against the inner wall of my chest, and my palms grew clammy against my knee. I closed my eyes as I waited for the sensation to come to an end. She asked me again, and this time, I nodded and stood. As I headed for the door, I felt heavier than I was a few moments ago. Maybe the air would do me some good.

Geneva got up and followed me out, and I observed the neighbors' reactions to my being there. The ones who paid any attention nodded, and the others kept going, like my presence wasn't unusual.

The air was warm, and the ground moved under my feet. The streets weren't like Anon, with the solid claylike matter, but loose, like sand. The people wore high-necked outfits, equipped with something that looked like nose masks.

"Do you have sandstorms here?" I asked Geneva. She was moving at my pace, keeping her gaze on me.

"Hmm." She smiled. "You have odd expressions on Earth," she said. "I think I know what you mean, though. The wind can get quite rough out here at times, and that's why the houses are so close; it protects us from the desert rage."

"Desert rage?" I asked. And she said *our* expressions were strange.

"What you call sandstorms," she replied.

"Does it ever rain?" I asked, shielding my eyes as I looked up at the sky. The sun was creeping to the center, signifying it was close to midday. The thudding in my heart continued, but I knew from experience that if I distracted myself enough, it would subside.

"About once or twice every month," she replied.

"What?" I asked. "That often?"

"Yes," she replied. "It is very hot here, and the heat attracts the rain."

It seemed every time I got something figured out about Jupiter, another oddity presented itself. We went along the street, and I noticed everything looked almost identical. It reminded me of an area in Queens, New York I had visited before, rows of buildings in an apartment complex that were only distinguishable by the number on the building. Were the numbers to be removed, one could easily mistake one for the other. Except here, there weren't numbers, but symbols and carvings on the doors.

"Where did Roan go?" I asked. I wasn't really interested, but it was something else to talk about.

"To perform his assigned duties," she replied. "He is a hunter."

That explained the machete-type weapon I'd seen earlier. "In the desert?"

"One does not hunt in the desert," Geneva answered and looked at me like I'd asked a stupid question. "There are forests west of here."

"Oh," I responded. I stopped when I realized we were at the end of the cluster of houses and she was no longer walking. "What's the matter?"

"I would like to go to Earth one day," the woman said.

"Why don't you?" I asked. "Your people sure visit Earth often."

She seemed to have caught my meaning, that we were continuously being kidnapped from Earth. "I am sorry you had to be a victim of that," she apologized. "But it isn't so bad being here, is it? We have a few humans here who are situated well."

"That's easy for you to say," I retorted. "I've received more than my share of hostility."

"That is not always the case," she defended. "I've met a few humans who seem to prefer being here, and there are others who have never been shown hostility. Jupiter is not as bad as you think." Her face grew blank then as she stared ahead. "Look!" she exclaimed and pointed to an object in the air that was approaching us.

"Gideon?" I asked. Actually, I was hoping it was him, and the thought that it was reanimated my heart and it started thudding once more.

The hovercraft circled ahead, and he indicated the house when he saw us. We started back, and I began jogging toward it. I could feel pressure building within me the closer I got to him. He would have news about Sekkol, and I hoped it would be good.

Geneva was lighter on her feet than I expected and got to the door at the same time as I did.

"Where's Sekkol? What happened?" I asked as soon as I got inside and she closed the door behind us.

"They've taken him into custody," Gideon replied.

"And?" I asked, when I saw he wasn't going to say anything else. I could feel the lump in my throat growing bigger the longer I waited, and my head began to feel heavy as anxiety filled me throughout. I tried not to visualize Sekkol in chains, or worse. Though I couldn't dismiss the feeling of dread that came with Gideon's very few words.

"That's all I know," he replied. "When we got to the Great Pike, he ordered Thorax and me to leave him. We did as commanded, but Brom informed us that when he was being released, he saw Sekkol being led away by the royal guards."

I stared at him, still waiting for more. When nothing else came, I grew livid. "So you mean to tell me you went all that way only to leave and not know what happened to him? What kind of soldier are you?"

"The very best," Gideon said and scowled at me.

"And you just left him there to die?" I could hardly believe any of this was happening. "He came back for one of you. He could have left Brom there to die and then flee and live happily ever after. But instead, he left me here so I can be safe. He replaced Brom so he can be safe. And you just left him? Without finding out what's going to happen to him?"

"I know what's going to happen to him," Gideon barked. "It's the same thing that happened to all the others before him who transgressed any of our laws."

"Oh, I see." I fumed. "So he is going to die, and that's it. You're okay with that." It was a statement, not a question. I folded my arms over my chest and stared at him. His mouth opened, but nothing came out. "Yeah, that's what I thought. At least he had the fortitude to fight for what he wants and believes in. I can hardly say the same about you. About any of you," I said as I stormed out, almost bumping into the door that was sliding open too slowly.

I was angry and hurt and needed once more to clear my head. I felt I would collapse when I thought about Sekkol dying, about not seeing him again. And I was afraid for him. But what was I supposed to do? I would likely be killed too if they ever found me, and then he would die in vain. But I couldn't just stay here, not knowing what would happen to him.

I was still heaving, my consciousness toying with several possibilities, when I felt someone behind me. I turned and saw it was Geneva.

"You are very passionate, woman of Earth," she said to me.

I didn't reply, but instead, I turned around again. I folded my arms over my chest and stared past the clutter of homes into the distance.

"I don't get you people," I said and turned again. "How can you just watch this and do nothing? He is supposed to be the next ruler of Jupiter. Why won't anyone fight for him?"

"You are right," she said.

"What?" I asked, hardly expecting that response.

"We are too set in our ways, driven by too many rules and not enough instinct," she admitted. "I guess it takes love to make one do otherwise."

"What does love have to do with this?" I questioned.

She reached out and placed her hand on my chest, and my eyes followed it and then found her smiling eyes after.

"It is strange how you can possess something so powerful yet be so oblivious to it," she said.

"What are you talking about?" I was already confused and could not handle any complicated thought.

"You love him," she said, and then she removed her hand and walked away.

I watched her as she did, and for the first time since I met Sekkol, I opened my mind to the possibility that I had fallen in love with him. And then I was saddened to think that as soon as I had found love, it was already being taken from me.

CHAPTER 21
SEKKOL

Her hands made slow movements across my chest and stopped to create circular patterns around my nipples. They gradually perked and grew harder the longer she played with them. Then she moved, and her lips took the place of her hands, and when she covered me with the warmth of her mouth, my body shook, and I grabbed a fistful of her hair as minuscule bumps decorated my body. Her tongue flicked over the hardened peaks, and when she looked up at me, her brown eyes taunting me, I pulled her upward and planted a firm kiss on her lips.

Her tongue did a strange dance with mine, and then she started sucking on it. I'd never experienced this kind of kiss before her, but something about it caused my body to vibrate and my member to dance in anticipation of what she would do next. I always liked being in control, relished in it, even. But when I was with her, I wanted her to lead; I wanted her to take control of me.

Her hands moved down to it just as it started pulsating, begging for her attention, too, and she wrapped her fingers around it and started stroking. Her pulling on my tongue while she did sent shivers up my spine, and I reached out and caught her breast that was pressing into my chest. She pulled back then and started kissing the rest of my body, making a trail down to where her hand still gripped my most sensitive region. I gripped both sides of her head when she guided my shaft into her mouth, the warmth of her threat-

ening insanity. I felt like mush inside, and my body grew limp and surren-
dered itself completely when she straddled me, guiding me home.

My eyes flew open, and I punched the bedding in frustration when I realized she was not there. It had been a dream, and my reality was the cold walls of the room that still held me prisoner. My heart was thumping in my chest, and my forehead was damp with sweat.

I had never been privy to the inside of a jail cell, but here I was, getting overly familiar with the gray walls and the bars that separated me from the life I knew. I had every reason to believe I would be put to death, but I also had every intention of fighting all the way. I knew the procedure well, having witnessed the event quite a few times before. The Tribunal would convene, and I would be given an opportunity to defend myself. There would be a discussion after the proceedings, where my fate would be decided. I did not intend to leave it in their hands, nor did I plan on dying today. I had too much to live for…and her name was Keira.

There was a loud beeping sound, and I sat up from the relaxed position I was occupying. I waited as footsteps echoed in the long hall-way, and then I stood and went to the bars.

"You have fifteen minutes," the guard said just before I saw Brom's face.

"What are you doing here?" I asked him. I had given them instruc-tions to stay away, fearing they would take on the same punishment for my sake.

"We weren't about to leave you here alone." Gideon's voice came before his face did.

"You should leave now and go back to your families," I told them and turned around. I closed my eyes and turned my face to the ceiling. I expected to hear movement, but instead, there was only silence. I turned back to them, the anger within me rising to greater proportions. "That was a direct command."

"I know," Brom confirmed. "But we refuse to obey that command, Sekkol."

"That human of yours is quite convincing," Gideon added and then smiled.

The thought of her sent my heart racing, and I rushed over to the bars. "She sent you?" I asked Gideon. My eyes searched his face, looking for answers to questions I could not utter.

"She has much fire." Gideon chuckled. "But yes, I must admit she was instrumental in my decision to come."

"She does not know of our custom," I replied, even though inside I was bursting at the seams with anxiety. I longed to be with her, and being locked away in this glass prison was made even more intolerable by her absence. I no longer desired to fight what I was feeling, to question the person my heart had chosen. Instead, I would make the world bend to my will, listen to my command, and follow in my footsteps.

"That may be true, but she will not be quiet," Gideon said.

"Was she secured when you left?" I questioned.

"She was," he responded.

"Good." At least I didn't need to worry about her. I knew where to find her after this was over.

"So we've been thinking…" Brom began and came a little bit closer to the bars. He glanced down the passageway and then looked to the ceilings as he tried to locate the hidden monitors. He held his hand close to his face so his lips were partially covered, and then he whispered, "There are only two guards out front and none along the way here. They will be the same guards that will accompany you to the trial. At midday, Gideon will wait by the door…"

The longer he talked, the more I automatically tuned him out. He was talking escape, but I knew that was by no means a solution.

"Stop," I ordered, and his words cut off instantly. "What do you suppose will happen if I were to escape? Would I flee and live in the wild with Keira? What kind of a future could I promise her, feeding off wild animals and scavenging off the waste of others? I am Sekkol. I am the heir to this planet. I will not run."

"You know they will take you to the disintegration chamber." Brom pleaded with me. "At least let us do this thing for you, and then you can figure out the rest."

"I appreciate the efforts you have made on my behalf, but I will handle this my way," I told them. "You may go now."

They stood there and looked from each other to me and then to each other again before they nodded and went out.

I went back to the bed, the only piece of furniture in the room, and folded my hands between my knees and waited. Soon enough, when the sun was higher in the sky, the doors opened again, and this time, another set of footsteps was heard. I got up and stood by the door with my arms outstretched, a willing participant to my fate.

"It is time," the guard said as he punched in the numbers on the keypad, and the bars slid open. One of them held the plastic device in the space between my extended arms, and my wrists were automatically clamped together and held in place by the threading that looped around them. I followed the guards down the passageway, listening to the ominous sounds of my footsteps as they neared the court. There was a small gathering inside, and at the front of the room, the members of the Tribunal sat, with my father placed above them on the second tier.

His face was like stone, and he avoided my gaze as I was marched to the front of the room. I was given a seat, at which time the guards took their places on either side of me. There was no introduction. No acknowledgment. Just straight to business.

The member of the Tribunal in the center of the three stood and tapped on the screen before him. "Sekkol, you have been charged with the transgression of laws that forbid any form of relation with humans except for the purpose of labor. By so doing, you have compromised the future of the race and, as such, must be held accountable. Do you deny these charges?" he asked and then stared at me through the dark hollows in his face.

Of course, I was not guilty of jeopardizing the future of Jupiter. I was not left solely in charge of all procreation. "Not guilty," I responded.

There was a slight stir in the back of the court, and I turned just in time to see Commander Styx and Nala entering the room. My breath started coming out raggedly, and my fists clenched even without my conscious permission. Nala glared at me, and I returned my attention to the Tribunal.

"Do you disagree that you have consorted with a human?" the man asked again, in a much simpler way.

"I do," I replied.

There was a round of murmurs and whispers coming from the back section again, but this time, I needn't check to see who it was.

"Commander Styx, is there something you would like to say?" the Tribunal member asked.

"Yes, my lord," he replied. I could see his huge frame as it rose above the other members present for the hearing.

"Proceed," the man prompted.

"I have personal knowledge of his actions with the human. Its very words betrayed him when it referred to him as 'companion.' Closer investigation by me revealed that not only was she being untruthful about being his possession, but that the act was being covered up by one of his Enforcers. My lord, he has shown blatant and utter disregard for the morals and systems in place here on Jupiter and should thus be duly punished."

That was it. I rose and turned my attention first to the commander. "Did you see me lie with her?" He could give no answer. "Did I ever claim her as my own?" Again, nothing. "I have done nothing wrong. According to the customs of our people, a man cannot choose his own mate. She will be chosen for him by way of imprinting. If such is the case—"

"Are you saying you have imprinted on her?" another member of the Tribunal asked.

I looked up at my father, to see his lips pursed and his fingers locked on the table before him. I wanted to deny that I had, but my lips refused to utter the words, to deny the woman I'd rather die for than live without. What I felt for her had been magnified, constantly increasing daily, and even as I knew I was defeated, I couldn't help feeling like I had won. I smiled and then looked to the Tribunal.

"That I did," I replied.

There was even more murmuring in the room, and the members looked from one to the other as they all speculated at the possibility that what I had said was true.

"It is impossible to imprint on a human. It has never been done before," the first Tribunal member said at last.

"Our laws forbid it, but there has been nothing preventing us from imprinting with them before—nothing except absolute separation from them," I told them. "How can I be held accountable for something I have no control over?" I asked, and then turned to the court.

"I can assure you what he says is true," my father uttered and then looked at me with reprimand.

The murmurs continued, but the contempt on some of their faces, like I was vile, was unmistakable.

"Your admission of guilt leaves us with no choice but to sentence you to extraction," the tribunal member said.

And that was it. I would not be killed, but I would be taken from society, to live out my days in solitude.

"What would convince you to revoke this decision?" I asked.

"Bring in the girl," the man replied and then sat. "We will determine the truth if we examine her."

I already knew that was not going to happen. If Keira came here, they would only lock her away, and we would both be condemned to spend our lives apart. That was not a thought that rested comfortably with me, considering what Gideon had mentioned earlier.

My father remained quiet, obviously content with the decision to watch his only child carted off to solitude. I became angry, and it swelled as the guards held my hands and attempted to take me out. I grabbed one by the throat as the other reached for his device.

"Sekkol!" my father shouted, but he did not have the same sway over me as he had before.

"Father," I replied through gritted teeth as I turned about defensively, allowing no one to have a strike advantage.

"Release him," he ordered me as he prepared to move.

"I'm afraid I cannot do that," I told them and started backing out of the room.

I spotted the commander, his hand placed firmly on his waist, waiting for an appropriate moment to attack. I swerved to my right, widening the gap between us, and kept going to the door. Styx growled at me, his eyes narrowing. I was halfway to the door when I heard a sound outside. A woman screamed just before there was a thud, and then something crashed against the wall. I was temporarily forgotten as everyone looked to the door.

It burst open, and my body went limp when I saw Keira standing there. Her chest was heaving, her hair wild and her face dripping with sweat, like she had run all the way from across the desert.

"It wasn't his fault." She panted, and then a surprised look crossed her face when she saw me standing there with the guard's neck locked under my arm.

"Take her!" I heard my father shout.

"No!" I yelled and instinctively let go of the man. He staggered away, and I lunged toward Keira before Commander Styx could get to her.

I had forgotten about the other guard until I felt something come down hard on my back. I doubled over in pain, though my eyes never left her frightened face.

"Why did you come?" I asked her just as I felt the sting from the needle as the guard jabbed it into my shoulder. It was likely sleep serum, and I was already beginning to feel woozy.

"I had to," was all she said as Styx grabbed her arm.

My eyes grew cloudy, and she disappeared behind the veil that grew thicker the more I blinked until she ceased to exist, and there was only the dark.

CHAPTER 22
KEIRA

I was panting as I raced up the steps that led to the Great Pike. Gideon escorted me past the guards; it would have been unnatural for a human to go there alone. When I reached the wide doors, my heart flip-flopped in my chest. I knew what was going on inside. Sekkol was being tried in what was similar to Earth's court of law. Tried like a criminal because he had fallen in love with someone the inhabitants of this planet did not approve of: me.

I shoved open the door, oblivious at the moment of all the spectators in the room, except for the robed men who would decide Sekkol's fate. I was not suicidal, but I'd be damned if he was going to suffer alone. Sekkol had left the desert to return here, to defend my honor. I had to come, even if it meant my death.

"It wasn't his fault," I yelled while gasping for breath, hair wild and face drenched with perspiration. My eyes widened when I saw Sekkol standing with a guard's neck locked under his arm. *What the hell?*

"Take her!" a man's voice bellowed.

"No!" Sekkol roared, releasing the man he had in his clutch. The man stumbled away, and Sekkol lunged toward me. A guard pounced on him, and Sekkol doubled over as if in pain. Shocked, I stared at him, frozen to my spot.

"Why did you come?" Sekkol asked me before the guard injected him with something in the shoulder. My breath moved in and out of my mouth raggedly at regular, gasping intervals as I watched Sekkol's body sway.

"I had to," I countered as Styx grabbed my arm.

I felt my pulse beating in my ears when Sekkol fell to the ground. Guards converged on me, pulling my arms back before I felt the sting as my hands locked behind me.

"Let me go!" I screamed and thrashed about, and my feet slipped as I did. "Sekkol!" I cried as I tried to move. *I'm too late.* That was all I could think about when I saw his motionless body lying crumpled on the floor. I couldn't take my eyes away from him. Nothing else mattered. The connection had to be held; if it broke, he would die. I'd never felt so certain of anything else in my life.

"Let me go!" I shouted again, and this time, I kicked the ankle of one of the men.

He dipped, and when he did, his hand loosened on mine. I wriggled out of the other's grasp and skittered across the floor, straight toward Sekkol, before I could be caught again.

"Sekkol," I called frantically. When I got to him, I fell to the ground next to him. Grabbing his arm, I turned him over. Relief washed over me when I saw the steady rise and fall of his chest.

Thank God he's not dead.

I draped my arm over him as tears sprang from my eyes and rolled down my cheeks. I could hardly believe I was risking my life for him when, not so long ago, I wanted nothing more than to be free of him. He had claimed me as his from the very beginning, even before I knew who he was or what he would mean to me.

The men got to me then, and one of them yanked me to my feet.

"You are spritely for a human," he snapped as he brought me to stand.

They spun me, and I faced the door. I was now able to see the other witnesses to Sekkol's apparent crime. The commander and his insane sister were seated close to the back of the room, and my eyes narrowed with rage when I became aware of them. They had been my ultimate demise. I'd been living with Sekkol for weeks, and had it not been for those two, neither he nor I would be here. The commander was envious of Sekkol's station and his sister jealous of the human he'd fallen for and chosen above her. They had kidnapped me from my home and had made everyone aware of what I meant to Sekkol. He had returned just in time to save me from their clutches, but he was far too noble to run. He had returned to face his "crime," even though it meant he could die.

But none of it would have happened except for Commander Styx. Rage coursed through my veins as I watched the evil smirk on their faces as they waited for what they hoped would be our end.

"You fucking bastard!" I screeched, lunging toward them. The hold the alien guard had on me had tightened, and I felt the pressure in my shoulders when I tried to move. He yanked me back, but my eyes remained fixed on the commander, who was now walking toward me.

"What did you think would happen, human? That you would show up here, and we would just let you go?" he asked, the smirk spreading across his face the closer he got.

When he was close enough, I spat in his face. His eyes narrowed before he slid his thumb down his cheek, removing all traces of my DNA. He raised his hand like he meant to strike, but the other alien guard held his hand in midair.

"That will not be necessary," the guard warned the commander.

Nala, the commander's sister, came up behind him like she meant to defend his honor. I remembered how vicious she had been when the two had taken me prisoner. She had planned to use me as a ransom for Sekkol's hand in marriage, and when it backfired, it had left her a bitter woman. She walked around me and observed me like I was a lab rat.

"Stay the fuck away from me, you vindictive bitch!" I shouted at her.

"I fail to see what all the fuss is about," Nala crooned.

"That's enough," I heard a voice say then. The alien guards relaxed their hold on me, and I turned and saw a man I didn't recognize. He was the one wearing the white robe, while the other three wore black, and he had a grim expression when he looked at me.

I looked him over, observing the long white garb and the braided silver hair that fell down his back. I glanced behind him and saw three men, like angels of death, dressed in black and standing as if they were in accordance with him. I looked at him again, and then it made sense.

"You're Lord Magnus," I whispered, and then I grew nervous.

I was dumbstruck for a few seconds, thinking I might not have given him a very good first impression. But I also found it hard to believe he would just be sitting there, watching as his son was tried for something he had no control over. I wanted to say something, but then my eyes caught Sekkol and the guards who were just now lifting him from the floor, and I stilled my wagging tongue.

"So you are the human." His eyes searched mine, but for all the confusion I was feeling, I doubted he found much there.

"And you are Sekkol's father," I countered. He didn't answer, but there was no need to. "He is your son, and you would sit by and watch this?"

I felt the sting even before I knew what had happened. *What the hell?* I winced when I felt a burning sensation at the back of my leg, and I wobbled before falling to my knees. I looked back and saw the blue light from the conical device the alien guard wielded.

"You will not speak to Lord Magnus in that manner, human!" the guard yelled.

"*Lord Magnus* may be your king, but he hasn't earned my respect just yet," I spat as I gazed at him.

The alien guard's face twisted into anger, and before I could move, he slapped the device against my hand. I could smell my flesh burn under its touch, and I pulled my hand back sharply and covered the spot with my other palm.

"Ouch. Son of a bitch," I wailed and sucked in a deep breath as I tried to ignore the pain. "Would you stop burning me with that fucking thing?"

"You will speak to our king with respect," the guard said as he held out the device, ready to give me another jolt.

Lord Magnus held up his hand, and the guards backed off. "Stand down. I wish to speak with the human."

I was still gripping my arm as I stood and glanced over at Sekkol, who was now propped up on a machine resembling a gurney. "Are you just going to leave him there? He's your son, for Christ's sake."

"Interesting. The human seems to care for my son," he said without looking at me.

What the fuck have we been trying to say this entire time? What does he mean by "the human seems," like we don't feel, too?

"More than you do, apparently," I shot back defensively. His head whipped around to glare at me, and he strode to where I stood.

"What do you know of the ways of Jupiter?" he asked. "You come from a world that is far different from our own."

"But it is a home that *your* people kidnapped me from," I stated. "If you mix the two, what did you think would happen?"

"We expected you to be our helpers," he replied. "You were not brought here to lie with our men. And especially not my son." He seemed offended that Sekkol had chosen me, almost regretful he was being tried on my account.

My fists clenched and unclenched themselves like they had a mind of their own. "And you think I actually came here to sleep with him? Do you think I wanted to come here at all? You snatch people from their homes and families every day."

I remembered the cruel way in which I had been kidnapped. Granted, I didn't have a family to go back to, being the only child to deceased parents. But I had a life and a home, and I damn sure didn't need this shit.

"No matter, human," he said as he walked back to the seating he had shared with the other robed men. "Our laws forbid any resident of Jupiter from consorting with any human, and to transgress that law is punishable by death."

"Well, maybe you should have thought about that before you started kidnapping humans!" I screamed as I walked after him.

He turned and arrested me with his eyes, and I froze in my steps.

"Human. You will hold your tongue," he commanded.

"I will not," I replied.

I had nothing to lose at this point, besides Sekkol, of course, who I might very well lose to death if I didn't at least try to save us. I was extremely cognizant of the hushed whispers in the room and how the guards seemed ready to fry me just for speaking to Lord Magnus. I had always been told *when in Rome, do as the Romans do.* But not when the Romans wanted to kill me. I would at least be heard before judgment was cast against my favor.

"Look at him," I demanded, pointing at Sekkol, who was now lying on the gurney. "Your fucking flesh and blood." I stared at Magnus until his eyes moved and he too observed his son. "He will be killed for something he did not do. What kind of a law is that?"

"He did do what he's accused of," Lord Magnus said.

"He had no control over this."

I felt flushed, like I was pushing water uphill. I could feel the weight of it in my arms, but to stop would mean a sure drowning. I could see it in his eyes when he looked at Sekkol; he was afraid, too. And I felt a glimmer of hope he might rethink his decision. I was being crushed between the rock and that hard place I often heard talk of.

"Please don't do this," I now begged as I stopped inches from him. Maybe it would serve me better to appeal to his sensitive side. They didn't receive force well in this place, so it hadn't won me any favors thus far.

He shook his head. "There is nothing I can do. The laws already exist, and he was found in breach of them."

"Then your laws are ridiculous and unfair," I said with disdain. "Where I come from, a man can only be held accountable for something he chooses to do that is against the common laws or practices. Sekkol imprinted on me, and that was pure instinct. Are you telling me it is a crime to act on instinct? To deny the very thing that makes you who you are?"

There was suddenly a chorus of murmurs in the room, and I looked around and noticed there were more people in the room than there had been before. Apparently, some others had stolen inside, anxious to view history in the making. Who wouldn't want to tell this story to their grandchildren?

"It is not, but it is a crime to lie with a human. Our ancestors made these laws with the intention that our bloodline would not get corrupted with that of other cultures," Lord Magnus explained.

"Laws can only be broken if a choice is present. Did your ancestors frequently kidnap people from another planet?" I challenged him.

"It was not a common practice at the time," he responded.

I could feel him beginning to fold, and he looked around the room anxiously. I had the feeling he'd never been challenged before, especially not by a human. Maybe that was the only reason I was still alive. The law enforcement on Jupiter was whimsical in its killings; people had been vaporized, disintegrated, or fried for far less than what I was exhibiting. But sentencing me to death for disrespecting or defying the king would be a far more just punishment than killing me for love.

"Then maybe you should either change the laws or stop commingling," I informed him.

A movement caught the corner of my eye, and I turned my head and saw it was Sekkol. My heart fluttered in my chest, and I looked back at Lord Magnus before rushing over to Sekkol. This time, no one moved to stop me. I leaned over him and brushed the loose hair that covered his face when I did.

"Hey, you," I whispered.

His eyes fluttered, but he still seemed heavily sedated.

"Keira?" he whispered. Then his head slumped to the side, and he fell back into his unconscious state once more.

I glanced back at Lord Magnus and the other alien guards who stood there looking on. A sweep of the room showed the commander and his sister sneering at us. Disgust festered within me like an old sore.

"Maybe you're right," I said to Lord Magnus as I rose. "Maybe you should kill him."

The murmurs in the room rang even louder.

"What?" he asked.

"You heard me," I told him. "Sekkol is willing to fight for something he believes in. He has lived by Jupiter's laws all his life, and what did it get him? He is lying there unconscious and waiting to die because he fell in love." I laughed then, and that seemed to take them by surprise. "Heck, just kill me, too, because if this is what it means to be a resident of Jupiter, then I'd rather die." I was addressing the room of confused and angry faces now, but I no longer cared. "For all your fancy technological devices and talking houses, you still don't know anything about love. No wonder you started coming to Earth."

"Earth is but a savage land of primordial beings," the commander said as he came forward.

"Maybe, but at least we don't kill someone for loving someone else," I replied. "Sekkol is better than all of you here. He is strong and compassionate and is exactly what Jupiter needs in a king." I was challenging Lord Magnus now, and I could see he was no longer pleased or welcoming of my debate. "Maybe he is better off dead than alive here and living with you dumbasses."

"Get her out of here." Lord Magnus's voice boomed now, his face a deep shade of blue.

It seemed the guards had been on their toes, waiting for the command. As soon as it came, I felt their hands on me. I knew it was over for me, and I could more readily accept my fate over that which would be meted out to Sekkol by his own people. Still, I struggled against them, fighting to catch one last glimpse of Sekkol before I was pulled from the room. My stomach twisted with agony when I thought that might be the last time I'd see him.

CHAPTER 23
SEKKOL

There was a blinding light as I opened my eyes and blinked. I gripped my head as a sharp pain cut across my forehead.

"Don't move too suddenly," a voice instructed me from behind.

I turned sharply and spotted my father leaning against the wall.

"What are you doing here?" I asked while trying to sit up. The pain in my head was increasing in intensity, and the ground began to move as I glanced down. Feeling groggy, I touched the spot on my shoulder where I had been injected with what I believed to be a sleep serum. Now I was struggling to regain control of my senses.

"I had to see you," Father said as he came over to me.

"You had enough chances out there," I told him, reminding him of the trial that had ended. "What time is it?" I had no idea how long I had been unconscious.

"It's a few minutes before five," he told me.

So I had been asleep for five hours. I planted my feet firmly on the ground, then tried to stand. I wobbled and almost collapsed. My feet, it seemed, were not awake as yet.

Father rushed over and grabbed me by the arm as he tried to help me to the bed once more. I shrugged him off, and the act caused him to stumble backward just as I landed on the bed with a thud.

"Just go," I instructed him, the thunder in my head sounding louder after each word.

My father was the one person on Jupiter who could overturn a ruling by the Tribunal, but he had insisted I be punished for my act. It was almost treasonous to lie with a human and even worse to imprint on one. And I had done both. But none of those decisions were my own. I had found myself incapable of resisting Keira ever since I had first laid eyes on her.

She had appeared frightened, and I had felt an overwhelming sense to protect her without understanding why. But that was before I had realized I had imprinted on her. I tried to escape the feelings and the thoughts that came with it, an insatiable desire to be with her. They had come on fast and strong and had winded me before I could fully grasp them. Now I was facing punishment for what my people believed to be an insult to the future of Jupiter.

Father regained his footing and stood before me, his arms hidden behind him. "I met your human."

Fury built inside me, and I remembered then that she had been in the room. I blinked rapidly as I tried to clear the mist in my mind, to capture the memories that had temporarily left me.

"What did you do to her?"

"Nothing," he said and walked to the bars of the gate.

I checked my surroundings and realized I was in a different holding area than the one I had been in earlier. This was an unfamiliar place to me, with its gray walls and steel bars.

"Where am I?"

"This is the pre-death chamber," Father answered without hesitation.

Of course. I wouldn't have seen this place before. Only those about to die would.

I thought of the last man I had witnessed being disintegrated. He had struggled, but the armed guards had been too much for him. My Enforcers were also on hand to ensure he wouldn't escape, and I wondered now if they would use my own men to safeguard me. Each time I thought I was ready to die, Keira's face would come into view, and everything would rearrange in my head and make me want to live. For her.

"I don't understand," my father murmured.

"Understand what?"

"What is it like with the human?" he asked and then turned to face me.

I was not in the mood for small talk, not right before my execution. I would rather spend my last moments with her. "Where is Keira? I need to see her."

She was all I cared about and wanted. I hadn't known how empty my life had been before her, and now that she had become a part of me, her absence was remarkably noticeable. She snuck in to my heart when I least expected it and had swiftly become my entire world.

"For centuries, no resident of Jupiter has ever imprinted on a human. There is nothing in our jurisdiction that provides for such an improbable thing and, therefore, no reason before to change the laws." I looked at him and saw genuine confusion written all over his face.

"You have the power to rewrite the old laws, and I am Jupiter's heir. I should not be here."

"Am I expected to change the laws because my son fell in love with a human?" he asked. "What happens next, when someone commits an act that is uncommon again? Do we keep changing the laws?"

"No, Father," I told him. "You simply make room for compromise." I heaved an exasperated sigh. "Especially when one doesn't have a choice."

"Interesting. That was the same argument your human presented."

I whipped my head around, the fog in my mind lifting a little more each time he mentioned Keira. "You spoke with her? I didn't think that was customary."

"It is not," he replied. "But she refused to be quiet. Fought off my men to get to you while you were still unconscious. Given her predicament…she's a very brave human."

I stormed over to him now, feeling stronger. "Where is she now? What have you done to her?"

"We haven't decided as yet what to do with her," he snapped. "You stand to die, and all you care to ask concerns her?"

"You speak like a man who has never imprinted. Surely you must remember what it's like."

"I do."

This time, I touched him on the shoulder. "Then how can you do this thing?" It was like he was killing me twice. "Do you remember how you felt when you first saw Mother? How you felt when she died, leaving you all alone?"

He did not respond. His face became even more serious.

"There is no difference in what I feel for Keira, except you got your chance to be with Mother, who only left you when she died. She was not taken from you. You were not denied being with her. What you're doing to us is cruel. Perhaps if I were not the one facing such a harsh judgment, I would feel no sympathy, too." I turned away from him then. "But I am the one."

This was my harsh reality, and there was no escaping it. Being so close to death gave me much clarity and, in a way, greater prepared me for a leadership role. The position I had long avoided and that my father had constantly thrust upon me. I was his only heir, and he had been waiting for me to create my family and take my position at the top. Now, when I was most open to it, I was also furthest away. Despair clung to me like an ally, and I returned to the bed and sat down, weakened by the weight of it.

"And I am the one burdened with the decision to overturn a law that has stood for centuries or watch my only child die," he retorted. "Do you understand the gravity of the situation?"

"Are you really trying to get me to understand and accept my own execution?" I could hardly believe the impossibility of his unspoken request. "I will not die here. You hear me?"

He lowered his head, but his hands remained neatly tucked behind him. In that small cell, he did not feel like my father. We had not been close of late, especially since I had rebelled against so many things he wanted me to do or be. This was my greatest rebellion, and it seemed to have driven an even greater wedge between us.

"Your human seems to care for you. And ready to die to protect you."

And what good would that do? I did not respond. But the thought that she had come to the trial to speak on my behalf had proven that she was worthy of me, as I was of her.

"Bring her to me," I told him and then lay back on the bed.

He sighed, but he didn't speak another word before he walked to the bars and went out.

As soon as he had gone, I sat up again and started pacing the room. I was growing frustrated at my limited possibilities of escape, and I punched into the wall. My knuckles throbbed with pain, and I saw the bruise that quickly appeared. But the sharp sting from the wound was incomparable to the pain I felt inside. I was so lost in thought I didn't hear the footsteps approaching in the hallway until I heard Brom's voice.

"Sekkol?"

I wheeled around. "What are you doing here?" I rubbed my hand down my face and went back to sit on the bed.

"I had to come. I saw Keira," he said softly. "She wants to see you."

"Where is she?" I charged to the bars and gripped them in my palms.

"They are holding her over at the Great Pike. Lord Magnus has not yet made a decision on whether to have her resold or…"

He didn't need to say. I already knew. My eyes bulged, and for the first time in my life, I felt helpless.

"Brom, you need to get her out of there," I implored.

"She is well guarded," he said. "There is no way for me to get in there."

"Then get me out." I shook the bars as I spoke. "She cannot remain there." I gritted my teeth and watched as my knuckles grew white. I felt sweat beads where there had been none. An enormous pressure descended upon my chest. I became dizzy, and I rested my forehead against the cold metal of the bars.

"I'm sorry, Sekkol," Brom said as he touched my fingers. "There is nothing I can do without joining the both of you on death row."

"I understand." I grimaced. It was senseless for me to return to Anon to save Brom, after he was held for ransom until I did, and then have him face the same fate still.

He walked off then, his head hung and his steps echoing off the walls, creating a sad melody that seemed to remain even after he had gone.

I went back to the bed and sat. My body began to shake as fear overcame me. But it wasn't fear that I was about to die. I was more concerned *she* would. The idea of her dying crippled me, and I felt my body grow limp as I fell against the bed. I closed my eyes, and when I did, I saw her standing there the first night she had been at my house. She had found me naked, and I remembered clearly the way her eyes had bulged before she had run off again.

I was not ready to let her go, but I had yet to find a way to keep her.

CHAPTER 24
KEIRA

"Guard!" I called as I pressed my head against the bars. "Guard."

I touched the spot at my neck where the communicator was still implanted and wondered if it had been dislodged. It would be the worst time for me not to be able to communicate when I needed them to understand me now. There were two guards posted outside my cell, which was somewhat different from the one I had seen when I'd first arrived on Jupiter. Jonas had tossed me and the other humans into a cell that seemed more like a dungeon. At least here, the walls were a pale shade of gray and the bedding was soft. But there was no toilet or sink or anything of that manner, which gave me the idea that this was not a place where one was held for any considerable length of time.

"Hey!" I shouted again, until one of them moved and looked over at me. "I need to see Lord Magnus," I called, but he just looked back around and kept ignoring me. "I want to see Lord Magnus. Hey." I started shaking the bars until the other guard stormed over to me.

"If you don't remain quiet, I will personally disintegrate you," he said. He glared at me with small, beady eyes that flashed with danger.

"Please, I need to talk to Lord Magnus."

My words fell on deaf ears as he walked off again. I was growing frustrated, and I slid to the floor as the first tears began to fall from my eyes. I wiped them back and closed my eyes as I tried to control my breathing. I could feel the tension growing inside, and I pressed my fingertips against my temples as I began to experience something that felt like a brain freeze from drinking cold water too quickly. I had been spirited for the first few weeks I had been here, fighting Sekkol the entire time and sometimes wishing I would die. Now that it was a real possibility, I no longer desired it. The difference was this was not my home; these were not my laws. I had no legal representation, nor would I have a trial. I was a stranger in a strange place, just waiting to die. I thought then that maybe seeing Sekkol would make this burden bearable.

I didn't even move when I heard footsteps approaching; they were probably those of the men sent to take me away. If I were lucky, I'd wind up a foot servant to the cruel commander. I was afraid to think of other ways to remain alive.

"Why is it so important for you to speak to me?" the voice asked.

My eyes flew open, and I twisted my body far enough for me to see Lord Magnus standing there. I clawed at the bars as I struggled to stand and wound up slipping a few times.

"Lord Magnus." I felt relief wash over me just before I realized he was possibly there to escort me to my death.

"I don't think we have ever had a human on Jupiter who was as stubborn as you are, or as vociferous," he said as he swung his hands behind him.

"Can I see him?" I was gripping the bars now as I tried to understand the meaning of his visit. I had been pressing my luck. I didn't think the guards would have actually passed on my request to see him.

"You stand here facing death or worse, as does he, yet the one thing you ask for is not for your freedom, but to see my son?" he asked.

"Yes," was all I could say.

"Hmm," he grunted.

"I don't want him to be alone," I told the man.

Up until that moment, I hadn't acknowledged how much I wanted that very thing. I was a social handicap back on Earth. I didn't have many friends, didn't go out much, and had little experience with men. It was ironic that it wasn't until after I was kidnapped from home that I found one where I belonged. It wasn't until I was made a slave to an alien that I realized how badly I wanted to be possessed, not until I was facing death had I ever felt more alive. And if I could share those last moments with the man who had triggered it all, then I was willing to risk it.

Lord Magnus stood there looking at me in an odd way that was beginning to make me feel naked. I looked down at my clothes, ones I hadn't changed since I had showered at Geneva's.

"Guards," he said after a while. One of the men hastened over, bowed, and stood rigidly beside Lord Magnus. "Release her." Then he stepped back and gave the man room.

I had been asking, but I was still surprised when he gave the order. I stepped back when the guard pushed the bars inward, sidestepped them, and quickly walked past.

"Follow me," Lord Magnus said as he started walking.

I looked around as I followed him, observing the plainness of the building. Like Sekkol's home, everything was of a uniform color, but instead of white, this was a shade of gray. There were bars connecting several cells down a long passageway, and I wondered how often they needed these. How often they killed here.

"Will I see him?" I asked as I skipped to keep up with his long strides.

He did not respond. His eyes remained trained before him as we went through a series of long passages until we wound up on a platform. There was an opaque tube of sorts that ran as far as I could see on both sides and resembled oversized pipelines.

"Where are we?" I asked as I looked around.

"Chute number eight approaching."

"What was that? What is this?" I asked. Suddenly, I got the odd feeling he was taking me elsewhere, and I started backing away, looking around me at the same time for someplace I could escape to.

Something whizzed along the tubes and then opened inches away from our feet.

"Get in," Lord Magnus said and moved away.

I was not inclined to do the same. I folded my arms over my chest and tilted my body forward as I tried to look inside the thing. He stepped inside and then turned when he realized I wasn't following.

"Do you think I would have entered if I had meant to kill you here?" he asked.

He had a point. I inched slowly toward him and stuck my neck in. The interior was empty of people, but there were seats embedded into the walls of the chute, and I sat in one across from him. As soon as I did, I was strapped in, but I relaxed somewhat when I saw the same thing happen to Lord Magnus.

The doors closed then, and the vessel shot forward, shifting everything within me as it did. I gripped the sides of the seat until I felt my fingers grow numb. I felt like I was on an amusement park ride, and I was beginning to feel nauseated. I closed my eyes and was relieved when I felt it slow down. As soon as it stopped, the belts slid back, and I stood. My legs were shaking, and I thought I saw a hint of amusement in his eyes before he turned away.

We walked across the platform and to a huge chrome-like door. He tapped the transparent screen, and numbers illuminated the surface. A few swipes across the device and the door whooshed open. I walked behind him down another corridor, passing a few other barred cells and guards placed strategically along the way, until I saw him stop before one. I hurried past him, and my heart did a somersault when I saw Sekkol.

"Sekkol!" I cried as I rushed to the bars.

He sprang from the bed and raced forward. Immediately, his hand came through, and he cupped my face with it. I leaned against it as his warmth seeped through me, and I closed my eyes as I reached up and held his hand there.

Then he looked over at his father, and his hand left my face. "Allow her inside," he said to the man.

"This can only be a brief meeting," Lord Magnus said as he stepped forward and entered a code on the screen to the right of the bars.

They had barely started to open before I charged inside and into Sekkol's arms. My act surprised even me as I flung my arms around him. Instantly, he started kissing my neck, all the way around, before he planted even more on my face. And when he found my lips, all the noise in my head died, and there was only him. I gripped his nape and pressed him farther into me as his hands wound tighter around me. I felt like I'd been drowning and he was my air, and I sucked him in with large gulps.

Then I pulled back and looked him in the eyes. I saw pain, and then I smoothed the loose hair falling onto his cheeks.

"Why is this wrong?" he asked as he began to kiss me again. His lips were harder than they had been before, like they were chapped, and I felt weak inside thinking of how much he had suffered for loving me.

When he pulled back, I saw him look intently behind me, and I turned and saw Lord Magnus standing there, observing us. He seemed in awe, and he jerked his head and looked away when he realized we were both looking.

There was so much I wanted to say to Sekkol, but he said it all when he pulled me to him and just stood there holding me. I never would have thought I would fall for an alien. For him. I had kept my heart guarded for so long, trying to block any possibility of pain. But little did I know when I built that wall around me, I was also keeping love away. It had found me still, when I least expected it, and I could feel the tears rolling down my cheeks when I thought I might need that wall again. If I was spared.

"That is enough," Lord Magnus's voice broke through, and I ran my hand down my face to rid it of the residual tears. I saw him signal to someone, and instantly, two guards appeared.

They entered the cell and stood by us. Sekkol looked at them and then at me, and then his lips dipped once more and connected with mine like a magnet to a steel plate. I could feel his resistance to let go, and I didn't think he would. Except the guards held on to my arm and pulled us apart. I reached out to him, and he gripped my arm as he tried to pull me back. The guard was strong as he pushed me, while the other braved Sekkol's wrath.

"Father, don't do this!" he shouted as I was pulled out and the bars slid into place again.

I looked around, but Lord Magnus had already walked away. I

stood there for a while longer, recognizing too well the anguish on his face. My head began to spin when I realized that might have been the last time I saw him. I clutched my chest when I felt like I was suffocating. Moments later, I heard Sekkol call my name in a faraway voice just before I crashed to the floor.

CHAPTER 25
SEKKOL

I kept my face pressed against the bars as I strained to see what they were doing to her. Keira had fallen, and the guards had taken her.

I called to my father, but they all kept walking until there was the loud whoosh as the doors closed and then silence as thick as a cloud enveloped me. My heart felt like someone was holding it in their palm and crushing it. I paced the floor, waiting for something to happen, though the likelihood of anything happening that would alter my fate was slim to none. The hours went by until I wasn't sure anymore if it was night or day. I went to the bed and fell backward onto it and stared at the ceiling until my eyes got tired.

"Sekkol," someone called, and my eyes fluttered open.

My eyelids were heavy, and I got the impression I had not been asleep for long.

"Sekkol," the voice came again.

I rubbed my eyes and sat up in bed. There were two guards standing there, and instantly, I was at the bars.

"Open them," I growled.

They looked across at each other, and then one of them leaned to his right and slid his hand across the screen. There was a click, and the bars rolled open. They moved to stand on either side, and I looked at them oddly. I felt like I was in a prehistoric game of "escaping the hunter," and though I wanted to be free, I also wanted to be alive.

"So, what? I run, you chase, I die?" I asked the men as I looked at them. "Is this a trick of some sort?"

"You are free to go," one of the guards said, even though he didn't look at me.

I had known of men who had been here before, but I'd never heard of one that was ever set free.

"Lord Magnus requests your presence at the Great Pike. We are only here to escort you," the guard added.

I needed no further information. I started running down the hallway, and the guards gave chase.

"Wait!" one of them shouted.

But I felt like I had been waiting for far too long. I needed to see her; there was no use in being free if I could not be with her. I got to the door, and I slid my fingers across the screen to open it. I had used it many times before, and I was glad it had not changed. I was out the door and down the platform before the guards got to me. The chute came after a few minutes, just before my pacing carved a hole into the metal flooring.

The chute could not glide fast enough, and I bounded out, rushed across the platform, and through the doors. I ran down the halls as I headed for the room where I knew I would find my father. I looked back and saw the guards were no longer chasing me, but they had taken to walking. They were not allowed to run through the halls except in extreme emergencies. I got to the large metal door and pressed the button shaped like an M in the center. The doors slid apart, and I rushed inside.

"Father?" I called.

I did not see them at first when my eyes scoured the room. But then I saw her head stick out from behind the column to my right.

"Keira," I breathed as I ran to her.

We collided somewhere in the middle, and I wrapped my hands around her. I pressed her against me until I could feel her heart beating against my chest, and then I pulled back and smoothed the hair down her face.

"Are you all right?" I asked, and then I kissed her before she could answer me. "Are you?"

She started laughing, and I was not sure if I had ever heard that sound before. It caressed me just as her fingertips did when she stroked my face. "You won't give me a chance to answer."

Then I realized she was here, in my father's room. I looked over at him, my eyes armed with a ton of questions.

"What does this mean, Father?" I asked, even as I kept my hands secure around her waist.

"Your human, she makes quite an argument," he said as he came over to us. Then he patted me on the shoulder and smiled. "I'll let her give you an update." Then he walked out, and I searched her eyes for the answer.

"Is this real? Is it over?" I probed. "What happened when they took you away?"

"They brought me here, but you know me. I don't shut up," she said and smiled. Her entire face lit up, and I felt her warmth traveling through me, and all I wanted was to take her into my arms and show her how much my spirit needed her.

"What did you do?" I asked, already sensing my freedom had been her doing.

"I simply asked him to let you go," she said and grinned.

My head snapped back as I looked at the amusement on her face. "That cannot be true," I replied. "I've asked that many times, and I was ignored."

"Well, you're not a woman from Earth with great influence," she continued to tease, and I pulled her closer to me.

"If you don't tell me the truth, woman, I will not be held responsible for what happens next," I warned as I played with her. I had never seen this side of her before, and where I had felt like I had wanted her before, I realized I could not have been more wrong. "Keira," I said in a husky voice, and I dipped my head as I prepared to kiss her again. My lips remained suspended in midair, held by her index finger as she broke my advance.

"Don't you want to know what happened?" she asked as she pried herself from my reluctant fingers.

"Must you tell me now?" I asked. Need was driving me insane, and all I could think about was stripping her right there and taking her.

She looked around the room and then moved closer to me. She had that look in her eyes, and when she stood before me, she bit her lower lip and started making trails down my chest with her fingertip. I felt the ripples on my skin as she moved, and a slight groan escaped me as my member began to pulsate and burn with desire.

"You think your father will be coming back in here anytime soon?" she asked.

She looked up at me with her large brown eyes, and I lost control. I pulled her to me and kissed her with such ferocity it made my head spin. Her tongue darted into my mouth and began exploring before my own joined hers, and the two engaged in a sensual dance. I gripped her ass and pulled her in even closer until I could feel her heart beating against my chest. I could feel my erection throbbing, wanting nothing more than to enter her, but I wanted to take every part of her.

I pushed her dress upward and covered her soft, warm breasts with my palms before finding her lips again. I squeezed her breasts and listened to her moan against my mouth. She gripped both sides of my head and forced me downward, and I followed her lead and caught her nipple through the thin fabric. I felt a sharp pain as she grabbed a fistful of my hair, and my tongue only moved faster, flicking over her firm peaks as I moved from one to the other. Even the pain she inflicted awakened my erogenous zones. I listened to her breathing and experienced a new level of pleasure.

One hand remained on her breast while the other moved down to her middle, and I felt her body as it melted under my touch and the liquid got sticky on my fingers. Slowly, I slid one inside her, feeling as her body opened to me, then closed again around my finger. I stroked her, and I could feel my own body begin to melt as my own liquid rose to the surface and balanced at the pinnacle of my erection.

She was breathing harder now, and I stroked even faster as her hold on my hair tightened. My manhood squeezed against the fabric of my suit, and I detangled myself from her long enough to rid myself of it. I lifted her in the air when I was done, and she wrapped her legs around me. Then I cupped both of her ass cheeks and slid her downward, where my impatient manhood wriggled its head as it tried to force its way into her. I gripped it around the middle and drove it home and felt as she clenched her core around me. I squeezed into her, slowly at first as I forced her to receive me, and then, as she grew hotter and wetter, I moved faster. I clenched my jaw as she enveloped me, and her back rubbed against the wall as I pounded into her. She moaned, and her legs spread wide, and I sank all the way in.

I felt like everything was right when I was inside her, and I enticed her into a kiss, wanting to take her everywhere at once. I was panting and my chest was heaving, and for that moment, I didn't care about the laws or that she wasn't even supposed to be mine. Each time I was inside her, she belonged to me, and I consumed her, as she did me, one stroke at a time.

Then I started to move faster, feeling the sensations building up all too quickly inside me, and though I wanted to postpone the moment, I was weak, too. Her walls were slick from her overflow, and as it filled the space around my member, my body responded in kind. I felt my engorged veins swell even more, and I was aware of the warmth rushing upward. I dug into her flesh and emitted a low moan as my legs tightened under me.

My body twisted and my knees grew weak as I felt myself spill into her. I rocked and buried my head against her neck as I tried to draw strength from her. She was sweating, and her aroma filled my nostrils and caused me to shudder even more. I stroked, much weaker now, as I emptied myself, and she clung to me as she took it all. I could feel her legs trembling still, and their hold on me grew slack as she slid one leg to the ground and then another.

"I think we need to get dressed," she said as she winked and pulled on her clothing.

I did the same, and in minutes, it was as if nothing ever happened. Sex with her was extraordinary, and I was still breathing hard as I went over to the seating and she took a spot next to me.

"Now you can tell me what happened," I prompted as I looked over at her.

"Well, your father spoke with the Tribunal, and they agreed to amend the laws. Now, as long as it's an imprint and not outright defiance, then it is possible for two persons to be together," she said.

"I bet that was not an easy thing to do," I replied as I leaned back in the seat. "There have not been many amendments to our laws over the decades."

"I think it was stupid."

"What?" I shot back.

"The laws. Back on Earth, laws are meant to protect people and to make sure no group shows any control over another. But here, how can there be a law about falling in love?"

"I don't think there was much thought about love when it was written. More of preserving the purity of Jupiter and its inhabitants."

"I'm sorry I spoiled all of that," she said with a smile.

"That does not look like a sorry face," I teased as I put my hand around her shoulder.

She leaned into me and sighed. "So now what?"

"What do you mean?"

"Do we have to wait for a while before...? Can we just move in now?"

"Would you rather go back to Earth?" I asked, though I dreaded hearing the answer.

"Not a chance," she replied. "Not unless you come with me."

"Not a chance," I said as we both laughed.

Then the great doors parted, and my father reentered the room. We both stood as he walked over to us. He gave us an odd look, and I felt naked thinking he suspected what had happened before, but I knew that was probably just my guilt nipping at me.

"I trust Keira has told you everything by now," he said as he stood before us with his hands behind him.

"She has." I confirmed as I felt the pressure leave my body. He stood there looking at us like he expected us either to be doing or saying something. "What?"

"I thought there might be somewhere else you might like to be," he said. Keira started giggling, and I blushed. "Was it something I said?"

"No." I held her hand and went to the door. I stopped inches away from it and then looked back at him. "Thank you, Father," I told him and smiled.

"I couldn't let my only son die," he replied.

He stood there like a god, in his pure white clothing and hair braided down his back, as the doors closed.

Then I placed my arm around Keira's shoulder as we went home.

CHAPTER 26
KEIRA

I woke up the same way I had for the last five months, with a smile on my face and the alien I had come to appreciate and love, known as Sekkol, right by my side. He was still sleeping, and I turned, causing his hand closer to me to twitch and, as if by instinct, pull me closer to his side. His eyelids moved, suggesting he was still engaged in deep sleep, and I traced the outline of his firm cheeks. The bluish color of his skin was even more beautiful at dawn, when the light was still soft and made delicate patterns on his body. I lowered my head and kissed his chest and his cheeks and then nestled up to him again.

For the last three months, I hadn't felt like the walls were closing in on me. I no longer jumped out of my sleep every night because I was plagued by demons I allowed to follow me home. I had thought when I'd first come to Jupiter that my life was over. It was ironic to think it hadn't begun before that point.

The device on the conical stand next to the bed sounded then, and he stirred. His eyes flickered open, and he immediately turned to stamp a kiss onto my forehead.

"I think Brom needs you," I told him as I detangled myself.

"How do you know?" he asked as he reached for his device and looked at the screen.

"Doesn't take a genius to figure out the codes," I replied and grinned. "Besides, what else do I have to do?"

"Genius, huh?" he asked. "Maybe you can figure out the secrets of civilization."

"I think someone else did that," I told him and laughed. "Now get up before he storms the house again."

"Maybe I can take the day off," he said as he pulled me down to him. "Then you can show me again what the Earth women mean when they say 'fuck me.'"

My mouth fell open, and I laughed when I heard the words come from his lips. I hadn't been aware he'd been taking notes, and it was hard not to laugh at how funny they sounded coming from him.

"What? Did I say it incorrectly?" he asked.

I fell on the bed now, rolling with laughter until the breath left my lungs. "Did I say it wrong?" I laughed still. Tears were falling from my eyes, which seemed to confuse him even more.

"Are you hurt?" he asked as his face grew serious with concern.

I looked then and wiped the tears away. "No," I said when I realized he was referring to my tears. "This happens sometimes when we laugh too hard." I went over to him and wrapped my hands around his neck. "And we laugh when we're happy."

"So you cry when you are sad and also when you are happy?" he asked, looking at me like I was a crazy person.

"When you say it like that, it sounds ridiculous," I replied. "But yeah, we have tears of joy, too."

"Strange humans," he said and pulled me to him. We got lost in a blissful kiss just before the device started beeping again. Sekkol growled into my mouth and then pulled away.

"Just go," I told him, though I hated seeing him leave.

"Not yet," he whispered against my face, and then he started kissing my neck.

It felt so good when he kissed the base of my throat, and I bit my lips as I rested my palm against his cheek. His mouth moved from my throat to my earlobes and then my lips. I caught them and embraced the rush that was quickly building up inside me. A yelp escaped my lips when he grabbed me around the middle, and we crashed onto the bed with me on top of him. His hands wrapped around my waist and then his fingers moved along the spot just above my ass. He set my body on fire when he touched me, and instantly, I started throbbing with need.

I gripped his member, feeling the heat that emanated from it. I squeezed it and felt him jump, and then he started to tremble. I looked over at him and kissed his stomach, his navel, and then ran my tongue up the length of his shaft. He froze as he watched me, and when I opened my mouth and slid him into it, stroking the base of his cock in a circular motion as I did, he jerked uncontrollably and grabbed fistfuls of the bedding. I moved my head swiftly up and down, and I tasted his salty, tangy flavor as he climaxed in my mouth.

"How did you do that?" he asked.

I smiled at him, pleased to see he was still hard, and then straddled him. I held his erection around the middle and guided it inside me, and he gripped my hips as he watched me pump. I pressed my palms against his chest, and he started moving. He was slow and purposeful at first, but when he started moving faster and going so deep, I felt my walls began to shake. He was hitting all the right places, and suddenly, I found it hard to retain my balance.

I pressed my legs against his chest, and he cupped my ass as he stroked me harder. My moans filled the room as pleasure took me over, and I felt my legs tremble as I climaxed. As soon as I did, I felt his rhythm change as he got jerky, and he increased in speed as he pounded against me until he bellowed and slammed into me one last time.

I was sweating, and my hair fell over my face. He looked at me and rested his hand on my cheek, and I kissed his palm when he did.

"Now I can go," he whispered.

"Yeah," I agreed and gave a mock pout. I rolled off him and drew the covers over me. I was no longer ready to leave the comfort of the bed.

He swung his legs over the side of the bed and went toward the bathroom. I remained there until he reemerged and went out of the room.

I knew what his responsibilities were, and as he was the leader of an elite team of warriors, it left me anxious every day he left. But I had seen him in action, and he was more than capable of handling his own. Further, I had seen how people shied away from him when we went on the streets; they feared him. Though, in that fear was inherent respect. His being with me inspired many of the residents of Anon, and soon, different races were mingling across Jupiter. I could hardly believe that a once insignificant person on Earth could have inspired so much on another planet.

I had already begun to settle here, too, but with the advanced technology and the flying vehicles, it left a girl with too much time on her hands. I was musing over what I would use to occupy my time that day when I heard voices in the other room. My brows instantly slanted as I slowly walked to where I could see who the visitor was.

Shit, I need to get some clothes.

I hopped into a fresh suit that was already waiting on the rack and then swept my hair back. I hoped she wouldn't smell the sex on me.

"Geneva!" I exclaimed and skipped into the room.

She glanced over at Sekkol before she stepped past him. "Keira."

I hugged her tightly, already happy she was there. She had become something of a mother figure to me, and I treasured her company. Now I knew what would consume my day; Geneva always had something interesting to do. We had developed a rare friendship since my time with her, and Sekkol continually expressed his gratitude to her and Gideon for allowing me the use of the hovercraft that day when I burst into the trial.

"What do you have planned for today?" she asked as she smoothed her dress behind her and sat on the oval stool that projected from the floor.

"Nothing before you got here," I beamed as I went before her. I turned when I heard the door slide open and was just in time to see Sekkol as he disappeared outside and the doors closed after him.

"Sari, could you make us something to drink, please?" I asked the automated helper installed in Sekkol's home.

"Would that be chilled or brewed?" Sari's robotic yet clearly feminine voice pierced the air.

"Brewed," I replied, knowing all too well Geneva loved nothing more than a hot beverage.

"I have something grand planned for us today," she said.

"The drinks are ready," Sari said shortly, and I went to the kitchen counter and retrieved the goblet-like cups from the tray that had slid from the wall. As soon as I took the cups, the tray rolled inward, leaving no evidence it had been there.

I was excited as always, now that I wasn't a wanted criminal, to tour the streets of Jupiter. Once outside, Geneva pulled me along, and I found it hard to believe she was over three hundred years old. She moved with great alacrity, and I couldn't help feeling like a child at a carnival. I watched as the world buzzed around me, as hovercrafts whizzed by, accompanied by the cheerful hooting of the young. I watched as a little girl, her skin much like Sekkol's and her dark hair braided and coiled atop her head, smiled and waved at me. I looked longingly at her, and when I looked over at Geneva, she was staring intently at me.

"You could make one of your own," she intimated.

"I don't know about that," I said, though my heart had begun to flutter inside me at the possibility of it. "Can that happen?"

"No one knows," she replied. "No human has ever conceived a child with a man from Jupiter before. If you do, you and Sekkol will be the first to parent such a child."

The excitement within me grew, especially because I never thought I'd ever have children. After my parents' death, my life had been plunged into what felt like a black hole in the Bermuda Triangle. I was lost, and I spent my days going through the motions, just existing until my number was up. Now, something better waited for me, and I was growing nervous at the very thought of it.

"Don't worry. You will make a great mother." She patted my hand as if she could read my mind. "And with a mother like you and a father like him…" She stopped there, but she said more with her silence than her words could ever do justice.

I laughed at what she was insinuating, but she had given me, at that moment, something I had not felt in years: hope.

We spent the day touring the science center, and I was overwhelmed by the leaps and bounds in technology afforded to the people on Jupiter. They could make food simply by directing a laser-like beam onto a flat, white surface, adding some necessary data, and presto! Which greatly explained what went on behind the walls in Sekkol's home. They had equipment that could recreate body parts, add or subtract memory, and, of course, weave information into their version of the DNA strand.

I touched the back of my neck, where my transmitter used to be. It had been my only way of communicating with the people, but Sekkol had upgraded my communication capability with a state-of-the-art technology enhancement, where my ability to speak their language had been infused into my brain. Now I thought as they did and desired the same things as them, but I had decided to keep my memories of Earth and my life before meeting the love of my life. I didn't want to lose any part of me, and forgetting my days on Earth would have left a void nothing could fill.

By the time I got back home, I was bursting at the seams with enthusiasm. I was anxious for Sekkol to get home, and I busied myself by getting ready for it. I hadn't seen anything like lingerie on this planet, but I could make something that would take his breath away. I got cutting tools from the kitchen, and my hands worked quickly to make a satin bodysuit that ended at my bikini line. Everything was visible to the naked eye, and as soon as I heard him enter, I stepped into the shower and let the water soak me through.

He heard the water and came in…and froze at the door when he saw the spectacle before him. He looked me over several times, and I stood there, biting my lip, as I waited for him to move. But he remained immobilized. I smiled and walked over to him, leaving wet footprints all the way. I got to him and held his hand. Only his eyes moved as I placed his hand over my left breast, feeling his warmth already seeping through me. Then I took the other hand and did the same, and when he had them both, I wrapped my arm around his neck and pulled him down to my aching lips.

His touch sent shivers down my spine, and I felt his hands move as they squeezed me now.

"About time," I muttered against his mouth, and I lost my breath when I felt his thumbs caressing my hardened nipples.

I traced my tongue along the outline of his lips and darted in and out of his mouth as I teased him. I heard him growl as he moved his hand and grabbed me around the middle, lifting me in the air and making long strides that brought us to the bed. He ripped the flimsy fabric from my body and tossed it aside before he stepped out of his dark suit, revealing hardened muscles that glimmered in the light.

"Let's make a baby," I said to him as he stood there.

He looked curiously at me, and then he pressed his palms on the bed on either side of me. "You do not even know what you ask of me."

"I know it's never been done, but we can try, right?" I asked and grinned sheepishly.

His face suddenly broke out into a smile. He grabbed me and rolled on top of me. I could already feel his manhood throbbing, and I reached down and caught it in my hand. It had only been a few hours, but it felt like it had been too long since we made love. I spread my legs and used his erection to rub against me. When he lowered his head and caught my nipple in his mouth, my hand fell. He grabbed his member and repeated my motions. My body quivered as it grew hot with pleasure.

"What are you doing to me?" he breathed against my neck.

"Giving you everything," I replied as I spread my legs and helped him inside me.

My muscles tightened around him, and when he stroked, he did so with a new purpose. We remained tangled in the sheets as the sounds of our moans filled the evening air and took us into the night. Sekkol seemed insatiable, and I was reluctant for him to leave my body. When I felt him shudder as he climaxed once more, I knew he was now spent.

Breathing hard, he rolled, pulling me with him into an embrace.

"Wow," I said as I locked my fingers with his.

"Do you think that might do?" he asked.

I laughed before kissing him on the cheek. "I have no doubt about it."

Before I fell asleep that night, my hand was planted on my

abdomen, feeling what I knew to be a new life within me. I had all but forgotten about Earth now. Here, on Jupiter, I had found a new home and love. Just the thought made me sleep soundly.

DEKKIR

CHAPTER 1
GRACE

"All right, Grace, you've entered the atmosphere. If you check out your left view-screen, you will notice the main continent coming up quickly. You will need to hit the braking jets in sixty seconds. Just keep calm and get ready to go on my mark."

"'Keep calm,' he says." Cradled in the control chair of my dropship, I hovered my hand over the ignition switch, watching the growing broad swath of green and brown landmass through the view-screen. My heart pounded as I waited. This was my first live drop onto Planet Lyra. My instructor, Chief Science Officer John Stirling, had run me through dozens of simulations. By now, I could do them in my sleep. The difference here was none of the simulations could have killed me. "Ready when you are, Dr. Stirling." *I hope.*

"Right, then, here we go. On one. Three... two... one... Go for rockets!"

I hit the switch and felt my stomach lurch. The red edges on the view-screen retreated as the rockets shook the ship around me, easing my catastrophic drop toward the forested land below. Soon, the dropship's wings would deploy automatically, and I would be able to fly the rest of the way in. Meanwhile, I had to trust the onboard computers to slow my descent enough that I wouldn't splatter all over the landscape.

It was the most nerve-racking part of the entire descent: twelve long minutes of sitting there doing nothing, hoping all the calculations the programmers had made back at base were correct. I trusted most of my fellow personnel at Command, but that was hard to remember when I was rocketing toward the surface of a foreign planet.

"Are you still with me, Grace?" Stirling's voice probed gently, the tiniest touch of concern coloring his tone. John Stirling, the only other human to make contact with the Lyrans, had a talent for putting me at ease. So much so that I had fought a totally inappropriate crush on him for nearly as long as we had been stationed together. Tall, lean, and pale, with white-blond hair and strangely impenetrable blue eyes, he had a velvet voice that soothed me as much as it got my attention.

"Oh, yes, Doctor, sorry about that. Descent rockets appear to be functioning normally. I'm just waiting for the wings to deploy." I glanced nervously around the tiny cocoon of a cabin. Had I left any of my needed gear behind? *Am I really ready for any of this?*

"All right, then, we've got a little bit of time to go over your orders. I'll be available to coach you if things get tight down there, but remember the Lyrans don't trust our technology, so it's best if they don't see you talking to your earbud too much."

That had been the biggest barrier to creating a treaty with the Lyrans: their almost superstitious wariness of our technology. Stirling had warned me that the first two dropships to approach one of their walled towns, known as forts, had been attacked on landing, mistaken for an invasion. Even now, he still had to land well away from any settlements and meet a guide to help him hike to civilization safely. I faced the same as soon as I disembarked.

"Understood, Doctor. Okay, so I'm supposed to meet this Chief Dekkir once I land, right? The briefing sheets Norcross gave me weren't very complete."

He snorted. "Well, that's because they came from Damon bloody Norcross. Everything's need-to-know with him, and in his mind, nobody needs to know. There are reasons I try to get you your data without his added filters, especially now that he has that grudge against you."

My lips twisted. Norcross, my immediate superior, was dark-haired and handsome in that plastic way that spoke of a rich family and customized genes. He fancied himself a ladies' man and had approached me with the most disrespectful case of jungle fever I had ever seen. At this point, I really could go my whole life without ever hearing a white man call me "exotic" again.

I had politely put him off, citing fraternization laws, while my stomach had churned with disgust. He had sulked ever since and kept doing childish things to trip me up—like supplying incomplete briefings on crucial missions. His hope seemed to be I would go directly to him to be filled in, but I always went to Dr. Stirling instead.

"Yeah, well, we may be out by the Crab Nebula right now, but Command rules still apply."

"Actually, if the lieutenant doesn't improve his behavior, a little bird may soon whisper in Commander Wickman's ear."

"Thanks for that, Doctor."

"Thanks for what?" came the reply, so smoothly I giggled a little. *Wow, that's not professional. I need to do something to get rid of this crush.*

Stirling sobered and went on. "War Chief Dekkir is the high chieftain's son, Grace, and he is likely to be a little bit brusque until he knows you. They are very suspicious of outsiders—understandable, being that we are the first space-faring race they have ever had contact with."

"If I were studying some lost Earth tribe instead, I would expect them to be wary at first as well." Though, all the "lost tribes" of Earth were truly lost now. My home planet was struggling along with massive overpopulation, resource depletion, and air that required breathers anywhere outside. *Welcome to the twenty-fourth century, where you have to go off-world to see a real forest.* Like the shimmering green canopy below me, growing vaster in my view-screens with every second. I would have marveled at its beauty if I weren't busy hoping I wouldn't crash into it.

I checked the chronometer: eight more minutes. Were the rockets stuttering a little? Could there be a fuel line problem? *Is this crate slowing down fast enough?*

"Anyway, I'm trying to figure out what my relationship with this Dekkir guy is going to be and how I should address him."

It was standard issue for all personnel working for Earth Military Command to have a universal language translator embedded in their neck just below the ear. The translator automatically interpreted alien language, in addition to converting English to the alien's native tongue, but I was wary of screwing up such an important introduction.

"Dekkir will be your guide and guardian while you are on Lyra. He will be responsible not only for your safety and basic needs, but also for any diplomatic situation that may come up. He will help you to connect with whatever goods and services you may need and will advocate for you among the other chiefs. You will live in his house-hold, and if Highfort should be attacked, he is obligated to protect you."

"Wow. Okay, well, that's a lot. Guess I had better be nice to this guy."

"To a point. Lyrans tend to appreciate it more if people are assertive and honest with them. 'Honeyed words often carry poison' is a rough translation of a local proverb."

"They'd *really* hate Norcross, then."

Stirling chuckled. "Yes, I dare say they would. Anyway, just use his title in any formal situation and follow his lead otherwise."

"Got it." I looked back at the rear view-screen, where Lyra's third moon shone a pale blue-green as it dwindled. The Earth base clung to its surface like a silver blister. That base had been my home for eigh-teen months, and though I didn't always like the company, I was going to miss it now that I was about to spend two years as the only human on Lyra.

I was the daughter of fourth-generation soldiers, and though I had gone for a doctorate instead, I still ended up working for Earth Mili-tary Command. I had spent my training period at the base eagerly looking forward to my first big assignment: the cultural evaluation of an entire species, which could lead to a possible trade alliance. I was proud to be part of it. But all I could think right now, as I waited for those wings to finally deploy and give me back control of my drop-ship, was I might be making a huge mistake.

I tried distracting myself again. "Do you have an image file of Dekkir?"

"Well, it's not likely you'll run into anyone else out there, but I did take a few images during our meetings." The forward view-screen flickered, and a secondary window popped up, showing an enormous, armored man bent over a stone table as he spoke tensely with a group of others.

I stared. He was well over two meters tall, with a long, top-knotted mane of white-blond hair and shoulders that could block a doorway. His scaly black armor contrasted with smooth, milk-colored skin that lay over massive muscles. His face was long and strong-featured with large, tilted eyes, pointed ears, and a wide mouth set in a focused line. His eyes caught my attention the most: almost metallic gold with a fierce wildness to them, like the eyes of a raptor-preserve owl. A black, long-bladed spear leaned against the table beside him; he kept one hand on its shaft as he pointed to a map on the table in front of him.

"All right," I managed breathlessly. "I don't think he's going to be easy to forget."

The image flickered out as the doctor chuckled. "Good. Now, once you make landfall, Dekkir should meet up with you within the hour. They are very careful not to leave people out in the wilderness too long. That would essentially be a death sentence thanks to all of the hostile flora and fauna around."

"Yes, I studied up on your ecological reports. I still don't understand why I can't bring my rail gun."

"I wouldn't worry about security too much. Dekkir himself will be acting as your bodyguard. Believe me, he is very competent and highly respected."

And a total stranger. "That's fine, but I really would feel better if I were able to protect *myself.*"

"I have included a selection of combat blades in your gear."

I sighed. *Knives...against predators that grow to the size of old Earth dinosaurs.* "I guess it will have to do. I just wish I understood why the Lyrans are so backward about technology."

"Grace, if aliens came to your world, would you be comfortable with them wandering around carrying weapons capable of leveling your cities?"

"No, of course I wouldn't. I'll…try to adjust." *And hope I survive.* "You're sure this Dekkir guy is that good?"

"He's the war chief for the entire planet. I think he probably knows what he's doing. Anyway, stay inside the dropship until he arrives. He will probably have some riding beast you'll have to get used to. Personality-wise, he is honorable and considerate and quite intelligent, but rather hardheaded. Fortunately, he is less so than his father, the high chieftain. I'm afraid *that* one is going to be a little bit difficult to win over. He is still convinced the humans from the sky are planning to take over his planet. Nor is he alone in this concern."

"I hope I can convince the Lyrans that's not true." Otherwise, studying their culture was going to involve a lot of tension.

"You may be successful in convincing them it is not *your* aim, Grace, but I am afraid convincing Lyrans to trust humans in general may be beyond your power. It certainly was beyond mine. Now that I have been promoted to chief science officer, I'm hoping you'll be able to continue my work fairly seamlessly. If we can make a good case to Command for creating this alliance, it will benefit both our worlds."

"I'll do my best."

"Just one more thing before you take over the controls again. Do you remember the emergency medical vial I gave you before you left?"

I reached up into the collar of my white jumpsuit, my fingertips finding the narrow steel pendant. "Yes, Doctor, I have it with me. What's in the vial, anyway?"

"It's nanite medicine of my own design. If you find yourself falling dangerously ill or are seriously injured, I want you to take the contents of that pendant. It will likely save your life, so keep it close."

"Of course, Doctor." *I'll just have to make sure none of the locals gets too curious about it.*

"Good. Now, you should be getting wing deployment within about thirty seconds."

"Got it." I grabbed for the steering column grips as they popped out automatically. Outside, the wings spread panel by panel to either side of the cockpit. "Okay, deployment's going clean, but I'm wondering about my velocity right now. It seems a little high."

"All right, let's have a look." A pause. When he spoke again, the tiniest note of tension had entered his voice. "You're considerably over the maximum speed for a safe landing. It looks like entry calculations were off."

"Oh, thanks, Norcross, you passive-aggressive pig. Okay. Looks like he expects me to work for a clean landing. How do we correct?"

"Increase the fuel to the braking jets to maximum. It will burn through your reserves, but we can always send another dropship."

"Done." I started flipping switches. "Let me know if my speed gets down enough, or else I'll have to pull up and circle back." The forest flashed past beneath me, and I fought hard to keep the dropship's nose up.

"You're in for a bumpy ride. Tighten your crash harness and get ready for it."

"Right." I adjusted my harness. The dropship shook from the efforts of the braking jets as it skimmed above the surface of an algae-greened lake. "I'm coming up on your landing beacon. Can I stop in time?"

"No. Looks like you'd best pull up and circle back."

I opened my mouth to reply, when I saw a massive green shape uncoil from the tree line ahead of me. The only thing I could think of was an octopus tentacle—except it was the size of a building. It reached for the dropship.

And I let out a quickly cutoff scream as the impact knocked me out.

CHAPTER 2
DEKKIR

I was waiting near the drop site when I smelled the familiar stench of beastvines coming out of dormancy and saw one's enormous green hunting tendril shoot skyward from its hiding place in the trees. The heavy thud that followed set my hackles on end. I bolted in that direction, knowing my guest was in deep trouble. *Get there fast, Dekkir, or you'll be burying the new human instead of greeting her.*

I had reservations about receiving another human guest, but my father, the high chieftain, had insisted on it. He claimed it was important for me as the future ruler to understand these aliens who inhabited one of our moons now. I knew he had a point, so I stepped forward. Now I regretted it.

I had no idea what power allowed the humans to live on our moon or allowed them to fly around in those metal crafts. However, I knew their devices could not be infallible. The sound of the collision and the ensuing crash of the vine and its metal prey to the forest floor only confirmed that.

Beastvines didn't move very often since it took a tremendous amount of energy for them to shift their gigantic bulk. When they did, it was a well-timed ambush, usually taking out some large land beast or as many as an entire flock of avians at once. Their skin and leaves were very sticky, helping them keep hold of whatever they slammed into. Unfortunately, that meant my visitor was probably trapped by the vine, no matter how wounded it was. If I did not get to her quickly, either the vine would crush the ship, or scavengers would arrive and tear into it. Either way, she would die.

Spear in hand, I bounded over deadfalls and dashed through a shallow stream on my way to the crash site. I could smell the wounded beastvine up ahead, as easy to follow as a flaming beacon.

I hadn't even run more than a minute before I saw part of the damaged vine sprawled out before me. The rotten green stink of it filled my nostrils, and I gagged as I hurried toward its far end.

In over a century as my father's war chief, I had faced many crises. Battles between villages, plagues, floods, hundreds of predator attacks. I had met all these challenges with distinction. I did not intend to do any less for this stranger, even if she was from a completely alien race. It was a matter of honor and pride as well.

Finally, I saw the gleam of crumpled metal up ahead and slowed down to take in the wreckage. The craft was very small compared to the one the doctor had used. It looked barely larger than a two-man handcart. The rear portion had ruptured, spilling a tangle of strange tubes and blocky instruments down the length of the vine, where it leaned against the splintered trunk of a massive tree. A sharp scent cut through the beastvine stink, and I saw amber liquid drizzling from the vehicle's rear.

Collapsing the shaft of my spear to a short grip, I dug the blade into the side of the tree, pulling myself upward and then using the deep notches it left as footholds. Eventually, I reached some of the remaining branches and pulled myself onto them. Above me, I could see through the windows of the strange craft. I felt a surge of relief as I noticed someone moving around inside. The impact had shattered some of the windows, allowing me to hear the person talking as she tried to salvage what she could from that small chamber. I listened closely. The alien female was speaking fluent Lyran. I'd learned from the doctor that their strange human technology automatically translated their speech to Lyran and my words to their alien tongue.

"No, Doctor, thanks to the harness, I'm only bruised, but I'm halfway up a giant tree, the vine's still wrapped around the ship, and I think we're leaking fuel. I'm trying to salvage what I can of my gear." She paused, bending over next to one of the two throne-like seats, and I peered in to get a better look at her. She was small and fetchingly curvy, with dark brown skin and fluffy jet-black hair. Even in bad circumstances, I had to admit this alien female was really quite beautiful.

I clambered closer as I listened, careful not to touch any of the vines, looking for a perch from which I could lever open one of the windows safely. *No luck so far. I may have to get creative.*

The human straightened finally, a small carry bag hanging from one shoulder, and took a final look around. "Okay, Doctor, I don't think it is safe for me to stay here much longer. I'm going to go do my best to climb down that damn tree—" She froze, staring out at me, wide-eyed. "Wait, I think my ride's here."

Her eyes were so dark and liquid that all I could do was stare back. It was like peering down into the bottom of two wells, but much more pleasant.

"Hello," I called over cheerfully in my native tongue. "I am War Chief Dekkir. Would you like to get out of there?"

She hurried up to the shattered window. "Well, your timing's good," she replied in a shaky voice. "I'm Science Officer Grace Bryant, your new Earth liaison. Thanks for coming. Do you have some rope? I can't find my descent line."

"No need. If you can cross the gap, I will simply carry you." I stowed my spear back in its sling. Grasping the branch above me, I leaned out as far as I could, testing the distance. It wasn't that far a reach; I could get her onto the branch with me without dropping her if she could get past the windows. "Can you get to me from there?"

Grace—what an intriguing name—stared at me speculatively then she nodded and reached for the rim of one of the windows. "Let me see if I can pop this thing out."

I heard a faint noise like a bird chirping, and suddenly, the entire cracked window burst from its frame and fell toward the ground. It startled me, but I managed to keep my grip on the branch and reached out to her. "Come, then. Scavengers will arrive soon to investigate the noise."

"Uh-oh." Her eyes widened, and she reached out to take my hand.

When her small fingers brushed against mine, I felt an unexpected rush of warmth, like the feeling when a hot drink went down my throat after I came in from the cold. It comforted me deeply, yet hurt a little, and left me with a strange feeling I had been without for far too long. The sensation stunned me, and it took all my will to keep my grip on the tree.

She seemed to feel something, too, her hand hesitating in my own. I worried she might draw it back while her balance was so precarious.

"Hurry," I told her. "I cannot hang on to this branch forever."

She hesitated and then firmly grasped my hand with both of hers. She jumped forward, and I pulled her across, wrapping an arm around her.

The feel of her soft, warm little body pressed against mine distracted me again, so much that I risked pitching forward and falling. But that might have hurt her, and the same strange instinct that gave me such pleasure demanded I *not* allow that to happen. "There," I muttered breathlessly. "Now hold on to my back, and I will climb down."

She clung to the back of my armor as I descended. I felt a little surge of disappointment when I reached the ground and she let go of me.

"We cannot remain here," I warned quietly. "Follow me." My heart beat very fast as I stared down at her. The warmth I had felt from her was still sinking into my bones, but I couldn't stop to think about why right now. "Our transport awaits at the lakeshore."

"I understand. Let's go." She sounded surprisingly calm for someone who had just nearly died. She had a strange air of quiet strength about her, and it intrigued me just as much as the warmth that passed between us.

I started back as she hurried along behind me, her shorter legs putting her at a disadvantage. I broke trail through the underbrush for her and did my best to let her keep up. We did not speak unless we had to, wary of drawing a predator's attention. Now and again, I looked back to check on her—and drink in the sight of her again.

Fortunately, nothing accosted us during our journey.

"Do you know how to ride?" I asked her quietly as we broke through the tree line.

"If you mean animals, I have never had the opportunity. Our world does not have this much wildlife. I'm not sure it ever did," she puffed as she followed me toward the water's edge.

"Is your whole world a desert?" I asked, intrigued. The doctor mentioned deserts during one of our brief conversations. What a strange idea: a place where rain never fell and plants never grew. Lyra had no regions like that at all.

Her voice went a little sad. "No, it's simply…used up. It is difficult to explain. But anyway, the answer to your question is no."

I grunted acknowledgment; this could be difficult. "My steed, Keer, is temperamental, but I will introduce you to her, and she should be willing to carry you as long as I am with you."

We walked out onto the muddy shore together. I pulled my spear back out, wary of what might be lurking under the water's surface. Lyra offered countless dangers. There was no such thing as a truly safe place here outside of the forts.

"I will try not to spook her," she promised, and I had to stifle a laugh. Full-fledged Sky Eels could not spook Keer.

"I do not think that will be a problem." I whistled loudly.

A dark shape burst from the treetops nearby, startling Grace into drawing closer to me. Powerful wings beat the air as the shape sailed toward us. "That is Keer." I smiled faintly. "Please do not be alarmed."

"'Do not be alarmed'?" she asked incredulously, and this time, I actually did laugh. She was funny as well as beautiful! Perhaps this would work out better than I had thought.

Keer landed nearby, close enough that the wind from her wings blew our hair around. She towered over us before settling down on her haunches. I couldn't really blame Grace for staring. Keer's long body rippled with muscle, her talons were the size of daggers, and her bright, golden eyes almost glowed against the velvet blackness of her fur. She stretched her narrow head toward Grace, sniffing curiously, and the human drew back a bit, her eyes widening.

"Keer is a Rilleen," I explained quietly as the creature continued to snuffle at her. "I have raised her since her hatching. You need not fear her." I stepped forward and patted Keer's neck. "Keer, this is Grace. Friend. *Not* food."

"Okay, War Chief, that is *not* reassuring. Are you sure she won't bite?" The skepticism in her voice almost sounded like sarcasm.

"She will not." Not usually, anyway. *Behave, beast.*

"Okay." Grace steeled herself visibly and stepped forward, holding out a hand, palm up.

I murmured to Keer soothingly as my mount sniffed at her hand. The Rilleen stayed calm, her wings folded placidly against her back and her tail relaxed. Then, to my absolute shock, Keer bent her head down and rubbed it very lightly against Grace's arm.

"Oh, wow, I think she actually likes me." Grace moved forward a little more, and Keer crouched down and butted her head against her hip.

"It appears so!" *So do I.* How could I feel so strongly attracted to a stranger that it distracted me from my mission? A possibility nagged at the back of my head, but I couldn't stop and contemplate it until we were safely aloft. "Can you climb onto her back? I will help."

She looked dubiously at the beast crouched in front of us. But then Keer let out a rumbling purr and squinted at her happily, and her worried look softened. "I'll manage."

"Do not be frightened. I will hold you." *Now there's a lovely prospect.* I climbed onto the narrow flight saddle perched between Keer's wings, buckling myself in before offering my guest a hand up. Keer barely shifted as Grace climbed up in front of me. "Here, use me as a backrest, and I will help strap you in—" I went silent as she sat back against me.

As her small body settled against my torso, I felt that warmth again —but a hundred times stronger. It went straight through my armor and roared through me like magma, leaving me shaking a little bit with its intensity. The suspicion lurking in the back of my mind gained strength.

Other Lyrans had described this feeling to me in joyous tones—its power, its sweetness, and the protectiveness that came with it. My head fell back, eyes closed to slits as the delicious rush of pleasure ran all through me. Her scent filled my nostrils, dispelling the stench of beastvine sap, algae, and mud, and I sighed with deep contentment. *This one is mine,* came the unbidden thought.

I shook myself out of my reverie and helped her buckle her straps. "Hold on," I instructed and then clicked my teeth at Keer. The Rilleen bounded skyward, wings unfolding to catch the air, and Grace let out a little cry of shock. I wrapped my arms around her reflexively, steadying her while struggling to contain another surge of delight.

How can this be? She is human. I cannot even breed children with her. Yet this was exactly how the others had described catching the scent of their True Mate for the first time. As we leveled off just out of beastvine range, and poor fish-out-of-water Grace slowly relaxed against me, I struggled with the idea.

Could this truly be her? My destined mate? An alien woman with an unknown agenda, who weathers a fall from the sky with stoic courage but cringes at the sight of my mount? And if so…how?

I held her as we flew, baffled and dizzy with unaccustomed bliss, drawing her scent in again and again as Keer carried us past the forest to the plains beyond.

CHAPTER 3
GRACE

This guy keeps sniffing me. What the hell?

I had finally relaxed enough to notice what Dekkir was doing about halfway through the flight. He was trying to be subtle about it at least, but it made my neck hairs prickle. There was nothing like having a guy three times your size getting touchy-feely while you're isolated with him and can't get away. Fortunately, all he did was hold me there against his chest and smell my hair. It might even have been pleasant, except he hadn't bothered to see if I was all right with it—and I wasn't, from a stranger. The doctor had reassured me that the kind of garbage Norcross pulled on women didn't happen as much with Lyran men. But if they were so much more enlightened, then why was Dekkir creeping on me?

Dekkir didn't seem like that bad of a guy. That just made his behavior all the more baffling. I was an alien on a diplomatic mission. He had to know cuddling me and sticking his nose in my hair without so much as a *by your leave* wasn't appropriate. But here he was doing it. *Oh, no way am I putting up with this for two years, no matter what's at stake.*

Norcross wasn't the only creep I had run into working for Command. There was always some guy around who was going to grope my butt at a party or hit on me drunkenly or generally act like a pig whenever he thought he could get away with it. It had left me very tired of horny idiots interfering when I was trying to work.

The worst part was I could have found Dekkir very attractive if he wasn't creeping—but that ruined it completely. When a guy moved in on you and didn't respect your boundaries, or even check to see if you had any, it was a giant red flag. Few things turned me off more quickly. But how was I to deal with this and save the diplomatic mission? Maybe the high chief would intervene if appealed to properly. *I just hope this problem doesn't continue long enough that I actually have to ask.*

We flew over the teeming forest—a gorgeous view, now that I wasn't worried about crashing into it. I liked Lyra, even though the planet had already tried to kill me once. I even liked Keer, and the giant, furry saurian certainly seemed to like me. But as for Dekkir? The very thought of him left me torn and worried. If he'd kept his hands and nose to himself, his instant crush on me would have been almost charming. But the eager sniffing just reminded me of the creeps back home.

Finally, something distracted him enough to give me a brief break. "There is Highfort," he murmured in my ear and pointed.

I looked out at the rolling, lightly wooded plain before us, and spied a tall, stone structure, a single building housing the entire town. Its broad shape circled a huge central courtyard, and all its doors faced inward except for the massive main gate. Arrow towers with slit windows sprouted from its outer rim, six in all. It shocked me to realize just how small Lyra's population was. I had looked at the numbers on paper, but it really didn't compare to seeing the capital of the planet and realizing it housed maybe ten thousand.

"We must hurry. My father is expecting us for an audience soon." We spiraled downward toward the crenellated top of the fort, heading for an area lined with thatched overhangs. A few long, gray heads poked out from the shelters. More Rilleen peering at their fellow as she back-winged above them. Keer landed with a thump and crouched down for us to disembark.

Dekkir unbuckled our straps and jumped down ahead of me, holding out a hand to help me down. I hesitated before taking it, but at least he let me go promptly. Keer head-butted me affectionately as we left. I turned back to scratch the beast briefly, glad at least something on this planet treated me well.

The war chief walked a bit too close as we hurried toward a sunken staircase near one of the arrow towers. I tried to ignore his proximity and focus on the meeting ahead. I had to make a good impression with the high chieftain, especially since he was so wary of humans.

We made our way downstairs into a crowded hallway that seemed to be some sort of indoor marketplace. Temporary wooden stalls lined the stone walls, with a narrow corridor in between. I could smell meat cooking, animal dung, sweat, and perfume. The overload dizzied me. A few of the merchants greeted us as we hurried past, but Dekkir held up an imperious hand, and they all backed off.

He led me maybe a quarter kilometer down the gently curved hallway, and eventually, we reached a heavy timber gate. The two leather-armored guards standing before it gave me curious looks as we walked up. One nod from Dekkir, however, and they bowed and pulled the gate open for us.

Beyond, I found myself in a clean, quiet hall. Multicolored banners and tapestries hung on the walls, oil lanterns and open windows on the outer wall provided light, and on either side, I occasionally saw a guard standing at attention. This place housed Lyra's decision-makers. I braced myself to spend the next hour or so on my best behavior, despite my crazy day.

Finally, the hallway opened out into a long, heavily bannered chamber that spanned from inner to outer wall. Rows of wooden benches sat with their backs to us, loosely filled with armored and robed Lyrans, all facing the single wooden throne of a tall, bronze-bearded man in slick-looking gray armor. He lifted his head as we came in and fixed his golden eyes on me.

"Come forward, my war chief," the high chieftain boomed.

I had to admit, High Chieftain Dorin really did look the part. Heroic build, Grecian curls… All he was missing was a golden crown. I slipped my pen-sized image capturer out of my sleeve and surreptitiously took a picture of him. *This will look great in my first report.*

He waved us forward. "Show us this new human who has come to our world."

Dekkir took me by the hand and led me down the center aisle to stand at the foot of the throne. "My Chieftain father, I bring before you today Science Officer Grace Bryant of Earth. She is to be our liaison with the humans above and a guest in my home, as you have ordered."

I sketched a bow as best I could with Dekkir keeping a grip on my hand.

Dorin nodded curtly. "I see. Good. This human is to be watched closely until she has proven herself to us. You will be responsible for her in every way." He didn't even look at me as he said this, focusing solely on Dekkir.

My heart sank. Apparently, in order to have any access to the high chieftain, I was going to have to go through Dekkir. I wouldn't have the chance to show my diplomatic chops, let alone ask Dorin to tug on his horny war chief's leash for me.

Maybe I'll get lucky, and he'll leave me be while he's back under his father's eye.

Dekkir nodded back and surprised me by smiling. "I will gladly do so, my Chieftain father, for I bring good tidings directly related to this matter."

Dorin leaned forward, chin on fist. "Oh? Please enlighten me."

"I have recognized her scent as that of my True Mate," Dekkir declared in a ringing voice, causing a ripple of turned heads and curious murmurs to go through the crowd. "She is my intended, and I will be petitioning for a permanent union."

I stared at him in shock, but given the awkward predicament, decided to remain silent.

"What in the hell was *that* about?" I demanded as soon as the audience had ended and the two of us were alone together again. He had brought me to his chambers at the far end of the marketplace: three large rooms, fairly plain, furnished in a masculine style of mostly heavy timbers. I stalked back and forth through the front room like a caged tiger.

He stood in a corner of the room, arms folded, his expression stern but a bit confused in the face of my anger. "You should calm down. There is no reason to be upset."

"You just announced to your high chieftain that we're engaged!"

"Yes, you should feel grateful I have accepted you as my mate so quickly."

Oh, he really does think he's God's gift.

"What is wrong with you? We just met. You never even asked me if *I* was interested in *you*. Why would you think it would be okay to go before your leader and tell him the two of us are...*mates*?" What an ugly word. It made us sound like animals in a breeding program.

Dekkir blinked at me. "I do not understand. I knew from your scent that you were mine. You must have sensed something from me as well."

"I don't even know what you're talking about. All I know is you just put me on the spot in front of the entire court. You have no right just to *decide* I'm yours."

His expression softened with even more confusion, the tight fold to his arms loosening. "But I did not make this decision. This was not under my control either. I did not intend to humiliate you by announcing what has been decided by fate."

I stared at him. *Is he crazy? I need to get to a private place and ask the doctor for advice.* "Look, I don't know what kind of romantic stories you guys wrap your ideas of attraction in, but you're missing the point. You can be interested all you want, but unless I agree, you get nothing. I am not your possession. I am a person!"

"I never said you were not. But it does not change the fact that you belong—"

I rounded on him, scowling. "Do you really think because you have power over me here and I give you a boner, you get to treat me like you own me?"

He just kept blinking, his expression so baffled I could have felt sorry for him if I hadn't wanted to rip his head off. "But...I belong to you as well."

"Did you ever ask if I wanted you? You don't even know if I'm single or married. You never bothered to ask. You just *decided.* Or tried to, because I'm not going along with it!"

His expression darkened. "I have declared myself to you in the ancient way, before my chieftain and my father, and in return, you refuse me in a most unnatural fashion!"

"I don't care what you think is natural. I choose whom I love, not you." I struggled to rein in my temper. "As much as I respect your culture, I refuse to be victimized by some sexist tradition that lets a guy lay claim to a lady without her permission. Don't make me have to report to my superiors that you are mistreating me."

He slowly lowered himself into one of the hide-seated chairs arranged along the far wall. "Mistreating you? I thought you wanted an alliance between our two peoples."

"Okay, let's put this another way. When Dr. Stirling lived here, did you guys try to marry him off to one of you to make an alliance?"

"No, of course not. He was not claimed."

"Then *don't* think that you can do it to me!" I pointed a finger at his chest. "I am a visiting diplomat from the only space-faring race that has bothered with this backwater, and I will be treated with respect. You don't touch me without my permission, you don't *smell* me without my permission, you don't walk around calling me your mate, and you *don't* try to get sex out of me. If you do, I will contact Command, and they will send an extraction team for me, armed with weapons you do *not* want brought to your fort. Got it?"

He scowled. Apparently, he wasn't used to taking orders from anyone but his father. "Woman, you defy the laws of nature! How can you claim to have no attraction to me?"

"I just don't. And that doesn't make me 'unnatural.' I'm sure a lot of girls think you're awesome, but I bet you never tried to claim them against their will!"

He shook his head in obvious frustration. "You are treating me as if I were some drunken fool accosting you at a festival. Is this your idea of diplomacy?"

"No, it isn't. But I'm disgusted that *your* idea of diplomacy involves me fucking you." I turned and walked to the hallway door, hoping I remembered the way back to the fort roof. "I'm going out to clear my head."

He got up. "You are under my protection. You should not leave my sight."

"Go to hell." I pushed the door open and stepped through, hurrying down the hall. I hoped I could lose myself in the market crowds before he could follow. I really needed a breather.

I got a lot of curious looks as I rushed through the marketplace, but none of the shopkeepers approached me this time. I supposed none of them knew what to make of me. That was fine. I didn't really want to talk to anyone right then anyway.

I felt like crying. I had looked forward to this job for the better part of two years, and now it was being screwed up by something as stupid as an oversexed, egotistical local. And somehow, the fact that it was *Dekkir* doing this bothered me the most. It almost felt like a betrayal, like maybe we *could* have had something if only he hadn't been such an ass about things. As it was, I felt like yet another woman who would end up being sexually harassed out of an important job.

I plodded up the staircase with the last of my strength. *What a day.* I didn't know how I was going to be able to rest safely in Dekkir's household. I didn't trust him not to try something while I was sleeping. Nor did I have any idea how I was going to work with him. I had endured Norcross, but this was potentially far worse.

I didn't catch sight of Dekkir in the crowd below, giving me hope I had escaped him. I made my way up onto the roof and looked around for a private place where I could sit. I finally found a clear spot near the overhangs that sheltered the Rilleen. I didn't get too close since, after all, only one of them knew me.

I sat against a haystack and pulled out my white, palm-sized uplink booster. It wouldn't be as strong as the one in the dropship, but I hoped for a clear signal anyway. I keyed it up, slotted my imager into it, and plugged one of its spooled cables into my earpiece. I heard the soft hum of the standby signal.

"Come on, you piece of crap," I muttered. I wanted to talk to the doctor first, for the sake of hearing a friendly voice. Too bad I was overdue for my first report to Norcross.

Fortunately, he was not a fan of long communications. I touched my earpiece as the tone in my ear finally cut off. "Lieutenant Damon Norcross from Science Officer Bryant."

The earpiece trilled softly, and I heard a click. "Miss Bryant!" Not

Science Officer or Doctor, of course—this was Norcross. His voice brimmed with obnoxious cheer. "How good to hear from you. How was your landing?"

"Your techs miscalculated my landing velocity to a degree that could have killed me. The dropship was then grabbed out of midair by an animate plant, and I barely escaped with my life." I spoke in a flatly professional tone, hiding my disgust with him. "Fortunately, my contact picked me up quickly. I am now at the Capitol."

"Is it really as tiny as everyone says?" No comment about his team's screw-up.

"I'm estimating the local population at roughly ten thousand."

He chuckled. "So what else do you have for me?"

"I have made contact with the high chieftain. His name is Dorin. He is highly skeptical of our continued overtures. It may be some time before I can earn his trust."

"Pick up any image files of their fort?"

"I have an image of Dorin and his court for you. You should find it educational. I'm drawing parallels with Britain in approximately the eleventh century."

"Upload this image for me immediately. I'm interested in finding out exactly what the high chieftain looks like." His voice held a strange note of anticipation, but I was too tired to wonder about it.

I uploaded the image. "I'm afraid that's all I have for you so far."

"That's fine. This is helpful. I expect to hear from you again in three days."

"Yes, sir." The communicator clicked back to the standby hum.

I sighed and sat back against the haystack, staring out past the crenellations at the cloudy sky. I noticed one far-off cloud that glittered strangely. I watched it curiously as I put in a call to the doctor.

"This is Dr. Stirling. Nice to hear from you again. How are you doing after that crash? Must have been very harrowing."

Of course, he *understands.* "It was, but I made do. Still, the dropship is a total loss."

"I'll send some salvage drones to clean up the mess. Are you missing much of your gear?"

"Pretty much everything except what I had in my jumpsuit."

"Maybe I can send you a supply drop at some point. At least your communications equipment didn't get damaged." There was a brief pause. "And how were you received by the Lyrans?"

I hesitated.

"Grace, is something wrong?" Concern had entered his voice, and I felt my throat tighten.

"Doctor, I have run into some unexpected social complications here. They may interfere with the mission."

"I'm sorry. What happened?"

I noticed the glittering cloud seemed to be growing closer. I realized it was moving against the wind. *What is that?* "I need to know about Lyran courtship customs."

"That's not something I had an opportunity to study. I do know they tend to have a good number of casual lovers but eventually settle down with permanent mates."

"And those mates… They get a choice in the m-matter, right?" *Damn.*

"Grace, tell me what happened."

Deep breath. "I just need to know what kind of recourse I have if one of the men will not leave me alone."

"I beg your pardon?" He sounded incredulous.

"Look, I know most men have never been in a situation where they feel endangered because there's a guy around who's three times their size and doesn't understand the meaning of the word no. Just take my word that it's a serious problem."

"I do believe you. However, I will need more details if I'm to be of any help."

The glittering cloud was definitely heading our way. I started to hear a faint hum coming from it. "Look, this would be less of a problem, but it's Dekkir. Did you find out how he and the other chiefs treat women before you sent me down here?"

"Your liaison?" He sounded shocked. "What has he been doing?"

"He went and told the high chieftain I was his…his *mate.*"

Stirling coughed. "Oh, dear."

"Do you have any idea what is going on? I can't work around

someone who is this sexually entitled. It's worse than Norcross ever dreamed of being!"

"It may not be sexual entitlement. You see, I don't know that much about Lyran romance, but I do know a few things. Their mates… It's called True Mating. They *imprint* on each other. It may be pheromonal, which would explain the sniffing, but there may also be a psychic component to it."

"Wait…wait… Do you mean Dekkir could be attached to me instinctively, like a…duckling?" It sounded so bizarre that some of my upset melted away. But it also gave context to some of the things Dekkir had said—especially his comment about having no choice in his strange infatuation.

The doctor let out a little laugh. "I doubt he would appreciate the comparison, but yes. Apparently, something in your pheromone balance may have triggered his mating instincts. He's no more in control of it than you are. But since you are not Lyran, you don't have the same response."

"So you're saying this guy is fixated on me, and he's expecting me to feel the same way and doesn't get that I don't, because no one in their race has any choice who they end up with. How in the world am I going to live and work with someone who is constantly obsessing over me? And what if he decides to force the issue?"

"He's not going to rape you. Trust me on that." I relaxed a little at the firm reassurance in his tone. "Even if he were that type of man, the same imprinting that makes him so attached prevents him from harming you."

"Well, that's a relief, at least." The humming was growing louder. I stood up, shading my eyes to peer out at the strange, shining cloud. I heard some of the Rilleen growing restless. "Hang on. I may have a situation developing here."

"Do you need to sign off?"

I suddenly realized what I was looking at as I stared up into the sky: a glittering swarm of flying insects, each the size of my dropship, with wings that hummed like generators. They were headed straight for us.

"Yes. I'll call you back." I signed off quickly, tucked my gear away in the jumpsuit's belly pocket, and waved my arms at a passing soldier. "Hey!"

He paused. "What, human?"

I pointed at the swarm. "Is that normal?"

He looked…and his eyes widened. He straightened and bracketed his mouth with his hands. "Sound the alarm! Swarm attack!"

An alarm gong started clanging somewhere, and further shouts of warning sounded up and down the rooftop. The soldier had already run off to join his fellows. The Rilleen screeched excitedly as they poked their heads out of their shelters. I noticed no one went to guard them or take them inside. Perhaps they were simply that good at fending for themselves.

No time to worry about Keer's safety now.

I tried to run for the stairs myself and suddenly saw a massive shadow fall over me. The humming almost deafened me; I threw myself to the side as a heavy body slammed into the stones where I had been standing. The swarm had arrived, and I was trapped out in the open.

CHAPTER 4
DEKKIR

She rejected me. How can she reject me? I know what I smelled. How is it that she does not feel the same things? How is it that she is so frightened and angry?

I sat in a guesting-room chair, trying to sort through my confusion. Her furious refusal of me had put me in agony. My whole body wanted to be as close to her as I could. I wanted her in my arms again. I wanted her in my bed. But I had let her go when she had run away, for the sake of her own comfort. I just didn't understand why she seemed repulsed by me instead of attracted.

Now and again, female friends and casual lovers had described to me the experience of an unwanted suitor who would not accept their refusal. There were so many fewer women than men on Lyra that now and again, a male would get frustrated and behave a bit irrationally. Most could be talked down, but once in a while, one would become overpersistent or rage at rejection. Women's reactions to such a man reminded me of Grace's reaction to me, and the comparison horrified me.

Why can she not sense what I sense? Is she crippled in some way? Are all humans? I had no idea. But I would have to find a way to work with her in any case, for the sake of the potential treaty.

I was just starting to settle down and weigh my options when I heard the clang of the steel alarm gong on the roof. Someone ran down the hall outside, yelling, "Swarm attack!" I heard booted feet running toward the stairs, my fellow members of the warrior caste, mustering for defense.

I cursed under my breath as I scooped up my spear and hurried out. Duty called, and I needed to find my guest as well. I had no idea where Grace was, but she would most likely have gone to one of the areas she was already familiar with. That would be either the market or possibly…the roof. *Oh, no.*

I ran through the market and bounded up the stairs, other warriors running to join me. Some bore spears like myself, some long torches, and some crossbows with their bolt-tips dipped in pitch.

"Bows, form up around the rear torchmen!" I bellowed, waving my arm. "Spearmen, with me!"

Despite having a job to do, I could barely think of anything besides the potential danger to Grace. I had no idea what I would do if she got hurt. Our bond was too new for me to fully sense where she was, but as soon as I got up the stairs, I must have caught her scent again. My head turned toward the Rilleen shelters.

There. She's there.

I would have to fight my way to her. Gigantic, dark blue insects swarmed all over the top of the wall, three-segmented, with jaws larger than swords. Their wings beat the air as they dove at the gathered warriors, trying to grab us and drag us off. The torchmen drove them back and lit the bolts of the crossbow wielders, who shot at the creatures' wings. Once they were grounded, it was up to us spearmen to end them. I drove my spear into one's back, pinning it down until a caste-mate could drive her spear into its head. I moved on to the next one and then the next, dispatching them methodically, only breaking my rhythm to dodge the odd mandible strike or flying body.

The Rilleen aerie was piling up its own insect corpses. I could see those winged gray and black shapes darting back and forth as they slashed through their mindless attackers. Their young and wounded would be safe. Hopefully, the same could be said for Grace.

My arms ached with exhaustion from swinging the spear before the last of the swarm gave up and flew off. The rest lay in twitching piles all over the roof. I took a quick look around, noting only a few warriors seemed to be missing. However, I didn't see Grace yet.

I turned to the Rilleen shelters, which had partly collapsed under the weight of the insects. I picked my way toward it around chitinous corpses and a single feeding Rilleen that didn't even look up as I stepped over its tail.

"Grace!" I called. "Are you in there?"

"I'm here!" Relief washed over me at the sound of her voice. She clambered out from under a collapsed overhang. A familiar black muzzle poked out after her. "Keer protected me."

A rattle of chitin nearby caught my attention. A wounded insect, drawn by our voices, dragged itself out of a pile of its dead fellows, its wings burned down to stumps and one leg missing. Before I could do anything, it tried to launch itself past me—straight at Grace.

I turned to face it, but it was too close for the spear. I was forced to drive the shaft of the spear crosswise against its mandibles to try to pin them, but one of them slipped and gashed open my bicep. I threw the thing backward with all my strength, turned, and as it launched forward again, drove my spear straight through its head. It collapsed instantly.

I straightened, my arm dripping blood, and looked over at Grace, who had cowered back against Keer. "Are you hurt?" I called out desperately.

"I'm not, but it looks like you are." Grace hurried over to me without hesitation. "Here." She pulled what looked like a hand-sized square of very white cloth out of her jumpsuit pocket and offered it. "Put this over the wound. It'll stop the bleeding."

I took it and examined it dubiously. *More of the technology these humans depend on so much.* But it also sounded like exactly what I needed right then. I slapped it over the wound and felt it sting a little. "Thank you."

"You wouldn't even have that wound if it weren't for me." The regret in her voice surprised me. *Perhaps she does not hate me so much after all.*

"What happened?"

"The bugs cut me off from the stairs, and the only safe place I could go was in with Keer. I think I'm really lucky she likes me." She picked a few bits of straw out of her hair and looked around at the mess squeamishly. The Rilleen were all gathering to feed now, chomping on insect corpses enthusiastically.

"Yes, to befriend a Rilleen is a rare thing, especially if you are not its normal rider." I hesitated, wary of upsetting her again, but cowardice in any arena did not suit a warrior. "Are you still angry with me?"

"I'm mixed. You've rescued me twice, but you also caused me a lot of awkwardness. I'm here to do a job, Dekkir." She frowned at the way I held the odd bandage against my arm. "Here, your whole hand's covering it. It needs more exposure to air to work."

She took the bandage in her little hands and pressed it against my skin, holding it by the edges. The stinging intensified and then became a sharp tingle. I held very still, delighting in that small gesture of kindness. The blood drizzling from beneath the edge of the opaque cloth slowed then stopped.

"Just helping put us even." Her voice was so much gentler now that it gave me hope. "Look. I know some of our problem is culture clash. I also know some of it you may not even be able to help. But what you don't get is how strange all this is to me and why it bothers me."

"I don't understand. Do humans not mate by instinct?"

Grace sighed. "I'm afraid our instincts have atrophied. We never know who's a good match for us. We make mistakes, we get with the wrong people, and we get abused..." She hesitated. "Some people, mostly men, feel like women owe them something for turning them on and get violent when rejected. Or they simply rape us."

Understanding dawned, horrifying me. "Someone tried this with you."

"Yes. More than once."

I drew a deep breath. "It is true you and I do not understand each other very well. But understand that I would rather never touch you again than hurt you. I have frightened you without meaning to, but I am not like these beasts you describe. I will do whatever I must to prove to you I am a man of honor."

She swallowed, and I saw the relief on her face—and the tears in her eyes. "I'm starting to see that," she said softly, not removing her hands from my arm. The tingling in my flesh there wasn't all from the bandage anymore, and I swallowed, suppressing the urge to embrace her.

"I will fight these urges and give you time to make your own choice about me." The craving would never leave me—but I was stronger than my instinct. I would not give her reason to fear me again.

"Thank you," she murmured, and her expression grew even kinder.

Perhaps I was the most fortunate of men and could somehow win her over eventually. But in the meantime, I couldn't help but move closer to her as she kept her hands on my arm. She lowered her eyelids but still kept her face tilted up toward me. I hesitated, enchanted by that soft little smile…and then bent down to kiss her.

She shivered as our lips brushed, but she didn't pull away from me. I felt my heart leap as I reached to take her in my arms.

Booted feet ran up behind me. "War Chief!"

Scowling in frustration, I turned to see one of the hall guards skidding to a stop and bowing. "What is it?" I demanded.

His voice cracked with panic. "Dorin has been poisoned! We found him unconscious on his throne!"

"What? How?" Now my heart was pounding for a different reason entirely.

"He is delirious and keeps mumbling about being stung by a metal insect."

"A metal insect?" I exchanged glances with Grace as her eyes widened.

"The seers are convening to investigate." The guard stared at her with a suspiciousness I did not like. "Only humans are capable of creating such devices."

I stiffened. "What are you saying?"

He bowed apologetically, but his voice stayed firm. "This woman is our main suspect. She is to be taken into custody immediately."

CHAPTER 5
GRACE

"The human, Grace, is confused as to why she is here," a female voice, low and fluting, commented.

"That is inaccurate. The human is aware of our legal customs, thanks to the counsel of her promised mate, War Chief Dekkir. Her confusion is moral in nature, not factual." This voice was male, deep and raspy.

The first speaker, a woman in a gray cloak that looked like embroidered doeskin, frowned slightly. "Correction. The human is confused as to how she could have become involved in a situation like this. Her training, occupation, and mission goals have nothing to do with sabotage, murder, or the attempted destabilization of our government."

Yeah, no kidding. I sat numbly in the blackened wood examination chair, clenching tense fingers in the slick white fabric of my jumpsuit sleeve. I had been in that small, lamp-lit room for about an hour, surrounded by a circle of six figures in pale robes and various colors of elaborately decorated leather cloaks. The Lyran seers looked typical of their species: tall, athletic, pale in coloring, their skin and hair ranging from light bronze to literally white. Their eyes were uniformly golden, like owls' eyes, and their pupils glowed when the light hit them. They towered over me—small, black, and curvy, with long, relaxed black hair that had gone frizzy in the planet's persistent humidity—so I contrasted with them even more sharply than most humans. Their hoods were pulled up, and some of them were veiled as well. They looked more suited to a religious ritual than a court interrogation.

When Dekkir told me I was going to an inquest into the attempted murder of Planet Lyra's High Chieftain Dorin, I had expected the seers to be something like lawyers. But as I sat there listening to them comment on things I had not spoken aloud, I realized seers were more like psychics out of Greek mythology. *It almost seems as if they're reading my mind.*

One of the speakers, the one who kept correcting the others for accuracy, stepped forward just slightly. He was very tall, even for a Lyran, but unusually thin. His long face smirked down at me from the shadow of his deep-blue hood. "That is exactly what we're doing, human. Hiding anything from us is pointless, so it would be best for you to remain honest."

Holy crap. I stared at him. His smirk widened slightly, and he stepped back into place.

Gray Cloak continued tiredly. "The human was not aware before now of the verified existence of telepathy, empathy, and prescience. Apparently, human society still largely denies the possibility. She's extremely confused by our use of our abilities."

Blue Cloak gave a single nod. "That is understandable under the circumstances. Please continue."

Did the doctor know about this? He mentioned a possibility of psychic connections in passing when he was talking about Dekkir involuntarily imprinting on me as his mate. But he never got this specific. And it's a huge omission. Was he worried I'd report their psychic powers back to Command?

The chief science officer had spent years on Lyra before me, prior to his promotion. He was our only real source of information on the world and its people, and I knew him for being cautious and thoughtful. Norcross, on the other hand, wasn't exactly known for ethics or professionalism and sought fame and commendations like an addict sought drugs.

Maybe Dr. Stirling was worried about what Norcross would do if he discovered this. I'd hesitate to tell him myself, even if the Lyrans hadn't taken away my communicator.

"The subject notes that her predecessor did not report on our abilities to his superiors. She seems inclined to follow his lead." Gray Cloak sounded mildly surprised—and pleased.

"Good. It is best the humans continue to underestimate us. Continue." The approval in Blue Cloak's voice shocked and gratified me. It scared me that they could sense my thoughts… Except their ability to do that could be a fast track to proving my innocence. These people weren't looking for a convenient scapegoat. They were looking for the truth.

"The subject is extremely alarmed by the attack on our high chieftain. She was not part of any plan to harm him. However, I feel a great deal of uncertainty and guilt from her." Gray Cloak tilted her head slightly. "Is it possible she is a pawn of another in this matter?"

A third figure in a dark green cloak and veil spoke up, voice feminine but low and smoky. "Even she is beginning to contemplate that possibility, uncomfortable as it is."

It was true. My mission was supposed to be completely benign: studying Lyran culture and making overtures toward a trade alliance. Their unspoiled planet was rich in resources depleted Earth needed desperately. But just as I had gotten over some initial problems in relating to the Lyrans, a silver metal insect had flown into the high chieftain's throne room and poisoned him with its hypodermic stinger.

Just hearing the description, I knew the thing in question was an assassination drone. They had been used in several Earth wars over the last twenty years. Someone on the Earth base on Lyra's third moon had just used one to try to kill Lyra's planetary leader. I, as the only human on the planet, had been left to take the fall. I was just fortunate the Lyran government wasn't satisfied with a mere convenient target.

Gray Cloak smoothed the front of her robe. "She wonders if one of her fellow humans decided to deliberately leave her to face the consequences of this assassination attempt or whether they simply did not care that she would."

This is really unnerving.

"The lack of any criminal intent in your case has saved your life."

Blue Cloak addressed me directly. "It also corroborates the war chief's claims about you. However, your presence here coincides with the attempted murder, which was clearly committed by a human among your company. We must determine whether you were involved in any way whatsoever. After that, we will decide how to deal with you and how to deal with the rest of the humans."

I nodded mutely. No point in talking much if they were reading my currently racing mind. *This is not good at all. If the high chieftain dies, the Lyrans will definitely not sign any kind of treaty with us. And the worst thing is, whoever is behind this is very likely sabotaging the peace process on purpose. Maybe they want to have an excuse to use Earth Command's bombers and attack drones.*

As I sat there listening to them discuss what was going on in my head and its implications for my future, my thoughts turned back to Dekkir. The one they referred to as War Chief had pledged himself to me, claiming I was his ideal mate. Considering we were from two entirely different species, I had no idea how he could have recognized me as his mate. But here we were.

When Dekkir first imprinted on me, I had taken it wrong. He was a dominant type, in a way that sometimes really annoyed me, no matter how much sex appeal he had. He had outright announced to the high chieftain and the entire court that we were to be married, before I even knew what was going on. Fortunately for me, he was the type of guy who was willing to earn what he wanted, and he backed off when I expressed my discomfort.

He was also the type of guy who stood up for me immediately when I had been accused of conspiring to kill the high chieftain that afternoon. He was putting his own reputation on the line to protect me from any serious consequences. Considering he was next in line to become high chieftain himself, it was a significant risk to take.

He had prevented the guards from taking me away and imprisoning me. Instead, he took charge of me and kept me in his chambers. Right now, I owed a lot of my safety to his strength and position and to his devotion to me. I was sure a good number of Lyrans wanted me dead right now, and thanks to Dekkir, they wouldn't have a chance at me. Even though I could not return the feelings prompted by his imprinting, right now, I truly wished he were with me.

"Let me ask you something," Blue Cloak queried in a hard tone. "If you were left to yourself, how would you react to this situation?"

I took a deep breath. "There's only one person at our moon base that I feel comfortable contacting about this. He is my predecessor and our chief science officer, Dr. John Stirling. He would not want this assassination plan to succeed, if he knew of it. I certainly don't believe he is the one behind it. Because he has such a comprehensive medical background, I think he would stand a good chance of knowing what the poison is and how to treat it."

"So your primary concern is curing our high chieftain? Despite the fact that you would be defying your own superiors?" Blue Cloak's head tilted slightly in curiosity. "Interesting. However, we cannot indulge the suggestion because of two issues. One, I am aware, Lady Grace, that conversations made on your communications devices can be spied upon. Two, although John Stirling has never caused trouble during his stays here, we still do not know what his connection is with those who have committed this crime."

"Grace is innocent in intent. However, her arrival coincided too closely with the attack for us to discount the connection. So the question is, did she assist the would-be assassins without knowing it?" Gray Cloak's expression was very thoughtful as she gazed at me.

I felt my heart start beating fast. The idea that I had been used by one of my superiors to help incite a war infuriated me. Was it possible? I went back over the few hours I had been on Lyra before the assassination attempt: my crash landing, Dekkir rescuing me, the brief audience with the high chieftain, the argument with Dekkir, filing my report with Command, an attack by a swarm of giant insects, Dekkir rescuing me again… *The drone must have gone after Dorin during the insect attack, which means if I did something, it happened before that… Wait.*

I swallowed. "When I had my audience with the high chieftain, I was overdue to give a report to my superiors. They had asked me to record images of Lyra to go with my reports. I took one of High Chieftain Dorin while he was sitting on his throne."

A rustle went through the assembled seers, and my fists clenched in outrage. *Someone used me, dammit.* Many of the drones operated on visual recognition to find their targets. Without my photograph, it might not have been able to find Dorin.

My lips trembled as I glared at the stone floor. *How could I have been so stupid?* I had trusted Command, forgetting even if there was no larger agenda to cause problems on Lyra, every organization had its troublemakers. It wasn't even my fault—I *should have* been able to trust them. But I still felt like a fool for doing so.

"I see," Blue Cloak said icily. I clenched my teeth behind my lips and sat silent. After a few minutes, he surprised me by chuckling. "It's become clear you have been used as a pawn by those truly responsible. As a result, we will continue to retain your communications device and other electronics until we know for certain we can trust you. In addition, you will assist us in finding a cure for High Chieftain Dorin."

I looked up at him in surprise. Dekkir and Dr. Stirling had both mentioned the Lyrans preferred that those accused of crimes work off their sentence in service of those they had wronged, but I had wondered if they would go the normal route with me. After all, I was an alien to them. It was almost a relief to hear I would be permitted to do something to correct my mistake. "How may I do that?"

"That will be determined after we take our findings to the chiefs' council, which is meeting now to discuss their portion of this inquest."

I swallowed. Dekkir was at that meeting, defending me to the others. He was putting his reputation at risk for my sake, despite the fact that his affections for me went largely unrequited. We had come close to kissing before my arrest, but that was it. That didn't stop him from protecting me time and again.

The possibility of Command itself having mandated this assassination left me torn in half inside. Justice, in this case, fell firmly on the side of the Lyrans, whose leader had been attacked without provocation. Nor did I plan to answer Dekkir's sacrifices with betrayal. Yet Earth Command was my home and my people. What was I supposed to think if they were suddenly committing unprovoked murder and fomenting planetary war? *It doesn't matter. I'll damn well do the right thing either way, no matter what it costs me.*

"If there's something I can do to help save the high chieftain's life,

I'll do it. Tell the chiefs that." I had many reasons to help now; it wasn't just about guilt or honor. The high chieftain was also Dekkir's father.

I looked around and saw the seers nodding approvingly. At least I had managed to prove to someone around here that I meant them no harm. I only hoped Dekkir too was finding success. I wasn't in love with him, but I didn't want him dealing with any more trouble because of me.

CHAPTER 6
DEKKIR

"The girl is being used," I stated calmly in Lyran as I stood facing the assembled chiefs. I stared around at them, fists on hips, standing at the base of my father's empty throne. "She came here in good faith. I'm absolutely certain she had no part in this assassination attempt."

"How can you be so sure?" The lank-haired, slightly chubby speaker, Brax, was chief of Twelvetrees, half a day's flight from High-fort. "We are aware you have a certain…bias."

"Be that as it may, the fact that we are mated also means I can tell when she is lying to me. Grace was as shocked as I was to learn of the assassination attempt. She submitted to examination by the seers without protest. I am certain they will find her innocent, or as close to it as possible given her associations."

The assembled chiefs muttered together; several heads nodded. I glanced back at my questioner. Brax fancied himself a rival of mine and was always picking at any perceived vulnerability—and always failing. The suspicions against Grace apparently looked to him like a prime opportunity. But I had spent decades earning the respect of the council, while he had inherited his position from his father barely two years ago. And I had faith in Grace. Fate would not have mated me to some craven backstabber.

"About her associations," Chief Reela of far-off Stonemountain mused, tucking one of her gold ringlets behind her ear. "Are you suggesting she is being used by her own people?"

"That is exactly what I am saying, and that is why I agreed to have her communications device taken away from her. Without the influence of her superiors, I have no doubt she will come to prove her trustworthiness to all of us."

Brax stroked his chin. "Still, someone on that base is indeed our enemy. That leaves your mate with divided loyalties."

"Unlikely." My voice was flat with disdain.

Brax looked startled. "How so?"

"It is her desire, as well as the desire of her predecessor, to learn our ways and develop a treaty between our two peoples. This has been the same effort the humans have consistently made with us for years. Whoever is behind the assassination attempt may not be the major power at this base. In fact, this person may be an enemy infiltrator of theirs who is attempting to sabotage the treaty to cause problems for Earth or for both of us. We will not know until the seers can gather enough information on the matter. In either case, there will be no division of loyalty." I kept my voice calm and matter-of-fact, though I wanted to punch that politicking opportunist through a wall. The others trusted my judgment; only he disrupted council unity.

"Then we once again await the seers' verdict." Reela settled back in her chair.

Brax scowled. "I do not believe our war chief has a clear mind on this issue. He should not be allowed to continue his leadership position until his own loyalties are confirmed."

Oh, not this again. "I suppose you believe *you* should replace me as war chief until this matter is resolved?"

"You have to admit that panting after this human girl affects your judgment. And of those left, I am clearly the most qualified." Brax smirked smugly, oblivious to the annoyed muttering around him.

Reining in my temper again, I looked him in the eye. "Well, Brax, if you truly wish to be war chief and acting high chieftain, tell me something."

His smirk weakened. "What is that?"

"How do you plan to deal with the uneven food distribution among the southern villages?"

Brax's smug expression crumbled into uncertainty. "Uh…"

"The insect raids on food crops must also be addressed. Do you have any proposed solutions?"

Brax's blank and slightly panicked expression caused a few chuckles from the other chiefs.

I smiled tightly. Brax was an adequate chief for his own village, but he never kept abreast of issues outside his own walls. "What about the humans? Do you have any idea what to do if they *do* attack?"

Torvin, whose fishing village, Steamcliffs, bordered on the Boiling Sea to the south, scratched his bronze-colored mustache. "Do you, War Chief? I would like as much lead time as possible to prepare my people."

"Yes, I have a number of contingencies in mind." I put my hands behind my back. "Remember, humans have little acquaintance with this world's hazards. We can use that. We can shelter in our more remote outposts and force them to face this world's predators and other dangers."

"Then we must prepare for evacuation." Torvin lowered his hand thoughtfully. "And what about striking back?"

"Sabotage and the use of our seers. The humans rely on technology. We now have someone with us who knows human technology and sciences, and from her knowledge, we can devise how to stop them." I smiled. If anything, I knew after this shock, Grace would be eager to find some way to fix things. She was like me that way: always looking for solutions, even in times of high emotion.

Reela clasped her hands before her. "You plan to get the human to help us against her own people?"

"The seers will confirm she opposes hostilities. And she *is* my mate." I held my confident tone, despite a twinge of doubt. Grace's stunted psychic senses prevented her from feeling the bond between us. But I had sworn to win her heart regardless, even if I had to learn the human modes of courtship from nothing. "I have no doubt she will assist us if it is needed."

Brax sat back, no longer able to look me in the eye. "We shall see," he growled petulantly.

The door to the seers' chamber opened, and a lean figure in a blue cloak stepped out. He folded back his hood, nodding to me briefly.

I called out to him, "Chief Seer Morion, the other chiefs and I are eager to hear your findings."

He strode over and took the floor from me with a small bow. I went back to my seat, fully expecting him to verify every word of what I had said about Grace.

Standing in front of the empty throne, the chief seer cleared his throat. "Well, the girl is innocent of intent and knowledge. That is certain. It appears she was used by an unknown number of her superiors back at the moon base she came from."

I heard faint sighs of relief from those around me and had to echo them, if only in my heart. The accusations of bias against me weren't far off the mark, although it was not my feelings for Grace that were causing me problems. Instead, it was my suffering that might affect my judgment

My head pounded. My mouth was perpetually dry. A painful craving grew stronger in me with every passing hour—not sexual frustration, not loneliness, but both mixed, and far more. I knew instinctively it was happening because Grace was rejecting our bond.

I could not blame her for doing so now that I understood she could not feel it herself. Among humans, there was no instinctive mating, and a man who claimed to possess a woman was merely being egotistical and cruel. No wonder she had assumed the same of me when I had first announced our bond to my father. Since then, I had restrained myself around her and thus seemed to be winning her trust. But it was starting to cost me.

I held the image of her in my head: small, dark, and smooth-skinned, with those enormous eyes and hair like a thundercloud. Just thinking of her left me forcing down a surge of desire. *Grace…voluptuous little alien…most unlikely and most perfect of mates. I'll win you yet. I just hope it doesn't take me too long, or I may go mad.*

Morion went on. "The girl sent an image of the high chieftain to her superiors at the base. We don't yet know if one of them was responsible for the order to assassinate, or whether someone on the base intercepted the communication and attempted it individually. Whatever the case, providing that image is the one thing she can be held responsible for. She has already expressed the desire to make amends. She is uninterested in being returned to her base or making any contact with her fellow humans at this point. She is just as shocked as we about the attack, if not more."

More muttering. Some of the tension left the room. Even Brax looked a bit calmer. *Told you so, idiot.* But I was too tactful to gloat aloud.

"It is our recommendation that she be taken on the pilgrimage to the Master Healer Neyilla, who holds our best hope of healing the high chieftain. Grace's experience with human technology and medicine should be useful, and we predict her presence will be required. She will act as an assistant to the healer until such time as Dorin recovers or dies." Morion lifted his chin officiously.

I looked around and saw heads nodding. "Who else is to go on the pilgrimage?"

"Neyilla has specifically asked that you accompany the caravan, War Chief. Our prescients have confirmed the necessity. You must go, sir."

Wait, what? "What about my duties here?"

"It is suggested you choose a proxy for the interim, as you cannot be expected to maintain your duties from a distance."

I looked around at the other chiefs and then nodded, standing again to address them. *Fine.* "Decisions of war and security will be made by general council vote until my return. Chief Morion, I ask you to handle domestic matters in Highfort for now." I fought the urge to laugh as I saw Brax deflate visibly. "Are there further questions or statements before we adjourn?"

There were none, so I ended the meeting. As the others walked away, Morion walked up and spoke quietly. "You are not well, War Chief."

I hate mind readers sometimes. "I am well enough to perform my duties."

"Your performance is not being questioned. But it seems you suffer from being mated to a woman of their kind." He gazed at me and then spoke quietly again. "Tell Neyilla. If any of us can determine a way to assist you in your affliction, it will be her."

I nodded distractedly, thanking him for his advice. I did not know why the healer had called for me to accompany the caravan, but at least it meant Grace and I would not be separated. I suspected if that happened, I would become even sicker.

In the morning, after breaking our fasts, I led Grace down to the courtyard, doing my best, as usual, to ignore how her jumpsuit clung to her curves. A familiar caravan waited for us at the gate. The sight of it, and the slim woman standing beside the burden-beasts at its head, made me smile through my headache as we approached.

Hello again.

It had been a quarter of a year since I had seen Elorie last, but nothing had changed. She was almost as slight as a human, her clothes the plain leathers of a gatherer, and she still kept her dark gold hair cut to shoulder-length. I remembered gripping that hair by the roots as I pinned her against a wall and her cries of delight—and hoped meeting Grace wouldn't be too awkward for her.

Grace gasped as she saw the creatures hunkering obediently beside the caravan master. "What are those?"

"Those are Grogs. Did your mentor not tell you about them?"

"Only a little. I expected them to be four-legged, but they're more like giant apes. Are they intelligent?"

"Somewhat. Our Rilleen are cleverer, but Grogs are more obedient. They will bear the caravan through the jungle for us."

She nodded, staring at them with one arm looped delightfully through mine. She had stuck very close to me since her trial, which made me feel a bit better.

I raised a hand in greeting. "Elorie!"

The caravan master grinned as she saw me. "Well, there you are. I almost left without you," she teased. "Who's this?" Her gaze fell on Grace, who nodded distractedly and went back to staring at the Grogs.

What is it with you and animals, little one? I may have to get you a pet. "Elorie, this is Grace, my intended. She is also the human liaison. There's been—"

Elorie held up a hand. "I've been filled in on all the rumors." She gave Grace a small smile. "Hi. Like the Grogs, huh?"

Grace smiled back. "They're awesome."

"Glad you think so. I love the big fuzzies. I'll introduce you once we get to the retreat." Her expression sobered. "I know you've never been on a caravan like this before, so let me just go over the rules before we mount up. All right?"

Grace tore her gaze from the beasts and nodded. "Sure. I'm interested to know how you guys travel safely in that homicidal salad you call a forest."

As the two of them spoke, my gaze slipped past Elorie to rest on the three cargo sedans the Grogs would be carrying. They were enormous, with wooden sides and arch-framed hide roofs. Bench seats for the guards poked out from the front, sides, and back of each. The middle sedan held my father's makeshift infirmary, where two local healers would tend to him on the journey. The front one would be used as a bunkroom, where we would sleep in shifts as we traveled. The third held cargo and our gear.

I numbered our company at perhaps twenty, most of them members of my warrior caste, with a few gatherers, like Elorie, acting as beast tenders and camp organizers. I was glad she was the one transferring my father to the healer's forest retreat. She wasn't just a friend and sometimes lover; she was also the most competent caravan master I knew.

"It's just a few days to the healing sanctuary. Whatever happens, stay with us. If you get separated from the caravan, chances are we will not be able to help you in time." Elorie's tone was grave.

"Is the local forest that dangerous?" Grace looked calm on the outside, but I immediately knew better.

Elorie shrugged. "Compared to some regions? It's an easy ride. But from what Dr. Stirling told us of your world, yes. Compared to what you're used to, *any* forest on Lyra is that dangerous."

I felt a brief surge of fear that I identified immediately as not my own. It seemed my bond with Grace was deepening, and the empathy had begun. Barely thinking about it, I reached over and laid a hand on her shoulder. She relaxed slightly under my grip, and I felt the foreign fear recede a little. She *did* feel safe around me. It was progress. But as I stared at her like a starved prisoner might look at a plate of food held just out of reach, I knew it was not enough.

CHAPTER 7
GRACE

"I think I have something that could help your father," I said as I sat next to Dekkir on the swaying bench of the second sedan.

He looked over at me. "What are you speaking of? I thought your technology was all confiscated."

The caravan was nothing like I'd ever experienced. The three huge cargo sedans had no wheels, instead bearing massive handles on their front and back end, which the giant Grogs used to carry them through the forest. Our seats swayed as the creatures clambered over deadfalls and waded through rivers across the trackless landscape, where it was too dangerous to maintain roads.

As we jolted along, I gradually noticed Dekkir looked a little…sick. His skin was always pale, especially in contrast with his black-scale armor, but the shadows around his narrow, fierce eyes were new. He had the body of a god and the face of a superhero and radiated self-assuredness even now. The signs of illness stood out even more sharply in contrast.

Guilt gnawed at me as I watched him. I knew somehow that I was responsible for his suffering. Either it was my rejection of him, or the stress his father's poisoning and my trial had caused, or some combination. So as soon as I remembered, I spoke up about my possible solution to some of it.

"Everything was taken except for this."

I pulled the pendant Dr. Stirling had given me out of my jumpsuit collar. "This contains an emergency pill that was given to me in case I was seriously hurt or got very sick. I don't know how good it is against poison, but it may be worth a try to give it to Dorin. He needs it more than I do."

Dekkir took it and held it up, peering at the tube-shaped pendant. "I am not certain. That strange bandage you gave me did me good, and this may indeed help my father. But I suggest you show this to Neyilla when we confer with her and let her decide. She is the finest healer in our world. She will know better than I how such a thing may affect a Lyran."

I nodded…then reached over and put a hand on his shoulder. "Are you all right?"

A shudder went through him, and I saw his shining golden eyes hood, like those of a cat I was petting. "I will…endure. I mean to ask the healer about our…predicament…as well." His throat worked, and I stared at him sadly.

This is my fault. I hadn't meant for it to happen. I didn't want to see him suffer. It wasn't even that I didn't like him or find him attractive. But the urgent hunger he aimed at me, sometimes without even meaning to, completely overwhelmed me. I didn't feel the same. I *couldn't* feel the same, and so his passion came very close to scaring me off entirely.

As I looked at him, I honestly wished there were some way I could match his ardor. But whether it was pheromones, something psychic, or something else the Lyrans had that I didn't, I couldn't. My stomach boiled with a mix of shame, apprehension, and frustration.

"If she can help, I'll cooperate any way I can, okay?" I rubbed his massive arm soothingly around the armor straps, and he shivered again.

Maybe I should just sleep with him, I thought. The idea had some appeal. *I haven't gotten laid in a long time. If I could just get over these weird feelings, it could be nice.* But it was more than that. The longer we went on, the more he seemed to…pine for my love. He was so tough, so smart and brave, but I saw how this chewed him up from within. *He needs me. Maybe I should just make myself.*

But the idea of gritting my teeth through a sexual encounter I wasn't entirely into made me even sicker. In my younger years, men had tried to guilt me into sex or tried to make me feel obligated. Sometimes, it had worked, leaving me dissatisfied and in need of a long shower after. And what if once wasn't enough to satisfy this… imprinting of his?

I brooded on it as we spent our first day on the road. We traveled as constantly as we could; camping was out of the question. But every six hours or so, the Grogs had to rest and eat for a while. Each time, they would set down their burdens and then proceed to eat themselves a small clearing out of whatever vegetation was handy. It didn't matter if it was thornbushes the size of small buildings, masses of green tentacles that constantly moved on their own, or the ever-present vines. Into the Grogs' massive jaws, it all went, to be chewed up and swallowed with the same enthusiasm every time. Eventually, their vast bellies full, they would settle down for short naps and proceed to snore so loudly it scared birds out of the trees. Elorie explained that sleeping Grogs were so bad-tempered and destructive if forced awake, only the most dangerous or stupid of predators would disturb them.

We stopped again at sunset. Dekkir went off to speak to some of the other warriors, and I took the opportunity to jump down and cautiously stretch my legs around the small artificial clearing. My joints popped as I moved, and I immediately started feeling a little better. I walked carefully, avoiding the edges of the clearing. I was mindful of what Elorie had said, and I had seen what this forest could do. I was halfway through my first circuit when I saw the caravan master walking up to me.

"Hey," she said breezily. "I had been hoping to get a chance to talk to you alone."

I tensed slightly but gave her a smile. "Yeah? What about?"

"You know, Dekkir and I have been lovers off and on." Her smile got a little tight, and mine died. "Oh, it's never been anything serious.

Lyrans don't really get into anything serious until we find real mates. Which is kind of what I wanted to talk to you about."

"Oh." I didn't know whether to be relieved she wasn't jealous of me or annoyed about her sticking in her nose in general. "So what's up?"

"I was just wondering why you're not interested in Dekkir. I guess I don't understand it."

"Well, the short of it is humans don't have the same—mating thing? —that you do. Basically, he's suddenly crazy for me, and I feel guilty because I don't feel the same way back. I wish I could. Now that I know him a little better, he's a great guy. But I don't have the pheromones or the psychic powers or whatever causes True Mating."

Elorie's face fell. "Oh. Well, that makes a little more sense. Except I don't get how he would fall for a human anyway, if that's the case." She walked alongside me, keeping her crossbow propped on her shoulder.

"We're going to talk to the healer about it. I don't want him to suffer. I really do like the guy."

The caravan master looked at me seriously. "He *is* suffering, though, Grace. When a True Mating is denied, those connected by it become sick. Dekkir could *die* without you if this goes on too long. I know he's a tough guy, but he can't do this forever. We need him. I know you can't force yourself to love someone, but you should really think about that." She looked me right in the eyes and then turned and walked back toward the caravan.

I stared after her, my eyes stinging. *Well, crap. Now, what do I do?*

Dekkir could not eat his meal of dried meat and fruit. I watched him force down a few bites and some water and then give up, tucking the remainder back into his provision pouch. I remembered what Elorie had said to me and felt a fresh surge of shame. What the hell could I do? Just sleep with the guy because I felt bad and was being pressured from every side about it? It wasn't fair to me, and if I actually went through with it, it wouldn't be fair to him either. I could screw him, but I couldn't love him in the same way.

I hate this place. Political problems, things trying to eat me, someone at the Command base deciding to try to start a war, and then this. I turned away from him and surreptitiously wiped away a tear. All this time, all this training, all these aspirations, and it was all being ruined by other people's agendas and instincts. *I should have stayed back on Earth.*

"Are you all right?" He looked at me with concern.

"Oh, nothing. It's fine." The corners of my jaw ached from holding back an angry, weepy tirade. He was the one suffering the most here. He had put everything on the line to try to protect me, and it was his father who might be dying only a few meters behind us. I couldn't just smile and spread my legs for him like a dutiful Victorian wife, but I wasn't going to dump my problems on him. "I'll manage." I just didn't know how.

"You regret coming to my world." His voice was filled with tired resignation.

My eyes brimmed over again, and I turned away. "Yeah, good guess. Look, we're both in a bad state right now, and I really don't want to bring up my problems."

"I can feel them whether you bring them up or not," he rasped.

"Oh, great. That's just wonderful. Well, I'm sorry I'm not all sunshine and fucking roses, then." I didn't even know if that translated correctly, and I was too upset to care. I gritted my teeth, but the tears just kept sliding down my cheeks no matter what I did.

He reached over and started stroking my hair gently. "What can I do to help you?"

Oh, God. Please don't do that. I don't understand why there's no spark there for me, but the more you act like someone I actually would want to date if I felt anything, the harder it is for me to live with myself. "You're great. You've already done a lot. You really shouldn't have to worry about it."

He opened his mouth to answer—just as the Grogs up front let out rumbling cries of alarm.

"Stay here," Dekkir warned in a sharp voice as he leaped down from the sedan. I saw him whip that telescoping spear off his back and open it fully with a flick of his wrist. He hurried toward the disturbance at the front of the caravan, shouting orders to the other warriors as he went. "It's a Raptor ambush! Bring them down quickly. Their hunting cries will call others!"

I stood up and craned my neck to try to see what was going on. The lead sedan toppled to the ground suddenly, landing on its side as several Lyrans leaped free. The rest ran forward to rank up behind Dekkir as he strode toward the pair of Grogs that had taken the lead of the caravan.

The two hairy giants flailed at the ground in front of them, then I caught sight of some sort of two-legged, birdlike creatures roughly the size of men, milling around, snapping at their legs. Wailing cries rose from the pack, so high-pitched they stung my ears.

The warriors formed a crescent shape around the Grogs and started moving forward, killing the Raptors as they went. I heard the grunts and shouts of battle and the heavy thud of steel on leathery hides. Dekkir waded into the middle of it, and I felt an immediate surge of fear for him. He wasn't well. He wasn't entirely himself. And worse, it was my fault. What if he got hurt?

In the sedan at my back, I heard Dorin let out a loud moan as the sound of battle roused him some. A number of the warriors had stayed behind to guard his sedan and looked at each other as he cried out. I pressed my back against the stretched-hide cover and wondered if I should step out of sight inside.

They had left me with no weapons, not even my knives. I finally decided hiding was the smartest course of action and grabbed my carry bag, along with Dekkir's, planning to duck into the high chieftain's sickroom. But then a familiar deep voice shouted a battle cry, and I looked back at the fight, only to be completely captivated by what I saw next.

Dekkir had closed with three of the creatures on his own, spinning the long-bladed spear in a circle before lopping off the first one's head. A second beast tried to jump him from the side, only to get the butt of the spear in its gut. It staggered back, and the third lunged and then took the blade through its chest as he turned so fast I could barely track the movement.

I stared. *This is how fiercely he fights when he's not well? Holy crap. Dekkir is a badass!*

Suddenly, shouts rose up around me. I turned my eyes away from the fight ahead and found myself staring unexpectedly into the green eyes of one of the bird creatures. A trio of them had snuck up on the middle caravan while I was captivated, watching the fight.

Oh, crap! I ducked as the one in front of me snapped at me and then jumped around the corner to the side bench, running down it as fast as I could. It gave chase, letting out that skirling cry as I scrambled to get away from it.

I looked around as I ran for my life and noticed none of the guards was coming to help. One or two of them actually looked my way as they continued fending off the other birds, but none made a single move to protect me. I saved my breath for running, suddenly understanding calling out for help was pointless. Sheltered and treated kindly by Dekkir, I had forgotten for a while that I had become a pariah. And now that was going to kill me.

I swung around the corner of the sedan, jumping onto the next bench. But before I could get any farther, the creature darted under the sedan and popped up to intercept me. Nearly running into it, I backpedaled, holding my hands up in a futile warding-off gesture as it crouched to spring.

It was midair when suddenly a black spear slammed into its side and pinned it against the sedan. It went limp immediately, and I looked up to see Dekkir standing empty-handed, staring at me with his chest heaving. He had just thrown away his weapon to save me.

I got over the shock just in time and screamed, "Duck!" He did, and one of the things sailed over his head. I saw him draw a pair of short blades from his belt and leap onto the bird's back, driving the weapons into its flesh.

I drew a deep breath of relief and then turned to try to pull the spear out of the dead bird next to me. It took all of my strength to yank it free, but I had to get his weapon back to him. Those short blades forced him too close in with the creatures instead of keeping him out of biting range.

I had barely managed to pry it free when I looked up and saw two of the creatures jump on his back at once. His companions turned to pry them off and stab them to death, but as they were in mid-motion, one of the birds sank its teeth right through his scale-armor and into his arm.

I screamed as if I had been bitten myself. Blind with anger, I ran forward, only vaguely aware I was holding the spear in front of me in a desperate charge. The men made short work of one of the creatures, but the one with its teeth in Dekkir's arm hung on doggedly as he shouted and stabbed at it with his good hand. Forcing myself past hesitation, I ran smack into it, spearhead first.

Its teeth popped free of his flesh as it squealed. Dekkir immediately turned as I pinned it to the ground with the spear and drove his knife into its throat.

The air was suddenly quiet as the other creatures fled into the underbrush. I looked around, getting my bearings. One of the Grogs was bleeding, and two guards lay dead. About half a dozen others appeared to be nursing wounds besides Dekkir. We had won, but it had cost us.

I let go of the spear and turned to him. "Are you all right?"

He grinned, panting as he struggled to stanch the bleeding wound in his arm with his other hand. "You have survived and are unhurt. Because of this, yes, I am fine."

That night, wounds tended, he lay resting in the infirmary sedan with his father and the other injured. I sat outside, alone on the bench, as we moved along through the dark. Thinking of his exhausted smile as he had seen I was safe, I felt tears fill my eyes again. He deserved something from me in return for his devotion and all he had done. But all I could feel when I thought of him was guilt, stress, and that smothering feeling of being trapped. I asked myself again as I rode through the dark, weeping, *What's wrong with me?*

CHAPTER 8
GRACE

"The high chieftain is resting comfortably." Neyilla glided toward us across the polished hardwood floor, her silver-gray robes rustling slightly. Her hair was very white and was pulled back from her high, olive-skinned forehead in an elaborate mass of braids. "Now that I have him stabilized, I can have a look at the medicine your mentor Dr. Stirling gave you."

Beside me on a wooden bench built into the wall, Dekkir nodded. His arm was still bandaged, but after a few more days on the road, I no longer saw blood spots seeping through the white cloth whenever he moved too much. "We wished to see if it might assist my father. Using one part of their technology against another, basically."

"It's an interesting idea. Let me examine the medicine."

I removed the necklace and twisted the vial pendant open, shaking the single capsule out into my hand. The golden powder inside shimmered as I handed it over to her. "I was instructed to take this if my own health was badly compromised."

She peered at the tablet, then walked over to a small desk in the corner and sat down at it. Pulling over a white porcelain tray, she opened the capsule and tapped out a bit of the contents. "You say your mentor claimed this to be human technology?"

"Yes. Nanotech. Tiny machines that fix people from inside, basically."

Her lips quirked. "Well, it has been known to perform in such a manner. But I am afraid your mentor misled you, Grace."

"What's that? Is it dangerous?" Dekkir stepped forward to look at the powder. "It almost looks like—"

"It is." Neyilla peered at me curiously. "And you say you received this from Dr. Stirling?"

"I did. He told me to use it in case of emergency." I came up beside Dekkir and looked down at the plate. "Why?"

"Because this is no modern technology of Earth. It is instead a technology of our world. If you want to call it that." She smiled at my startled look and carefully scraped all the powder back into the capsule. "This is a purified form of a symbiont that is essential to our health, culture, and environment. It is known as the Golden Strain.

"Long ago, our people were reliant on technology just as yours are." Neyilla finished replacing the powder and closed the capsule. "When we decided to change our ways, one of the last things we invented with our biotechnological skills was this symbiont, which was meant to help our descendants adapt to our world more organically. The symbiont colonizes our neural tissue, as well as certain muscle groups. As a result of this, our eye color is uniformly golden."

I looked up into Dekkir's eyes, meeting a gaze so soft and wistful that I blushed. "What does it do?"

"It strengthens the immune system, assists in wound recovery, enhances our sensory processing abilities, and awakens the inherent abilities of the pineal gland."

"Such as?"

"The gifts used by those of us in the seer caste."

I quickly put two and two together. "You are saying this Golden Strain gives its carriers psychic powers?" *That's impossible.*

"Might I remind you, about a week ago, you believed psychic abilities in general were 'impossible'?"

I stared at her. "Does that mean every single animal on the planet is psychic?"

"No. The Strain only colonizes the brains of creatures with at least some intelligence. For example, you have encountered the Rilleen we use as mounts. You may have noticed their eyes are the same color as our own. They have some minor empathic ability, which helps us to communicate with them. They also have a strong psychokinetic power, which allows them to counter their weight when they fly. That is how they can not only keep themselves aloft, but bear multiple riders."

"Wait a second. So you're saying Dr. Stirling wanted me to inoculate myself with this symbiont?"

"That certainly appears to be the case. I am not surprised he developed an interest in the symbiont without telling the rest of his fellow humans. He explained to me once that he did not believe humans were ready for some of the knowledge he had gained here."

I thought of Damon Norcross and had to agree. "If I swallowed this, what would happen to me?"

"If humans react as Lyrans do, your brain would take about a week to adapt. You would slowly manifest whatever abilities are intrinsic in your nature. It could be empathy, it could be prescience, and it could even be a form of telepathy. In addition, any injuries and illnesses would be dealt with rapidly by the symbiont."

"So Dr. Stirling wanted me to inoculate myself to protect me." *Doctor, what were you trying to do? I wish I could talk to you right now.*

"If I know Dr. Stirling, I would say rather that he was attempting to help you adapt to our world and culture. I am surprised, in fact, that he never inoculated himself."

Adapt to our world. I turned and looked at Dekkir again, who was suffering because I did not have the sensitivities he had and could not sense the bond he swore existed between us. I looked down at the pill again, and I had to fight the impulse to simply swallow it down. If I could feel what he felt, then this messed-up imbalance between us would no longer exist. "What are the side effects of having something like this in my system?"

Dekkir's jaw dropped. "You are actually thinking of inoculating yourself?"

"I've got a lot of reasons to." *Including you.* I hesitated. If he realized why I was considering it, I didn't know if he would feel flattered, grateful, or guilty. After all, if I did this, I was basically going to be rewiring my brain. Neyilla had already warned that it would be an ordeal that lasted at least a week. I turned to her. "Look, just answer the question, okay?"

She smiled. "I cannot tell you what powers may be bestowed upon you, but during the adjustment, they will run out of control. If you are telepathic, you will overhear thoughts from all around you. If you are empathic, depending on who you're close to, you will have similar problems. Other abilities have other side effects. You will have to be watched over and mentored until you adjust."

"Do you think if I follow what the doctor wanted me to do that it will prove some help in curing the high chieftain? The seers seemed certain I would be useful to you, but so far, I'm not sure how. I know nothing of poisons from my world. I'm an anthropologist, not a chemist." And I was tired of feeling useless. I was ready to take a serious risk just to get a chance to help make things right.

"This may be what the prescient among them sensed. It surprises me that another human recommended you do this. As far as I know, the doctor never inoculated himself."

"I see."

"There are certain other issues that you and Dekkir are facing that this inoculation would help to solve," she added very gently.

I looked back at Dekkir. Big, hunky, brave Dekkir, who kept saving my life and shrugging off pain for my sake. *That may be worth it just by itself.*

"There would be no additional side effects. You do not have any of the mental or biochemical issues that can interfere with adaptation."

"Thank you, Neyilla. You've given me a lot to think about."

She got up from the desk, smoothing her robes. "I will enter a trance soon to investigate the toxin used on the high chieftain. I am hoping my knowledge is sufficient to affect a cure."

My head spun as we bowed and left for the room she had given us. *Should I take this pill or not?* It seemed like the best course of action, but the whole prospect was so strange it left me wary.

Later that night, I woke up to discover Dekkir was getting worse. When I opened my eyes, I saw him lying on the bed across the room, bathed in sweat, his eyes clenched closed and his teeth gritted. His breath came in short pants, like those of a man in a fever. I remembered Elorie's words and felt a cold finger of fear run down my back. *I'm killing him.*

I grabbed the pendant and hurried out. I had no time to hesitate. I didn't want Dekkir to die. If the only thing standing between him and me was my inability to feel what he felt, then maybe it was time I fixed that.

The retreat had been carved out from the heart of a gigantic tree, like a living tower. I found Neyilla meditating in a large round chamber at the very top. I hesitated in the doorway, worried about interrupting something important. She opened her eyes and beckoned me in.

"I have been preparing myself for your journey," she said simply, shocking me again.

"You *knew* I would choose to do this?"

"I sensed a strong possibility. It's Dekkir, isn't it?" Her smile was soft.

I nodded. "He's suffering because I can't feel what he feels. I thought more than once that if there were some way I could, I would do it. Now the opportunity's presented itself."

"You are an extraordinary woman to undergo this for the sake of the man who loves you."

"He's willing to die for me. He's proven it more than once. But he shouldn't have to. This world needs him. And he needs me. You're really sure this stuff will do the trick?" I removed the capsule and held it up.

"I have little doubt."

"How will I know if it's working?"

She just smiled. "You'll know."

I swallowed the pill before I could second-guess myself out of it. Then I sat down to wait. I could only hope this was the right call. The idea of gaining psychic abilities intrigued me. And if it meant I would spend the rest of my life mated to an alien, then so be it. Better that than stand by and do nothing while he and his father struggled on the brink of death.

I waited. And waited, my stomach churning with nervousness.

After a while, I started to get frustrated. *Maybe it doesn't work on humans after all.* I looked up at the healer to ask her how much longer it would take to kick in—and then stared at her.

Neyilla had become a statue of golden light. Her flesh and clothes seemed to have become translucent, like a pale mist, and inside, her whole body was inundated with threads of gold. I looked down at my hands and was shocked to discover they looked almost the same way. In my case, the gold was still spreading, running down my nerve endings and sliding into my muscles and skin. I was filling up with light.

"It's working," I mumbled in astonishment.

"Can you sense anything?"

I closed my eyes then felt my mind stretching out, downstairs, back to my room, where a mass of loneliness, exhaustion, and frustration thrashed on the bed in delirium. "Dekkir. He's in trouble." My heart started pounding. I remembered that when I thought the flightless bird was about to bite off his arm. That moment when it felt as if I were screaming in pain for him. "He needs me."

"Can you walk?"

I got up unsteadily. "I think so."

"Good. Go to him."

I had no idea how I made it down the stairs so fast. Before I knew it, I stood at his bedside, looking down at his pale, drawn face.

I smoothed his tangled hair back from his brow, and gentle warmth swelled inside me. Perhaps the bond was not completed, but I could feel it now. And it was time for me to do something about it.

I took off my boots and settled on the bed with him. After a moment, he stirred, and his eyes opened.

He sat up, startled to see me leaning over him, and then stared at my face. "Your eyes," he murmured. "What have you done?"

"What I knew had to be done. Anything else wouldn't have been fair to either of us."

"But—"

I laid a finger on his lips and then moved forward and put my arms around him. It was like embracing a sun-warmed statue. There was nothing soft about him but his skin and hair. I ran my hands over his muscled back through his tunic, eagerly mapping the contours of his body with my fingertips. He shuddered, his eyes hooding again, but held himself still, as if wary of frightening me off. I reassured him the best way I could think of, leaning up and pressing my lips to his.

He caught me in his arms, pulling me against him hungrily. The kiss ignited suddenly as we clung to each other, intensifying until my lips stung, stealing our breaths until we finally had to lean back from each other just to catch them.

"I…do not wish to hurt you," he murmured. I could feel his muscles tighten with restrained strength as he held me.

I smiled. "You've bled for me twice, Dekkir," I purred as I ran the back of my hand down his cheek. "I'm not worried about you hurting me in any way I wouldn't like."

He licked his lips and had that gleam back in his eyes. He knew I wasn't lying. I didn't give a damn if I woke up with all-over finger bruises and bite marks tomorrow. In fact, gazing into his feral eyes, I thought I might enjoy it.

I stood and unzipped my jumpsuit, folding the fabric aside and watching his eyes widen as they lingered on my chest. I smiled. *Breast man, huh, Dekkir? Well, you've hit the jackpot.* I cupped them and pushed them together, displaying them as I held my smile. "Like what you see, big guy?"

"More than you know." He stared in fascination as I slipped my arms from the jumpsuit sleeves and let the fabric fall to my waist.

"Oh, I think I know…*now*. And I'm sorry to have kept you waiting." I unzipped the jumpsuit farther and pushed it down over my hips, shimmying slightly as his eyes tracked the movement.

"Worth it," he rasped in a voice heavy with need. I could tell he was still stunned I had taken the symbiont—for *him*. "I would have waited a lifetime for you."

"You shouldn't have to." Gazing at him as I stripped, I felt that warmth inside me strengthen, and I knew. I did not love him because I had taken the symbiont. I had taken the symbiont because I loved him. He had always been attractive, and I had quickly come to care for him, but his desperation and the imbalance in our feelings had scared me off. But now the scales had finally balanced, and his declaration that we were bound together by fate suddenly made perfect sense.

The fabric slid down my legs and puddled at my feet. I stepped free of it and stood there in my sheer undertights. "Lose some clothes. I want to see you, too."

He stared a while longer—and then tore off his tunic, revealing gleaming skin and muscles that rippled with each heaving breath. I slid my hands over his chest and then down his belly, teasing at the thin scattering of tiny white-gold curls that started just above the belt of his heavy suede trousers. His abdomen flexed under my fingertips, and a shiver went through him.

He pulled me onto his lap and bent to cover my breasts with kisses. His breath shuddered against my skin as he ran his tongue over them and then gently took a nipple into his mouth. So delicate, as if I were made of soap bubbles. His tenderness touched my heart—but I craved more and knew he did as well.

"Harder," I whispered as I pushed my breasts against his face. "It's okay. *Please*." He rumbled contentedly and answered with a deep pull, his tongue lashing against my nipple as he suckled me. I let out a sharp moan and ran my hands through his silky hair, murmuring encouragement between gasps.

Caressing his satin-over-stone flesh gave me a melting sensation inside, as if the skin I touched were my own. His mouth was hot over mine; calloused hands that could have crushed the life out of me glided over my body gently, leaving tingling trails behind. As we helped each other out of the rest of our clothes, I became aware of a sort of double sensation inside me. My pleasure and growing excitement overlaid a second set of feelings: hunger, joy, and anticipated relief. He had told me once that he could feel my pain. Now I could feel his ebbing away with every kiss and caress.

As he pinned me down gently, one powerful thigh sliding between my own, I could feel the almost agonizing tightness of his loins as he restrained himself from thrusting into me yet. I could feel his heart pounding in wild joy at my acceptance. I could feel his pleasure at finally touching me as much as he wanted to. The taste of my skin intoxicated him. The smell of my sweat and my growing arousal drove him wild. I was an oasis in the desert to him.

At last, I realized just how much he had been suffering from my refusal. His great strength and will had allowed him to bear up when others would have faltered. But as the last of the pain left him, I knew he had been far closer to collapse than he would have ever let on.

We rolled back and forth on the mattress, tangled up together, mouths working against each other's as we felt our pleasure and craving grow. His body shuddered under my hands and mouth; mine squirmed under his, my voice gone to breathless whimpers as his hand slid between my legs to knead and stroke me. My hands trembled on his skin and then clung to him, nails digging into the muscle of his back as I rocked my hips against his hand.

Finally, neither of us could stand it any longer. He sat back against the wall while I climbed over him eagerly, raising myself on my thighs and then settling slowly over his length. The pleasure of filling myself with him was edged with pain, my flesh stretched to its limit around his thick girth—but I pushed downward eagerly, feeling his intense bliss as he entered. I could barely take him all in, but his long groan of pleasure encouraged me just as much as the feedback from his nerve endings.

He dug his heels against the mattress and grabbed my hips, arching up into me roughly. We moved together feverishly, his grip on me almost bruising as he rose to meet me every time I bore down. The tension gathering in his body intensified my own and fed back to him, until shudders rolled through both our bodies and our joints cracked with the effort of riding against each other. Our shivering breaths sounded together, each thrust pushing the air from us, leaving us gasping at each withdrawal. I couldn't speak anymore; as I looked up at him, I saw him in the same state: golden eyes hooded, lips parted, the strain of holding off deepening on his face.

Our bellies slapped together rhythmically as I kept riding him, the ache in my thigh muscles almost lost in my growing pleasure. The sensations ramped up until I lost control of my voice, moaning and gasping loudly as I moved. His muscles tightened, fingertips digging against my hips, and sharp little shouts of pleasure started escaping him with each thrust. Our voices grew louder and more desperate as we galloped toward climax. No fighting it now.

My back arched and I went rigid, my voice rising in a wail as my sex contracted around his. My climax tore through me, reflected in his own nerve endings, and he threw back his head and roared with pleasure. I felt a second wave of ecstasy rush through me on the heels of the first as he crushed me against him, hips lifting me off the mattress as he emptied himself into me. A few more convulsive thrusts… and he settled back down, legs stretching out under me as his cry died down to a soft rumble. We held each other tightly for several heartbeats, shaking and gasping for air.

Finally, his grip loosened as he let out a contented sigh. "Grace," he murmured, nose buried in my hair. I leaned my head back and kissed him softly, too overwhelmed to speak yet. He saw it and chuckled, stroking my back and setting off tingling aftershocks through my body.

He settled back against the pillows, cradling me against his chest. His pain was gone, and amazingly, so was mine, though I had never been aware of it before. When the last of my shudders had ebbed away and I had my breath back, he looked down at me. "Are you all right?"

"More than." I laid my head on his shoulder, closing my eyes. I had never felt such contentment. I knew I might pay for this tomorrow in sore muscles and bruises, but I didn't care. The ordeal was over. Whatever madness someone at Command was cooking up, whatever consequences I would face for taking the symbiont and siding with Dekkir and his people, I could bear it just as long as I had him.

"I feel the same," he murmured drowsily as his grip on me loosened.

My eyelids grew heavy as I tried to sort out if he was answering my words or my thoughts. As I drifted off, I wondered if it mattered.

I dreamed I had my earbud communicator back and could hear Dr. Stirling's reassuring voice in my ear. He was giving me a list of what sounded like local herbs. *Beastvine sap. Thorntree bark, powdered. Janna nut milk, all in equal proportion. Heat until the mixture turns white and apply in thumbprint-sized dollops beneath the tongue every two hours.*

I sat up suddenly in the dark. I could still hear the voice. Not in my ear, however. In my head. "Doctor?" I mumbled.

I'm here. Bring the formula to Neyilla. I determined which poison they used on the high chieftain. This will help his body purge it.

My heart started hammering. *But how are you talking to me this way?*

It is a long story, the thought came, colored with amusement. *Suffice it to say, I inoculated myself quite a long time ago. Now, it's best you hurry.*

What if she doesn't believe me?

Tell her Tabirus supplied the formula. She will know it to be genuine.

Tabirus?

But the voice didn't answer. Stunned, I got up and started dressing.

Dekkir opened his eyes and looked at me curiously. "Is something happening?"

"Someone named Tabirus is talking to me in my head. Apparently, Neyilla knows him. He just gave me a formula he said will help cure your father."

He immediately jumped up and started pulling on his clothes. "Let us go, then, and see what Neyilla says."

We hurried out together, hand in hand. I didn't know what the symbiont would end up doing to me any more than I knew what would happen now that I had aligned myself fully with the Lyrans. But as I felt the quiet joy radiating from Dekkir and my own strange new sense of wholeness, I knew I had done the right thing. Heart full of hope and head full of a formula I hoped would cure the high chieftain, I rushed up the stairs with my mate.

CHAPTER 9
GRACE

I woke slowly, vaguely aware of the warm, hard body curled around me from behind. My dreams, wild and vivid, faded quickly to dim memories as I opened my eyes. The large, organically rounded wooden sleeping chamber was beginning to look familiar after my first few days of waking up to it, and I relaxed, starting to get my bearings at the sight.

I had woken up in a lot of different kinds of bedrooms during my short life. The living pod I had shared with my mother, father, and two brothers back on Earth had been cramped, despite my father's high rank. Five of us had shared two bedrooms, each one barely large enough to cram us all in. From that, I had gone on to the enormous, crowded Science Academy barracks, with one hundred students to each cavernous room. Doctoral candidates had it a bit better, and so for the last three years of my education, I had shared a smaller bedroom with three other students instead.

Then, a treasure. During my internship on Mars, I had finally gained my own living capsule, with no roommates. Sweet solitude. Granted, the capsule had been small, but it had been mine. Finally, a similar living capsule awaited me on Lyra's third moon, where our Earth base was located. And then, eighteen months and two weeks later, this room, hollowed out of living wood by unknown means within the gigantic tree that served as Lyran master healer Neyilla's hospice. This time, however, I was back to sharing space with another person. The difference was, this time, I wouldn't have traded that for anything.

I could hear Dekkir breathing softly in sleep behind me. We had exhausted each other again. I smiled slowly, remembering why exactly I was a mix of slack-muscled and slightly sore. I had already known Lyrans tended to have higher sex drives than humans, but Dekkir was something else again. Once he got started, he didn't let go until both of us were so completely satisfied that we couldn't do anything but sleep. It was interfering with my training a little bit, but fortunately, Neyilla didn't seem to mind much.

Ever since I had deliberately exposed myself to the Lyran symbiont known as the Golden Strain, Dekkir and I had joined as what the Lyrans called True Mates. Before that, I had not been psychically aware enough to understand why it was that Dekkir had become so infatu-ated with me on our first meeting. Once the Strain had inoculated my body and awakened the psychic receptors in my brain, I hadn't only known what he had gone through; I started feeling it for myself. We didn't quite do everything together since, after all, I was still under-going training and he still had messages to run back and forth to the capital at Highfort. But as my body and mind adjusted to the symbiont and to the new mating, I found it uncomfortable to be without him for very long.

No one at Neyilla's sanctuary, including the healer herself, could explain to me how it was that a purebred Lyran nobleman had somehow imprinted on a human instead of one of his own kind. Like many things about the planet, its culture, and my mission there in general, it remained a mystery. Nor could anyone explain to me how it was that once I accepted the symbiont myself, I immediately imprinted on him in return. The idea of such intimacy had frightened me before now. I simply had not had the capacity to be receptive to it. But once it had been accomplished, I had started…changing. And now, nothing felt more right.

I rolled over in the circle of his arms and looked up at Dekkir as he snoozed away in happy exhaustion. I never got tired of looking at him. He wasn't just bigger than any human I had ever seen—he was beautiful. He had strong, sharp features, very close to human but on a larger scale, and huge hands that clutched at me gently as his heart beat slowly against my breasts. Smooth, pale skin gleamed over hard muscle in the faint light from the single night lantern as his broad chest rose and fell. His hair was long and silky and almost white, tangles of it falling across one high cheekbone as he dreamed away.

Now that I understood the power of the feelings he had been fighting, I realized just how patient he had been with me back when I hadn't been able to feel the same thing in return. Since then, he had seemed determined to make up for lost time. I could feel his contentment right now, his emotions brushing up against my own and strengthening those we had in common. It was more intense than being in love had ever been for me before. Sometimes, like the rest of my adjustment period, it did frighten me a little bit. But all I had to do was look at his face and feel the happiness radiating from him, even in his sleep, and I knew I had made the right decision.

My skin was starting to itch from all the sweat that had dried on it. Slipping free of his arms reluctantly, I stood and moved somewhat stiffly over to the shower pod at the far end of the room. I had to lean against the wall inside the pod as I rinsed off. I could feel the marks he had left on me: hickeys, little scratches, and finger bruises where he had lost control of his strength. The water made them sting, and that made me smile. I loved it when he lost control a little because of what I was doing to him.

Grace, are you there? Can you hear me?

The voice in my head sounded familiar, but I was still more used to hearing it from my communications earpiece.

I'm here. I just woke up. Hope I didn't leave you waiting.

I didn't know how long he had lived with the Golden Strain in his system. Over a year? Several months? He had hidden its presence from everyone, including wearing undetectable realistically colored contacts to hide irises that the symbiont always stained a metallic gold. The Lyrans, particularly Neyilla, called him Tabirus. Apparently, he was well known among some on the planet, and not just as the human representative of two years. I had no idea Stirling had "gone native." No one had. It was a mystery to me that, given his newfound close connection to the planet, he hadn't chosen to stay here. Instead, he had taken the job of chief science officer and returned to base, leaving the task of approaching the planetary leaders to a subordinate: me.

No, no. I pretty much just woke up myself. I wanted to check in with you. I know the adjustment period can be somewhat disorienting.

I could feel the almost paternal warmth of his feelings for me transmit down the communication and smiled. I could still remember having such a terrible crush on him and knew now he had known of it the whole time. He did care for me, but his feelings were such that desire would have been...somehow inappropriate.

I washed and oiled my waist-length, relaxed hair as we "talked." *My dreams are wild. Unfortunately, I haven't been getting enough sleep to remember them. Other than that, well, I would probably be having more problems if I were back at Highfort. I only really get disoriented in crowds.*

That makes sense. Your abilities seem to be telepathic and empathic in nature. On the one hand, you'll never be able to fly or lift more than your weight. On the other hand, telepathic and empathic abilities can come in very handy. Just as they are doing now.

I could sense his amusement as he communicated with me. Emotions were very easy for me to sort out now. Besides doing it through telepathic contact, I could sense people's feelings from as far away as two floors above or below me. It made it very easy for me to determine whether someone was lying or trying to hide his or her true feelings. The downside was if someone was having an argument with his or her lover, which had happened a few times so far, or if they were having sex, I would feel all of it. It was a bit of a roller coaster ride because I never quite knew what was causing the sudden surge of emotions. At least now, after three days of adjusting, I could pick out when the emotions in question were someone else's instead of mine.

He went on. *I am taking the liberty of fabricating some communications between the two of us in order to satisfy our superiors that you are still in contact. They aren't aware that your communicator was confiscated after the assassination attempt on the high chieftain.*

I heaved a small sigh of relief. I had no doubt I would get my communicator back as soon as the Lyran leaders were satisfied I had done all I could to rectify the situation. Meanwhile, though, I didn't want anyone showing up by dropship to check in on me. *Thank you.*

It's no problem at all. You would be surprised just how easy it is to recycle an old report, doctor it a bit, and pass it off as yours. The flash of amusement he sent reminded me of a mental chuckle.

Have you had any luck finding out who is responsible for the drone that poisoned the high chieftain?

I reached for the small bottle of scented oil the healer had gifted me with yesterday. I seemed to be the only person on the planet who naturally had tightly curled hair, and in the constant humidity, I had been looking for something that would keep it from frizzing. Neyilla had put together the combination of nut oils for me, and ever since I had tried it last night, my hair was suddenly manageable again. It made the synthetic stuff I used at home feel and smell about as pleasant as rancid bacon grease.

Dorin is finally recovering, thanks to that formula you recommended, and may even be leaving in a few days. But I'm pretty worried that whoever is responsible will try again.

That's completely understandable. Whoever it is, they don't exactly have anyone's best interest in mind here. I will continue to search for them. Just suffice it to say that whoever they are, they're going to have significant difficulty slipping any major plans by me. His mental voice radiated confidence and reassurance. I couldn't keep the doubt out of my own thoughts, however. Neither one of us had expected the poisoning attempt, after all.

So, no suspects yet? I sat down on the little stool in the shower pod, working the oil through my hair with my fingers.

I have my suspicions. I do know, however, the commander himself is not responsible. He's hard to read when he's drunk...but none of the drone operators have received any orders signed off by him for months. What that means is either the order came from above him or below him.

What about Lieutenant Norcross? I winced even thinking of the name. He had intervened in my training, sexually harassed me, and made sure my trip to Lyra was as bumpy and unpleasant as possible by giving my dropship computer poorly calculated landing instructions.

He was petty, he was power crazy, and he had no real grasp of the gravity and importance of creating an alliance with the Lyrans. It was one of the reasons I always went to Dr. Stirling first. Between the two, the doctor was the one who always came up with good answers and advice. Norcross, on the other hand, could mostly be relied on to do whatever he considered to be in his best interest.

The problem is Damon Norcross's mind is unreadable. Certain mental and physical conditions can make minds impossible for me to reach. For one thing, his emotional states tend to be extremely shallow, and he has no sentimental attachments to anyone outside of himself. There's very little for me to latch on to, unless he is angry about something.

My eyes widened slightly as I sat there letting the oil do its work. *Shallow emotional states? No sentimental attachments?* It set off an alarm bell in my head. *What kind of mental disorders make someone unreadable?*

Certain forms of extreme psychosis will do it. Extreme autism can as well. Essentially, the mind is shielded. But the commonest sort of person that remains unreadable by us is the sociopath. Especially if he is also a narcissist, which we both can tell is true with the lieutenant. Across the gulf of space between where I sat on Lyra and the doctor's room up on the moon base, I could feel his concern deepening. *I had not considered Norcross to be effective enough to pose much of a threat outside of his petty acts of revenge. But he does have some power, and for all we know, he has friends on the base that I had not considered.*

Damon Norcross, friends? Unless he's providing them with very good drugs, or paying them, I can't imagine anyone keeping company with him voluntarily.

He sent back a brief flash of amusement. *Well, not everyone has taste, and some are more easily manipulated than others.*

I guess that's fair enough. So where does that leave us?

Well, your first priority right now will continue to be completing your adjustment period and your subsequent training with Neyilla. I may need you to take her some messages. Other than that… Well, there is always your new lover. His mental tone was gently teasing, and I blushed. He simply went on excitedly. *The prospect of interspecies mating is unprecedented. I will be very happy to see what comes of it.* Then he sobered. *Be careful, Grace. Once you've adjusted and trained, and once you and Dekkir have settled in together, we still have an enemy among us. I don't imagine he'll be able to slip anything else past me, but I know I'm not perfect. Keep an eye out. I will keep in touch.*

I'll do that. Thank you. We broke mental contact, and I turned the water back on to rinse the residual oil out of my hair.

Dekkir stirred and opened an eye as I stepped out of the shower pod. Seeing me approach wrapped in a towel, he smiled widely and sat up. "What did I miss?" The universal translator embedded in my neck just below my ear interpreted his native Lyran into English fluently.

"No news is good news, I guess." I came to perch on his lap, sitting sideways across his massive thighs. Dekkir was a big guy, even by Lyran standards. The size difference between us was sometimes a little alarming, but I was learning to enjoy it a great deal. "Tabirus will check in with us when he has some real information."

He wrapped his arms around me and nuzzled my drying hair. "I suppose I should be disappointed, but I'm glad there are no new developments yet. I'd prefer to be spending my time and attention on you."

His hand slipped under the towel and caressed my lower back, then slid down the curve of my ass familiarly. I shivered and then smiled up at him. "Well, I really can't argue with that."

CHAPTER 10
DEKKIR

In the last three days, I had discovered there were very few things as satisfying as waking up to see my mate walking toward me across the room, wearing only a towel. The rough, white cloth against her smooth, dark skin, the way the dampness made her gleam and turned her hair into a wavy ink spill, those bottomless dark eyes, and that shy little smile she always wore when she saw what the look of her did to me. She was so small and soft and warm that embracing her felt like a luxury. And whatever struggle was now behind us, or still lay ahead, the best part of all was she was now mine.

Cuddling her on my lap, I breathed in the scent of that perfumed oil the healer had given her for her hair and smiled, feeling my desire stirring. "How much longer do we have before you go for your next lesson, my love?"

"I'm supposed to meet Neyilla two hours after dawn today." She shivered and turned her face up to me invitingly as I gently pulled the towel away from her and dropped it to the floor. I could feel her sleepiness and mild worry giving way to affection and arousal as I nuzzled her neck and ran my hands over her.

"Well, good. Because once I'm done with you, I'm afraid you'll have to take time out for another shower." I started kissing her neck and the side of her jaw and then bent her back so I could get at her breasts. Her skin was so sensitive. All I had to do was lay a few kisses around her nipple to have her trembling constantly, her breath starting to come in sharp pants.

I ran my hands over her rump and up her back, through her damp and scented hair. We kissed, and I scooped her up and pulled her against me, supporting her in my arms as I drew her nipple into my mouth. She whimpered and wrapped her thighs around me, cupping the back of my head encouragingly and squirming as I suckled her. So easy now to know what she liked when I could feel the faint echo of her pleasure in my own body. The only problem was holding back against both my own urgency and hers as things heated up.

Her low moans rose and fell as I held her up to my mouth, moving from breast to breast until both her nipples stood out in points. I heard her breath catch and shiver, and the way her hands and thighs clutched at me…and faintly, the hungry ache I had woken in her loins. Grinning, I shifted her position in my hands and then arched against her as I lowered her onto my equally aching erection.

Sinking into her hot, clinging softness nearly undid me right there. I groaned, setting my teeth in her shoulder as I pressed up against her until our hips touched. She started to rock, rolling her hips as she clung to me, and I gasped and held her, raising my hips to each downstroke. Each soft engulfment drove me toward the inevitable edge, and I slid a hand between us to caress her and take her along with me.

I felt the warmth between us dry the last of the water from her skin as we rode together. The pressure built within us, between us, pleasure running through us, echoing back and forth and driving each of us to greater and greater frenzy. I heard both our voices spiral up in louder and louder cries as we thrust against each other. Then her body clenched around me. She sobbed, arching and trembling as electric jolts of ecstasy ran from her body to mine. I threw my head back, shouting with joy at the ceiling as my seed rushed out of me and deep into her body.

We caught our breath in each other's arms, lying on our sides with our legs still tangled up. I pushed the tendrils of hair from her face and kissed her forehead, and she smiled up at me drowsily.

"We're going at it so much that people are going to think we're trying for a kid," she teased me softly as I settled in beside her.

I chuckled, my eyelids feeling heavy. It was still at least a good hour before dawn. And a good thing, too, for I had exhausted myself with her so many times in the night that I was actually starting to feel sore. "Would that be such a terrible thing?"

"I don't know. All of this is happening so fast that I haven't even thought about that yet. Is it even possible?"

I looked down at her thoughtfully. "We should ask the healer. She's the only one in a position to know."

"If she does know. This seems to be pretty unexplored territory for your people and mine." She stifled a yawn behind her hand. "But I agree. We should definitely ask."

I sensed the conflict inside her and looked at her curiously. "Is everything all right?"

"I'm just thinking if we ended up having a child of our two races, I'm not sure I would want Earth Command to know. I would have to find a way to hide it from them."

"Are you...expected back anytime soon?" I squashed a surge of apprehension. It was the one thing I had not gotten around to asking her. I had only assumed, since we were now together, that she would be staying on Lyra. Especially since, right now, she had no idea who among her own race she could actually trust. At least, aside from Tabirus.

"I was supposed to be here for two years straight, same as my predecessor, but I don't know what will happen if some kind of active conflict breaks out. They might recall me. And then, I can either defy orders or end up..." She hesitated. "I don't know. I know there's no way I'm going to work for whatever crazy bastard is trying to engineer a war between us. I know I don't want us to be separated. And besides, if they found out I have the symbiont in my system, I'd probably end up a lab experiment. But...that's the thing. If I fall into their hands and I'm pregnant, our child could become a lab experiment, too."

A jolt of adrenaline went through me, and my eyes flew open. I held her close, stroking her hair back from her face. "Then you must stay with me. If you face that sort of insanity otherwise, just from having the Golden Strain within you, then the answer is obvious. Stay with me. Stay here. Let Lyra be your home from now on."

She licked her full lips thoughtfully. "I want to. As much as I miss my family, I can't even think about returning to Earth Command until I know this…madness…of an interplanetary war isn't going to come to pass. Whoever is doing this to us, he has to be caught and stopped. Until then, there's no point in even discussing my going back. I simply can't do it."

"Well, then let's not discuss it. Let us focus instead on what is immediately ahead of us, until Tabirus gives us something to go on." I kissed her forehead, and she tucked her head under my chin and let out a sigh as her body relaxed.

"That sounds like a plan."

We were drifting off, my eyelids growing heavy and her breathing going soft and even, when suddenly her whole body tensed against me. She gasped aloud and leaned back, her eyes flying open. "Airships!" she cried out.

I looked down at her. The Strain had left bronze threads in her irises, which seemed to grow more numerous with each day that dawned. Now I saw them sparkle and gleam. I had seen that look before. "Are you having a vision?"

"I think so." Her eyes were very wide now and focused on something I could not see. It had happened to her off and on during her adjustment: visions, insights, and flashes of intuition. Fortunately, I was around enough that I managed to catch her the few times when the distraction of a vision made her stumble on her feet.

"Tell me what you are seeing." I watched her face intently. Her emotions had gone ragged and spiky, adrenaline running through her as her eyes tracked around, watching nothing.

"They're not Earth airships. The design's wrong. I've never seen anything like them. They don't make any noise as they fly around. I don't know what they're using for propulsion, but it's nothing like dropship fuel." She blinked several times. "They're having a battle over some kind of… It looks like the place they're fighting over got hit with a volcanic eruption. There's no vegetation. The ground's black… I wouldn't even think it's on Lyra, but I can see the moons."

"I've seen places near the Boiling Sea that look a little bit like that. Is it on an island?"

"No. It looks more like a plain somewhere. I can see a dry riverbed running through it." She squinted into the darkness. "The sky looks strange. It's got a yellowish tinge. It almost looks polluted. But the air on Lyra is so clean."

I wet my lips. "It was not always so. There is much you do not know about our world. I believe you are seeing a vision from its distant past."

The gleam in her eyes faded, and she peered up at me curiously. "What do you mean?"

"The Lyra you have come to know was not always thus." I stroked her hair absently as I spoke. "Two thousand years ago, our world much more closely resembled what you have told me of your own. There were too many people, too many machines. Our chroniclers have carried the memory of those times forward for us across many generations."

"What was it like then?" She watched me intently, her brown-bronze eyes full of curiosity.

"War was constant. Famines, epidemics, overcrowding in every fort. The air was difficult to breathe, and the poisons in land and water made many of our offspring born...wrong." I rubbed my face, the uncomfortable subject dispelling the sweet lassitude that had lain over me before.

"That does sound like what Earth is facing. It's one of the reasons we came here looking for a trade agreement. We're running out of critical resources. The moon, Mars, and the asteroid belt... they're all mined out. When I left, they were estimating pollution levels would surpass what atmosphere scrubbers can handle within two decades." She shivered, and I rubbed her back soothingly.

"If that is so, would it not be in their best interests to avoid all conflict with us?" I frowned. So many decisions made by her superiors at Earth Command seemed to be tactically nonsensical.

"You would think so. But it depends. I don't know if it's Earth Command or someone in its hierarchy acting on their own. I don't know their motives or their plans. That's why Dr. Stirling—Tabirus—may be our only hope of getting answers."

I nodded, rubbing her back still. She was finally starting to relax again. "You trust him, and so does Neyilla. I shall try to as well. But I hope we hear good news from him soon."

"Me, too." Her brows drew together. "How did Lyra go from the kind of environmental mess Earth is currently into this? If Earth could do the same…"

"Neyilla will be better at explaining the science behind it than I would. Let us ask once your lesson is done."

We managed to get some rest, and I woke to rain pattering on the edges of the round windows. A Glow Beetle the size of my fist sat on the edge of one of them, drinking rainwater with its proboscis while it shed yellow-green light around it. I watched it rest there until the rain thinned out, and it lifted off heavily to fly out of sight. Glow Beetles were peaceful creatures; their presence was considered a blessing. Turning my gaze back to my new mate, I hoped that would be true here as well.

I let Grace sleep while I washed and dressed, leaving off the armor in favor of a soft under-tunic and drawstring leggings. I grinned a little. The armor wasn't needed in this place, which was guarded by Neyilla's three enormous trained Grogs and her own powers. Besides…it got awfully inconvenient to take off when things between my mate and me heated up. Which, to my delight, was nearly every waking minute Grace and I were alone.

We broke our fast in the communal dining hall on fruit, a loaf of bread, and pale slabs of river eel. The caravan workers who had brought us to Neyilla's hostel chattered and laughed at the tables around us. The caravan master, my friend and former lover Elorie, exchanged waves with me before going back to chatting up the bronze-haired guard she had designs on lately. They all looked restless, bored. I heard a few talking about their eagerness to get back to traveling. Fortunately, they would not be waiting long.

Tomorrow, my father, the High Chieftain Dorin, would undergo a last few physical tests and return with the caravan to Highfort to resume his duties. He still refused to eat with us, as his illness had left him with a touchy stomach, and he would not humiliate himself by losing his meal in front of others. I, for one, was just glad he was alive, but aside from saying that to him once, I could not express it. My father was not exactly demonstrative.

Grace tasted a little of everything, a bit gingerly. Some of our food had turned out to be far too spicy for her. I just stopped and watched her sometimes, forgetting my own food to do so, a little smile playing on my lips.

She had finally tried the eel and was happily munching on a bite of it when she blinked and her eyes widened. She set her fork down and turned to look at me. "It's Tabirus. He's found something."

I set down my fork as well. "What is it?"

She stared off into space. "He was reading Commander Wickman's mind…and he found something. He says it's nothing good."

I reached over and folded her tiny hand in my own, feeling her trembling as she sat there receiving the message. Her face went ashen, horror creeping across her features.

"The commander…drinks. A lot. Tabirus could never read his mind when he was drunk. He just caught him sober for a teleconference with Earth Command headquarters and 'listened in.'" A long pause, and then she pressed her free hand over her mouth, and her trembling intensified. A glaze of tears brightened her eyes. "Oh, God."

"Grace, speak to me. I cannot help you if I do not know what is going on." I had been war chief of this world for many decades. I was a man of action. If there was one feeling I despised the most out of all of them, it was helplessness.

Her eyes held misery and horror as she looked up at me. "We need to talk to Neyilla and your father right away. Earth Command has ordered them to *look for an excuse* to go to war with Lyra and take it over. They want to strip-mine this world. Take *everything*. By any amount of force that's necessary."

CHAPTER 11
GRACE

I sat numbly in my seat in Neyilla's practice room, staring off into space. My only tie to reality right now was Dekkir, who kept gently rubbing my back as I struggled against a breakdown. *I have been used. This entire time, Earth Command was using me. Not just me, but everyone at the base. We're all sacrifices to greed and political expediency.*

Across from me, Neyilla sat placid in her own seat, as her most recent patient, High Chieftain Dorin, paced the floor between us. The two were a study in contrasts. The healer, slender to the point of emaciation and with her pale hair caught up in elaborate braids, watched the scene before her while showing little emotion. Her questions, when they came, were calm and pointed. Draped neck to foot in embroidered blue robes, she only moved now and again to reach out, placatingly, to her patient, who grew more and more agitated as time went on. It was not good for his health, not so soon after being poisoned.

Dorin, nearly as big and broad as his son, olive-skinned and sporting curly, bronze-colored hair and beard, stalked back and forth like a caged tiger. Every once in a while, his golden eyes would fix on me, a mix of anger and suspicion riding in them. I always stared back as calmly as I could. If he felt like making me his personal scapegoat in this matter, I was pretty much ready to tell him to go to hell. My life was falling apart around me, and the last thing I needed was some egotistical alien nobleman trying to tell me I was the one to blame in this situation.

"You say they gave you no idea at all that this was their aim." His voice was hard and angry, and I felt Dekkir tense beside me. He had already started arguing with his father twice, and I was glad he was there to step in on my behalf. "What else did Tabirus say?"

"He said their plan is to manufacture a conflict the people of Earth will accept as sufficient excuse to take over this planet. They've been planning it for years, but they did not even bring it to the commander's attention until recently. Everyone on that base has been operating under the same lie. We all believed what Command's leaders wanted was a treaty and trade agreements." I wiped my eyes. I had managed to keep my voice even, at least.

He turned and stared at me hard, standing still for a while. I could feel his rage and worry pecking at me from the outside, like small, sharp-beaked birds. "And if we took you hostage, would they still feel comfortable in attacking?"

"Excuse me? Are you out of your mind?" I was getting thoroughly sick of his posturing. He might be important in this world, but right now, I didn't care what happened to me. "I've technically *been* your hostage for over a week and a half. You may or may not have noticed that no one has come to rescue me." He had no need to know Tabirus was covering for me. It didn't change the truth of what I said next. "My death would be considered an acceptable loss. I'm absolutely certain of it."

He blinked at me in shock, and Dekkir quickly spoke up. "Father, may I remind you of the risks Grace has already faced in order to thwart those who sought your life?"

His anger faded slightly from both his manner and his face. "That, at least, is true. But how do we know where your loyalties lie?"

I glared at him, tears running down my face. "I've been betrayed by Earth Command. I just found out they have decided to use me as a pawn in their long game of screwing up everything I intended to come here to do. Do you really think, even though my family and people are back on Earth, that I could possibly have any loyalty left to my former employers?" I knew it to be true even more once I said it aloud. After this, any respect or consideration I showed to Earth Command would be an act. As theirs had been to me.

Dorin went quiet. Neyilla spoke up. "I recognize your grief at this betrayal. But I do not understand. Why would they have you gathering information on us if they had no intention of releasing it to the general public?"

"They did release it to the general public, just as propaganda. According to Tabirus, they took all of my reports, and all the reports he did before me, and edited them so heavily they pretty much became fiction. They left our names on them and sent them back to Earth. Their aim was basically to make your people seem like uncooperative savages who would have to be forced to give us the resources we need to survive."

The healer steepled her fingers. "And don't you think anyone back on Earth would raise any sort of protest if they killed you in the course of their actions?"

My face crumpled, and fresh tears filled my eyes. I had to stay silent for a minute while I pulled myself back together.

Dekkir spoke up for me. "It seems likely that her family, which is important amongst the warriors of Earth, would lodge some sort of protest. We have not yet determined how it is that Command intends to get around this complication."

My heart ached. I tried to imagine Mom, Dad, and my brothers getting the news that there was war with Lyra and that I was trapped planet-side with no possibility of rescue. They would all be furious. They would definitely protest. They would even go to the press if they felt they had to, oaths of loyalty or no. But...it wouldn't change anything. Earth Command had too much power to challenge directly unless there was truly widespread outrage. My one death would not be enough to stir that.

"So," Neyilla said in that same calm voice, "what can best be done about this?"

Dorin glared at me again. "If you weren't my son's mate, I would exile you from this world immediately. I know you are conflicted. You cannot hide it from me. You may despise those who give the orders, but that is still your world, and this is not. I also know your people are desperate. You must sympathize with them at least somewhat. Your world is dying."

I managed to focus enough to answer. "Yes, and even from a purely logical standpoint, no one in their right mind would support war with your world. We barely have any resources left. The idea we should waste them all in a gamble to take over this planet is ridiculous. We needed this alliance. We can't afford to have Lyra as our enemy. I don't understand how Earth Command came to the decision to manufacture a conflict."

Dekkir turned to me, his brow furrowing. "What would happen if the general public of Earth learned of Command's scheme?"

"It would create scandal. Those currently in power would find themselves challenged. It would create a period of extreme upheaval if enough people reacted violently enough. And I suspect they would. I don't know whose bright idea it was to do this, but I don't think my people in general would be in agreement with the move if they understood the entire war is being manufactured to take advantage of Lyra's resources."

Dorin frowned thoughtfully. "And if they determined your life was put at risk in order to further their plans, would that not cause even more scandal?"

"It would if the information got past Command censors and reached Earth." I felt a touch of hope. It almost sounded like Dorin was slowly forming a plan.

"Can Tabirus get that information past the censors?"

"I could find out."

He rubbed his face. Then he turned to his son. "I will return to my duties tomorrow. In the meantime, I strongly suggest you find out everything you can from your new mate about Earth's military, the weapons, their technology, and their tactics. We need to know what may be coming at us."

Dekkir bowed his head. "It will be done."

Dorin glared at me one last time and then turned on his heel and strode out. I stared after him, shaking my head. I hadn't exactly expected him to be grateful after I had to defy my own people to make sure he had a cure for the poison someone in Command sent. But it would have been nice if he'd at least acknowledged I was more or less trustworthy after that. Instead, since I was human, I remained persona non grata.

Once he was gone, my shoulders sagged and I dropped my face into my hands. Dekkir slipped an arm around me, and I just cried quietly for a little while in his embrace. Finally, I gulped air and mumbled past my hands, "There's nothing I can do. I can't fix this. I have no idea where to begin."

"Let us begin, then, with what my father requested." My mate's tone was gentle but pointed.

I hesitated. If my parents ever found out I had given up crucial military information about Command to an extraterrestrial power, they probably would disown me. But now…it was the only thing I could do to prevent what could play out as a planet-wide atrocity. "I'll tell you everything."

It took me roughly an hour to go into all the details I thought could possibly be relevant. The dropships, the drones, the fuel they used, and the weapons they tended to carry. How many soldiers the base housed. The possibility of a bombing. The possibility of another assassination attempt. Every bit of it made me sick to talk about, but I kept on until it was all done.

As I finished, Dekkir stared at me, and Neyilla sighed. "Our fearless leader seems to have forgotten his manners, but I assure you he will be grateful for the information. As for me, I am more concerned about you. Perhaps it is time to change the subject. I know you came in here with questions for me."

I swallowed and looked up at her, nodding gratefully—then forced myself to move on. "I've started having visions about how Lyra used to be. It reminded me a lot of Earth now, although, from the airship designs, it looks as if your technology actually advanced past ours."

"Very likely. At the time of the Great Transition, we had mastered space-fold technology and had traveled to several other star systems. We actually have a few colonies of Lyrans living in other worlds. We have not been in contact with them in over two thousand years."

I leaned on Dekkir, who was slowly relaxing. "But why would your people give up all that technology?"

"Technological dependence almost ended us. The pollution it created nearly destroyed our world. The constant demand for resources caused us to mine out our planet, along with our moons. As resources became scarce, we struggled to discover a form of technology that was 'clean' enough to be sustainable. But nothing we came up with allowed us to truly live in harmony with our world. Especially at our population levels."

Wait. "So your solution to your problem was to give up technology?"

"In part. The decision was made to alter both the remaining life on the planet and our own gene sequences in order to adapt to a new way of living. Back then, we were not significantly larger or stronger than humans, and neither were we psychically active. We created the Golden Strain during that time. We developed plant life and bacteria capable of metabolizing the pollution and restoring the ecosystem. We also changed our level of fertility so we would not reproduce as quickly. Because of this, our population eventually dwindled to sustainable levels."

"I wonder if something like that would work on Earth." I kissed Dekkir on the cheek and then got up to go and look out the window. It was raining again, and I could see fat droplets bouncing their way down the leaves of the tree that surrounded us. "If this world was once a wasteland like Earth has become, I would have never been able to tell."

"Ironically, records of the biotechnology we used to accomplish these things do still exist. If Earth Command was not attempting to destroy us, we could supply this information and assist you in saving your own world." Neyilla offered a sad little smile, seeming almost apologetic.

"What if I sent that idea along to the doctor—I mean, Tabirus?"

"He is quite aware of the origins of our world. However, it may not have occurred to him to use this information as a bargaining chip among the humans. By all means, let him know." She came up behind me and laid a long-fingered hand on my shoulder. "You are too distraught now for further training, and this is understandable. I'm going to suggest you take some time away with your mate and leave everything else behind for a while. We have a whole month together until your training is completed. By then, perhaps we will have come up with some way of fixing this…situation as well."

I nodded, wiping my eyes. She stepped away, and Dekkir moved up beside me. "Come, let's go into the Meditation Temple."

I followed him mutely up the spiral staircase that ran the height of the tree, not really seeing anything around me. I wished I could close my eyes, open them again, and—like waking from a bad dream—all of this would dissolve. I just wanted to go back to the job I had when I first came here. I was supposed to be a cultural attaché. I was supposed to be studying Lyran customs and their world. Instead, here I was caught in the middle of not only an escalating conflict, but also a plot to plunge both our worlds into war.

I still hadn't heard from Tabirus. I had known him to be very troubled by what he had learned, and I imagined he was spending all of his time right now following up on it. I just wished he would check in. He was the only friendly voice from Earth I had left.

Dekkir led me to the very top of the tree, above the tree line. We came up into a dome-shaped room, its entire outer wall carefully shaped from branches that formed a web-like pattern as they arched above us. Set in the gaps between branches, panels of some kind of plastic material—perhaps thickened, translucent cellulose, but in a dozen different colors—let in the dim, storm-filtered sunlight, splashing the polished wood floor in rainbow fragments. Several large cushions were scattered across the floor, dyed the same colors as the skylight panels. It was so beautiful it shocked me partway out of my dark mood, and I looked around with quiet amazement.

"It's raining too hard for us to dare explore outside. The night predators come out as well in such a storm, which makes it twice as deadly out in the forest." He took my hand and led me to a pile of cushions in the center of the room. "I thought perhaps bringing you here would be the best compromise."

I settled onto the cushions, and he crouched down next to me, caressing my shoulder through the white fabric of my jumpsuit. I looked down at it, and I felt my sadness stab a little deeper. "I'd like some clothes from Lyra," I said quietly. "Every time I look at this getup now, I am reminded of what I once had. Or…thought I had."

"I will have one of the gatherers fashion you a tunic and trousers." He reached down and unfastened both of my boots, then pulled them off me and started rubbing my feet. He had become good at it in a few short days, good enough that my head lolled and my anguish slipped away a little bit.

"Thank you. Mmm. Magic fingers." I lay back against the pillows, knowing he had not brought me here to meditate, but minding not one bit as my body relaxed. He stopped only to slip off his tunic, and I looked up to see the multicolored blobs of light splashing across his skin like watercolor spreading across fresh paper. His eyes gleamed down at me, and I reached up to run my hands over his shoulders.

He knew I was mourning the loss of my world and all I had known, so he was gentle with me, moving slow caresses through the jumpsuit, giving way to the soft glide of his mouth as he slid the fabric off my shoulders and pulled it down inch by gradual inch. Sometimes, tears would still come sliding down my cheeks or catch in my hair as my head tilted back. He would hold me then and kiss them away, waiting until I was ready before moving on with his delicate seduction. So strange that someone so huge and built for carnage could be so gentle. It made me count my blessings as he laid his mouth against my neck and pulled me into his arms.

We rolled back and forth on the pile of pillows, mouths ravaging each other's and hands exploring skin, breath gone to harsh pants in the cavernous quiet of the room. The only sound we could hear outside our breaths and the heartbeats in our ears was the soft tap of rain on the panels. He kept his trousers on, even as he shuddered and his desire for me pushed the cloth of them firmly outward.

I ended up pinned under him, his hands gripping my wrists as he slid downward, trailing kisses down my belly. His lips brushed against my sex, and then he nuzzled me and started to kiss me there as well. I moaned, struggling reflexively, but he held me firmly as he darted his tongue into me and started slowly licking.

He kept at me as I writhed in his grip, the feeling almost too intense to bear. Pleasure won soon enough, and my struggles slowed, changing to rhythmic thrashing and slow rolls of my hips. I crooned, eyes going blurry, the shimmering light above me seeming to run together as I went up on my heels. I heard my own high, ecstatic wail echo off the dome, and then pleasure roared through me like a tidal wave.

I collapsed back to the pillows, staring up at the dome as I grappled to catch my breath. He sat up, a feral gleam in his eyes, as he kicked off his boots and took his trousers down. He threw himself over me, arching his back to sink his erection deep into me. He shouted into my shoulder, two short, hard cries, and then started to move fiercely.

I clung to him, whimpering and sobbing as he pounded away. He took hold of me and pushed us forward across the mound of pillows so my head lay back against them, dangling a little, lower than my heart. It made me feel a little dizzy, but as I saw the faintly wicked smile on his face, I knew it was quite deliberate. Gasping afresh, I gazed up at him as he thrust into me again and again.

His face transformed from impatient lust to wild bliss as the harsh slap of our bellies broke the quiet. His voice spiraled up slowly, from low grunts of effort to short groans, his head thrown back, lips parted, and his magnificent chest heaving.

The lightheaded feeling grew and grew as his thrusts aroused me again. I dug my nails into his back and panted, clinging tight. Then suddenly, the aftershocks he had roused in me rushed together into another powerful climax, and this time, a head rush intensified the sensation until I all but screamed in his ear.

"Aaah! Ah—" He thrust deep and groaned, and I felt his member jolt hard inside me. He stayed rigid as his body trembled, and then he collapsed over me with a sigh.

We held each other after, staring up at the glowing ceiling. "I have no world," I murmured sadly, but the sadness was much muted now.

"Then let Lyra be your world." He rolled over to look at me. "Let their betrayal make the decision for you. Please, my love. Stay with me, where you belong."

I looked up at him and then swallowed, nodding. "I will."

CHAPTER 12
DEKKIR

"So how is she doing?" Elorie asked as her massive, bipedal Grogs bore the single travel sedan between them through the trackless forest.

I glanced back; Grace was napping in the sedan's bunkhouse interior, tired and aggravated from the constant sway of our travel. I wasn't altogether surprised. She had felt queasy the last few mornings —in a way I was trying not to get too hopeful about. Too bad we had left Neyilla's tower behind before it had started, or we would know for certain.

"Neyilla trained her well. She is a formidable psychic, in her own way. She continues receiving communications from our spy on the humans' moon base and has learned to broadcast as far as the seers in Highfort. She is accomplished as an empath as well and can detect lies on hearing them. And according to Neyilla, who monitored her for the whole moon cycle, her abilities continue to grow."

"That's a lot of potential for a race that doesn't normally have psi abilities." The slight, blond gatherer smiled up at me wryly. "But it's not what I was talking about, and you know it." She turned her head to click her tongue at the Grogs, who grunted a reply as they kept moving. The beasts clambered over obstacles, waded through them, or sometimes simply shouldered them aside, snapping off branches and uprooting brush. Now and again, they grunted to one another and shifted their path slightly to more easily bear the sedan over the broken ground.

I sighed, rubbing my face. "Well, she's no longer so depressed, but I know she's still angry about this and still misses her family. Once we return to Highfort and she regains her communications equipment, she's going to be very careful about what she transmits. We will be meeting with my father and the council of seers about our next moves." Poor Grace had been in the doldrums for over a week after learning of her commanders' betrayal of both herself and the principles by which they claimed to operate. But slowly, with my help, Neyilla's training, and a lot of pleasant distraction, she had improved and could now go a whole day and evening without my catching tears in her eyes.

"Well, I have to admit I like her better after seeing the risks she was willing to take for you. For all we knew, the Golden Strain could have killed her."

"No," I replied, though I certainly valued what Grace had done— and it had involved risks of a different sort. The Strain was reason enough that her fellow humans might not accept her anymore. "Her contact on the moon base, Tabirus, was the first human to inoculate himself. Once he knew it was safe, he recommended she do the same."

"Tabirus. Now, where have I heard that name before?" The corner of her mouth drew up as she mulled it.

"He was the first human to keep company with us. He is also apparently a friend of Neyilla's."

"Hmm. I didn't know she spent much time with the human when he was here." She pressed her lips together. "Did you have much inter-action with him?"

"Only a few conversations. He traveled around the planet a great deal." Something about that tickled at my mind. How had a human lived among us for two years as a liaison and made so little real impression, save on a few? And where had he gained his Lyran name? I knew my father had not granted it to him. *So where did he get it?*

"Sounds like an interesting guy. If he ends up coming back here, I'd kind of like to meet him." The Grogs were slowing, and they snuffled hungrily at the vegetation around them. "Time for a rest break for the fuzzies. You think Grace would like a chance to stretch her legs?"

"I'll go check on her." I turned to scramble along the side bench bolted to the wood and stretched-hide sedan, found the lashed-shut entry flap, and untied it, sticking my head in.

Grace was already sitting up, blinking sleepily. "Grogs get hungry again?"

I smiled. "Yes, time for a rest break."

"I'll put my boots on."

We ate dried eel meat and fruit leather as we wandered the small clearing where the Grogs had set down the sedan. The great beasts were currently widening the clearing, yanking greenery from the trees and ground and shoving it into their maws. The plants would grow back in a few days, but meanwhile, it gave us a little room to stretch our legs.

"I've got to admit, and I hope you'll forgive me, but the high chieftain's a better passenger when he's unconscious. He kept arguing with me over everything: the route, the meals, the rest breaks. I'm a patriotic type, but..." Elorie trailed off, smirking tightly. Her crossbow was propped on her shoulder as she walked.

I laughed. "Say no more. He's always moody after an illness, and bossy, too. It's how he gets his sense of command back."

"Well, at least you're not like that when you're recovering from something." Grace rubbed her hand down my arm, leaving me tingling even through the sleeve leather.

"Oh no, I just eat like a Grog—" *Wait. What was that sound?*

Humming. I quickly exchanged looks with the two women. "That sounds like an insect swarm."

Our trio broke up immediately. Elorie started shouting orders to her men, while I turned and bustled Grace back toward the sedan. But before we could get more than ten paces, Grace looked up and gasped. "War drones!"

I followed her gaze and saw a dozen silvery shapes descending toward us on fragile-looking wings that spun instead of flapped. "Get the crossbows!" I shouted to the others as we ran to retrieve our own from the sedan.

"Those things have blasters." Grace raised her voice, surprising me. "They have projectile weapons! Take cover!"

Chaos erupted throughout the caravan as people did their best to grab for their crossbows, just as shining bolts of pure energy started slamming into the ground all around us. I shielded Grace with my body as we ran the last few desperate paces, the ground erupting in puffs of dust and burning leaves behind us. I heard a scream of agony, and at least one body hit the ground. Cursing, I pushed her inside and then dove in myself, going for the weapons rack bolted to one of the ribs of the hide frame. I grabbed one crossbow and tossed her the other, shouldered a quiver of bolts, and turned to run back outside.

"How are these things controlled, Grace? We need your intelligence now."

"They're controlled remotely. Usually, it's one person piloting up to four of them."

I turned and gripped her shoulder. "Right. Then what I need from you is to leave the crossbow, stay here, and do everything you can to contact Tabirus. If he can shut them down at the source, we'll win the day. Otherwise, we'll have to get lucky shots in on their wings."

Grace nodded and sat down in the middle of the sedan floor, closing her eyes. I saw her lips moving as she tried to project her thoughts all the way up to the moon base and the only friend who could help us now. She glanced up at me worriedly as I stepped back toward the entry flap, but she knew I had to go. I looked back once and then ran outside.

We had two men down, and everyone else was fighting for their lives, firing bolts and dodging blasts from their darting, hovering foes. Each drone was barely as long as my arm, but what fired from their proboscis-like projectors cut a man in half in front of me seconds after I emerged. I fired and managed to foul one's wings but then ducked quickly away as another turned to fire on me.

In the back of my mind, I could feel Grace's strain as she struggled to reach Tabirus. All I could do was protect the caravan until she could get through, but we were taking losses. Our weapons, which had fended off insect swarms and marauding predators of every size, were no match for these lifeless, murderous…things.

More of them poured down at us from the sky; the reinforcements put them at perhaps two dozen to our handful of remaining unwounded. I fought to keep my heart from sinking, knowing Grace would feel it and lose morale. Elorie and I ended up back-to-back as we guarded one of the wounded Grogs, who groaned and rolled as it gripped its singed arm.

"If this is it, Dekkir, you always were a good fuck," Elorie quipped before one of her shots crippled another drone.

"Uh, thanks, and we're *not* dying. Also, don't let my mate hear you talk that way." I fired again, and this time, the drone danced aside impossibly and then oriented on us to fire.

I felt a surge of relief that wasn't mine, and then was, as the drones suddenly stopped firing. They all hovered in place then rose up again, disappearing rapidly into the sky.

Ragged cheers rose up as I turned and ran back to the sedan. I jumped up onto the bench and went inside, only to see Grace smiling up at me tiredly. "It's done," she said, and I sagged and pulled her into my arms.

"What happened?"

"Six drone pilots from one of Norcross's divisions got the order to come after us. Tabirus found them with his mind and managed to convince them their target had been destroyed. He doesn't know if the order came from Norcross, the commander, or someone else. He's trying to find out."

"So they think they killed us?"

Her smile became tight and troubled. "No, me. I was their target."

I stared. "But why?"

"He's trying to find that out, too." She wiped sweat from her brow and went back to hanging on to me tightly. "Best guess either of us has is they wanted to kill me and then pin the deaths on you guys to strengthen their position that Earth must attack Lyra."

I cupped the back of her head and held her against my shoulder. "So now they think you are dead."

"Yes. Tabirus is trying to determine who among the superiors should be told I am actually alive, if any. Right now, neither of us knows who up there can be trusted." She shuddered violently.

I closed my eyes, just holding her. "We will find a way to deal with all of this," I promised her as her shivering eased off. "And I will protect you in the meantime."

"I know," she murmured. "I'm just glad they had already lost my loyalty. Otherwise, I would never have had the strength to reach out to Tabirus."

I kissed her forehead. "From now on, you will be keeping company with those who value your loyalty as you deserve. And as for the Earth Command leaders… If they think they can rain death down on Lyra with impunity, they are about to get a very large surprise."

A storm was coming. But on Lyra, we had much experience in weathering storms. The humans, on the other hand, had no idea what they were in for now that they had threatened both my father and my mate. *I will take revenge…for all of us.*

CHAPTER 13
GRACE

Grace! Wake up, young one. There's trouble.

My eyes flew open, and I stared in confusion at the friendly darkness of the bedroom I shared with my mate. I could hear Dekkir breathing softly beside me, soundly asleep. His mind projected contentment, sexual satisfaction, and the vague confusion of his dreams. The voice in my head had not come from him. I squinted, trying to focus. It was still difficult for me to project telepathically, and my lips moved as I sub-vocalized my answer. *Doctor, is that you?*

It is. I could sense the urgency in his mental contact, real fear behind it. Not fear for himself. Fear for us. Fear for me. *We have a serious problem, and the sooner you and the others can ready yourselves, the better.*

I felt my muscles tense as I focused on that mental voice. The man on the other end of the contact was supposed to be on the moon base where the humans were located. All except for me, anyway. But for all intents and purposes, including bonding myself to the future leader of this planet, I had completely gone native. *Tell me what's happening.*

Our dear friend, Lieutenant Damon Norcross, stormed out of an argument with the commander perhaps half an hour ago. Ever since then, he's been gathering his troops. He's taking a contingent of one hundred men down to Lyra by dropship. He intends to attack Highfort within two hours.

Adrenaline surged through me like icy water in my veins. *I don't understand. The commander is just letting him do this?*

The commander is emotionally compromised and has been compensating with an awful lot of alcohol. The doctor's mental voice went very grave. *Norcross has been able to do a great deal under his nose because of this. He is responsible for the drone attack on your caravan. He is very likely responsible for the assassination attempt on High Chieftain Dorin. I don't know if he's under orders from the higher-ups in Earth Command, but either way, he is bringing trouble to Lyra.*

That absolute son of a bitch. I slipped quickly out of bed, rearranging the fur blankets so the chill of the room would not reach my mate's back. *Do you have any idea what his aim is?*

If his mind were not unreadable, I would know for certain. However, it stands to reason that he intends to kill the high chieftain, the chieftain's successor, Dekkir, and you. Killing all three targets and destroying the capital would go a very long way toward crippling Lyran society. We already know Earth Command wants to take over the planet. If they level Highfort, they may just manage it.

Not a chance. Dekkir and I won't allow it. I scowled as I pulled on the pale brown leather trousers and tunic my mate had sourced for me.

Well, that's an excellent attitude, but it won't change the fact that a small army will be headed your direction very quickly. I would suggest waking up your mate and getting to work on warning the others. His mental contact had a touch of bitter humor. *I will arrange to follow the dropships. I have ideas on how I can toss an auto-spanner into their plans. But meanwhile, you need to deal with all of those human soldiers headed your way.*

Any chance of you being able to slow them down? I stomped into my boots, making a little bit of noise. Dekkir started to wake up, rolling over and letting out a soft grunt.

I will do my best, but I cannot make any guarantees. It's simply too uncertain, and unfortunately, I have to reach my stash of equipment planet-side before I can do them any real damage.

I felt his regret and another slight surge of fear. *Okay, then. I'll do my best. I'll let them know the warning came from you. I suppose I need to remember to call you by your Lyran name when I'm talking about you to them.*

Yes, well, to be completely honest about it, my dear, Tabirus is the name I was born with. Dr. Stirling is the alias.

I gasped so loudly that Dekkir opened an eye. *What? How is that possible? You don't look anything like the rest of the Lyrans.*

I couldn't believe it. Dr. Stirling had been my mentor and friend for two years. He directed the science division at the base. Next to Lyran men like Dekkir, he looked completely human. Blond, yes, tall, yes, well-built, and, thanks to his symbiont inoculation, telepathic. But Lyran? How was that even possible? He was at least a foot shorter than any Lyran male I had ever seen.

No, I do not. There's a very good reason for that, and I will explain once you and the others have prepared. A pause. I felt a trickle of guilt from him. *For the record, I apologize for deceiving you. But someone had to watch out for what went on at the Earth base.*

I sighed. Dekkir blinked and sat up; I went to him and slipped my arms around him, laying my head against his massive chest for comfort. He held me, radiating curiosity and mild alarm. *Tabirus it is, then. I would be angrier with you if your infiltration had not just given us the warning that may save our butts.*

His amusement brushed against my mind. *Fair enough.*

Dekkir stroked a big hand down my back. I shivered. "What is it, my love?" he rumbled gently.

"It's Tabirus. He just sent a warning." I relayed the information the telepath had sent me and watched his golden eyes widen and then narrow in anger. "Looks like it's time to put your war chief hat on."

He stood, towering over me, his arm still around me protectively. I could feel the heat radiating off his bare skin, warming my back soothingly. His muscles were taut, though, with readiness for battle. "Indeed, it is," he growled softly.

Twenty minutes later, Dekkir stood before High Chieftain Dorin and his assembled court. I let him do the talking while I sat in the front row of seats, maintaining a tenuous mental link with Tabirus while I held on to some of Dekkir's gear for him. Now and again, I relayed updates on the humans' progress toward the planet's surface, but that was all I could do to help. I had no fresh ideas. I had already given the Lyrans everything I knew about the technology that would soon be arrayed against them and the tactics most commonly used by Earth Command. Other than that, I was useless to them, and I felt it. This was Dekkir's show now. And for all my faith in him, I was terrified.

"We must act now. The humans are approaching rapidly. Their ships will land as close to us as they can manage. Tabirus will attempt to manipulate them mentally into miscalculating their landing. If he does, they will land in the jungle and be subject to the local hostile wildlife. But even then, at least some of them will make it this far." Dekkir's deep voice rolled commandingly through the guesting hall. He folded his arms over his armored chest, his broad, handsome face set in determined lines and his silver-gold hair caught back in a braid to coil under his helmet, which I held for him as he spoke bare-headed to the assembly. He glanced up at the throne behind him, and his father looked on and nodded.

"The seers must work to assist Tabirus in monitoring and deceiving the humans," Dorin rasped and then coughed into his fist. He was still recovering from being poisoned. His skin was ashen under its olive tone, but the determination in his eyes matched that of his son. "The gatherers who know the jungles will act as guides for the warriors."

Dekkir nodded. "A second contingent of warriors will protect Highfort. Half that number will attack from the air using our Rilleen mounts as empathically controlled proxies. The rest will arm the walls and strike back with projectile weapons. We will coordinate with the seers' guidance. I will keep direct command."

I listened and did my best to stay calm…or at least look that way. Inside, my stomach was in knots. My heart pounded, and I wanted to cry. I had come to Lyra in the service of Earth Command. Now they had betrayed me, along with the principles they supposedly stood for. They came to destroy, conquer, and pillage this world of everything they could.

Maybe it should not have been a surprise. Humans had a reputation for preying on each other; why wouldn't they do it to aliens? *I'm an idiot. A damned idiot.* And suddenly, in the middle of everything, I found myself fighting tears.

Dekkir turned his eyes to me as he fielded questions from the assembled court. He couldn't reach out and hold me in the middle of everything, but I felt a strong, fierce wave of his love and protectiveness wash over me. He would not let me be hurt. He would look after me, just as he aimed to look after all his people. Just...much more personally.

I love you, I thought at him gently with my still slightly inept telepathy, trying to push aside my anguish. But even with his love burning inside me like a brilliant flame, I couldn't manage it.

"How do we counter their weaponry?" The speaker was a warrior armored in gray scale, with a shock of dark blond hair that was cropped close, unlike most of his brethren.

"The seers will foul their aim while aiding us in aiming true. Telekinetics will disable what they can of their machinery. Telepaths will misguide them using illusions. Empaths will disable them with nausea, pain, or other strong emotions or sensations, as well as disrupting morale." Dekkir paused to aim a glance at the willowy, hooded chief seer, who nodded back curtly. He then looked up and addressed everyone. "Unless we work with unity and courage, we will not win. I call on each one of you to accept the roles assigned to you and give your very best to the effort." He looked back at his father, who nodded at him proudly as he gave his beard a thoughtful tug. "Do it for your people, your high chieftain, and yourselves. The freedom of our planet is at stake."

Shouts of affirmation rose as he turned on his heel and strode back to his seat beside me.

CHAPTER 14
GRACE

"I'm scared," I admitted softly as soon as we were alone together. He had sensed my suffering the entire time he had addressed the court, and as soon as he had gotten everyone's orders out to them, he had taken me aside into one of the small meeting rooms. Now he cradled me against his chest, stroking one hand through my hair. I drew in deep breaths of his warm, woodsy musk and laid my cheek against his heartbeat, my arms wrapped tight around his solid, powerful torso for security.

"Have faith in your new people, my love." His voice was so gentle it was almost a purr.

"I do. I understand we're not helpless and that we've got more than one surprise for them when they get here. But there's more riding on this for me than just survival. No matter who dies today, they will be people I don't want to die. It doesn't matter which side they're on. With the exception of Norcross himself, I don't want *anyone* dying."

He tilted his head, gazing down into my eyes, his adoration and support tinged with curiosity. "Are you that merciful, even to those who make themselves your enemies? They will not be merciful to you."

"I know, but...my tie to them still exists. You talk about the Lyrans being my new people. But...*these* were supposed to be my people as well. Humanity, I mean. My family is human. Humanity is still my race. With the exception of people like Norcross, I thought they were basically good. Instead, they're suddenly the bad guys. But they won't see it that way. The people back home, the people I care about, I... I'm alienated from them now. I'll be branded an enemy of the planetary regime. There's no way I can ever go back to Earth after this. I...I'm never going to see my family again."

I didn't realize how much that very idea upset me until I spoke it aloud, and suddenly, I started sobbing. From now on, I was an enemy of Earth. Even if we survived, one day, it was going to get back to my family that I had betrayed Earth Command and joined an alien enemy. They would hate me then. My parents would be so disappointed. My mother would cry. Instead of being able to introduce the love of my life to them and invite them to the wedding or present their grandchildren to them one day, I would be a pariah who was better off never seeing them again, because if I did, they would hate me.

"This isn't right. I don't know why this is happening. I never wanted to be part of a war on another race. I would give anything to make this not be happening." I was clinging to him, mumbling into his chest as my tears soaked through his shirt.

"Do you wish you had not come here?" His query was very gentle, but I could tell there was real concern behind it.

I shook my head rapidly. "If I had not come, I would never have met you. I wouldn't give you up for anything. But I really am going to miss my family. I wish humanity weren't on the wrong side of a war again. I know we're desperate. I know Earth is dying. But if they just stopped and listened… The Lyrans once saved their own planet from a fate like Earth is facing. Your people could help us. We don't have to be enemies. But...how in the world could I ever get anyone at Earth Command to understand that?"

"You don't. It is not your task to change the minds of your people by yourself." He nuzzled the top of my head.

"I know, I know." I blinked back tears. *I knew it was irrational to hope things would turn out better than this once I found out about Earth*

Command's plans, but it still hurt. "How…how am I supposed to cope with this?"

"Handle one thing at a time, my darling. First, we must determine the best way of getting through this siege alive. After that, perhaps Tabirus will have some ideas. We still have a chance. As long as we're alive, we have a chance."

I struggled to calm down within the circle of his arms. It would be so easy to let go of control and just panic and cry on him. But right now, the only reason we had any time alone was that the entire fort was currently waiting for the humans to arrive. Once they made landfall, we would know where to strike out at them. Once they made landfall, everyone would be scrambling again. But for now, and perhaps the next half hour, I was with him, safe and private. And as I drew in deep breaths of his clean male scent and basked in the warmth of his body, it struck me: I could spend that time crying on his chest and despairing over the loss of everything I knew. Or I could take what might be our last chance to make love.

The same thoughts seemed to occur to him at the same time. He didn't need to be psychic for that. Instead, he stroked my head until I tilted it back, and then he bent down to claim my lips, his mouth moving hungrily against mine. The coppery taste of his mouth distracted me; the sweet friction and minty smell of his warm breath left me suddenly craving more.

I responded slowly as my terror started to melt away like an icicle in a flame. My hands slid up his muscular back. He lifted me, then walked over to the nearest wall and pressed me against it. One powerful, armored thigh worked its way between my own to help prop me up as our kiss intensified until we ravaged each other's mouths. My fast heartbeat now thundered in my ears for another reason, and I embraced the distraction with relief.

His hands found the laces on my tunic and slipped them loose, parting the leather to expose my breasts and belly. I stiffened slightly, vaguely aware of the milling crowd just outside the door. They were discussing the situation in loud voices, sorting out the minutiae of his orders before going to their posts. It wouldn't take much for one of them to walk in on us. But Dekkir did not seem concerned. He simply kept on, running his hands over my freshly bared skin. I didn't realize he had locked the door until someone tried the handle and could not open it. I blinked up at him, and he smiled…then winked. "They can wait a little while," he rumbled in my ear. Then he lifted me farther against the wall and started kissing my breasts and throat.

I cooed, clinging to him, the beast-scale armor strange under my fingertips. I wanted to feel his skin against mine, but there was no time. Even as he licked and suckled my nipples into hard points, even as I started to tremble as he pressed me against the wall, I felt the sense of urgency in the crowd beyond the door, in Dekkir, in myself. It never quite went away, no matter how sweet the distraction, and I cursed it in my mind. *Damn you, Norcross.*

But then the despairing thought swept away as Dekkir's emotions reached out and entwined with mine. His empathy was not as strong as a seer's, but he had honed it through many years of working with the Rilleen. Those ferocious beasts would not allow anyone to ride them whom they did not love, and so he had ensured a strong rapport and strengthened his mind in the process. Now I could feel an urgency of a different sort from him: the hunger of his skin, trapped in armor, and his sweetly aching length, feeling more and more confined within his codpiece.

I moaned softly as he reached down to knead and stroke my slick, throbbing mound through the crotch of my leggings. I was starting to ache for him, to need him inside me. His breath started to shiver as he felt my need mix with his own and stoke it upward. To be a True Mate to a Lyran was to weather passions stronger than humans could manage. He growled against my throat, then settled me on the floor just long enough to strip off my leggings and boots. Naked save the parted tunic, I reached for his belt with trembling fingers—only to have him push me away and unfasten the codpiece itself, lifting it aside.

He scooped me up and thrust into me, pinning me to the wall again. I gasped aloud at his rough entry, but my body was already too aroused to be hurt by even his prodigious girth. He went taut and pushed deeper, powerful thighs holding us firmly as I clung to him. Our shouts of pleasure rose as one, my own soft and breathy and his hard and harsh. The hand not clinging to his shoulder gripped his buttocks, which tightened rock hard with urgency as he ground against me. He drew out, and I felt his bliss at our flesh sliding against each other echo in my own nerve endings. The edges of the armor dug against my inner thighs as I wrapped my legs around him. I didn't care. *Do it. More. Harder. Oh, yes…please. Don't stop.*

He thrust back in, growling softly as he stretched me open and sank his whole length inside me, a jolt of pleasure running back and forth between our bodies. He picked up a rhythm, slow and gentle at first, just rocking against me, shuddering each time he sank his shaft. But his instincts made their demands soon enough, and he sped up, grinding against me harder as his armor creaked, and I gasped and clung to him.

My body responded to his pleasure and my own, writhing against him despite the hard, nerveless plates of hide between us. His grunts became sharp groans, voice guttural and a little breathless, hands gripping my back and hip hard as he pounded against me. I could feel my flesh tightening around him, more and more, tingling, aching, craving completion. I whimpered, nails digging against his armor, head falling back against the wall as he ran his mouth over my neck.

His voice rose in slow crescendo, deepening, growing louder, the strain in it intensifying until every throaty pant sounded like he was being tortured. Shocks of doubled pleasure ran through me; my muscles locked, body tightening until I could hardly bear it. I let out a long, panting cry—which rose into a wail I had to muffle with my hand as waves of pleasure overtook me.

He groaned through his teeth as I came and sped further, belly flexing, armor creaking and digging into me, the tips of his fingers gripping me, bruising. I gasped with pleasure, his rising ecstasy and the little edge of pain he gave me driving me quickly toward another climax. His head fell back, and he shouted as his orgasm spiraled outward to include me. I felt him release from within and without, the rush of warmth filling me even as his pleasure sent me into spasms of delight.

We came back to ourselves slowly, him panting into my shoulder, barely holding me up as he leaned against the wall. He let out a purring rumble and ran his teeth over the side of my neck, nipping affectionately. Slowly, he disengaged from my body before gently lowering me to the floor. He steadied me as I got my wobbly feet under me. "There. Now at least my head is clear, lovely one."

Our lips brushed as I gasped for air, feeling little aches and pains where his armor or his hands had left me bruised. The thought made me smile; I would wear his marks proudly. It would remind me that whatever else happened, I still had love in my life, even if I never saw my blood kin again.

I brushed my hand over my belly before reaching for my leggings. *Perhaps there's a chance we can make our own family here,* I thought wistfully. The idea I might carry Dekkir's child even now already filled me with an easy joy. I had been queasy a lot these past mornings, but there had been no time to trouble a healer with pregnancy testing while we had been scrambling to recover from the last Earth attack and prepare for the next. The battle to come would be a horror, and I knew it would hurt me no matter who died. But at least with Dekkir around, and the possibility of a child on the way, there was hope and something to live and fight for without second-guessing myself.

You must live, my darling. We both must live, I thought as I finished dressing. I laced my tunic back up, and we shared a last soft kiss as he fixed his armor back around his loins.

"It is time, Grace," he murmured. "The humans land soon. We must prepare."

I nodded, still catching my breath. "I'm with you." When he turned to leave, unlocking the door finally, I followed him out.

CHAPTER 15
DEKKIR

Grace was not doing well. I sensed it in my mind, my heart; she grieved for the upcoming battle. And no wonder. Either her adoptive people would die or the people of her blood would. No matter what, she would suffer terrible loss before this fight was over.

I watched her as we took our places at the crenellated outer wall of Highfort's rooftop. She was ashen beneath the brown and golden tones of her skin. Her bronze eyes threaded with deep brown and sparks of gold held a deep fear and an even deeper sadness. I knew in my heart her instinct was right: this battle was pointless and a tragedy for both sides. But sadly, that was often the case with wars.

For centuries, I had fought in skirmishes between forts when diplomacy had failed. It was always tragic. Always a horror. But I could hardly tell her to get used to it. She had the heart of a seer. Not a warrior. She had the ability to sense the interconnectedness of all things, but like some empaths before their training, it left her vulnerable to the suffering of others. My lady had no armor against the world's harsh realities.

"I need you to be focused for this, my love, and I apologize. But with Neyilla monitoring our troops in the jungle and the rest of the seers preparing their defenses, I need someone to monitor our troops here." At her nervous look, I smiled reassuringly. "Do not worry about your inexperience. I just need you to 'watch,' not relay messages."

She swallowed. "Neyilla trained me to monitor single individuals and small groups. What if I get overwhelmed?"

I offered my most reassuring smile. "Have some faith in yourself, my love. I have no doubt you can handle this. Just reach out with your mind and feel the men on the walls and the ones beside their mounts." None of the Rilleen riders was airborne yet. "Once you make contact, they can engage your stream of consciousness and feed you information on what is going on."

"I'll try." She closed her eyes, leaning on one of the fuel barrels we used for fire arrows. Her brows drew together, and she twitched slightly. I reached out to her with my heart and felt the strain of her connection with multiple minds at once. "I think I've got it," she mumbled, her voice light and dreamy.

"The men on the battlements?"

She frowned thoughtfully. "Yes, and the Rilleen riders. They're impatient. It's what they are letting themselves feel instead of fear."

I nodded, stroking a thumb across my chin. "Any word from Tabirus?"

"I'll check in with him. Hang on." The strain deepened on her face. She drew a few deep breaths and struggled to focus.

As I waited, I looked up and down the row of battlements and the men and beasts manning them. Warriors—my people. Tabirus had warned that the attack would be coming from the west. He didn't yet know how deep into the jungle he could mislead them or what tactic to use once he did. Perhaps he could lead them into a beastvine field or near enough to a giant insect nest. I could only hope it would be enough to slow them down and let some of our guerrillas pick them off.

My hand reached out by itself to stroke down the soft, dark cloud of her hair, and she smiled slightly, then relaxed. "I've got Tabirus. He says he's leading them to the swamps half a day's march from here. He may be able to convince a few dropship pilots that the jungle is several meters lower than it actually is."

"He plans to crash them?" *Not bad.*

"Some of them." Her lips trembled, but she set her jaw and focused. "He can't manage it with all the dropships. Some of those pilots have unreachable minds, including Norcross himself."

"I see." I squinted out over the rolling plain to the west, where the jungle started thinly and rapidly thickened. Far off, I could see something sparkling high in the sky in that direction. "Then he should focus on misleading those he can to as deadly an effect as he can. The seers monitoring the jungle can aid him in the effort."

She nodded, and I saw her lips moving as she relayed the message. A pause, and then a flicker of sadness crossed her face. "He says he may be able to remove a quarter of them by this method, and then they will be forced to hike in. That is when our troops in the jungle can start picking them off."

"That should thin their numbers considerably. Under the cover of the jungle, we will have the advantage. We can pick a good number of them off and lead survivors into the various jungle hazards." I put a hand on her shoulder. "Keep monitoring. See if you can reach the men in the jungle."

She closed her eyes again, and tiny droplets of sweat misted her forehead. "They're pretty antsy over there. I think they're almost too close to some of the insect colonies." She paused and gasped aloud. "Neyilla says she's anticipating a crash site with her precognition. The other dropships will land in the same area to attempt rescues." She shook her head slowly, anguish twisting her features. "Of course they will. They'll even defy Norcross to retrieve their own."

"Do you have any idea why none have thought to try to rescue *you* while they are at it?"

She bit her lip softly, in a way that distracted me. It wasn't the time for desire, but need flared inside me regardless. But then the sadness on her face deepened. "Norcross claims I was either killed in the last drone attack or have gone over to the other side. If they see me, I'm to be killed, not rescued."

A tear tracked down her cheek, sending a small pang through me. I hated seeing her cry. And more than that, I hated the man responsible —this Norcross, supposedly a leader of men but actually a coward whose face I longed to smash open with my fists for his audacity. *How dare he seek my mate's life? In fact…how dare he make her shed even a single tear? I'll destroy him.*

"I am sorry. Just remember…despite what fools like Norcross may think, you did not betray them. You responded to their betrayal of you. They used you to gather information on us so they could defame us to your fellow humans and then gain justification to wipe us out." I brushed the tear away, but more joined it quickly. *Yes, definitely going to kill this Norcross. Slowly, if I can manage.*

Still, Grace kept focused, despite her grief, impressing me. "I understand that. It's just one thing to understand it intellectually and another to…feel it. The humans on that base that suspect I'm alive, they hate me, Dekkir. They think of me as the traitor."

"Don't absorb their hate. Don't turn it against yourself. There is no need. You know you don't deserve this." I couldn't keep the urgency out of my voice any more than I could keep the love out of my heart.

"Some of the ones being sent after us don't deserve what we have in store for them either." She swallowed, and I felt her grief pricking at my heart.

"That is war, my darling. It is hideous and nonsensical, and one ends up mourning the innocent more than rejoicing that the guilty are gone." I stroked her hair again and felt her shivering. "Keep monitoring."

"I'll try." She took several deep breaths and tried to focus again. "I can feel what Tabirus and Neyilla are doing. I'm afraid if I look too closely, I'll mess it up somehow."

I chuckled. "You worry too much. You would have a difficult time doing that when, from what I gather, they are far more advanced in experience than you are."

"All right," she mumbled in reply and then tensed. "They're nearing landfall."

"Keep watching. We need to find out how many survive this so the jungle forces may be warned. Any humans who find a hole in our outer defenses must be confronted here."

She panted softly, eyes screwed shut. In the distance, the sparkling motes grew ever larger. They were streaking toward the jungle, barely slowing yet. I was reminded of her own precipitous landing, which had come to an abrupt end when a beastvine had grabbed her drop-ship from the air. Back then, I had not yet realized what she was to me, but I had felt a surge of panic I realized now had not been my own.

"They're coming," she whispered. "He's convinced most of the pilots that you and your father are hiding in the jungle in that area."

"Good." I watched as the shining dropships headed for the jungle canopy. Seconds later, the lead ones penetrated it, and a heartbeat later, I heard a ground-shaking explosion.

"Ohh!" she cried out, fresh tears suddenly tracking down her cheeks. "Oh, the panic, the panic, they're so scared." She buried her face in her hands, and I suddenly realized she had felt the deaths of the fallen humans. "They're gone…"

"No." I shook her gently by the shoulder with one hand and then cupped her face with the other. "No, don't get entangled with them. Come back. Draw back to me and to the living."

She sobbed, her skin alarmingly cold under my hands. "I trained with those guys in my self-defense classes. Some of them were just teenagers—"

I shook her firmly. "Stop. Come back. Do not dwell on them. The living need you! I need you."

She nodded convulsively, and I sensed her struggling. *Tabirus*, I thought as I radiated love and support toward her. *Neyilla. Help me.*

I heard their voices overlaid in my head briefly even as my broad-cast left my temples stinging. I was no telepath, but fortunately, they were monitoring us all. *Dekkir, we cannot… You must bring her back! The survivors are emerging. They wear power armor. Most survived. Most are uninjured. They are gathering their forces in the jungle, and we must act!*

I pulled Grace into my arms and hugged her tightly. "Come back, love. Come back."

Slowly, she did, her shaking easing off and the warmth slowly returning to her skin. "There are still…many. So many. Seventy, eighty…"

I nodded and sighed. "Tell Neyilla to coordinate the jungle teams. We will try to lead them into an ambush."

She swallowed. "Okay. Okay." She squinted then nodded. "The lead warrior is making contact—"

A thud and a flash of light from the jungle startled me; Grace flinched. "They're shooting! The warriors have no armor against pulse rifles. Bodies falling—it burns…" Her tears started flowing again. "This is crazy. So craz—"

"How do they fare?" I shook her again lightly, and her eyes flew open but stared sightlessly.

"Neyilla says some of the men are leading about twenty of them off into the jungle. Norcross ordered them to stop, but these are impulsive and angry about the crash." She started trembling. "If they go too near the hives—"

"The warriors will die, too. I understand that. Darling, so do they. This is acceptable risk to them. Lose one's own life, save the world."

"Oh God, they're doing it. They're doing it… No. No, please, don't go near there!"

More flashes and thuds of pulse rifles going off, this time, in rapid succession. Suddenly, several dozen gigantic wasp shapes, almost black, rose above the tree line and then dove back downward, stingers first. I couldn't see the siege, but from the horror twisting Grace's features and making her sob, she could feel it.

"Too many. The bugs… The warriors… They're being over-whelmed. They pick off a few, but not so many. They can't get through that armor!"

I frowned. "Tell Neyilla I want her and her seers to find a way to convince them to take off their armor."

"It will only work on some," she warned. "Norcross—"

"It will have to do," I replied quietly. "It will at least thin them out."

"O-okay." She wiped her own cheek this time and just focused. "She says it's possible. They're working on it now." But a few seconds later, she stiffened and started clawing weakly at the front of her tunic. "Hot… Oh God, so hot…"

"Not you," I chided, snapping my finger an inch from her ear. She flinched slightly and then opened her eyes, which offered only that terrifyingly empty look again. I tugged at her hair lightly. "No, darling girl, no. Come back to me."

"I'm sorry," she gasped. "I can't just ignore their suffering. I know they are the enemy now. But they're also young men who have barely gotten to live yet." She drew a shuddering breath to steady herself.

"Of course they are. I'm not angry that you remember they are some mother's son. But you must comply. I need you focused on the task at hand, not its emotional impact." I stared into her eyes until they focused on me.

"Yes… I understand." She didn't seem happy about it, but she lifted her chin and struggled to focus.

I sighed relief, but prematurely. For the next second, just as the pulse rifle fire erupted again, she went rigid, going ashen again. "No… no! The arrows… Those bugs… *They're stinging me!*"

This isn't sentiment or lack of nerve. She has more psychic power than she has self-control yet, and it's turning on her. "They aren't! You're right here with me, Grace. You're not out there! You're not dying!" I did everything I could think of to get her attention, shaking her, holding her. But all she did was go completely slack, sliding down to her knees at my feet. The emptiness in her eyes had gone from blankness to a sort of void, as if her soul were falling down a deep well. "Grace? Grace! *Grace!* Wake up, love. Don't leave me!"

Deep inside, I could feel her struggling against the tide of pain and death flooding into her inexperienced mind. But then all she did was fold up into a ball and cover her face with her forearms. Her mind was retreating into itself, away from the pain, away from this ugly reality… away from me. And I wasn't sure how to call her back.

CHAPTER 16
GRACE

The remaining troops are reaching the edge of the forest.

How did they move so fast?

Their suits have some sort of jets they can use for leaping. They're just bounding over deadfalls and everything else and heading straight at us.

I struggled to make out all the brain chatter in my head, knowing I was supposed to be doing something with it. *Dekkir. I need to tell Dekkir.* But my lips wouldn't move. It was if I were frozen in a block of ice and could vaguely hear him banging on it and shouting in at me, trying to help me break out. I tried to struggle…but pain lay that way. The pain of so many losses. The knowledge that so many more were to come.

A bolt of white light rips through my chest, and the world goes black. An insect stinger as long as my arm pierces my shoulder. I scream, try to fight, seconds before its massive mandibles close on my head. Arrows thud into my back, three, four, five—the last one pierces something vital, and the ground swings up and hits me in the face. I'm dying. I'm dying. I'm dying, over and over, human and Lyran, no difference, really, in that final moment, when I go from a living, vital person to a twitching sack of meat.

Dekkir… Help me…

He was holding me, as if trying to bring warmth back into my body with his own, his broad chest heaving against my face. *I love you,* his voice said into my ear and into my heart. *I love you. Come back to me. Please, come back…*

Dozens of dead hands clawed at my mind, gone too young, gone in the midst of fury and terror, their souls still outraged. Wanting to know why. Souls on both sides gone too soon, some of them hundred-plus-year-old Lyrans, but still—too soon, too soon. I wanted to tell them how sorry I was. I wanted to tell them I wished it had not happened. But their grief, pain, and anger were mindless, clawing at me in dead reflex, like the echo of a scream.

Grace.

I heard the voice, Dekkir's voice, calling me back, shouting with all his strength and straining his mind. Other voices joined it in chorus: Tabirus, Neyilla, even Dorin. Joining together, boosting the strength of Dekkir's call. *Grace. Come back. Don't stay with the dead. Don't. You must come back, Grace.*

I could feel love and concern in their mental voices, even if Dorin's was a bit grudging. Their voices were like a beacon to me in the icy dark. I rose toward it, fighting against the clawing souls that tried to drag me down with them. But there were more important people waiting for me. Dekkir waited for me. He was my strength…but I was his as well, an endless wellspring the psychic backlash of so many deaths was threatening to rip away.

Come back, precious one. Come back.

Dekkir?

I'm here. His mental contact overflowed with relief, and I rose toward it, toward my skin, which itched and tingled, toward my face with its tears wet and dried, my aching eyes, and my aching head. Toward my fallen body, which he held so tenderly.

I gasped awake, eyes flying open, and looked up at him. "Dekkir—Dekkir! They're coming!"

He sighed his relief and then set his jaw grimly. "I know, my love. I know. We've only been able to kill a few of them. The beasts and our weapons are no match for their armor, and the seers can only convince some to disrobe or attack each other. Most of Norcross's force is still on its way."

I sucked in air and sat up painfully, fighting a wave of dizziness and terror. He helped me to my feet, and we looked out beyond the battlements. A wedge-shape of armored Earth soldiers bounded across the plain toward us, rifles at the ready, faceless in their heavy helmets. It almost felt as if I were back in the nightmare in-between place again, but my eyes were wide open, and these antagonists were all too alive.

"What do we do?" I whispered breathlessly.

He set his jaw. "We fight," he replied. "We fight down to the last man."

Keer squawked happily as she saw us, bounding out of her aerie atop the wall and crouching down in front of us. The gigantic creature was equal parts lion, bird, bat, and lizard, covered in jet-black fur, with golden eyes and claws of shining ebony. She had gotten a little chubbier since I had last seen her—but that might have been my imagination. She rubbed her head against Dekkir's legs, then against my belly, and crooned.

"Is she excited to go to war?" I asked incredulously. I understood Rilleen were powerful, violent predators. I had seen her and her companions tear apart an entire swarm of giant insects and even eat them. But armored humans with pulse rifles were something else altogether.

"She always craves battle. But I fear even the Rilleen may be no match for their weapons." Dekkir sounded grim. "Today, the riders hold the walls while the Rilleen attack on their own. We will direct them from the walls."

"But they'll be slaughtered."

"Yes. But this is what they are born and bred for. This is what they live for. Battle and protecting their home."

Dammit, that's no fairer than sending heavily armed teenagers. I hugged the beast around the neck suddenly. "Please don't die, Keer."

Keer just crooned and licked my cheek before moving to the edge of the outer wall with the others. Her tail lashed with excitement.

Dekkir slipped an arm around me gently. "I will guide her. But I will need your help anticipating any who might aim at her. Without a seer, she has no chance of dodging those weapons."

I closed my eyes. *Tabirus. Where are you? Please, you said you'd do something. There are still dozens of them and they're all armored, and they'll fire as soon as they are in range. Please—*

His voice came to my head grimly. *I'm on my way. Just hold the wall until I get there. I had to take a little something out of mothballs for this particular battle, and it took me some time.*

I took a deep, shivery breath and looked up at Dekkir. "Tabirus is on his way. He says he has a surprise for our enemies. All we have to do is hold the wall until he gets here."

The heavy thud of a pulse rifle sounded, and a bolt of light slammed against the fort's outer wall. Dekkir turned and whistled to the other riders, and suddenly, dozens of Rilleen bounded into the air.

I closed my eyes, focusing past Dekkir's mind and the warriors' minds, past the wildly delighted Rilleen, down onto the plain, where the human soldiers saw the Rilleen rise and started taking aim. I sensed a finger tightening on a trigger and gunsights locking on Keer. *There—dodge! Dodge now!*

I felt Dekkir's mental command, and Keer swooped sideways, a sizzling beam of light darting past her. Around her, other Rilleen were doing the same—but one didn't dodge in time and dissolved in blinding light and a final shriek. The rest continued circling down toward the soldiers, dodging fire, a few dying on the way. My head pounded as I struggled to anticipate each shot.

"I'm not sure I can focus much longer," I gasped, exhaustion clawing at my mind. I was proud of how far I had come with my new powers, but I knew my limits. I didn't want to fail him at a crucial time.

"You *can* do this, my darling. Keep trying!" Dekkir's voice was firm and brooked no refusal. I felt his strength add to my own again and reached out to the minds of the humans. Keer wheeled, dodged—and tore the head off one of the soldiers as she swept past, helmet and all.

The battle raged for minutes as we helped the Rilleen dodge and strike between the beams. Cheers rose from the walls as the line stopped advancing—but the humans fought back doggedly, holding their ground. I did my best not to involve myself emotionally in the chaos below—but sometimes, the human I was "watching" would die suddenly, and I would get that same cold, panicky feeling of being pulled down after him. When that happened, Dekkir would reach a hand out and lay it firmly on my shoulder, and my mind would settle again.

I closed my eyes and focused again and felt something on the edge of my consciousness, a powerful soul—Tabirus, flying high. I expected that when I opened my eyes, I would see him on the back of a Rilleen. Instead, I saw the silver, vane-winged airship from my visions of ancient Lyra.

It extended two glittering prongs toward the line of armored men, and I heard a low thump as something shimmering and colorless rolled through the air toward the enemy line. It detonated when it hit, sending twenty of them scattering in pieces.

I stared. Dekkir slipped an arm around me, staring upward as well, but his face was grim.

"What is that?" I breathed.

"Forbidden technology," he rumbled gravely. "A device so ancient it should have fallen to pieces by now, save for its accursed brilliance of design."

I stared at him as he scowled, then nodded slowly. Lyran technological excesses had led them to ravage this world. Of course, he would be wary of something like that, "brought out of mothballs."

But profane or not, the airship did the job and, with a few more shots, broke the human line and sent them fleeing toward the pitiless jungle. I knew they would not survive there; the others would pick them off now that the concussive wave from even glancing blows from the ship's fore weapon had shattered their power armor. The airship soared overhead as the Rilleen turned back toward the wall, and the cheer that went up from the assembled warriors boomed like thunder.

Tabirus had the good grace to abandon the airship before walking in through the gates of Highfort. He was met with fanfare… Until the cheers died out, as everyone realized they were looking at a man who was neither human nor modern Lyran.

Helmet under his arm, the figure who strode toward us in the silver jumpsuit of his human disguise had close-cropped white-blond hair… and the golden eyes of a Lyran. He smiled around at the assembled court, Dorin, willowy Neyilla, Dekkir, and myself and then walked up to the high chieftain and bowed. "Tabirus, at your service."

Neyilla stared. "You…you are one of the Ancients!" She took a step forward, looking him up and down. "Are you not?"

The Ancients were legendary on Lyra. Over two thousand years ago, they had chosen to alter their race's genetic structure, to adapt them to survival without the overreliance on technology that had nearly killed their planet. Thanks to them, the planet was currently thriving, its ecosystem pristine and its people, though low in population, both long-lived and almost impossibly healthy. Apparently, the older version of the Lyrans was so close to human in appearance that he had been able to pass for one of us.

Tabirus nodded once. "I am. I was alive when the great adaptation was made. I was part of the team of scientists who developed the Golden Strain and one of the first to inoculate myself with it." He bowed to us. "I apologize for my deceit, but it was necessary in order to make my infiltration of the humans that much more convincing." He offered a charming smile.

Dorin didn't seem entirely convinced, but he simply lifted an eyebrow. "Your assistance is welcome," the high chieftain said and then started coughing, leaning hard against the wall as his son put a hand on his shoulder.

"What my father means is your assistance is welcome, *but…*" Dekkir frowned. "Do not bring that flying machine within range of any of our forts again."

The Ancient smiled. "Understood. It was a desperate time for us."

Tabirus sat with his brandy by Dorin's hearth, as everyone perched around nearby, listening to his story. "We watched our world dying around us while most of us busied ourselves warring over the scraps that were left. It was the biological sciences that saved us, where mechanistic science had failed. By engineering ourselves and our world, we slowly healed this world and made it strong again."

"Any particular reason you filled it up with horrible flesh-eating monsters?" I couldn't help but sound a little sarcastic.

"All right, well, perhaps we made it just a bit *too* strong." He smiled ruefully. "But the powerful genetics that allowed this world to heal simply made everything that much more…vital."

"And aggressive." Dekkir smiled a bit, though. Keer had come through unscathed, and he was clearly happy about it.

"But even though our world is dangerous and our numbers small, we live in balance with it and thrive. That was what we Ancients set out to do, and I see it in what the humans now covet." Tabirus looked around at them calmly. "You have done well with the tools we have given you. That is why I chose to aid you by infiltrating the humans."

I frowned thoughtfully at him. "Were you among the developing Lyrans this entire time?"

"Actually, I was in stasis for a significant portion of that time. I had deliberately absented myself in order to let our descendants develop without as much meddling. But the approach of the humans awakened me, and I chose to intervene." He smiled around at their stunned expressions. "Dear me, you're an interesting lot when you're quiet for once."

"Very funny." Dekkir tilted his head slightly. "What are your intentions now?"

Tabirus smiled. "Take one of the dropships back, continue the charade. I have a project…growing…back at Earth base, which should help us tremendously."

He looked straight at me and then gave me a conspiratorial wink. I blinked at him, wondering what it meant, but he just went right back to telling stories of ancient times.

CHAPTER 17
DEKKIR

That night, my mate and I celebrated in the most appropriate Lyran fashion: in the baths. The enormous, frothy tub of steaming water smelled of night-blooms and washed against us softly as we embraced in its depths. I stood in water up to my chest, cradling her soft, warm, deliciously lithe body against me as we bobbed and writhed and nuzzled together. My muscles were beautifully slack after the second climax, and she sobbed with pleasure and happy exhaustion as she clung to me.

Resting half afloat between bouts, her head pillowed on my chest while her hair floated around her, she radiated contentment, love, and relief. We were all relieved. We had survived the siege, the humans were routed, and Tabirus had shared his secret—and hope for the future, not only for Lyra, but for Earth as well. For if a scientist of the old times chose to intervene in Earth's accelerating decline, then perhaps there was hope for humanity and for peace between them and the Lyrans.

The very idea had Grace much happier and more excited than I had seen her since she had discovered the true aims of Earth Command in this sector. I was so happy to see her smiling wholeheartedly instead of fighting tears.

I drowsed against her for a little while as we leaned on the side of the tub, my eyelids growing deliciously heavy. But then… I sensed something.

Normally, no one could slip up on me. I would sense their emotions, if not the noise they made. I realized we were not alone in the columned bathing chamber. A shadow with no feelings at all stepped out from behind a partition and pointed a silver hand weapon at me.

"Well, isn't this cute?" the dark-haired, icily pretty human male sneered as he walked toward us. He wore one of the silver jumpsuits, this one with black piping, and his blue eyes were empty despite his broad smirk. "Didn't think you had an alien fetish, *Grace.*" His tone turned childishly mocking.

Grace stiffened against me, and I tightened a protective arm around her, knowing from her disgusted rage who this man had to be. "What is your game, Norcross?" I spat the name.

"It's quite simple. I've got a dropship waiting. I'm taking this little infected traitor back with me for experimentation…and then trial and execution." He licked his lips. "Now. Let go of her. The two of you get your clothes on. I'm sure Earth Command will be happy as hell to see me take the war chief back as a captive." He grinned.

I glared at him and then let her go. We quickly scrambled for our clothes, while he pointed the pistol straight at Grace to ensure my good behavior.

I growled with frustration under my breath but complied. I wouldn't risk him wiggling his finger and sending my mate into dust with that…device. He would smile as he did it—of that I was certain. So I stood there, forced to tolerate it as he eyed her up and down, staring at every flex and curve of her as she pulled on her tunic and leggings.

He led us to the back of the bathing chamber, where a single open window dangled a silvery rope ladder down the outer wall. I wondered how we had missed his entrance and then ground my teeth in embarrassment. *Oh.*

"Climb. No messing around."

I went first, testing the strange, thin, but terribly sturdy rope. I climbed along slowly, trying to keep within grabbing range of an exhausted Grace should she slip. When we were most of the way down, Norcross looked down at me coldly and then leaped out the window. The retro-rockets on his boots hissed a few times, and he landed on the ground and trained his pistol back on Grace. "Move."

"This is foolish, Norcross. Listen to me." Grace was struggling to reason with him, her voice a little shaky, but her tone and expression earnest. "You don't have to do this. The Lyrans are preparing to offer their assistance in revitalizing Earth. That's not an opportunity you want to pass up!"

He stood over her with his fists on his hips, laughing as I helped her the rest of the way down. "Wow, that's funny. You actually believe that. You have an awful lot of faith in these aliens, Grace! But we all know it's bullshit.

"Earth is dying! Our homes…our families…everything back home that we love is going to be gone in under a generation. It's all gone to shit. Poverty and wars over tiny scraps of half-fertile land where everything mutates because of radon or chemical poisoning, people starving to death, standing up in cities so crowded there's no lying down. Earth is a rotting corpse, and we're still trying to suckle from her teat, and look what that shit is getting us! Sick, dying, and fighting each other over the last rotten drops. We have three choices: take over somewhere else, die out, or let the Lyrans help out. And guess what? I don't plan to die!"

He marched us away from the wall, toward a little canyon dug by a rushing creek. The three moons rode high in the sky, casting blue, greenish, and golden light over the wavering grass, but it seemed none of their light could reach far into the cleft between those rock walls. I could see gleams of silver in the darkness of the canyon: a dropship.

Norcross started talking again as we entered the canyon of shadows. "Now here's the deal. Grace pilots, you'll be in the passenger seat, and I'll be sitting behind Grace with my gun to her head. We're headed back to Earth Command Base up on that moon, Grace girl, and you're going to face the music." He gestured with the gun, and we mutely descended into the dark of the canyon.

My eyes adjusted quickly to the darkness and narrowed as I saw

Norcross stumble slightly on the path. He was at a greater disadvantage here. My muscles tensed as I gauged how closely he was following Grace with the pistol.

He stumbled again, and his aim wavered. I dove forward at once, knocking his hand away from her direction. The pistol went off with a hard thud and knocked a skull-sized chunk of rock from the canyon wall. Then I slammed into him with my full weight, and we both went over and started rolling down the steep path toward the creek bottom.

He fought the whole time, even after the pistol slid down the slope before him, squirming and kicking under me with the tenacity of one too proud to give in. Of all his traits, that one I could admire, though I wasn't about to admit that to him. Instead, I wrestled back and forth with him as we slid farther down the slope, while Grace ran after us, trying to get past our tangled, angry, dust-smeared mass to grab the fallen, sliding pistol.

I grabbed him by the head and pinned him down briefly; she darted past, but he stuck out a leg and kicked hers out from under her. She went down with a yelp and then scrambled back up, only to have us slide into her and knock her over again. The rough canyon scree flew up into my face and ground against my shoulder and arm as I slid downward. Norcross kneed me in the stomach and then gasped when it hurt him more than me. Growling, I flipped him over and rode his face partway down the canyon.

Finally, we fetched up against the landing gear of the dropship with a hard clunk. Grace got up with a sigh, brushing herself off, while I pinned down Norcross with one hand and started punching him hard in the face.

"How dare you! How dare you threaten my mate! How dare you burst in on us when we're enjoying ourselves, you perverse beast! How dare you look at her like that!" *Slam, slam, slam...* Each blow bounced his head off the stone and forced a little grunt of pain and surprise out of him, but I wasn't satisfied. His gaze had oozed all over Grace like a slug when he had watched her dress. I wanted him dead. And doing it by punching his brains half out of his head first seemed like the best method possible. "Grace, get the firearm!"

"I'm looking for it," she started as she scrambled around the creek shallows beneath the dropship.

Norcross shouted in outrage, his voice slurred by bloody lips and loose teeth, and kicked me hard in the thigh. His hands lashed out and dug against my face, gouging at my eyes. I reared back, prepared to punch him in the face again, and suddenly, I heard Grace's voice in my head. *Stop!*

What? I raised my head to look at her, and she nodded at me.

Play along. Just trust me. She winked with a strangely mischievous little smile. I wondered why it looked familiar.

Norcross clawed at something in the shadows, just catching it with his fingertips, and abruptly, he had the pistol in his hand. He trained it on Grace again, and I froze.

"That's better," he chuckled as he pushed his way up, wriggling free of my grip like a lizard and jumping to his feet. Blood streamed down his face, but he simply grinned. "Now get into the damn ship."

We climbed inside, Grace sliding into the pilot's seat and me sitting down beside her. The copilot's seat was tiny under me, cramped. The padding was inadequate. Norcross clambered in after us and slammed the hatch shut, making the egg-shaped compartment feel even more claustrophobic.

"Now. Let's get out of here." He gestured with the point of the gun, and Grace started flipping switches, her back completely to him.

She was smiling.

I didn't realize why until I glanced behind me for a second. I noticed a shock of blond hair and a silver jumpsuit and realized Tabirus was sitting behind me.

Norcross laughed. "I almost had to call you out to help me subdue this one, Stirling. He's a real wild animal."

"You have no idea," I broke in dryly.

"Quiet, you," Tabirus snapped and winked at me with the eye farthest from Norcross, a tiny curl to his lips. "Adults are talking."

He says he wants us with him so we can infiltrate the base. He has a plan for when we get there. Just play along for now.

I fought a smile. *Well, that's different.*

I sat stoically, faking silent indignation as the engines cycled up with a whir. I was going to fly high tonight, higher than Keer could take me, all the way up to that place on the moon where the humans dwelled and schemed under domes. And when Grace, Tabirus, and I got there, we were going to give the humans at Earth Command Base the surprise of their lives.

CHAPTER 18
GRACE

I had never imagined in my life that I would be brought before my commanding officer in manacles. They chafed my wrists as a pair of guards led me down the hallway toward the commander's office. I felt sick. Dekkir had been separated from me, taken away to be imprisoned somewhere else. My only hope was that the spy who had gone with them, the Lyran Ancient the Earth base members knew only as Dr. Stirling, really did have a plan to help Dekkir and me escape.

I had known from the beginning there would be consequences to siding with the Lyrans against the corrupt war Earth Command was attempting to impose on them. I'd known from the beginning there would be consequences to binding myself for life to Dekkir, future leader of the planet. But it didn't make it any easier for me to take that long walk down the hall, led roughly between two guards who glared at me with a mix of anger, suspicion, and fear. I knew I had done the right thing, but now I had to explain myself under hostile circumstances, and I didn't know if I could manage it.

My whole family had served the Earth military for generations. I myself had looked forward to becoming one of their premier science officers. And certainly, I had started out well. I never could have imagined it would turn out like this.

I couldn't help but feel cold waves of fear as we neared the doorway of Base Commander Aaron Wickman's office. The boot steps behind me were half the cause. The guards were none too kind with me, assuming I was a traitor. Technically, I was. But I knew if the people of Earth had known about Command's plan for Lyra and its people, they would not have gone along with it. Earth's leaders were supposed to be representatives of the will of the people. But they weren't anymore. Especially not out here, in a far corner of space, where they were trying to start a resource war that would leave as many Lyrans as they could manage dead.

I heard a faint chuckle behind me as I walked, and the hairs on the back of my neck prickled. My mission commander, second-in-command at the base and one of the most terrifyingly sociopathic men I had ever met, Lieutenant Damon Norcross, gloated as he followed me toward the room. This was all wonderful fun for him. I knew he was enjoying watching me as a captive. I wondered if there was any way I could get out from under his control. Perhaps the base commander would be willing to do something if I gave him a strong enough dose of the truth.

The guards stopped me before I reached the door, and Norcross stepped past me, knocking on it.

"Come in," a tired-sounding male voice called from inside. Norcross pushed the door open and strode in, head back, chest puffed out, looking tremendously proud of himself.

"I brought you our little defector, Commander. I thought perhaps you'd like to interrogate her yourself before we throw her into a cell. The Lyran garbage she's been keeping company with is already captive down in the brig. Dr. Stirling will be performing a few tests on him. I imagine he'd like a crack at this one as well, as that disgusting alien has managed to...*infect* her." He looked me up and down with dramatic disgust while I stared back impassively.

"Infect her?" Wickman's voice sounded more tiredly incredulous than anything.

The guards gave me a shove, and I stumbled through the door just ahead of them. "Nice touch. Very theatrical," I muttered as I caught my balance. Norcross was rubbing off on them—badly. I looked around, seeing shelves full of old, real paper books lining the walls and up to the ceiling of the enormous office. A steel and wood desk of a very old design dominated the room. A row of four chairs sat before it, and behind it, the base commander sat in his office chair, slouching slightly, his eyes sunken and dull with exhaustion.

Wickman's eyebrows rose as he looked at me. He was a tall, older man, slightly weak-chinned, his brown and gray hair thinning at the temples. His watery gray eyes had snaps of red in them, which I had long since learned were the direct result of all the drinking he did. A wet bar was set into the wall behind him, and I saw its row of bottles was largely dry. I almost felt sorry for him, except I couldn't. If he had actually been doing his job instead of crawling into a bottle regularly, he would have noticed what Norcross had been getting up to behind his back.

"Dr. Bryant, what is this? I only know what Norcross has told me. He claims you defected and you have taken one of the Lyran upper class as your lover. He claims you have betrayed us. Is there any truth to this?"

I took a deep breath and reached out psychically to the Lyran noble in question. Dekkir and I had a strong bond, strong enough for me to seek his mind on a whole different level of the complex. I sensed him faintly: awake, calm, waiting. He sent me a strong current of love and strength, and I felt my fear melt away in its warm torrent.

I squared my shoulders and looked Wickman in the eye. "Commander, this is a much more complicated situation than Lieutenant Norcross is letting on. I will gladly explain the entire situation to you. I will provide you with proof of my assertions as required. But I'm going to have to ask that I do this without Norcross being present. It is in his best interest to muddy the waters as much as possible, as he has been committing war crimes behind your back." *Fuck you, Damon.*

The commander sat back in shock, gripping the edge of his desk. Norcross, meanwhile, simply let out a high, nervous laugh. "Will you listen to this little bitch? Lying to save her own skin. So typical of a woman. But look at her. Look at her eyes. She's gone native. It's disgusting. She can't be trusted. You don't want to be alone with her, Commander. She's crazy and probably dangerous!"

Wickman held up a hand. "That's enough, Lieutenant. I'm very interested in hearing what she has to say, but if she will not speak in your presence—"

Norcross started talking very fast as he fidgeted nervously in his seat. "Then we can go straight to assisted interrogation. I'm sure an electroshock device connected to her brain would provide proper punishment for when she tries to lie again. And if she won't talk, we can hit the button a few times to get her going."

I thought of Dekkir's calm strength, drew a deep breath, and turned my head to look at Norcross. "You know what? Go ahead and hook me up. You won't hear a single lie from me, so the device will never be set off." I looked him deep in his empty blue eyes, watching them widen in surprise at my show of backbone. Before Dekkir and all this strife, I had always been as diplomatic as possible with Norcross, understanding he essentially had a personality as unstable as badly stored explosives. But now, I simply didn't care anymore. The only liar in the room was Norcross. And I intended to make sure the commander knew that fully.

The commander frowned but looked mildly impressed. "That's a very big show of confidence, considering the circumstances you're in, Grace. But since you have had an exemplary performance record up until now, I will consider what you have to say. However, Norcross stays, at least for now. He *is* your immediate superior, and if Dr. Stirling were not currently busy with our other captive, I would want him to be here as well."

Shit. "Understood, sir."

He gave me another surprised look. "I was expecting a lot more insubordination."

I smiled tightly. "I'm afraid you'll have to look to Lieutenant Norcross for insubordination today, sir. And I'm sure he's going to come out with it quickly enough." I gave Norcross a glance as he reddened. "You see, there was no conflict between ourselves and the Lyrans until he decided to act on his own."

Norcross tittered nervously again. "Will you listen to this woman? There's no end to her lies. Commander, she's trying to manipulate you before the machine can get here."

Wickman looked between the two of us. "I see. Well, fine. Let's attach the interrogation unit to her before we go on. If she lies, she will receive an electric shock, and we will know. If she does not lie, then, Lieutenant Norcross, we're going to talk a lot more about what you've been doing while I have been otherwise occupied." He drummed his fingers on the desk. "For example, your unauthorized visit to the planet's surface to capture her in the first place. I also happened to notice we are missing several drones and *scores* of our soldiers."

Norcross stiffened, his mouth closing suddenly. I fought down a smile. Norcross had already organized three attacks on the world below us, and apparently, none had been authorized. I could only wonder how much Wickman had been drinking not to notice…or what drugs Norcross had slipped into his drink to ensure his obliviousness.

The guards sat me down in one of the chairs in front of the commander's desk and fastened my manacles to its arms. I couldn't help but tug at them a little bit, but they were on firmly. *Calm. Stay calm. What would Dekkir do? Stay in control.*

As we waited for the interrogation device to arrive, Wickman looked at me curiously. "What has happened to your eyes?" he finally asked.

I smiled a little awkwardly. My once dark brown eyes were now threaded with gold and bronze, signs of the aliens' symbiont I now carried in my system, just like every Lyran did. "Well, sir, it's a symbiont native to Lyra. It ended up in my system after being exposed in an infirmary, and I've adapted to it. It's not hazardous. Dr. Stirling can back that up."

"You know that means I'll want to see the results of a full physical and blood workup once we're done here."

"Of course, sir. Dr. Stirling already did a blood draw on me before he left with Dekkir. It was not actually known by any of us that this symbiont could adapt to a human's system. I was as surprised as everyone else." Which was to say, not surprised at all.

Wickman steepled his fingers. "What does it do?"

I smiled and chose my words very carefully. "Well, for one thing, it's helped me adapt physically to the stresses of life on the surface. People with the Golden Strain in their system will heal and recover from illness a lot faster than normal. It's much more efficient than nanotech, as a matter of fact."

His brow knit. "Are there any side effects?"

I smiled sadly and, instead of answering immediately, reached into the commander's mind. I was still getting control of my empathic and telepathic powers, but I had enough command of it. Now, reaching out to the open book of a man in front of me, I felt a mind that was full of doubt and grief.

He knew Earth Command wanted to take over Lyra. He also knew the conquest would be costly, that it was morally insupportable, that it went against the charter of the Earth Command military, and that it wasn't even necessary if they had managed the proper trade arrangements. But Earth Command did not care. They saw Lyra as a fresh store of natural resources the depleted and dying Earth desperately needed. The commander had struggled for over a month with these new orders, refusing to go forward with anything that would destabilize the planet or risk the peace. He was under tremendous pressure from his higher-ups, and he suspected someone on the base had been working on the plan behind his back. Now that I had brought Norcross to his attention, he was starting to suspect. It was a hopeful sign.

Dekkir, Tabirus, I sent telepathically. *Had a look in the commander's mind. He's been suspecting Norcross for a while now. I think I am giving him enough reason to investigate fully.*

Tabirus answered, his cultured voice translating into calm thoughts. *I'm here with Dekkir, faking an interrogation and medical examination. Keep playing Wickman. He's much more open than Norcross, now that he's mostly sober, and it's time we got more humans on our side.*

Dekkir was no telepath, but he simply sent me an awareness of his presence with Tabirus, his calm security, and his faith in me. It was enough. I had to fight a smile. "Sir, the full effects of the symbiont are somewhat difficult to explain because they vary from individual to individual. I will happily give you and Dr. Stirling a demonstration once he is free."

Wickman scratched his chin. "That could be interesting. Let's just finish the formal interrogation first."

I reached out to the commander's mind again, soothing and reassuring him as subtly as I could as I infused my thoughts into his mind. He was so exhausted that it was easy. *It's all right. Grace will cooperate. She always has before. There's no need for this to become drama just because Norcross wants it to. You can handle this no matter how bad he gets. There's no need to reach for the bottle behind you.*

It worked. The commander seemed to relax slightly, and some of the light returned to his eyes. I wondered how long he had dealt with Norcross's crap that it had worn him down so much.

Just then, one of the science officers arrived, a tall, gawky redhead who blinked at me in surprise as he wheeled the blocky, trash can-sized interrogation device ahead of him.

Norcross stood and gestured a bit grandly. "Ah, now the interrogation can begin."

He turned to leer at me...and his smile faded and died as I looked back at him impassively. Suspicion glinted briefly in his still mostly empty eyes, but I didn't change expression. I had a plan now, and Dekkir and Tabirus were together and safe. The calmer I was, the more worried Norcross got. And the more likely he would make a mistake in front of the commander.

"Hook me up," I said calmly and saw even more of the color drain from Norcross's face.

CHAPTER 19

DEKKIR

"What are you doing with Grace's blood?" I asked as soon as "Dr. Stirling" ordered the guards outside into the hallway. The manacles they put on me gapped open on my wrists; they had not been able to fasten the puny things properly, and after a nod from the white-garbed man in front of me, I slipped them off and set them aside.

"The Golden Strain adapted perfectly to her human cells for the same reason she is so compatible with you. It took only a minor genetic mutation for her to bridge the gap. But now that she has, the Golden Strain in her system has been altered by interaction with her human DNA. I'm culturing the human-variant Strain now, in large quantities, outside her body." The slight Ancient Lyran with his human-like cropped haircut and blue contact lenses winked at me.

I frowned at him, folding my arms over my chest. Even now, Grace was being interrogated by her former superiors, one of whom was hostile, a liar, and mad. Lyrans never trusted those whose minds could not be reached by seer powers. They felt no connection to other people, and thus, they had no reason to care for or consider other people. Norcross was like that. Even I, whose mind was more adapted to communicating with my flying mount Keer than contacting other thinking minds, had felt the alarming *blankness* behind Norcross's eyes and smile.

"When are we rescuing my mate?"

"Rescue should not be necessary. She is not currently in any danger. I am helping coach her through her interrogation. She is drawing the commander's attention to Norcross's bald insubordination and attempts to foment war. The commander is not actually acting on behalf of Earth Command, you see, though he received orders to soften up Lyra for a mass takeover." Tabirus smiled reassuringly, but my eyes narrowed.

"That's a dangerous gambit. Yes, you have explained the troops have more loyalty to the commander than this lieutenant, but you're ignoring simple facts that any warrior would understand." Seer's blindness, I had heard it called. Those whose livelihoods centered on their psychic powers tended to rely on them too much, ignoring their instincts and sometimes common sense. Tabirus had shown signs of this before, and I wasn't having it.

He blinked and sat back in his office chair before the bank of medical computers. "You think so? Would you mind elaborating?"

I sighed and tossed my blond hair back over my shoulder impatiently. Upstairs in Wickman's office, Grace *was* in danger, for she was in Norcross's presence. The thought of her small, curvy, wide-eyed form surrounded by Earth soldiers, Norcross close enough he could touch her soft cloud of black hair before I could again, made me seethe inside. *She must be protected.*

"Their supreme leaders have sent down orders to destabilize our world and make war on us. This base commander has resisted the orders. His subordinate, the lieutenant, is carrying them out anyway. First, how do you know Norcross was not installed specifically for his lack of conscience so he would carry out orders like this without protest? You cannot read his mind, and Earth is too far away for you to parse psychically." I looked into Tabirus's blue-masked eyes sharply until he glanced away.

"You have a point." He frowned as he continued tapping away at one of the tablet controls he was working at, staring at the big screen in front of him.

I peered at it briefly. "I can't read that."

"Ah, give me a second." I felt a slight tug at my mind, and the incomprehensible symbols in front of me blurred, then suddenly became readable. I wondered if he was translating for me telepathically or if this was some other ancient trick.

I read the screen quickly, noting something mentioning propagation vats and a percentage: 10%, rising to 12% in the brief time I watched.

Tabirus adjusted a dial and pressed a button. "Go on."

"Norcross was able to get a room full of drone operators to go along with his plans. Then he was able to go behind Wickman's back and tap a hundred men to come down in dropships to try to take Highfort. To do that, he must have both a talent for persuasion and at least some outside help. Someone from Earth is helping him move around his superior and use people to get what Earth Command wants done. And at least some of the troops support Norcross far more than Wickman. If they find out Wickman is rebelling against Earth Command, even more will turn against him. Even if he is ethically in the right." *And my mate is caught in the middle of all of it.*

Tabirus blinked slowly and then offered a faint smile. "I believe we can sway the bulk of the humans here against Norcross," he insisted.

I scowled at him as I stood beside his chair, watching the screen. Its mostly black surface gave back a shadow of my long, pale face and hair, reducing my eyes to a pair of gold crescents. "Explain. And your plan had better not involve an appeal to their consciences."

He smiled slowly. Over his shoulder, I saw the readout reach 18%. "It is not human consciences, but human *consciousness* I seek to appeal to today."

Before I could ask what the cryptic Ancient meant, the door to the lab opened, and a man in more of those laboratory whites strode in with his coat flapping. "Dr. Stirling!" the man called as he looked around. He reminded me a bit of Grace with his dark brown eyes and short, tightly curled hair. His skin was paler than hers, a bit like my father's, and he spoke with a slight, drawly accent I could not place. "You called for my assistance?"

He drew up short as he saw me standing unmanacled by the doctor. "What...what's this?" he asked in shock.

"There's no reason to be alarmed, Dr. Eastman. Our captive has been given a fail-safe injection to ensure his cooperation." He glanced my way, and I sensed his thoughts at once. *He will think I have injected you with destructive nanites that will kill you if I use a remote signal, so try not to look too comfortable.*

I thought of Grace facing our enemies alone and manacled upstairs, and my mouth worked. *That will not be a problem.*

The man blinked as I glowered at him. "You're...sure?" he asked the doctor, keeping a wary distance.

"Absolutely. Now please, come have a look. I've isolated and cultured the Lyran symbiont they call the Golden Strain." He gestured toward the screen, and the man's eyes lit up.

He stepped forward beside us to peer at the readout. "What kind of proteins are these? I've never seen anything like them."

"This is completely new, my dear Eastman. It's an adaptive organism, which has proven compatibility with humans. It can even adapt to animal systems and enhance their survival ability in hostile environments." He laid a hand on the man's shoulder, and I felt his mind push against the other's in a way I couldn't quite comprehend.

"That's amazing! Something like this... It could really help back on Earth. We have entire ecosystems decimated. If something like this could shore them up...." He moved toward the screen, like a night insect dazzled by a flame.

"It could do a lot more than that." Tabirus pointed at the readout. "I'm currently propagating a large sample in medium for study. We don't know how stable the symbiont is outside of a living system, so we're going to need as much as possible to work with."

"Did this come from his blood?" He paused to glance at me again, and I deepened my scowl. He looked away quickly and edged a bit closer to Tabirus.

"No, it came from Dr. Bryant's. She was exposed while planetside."

Eastman's jaw dropped. He had little bits of gray in his hair, I noticed, but his large eyes and enthusiastic manner reminded me of a much younger man. "She was? Oh, my—what did it do to her? Is she all right?"

I closed my eyes, my mind drifting back to the night my Grace had chosen to inoculate herself with the Golden Strain. She had not done it for science or survival, or by accident, as many of the humans might assume. I felt my heart lift despite the current circumstances, and a warm wash of desire flooded me simply at the memory. She had done it for me. She had introduced the Strain into her system to awaken the senses she needed to feel the mating bond that existed between us. And then…

My hands flexed at my sides. It had been only hours since I last held her in my arms. Only hours since we had shuddered together in the climax of the ancient dance. But I needed it again. The softness of her body, the smell of her hair, the little musical sounds of pleasure she made as I thrust into her. The link would always feed her pleasure back to me, and her desire, guiding my hands and body even as they echoed delightfully in my own nerve endings. When the time finally came, one release would drag the other over the precipice in a feedback loop of pleasure so intense it made us scream. Even in the midst of an interplanetary crisis, the thought of her made me crave her so badly that my nails dug into my palms.

"May I have a look at one of the samples?" Eastman asked eagerly.

Tabirus nodded and moved over to the propagation vat, tapping the controls. A clear, covered dish the size of his palm slid out of a slot. I saw him grab it and turn around, and when his hands were out of Eastman's sight, he flipped open the lid and dipped his finger into the sparkling golden powder within.

I watched impassively, despite the sudden surge of shock and curiosity that ran through me. Tabirus's amusement brushed against my mind, tickling. *What are you up to?* I thought at him suspiciously.

Just what I said. These soldiers and scientists are in need of…enlightening. Once I'm done with them, not a single one of them will be willing to follow a monster like Norcross.

My brows drew together as Tabirus came back with the sample. *What do you mean?*

Watch and see, my warlike friend.

I watched him bring the sample to the fascinated human scientist, who took the little dish in hand and bent his head over it in fascination. "How does it work? Is it airborne?"

"Ingested, introduced through a wound or through the pores, actually. I suppose it could be aspirated, but it dries out easily in open air." A lie, which I noticed but did not comment on. He laid that paternal hand on the younger scientist's shoulder…and I saw the finger he had dipped into the Golden Strain sample tap once against the bare back of Eastman's neck. He left a single golden fingerprint behind, which sparkled and started to spread.

Eastman didn't notice. He took the dish over to another of the machines and set it down on a tray set into the machine. He put his eyes to a viewing scope of some kind in the top and hit a few buttons. "This is amazing," he breathed in something almost like joy. "It divides so fast in medium. I only wonder how long it takes to propagate in a human body."

"Several minutes, if that," Tabirus said with a smile. On the back of the man's neck, the golden patch spread and spread, gleaming as it sank into his skin. "Of course, it takes the human body and brain about a week to adjust to it."

"What happens during that adjustment period? Will Grace, I mean, Dr. Bryant, be available for questioning?"

"Once they're done with her downstairs, she's all ours," Tabirus reassured. "But suffice it to say the adjustment period tends to be a bit…disorienting."

I exchanged glances with the Ancient, who winked, and I suddenly started to suspect what at least part of his plan was. My eyes widened and then went back to the propagation vats. They were huge, taller than I was, broader than the span of my arms, eight in all. And according to the computer, he was filling every last one of them with Golden Strain spores. The readout now read 25%. It wouldn't be long before they all filled completely.

Grace, my darling, I thought with a surge of hope. *Hold on. Soon, we will be together again…and starting to engineer our enemies' defeat.* Or better yet, make them simply not be enemies anymore.

CHAPTER 20
GRACE

They got me hooked up to the interrogation machine, sensors on my temples and the back of my neck, as well as my wrists. I knew if I lied or allowed myself to get too nervous, I would end up violently shocked by the device, which would also set off an alarm. I struggled to focus, knowing now was the time for me to really come through. We had one chance to get Wickman's ear. Without it, I had no doubt I would have to make every human on the base my enemy in order for us to escape. And after that, war would be inevitable.

"All right, now…" The commander leaned back in his chair. "I want a full accounting of your actions on Lyra."

"Yes, sir." He had already made a mistake; the machine could not detect lies of omission. *Good, because I'm not describing to him all the time I've spent screwing the local high chieftain's heir.* Now and again, Dekkir's mind brushed against mine reassuringly, bolstering me. I felt it again and lifted my chin, speaking in an even tone.

"I entered Lyra's atmosphere at the appointed time, only to discover the calculations Norcross's team had made for my landing speed, trajectory, and wing deployment had left me coming in at an almost fatal speed. With the assistance of Dr. Stirling, I was able to correct, but I was attacked by some of the local wildlife while distracted with this and crashed."

He blinked slowly. "Local wildlife? I know your dropship was small, but one animal managed to take it down?"

"Plant, actually. It's called a beastvine, sir. It's basically a gigantic version of one of Earth's carnivorous plants. It senses vibrations. When it detects prey, it lashes out a very large tendril, which is covered in a sticky sap. Once it grabs its prey, it cannot move again for a significant period, so the sap holds what it catches until it can absorb it. I was just unlucky enough to fly within its sensing range, and…*bam*."

He winced. "I'm surprised you weren't killed."

"I was just as surprised at the time, sir. At any rate, Lyran War Chief Dekkir had been sent to rendezvous with me. He managed to get me loose of the vine and helped me return to their capital, Highfort, with him." *And that was when he recognized me as his True Mate. But at the time, my senses weren't awakened, and I had no idea what he was talking about. Even if I noticed how hot he was then.* He really was. Almost seven feet of muscle, silky pale skin, flowing white-gold hair, golden eyes, and rumbling voice, usually in black armor, with a giant spear across his back. He was a sight that would make any girl who was into guys get all curly-toed…and he was mine.

Norcross fidgeted in his seat. Wickman eyed him, and he subsided.

The commander looked back at me. "How were you received?"

"With suspicion. The Lyrans are nearly as xenophobic as we are. Dr. Stirling had made some headway with them, but they tend to take us as individuals only and suspect us highly as a group. If you prove yourself to them, they can be very good allies. If you make an enemy of them, as the lieutenant has done—"

Norcross scoffed again, only to fall silent when he saw the commander raise an annoyed eyebrow.

Wickman coughed into his fist. "I understand. So you were not well received."

"Not by all. High Chieftain Dorin is very suspicious by nature. But his son Dekkir received me warmly enough." I glanced over at Norcross, amused when he turned purple.

"*Too* warmly, apparently, you little whore."

Wickman slapped his palm down on his desktop. "Norcross. This is not the time for your sexual jealousy. You were written up three times for unwanted overtures during her time on base. It may surprise you to know I remember that. Now stow it." He turned back to me. "Go on."

"I had some difficulty adjusting to some of the local customs." *Like a besotted Dekkir announcing me as his intended before the entire court barely an hour after I arrived.* That had been horribly awkward at the time, but looking back on it now, I could almost laugh. Poor Dekkir, so aroused and delighted by his discovery of me as his True Mate that his normal iron control hadn't done a thing to curb his enthusiasm. "But before I could find a resolution for this, Highfort was attacked by an insect swarm. To give perspective, each one was roughly the size of a two-person dropship. I was able to witness examples of Lyran military prowess as a result of this, as I mentioned in my second report." A report filed by Tabirus in my stead, the contents of which he had briefed me on telepathically on the way over. "The swarm was taken care of with few casualties, but during the attack, I was trapped out in the open. If it were not for the Lyrans, I would have ended up bug food."

The commander had pulled out his tablet and was keying in notes as I spoke, his expression both fascinated and a bit horrified. "I see. So what happened then?"

"By that time, I had filed my *first* report. I believe a copy of it should be on your server. It contained image files of the Lyran throne room, including where High Chieftain Dorin sits and what he looks like. I got a very good image of him. Unfortunately, this turned out to be a mistake. You see, as I was attempting simply to do my job of extending friendly overtures and documenting Lyran society and customs, someone else back here on base intended to foment war with Lyra as quickly as possible."

I spoke on quietly, describing the chaos that happened when Dorin had been found poisoned by an assassination drone sent from the moon base.

The commander listened to my description of the scene with shock slowly widening his watery eyes. "I never gave the order for that." He glanced at Norcross, who looked away quickly.

I sighed with relief. "I'm actually glad to hear that, sir. But it happened. And because I was the only human around, I was taken captive and interrogated."

The red-haired science officer next to me gasped. The guards shifted uncomfortably, and Wickman's eyebrows rose. Only Norcross seemed completely unaffected by the mention that I had been, as far as they knew, tortured. They didn't know about Lyran empathy or telepathy, and I wasn't about to let them know.

When I looked over at Norcross, though, I realized he wasn't indifferent; he was *smiling*. Disgusted, I turned away. Let him think his petty sadism hurt me. In reality, I just hoped I got to see Dekkir put a spear through his black heart soon.

The commander looked between me and the interrogation machine that had not given off so much as a blip so far. I drew a deep breath, preparing to be very selective with the truth for a while. The last thing they needed to know right now was that the Golden Strain had granted every single Lyran, as well as myself, some form of psychic ability. That was the way in which I had been interrogated. It had been awkward and uncomfortable but painless, and they had gotten at the truth, which had exonerated me.

"I'm surprised they allowed you to keep making reports at that point," Wickman commented. "Did they imprison you?"

"No, sir. I was placed under guard, but not jailed. The Lyran way tends toward forced labor instead. I was brought to a hostel run by their most famous healer and became her assistant, aiding her in discovering a cure for the poison. It took about a week, but we were eventually successful." I didn't bring up that was when I had inoculated myself with the Golden Strain in order to both awaken my psychic abilities and feel my half of the mating bond I shared with Dekkir. All Wickman really needed to know was I had been forced to work for the Lyrans.

He cleared his throat. "So the assassination attempt was unsuccessful, and you were forced to assist with the high chieftain's convalescence. Obviously, you were not allowed to provide us with any information about your captivity or punishment at the time."

"No, sir, that was not permitted." Although, that was technically only because my communications device had been taken away as soon as the assassination attempt had been discovered.

"What happened after that?" Wickman took a few more notes.

I spoke very carefully. "Lieutenant Norcross has asserted that I betrayed Earth Command. In reality, I was still attempting to do my job and pave the way for a potential trade agreement and alliance. At the time, all of my commanding officers, including you, had led me to believe that was what Earth Command wanted." I stared into his eyes until he couldn't hold my gaze, then went on. "By that time, the symbiont that exists on Lyra had entered my system. Upon discovering I was genetically compatible with the symbiont, and thus with Lyrans, an arrangement was made to solidify a more formal alliance. I became engaged to their war chief, Dekkir."

More like, I finally admitted to the bond that already existed once I was able to finally sense it. The symbiont only made me aware of it, and then we… formalized things. I looked over at Norcross, who was squirming in his seat with a petulant look. *Eat it, you. I've never climaxed so hard in my life, and you weren't even involved.*

Wickman looked up from his tablet with a frown. "Wait a second. How come you didn't report in to us about this development?"

My cheeks got hot, and I looked down. "Partly because my communications were restricted." As in, nonexistent. "As for the rest, that's honestly kind of awkward to talk about. But if you really want to know the details, I'll explain it. Just not in front of the man who has sexually harassed me for my entire stay."

Lieutenant Norcross stood up so fast that he knocked over his chair. "I've had about enough of this. Clearly, the interrogation device is malfunctioning. She's been feeding you lies and manipulations this entire time!"

The commander stared at him, his expression deadpan. "You know, Lieutenant, I haven't noticed any signs of malfunction, and the machine was tested prior to being brought up here." He glanced at the redhead, who nodded confirmation. "I have, however, noticed that you've gotten increasingly agitated the longer Grace has talked. Apparently, you don't want her telling me the truth. Maybe it's because she knows more than you thought. Or maybe it's because she never committed any kind of betrayal aside from attempting to carry out her orders the best she could in a shifting situation."

Norcross stood there glaring mutely at his superior. I blinked at the commander in shock. I had never expected he would come to my defense. I had hoped he would listen, especially when I had risen to the challenge of submitting to the interrogation device. "Sir, we can go over that later, if it is more convenient."

Wickman nodded thoughtfully. "I understand. We will discuss that later. At this point, you had this symbiont in your system, you had already dealt with one crisis and an interrogation, and you had become subject to an arranged marriage with a man who, apparently, is not that uncomfortable a companion for you. Is that correct?" I nodded, and he made a few more notes. "What happened next?"

"I returned from the hospice with Dekkir and the others in a caravan commanded by one of their local travel specialists. On our way back, we were attacked by a swarm of combat drones. Several members of the group were killed before we were able to fend them off." I stared at Norcross, who stood still, a single muscle jumping repeatedly in his cheek.

Once again, the machine didn't let out so much as a beep. The commander looked between it and myself and then sighed. "The missing drones. I assume the missing men have a similar story behind them?"

I opened my mouth to speak, only to hear Tabirus speaking to me in my mind. *Grace. You cannot read Norcross's mind or emotions, but you can get him to expose himself. Empathy works both ways. His emotions are entirely self-centered, so you cannot read them. But you can still manipulate them, just as they have been manipulated with words. Listen closely, for my part of the plan will soon be unfolding. Remember he loves to gloat. Also, remember he keeps getting more nervous the more he is caught at what he's been doing.*

I took a deep, steadying breath and decided to give it a try. I focused on Norcross: all that peculiar absence of connection, like a hole in the world. I watched his face as I started pouring my own batch of emotions into his emptiness. Pride, fear, the urge to brag. *Come on, you damn fool. You've been quiet most of this time. You know you can't take it anymore. You have to say something.*

Norcross cleared his throat. "I am not responsible for the drone strike," he blurted suddenly. Then he realized how suspicious that sounded and reddened.

Wickman rolled his eyes. "Were you equally 'not responsible' for our almost one hundred missing men? According to the latest bunk check, as of a few hours ago, over a quarter of our complement of soldiers has apparently vanished into thin air. Did you have something to do with this, or do you want to tell me that you somehow infiltrated Lyra by yourself and captured the doctor here and this Dekkir fellow on your own?"

Norcross scowled and shoved his hands in the pockets of his dress uniform. "Fine. It's true. I was seeking to follow our original orders and work to destabilize Lyra."

"Without my knowledge or permission? And using tactics that failed at every single turn, with the exception of taking hostage two people who would likely have come here willingly if asked in a peaceful fashion?" I could feel Wickman's craving for a drink, and this time, I really couldn't blame him.

I concentrated harder on Norcross. *Come on, then, keep flapping your gums. Dig your career a grave. It doesn't matter what Earth Command had in mind; you still jumped the line, and you messed up while you were at it. It's about time Wickman realized what's really going on here.*

Norcross glared at him. "You have been ignoring orders from Earth ever since they gave the command to start the destabilization of the planet. This stupid idealism of yours was going to get us nowhere. You and this silly little bitch have only succeeded in delaying the inevitable. It was time someone got things moving!"

"Yeah, except you failed every single time, bright boy," I snarled at him. "Just like the man said."

The commander waved at me to be silent. "I see." He made another note, then looked up at Norcross. "Lieutenant Damon Norcross, I'm hereby relieving you of your duty. You will be returned to Earth on the next shuttle, and I will be contacting Earth Command about these developments. I will also provide them with the new information I have received on both the costliness and the pointlessness of Lyran occupation."

Norcross stared at him for a long time, his face dark purple and his eyes temporarily full of fury. "I see. Well, then. You leave me no choice."

The lieutenant pulled a small energy pistol from his pocket and fired, flash-burning half the commander's chest. Wickman stiffened, eyes widening in shock, and clasped the wound before slumping over and sprawling across his desk. The four guards turned immediately, drawing their weapons, but Norcross was already out the door.

CHAPTER 21
DEKKIR

I was watching the culturing tanks fill with Golden Strain and the human scientist slowly sink into a trance as his body started to adapt to it, when a current of alarm and anger ran down the link I shared with Grace. I sat up suddenly and turned to look at Tabirus. He nodded and immediately sent out a telepathic beacon to link us all up. *What is it?*

Grace's message back was controlled but edged with fear, frustration, and rage. *Norcross shot the commander and escaped. I'm sure he's gathering whatever sympathetic forces he has right now. Meanwhile, one of the science officers and I are trying to keep Wickman alive. He needs medical attention, and now, or we're going to lose him, and with him, any chance of winning the base. He has command codes we need to cut off Norcross's access to escape craft, combat drones, and everything else.*

Well, I wouldn't actually say we can't win the base without him, Tabirus sent rather casually, and I elbowed him hard in the ribs. He blinked at me.

I scowled back. *Stop second-guessing my mate. She's right at least as often as you are.*

He sighed and nodded. "All right, then." He turned to the assistant he had drafted, who was sitting there wearing a vacant smile as the first threads of bronze and gold crept into his irises. "Dr. Eastman, we're needed upstairs. I'd like you to monitor the culturing tanks and let me know when they're completely full." He went over to the machine that Eastman had put the small dish of Golden Strain culture in. Scooping the dish up, he turned on his heel and strode toward the door. I trailed after him, pretending reluctance.

As I left, I heard a dreamy voice behind me say, "Sure. No problem." I hoped it wasn't. He was clearly sinking into an adaptation trance already, and whatever Tabirus's plans were, the Strain was an important part of it.

Upstairs was in chaos. I pretended to be the docile prisoner again, trailing closely behind Tabirus as soldiers and technicians ran past us in what looked like a panic. A large crowd had gathered outside one of the offices. I could sense Grace's presence in that room.

Tabirus pushed through the crowd, saying calmly, "Chief science officer here. I have medical equipment en route. Please let me pass."

The crowd parted for both of us, though I got a few startled looks. Inside, Grace radiated regret and anger as she labored to keep the tall, aging human commander's heart going with her palms. "We're going to lose him," she called out sharply. "If you're going to do something, Dr. Stirling, do it quick!"

The room was deserted except for her and a single technician with the reddest hair I had ever seen. Tabirus hurried over to bend over the commander with her. He looked up at the technician. "Get that interrogation unit out of here. Bring the crash cart down, along with a stasis bed. We have to get him stabilized before I can do anything."

The tech grabbed the machine, sparing us all one last look before he hurried out. I walked over to my Grace and gently put my hands on her shoulders. "Stay calm," I murmured in her ear. "I'm here now." She relaxed slightly under my hands, and I smiled despite the circumstances.

I could see why it was hard for her. The man in question hovered on the brink of death, his face absolutely white, the right side of his chest and belly burned down to red and black meat, the skin completely gone. "Can anything be done for him?" I asked.

Tabirus nodded grimly. "There's only one thing. The Golden Strain works faster when it's trying to save its host's life, and I'm about to give him a massive dose." Opening the sample dish he had kept in his hand, he stepped forward and unceremoniously dumped the entire contents into the wound on the commander's chest.

Wickman's eyes flew open, and his back arched slightly. He let out a low groan, and golden light started to sparkle and dance inside his wound as the pile of spores sank into it. Grace gasped and backed up against me, and I wrapped my arms around her from behind. I murmured reassurance in her ear, but I could feel her shivering as she watched the skin across the man's chest start to knit together.

A minute passed. I stood tensely, wishing I knew what was going on outside. Chances were Norcross was going to take advantage of his superior's supposed death in order to take over. "What are the odds the soldiers will side with him?" I asked, wishing I had my spear with me.

Grace sighed. "On the one hand, he doesn't have control of them all, or the ones guarding me wouldn't have flipped when he shot Wickman. But protocol says he's in charge if the commander's incapacitated, and only three witnesses saw him shoot Wickman besides me. If he silences them and tells the others I killed Wickman, they'll do whatever he says."

"Then we will have to expose the truth to all of them at once," Tabirus said as he monitored Wickman's healing. The man was breathing on his own again, and the blackened, raw look to his flesh was fading. "Once he is stabilized, I will need to part company with you for a while and put the next phase of my plan in motion. Once that is done, we can use the chaos to locate Norcross and take him out. Protocol will have command here fall to me at that point."

Grace nodded, still clutching my arms as I wrapped them around her chest. "We'll get him back on his feet. Once that's done, he can help us shut down internal controls and start winning back the locals."

Tabirus let out a soft laugh as he straightened up. The color was flowing back into Wickman's face, and his eyelids fluttered. "Believe me, by the time this fellow is back on his feet, human awareness on the base will have...expanded considerably." He winked, looking

Wickman over one last time. "If he doesn't regain consciousness within twenty minutes, contact me."

We stared after him as he turned on his heel and strode out. Grace turned to me, eyebrows drawn together. "What's he up to?"

"All I know is he inoculated one of the other science officers, and he's culturing gigantic amounts of Golden Strain down in his lab."

My fingertips slid up and down her arm. I was so happy to be alone with her again that my mind went straight to my desires. Perhaps it was the desperateness of the situation. Perhaps it was watching her come into her own. I had sensed the way she stood up to Norcross and the way she conducted herself with the commander. This was the woman I had known she could become from the beginning— strong enough to handle any situation. I leaned down and buried my nose in her hair. But then I realized she had gone rigid in my arms and was staring off into space as she weighed what I had just told her.

"There's only one thing he could need all of that Golden Strain for, Dekkir. If he makes enough, he could expose everyone on the base." Her voice was low and a little shaky with wonder. "He could force open all their minds."

It made sense in more ways than one. My heart started to pound as I contemplated the possibilities. "That would incapacitate everyone with their adjustment period at once!"

She nodded, running a hand up my chest almost subconsciously. "It would also immediately make them aware that Norcross is lying about who attacked the commander. And it would make it much more difficult for him to deceive them into doing anything else, even if they can't read him directly." She hesitated. "But what will exposure to the Strain do to Norcross?"

I shook my head, then leaned down to nuzzle her hair again. "I don't know, my love. When a Lyran who is incapable of connecting with others emotionally comes in contact with the Golden Strain, it kills them. It acts as a deadly poison. Most with this defect of mind and spirit who are inoculated as children do not see more than a handful of birthdays. But I do not know about humans. Norcross may drop dead. Or something unforeseen may happen to him."

I looked down at the commander, who was improving minute by

minute. I wondered what I would say to him when he finally woke up. I didn't know whether to blame him for letting Norcross get away with so much or thank him for standing up to his superiors and trying to prevent a war. Humans could be such contradictory creatures. If Grace mystified me, this man was a puzzle beyond all interpretation.

The man's breathing became more even and stronger. I had seen the Strain save lives this way, but I had never seen it act so quickly. I wondered if Tabirus had altered it somehow in order to have it work faster and more powerfully.

I leaned down and kissed my mate's lips lingeringly, stealing a few precious moments before we were forced to focus back on the crisis at hand. "When we get out of this, my darling, I'm going to spend many nights making up to you the time we've been apart."

She laughed huskily. "Well, we were only really apart for a few hours, but if you want to make up for lost time, I'm all for it." She leaned up and kissed me again, and I saw the faint smile on her face. Soon, everything would be all right again, and we would spend our time making love and planning for the future instead of worrying about how we would survive the next few hours.

Our kiss intensified suddenly, both of us feeling feedback from the other's arousal that drove me especially into an impulsive frenzy. I knew for a fact the man lying across the desk would not be conscious for at least another quarter hour. I sincerely considered pinning her up against the bookshelf beside his desk and seeing how much pleasure I could give her in that time.

Several sets of booted feet approached outside. I stiffened, and so did Grace. Before we could do anything, I heard pounding on the door, so hard it rattled on its hinges.

"Dammit. They've got to be on Norcross's side." Her eyes narrowed. Hastily, she reached for the uniform jacket hanging off the back of the commander's office chair and quickly laid it over his face and chest. It hid both his healing wound and the fact that he was alive.

Clever girl, I thought admiringly before someone kicked in the door.

I whirled, trying to shield Grace bodily, but six rifles were suddenly pointed in my direction. I froze, shaking with anger, too aware I was unarmed and had no choice but to surrender. Grace put her hands up as well, and I heard them shouting at her to step forward.

I tried to go with her. I had barely reunited with her, and here she was in peril again and about to be taken away. But before I could do anything, four of them stepped forward and closed in on me, raising their rifle butts.

I flew into a rage, seizing one of the rifles and slamming it into the skull of the nearest soldier. He went down like a sack of meal, and the others immediately panicked and went back to pointing their weapons at me instead of trying to beat me with them. I pointed the rifle back at them. I had never fired one, but they didn't have to know that.

"That's enough!" It was Norcross's voice, his tone mocking. I looked up and saw him standing in the doorway, pointing his pistol straight at Grace. "Drop your weapon, or I'll gun her down right here."

My mate and I looked at each other, and a silent current of understanding ran between us. We had several wild cards Norcross was not aware of, from our powers to Tabirus's plans. And even the man they mistook for a corpse, lying on the desk behind me. *We will win this*, we swore silently to each other. I refused to lose my temper, and she refused to panic.

Norcross stepped forward and took hold of Grace by the wrist. He glanced at the guards. "You four, guard him here. Send Michaelson to the infirmary when he wakes up. I'll be back to take care of this alien as soon as I show the rest of our men the traitor in our midst. I'm sure they'll enjoy having some…*fun* with her. I sure will." He spat the last part in her ear and seemed startled when she barely reacted.

Grace didn't say anything. All she did was stare back at me as he dragged her away. The last thing I saw before the door closed was her gleaming bronze eyes, full of determination, trust, and love.

CHAPTER 22
GRACE

"I'm going to fuck you onstage in front of everyone," Norcross gloated as he dragged me down the hall. "It's what you deserve. Running off and spreading your legs for that filthy alien. Oh, yeah. I'm going to punish you good. Then, after I tell them everything you've done, I'm going to give you to them. You'll be dead by the time they're done with you."

I didn't say anything. Having his hand on my wrist made me sick. The things he said disgusted me. But I knew he was not going to win. I had faith in Dekkir, and I had faith in Tabirus. There was no damn way Norcross was going to win this one. But I still couldn't stand the thought of the public humiliation I was about to experience.

He was taking me to the main briefing room, a large auditorium capable of holding all four hundred of the base personnel. At the front of the room, a tall, narrow stage glowed, bathed in a spotlight. I knew what he planned to use it for tonight. I just hoped Dekkir and our allies would make their move before he managed any of it.

He marched me in, the two soldiers flanking him looking at me with a mix of wariness and curiosity. They didn't seem to understand why I wasn't crying or begging. Norcross didn't either.

"What's the matter, honey? Cat got your tongue? This is your last chance to beg me to change my mind. You should probably take advantage of it." I stayed silent, so he angrily dragged me forward with more force, taking me up the stage stairs and towing me out to the middle. He then raised his hand to address everyone, and the muttering crowd went silent.

"People, I've got an announcement to make." He grabbed me by the hair and forced me to face the audience. I looked out at them, keeping my expression neutral. There were science officers I had trained with, some I had even considered friends. There were soldiers I had eaten lunch with in the mess hall, soldiers I had gone to physical training courses with, even a few who had flirted with me—with a lot more respect than Norcross had, now that I thought about it. But each and every one of them stared back at me now without a single scrap of sympathy or understanding in their eyes. They were eating up what Norcross was saying. He had already poisoned them against me, and I knew no matter what I said, until something happened to make them more persuadable, there was no point in saying anything.

Norcross raised his voice in the emphatic tones of a vitriolic preacher. "This little traitor bitch is the reason a hundred of our men did not come back from Lyra today. *She* told them all our secrets. How our weapons work, what our tactics usually are, everything. It's her fault your brothers-in-arms are dead. And then, when we brought her back to interrogate her, she murdered Commander Wickman!" His voice brimmed over with false horror. An angry buzz rose from the crowd, and Norcross smirked down at me.

I looked out at all of them and suddenly noticed a change in the room. As they stood unaware, taking in their new superior's lecture about what a traitor I was, something was happening no one had seemed to notice yet. High above, amid a nest of exposed ductwork, several ventilation grates opened directly above the crowd. As I watched, what looked like a sparkling golden mist started blowing out of the grates, slowly drifting down toward the crowd in a thickening cloud. My eyes widened slightly as I recognized spores of the Golden Strain, more than I had ever seen in one place. *Tabirus put it in the ventilation system!*

Norcross went on obliviously, his hand like a steel manacle on my wrist. "It's become clear this woman is too much of a liability to allow her to continue to survive. Therefore, it is my decision that she be punished in front of everyone, right here, right now. And once I'm done with her, boys, you can do *anything* to her you want. Just make sure she doesn't survive it."

Another rustle went through the crowd. To their credit, most of the soldiers looked immediately uncomfortable. A few men pushed to the front, grinning eagerly. Others stared in horrified sympathy, understanding at once what the less-than-subtle lieutenant planned to do. But in any case, all eyes were on me. None of them noticed the shower of gold descending from above.

Norcross twisted my arm behind my back painfully and drove me hard to my knees. "Now, bitch," he hissed as he reached to unzip his fly, "you're going to suck my cock in front of everyone, and that's just the start."

"You get that filthy thing near me, I'll bite it clean off," I hissed back. "You're going to kill me anyway. I may as well leave you bleeding out through a groin wound."

A ripple of laughter went through the crowd, and Norcross looked up in horror. The stage speakers had picked up and broadcasted our conversation. He angrily yanked on my arm, sending jolts of pain up my shoulder. "No, you won't. You don't have the guts."

"You wish I didn't have the guts. Truth is it will probably take less than a second and only a tiny effort to bite off your dirty dick. Thing's probably got the dimensions of a toothpick."

The ripple of laughter grew louder. As I looked out at the crowd, I saw the women laughing the loudest and wondered how many of them he had harassed during his tenure at the base. From their expressions, it was most of them.

Norcross started to huff and hiss through his teeth. He threw me against the stage and started kicking me. His boot slammed into my ribs, making me wince from the pain, but I refused to make a sound. I rolled away from him, and he chased after me, starting to yell and swear. My eyes narrowed. *Had about enough of this crap.* With nothing to lose, I chose to act.

When he kicked me again, I grabbed his leg suddenly, locking it up with my arms and rolling over. He went down with a yell; the crowd gasped. A few guards ran for the stairs to intervene. Meanwhile, I got up, hauled off, and drove the heel of my boot into Norcross's groin.

He sucked air and choked, for the air was now full of golden motes, and he had just gotten a lungful of them. His eyes widened. The guards stopped dead, and I heard shouts rise up randomly from the crowd, none of the voices recognizable.

"What's this shit?"

"Is it an attack?"

"It looks like glitter! Is somebody playing a joke?"

The crowd started to fall apart, some trying to filter their breathing through their uniform jackets, some already inoculated and collapsing under a wave of euphoria, others staring up at the descending golden cloud in wonder. Norcross gagged, curling up and cradling his wounded balls, and then started to choke and wheeze as the Strain hit his system.

I got up and looked around at all of them. "Don't panic. This substance is benign in nature. You will be all right. Please, just listen to me. Lieutenant Norcross has been lying to you from the start. He's the one who tried to kill the commander!"

Someone in the crowd tried to take a shot at me, but the bolt went wide. I ducked, looking down at Norcross as I did so. His eyes were rolled back in his head, and the golden motes were turning black as they settled over him. I could see blackness moving through the veins under his skin. He convulsed, drool gathering at the corner of his mouth. *Serves you right, asshole.*

I bolted for the stairs. No one stopped me. Two of the guards looked my way, but their eyes were wide and dilated. I could hear the psychic chaos being unleashed around me. Soldiers and scientists alike were panicking or trancing out or falling to fascination; a few even wept with joy as their minds expanded and started to connect. It was like a slow explosion, a wave of psychic energy so powerful it staggered me. I felt a soldier's mind expand empathically, radiating confusion. I gave him a gentle nudge. *Be calm. Tell the others to be calm. You're not hallucinating. You're not dying. You're getting superpowers.* And in the process, learning the truth, the truth that would hopefully end this conflict.

I ran out the door and into the hallway, stepping over a lab-coated tech who lay on the floor dreamily, staring up at the downpour of golden spores from a ventilation grate as her eyes slowly went from green to gold. "It's beautiful," she murmured. "Am I dying?"

I paused, crouching by her. "No. You're just adjusting. You're fine. Soon, you'll be better than fine."

She rolled her eyes toward me. "What is this stuff?"

"A gift from the Lyrans. It's going to help you understand."

She blinked, and when her eyes opened again, the golden threads had multiplied again. "Understand what?"

"That we and Lyra don't have to fight for us to get what we need."

She stared after me as I hurried down the hall, reaching out to Dekkir as I did. I could barely feel him through the cacophony of awakening minds, but finally, I found him, heading my direction. He was not alone.

I broke into a run, squinting through the gold-dust-filled air, my head starting to pound from the psychic chaos radiating from the auditorium behind me. It took a minute, but I reached the elevators at the end of the long hall and waited.

The doors opened, and Tabirus walked out with a weak-looking but very conscious Wickman leaning on him heavily. His blue eyes were threaded with gold, and a look of hazy wonder filled his expression.

He focused on me and blinked. "You all right?" he mumbled.

I laughed. "You nearly got your heart flash-burned, and you're worried about me? I'm fine."

Tabirus helped him out of the elevator, followed by his second, Dr. Eastman, whose eyes were slowly turning the same bronze as mine. He too had a look of wonder on his face. And behind him…

I saw Dekkir and ran for him, ignoring the pain in my arm and ribs, thinking only of being in his arms again. But before I could get more than a few steps, a look of horror crossed all four of their faces.

A hand closed on my shoulder and yanked me backward with such strength my feet left the ground. I heard more than felt my collarbone snap and gasped as I was flung back against the wall and pinned.

Norcross held me there with inhuman strength, his lips twitching up into a leering grin. "Got you," he gurgled, the inside of his mouth as black as his eyes, and threads of darkness turning his skin gray. "Whore. Told you I would."

Eastman stumbled back in horror. "What the hell is that thing?"

"It's Norcross," Wickman muttered, pulling the pistol from his belt and aiming at what his second had become. "Let her go, Lieutenant. Your murder and coup attempt have failed."

"Never! I… I… I… Bitch poisoned me… Poisoned us all! I'll take her with me! I'll take her with me when I die!" His clawlike hand dug into my wounded shoulder, making the broken ends of bone grind against my flesh.

Tabirus started to say something, but it was lost in a roar of outrage from Dekkir. Before anyone could do anything else, he bulled forward, and I saw he had his black spear in his hands. Tabirus must have retrieved it for him on the way up.

He drove the spear through Norcross's midsection. It thunked home in a spray of black, acrid-smelling blood, knocking him away from me. I stumbled back, and Tabirus and the others moved to surround me protectively. But all I could see was Dekkir and the thing he was fighting.

Norcross seemed to have swelled in size. His muscles bulged enough to tear his clothes, black fluid drooled from the corners of his mouth, and his breath came in a wheeze. He grabbed the spearhead and yanked it free. Dekkir twisted it out of his grasp and then stared as the wound knit together in seconds. Norcross shrieked out a laugh. "You can't kill me!"

"We'll see about that, abomination," Dekkir growled.

Norcross hissed and charged him. Dekkir knocked him back with the spear and raked the blade end across his throat. More black gore flew, but the wound still knit together in seconds.

I looked to Tabirus, who was gaping in horror along with the others. "How do we kill it?" I demanded.

"I…" He shook his head slightly, staring at the thing circling and lunging as it tried to get at Dekkir. "I have no idea."

Wickman aimed carefully as Dekkir pushed the thing back again and fired at its chest. Norcross staggered, clutching the wound, but I could see the skin rolling closed almost immediately. "Damn. How is it that everyone else is getting powers and healing old injuries, and he's turned into a monster?"

"It's because he was one to begin with," Tabirus said solemnly. "The Strain's effects depend on one's brain chemistry, for that is the seat of its colony within a living thing."

Dekkir's eyes narrowed. He had already stabbed the thing and even lopped off its arm. Only to watch a new one sprout in its place in seconds. Norcross laughed madly, clawing at Dekkir's face. The two were at a stalemate: Norcross couldn't land a solid hit, and Dekkir could not make one count.

I stared at them. *The brain is the seat of the Golden Strain's colony within a living thing. The brain. The brain.*

I focused as hard as I could and called out to Dekkir's mind, *Destroy his brain!*

Dekkir kicked the creature away with a booted foot and then swept his legs with the shaft of his spear, knocking Norcross onto his back. Before the abomination could recover, he whirled, raised his spear, and drove it through its head, cracking bone and sending its brain splattering. Norcross convulsed, and his screeching went silent then his body went slack.

I sighed in relief as Dekkir straightened. I wanted to run to him, but he held up a cautious hand, watching the corpse. Finally, satisfied it was dead for good this time, he sighed his own relief and walked toward me, leaving his spear embedded in the floor behind him. "It must be burned," he told the others.

I noticed Wickman nod.

Then I was in Dekkir's arms, breathing in the clean smell of his sweat and shivering with relief as I clutched him closer. "It's done, my love," he murmured. "The battle is over."

CHAPTER 23
GRACE

A few days later, Dekkir and I stood at the window of our small, carved-wood suite in the heart of master healer Neyilla's tree tower, watching clean rain bounce down the leaves of the trees around us. My shoulder had healed in an hour once properly set. The only reminder I had of my captivity was the set of manacles that sat on the table as a souvenir of what Dekkir and the others had helped me win back. He and I stood at that window, naked, his warm, muscled form pressed against my back as his arms circled my waist and shoulders. His nose was in my hair, and his breath blew softly against my scalp as we stared thoughtfully out the open window.

"So what did Tabirus say?" I asked drowsily. My muscles still ached a little from the last bout of lovemaking, and I wanted more, but I was also dead curious. My mentor had been too busy training the hundreds of newly inoculated humans in the use of their powers to spend much time contacting me telepathically.

"Once everyone at the base is adapted properly, he will return with Wickman to Earth with the proposal of a further peaceful exchange of resources and knowledge. He will also be explaining the Golden Strain to them and bringing several people with him to demonstrate its ability to enhance humans and other organisms. It is his and Wickman's hope that they will be able to negotiate peace. He also plans to use old Lyran science to help them repair your world."

I smiled hopefully. "Good."

He hesitated. "It was suggested that you return with them, to aid in facing the inquest. But Tabirus said he would understand if you stayed."

"Good," I replied, voice firm. "Because I'm not going anywhere."

Earth was not withdrawing fully from Lyran space, but most of the soldiers were being recalled. In their place, more scientists and technicians would be sent, along with transport ships. In just a day, they had negotiated with Dorin the right to mine silicon and iron from one of the moons. In return, Earth had signed a twenty-year nonaggression pact. It stunned me that it had all happened so fast and filled me with hope that I would soon be able to introduce Dekkir to my family after all.

For now, though, all I wanted was more time with him.

I turned in his arms and ran my hand up and down his chest, leaning up to kiss him. He responded with a little rumble, his hot mouth tasting of the minty tea we had shared and his hands starting to slide over my body. His warm, slightly rough palms left tingling trails behind, and he shivered in turn as I caressed his chest and sides, then ran my nails lightly over his back. His sex stirred against my belly, and I smiled up at him.

Peace between our planets meant the last great challenge to our union had finally died. It could not have come at a better time, for now, I was under the master healer Neyilla's care for a unique reason. In my belly, which had been unsettled for weeks, now grew the first hybrid child of our two races.

When I finally saw my mother, I could tell her of my adventures with a clear conscience. Wickman had promised to advocate for me with Command. Both our actions had been maverick and even a bit defiant compared to protocol, but following protocol had led Norcross to cause the deaths of dozens of innocent soldiers and even more innocent Lyrans. And now a child would be born. Mom would be a grandmother in under a year. If she shed tears now because of all of this, they would be tears of joy.

I looked up at him, at his golden eyes gleaming with love and arousal, at the flow of his white-gold hair, his rugged face set in a soft smile as his hands slid over my breasts. He gently rolled my nipples between his fingertips, then pinched just a little, making me gasp and whimper. My skin had grown even more sensitive with pregnancy, but as with the rest of our union, he knew just what to do and just how to touch me. Tenderness from this powerful, sexy warrior always made me melt.

I gasped softly as he lifted me, settling my bottom on the edge of the windowsill and moving forward between my parted thighs. He leaned me back in his arms a little so I was able to stare up at the dripping canopy as he ran his lips and tongue over my breasts. I felt his member against my thighs and reached down to grip it, running my fingertips up and down his length teasingly until he started to gasp for air.

I scooted forward, bracing one hand on the windowsill, and wrapped my legs around his hips, taking hold of his sex and fitting the head inside me. He thrust forward, his eyes squeezing closed and his back arching, and then kissed me fiercely as he started to move. The hand not braced against my back slipped between us to caress me expertly, in time with his slow, firm thrusts.

Our bellies slapped together, the sound mixing with the rain and our softly labored breathing. I rolled my hips against him, feeling my body tighten around him slowly as his skilled fingers drove me stroke by stroke toward the precipice. We had made love even more often and more fiercely since the battle on the Earth base, reminded by those horrors of the preciousness of what we had. I was his now, forever, and though we would not formalize the union until my parents could visit in a few months, it mattered little. I felt our union all through me: in heart, in mind, all the way down to my bones.

I felt the tension gathering in his loins, his pleasure as my flesh embraced him again and again. I felt his struggle not to tighten his hands too much, to keep the rhythm of his fingers between my thighs.

I felt his joy, his hunger, the eagerness with which he looked forward to doing this with me again and again, every night, for however many centuries the Golden Strain would let us live.

My grip on him tightened. I dug my nails into his shoulders, rocking my hips back and forth as I braced my feet against the back of his thighs. My soft moans spiraled upward, punctuated by his low, sharp grunts, which gradually evolved into shouts of pleasure. Outside, the rain intensified. I closed my eyes and felt his fingertips take me over the edge.

My climax touched off his, and the two mixed together, bearing us up toward bliss together. Our voices chorused; my flesh clenched around his, and his shuddered inside mine, and pleasure roared through us in long waves while we clung to each other and cried out in ecstasy and joy.

As the climax wore off, I opened my eyes onto the Lyran sky and saw the glow of an Earth dropship ascending from the hastily constructed landing pad near Highfort. Soon enough, such sights would be common as trade opened and visitors became more frequent.

He pulled me back inside, carrying me sleepily to our shared bed, and laid me down on it before settling in to curl around me from behind. I smiled as I drifted off, feeling his hand slide around to caress my belly. The little one inside, a girl, already had a name, which carried the contents of our hearts as we looked forward to the brighter future ahead: Hope. A child of both worlds.

As was I…now and forever.

IF YOU LOVED **GALAXY ALIEN WARRIORS BOX SET**, YOU'RE going to devour this next hot standalone SciFi Alien Abduction romance. **BEAUTY AND THE ALIEN BEAST!** is a hot SciFi alien warrior romance, starring one stubborn human and the Alien Warrior strong enough to master her.

Disclaimer: the author is not responsible for any actual alien abductions that may result should you purchase this book. ;)

GET A FREE SEDONA VENEZ BOOK!

https://sedonavenez.com/free-book

SNEAK PEEK AT BEAUTY AND THE ALIEN BEAST

ELLA / CHAPTER 1

My eyes snapped open as I woke from the weirdest nightmare I had ever experienced in my life.

A moment later, I discovered I was in a cage. Pale metal bars, very shiny and set in a wide mesh pattern, surrounded me on five sides. The sixth was a narrow door and frame made from some thick, transparent material. The bottom, made of the same stuff, was on casters and seemed locked in place.

Oh God, what the fuck is this?

I was too uncomfortable for it to be a dream. My knees were tucked too hard against my full breasts. My belly, back, and shoulders ached stiffly.

My heart started to pound with terror, and it took all I had to keep quiet and not panic.

I've been kidnapped… but by whom?

Using the bars, I pulled myself to my feet and felt my joints crack from being balled up on the bottom of the cage. Seeing a small fold-down seat attached to the inside of the cage, I flipped it down, perching my ass on it uncomfortably, barely fitting a cheek and a half on the damn thing.

Fear died back a little as I caught my breath, eyes still blurry. I felt off-kilter.

Have I been drugged?

I looked down at myself and realized the tank top and fleece sleep shorts I remembered going to bed in were gone. Now I was dressed in a translucent cream-and-gold gown that accented my dark skin perfectly and clung to my ample curves. Beneath the dress was a gold harness that held up my large breasts, while a gold-belted loincloth matching the gown was the only thing that covered my ass—barely.

Shit. I've been kidnapped and turned into eye candy.

To make matters worse, I couldn't remember how I'd gotten here. My last clear memory was of dozing off under my fluffy comforter with an open book on my chest.

I gave myself a quick once-over. No injuries, but I could tell I'd been bathed, perfumed, and my thick, curly hair was now pulled back from my face, allowing the tendrils to tumble loose down my back. My nails were clean and gilded. My feet were bare, and someone had painted my toenails gold.

What the hell? I felt like an involuntary model in a lingerie show.

I looked out through the bars at a gleaming, well-lit space with a mirrored ceiling, shiny black floor, and walls made up entirely of flat-screen panels.

For a moment, I looked up at my reflection. I was covered in sparkly gold dust, with more of the glittery substance coating my lips and eyelids.

I focused back on the walls. Shimmering golden lettering in a language I didn't know scrolled across some of the panels, and other surfaces displayed scenes of a beautiful, pristine landscape. Drinking it all in, I tried to glean some information on where I was being held.

The scenes being shown on the walls didn't look like Earth.

My stomach plummeted.

The scape depicted towering, conical mountains and a purple-tinged sky set with a small blue-white sun. A cluster of four jewel-colored moons rode the track of a faint, shimmering Saturn-like ring. In the foreground, there was a shining city with slim towers composed of a reflective metal-like surface studded with multicolored lights. And a flock of heavy-bodied, alien-looking four-legged birds soared through the air.

My body shook, and the dizziness intensified.

Oh God… am I dreaming? Or… am I really on an alien world?

I shut my eyes, trying to gather my shattered memories.

Okay… think, Ella…

I remembered lying in bed at Mom's cabin upstate, where I'd come to enjoy one of the last warm weekends of the year. I had been sleepy from too many glasses of wine and a lot of good food, so I'd decided to go to bed earlier than usual. My mind locked on to those memories of normalcy.

I smiled slightly just thinking about Mom. Coming up to the cabin with her had done a lot to help me decompress from a long week of work in Manhattan. She and I had spent hours just sitting on the porch, talking and sipping wine while quietly regretting that summer had faded. We shared hilarious yet nostalgic stories about Dad, who had been gone three years now.

Of course, true to form, Mom had asked if I was happy being single. It had been the subtlest, most easygoing sort of pressure I was used to, so I didn't complain. Mom just didn't get why I hadn't dated in years, and she refused to accept my insistence that I just plain didn't have time.

At twenty-nine years old, I'd made my career a priority, and I didn't have time for the bullshit drama associated with dating in Manhattan. I had stopped looking for a Sunday-afternoon man in Saturday-night places. It didn't help that I was picky as hell and was simply exhausted of suited, thirtysomething men who were still trying to fuck everything that moved and wanted nothing to do with relationships. I wanted something "real" with a partner that was interested in me. A man I'd feel safe with at all times and who could accept me as is, not constantly trying to upgrade or improve me.

I closed my eyes, leaning against the bars, trying to remember more about last night. We had retired early, maybe nine o'clock. I sat up a while in my room, working on my curriculum for my next public health seminar—a presentation on the real effects of health care legislation in the Tri-State area over the last ten years. I'd drifted off with one of my reference books on my chest, still sorting facts and figures in my head.

My breath hitched when I recalled how I'd gotten here...

I was lying in bed, sleepy as hell, when a faint light shined through my bedroom windows. Yawning, I rolled away from the illumination, determined to grab some rest while I could.

The light got brighter.

I mashed my face into my pillow, desperately trying to get some sleep.

Then shit got so weird and scary when I was plucked right off the bed by some invisible force. I screamed, but there was no sound.

I tried to move my limbs, but I was paralyzed while my body floated through the air and right out the open second-story window.

My vision blurred from the bright glare before I felt a bruising pressure against my body, as though the energy were trying to skin me alive.

My heart raced as I screamed again, and again, there was no sound. The light flashed several times before I felt myself floating lower and lower until the force against my body released.

I was free... sort of.

I stared at my surroundings in disbelief.

This was my worst nightmare come true.

I was inside a tiny metal room with no doors.

On my hands and knees, I scuttled around like a cornered animal because there was no doubt in my mind what had just happened...

I'd been abducted by aliens.

***

BEAUTY AND THE ALIEN BEAST! is a hot SciFi alien warrior romance, starring one stubborn human and the Alien Warrior strong enough to master her.

WANT FREE SEDONA VENEZ BOOKS?

Sign up for Sedona Venez's Newsletter and receive FREE BOOKS. In addition to the free stories, you will also get special pricing, exclusive previews and news of new releases.

GET A FREE SEDONA VENEZ BOOK!

Join Sedona's mailing list to be the first to know of new releases, free books, special prices and other author giveaways.

https://sedonavenez.com/free-book

ABOUT THE AUTHOR

USA TODAY BESTSELLING AUTHOR SEDONA VENEZ lives in New York City with her former military hubby—hooah—and their fur babies. She loves writing sizzling, sexy intricate stories about strong but broken characters who push limits, overcome their fears and risk it all for love.

Sedona loves to connect with readers!
www.sedonavenez.com

www.ingramcontent.com/pod-product-compliance
Lightning Source LLC
Chambersburg PA
CBHW060740210726
48292CB00012B/17